CEZAR'S LAST MARK

ALSO BY THE AUTHOR

Mark to Murder: Death in Budapest – A Mark Kent Mystery

Appassionata: and other stories of lovers, travelers, dreamers and rogues

Dogmeat: A Memoir of Love and Neurosurgery in San Francisco

CEZAR'S
LAST MARK
DEADLY RENDEZVOUS FOR TWO

A MARK KENT MYSTERY
MORIS SENEGOR

KAYMAK
PRESS

Published by Kaymak Press, Stockton and San Francisco, California

Copyright © 2022 Moris Senegor. All rights reserved.

ISBN:

Electronic: 979-8-9854570-0-1

Paperback: 979-8-9854570-1-8

Cover design by Tabitha Lahr, www.tabithalahrdesign.com

Map by Zoe Simon

Author's photograph © Julie Anne Senegor

*To my freshman English professor at the
University of Chicago,
who, after commenting on my dismal prose,
advised me to quit thinking in Turkish.*

"Then one day, when you least expect it,
the great adventure finds you."
—Ewan McGregor

CONTENTS

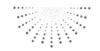

Map of where the story unfolds is on the following page

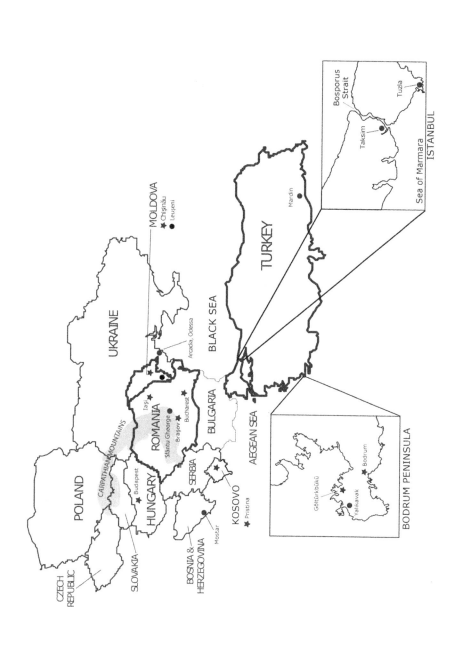

PROLOGUE

BRAŞOV, MARCH 29 ... AFTERNOON

Enver did not know that they were waiting inside. He had been up all night, bringing fresh meat for harvest. The job had left him dead tired, with a late start out of Chişinău. His recruit got cold feet and disappeared. Enver had to search for him and then convince him to return, losing precious time. As a result they drove all night from Moldova to Romania, arriving in Braşov early Saturday morning instead of Friday afternoon.

Enver unlocked the door to his second-floor apartment. A slim, diminutive man in his thirties, his thin face was itchy with the days-old beard that threatened to compete with his moustache. His long dark hair, which parted down the middle and hung over his ears, was greasier than usual.

His door had two locks, both usually engaged. He did not notice, as he would have if he had been more alert, that he needed to unlock only one.

He'd been away for several days and the apartment should have been cold. Instead it was warm, downright hot. Enver threw his keys on the dining table and cursed his landlady. The old woman must have turned on the heat when she checked up on the place. He unzipped his parka and threw it on top of his keys. It was ungodly hot. He pulled off his wool sweater and threw it on top of his parka.

The small apartment was situated along the ancient Strada Sforii in the Schei district. It had a tiny bedroom and kitchen, and a space in the front that served as both living and dining room. Enver was too tired to notice that his bedroom door, usually closed, was slightly ajar. A set of window blinds to one side were closed tighter than usual. Besides, the place was always in a state of bachelor disarray.

A black cat slid out of the kitchen and quietly rubbed against his ankle. Enver pulled out a chair and sat down. The cat circled around once and looked up at him. Enver picked it up, placed it on his lap and ran his fingers through its smooth fur. "Hello, little one, did you miss me?"

The cat purred and sat still, enjoying the attention. Enver continued rubbing it while he contemplated the news on the overnight journey. It had come from Iancu's bodyguard, who had called Enver's driver and announced that Iancu had been murdered in Budapest.

Enver could not comprehend the news. Iancu Negrescu was his boss. Not just a boss, but for all practical purposes, his father. A distant relative of Enver's mother, Iancu had offered to take Enver away from the civil war in Bosnia when Enver was a boy. Enver was shipped to Romania, saying goodbye to his father and two older brothers, whom he never saw again. They perished at Srebrenica.

Iancu treated the ten-year-old boy like another son, and eventually introduced him to the business. Enver became a master recruiter, a crucial cog in the kidney business that Iancu ran with his associate, Nicolae Radu.

Nicolae was also dead, assassinated in a fancy Budapest hotel. Iancu had gone to Budapest to collect Nicolae's body. And now he, too, was dead. Enver had a notion about who might have done in Nicolae. After all, he was the one who had alerted Nicolae Radu to the threat. Nevertheless, it was still a surprise. He did not expect a hit to occur outside Romania.

Enver understood Radu's fate, but not that of Iancu. Iancu knew nothing about the mess Nicolae had gotten into.

Enver gently placed the cat on the floor. The animal stood still, eyeing the kitchen door.

"What's the matter, little one?"

The cat usually hung out in the kitchen near its food plate. Fast and wiry, it always ran to the kitchen whenever Enver returned from a long absence, meowing and demanding food. This time, it didn't.

Enver stood up wearily. He could not think things through. He needed some sleep first, then a good shower and shave. He always thought most clearly when he was facing himself in the mirror, shaving. He would have to sort through the news later.

As Enver took a step toward his bedroom, they emerged suddenly, one from the kitchen, the other from the bedroom, approaching Enver from each side. They wore dark paramilitary uniforms with thick black leather belts that held empty holsters. They were slim and agile, and held pistols at waist level, pointed at him.

Enver's fatigue was suddenly erased by an adrenaline surge. He instinctively raised his arms up. Even though he had served in the Romanian army, he was not a skilled fighter. There was no way he could combat two armed men. Enver recognized their pistols: MP-443 Grach, standard Russian military issue, affectionately known as *Yarygin*.

"*Arme către partea,*" one of them ordered in Romanian. He had a raspy voice. Enver recognized a distinctly Moldovan accent. *Arms to the side*. He lowered his arms.

The men were now nearly at his face. They looked alike, both with thick black hair and moustache, the one who had issued the order slightly taller than the other. The shorter one had a black leather bag around his shoulder that he swung forward. Reaching in, he produced an industrial tape gun. He handed it to his partner and removed another for himself.

"*Ce este asta?*" Enver blurted, in alarm. *What is this?*

They didn't answer. The taller one began wrapping the tape around Enver's arms and body, starting at the shoulders and

3

working his way down, while his partner held a gun to Enver's head. The man worked efficiently, wrapping Enver like a mummy around his upper body. He stopped at the waist, tore the tape and stood back. His partner knelt down and began wrapping Enver's legs with equal ease.

Panic rising within, Enver screamed. His yell was quickly cut short with gauze stuffed into his mouth. Some duct tape followed, sealing his lips. The two men dragged Enver toward the open kitchen door and held him against it, upright.

Enver felt something go down around his head. It came to rest on his shoulders. It was a thick rope. He felt a noose behind his neck as it tightened. He struggled to no avail against his bindings, his screams muffled by the mouthpiece.

Suddenly a flash went off, temporarily blinding him. When his vision cleared he saw that the tall one was examining an iPad. He had taken a photo of Enver. As the noose tightened further, Enver could no longer make sense of any of it.

PART ONE

CHAPTERS 1–30

CHAPTER 1

ISTANBUL, MARCH 29 ... MORNING

M ark Kent awoke to the desperate sound of a foghorn wailing in the Bosporus. He was momentarily disoriented in pitch darkness, the heavy shades of his hotel windows drawn. He imagined he was still in Budapest, at the luxurious Gresham Palace Hotel. He had to catch a plane to Istanbul. He hoped he wouldn't run late.

More horns. This time it was street traffic, Istanbul drivers always loose with their Klaxons. Mark stumbled out of bed and pulled up the shades. He stared at the Architecture Faculty of Istanbul Technical University across the street, and beyond, downhill, the old soccer stadium that he knew as Mithatpaşa. It stood by a Bosporus shrouded in fog. He was in Istanbul, Mark realized, no longer in Budapest.

The foghorn howled again. On days like this there had been spectacular accidents in the narrow strait, giant ships crashing into *yalıs*, historic seaside villas that lined the waterway. Their inhabitants woke up to the bow of a ship in their living room. Mark hoped that the foghorns did not portend calamities. He'd had enough in Budapest.

He turned back inside and checked the bedside clock. Ten a.m.

He was famished. He wasn't sure how long he had slept. The hotel offered breakfast until eleven. He'd better hurry up.

Even so, he made his sleep-fogged way slowly into the bathroom. It was a spacious, marble-lined affair with a huge walk-in shower, nothing like the bathrooms of his childhood in Istanbul—tiny, squat toilets with showers that ran dry most of the time. This one also had a Jacuzzi bathtub. Mark shuddered as he recalled finding his old high school buddy Ahmet dead in a similar bathtub at the Gresham Palace. How long had it been? Not more than a week. It had plunged him into a misadventure from which he hoped he would recuperate in Istanbul.

Mark pushed back his charcoal black hair and stared at himself in the mirror. He had always been tall and lanky, but now that he had lost weight in Budapest, he looked downright gaunt. The purple shiner on his right eye, acquired during a foiled kidnap attempt, had faded but was still visible. He had a two-day-old beard and dark rings under his obsidian-dark eyes. He felt as tired as he looked.

At the spacious counter with a double sink, Mark reached for shaving cream. Nearby he spied his wallet atop his American passport. He had casually thrown them there the night before. They provoked another dreadful flashback, Ahmet's lifeless body surrounded, at the edge of the Jacuzzi tub, by two passports, Turkish and Romanian. The latter sat upright, open to the page with Ahmet's photo. The enigma of these passports had confounded police investigators. Mark himself discovered why they were there when Ahmet's killers gave Mark the same treatment with Mark's own passport. They took his photo with an iPad, the open passport next to his face. It was proof that they had gotten the right guy.

Mark picked up his worn-out passport and leafed through the pages. He stared at the entry stamp issued at Ferihegy Airport in Budapest, proof that he had entered Hungary. There was none marking his exit. Nor was there an entry stamp into Turkey. Mark wondered if he could take a commercial flight out of Istanbul without that entry stamp. Would he be detained at passport control?

He had been smuggled out of Budapest and into Istanbul in the back of a truck loaded with illegal car parts. Arranged by his new

Turkish friend—and partner in crime—Mustafa, it was the cleanest, most expedient exit from Hungary.

As Mark lathered up and began running a razor across his face, he pondered his predicament. He had been born and raised in Istanbul as Metin Özgür. After moving to the US, he changed his name to Mark Kent. Since then, he had rarely visited his country of birth. Now here he was, back in Istanbul, seeking a respite from his Hungarian misadventure, but on a mission as well. Her name was Günsu. He felt a sudden sting on his chin and a red blotch appeared, soiling the white cream on his face.

"Shit!" He reached for an elegant crystal jar full of cotton balls and blotted the cut. He stared at his half bare, half lathered face and realized that he might be trapped in Turkey. He had been smuggled in. He would have to find a suitable way out.

The breakfast buffet at the Hyatt was obscenely lavish, numerous tables full of unimaginable variety. By contrast, a typical Turkish breakfast was simple, some bread and cheese, black olives, perhaps some cucumber and tomatoes, and tea. Mark stared at the endless plates of hot and cold meats, eggs of every sort, smoked fish, cheeses galore, a special table of breads, nuts and dried fruit, and desserts—cakes, puddings, ice cream, chocolate.

A young waiter formally dressed in a black bow tie politely asked him for his room number and took a coffee order. Mark helped himself generously to scrambled eggs and fresh rolls that smelled divine, and a slice of ham.

Ham…in Istanbul! He cut a piece and stared at it on his fork. Back in his childhood, there was no way he would have access to pork of any sort. Natural as it was for Hyatt to serve it to foreign guests, Mark still found it odd to be eating this in his birthplace. He hesitated only a moment before gulping the ham. He then dove in for the rest, with much gusto.

There was one uniquely Turkish item on the dessert spread that Mark absolutely had to try. *Kaymak* was an ultra-smooth clotted cream with a consistency like butter. He had not tasted it for decades. As Mark took it with a drizzle of honey, he was interrupted by the waiter bearing a seemingly empty silver tray.

"This *kaymak* is excellent," Mark said, licking his fingers. "I haven't had it in many years."

Impressed that this American had acquired a taste for such a uniquely Turkish delicacy, the waiter smiled. "Yes, sir. And ours is the best in the city." He then extended the tray to Mark, displaying a business card atop.

Mark licked the last remnants of *kaymak* off his knife and let its fatty, creamy richness linger on his palate. He stared at the young man quizzically. The waiter brought the tray closer.

"You have a guest at reception."

"*Misafir?*" replied Mark in Turkish, with surprise in his voice. *A guest?*

The waiter drew back, startled with Mark's perfect Turkish. For a moment they stared at each other in silence, both surprised.

Mark finally took a closer look at the card and read the name. *Mahmut Erkan Gazioğlu.*

Mark stared at the card for a long moment as he recalled that name. It had begun when police interrogated him at Gresham Palace after his discovery of Ahmet's body. Commissaire Jean-Claude Gérard of the French Interpol had asked Mark if he knew this Dr. Gazioğlu. Mark didn't.

Later, when Mark had looked him up, he discovered that Gazioğlu was an infamous Turkish surgeon who acted as a crucial cog in illicit kidney transplants all over Eastern Europe. There had been an Interpol Red Alert issued for his apprehension, and yet he hid in plain sight in Istanbul. Mark discovered a candid interview that Gazioğlu granted to an American newspaper at his seaside villa, portraying himself as a skillful surgeon dedicated to improving human life.

Mark nodded to the waiter. Together they left the dining room toward the hotel's spacious two-story lobby. It was sumptuously appointed with a marble floor and imposing vertical columns, ornamented with Ottoman art redolent of the Topkapı Palace. The lobby was busy with tour groups checking out, piles of luggage interspersed among animated clusters talking in different languages.

Mark scanned the faces in the lobby but could not make out the Turkish doctor whose visage he remembered from his research. The waiter gently squeezed his arm. *This way,* he said in Turkish. They approached a figure sitting at a secluded armchair behind one of the giant pillars. The waiter stooped and whispered into the man's ear. The man rose. A cashmere driver's hat, pulled down on his forehead, partially concealed his face.

As the waiter departed, politely nodding to Mark, the man removed the hat and approached Mark. Mark recognized the bald shaven head and elongated face. Gazioğlu had narrow, angular eyes that gave him a Central Asian look. He wore rimless glasses that rendered his eyes peculiarly small.

Recognizable as he was, Gazioğlu appeared different from his internet photos. His gaunt cheeks now had new wrinkles, and his dark Genghis Khan moustache had morphed into a snowy goatee. Whatever Gazioğlu had been through had taken its toll on him. He looked older than Mark, even though Mark knew that he was younger.

"Dr. Mark Kent," he said in a baritone voice, as he extended his right hand. "I am Mahmut Gazioğlu. You probably don't know me, but I know you."

He wore an Adidas track suit and running shoes that clashed with his fancy hat. His body was leaner than in the photos Mark had seen. Mark shook Gazioğlu's hand and did not let on that he knew him.

"Nice to meet you. What can I do for you?"

"You and I have a mutual friend," said Gazioğlu, then he hesitated and looked down at the floor. "Well, *had,* I should say."

Mark knew whom he was referring to, but he stayed silent.

"Ahmet Gürsen," Gazioğlu continued. "He had a different name in Romania, Nicolae Radu."

"Yes. What about him?"

Gazioğlu was momentarily puzzled. "You know him, right? He

was your high school mate. You found him dead in Budapest last week."

"I know." Mark sounded cold and uninterested. "Once again, Doctor. What can I do for you?"

"I would like to invite you to dinner at my house, tonight, tomorrow, whenever you like. I'd like to discuss some sensitive matters regarding Ahmet's death. I'd rather do it privately."

Mark pondered the question. He had come to Istanbul to meet old friends, one in particular, a woman he had had a teenage crush on, and who, as Mark recently discovered, had been Ahmet's mistress. He also intended to use the occasion for some R&R. Now, this fugitive doctor was inviting him back into the perilous world Mark had left behind in Budapest. He wondered if he should go.

Sensing his hesitation, Gazioğlu spoke more emphatically. "*Rica ederim*," he said. *I plead with you.* "This is a matter of life and death."

Gazioğlu had unknowingly provoked Mark's dilemma. Mark's adventures in Budapest that included several near-death experiences, while tiresome and fearful, had also been exhilarating. He shunned them, but he also craved them.

The Turkish doctor pushed on. "I have a villa in Tuzla," he said. "At the seaside."

Mark raised his eyebrows. Tuzla was across the Bosporus, on the outskirts of the Asian side of the city. Istanbul traffic being what it was, Mark was reluctant to trek all the way out there. As he was about to reply, Gazioğlu interjected.

"I have a private chauffeur," he said, "part of my security detail."

Mark looked beyond the doctor, his eyes quickly scanning the lobby for anyone who looked like a bodyguard. No one.

"He can pick you up from here or anywhere else, and take you back. Don't worry about how far it is."

Mark knew he should stay away from this man. But he was curious about what Gazioğlu had to say, and even more curious about how this Turkish man, a fellow doctor, had strayed from what could have been a placid, prosperous life to become an international criminal. Mark also wondered how Gazioğlu was hiding in plain sight in Istanbul without getting apprehended.

"All right," said Mark. "How about tonight? Six p.m."

Gazioğlu let out a toothy smile, one side of his mouth curved farther than the other. He extended his right hand to Mark.

"*D'accord*," he said in French. *Agreed.*

They shook hands, Gazioğlu firm, Mark hesitant.

The Turkish surgeon put his hat back on and brought the visor down over his eyebrows.

"I've heard some interesting things about you," he said to Mark before turning around. "I can't wait to hear how you strayed away from a quiet, prosperous life—a doctor in America—to become James Bond."

CHAPTER 2

CHIŞINĂU, MARCH 29

Vadim Rusu stared at the Nativity Cathedral from his tenth-floor window, admiring its slender central dome atop a colonnaded Greek temple. The church was surrounded by a canopy of green in Chişinău's main park. Skytower, the glass high-rise Rusu stood in, was a new sort of temple, one dedicated to Western capitalism.

Rusu turned inside and gazed at the large emblem adorning the wall behind his spacious desk. It was a Classical depiction of a muscular hero holding the world above his shoulders. Below the figure was the name of his company in Cyrillic and English, Hercules Security Group. He marveled at how much things had changed.

Capitalism had recently arrived in Moldova, formerly under Soviet control. Rusu, who had spent most of his life fighting for communism, now fully partook in its antithesis. His recent move into Skytower was a final affirmation of his success with HSG.

Rusu brushed his slim goatee with his fingers. It had turned white over the years, as had his well-cropped hair. With a receding hairline, this gave him a nearly bald look. His once brawny body was turning flabby. Regardless, compared with other sixty-somethings, Rusu was still trim and fit. But he knew well, every time he faced the mirror, that he was no longer his former self. The years had left their scars. So had the abrupt, unexpected loss of his only son, Dima.

The door to his office opened, interrupting Rusu's thoughts. "Hello, Boss," said the visitor.

There was only one person in the Hercules organization who was allowed to enter Vadim's inner sanctum unannounced. "Boris, how are you."

Boris Petrov sat down on one of two armchairs in front of Rusu's desk and placed his black laptop bag on it. He was slim and athletic, in his early forties. He wore a well-tailored dark suit and starched white shirt, collar open. Fancy cuff links shaped like earphones protruded at his wrists. He looked like a younger version of Vadim, but without the goatee.

Back in their Tiraspol days, Boris had carried an attaché case. Now it was a computer bag. He pulled his laptop out of it and after several taps on the touchpad, produced a large color photo that he displayed for his chief. "Enver Muratovich," he said. "We got him in Braşov, at his apartment."

Rusu came around to examine the picture. It was of a young man with dark, greasy hair covering his ears, and bony, unshaven cheeks. His lips were taped shut. His eyes, wide open with fear, reflected the camera's flash. At the bottom, the photo displayed a thick rope wrapped around his neck.

"Is this the recruiter?" Rusu asked. Boris nodded.

"That photo is secure I hope," said Rusu. He was a stickler for discretion.

"Yes, sir," Boris assured him. "Our team sent it through our own proprietary onion routing." It was a traffic anonymization technique used in the Dark Web.

Vadim opened a desk drawer and removed a print photo from a folder. It was of a balding middle-aged man in a dry bathtub, his head slumped. To his right was a Romanian passport open to the page displaying his name, Nicolae Radu. He brought the print next to the laptop screen and silently examined the two.

"I hope they didn't botch this job like they did with Radu and Negrescu in Budapest."

Back in the day, when he served with OMON—the Soviet internal security service—in Riga, Vadim did not care how his assassinations were conducted. The special police unit within the Soviet National Guard had excellent political cover. If a killing was messy, it could easily be cleaned up after the fact. But nowadays, this too had changed.

"No, Boss. It was a clean job," Boris assured him. "Made it look like suicide. No forced entry, no struggle, no blood."

Boris Petrov had been a talented newcomer to Vadim Rusu's Latvian OMON team. Vadim took him on as a young protégé. But despite all their efforts, in 1991 Latvia managed to gain independence from Russia. When the new government began hunting down OMON operatives, Boris followed Vadim first to Moscow, then to Tiraspol, capital of the breakaway Republic of Transnistria. There they provided assistance to rebels trying to gain independence from Moldova. Vadim was the Republic's security chief and Boris, his main assistant. The effort did not succeed.

Vadim and Boris then moved on to nearby Chișinău, the capital of Moldova, where they started Hercules. The company provided sophisticated guard teams to wealthy Westerners and Russian oligarchs, as well as mercenaries to any government that needed them. It was a lucrative business that grew fast. They hit the jackpot with the Syrian civil war, where Hercules Security Group provided mercenaries all over the country for the Russian government.

Dima's death had caused Rusu to orient his company resources toward avenging his son's killers. Hercules could handle such an operation with little interference of its main business, especially since they subcontracted some of the work to local gangsters. But for Vadim Rusu it had become a major distraction, his quest for revenge taking his hands off the tiller.

"How did the team get into the apartment?" Vadim asked.

"The landlady." Boris smiled. "She let us in. It was like our inside connection at the Budapest hotel."

"Wasn't the one in Budapest a masseuse, Cezar's wife?"

Cezar Kaminesky was an independent contractor in Romania, working with, among others, the kidney transplant ring that had killed Dima. It was Cezar who tipped Vadim Rusu and Boris Petrov to what had happened and provided them with a list of the ringleaders.

"Correct. Olga," said Boris. "She did a nice job. Helped us bypass the security system of the hotel."

"But she also leaked our plans to that American agent," Vadim said acerbically. "What was his name?"

"Mark Kent," said Boris. "I am not sure that she did that. We don't know how the American latched on to Olga."

Rusu made a dismissive wave with his arm. He did not want to think of the fiasco caused by the American intruder. He pulled out his chair and sat down. "So who do we have left?"

"We'll be directing our efforts toward Turkey." Boris opened a screen and showed Vadim a *New York Times* article headlined: "Trafficking Investigations Put Surgeon In Spotlight."

"The doctor," Vadim murmured.

"Gazioğlu. We have a contact in Turkish police who says that he is still in Istanbul. Son of a bitch is hiding in plain sight. Interpol wants him but they can't get him."

"Crafty and slippery," muttered Vadim, as he examined the surgeon's photo. The man was slim, had a clean-shaven head and, like Vadim, a goatee. His eyes were hidden behind aviator sunglasses. "Slippery is no problem for us." Vadim turned the laptop screen back toward Boris.

"Then there is Latif Gürsen."

"Radu's father," said Vadim. "Where is he?"

"In the Bodrum Peninsula. Supposedly retired. He is the one that started the whole enterprise."

"Right," said Vadim. "Make sure the hits take place in proper sequence and with discretion."

As Boris slid the computer back into its case, they briefly fell into silence, contemplating the task ahead.

Rusu broke the silence. "You know, Dima was a screw-up but he was a good boy." He was somber as he contemplated his son's demise.

"Yes, Boss. He was a kind-hearted kid."

"He didn't deserve to die like that, like a Gagauz peasant." The Gagauz were a Turkic minority, a much scorned ethnic group, who lived in southern Moldova.

Boris played with his cuff links, rubbing his fingertips on the tiny headphones. He avoided eye contact with his chief.

"Tearing out his kidney like he was a laboratory pig!" Rusu's voice rose in anger. "Then letting him die in a shitty hotel room."

"He was a good boy," Boris repeated, still preoccupied with his cuff links. He then looked up at Vadim. "But he had a weakness for women. Tramps! That's what got him killed."

"And cocaine," Vadim added glumly.

They never discovered precisely who had drugged Dima. It did not matter. Whoever lured Dima into a trap was a mere pawn. Rusu was more interested in the organization that had preyed upon his son. He wanted those in charge.

"That doctor, the Turkish one. He is the one who trained them all. Correct?"

"Yes. He was recruited by Latif Gürsen and sent to help Radu set up the business. He trained Radu's surgeons in Romania. We'll be taking him out first."

"You better do a clean job, like you did with the recruiter in Braşov," Vadim commanded. "I don't want trouble with Turkish police."

"Yes, Boss." Boris stood up, ready to leave. As he turned the door latch, he hesitated. "I almost forgot," Boris said, turning to Vadim. "We have a report that the American, Mark Kent, is also in Istanbul."

Vadim looked at him sharply. Boris stood by the door, his hand on the latch. "Our Turkish police contact ran across the name during a routine scan of registered passports in Istanbul hotels. He might be at the Hyatt Regency in Taksim."

Vadim stood straight, his hands folded behind his back. "Well then. We have another chance."

"Yes, sir."

"I want to talk to that son of a bitch."

"You know, Boss, we checked him out pretty good. He appears to be a doctor in San Francisco, a radiologist."

"Give me a fucking break!" Vadim's voice rose. "This asshole outfoxed us, not to mention those inept Slovaks you hired in Budapest. He sent two of their men to the hospital and had two of our best killed. You don't seriously believe he is a real doctor, do you?"

"If it's a cover, it's a well-crafted one," said Boris, somewhat defensively. "We could not find any connection to American law enforcement or spies."

"Seems to me that the only way to blow his cover is to get him here and interrogate him." Vadim was firm. "You know how soft these Westerners are. Once we get our hands on him, he'll sing."

"Yes, Boss." Boris turned back to leave.

"Make sure you get this Kent guy alive," Vadim yelled after him.

CHAPTER 3

BRAŞOV, MARCH 29 ... AFTERNOON

Andrei Costiniu jumped as a black cat slithered around his ankles, rubbing itself against the pleats of his pants. His hand instinctively went for his gun, holstered under his left shoulder. Maries Boboc, his partner, let out a coarse laugh.

"What now! You're scared of cats?"

The cat meowed and moved onto Boboc's legs, sharply arching its back. Boboc picked it up and examined the animal, gently running his fingers along its back.

"I think it's hungry," he said, putting the cat down.

Andrei moved deeper into the apartment. It was warm inside. He headed toward the body hanging by the kitchen door, a giant noose around the neck attached to a thick rope stretched over the door. It was tied securely to the opposite door knob.

The man was obviously dead. His face, slumped to one side, was purple and bloated. He had greasy hair parted down the middle that covered his ears and a beard several days old. His swollen tongue stuck out of puffy lips, almost concealing a thin moustache. Andrei couldn't tell how old he was. Death had a way of making its victims look older.

Boboc looked around the back of the dead body. "Let's check the kitchen. See if there's any food for this poor thing."

Andrei gave his partner an annoyed look as Boboc slid by the dangling corpse without giving it a second glance. Andrei unzipped his uniform windbreaker and took it off, casually laying it on the floor.

Andrei was a *Subinspector de poliție* in the Sector 1 station, a brand new detective. Still in training, he was a fast learner, having previously spent time as an agent of SRI, the Romanian Intelligence Service. He lived in the Schei quarter not far from this apartment. The neighborhood was a small valley at the foot of the Carpathian Mountains that formed the backdrop to Brașov. In his early thirties, lean and athletic, Andrei was an avid runner, traversing the solitary dirt trails of the nearby foothills.

He examined the dead man more closely. The body was facing the living room, the noose slightly askew at the base of his neck. "No scratch marks," he murmured. The man had made no effort to fight the rope that strangled him.

Boboc returned from the kitchen empty-handed. "Pantry and refrigerator are nearly empty. No food for the cat."

He stood behind his partner, who was still examining the lifeless body, and watched Andrei impatiently. Boboc was in his late fifties, tall and stocky, a large belly bulging out of his pants, his belt invisible. He had a pockmarked face and receding hairline, his cheeks and nose permanently pink from years of drinking. He was an *Inspector de poliție*, a lieutenant, having never risen higher in rank despite his decades of service. Boboc reached for the rope stretched over the door and felt its tension.

"No," exclaimed Andrei, suddenly alarmed. Boboc withdrew.

"We may need forensics to look this over," Andrei added more calmly.

"What forensics?" Boboc was irate. "It's obviously a suicide."

Boboc had been annoyed all the way from headquarters as they drove to the Schei district. What a waste of time for a pair of detectives to be called on a self-inflicted hanging. As if they had nothing else to do. Andrei, who was driving, had tuned him out, even though he had hoped to get home early to his wife and their new baby girl. Boboc was always complaining about something.

"I think I know this guy," said Andrei thoughtfully. "His name is Enver something." He looked up at Boboc. "He lives near us. Quiet guy. Keeps to himself."

"Who called this in, anyway?" asked Boboc, still irate.

"The landlady. She found him. She checks on the apartment regularly to feed the cat. Apparently he goes away on business frequently."

Boboc looked toward the kitchen again. "Well, she obviously hasn't done that today."

Andrei surveyed the apartment. It was messy, a typical bachelor pad, but no evidence of any struggle. His eyes fell on a wool sweater atop what appeared to be a dining table, the only table in the apartment. It lay over a thick parka. He lifted the sweater, then the parka. A set of keys lay underneath.

"Looks like this guy just returned home before hanging himself," he told Boboc. "Maybe we should question the landlady, what time he arrived, if she heard anything unusual."

"We're not doing any of that!" Boboc was frustrated and firm.

Andrei understood his partner's annoyance. Ordinarily such suicide calls were looked over by uniformed patrol officers for any evidence of foul play. If not, the coroner was called to dispose of the body and the case was closed without any investigation. Today *Secția 1 Poliție*, the first police district, was short on patrol officers. Too many sick calls. So they had kicked the call up to Costiniu and Boboc.

"Look around," Boboc continued. "Do you see any sign of forced entry? Any struggle?" He swept an open hand around the room.

Andrei followed his partner's hand.

"Any sign that he was assaulted? Bruises, cuts? Any sign he was shot, stabbed? Any blood?"

Boboc was right. But Andrei still felt uneasy. "Let's look for a suicide note."

"Oh, give me a fucking break!" Boboc was exasperated. "Let's just leave it alone."

Andrei gave up and dropped the sweater and parka back over the keys. He took another look at the dead man while Boboc called headquarters, telling them to summon the coroner.

What led this man to take his own life in this manner, Andrei wondered, coming home from a business trip, taking his coat and sweater off and promptly hanging himself. On the few occasions when he had encountered him, the man didn't seem like the type to commit suicide. But then, what did he know? People concealed a variety of hidden lives behind placid facades.

"All right," said Boboc, turning toward the entrance of the apartment. "Let's get out of here."

Andrei put on his windbreaker and zipped it up.

"Where is that landlady anyhow?" he heard Boboc mumble as he exited. "We need to find some food for this cat."

* * *

Andrei plunged into his apartment hot and sweaty, returning from a brisk run. The noise he made woke up the baby, who began to cry. Ana came out of the kitchen, apron tied around her neck, and picked the baby up, rocking her on her chest. His petite wife was strikingly beautiful, with shortly cropped dark hair and deep blue eyes. Her curvaceous figure had enlarged after pregnancy, and she was trying to shed the extra weight. She was on maternity leave from her job as a nurse at the Braşov County Hospital.

Ana looked up at her husband, who kicked off his shoes, removed his sweat jacket, and dried his face on a towel he kept by the door. It was a familiar routine before dinner. They kissed afterwards and Andrei kissed the baby's forehead.

They ate quietly, Andrei deep in thought. He was still ill at ease about the suicide in nearby Strada Sforii. Boboc, his assigned mentor, despite his dismissive ways, had probably made the correct call, a self-inflicted hanging. Yet the scene at the man's apartment, seemingly rushing to kill himself soon after arriving there, didn't sit right with Andrei.

Ana left her husband to his thoughts, patiently waiting for him to open up. Later they cleared their plates together. Standing next to her husband at the kitchen sink, Ana asked, "What's the matter, Andrei?"

"Boboc and I looked into a suicide case today," he said. "Nearby."

"Why?" asked Ana. "Was there foul play?"

"Didn't seem like it."

"So what then?"

Andrei washed his hands and dried them on a towel. "It was that Bosnian. Enver." After returning to the station, Andrei had confirmed the identity of the body: Enver Muratovich.

Ana stopped and stared at her husband. "Really?"

"It's that guy whose sister you treated…when was it?"

"The young Muslim woman?" She hung her towel and thought for a second. "More than a year ago. I wasn't pregnant yet."

The woman had been admitted to Ana's ward with acute abdominal complaints. They turned out to be nothing dangerous, just a ruptured ovarian cyst. But she was hospitalized for two days. Ana would not have remembered this case were it not for the fact that the woman did not speak Romanian. She was from Bosnia, visiting her brother in Braşov. The brother had gone away on business when she became sick. Ana got involved, along with a social worker, in locating the brother, whose address turned out to be close to where she and Andrei lived.

"That's a shame," said Ana. She was puzzled but not surprised. This sort of unexpected news was common in her job. "He was a nice man."

Andrei sat down on a stool by a small table they kept in the kitchen. Ana joined him on a nearby stool.

"I think her name was Emina," said Ana. "Enver came to fetch her from the hospital. He was very polite."

Enver had apologized for his absence and hoped that he had not put the hospital staff through too much trouble. Emina was visibly relieved to see him there. When Ana told Enver that they both lived in the same neighborhood, Enver had smiled at the coincidence.

24

Later, as the brother and sister departed, Enver had shaken Ana's hand and told her that he hoped they'd run into each other from time to time.

"I used to see him in the market," said Ana. "He always bowed to me and exchanged a few pleasantries."

"Yes, I do remember." Andrei had been with Ana on one such occasion and she had told him the story.

"He didn't seem like the type to commit suicide," said Ana, mystified.

"Indeed." Andrei momentarily stared into blank space. "But then, who knows? How can we tell? We didn't know him well."

"How did he do it?"

"Hung himself off a door. With a rope tied to a doorknob."

Ana gasped. "I just saw him last week, at the Sanpetru market," she said. "He was waiting behind me in line and he patted the baby. He was so kind."

"Did he say anything to you?"

"Just idle chat." Ana thought for a moment. "I asked him what he was doing at the grocery store. At that hour it's only housewives or mothers with babies, like me. He told me that he was taking a few days off from work before leaving town for a while."

"What work?"

"I don't know," said Ana. "I had the impression that his work is mostly out of town. That's why he was away when his sister got admitted. Remember?"

Andrei nodded. "It's funny," he said, "how we bump into people regularly and we have no idea what their lives are like."

"Modern city life," said Ana thoughtfully. "It wasn't that way in my father's village outside Craiova. Everyone knew each other then."

They moved back to the living room. The baby was still peacefully asleep.

"Will they notify his sister?" Ana asked.

Andrei sat on the couch and stretched his legs. "I don't know," he said. "We're off the case."

CHAPTER 4

BRAȘOV, MARCH 29 ... MORNING

The outpatient annex of Spitatul Martinu was dark and deserted. Elsewhere the colossal hospital was humming with activity, but not here at this early hour on a Saturday. Enver hastily walked Yoet, his recruit, down the hallway that connected the desolate annex to the radiology department. They should have been here yesterday for Yoet's scheduled CT scan. After that there was yet another task, a final blood test, a serum crossmatch.

Yoet was in his mid-twenties, a slim youth, still lanky, like a teenager. His long dark hair was disheveled into unruly curls. He shuffled down the hall with his head down, eyes half-mast. Enver had spent months cultivating Yoet in Răspopeni, a village an hour north of Chișinău. The area was Enver's favorite hunting ground in Moldova.

The young man lived there with his thirty-something wife, who also happened to be his sister-in-law, and their five children. Four were older and belonged to Yoet's older brother, now deceased. As custom demanded, Yoet married his brother's widow, and the two of them had a new baby together. They were piss poor, living in a small dilapidated house, cohabitating with chickens, goats, and a much prized heifer, donated by her father.

The thousand dollars Enver offered Yoet would go a long way toward supporting his family. In return, the young man had readily submitted to a battery of blood tests. Enver had given him 10 percent down for the prelim. With an O blood type, Yoet was an ideal donor, a universal donor, as the doctors called it. Another crucial test was Yoet's tissue type, the HLA. Yoet was one of several recruits held in reserve, along with others on Enver's list, waiting for a client that matched.

The complex data involved in matching kidney donors with recipients was contracted out by Enver's bosses, Iancu Negrescu and Nicolae Radu, to a company owned by a certain Cezar Kaminesky, whom Enver had never met. Enver received news of a suitable match from Kaminesky's team by text or email. He then picked up the standby recruit and personally oversaw his delivery to the hospital and his final tests.

The donors were always men. The recipients, Negrescu and Radu's customers, mostly Israelis and Western Europeans, refused kidneys from women. When it was all over, Enver returned the donor to his home and issued the balance of the promised payout in cash.

It was a well-oiled, efficient machine, although occasional glitches did arise. What happened with Yoet was the most common. When Enver came calling for the final screening and surgery, the young man got cold feet and disappeared. It took an entire afternoon and evening for Enver and his driver, Kyril, a Ukrainian who knew the locals well, to wear down Yoet's wife and learn the fugitive's location. Yoet was hiding in a neighbor's barn.

Enver and Kyril then cajoled Yoet into delivering what he had promised. But it had wasted precious time, delaying their arrival in Braşov. During their drive, Enver gave Yoet sedatives, with the ruse that these were pre-op antibiotics. Yoet remained subdued while Kyril drove all night over treacherous mountain roads.

Now Enver was rushing to complete Yoet's final screening before the transplant, scheduled within a few hours. The final serum crossmatch was essential. If the receiving client developed new antibodies to the donor and the crossmatch was positive, the transplant was off. Enver didn't fret this. It was not his problem and he would not be blamed for it.

An abdominal CT scan was what he worried about. It screened for anomalies in the donor's kidneys and ureters, evaluated the arteries feeding them, and revealed any other unexpected pathology such as tumors. There were no radiology facilities with CT scanners in the distant rural areas where the donors lived. Thus, this crucial test had to be conducted immediately in advance of the scheduled surgery, preferably the night before. Any problems revealed by the CT could also scuttle the transplant. This was uncommon because the donors were mostly healthy young men. Still, it was not unheard of. On occasion, Enver had had to make last-minute adjustments, bringing in an alternative donor.

Now, if the CT showed a problem with Yoet, the procedure would be off. Enver's bosses did not like last-minute cancellations. Their clients were wealthy foreigners, paying cash, in the vicinity of $200,000 to $250,000. Inviting them to Romania and then turning them back without a new kidney was not good for business.

Enver's bosses had contracted the pre-op radiology to Cezar Kaminesky's outfit. Spitatul Martinu had two CT scanners, both busy during the day. Overnight and after hours, one scanner was down. Cezar had arranged the scans for this one. It was an older scanner located in an otherwise abandoned corner of the radiology department. The clandestine scans were run by Nicoleta Ciobanu, a technician already employed by Martinu that Cezar had hired. Enver walked the still-drugged Yoet down a dark hallway into a small waiting area outside the scanner. He left Yoet there, slumped, while he went looking for Nicoleta.

* * *

With Yoet safely strapped into the scanner, Nicoleta returned to her control booth and joined Enver, who was keenly observing the scene through a glass partition. As she booted up her computer, Nicoleta turned around to a small fireproof filing cabinet, entered a code into its electronic lock, and removed a log book. Opening it to the current page, she murmured "eighty seven" to herself. Enver glanced at the page, which was nearly full. Each log entry was a "CK" with a number that followed. The last number was eighty-six. Next to it were a date and time, and the real name of the subject being scanned.

Nicoleta returned to her console and typed a name into the CT computer, each letter immediately appearing on the scanner's monitor screen: Cezar Kaminesky 87.

After some preliminaries to adjust the table position and gantry angle, she tapped a command button and the computerized tomogram whirred into action, its gantry frame rapidly rotating around the patient as it acquired countless X-ray images to be sorted by a computer into intelligible slices of Yoet's abdomen. Nicoleta checked Yoet through the glass partition between the control room and the larger area that housed the scanner. All was quiet, her subject visible through the large round opening of the scanner, motionless on the table. Satisfied, Nicoleta sat back at her console and gave Enver a side glance.

Enver knew that the scanner, while in action, emitted a large dose of radiation. He retreated to the back of the control room, leaning against the wall, eyes closed.

"Long night?"

Enver opened his eyes and nodded with a slight, sideways smile. He rarely spoke to Nicoleta, preferring to conclude his pre-op business quietly and efficiently. He watched her as she oversaw the scan. She was in her thirties, curly red hair pulled back tightly into a bun, her plump body unabashedly revealed by tight scrubs. She was businesslike and competent.

Enver closed his eyelids and massaged them with his fingertips. His fatigue was overwhelming him. He couldn't wait to get home and into his own bed.

"I had expected you here yesterday," said Nicoleta. She gave him a sympathetic glance.

"He had cold feet." Enver opened his eyes and nodded in Yoet's direction. "We had to run after him."

Their conversation was cut short by preliminary images that

began appearing in the console's monitor. Nicoleta turned her attention to them. Enver too approached the console, studying the images. He had seen these before but had no idea what they showed.

"Any problems?"

The technician was not the final arbiter of CT results. That was up to the surgeon. Yet Enver knew that Nicoleta was experienced enough to spot trouble. She did not answer him and kept looking at the steady flow of axial cuts running through the monitor.

As the images concluded, she took another glance at her log book, confirming that she had entered the correct name and number. Finally she tapped a stop command and looked into the scanner room to make sure her subject was still lying quietly.

"Looks good," she said, and closed the book.

Enver wasn't sure if Nicoleta was referring to the scan or the log book. He stayed silent as Nicoleta returned the book to the filing cabinet and re-entered the locking code. She turned back, glanced at Enver and rolled her eyes.

Nicoleta knew that what she was doing, performing secret scans under assumed names, was illegal. But Cezar Kaminesky's organization paid her well, under the table and tax-free, and she had nothing to do with all else that happened. She remained discreet.

Enver knew that she knew. He understood Nicoleta's eye roll. All the donor recruits were registered as Cezar Kaminesky, with a number next to their names. Cezar had a deal with the hospital's administration to keep these cases off their routine medical records, and in separate logs. Enver didn't know who in Administration facilitated these scans, and he didn't care. He was sure that they too were well paid.

Enver received a small packet of records at the end of each transplant: CT report, lab results, operative records, all with the "Cezar Kaminesky" heading plus the patient's number. He delivered these to Iancu Negrescu or Nicolae Radu.

Enver had heard through the grapevine that Nicolae Radu had used one of these CT reports to summon an American friend to

Budapest. Nicolae had traveled to Hungary to meet this friend and ended up dead. Enver wondered if the American had something to do with Nicolae's death.

Nicoleta motioned him into the scanner room, interrupting his thoughts. He joined her and together they unstrapped Yoet and helped him off the table.

CHAPTER 5

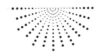

BRAŞOV, MARCH 29 ... MORNING

Irina hooked an IV bag to a pole on Yoet's gurney and turned to greet Enver. They were in the outpatient surgery annex of Spitatul Martinu, in a small, drab room that used to be a storage area, now unused. It had no windows and dim lighting that concealed peeling paint on its dirty walls. This was their makeshift pre-op holding area. Later, it would also serve as a recovery room.

Nicolae Radu and Iancu Negrescu had an arrangement with Martinu's hospital administration through Cezar to use an operating room in the outpatient surgery annex. The room was off the beaten path and accessed by an unused back hallway, thus avoiding the daily buzz of the otherwise busy outpatient suite. Besides, they scheduled their illicit transplants on weekends when Outpatient Surgery was inactive. Hospital administration made sure to keep their regular employees out of the area.

Irina, a seasoned operating room and recovery nurse from Bucharest, was a diminutive figure, like Enver, but older, in her forties. Her crisp blue scrubs revealed a shapely body that appeared younger than her actual age. Her blonde hair was neatly bundled, her makeup light. Irina had a businesslike air, projecting confidence that put patients at ease. With Yoet still drugged, she didn't have much challenge.

Irina adjusted the flow valve of the IV, gave the drip chamber a quick look, and turned to Enver. "You look like shit." She reached over and caressed Enver's cheek, making a face as his stubble rubbed on her soft palm.

Enver smiled and placed his hand over hers, letting it rest on his cheek. He lightly kissed her wrist. "Long day yesterday, and long night," he said. "You know."

She did know. She had seen him this way before. Irina gave him a sympathetic smile.

A few years earlier, Irina and Enver had had a fling. It was during a rough patch in her life, while separating from her husband. It ended soon and they went their separate ways, but they remained friends.

"I worry about you," said Irina. "You need to slow down. Take some time for yourself."

Yoet moaned, interrupting them. Irina went over to him, rubbed his hair and whispered into his ear.

She would soon be helping in Yoet's surgery, assisting and circulating at the same time, and subsequently overseeing his recovery. These were daunting tasks that normally required three different people. Irina was a one-woman dynamo, doing it all.

A short, stocky man in green scrubs entered the room with a lit cigarette between his fingers. He was in his late thirties but looked older. He had a thick black stubble on his meaty cheeks and stringy, shoulder-length hair hanging down from his surgeon's cap. Enver eyed the man with trepidation. Dr. Bekim Zhulati did not seem ready for a full day of surgery.

"How are you coming along?" asked Zhulati, turning to Irina, his voice raspy.

"Put that out!" Irina ordered him, pointing to his cigarette.

The man obediently turned away and waddled out.

"Son of a bitch," said Irina after him, shaking her head. "That sloppy bastard will get us in trouble one of these days."

Zhulati returned without a cigarette and gave Irina a kiss on the cheek. She tried to withdraw but could not avoid the wet peck.

"My dear Irina," he said, smiling. "You look ravishing as ever."

She pushed him away. "And you are a mess, as always."

The doctor approached Yoet and looked him over, lifting his bedsheet and gown and giving his abdomen a cursory look.

"We'll do the left kidney," he said. "The right one is not worth it. Double blood supply. Too much work."

He had obviously checked the CT scan. Enver was thankful for that. Zhulati then announced that the crossmatch results were favorable. The gig was on.

Irina told the surgeon, "I have the instrument trays opened and ready to go."

Zhulati blew her a kiss. "You're the best, darling." He turned around and staggered out. "Let's go."

Zhulati would start by removing—harvesting—Yoet's kidney. He would then proceed to transplant the harvested kidney into the client. Irina and Enver stared after him as he left the room, stumbling.

"Is he drunk?" asked Enver.

"Who knows! I wouldn't put it beyond him." Irina turned back to Yoet and took his vital signs, recording the numbers into a log. She unlocked the wheels of the gurney.

"It used to be so much better when the Turkish surgeon was here," she said to Enver, standing behind the gurney, ready to push off.

"Gazioğlu?" Enver pronounced the Turkish name correctly.

"He was a prick, but he was good," said Irina. "Kept everyone in line."

Enver remembered the man. Nicolae Radu had brought him over from Turkey. Gazioğlu was his father's doctor, he said. Enver never quite understood that. Radu's father, who lived in Turkey, had not needed a transplant.

Regardless, when the Turkish surgeon took over, a certain discipline descended upon the Braşov team. Gazioğlu sharpened the

34

surgeons hired by the organization. Zhulati was not a mess when Gazioğlu was supervising him.

"It's a shame what happened," Irina continued, "that fiasco in Kosovo."

A young Turkish man, a donor as it turned out, had been discovered unconscious at Pristina International Airport. He was in shock from internal bleeding. Investigation soon uncovered that a transplant ring in Kosovo, another one that Gazioğlu oversaw, was responsible. Gazioğlu had in fact harvested the young man's kidney himself.

"Complications happen," said Irina. "Even to the best of surgeons."

The affair led to Gazioğlu's downfall. He became a fugitive as Interpol widely circulated his name in a Red Alert, seeking his apprehension.

* * *

A young man entered the room, his head covered with a cap, his surgical mask drawn up. Enver did not recognize the newcomer.

"Here," said the new man to Irina, taking a quick glance at her log. "I'll take him in." He had a polite tone. He began pushing the gurney out. "Take a ten-minute break," he told Irina.

Enver and Irina were left alone in the grimy room. "Nurse anesthetist," she said to Enver. "He's pretty good. We can be thankful for that."

"He looks like he is still in school."

Irina chuckled. "No," she said. "We're getting old. They are looking younger and younger. Believe me, he is well trained."

Enver too smiled for a moment. Then his face got serious. "Irina," he said, his voice lower. "I'm afraid I have some bad news."

She looked at Enver with a mixture of curiosity and anticipation.

"Nicolae Radu is dead."

Irina exhaled loudly and covered her mouth with her hand. "No, that can't be. He is too young."

"He was murdered. Assassinated in Budapest."

"Oh, my God!"

"That's not all."

Irina gave Enver a *please don't tell me* look. Enver continued.

"Iancu is dead too. Also in Budapest."

"Iancu Negrescu, your father?"

"Well, he is not my father, but he is, in a manner of speaking."

"What happened?" Irina's voice was now a whisper.

"I don't know for sure," said Enver. "I had heard some rumors in Moldova that there was a plot afoot to kill Radu. I sent him a warning. But Iancu...I don't know what happened there. I got the news early this morning as we drove here."

"I can't believe it," said Irina, her hands covering her cheeks, her head shaking sideways. She looked about the empty room at the peeling paint and dirty walls. She swept her arm around the room. "Does it have to do with all this?"

"I think so," said Enver. "But I am not exactly sure what, or how."

Irina straightened her scrub top and retied her pants tighter, thinking all the while.

"That does it!" she said to Enver. "I'm done. The money is not worth it."

Enver gave her a nod.

"What are you going to do?" she asked him. With his bosses gone, Enver had no organization to work for. There were others who needed a recruiter, most notably Cezar Kaminesky himself, who had started his own transplant venture in addition to his consultant services.

"I don't know," he said. "The news is too fresh. I need to process it. I am too tired. I am going home. I'll get some sleep first. Then we'll see."

Irina gave Enver a hug and held him for a moment, her cheek touching his. "Be careful," she said.

They disengaged and she turned toward the hallway that connected to the operating room. Enver stood alone and stared after her.

Just before disappearing, she turned back to him. "Let's meet when I'm done today," she said.

"Okay," said Enver. He knew from experience when the job would be over. "I'll call you."

CHAPTER 6

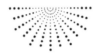

ISTANBUL, MARCH 29

Günsu threw her arms around Mark, sobbing. "Welcome back," she said in Turkish. "I'm so happy to see you."

Mark hugged her back, staring behind her at the busy traffic at Valikonak street. She had suggested that they meet at a café in the Nişantaşı quarter, near where she lived and near their old high school.

Günsu withdrew and took a step back, eyeing Mark up and down. "You haven't changed much," she said, drying her tears with a tissue, breaking into a slight smile.

Old friends from decades ago always seemed to say that. In fact, he *had* changed. A lot. He was in his fifties, for heaven's sake. Married twice, one wife dead, the other divorcing him, almost murdered twice in Budapest. Oh yes, he had changed. So had Günsu. She was no longer a beautiful teenager on the cusp of womanhood, as she was in the photo he had taken decades ago. He had kept that photo with him, always nearby. It reminded Mark of a bygone time, happy and innocent, and rekindled the heartbreak of his unrequited teenage crush on Günsu. In those days, she had only had eyes for Ahmet.

Mark had looked forward to reconnecting with Ahmet, his best friend from high school. Finding him dead in Budapest had been a major blow. Soon after, he received a startling call from Günsu. They had not seen each other much since their high school days. How had she found him? How did she know that Mark was in Budapest?

He was even more astonished when Günsu told him that Ahmet had carried on a long-distance affair with her, secretly visiting Günsu from Romania.

Günsu had been devastated by the news of Ahmet's death, which Mark had to deliver. He then inadvertently let it slip that Ahmet had a new Romanian wife and young children. Günsu was inconsolable and implored Mark to visit her in Istanbul. So, rather than doing the sensible thing and getting on a plane back to his home in San Francisco, here he was.

"You haven't changed much either," Mark replied hesitantly, hoping that she wouldn't detect his lie.

Günsu was a mature woman now, with prominent wrinkles on her forehead and a matronly, middle-age spread. But she still had those striking dark eyes that he admired back then, and they still sparkled with life.

Günsu noticed the fading bruise over Mark's eye. "What's that? What happened?"

Mark gently touched his eye. "Long story," he said. "I bumped it against a car door." He omitted the part about being kidnapped by Slovak thugs.

Mindful of more questions, he put his arms around her and led her toward the café. "Come on," he said. "We have a lot to talk about."

It was an Italian place that also sold Turkish tea and coffee, typical of Nişantaşı, a European neighborhood that resembled a slice of Rome. They sat at an outdoor bistro table facing Valikonak street. She ordered a cappuccino, he a double espresso.

"Well, what do you think?" she said, pointing to the boulevard in front of them named after the residence of Istanbul's mayor. *Same old apartment buildings, same old sidewalks*, thought Mark. But the cars whizzing by were new, much smaller than the 1950s American *dolmuş*—shared taxis—that dominated his memories.

"Hasn't changed much," said Mark. "You live nearby, right?"

"Yes," she said, pointing toward the left. "A short walk in that direction. My late husband's apartment."

She had not moved an inch away from her teenage life, Mark realized with wonderment. By comparison, he had gone off to another planet.

"I haven't done much with my life," she said, slightly embarrassed, as if reading his mind. "Not like you."

Mark wondered what happened. She was one of the brightest, most promising students back in high school. But he decided that this was not an opportune moment to explore how Günsu's life had derailed.

"Tell me what happened in Hungary," Günsu said.

"I don't know where to start," he said, taking a sip of his coffee.

"Start with Ahmet. What was he like in Budapest? You hadn't seen him in years. What did you think of him?"

Mark stared at her, trying to compose an answer. He couldn't bluntly describe Ahmet's dead body, naked in a dry bathtub, bearing handcuff marks on his wrists and tape marks all over from being tied up like a mummy.

"I...actually, didn't talk to him," he said tentatively. "He was already dead when I saw him."

Günsu's eyes teared instantly. She looked down at her coffee cup and picked up a napkin from the table. "I'm sorry," she said as she dabbed her eyes.

"Tell me about you and him." Mark figured it might be best to let her recount her own story first.

Günsu composed herself as she stirred sugar into her cappuccino. "It's a long story," she said, her eyes on her coffee cup. Then she looked up at Mark. "We were lovers."

Well, that's obvious, thought Mark, impatiently. "Since when?"

"Since forever." She took a sip from her cup. "It began in high school, our senior year."

That was a surprise to Mark. They were a tightly knit gang that year—Mark, Ahmet, Günsu, and several others. Neither Ahmet nor Günsu had given any indication that they were sexually involved. Those days were not like the freewheeling times of today. Sexual relations between teens were strictly forbidden. The few couples who did so kept it secret. But Mark was so close to both. He should have noticed it.

"It went on from there."

"But what about him getting married?" Mark was bewildered. "What about *you* and your marriage?"

"Yes," said Günsu, her expression grim, "it happened through all that, through his college in England, through both our marriages, through his time in Romania."

Mark stared at her, speechless.

"You must think I am a total slut."

"No!" Mark objected, a bit too loudly. "No," he repeated, more quietly. "I get it."

He reached for her hand. "I was there at the very beginning, remember?" He gently rested his hand over hers. "It's just that the part about Romania was unexpected. He was hiding there. I was stunned when I discovered that he was visiting you."

"Well, it wasn't all the time," she answered, letting his hand rest on hers. "It was every so often and it was very intense. Have you ever been in a long-distance relationship?"

Mark hadn't. He didn't answer.

"It's feast and famine," she continued. "When he wasn't here I was miserable. Then he came and it was ecstasy." She took another sip of coffee and added, with a stern expression, "It was mostly miserable."

"Did he discuss any of his business with you?"

"No. We mostly went out, you know, ate and drank, and had sex. A lot of sex."

Mark withdrew his hand, startled by her candor.

"You know how horny he always was."

In spite of himself, Mark smiled.

"Did he ever tell you about this whorehouse he used to frequent in Tarlabaşı?" She hesitated. "What was its name?"

41

"Varol?"

"Yes, that's it." Günsu broke into a smile. "Did you know that he had a regular there? And everyone called him her boyfriend?"

"Yıldız," said Mark, with a chuckle.

She slapped his hand playfully. "You too?!"

Mark laughed.

"I took you to be a well-behaved boy, not the sort to mingle with prostitutes."

Mark raised his hands, pleading innocence. "I was, I was," he said, still laughing. "But I did go there, once."

"Aha!"

"Ahmet took me."

She shook her head in fake disapproval. "It figures."

"It was a miserable experience," he added seriously. "It scarred me for life." She gave him a sideways glance, in disbelief. Mark didn't push the point. It had indeed been so.

Mark stirred his coffee cup. "He was a piece of work," he murmured.

"Yes," she agreed. "I too was a piece of work, wasn't I?"

Mark looked at her quizzically.

"For wasting my life with him."

Mark could not find a consoling answer. She was right.

They finished their coffee. Günsu produced a credit card and insisted that she pay.

"Let's take a walk to the old high school," she suggested as she waited for the electronic card reader to print a receipt.

It was early afternoon, breezy but sunny. They walked toward the heart of the quarter, the intersection of Valikonak and Rumeli streets where traffic was tied up into an impossible knot.

"So," he said, as they strolled along the crowded sidewalk. "I had an unexpected visitor at my hotel this morning."

"One of our old mates?"

"No. A doctor named Gazioğlu. Have you heard of him?"

Günsu thought for a moment.

Mark clarified. "Mahmut Erkan Gazioğlu. He is a surgeon. He's been in the papers."

"No," she said. "I don't read the papers much."

They crossed the intersection and came upon a small obelisk erected by the Ottoman sultan Abdülmecid. Mark wanted to stop and examine it, something he should have done when he was a kid. The stone gave the neighborhood its name. Nişantaşı meant "aiming stone."

Back then, in the late 1800s, the area was a barren hill that the Ottoman sultan and his army used for archery practice. The obelisk was inscribed in Arabic letters, giving information about the date, the shooter, and the distance the arrow traveled. By Mark's generation, the Turkish alphabet had changed into Latin, and Mark could not read the inscription. Nevertheless he stared at the small monument, dwarfed by the city that had grown around it, amazed that he had passed by it day after day in his youth and never even so much as glanced at it.

They moved on downhill, along Valikonak street. Here pedestrians were sparse. "Gazioğlu treated Ahmet's father, Latif Bey," Mark continued. "Do you remember Latif?"

Günsu smiled. "Of course I do. Charming man."

"Latif had some sort of heart problem. When Ahmet checked up on him, he met this doctor."

"I do remember when Latif had his heart problem. They placed stents in his blood vessels."

"Did Ahmet tell you what happened with this doctor?" asked Mark.

"No. What about it?"

"Gazioğlu and Ahmet formed a business relationship."

Günsu stopped and looked at Mark quizzically. What business would Ahmet have with a doctor?

Mark read her mind. "A clandestine kidney transplant business."

Günsu's jaw dropped.

"He didn't tell you?"

"No," she said quietly. "I had no idea."

Mark wondered about the nature of their intimacy. Was it just sex?

"He did not discuss business with me," Günsu explained, she in turn reading his mind. "I had a feeling that he was trying to protect me because most of what he did in Romania was not," she hesitated, "well, was not legal."

They stopped in front of a shop that sold nuts and dried fruits. Mark was momentarily distracted by the rich display of hazelnuts, pistachios, cashews, and walnuts, all shelled and ready to eat. Each display of nuts was decorated along the edges with a colorful array of dried apricots, figs, prunes, and pears.

He turned back to Günsu. "Look," he said, his voice serious. "This kidney transplant business is what got Ahmet killed. They also assassinated his Romanian business associate. I personally witnessed that. It was horrible."

"Who?"

"Iancu Negrescu."

Günsu thought for a moment. "That name rings a bell," she said. "Iancu used to regularly call him when Ahmet came to visit me. But I thought he was just a friend."

"He *was* a friend," Mark said. "But much more than that."

They began walking again, past the swank boutiques and intimate restaurants that this part of Valikonak street was known for. "I met Iancu in Budapest and got to know him a bit before he was killed. He was a decent man."

Instantly the image of Iancu's pinky ring crowded Mark's consciousness. An ostentatious ornament, how it had shone at the rooftop of the Rudas bathhouse, still on Iancu's severed hand. The hand lay atop some steps leading to a giant outdoor Jacuzzi. Iancu was floating in it, dead.

"You sound like you've been through a lot in Budapest."

"I can't even begin to tell you," said Mark. "Anyhow, this Gazioğlu is most likely also being targeted by those who killed Ahmet and Iancu. That's why he contacted me. He wants me to have dinner with him in his villa in Tuzla."

"Will you go?" Günsu gazed at Mark with concern.

They came upon the walls of the old English High School, nowadays renamed Istanbul Anadolu Lisesi. They walked up a steep side street that led to the main entrance and stared at the old four-story building through a padlocked wrought iron gate. The building looked to be freshly repainted, a huge Turkish flag hanging from its second floor near where their Turkish headmaster Mustafa Bey had his office.

Günsu's phone rang. Mark did not pay attention to her conversation, his eyes on the old school, memories flooding in. As she concluded her brief conversation, Mark asked, "Can we go in?"

"I am afraid not. We have to have advance permission to visit."

They both stared at the old school in silence. Günsu then dropped her phone into her purse. "That was Tarık," she said briskly.

"Who?"

"Tarık, my son. He is the one who located you in Budapest, remember?"

Mark vaguely recalled her saying that her grown son had run an internet search, looking for Ahmet in Budapest, and had serendipitously run into Mark on Facebook. He had then traced Mark's mobile number and given it to his mother.

"Come," said Günsu, putting her arm into his again. "Let's go meet him. He is at my apartment."

CHAPTER 7

ISTANBUL, MARCH 29

"*Hoşgeldiniz.*" Tarık extended a friendly hand, welcoming Mark.

As the two shook hands, Mark was speechless, unable to utter the customary *hoşbulduk*. He stared at Tarık, trying to hide his astonishment.

Tarık was of medium height, lean and solidly built. Considering his mid-twenties age, his hairline was fast receding. That and a dense, dark moustache made him look older. He wore prescription glasses that magnified his eyes.

Mark mentally wiped out Tarık's moustache and placed wire-rimmed John Lennon spectacles on him. There was no doubt about it. Tarık was a spitting image of a youthful Ahmet.

Tarık raised his eyebrows as Mark's silent handshake extended longer than expected. Günsu interrupted them, awkwardly hugging her son and separating him from Mark. Mother and son kissed once on each cheek, Turkish style. She then turned to Mark, giving him an anxious, expectant look.

"Glad to meet you," Mark managed in Turkish.

Tarık chuckled. "For a moment," he said, "I thought you had forgotten Turkish."

Mark smiled. "I nearly did," he said in a friendly tone, "but it comes back fast."

"Tarık is the one who found you," Günsu said to Mark.

Mark pretended to be surprised. He raised his eyebrows and uttered a phony, "Oh, yeah?" He then grabbed Tarık's right hand and shook it again with both of his hands. "Thank you."

Günsu ended the awkward introduction by offering to show Mark her apartment. Tarık tagged along behind them. It was spacious, occupying the entire fourth floor of an eight-story building. Up front was a living room, classically decorated as if it were a Parisian apartment, with big picture windows that opened to Valikonak street, the incessant din of the traffic down below filling the room.

The walls were decorated with European landscape paintings and a few old black-and-white photos of what Mark took to be Günsu's family. Off to the side, above a luxurious armchair, was a wedding photo. Curious, Mark sidled to it. Günsu was radiant in the photo, probably in her early thirties, decked out in a fine wedding dress with an elaborate headpiece, veil lifted. Her groom was surprisingly older, a square-jawed handsome man with thinly cropped white hair. His cleanly shaven face was creased with numerous lines. He stood considerably taller than his bride.

"That's Ilhan Bey, my father," Tarık said, noticing Mark's interest. "May he rest in peace." He paused with respect. "He was a *beyefendi*." A fine gentleman.

Mark eyed Günsu, eyebrows raised. She avoided his gaze. "He was indeed," she said firmly. She squeezed her son's arm. "And now, that's what you have become."

"Come," she said to Mark, drawing him away from the photo. "See the rest of the apartment."

A large, dimly lit hallway connected to a set of bedrooms in the back. On the way, they passed by a kitchen and spacious bathroom, and across from them a formal dining room that looked like it had not been used in years. The hallway was lined with numerous photos, Tarık at various stages of childhood, either alone or with his parents. One photo caught Mark's eye. It was of the family, Tarık with his mom and dad, taken on what appeared to be the deck of a sailboat.

"That was in Bodrum," said Tarık. "Dad used to take us there in a sailboat."

Günsu and her husband looked fit in swimming suits, leaning on the gunnel, Tarık a little boy with an inflated floaty around his waist.

"Do you still sail?" asked Mark.

Günsu answered curtly. "No. That was Ilhan's passion. We keep the boat in Bodrum and hire a captain to sail it." She beckoned him forward.

Mark superficially toured the bedrooms. The master was only slightly larger than the other two and lacked an adjoining bathroom. Everyone had to share the spacious bathroom in the hallway. It was typical of Istanbul apartments of that era.

Mark studied the photos on the wall and atop the bedside tables. He searched for a face that was nowhere to be found.

"Would you like some tea?" asked Tarık as they headed back to the living room.

"We just had coffee," said Mark.

"Oh, a little tea won't hurt anyone," Günsu interjected, polite but firm. "Turkish hospitality!"

* * *

Mark bit into a *simit*, a round bread covered with sesame seeds, classic Turkish street snack. Tarık had cut two *simits* into bite-sized pieces and presented them with tea served in traditional tulip-shaped glasses with sugar cubes aside. The *simit* was fresh and delicious.

"How come you have no photos of Ahmet?" Mark asked Günsu.

The question instantly changed the mood of the room, clouding Günsu's expression. She threw an anxious glance at her son.

"He was a friend of yours, was he?" asked Tarık with an aggressive tone in his voice.

Mark felt the tension. Puzzled, he had no choice but to answer.

"Yes," he said calmly. "Ahmet and I were best friends in high school. So was your mom. With both of us."

Günsu nervously alternated her gaze between the two men.

"I heard that the *pezevenk* is dead." Tarık had called him a pimp, a common swear word in Turkish. "Good," he added. "*Cehenneme.*" *May he go to hell.*

Mark was taken aback. He looked at Günsu for guidance, but none was forthcoming. Mark had broached the subject, now he would have to deal with it.

"I take it that you did not like Ahmet?"

Tarık laughed acerbically. "That's an understatement."

"Honey," Günsu finally said, "Metin Bey has not been to Turkey in many years," referring to Mark by his original Turkish first name. "He does not know our history." She laid a hand atop her son's.

Günsu's touch had a strangely calming effect on the young man. His voice softened and he apologized.

"I can't help myself," he told Mark. "After all that my mother suffered because of that…" He was about to utter another obscenity but he held himself. "Man!" he managed to finish.

Mark defused the situation. "No need to apologize," he said calmly. "I knew him in a different context than you and your mom. For me he was a charming but mischievous old friend. You understand?"

"Let's drop it," Günsu said sternly.

They talked about neutral subjects for a while, discussing America versus Turkey, how much Istanbul had modernized, and Tarık's visits to America, mostly New York City, to see old friends who had moved there.

Günsu mentioned that Mark had been invited by a fellow doctor to Tuzla. Like his mother, Tarık did not recognize the infamous Gazioğlu's name. He kindly offered to drive Mark there. Mother and son were both impressed when Mark told them that Gazioğlu was sending a private chauffeur.

Finally Tarık got up and told them he had to leave. He handed Mark a business card with his name and mobile number. "If you need anything, call me."

They shook hands again, this time warmly.

"Once again, please accept my apologies for my outburst."

"No problem," said Mark.

Mother and son kissed, and Tarık was gone.

Mark and Günsu returned to their seats near the picture windows. Günsu sank into one and let out a big sigh. She stared at Mark with raised eyebrows, as if saying *it is what it is*.

"Tarık is his son, isn't he?"

Günsu's eyes teared. "Yes," she said meekly.

"And he doesn't know it?"

She looked up at him, pleading. "Please don't say anything."

"What about your husband? Did he know?"

Günsu stared beyond Mark at her wedding photo on the wall. "Ilhan," she said quietly, "was a saint."

She then looked Mark in the eyes as she recounted her story. "Back then, I used to work in his architectural firm. He was in love with me from the very beginning."

"I can easily imagine that," said Mark.

Günsu patted Mark's hand. "How lovely," she said. "Thank you. Anyhow, he knew all about me and Ahmet. He couldn't understand it, but he carried a torch for me anyway."

Günsu stiffened. "Then I got pregnant. It was an accident. Ahmet wasn't around. He was working in Gaziantep, by the Syrian border. So Ilhan stepped in and made an honest woman out of me, as they say."

"And he continued accepting you and Ahmet afterwards?"

"Yes." Günsu shook her head. "He recognized how irresponsible Ahmet was and what a bad influence he would be on the child. So he continued with one condition."

"That he be Tarık's father?"

"Yes."

Mark raised his eyebrows in disbelief. The man must indeed have been a saint. Mark would not have put up with that. "How come you didn't tell Tarık after Ilhan passed away?"

"By then my boy was in high school. Seventeen, as I recall."

Günsu looked at Mark beseechingly. "It was too late. Do you understand?"

Mark nodded, deep in thought. He imagined his own teenage crush for this woman, a naïve love that, over decades in America, had petrified into something that belonged in fable. The ugly reality of Günsu's actual life struck him deeply. He felt stupid for having obsessively clung to fantasy.

"It's a sad story," Mark remarked, realizing now how Günsu's life had derailed.

"Isn't it?" Günsu too was deep in thought. She did not tear up. "Fate," she said. "We have to live with whatever fate has in store for us."

CHAPTER 8

BRAŞOV, MARCH 29 ... MORNING

D r. Zhulati made a long incision along the patient's left flank
with a 10-blade. Irina, standing across, dabbed the erupting
blood with a sponge. He controlled the skin bleeders with Bovie
electrocautery and continued on, through the subcutaneous tissues
and in deeper.

Yoet was positioned on his side, with the operating table cracked
into a reverse-V shape, bending his body at the waist. A standard
position in all nephrectomies, or kidney removals, it allowed easier
surgical access to the kidney.

As Irina leaned in toward the wound, suction in hand, her head
almost touched Zhulati's. He smelled of sweat and cigarettes.
Nauseated, she withdrew and turned her face away from the
operating field.

"Suction!" Zhulati ordered, looking up at her.

He was moving fast and would soon need a retractor to
maintain his exposure. Irina suctioned with one hand while with the
other, she reached over to the Mayo stand for the bulky retractor.
She was ready with it before Zhulati asked.

"You're the best, baby," he said, as he placed two huge blades
between skin edges and cranked the retractor open. "What are you

doing tonight?" Irina did not answer. He again looked at her. "How about dinner in my apartment? We'll get take-out."

Irina nodded toward the wound, gesturing him to move on.

"As you wish."

Zhulati, a Kosovar Albanian, had been hired by Cezar, whose scrutiny of surgeons was, in Irina's opinion, quite lax. Cezar paid them commensurately. By comparison, Iancu Negrescu and Nicolae Radu brought in higher-quality professionals, well vetted and well paid. Like the Turkish one, Gazioğlu.

"Clamp," Zhulati barked, interrupting her thoughts. He took it from her without looking up. Irina wondered what would become of the enterprise now that Nicolae and Iancu were dead. She presumed that Cezar would fully take over. She shrugged her shoulders. What did she care? She was done. This operation was her last job.

She worried about Yoet, draped off under her, a young man barely beyond childhood. He could have been her son. What would become of these poor donors?

Zhulati was slick. He moved through tissue planes swiftly. Soon the peritoneum was open, colon dissected off the kidney, and he began working on the spleen, separating it out. Irina pushed her thoughts away and focused all of her attention on the operation, accompanying him with ease. The nurse anesthetist remained quiet behind his curtain. They would hear from him only if there was trouble.

As his exposure deepened, Zhulati kept repeatedly adjusting the overhead lights, trying to illuminate hard-to-see corners. He finally gave up and said, "I need a headlight."

Irina let out a frustrated sigh. "I asked you at the beginning, didn't I?"

Zhulati stopped and stood back from the patient, arms apart, one hand still holding the Bovie. "Sorry." He had the tone of a scolded child.

Irina tore off her paper gown and stripped her gloves. She had to switch from scrub tech and assistant to becoming a circulator, the latter requiring a break in sterility. It was an unnecessary move that could have been avoided if Zhulati had accepted the headlight earlier, before the operation began. He could have put it on himself as many surgeons did, but he would never do that. The bastard enjoyed Irina's hands on him, her body in close proximity.

Irina plopped the plastic headpiece atop Zhulati's head roughly. She ratcheted the closing knob several notches beyond usual, squeezing Zhulati's head too tight.

"Ouch!"

Irina ignored him and moved over to the scrub sink to re-wash and gown. Zhulati momentarily watched her, then turned back to his work, resigned to his discomfort.

The dissection slowed down as Zhulati identified and freed the ureter, the tube that delivers urine from the kidney to the bladder. It often had a lot of blood vessels around it. Irina helped the surgeon place a sling around the ureter. Zhulati moved on to the adrenal, a hormone gland located atop the kidney. It had to be carefully separated in a tricky dissection that required careful ligation, or tying off, of several blood vessels.

Suddenly the field filled with blood. Zhulati cursed and shouted more emphatically. "Suction, suction!"

Irina remained calm and did as she was told. Zhulati had a tendency to panic in moments like this. Admonishing him would worsen the situation.

"Hey, what's going on down there?" the nurse anesthetist bellowed, poking his head above the anesthesia curtain. "The blood pressure just dropped."

Irina looked at him and shook her head in a *don't do that* gesture. "It's all right," she said, "it'll be over soon."

She continued to suction Zhulati's field, allowing him to locate his bleeders. The surgeon asked for a clip gun. It was in his hand instantly.

After a few minutes, as Irina predicted, the bleeding was under control and the patient's blood pressure rose back up, partly thanks to the extra fluids and pressor that the anesthetist administered.

Zhulati and Irina exchanged another glance. "You are the best, sweetheart," he said blowing her a hand kiss. He almost touched his sterile gloved hand to his mask, provoking another outburst from Irina.

"Come on! Move!" Irina ordered.

The remainder of the dissection went smoothly, Zhulati freeing up the kidney, taking care not to disturb the connective tissue that enveloped it. "Gerota's fascia," he murmured to Irina, naming it. Irina knew this, of course, but she didn't say anything.

He looked up at her. "You know that Gerota was Romanian, don't you?"

She sighed. Zhulati always reminded her of this fact.

"A great surgeon and urologist. A radiologist, too. The pride of Romanian medicine."

Considering that Zhulati was an itinerant Kosovar who practiced in various Balkan countries, Irina found his Romanian pride rather peculiar.

He moved on, rapidly ligating the ureter, the renal artery and finally the renal vein. The kidney was about to come out. Irina again removed her gown, this time according to plan. "I'll get the University of Wisconsin solution." It was a concoction of various chemicals, designed by the institution after which it was named. The solution kept the donor kidney in a nurturing environment until it was transplanted.

Zhulati delivered Yoet's left kidney as if it were a newborn baby. They both examined it in wonderment as though they had never seen a healthy kidney outside its owner's body. They threw each other thankful glances, Zhulati grateful for Irina's assistance, Irina pleased that Zhulati had not screwed up.

Irina opened the plastic bag full of clear Wisconsin solution and Zhulati dropped the organ in with uncharacteristic delicacy, as if it might otherwise shatter. Irina closed the bag and placed it in an ice-filled container.

"In Bucharest, they remove kidneys laparoscopically," said Irina, referring to the minimally invasive technique now favored by many surgeons.

Zhulati took a sip of coffee and made a face. "This is horrible. It's burnt."

They were in the small kitchen near the operating room, taking a break while the nurse anesthetist oversaw Yoet's awakening. They would not start the next operation, the transplant, until the anesthetist was ready.

Irina did not offer to make fresh coffee.

"I know," Zhulati said, returning to Irina's comment about laparoscopy. "That's pretty much standard in all donor harvests nowadays." He ran his hand over his stringy hair and shook his head to get some strands off his eye. "We can't do that here," he added. "It takes too long. Besides, we don't have enough crew to help with laparoscopy. It's tough enough as it is."

He took another sip of the coffee, this time without complaint. "If it weren't for you," he looked at Irina with lusty admiration, "Wonder Woman, this whole operation would fail." He was referring to the overall transplant organization.

Irina ignored his gaze and drew a bottle of orange juice from a small refrigerator. "Where else do you work these days?" she asked him.

Even though they had done a number of cases together, Irina did not know much about the surgeon. This was the first time they were chit-chatting.

"Oh, wherever," Zhulati said vaguely. "I am here for the next three months. Cezar scheduled a whole bunch of these for me. Usually, though, I am mostly in Pristina, in Kosovo."

"Is that your hometown?"

"No. I was born in Tirana." It was the capital of Albania. "But my family escaped to Kosovo, where communism was not nearly as bad." He shook his head, remembering his early years. "We lived in Gjakova, near the Albanian border. Do you know it?"

Irina said no.

"I'm not surprised. Wild, mountainous country. Middle of nowhere."

"How did you become a doctor?" she asked, with a tone of disbelief. She had been wondering that for a while.

Zhulati was not offended. "Stroke of good luck," he said. "My school was offered a university slot in Belgrade. In those days, Kosovo was part of Yugoslavia, as you know."

Irina nodded.

"Anyhow, they chose me. I don't know why. I was a screwed-up kid but I excelled in math, and they thought I had promise."

"Somehow I do believe that you were screwed up as a child," Irina said dryly.

Zhulati emitted a big laugh, his belly quivering beneath his scrubs. He pointed his index finger at her. "You devil, you! How about a night with me, sweet lady? You'll never forget it."

For once, Irina agreed with the man. She finished the rest of her juice in one gulp and decided to change the subject.

"Iancu and Nicolae are dead," she said abruptly.

The statement caught Zhulati by surprise. "What?"

"They were assassinated in Budapest."

Zhulati's eyes went wide. He stood up from his chair, momentarily speechless.

"Who told you that?"

"Enver," said Irina. "Just before we started our case this morning."

Zhulati looked around the room. "Where is Enver, anyway?"

"He went home to get some rest. He was up all night, bringing the donor."

Zhulati sank back in his chair. He rubbed his forehead.

"Enver thinks that it is related to what we do here." Even though she did not care much for Zhulati, Irina felt that he needed to know.

"Someone has a beef with what we're doing here." Irina was somber. "Do you have any idea who that might be?"

"No," said Zhulati. "I just do what they hired me to do. I don't get involved with anything else."

"Well, I think *this organization*," Irina put a sarcastic emphasis on the phrase, "may be kaput!"

The nurse anesthetist peeked into the kitchen. "Are you guys ready?"

Irina turned her attention to the anesthetist. "Do you need a break?"

"No," he said. "Let's move on. I'd rather finish early."

Zhulati got up and shuffled toward the door, his head slumped forward.

As they followed the anesthetist in the dark hallway toward the operating room, Irina whispered in his ear. "Don't think about it now," she advised him, "just focus on your case." Zhulati nodded in submission.

"This may be your last." She added, "I know it is *my* last."

CHAPTER 9

BRAŞOV, MARCH 29 ... AFTERNOON

Irina gazed at the house, wondering if she should ring. It was late afternoon and she had not heard from Enver. It was unlike him when he had promised to call.

Irina had texted him multiple times from Martinu Hospital and received no response. The day had ended uneventfully, Zhulati completing the transplant on a wealthy Israeli who, thankfully, had brought along his own private nurse to oversee his recovery at an Airbnb apartment he had rented. This freed up Irina early. Impulsively, she decided to go to Enver's without changing out of her scrubs. She hoped that maybe he had overslept.

Now, standing across the street from Enver's door, she hesitated.

The house was an ancient, rickety two-story building on a narrow, slanted cobblestoned street, not unlike most others in this neighborhood. The area was residential and quiet. Irina noted a car parked in front of the house, a small dark Škoda sedan. Most of the inhabitants in the quarter did not own cars, and if they did, rarely parked them on this narrow street. It impeded traffic. Irina had parked her own car two blocks away on a wider street. She did not know what to make of the Škoda.

Irina knew the house well. She had stayed there, spent some nights with Enver. There were only two people who lived in the building, Enver upstairs and that old hag, his landlady, downstairs.

She'd had a run-in with the woman one morning when the landlady let herself into Enver's apartment after he departed and discovered Irina coming out of the shower. Words were exchanged, the old woman calling her a slut and a whore. Irina had practically thrown the woman out, dragging her by the collar, calling her a witch.

Afterwards, Enver installed a chain lock on the door to prevent a repeat confrontation. Irina did not understand why Enver gave the old woman such free rein over his apartment. There were other ways to feed his cat. But she did not argue with him on the issue. Enver's life was his own, and what they had with each other, Irina knew well, was a passing fling. Let him live as he wished.

Now, amid the calm and silence of the neighborhood, Irina was concerned about running into the old lady if Enver did not answer. And what was that car doing there? Did the old lady have a visitor? There was only one way to find out.

Just as Irina mustered enough courage to start across the street, she was stopped by another vehicle that gave her a chill. It was a white van with black trim and no windows aside from its cab. It sped around the curve and stopped behind the Škoda. On the side, where the windows should have been, were large black block letters: CORONER.

Two officers emerged from the van and opened its back door, pulling out a stretcher. Just then, the door of the building opened and Irina saw the unmistakable visage of her nemesis, the old hag.

"What's all this?"

Startled, Irina turned to find a corpulent middle-aged woman wearing a tent-like dress and house slippers, her hair disheveled, standing by her side.

"I don't know," she answered. "Do you?"

"Me neither," the woman said. "I've been watching the house." She pointed to a window in her own house, close to where Irina was standing.

"That car," she said, pointing to the Škoda. "I think it is an unmarked police car."

"How do you know?"

"I saw the two guys that came out of it. They went into old Rădulescu's place."

"Who?"

"Elena Rădulescu, the old woman who lives there."

Irina realized that she had never found out the witch's name.

"Then you show up," the woman looked Irina up and down, "in your uniform."

Irina regretted not changing out of her scrubs. It made her stand out.

"And now this." The woman concluded by pointing to the coroner's van.

Irina realized that this woman would be less problematic if Irina could persuade her to go across the street and check up on what was happening. She forced her face into a smile.

"My name is Irina Cernea." Irina extended her hand to the fat woman. "I am a friend of Enver, the landlady's tenant."

The woman did not shake Irina's hand, and eyed her suspiciously.

"You see," Irina continued hesitantly, "he and I were to meet this afternoon." Irina tilted her head and looked down at the ground as though ashamed.

When she looked back up, the woman's expression had changed from suspicion to curiosity. Her lips parted into a slight smile.

"And he didn't show up," Irina added.

"You and that young guy," said the woman, her smile now more prominent. "I wouldn't have guessed."

"The landlady," Irina tilted her head in the direction of the house, "she doesn't like me."

The woman let out a laugh. "So what else is new? She doesn't like anyone. She is a crotchety old bitch."

Irina responded to her laugh with one of her own, though forced. "Do you mind going across and finding out what's going on?"

The woman needed little persuasion. She marched across the street, her long mumu sweeping the street, her slippered feet stumbling in her haste.

As it turned out, she did not need to ring the bell of the building. Two men emerged from the door and almost bumped into her. One was old and pudgy, the other young and handsome. They both wore dark suits, the older man with a short, loose tie that highlighted his prominent gut, the younger man with an open shirt collar and a half-zipped windbreaker with a police insignia on the chest.

Irina watched as the neighbor woman conversed with the pair. The older man quickly brushed her aside and entered the passenger seat of the Škoda. The young one, however, talked to her for a bit and handed her something before entering the driver side.

As the Škoda sped off, the woman waddled back across the street.

"Well," she said, in a satisfied voice. "It appears that your concern was not unfounded."

She looked at a business card she had in her hand. "I was right. Those two were police." She paused and waited for Irina's reaction.

"Yes?" asked Irina impatiently.

"They didn't tell me much but they confirmed that a dead body was found inside." She looked back at the house. "Suicide."

Irina's heart sank as the big woman continued. "It's not Elena," she said smugly, "so it has to be your friend."

"Thank you," Irina whispered, trying to hold back tears. She stared at the house as she pondered what the woman said. Suicide? Enver? It did not make sense. She wondered if she should still go in. No use, she thought, neither the landlady nor the coroner's people would allow her in.

As Irina turned back to walk to her car, the neighbor woman stopped her. "Here," she shouted. She held out her right hand. "That policeman I spoke with gave me this. You might have more use for it."

It was a business card with the insignia of Braşov Police. Irina took it and looked at the name. Andrei Costiniu.

She turned around without thanking the woman, and got in her car.

CHAPTER 10

TUZLA, MARCH 29

A s the late-model BMW inched along heavy traffic on the way to the suspension bridge, Mark looked down at the Mosque perching on its European pillars. The Ortaköy Mosque, with its slim, ornate minarets that resembled lit candles, was an iconic Baroque gem. It had been there since 1856. The bridge, the first to span the Bosporus, was completed in 1973. Together they became a symbol of Istanbul, old and new, Eastern and Western.

Mark thought about the photo of the Ortaköy mosque and Bosporus Bridge on a Budapest van that had helped save him from a kidnapping. It belonged to an illegal business, a chop shop operated by a group of affable Turks. *Bosporus Autojavitas*, it was called, Bosporus car repair. The men had smuggled Mark into Turkey in one of their larger trucks amid numerous car parts.

A month ago, in his ho-hum life as a radiologist in San Francisco, Mark could not have imagined being associated with people like that. Now here he was, heading to dinner with yet another shady character.

The back of the BMW was accoutered with plush leather seats and a spacious armrest. The driver, a dark-skinned man, polite and quiet, appeared to be Arabic. He spoke Turkish with a heavy accent.

Aside from a greeting at the Hyatt, he said little, leaving Mark to his thoughts during the long drive to Tuzla.

Traffic over the bridge was slow. Mark viewed the majestic body of water below, numerous large and small sea vessels crisscrossing the strait in all directions. The Old City stood in the far distance, its hilltop mosques gleaming in the late afternoon twilight.

Mark remembered that not so long ago he had crossed another majestic bridge, the Elizabeth, which spans the Danube River in Budapest. He had traversed the Elizabeth in the middle of the night, heading toward what turned out to be a violent bloodbath at a bathhouse called Rudas. The scenes would be etched forever in Mark's memory. Iancu floating dead in a Jacuzzi, his severed hand on the steps nearby. Iancu's guard Iosif, bleeding to death at the edge of the Jacuzzi. A Slovak gangster with his throat slit in the *hamam*, the historic Turkish section of the bathhouse.

Mark was eventually captured and imprisoned by the Slovak gangsters who killed Iancu. They then turned Mark over to Moldovan paramilitary operatives, who were to transport him to Chișinău.

Now as the BMW crested the curve of the Bosporus Bridge and began descending toward the Asian side of the city, Mark shuddered at the thought of all the havoc that his crossing of the Elizabeth had wreaked. Was he headed for further trouble at his dinner with Gazioğlu?

Mark knew this would be more than an evening at a luxurious seaside villa with a fellow doctor. Gazioğlu was not just any physician—he was an international fugitive, wanted for performing illegal surgeries. Having studied the man, Mark was curious about Gazioğlu. He looked forward to the dinner.

The BMW cleared the bridge and plunged into a dense urban landscape. Mark no longer recognized where he was. The Asian side used to be mostly barren hills during his childhood, when there were no bridges crossing the Bosporus. In those days the two continents were connected by slow, cumbersome car ferries that required long waits at their respective piers. Istanbul was a split city then, its

European and Asian sides distinct from each other geographically and culturally.

It was not unlike San Francisco, which, before the Golden Gate Bridge, was similarly disconnected from Marin County. Mark found San Francisco, his adopted hometown, peculiarly redolent of Istanbul, his city of birth. Both were pairs of peninsulas facing each other across narrow straits. Marin County blossomed into a plush, luxurious collection of suburban towns, thanks to the bridge. Sausalito, a sleepy fishing village at its foothills, turned into a swank, scenic tourist resort with super-expensive houses terraced along its steep hills, a Côte d'Azur by the Bay.

The Asian side of Istanbul, however, unlike Marin County, seemed to have experienced wild, uncontrolled growth. High-rise residences had sprouted everywhere like mushrooms, covering those barren hills with a dense tapestry of ugly urban architecture. Two more bridges had been built across the Bosporus, continuing to fuel the incessant sprawl.

Mark stopped surveying his surroundings, settling back into the seat and closing his eyes. He thought about Tarık, Günsu's son. Tarık had offered to drive him to Tuzla but Mark had refused. He did not want this young man embroiled in any potential misadventure.

Mark recalled Tarık's appearance, still startled. The youngster was a spitting image of his biological father, of whom he was unaware. He seemed to hate Ahmet with a passion. Mark wondered if Ahmet had known that Tarık was his son. He had neglected to pose the question to Günsu. Anyhow, it no longer mattered, now with Ahmet gone.

Mark felt that maybe he should set the score straight with the young man and reveal the truth. But was this appropriate? Mark had appeared out of nowhere after decades of absence from Turkey. He would soon disappear—he hoped—back to America. What right did he have to disrupt the order that Günsu had imposed on her own life and that of her son?

The BMW turned off the freeway and into less crowded streets, heading toward the Marmara coast. They were getting closer to Gazioğlu. Mark scrutinized his whereabouts with interest.

The driver entered a small two-lane road, not far from the seashore, surprisingly devoid of the dense housing prevalent everywhere else. Clumps of vegetation lined the road with gaps here and there, affording brief glimpses of the sea.

Soon tall cypress trees lined the road, darkening the landscape further. They passed large estates, each fenced off, some with huge mansions visible within the vast properties. They were obviously in an exclusive seaside enclave.

* * *

Gazioğlu's house was not visible from the road. The driver used an electronic remote to operate a large wrought iron gate that opened onto a narrow road. Mark noted two prominent closed-circuit TV monitors on each side. The BMW then traversed a vast orchard via a packed dirt road, faintly lit with low-lying lanterns inserted into the ground.

As they drew closer to the villa, with the road now paved, they encountered a security guard who bore a rifle slung across his right shoulder. He and the driver exchanged a few words in Arabic, and the driver chuckled. The guard saluted Mark as the BMW proceeded to the main door of the villa. Mark again noted video cameras at each end of the driveway, mounted atop slender light fixtures.

The large walnut door of the house, richly ornamented with detailed hand-carved woodwork, opened to reveal a strikingly statuesque woman. She nodded to the driver, who discharged his passenger, and then extended a welcoming hand to Mark. Her arm was long and pale, her hand delicate, with well-manicured red nails. Several gold bracelets gleamed around her wrist.

"*Hoşgeldiniz*," she said, with a slightly hoarse voice that instantly enthralled Mark. *Welcome.*

Mark shook her hand and stood still, eyeing the woman up and down. She was surprisingly tall, almost reaching Mark's own height of six feet. She wore a long white evening gown with thin straps on the shoulders and a slit running down the left from waist to foot. It afforded a provocative glimpse of her pale, shapely leg. Her face was also elongated, dark eyes highlighted heavily with eyeliner, black hair pulled back into a bun. She was an Erté, Mark thought, an elegant Art Deco statue, with ample breasts despite her slender figure.

"*Doktor* Mark," she said, "I am Semra." She smiled, revealing two slight gaps in her front teeth that somehow added to her allure. Her lips were thin and wide, bearing a subtle shade of red lipstick.

Mark stood frozen in place, staring at this unexpected apparition, finally returning her greeting in Turkish.

Semra turned and extended her long arm in the direction of the interior. "*Buyrun.*" She beckoned him in.

The house had a large, well-lit foyer with a grandiose staircase that curved toward the second floor. Beyond the foyer was a living room with picture windows that, even from this distance, afforded striking glimpses of the Marmara coast, with the lights of Büyükada, the largest of the Princes' Islands, twinkling in the distance. On one side of the grand room was an American-style bar and off to the other, an open kitchen with modern amenities. The house was obviously not an old Ottoman relic but rather, something recently built.

Semra walked ahead of Mark, revealing a deep décolletage on her back down to the curve of her buttocks. She had exquisitely pale, delicate skin. She moved elegantly on high-heeled sandals, her long toes as well pedicured as her manicured fingers.

"Ahh, here you are!" Gazioğlu was in a corner of the bar mixing drinks. His cheerful greeting broke Mark's Semra-induced trance. Gazioğlu walked over with two martini glasses that held orange-pink drinks and handed one to Semra, who towered over him. He reached up and gave her a delicate peck on the lips.

He then faced his guest and lifted his own glass in a silent toast, eyeing Mark up and down with a wide grin. He took a sip, set the glass on a nearby stand, and rushed Mark with a tight hug as if the two were long-lost brothers.

Shocked by the gesture, Mark stood like a statue—though not an elegant one like Semra—waiting for the hug to end. Gazioğlu smelled heavily of Old Spice. It made Mark queasy. He turned his head away, hoping that his gesture would not be taken as an insult.

The Turkish doctor finally disengaged and pulled back, Semra sidling to him. He placed his arm around her delicate waist. "I see you met my sweetheart."

In striking contrast to Semra's elegance, Gazioğlu was dressed casually in a short-sleeved khaki shirt and matching slacks. His small gut highlighted a prominent belt buckle shaped like an eagle. He admired Semra through wire-rimmed glasses. They made an odd couple, these two, thought Mark, Gazioğlu a man about his own age, and this striking young woman most likely in her late twenties.

"May I offer you a drink? Martini, daiquiri, cosmo?"

"A martini will do." Mark was wary of getting drunk at this encounter, but it would be rude to refuse. "Vodka. On the rocks."

As Gazioğlu turned toward the bar, a man appeared from the kitchen, carrying various food items. He wore a white chef's uniform with an exceptionally high toque that gave him a comic theatrical look. Semra glided over to him and exchanged some words that Mark could not hear.

Stuck by himself, Mark walked over to the picture windows and surveyed a nighttime scene of exquisite beauty. On one side, the horizon was lined with the Anatolian coast of the Sea of Marmara, its lights reflecting off the glassy water, evoking the Mediterranean Riviera. Mark gathered that the house was situated on a peninsula jutting into the sea to afford such a view. On the other side was a sea horizon in fading crimson as night descended. There, beyond the front garden, sparsely lit with lanterns, Büyükada loomed with its own lights, their reflections extending all the way to Tuzla in a striking tableau. A few vessels glided on the dark, calm sea, their blurry reflections moving in synch.

"Semra dear," Mark heard Gazioğlu shout, "why don't you show our guest the garden?"

Once more, Mark stood still as a statue, and the Erté floated toward him.

CHAPTER 11

TUZLA, MARCH 29

Mark followed Semra along a dim dirt path that curved around dark shrubbery. The evening was cool and crisp, the air salty with the smell of the sea. The front garden of the villa was vast, the shrubbery opening up to an empty lawn with a gazebo and benches. They faced the Sea of Marmara behind a low sea wall.

"Büyükada," Semra said, pointing her cocktail glass toward the dark mound in the horizon glittering with lights. Mark nodded. He stepped ahead of her, closer to the sea wall, and took in the view.

"Isn't it gorgeous here?" Semra moved closer to him. Her Turkish had a hint of Anatolian accent, suggesting a peasant stock that clashed with her urbane elegance. Mark caught an alluring whiff of her floral perfume. It melded well with the scents of the sea.

"How long have you lived here?" Mark asked.

"Oh, about a year." She was nonchalant. "Mahmut goes through girlfriends like shirts." She chuckled and took a sip of her drink. "I am the latest."

Mark eyed her curiously. "It doesn't bother me," she explained. "I am here to enjoy the ride, however long it lasts."

"You're not from Istanbul, are you?"

Semra curtseyed in a subtle gesture, as if congratulating him for his correct guess. "Mardin," she said.

Mardin was a godforsaken corner of southeastern Turkey along the Syrian border. Surprised, Mark wondered what her story was. How had she shed her rustic roots and transformed herself?

They were interrupted by Gazioğlu, who emerged from the dark with Mark's martini. He handed it over and raised his own glass for another toast. "*Şerefe*," they all said, clinking their glasses, a traditional Turkish toast.

Semra announced that she had to check on the chef's progress and headed back to the house. Gazioğlu offered Mark a seat at a bench near the sea wall and plopped down on the wall, between two lanterns, facing Mark with his back to the sea.

"You have a magnificent place here," said Mark. "I didn't expect to find such a property in Tuzla. It is more like villas on the Bosporus, or Moda."

Gazioğlu nodded modestly, then turned back to observe the seascape behind. "I bought this place soon after the 1999 earthquake."

Mark recalled the quake. Its epicenter in Gölcük, on the Asian outskirts of the city, the earthquake had been powerful enough to devastate that side of Istanbul and create a major scare in the entire metropolis.

"It was actually two estates, both old buildings that suffered damage," he continued. He turned back to Mark. "We tore them down and built this." He nodded behind Mark toward his villa.

"It's so peaceful here," Mark commented.

"Yeah," Gazioğlu confirmed. "It's a refuge. My safe place."

Gazioğlu's crouched figure formed a peculiar foreground to the magnificent night scene. The stark lights of nearby lanterns threw eerie shadows onto his sharply etched face. He seemed a tired, lonely figure in this light, not the arrogant, defiant rebel of Mark's internet research.

The man did indeed need a refuge, thought Mark. This remote spot in Tuzla, with its security guards, CCTV monitors, and who knows what else, was perfect for him. Yet Mark couldn't help but wonder how long Gazioğlu's peace would last. Storms were raging all around, international police hunting him, not to mention an Eastern European gang that had assassinated his past associates. Was the surgeon's life here in Tuzla as secure as he seemed to think?

Gazioğlu rose. "Come," he said. "Let's go back. The chef should be ready by now."

He took Mark through another path that led to the back porch of the villa through the side of the garden.

"I understand that you went to English High School," he said to Mark.

Mark nodded. Gazioğlu had obviously done some homework of his own.

"Where did you go to medical school?" Gazioğlu continued his query.

"UCSF," Mark answered. "San Francisco. And you?"

"For high school I went to Robert College." It was an elite private American prep school with a scenic campus on the hills overlooking the Bosporus. "Then to Cerrahpaşa for medical school."

"And where did you specialize in transplants?"

"Paris." Gazioğlu stopped and gazed at a distant side gate at the other end of the villa that separated the front driveway from the side of the house. "H'mmm," he murmured. "Someone left this open."

He proceeded briskly down a spacious path toward the gate. There was a prominent toolshed by the side of the house that partially obstructed the view of the gate. Mark waited near the shed and took a final sip of his now warm martini. He scrutinized the back of the villa, which was not as ornate as the front. More CCTV monitors were mounted along the edges of the house.

He soon heard loud clicking of metal on metal as Gazioğlu closed the gate.

"Sorry," he said as he reappeared, sliding his arm into Mark's. "This way." He led Mark into the villa via the back porch. "They should not have left that side gate open," he said to himself. Then, more loudly, "What were we talking about?"

"You trained in Paris," Mark prompted him.

"Oh, yes! At Necker Hospital, with Cukier and Beurton."

Mark had no idea who they were. Famous transplant pioneers, he figured. "How come you came back?" asked Mark.

The man was obviously ambitious. Mark figured his prospects would have been better in Europe. Gazioğlu disengaged Mark's arm and gazed at him thoughtfully. "I often ask myself that same question," he said ruefully.

The house was warm and humid. A strong aroma of onions and spices emanated from the kitchen, reminding Mark that he was hungry. He set down his martini glass and waited for his host to step in.

Gazioğlu continued with his train of thought. "You know, they did offer me a position in Paris." He led Mark toward the dining room off to one side of the kitchen. "Who knows," he said with an ironic smile. "Had I stayed there, I might have turned out like you."

* * *

Dinner began with escargot served within the shells, presented on six-hole escargot plates. They sat at one end of a long banquet table in the dining room, an alcove off the large living room. Still-life oil paintings lined the walls. Gazioğlu sat at the head of the table, Mark and Semra flanked him on each side.

Mark was surprised with the first course. Right before the meal, Gazioğlu had introduced him to the chef, who was also serving them in his white uniform and toque. He was in his sixties, tall and surprisingly slim, with a thick white moustache, formal and polite. According to Gazioğlu, the man was one of the best from Gaziantep, a southeastern Turkish city well known for its unique indigenous cuisine. Mark had expected a traditional Turkish meal, not French escargot.

Semra pushed her plate away with a revolted expression. "I don't know how you can eat such disgusting insects."

Gazioğlu delicately picked up a shell with a silver forceps. He then deftly extracted the snail within using a miniature fork, ceremoniously placing it in his mouth, his pinky finger extended in an exaggerated gesture.

"M'mmm," he said teasingly. He eyed Semra as though she were an ill-behaved child. "It's not an insect, my dear," he corrected her, "it's a mollusk."

Semra took a fresh roll and coarsely tore a large piece off it. She dipped it in olive oil and ate, petulantly staring at a painting. It featured a duck carcass in the foreground, decapitated, its bloody neck hanging off the table.

"Isn't she a lovely child?" Gazioğlu addressed Mark, still teasing.

Mark had already consumed most of his escargot. It was rich and buttery, seasoned with just the right amount of garlic, a perfect beginning to a banquet. He licked two fingers and turned an admiring glance at Semra. "Very lovely."

The remark melted away her sulk. She turned to Mark and gave him a wide, toothy grin, once again revealing her imperfect smile. "Thank you," she said with a polite nod. She turned to Gazioğlu and stuck out her tongue at him.

Gazioğlu laughed heartily.

"Where did you find such a gem?" Mark pointed at Semra with his escargot fork.

"In Beyoğlu, where else?"

"I was an aspiring star in Yeşilçam," she said proudly.

Beyoğlu was a busy entertainment district in the heart of European Istanbul, full of restaurants, taverns, coffeehouses, theaters, bookshops, and countless other, seedier offerings. Yeşilçam, a side street in the district, was synonymous with Turkey's once-vibrant movie industry, Istanbul's Hollywood. Mark didn't know if there was much moviemaking going on any more.

"Well," said Gazioğlu, "let's say that she had a long way to go." He winked at Semra. "A long, long way."

Semra raised a water glass and made a gesture as though she was going to throw it at him. Gazioğlu let out another big laugh.

They were interrupted by the chef, who presented them with the next course, another surprise. "*Kereviz kökü*," he announced. Celery root.

Mark stared at his plate. It featured celery root, peeled, cored and sliced, cooked in olive oil, served with diagonally sliced carrots, also cooked. It was a traditional Turkish dish that Mark had not tasted since childhood. He took a generous slice. The tangy flavor of the celery was perfect, its texture exquisite, its natural bitterness well masked by the oily sauce. Now it was Mark's turn to say "M'mmm."

The chef offered drinks, *rakı* or white wine. Mark could not refuse the *rakı*, a traditional Turkish liquor, similar to the Greek ouzo, with a strong anise flavor. Served in slim, tall cylindrical glasses, it was a strong and clear drink when taken straight up. Mark diluted his with plenty of water and ice. The drink turned milky white.

Gazioğlu took his *rakı* straight up, then plopped the glass down and stared at it contemplatively. "Isn't it amazing, Doctor," he addressed Mark, "that Turkey is the only Muslim country in the world with a national drink that is 45 percent alcohol!"

Mark had never thought of *rakı* that way. "Yes," he answered, chuckling.

"*Ne mutlu Türküm diyene,*" proclaimed Gazioğlu. It was a favorite saying of Atatürk, the founder of modern Turkey. *How happy it is to proclaim that one is a Turk.*

Perhaps it was the *rakı* taking hold, but Mark found himself thinking that this doctor he had scorned for his errant ways was actually a pretty likeable guy. In another world, under different circumstances, they could have been friends.

Semra ignored the two men and silently went to work on her celery root dish. She ate in a hurry, shoveling the food in large chunks that puffed her cheeks. Her manners betrayed her Mardin origins.

The main course was tournedos Rossini, a rich dish of filet mignon topped with foie gras and doused with a heavy sauce. A traditional red Bordeaux was served with it, poured from a crystal decanter.

Gazioğlu explained the history of the dish. Apparently the famous opera composer Gioachino Rossini had retired to Paris at a young age and become a gourmand, a glutton to be exact. This exceptionally heavy dish was created in his honor by a Parisian chef. Semra inquired what was atop the meat.

Gazioğlu cut himself a generous bite of foie gras, dipped it in the sauce and ate. "Duck liver paté," he told her. "It's a delicacy, very expensive."

She pushed the foie gras off her meat and cut into the tournedos. Gazioğlu reached over and picked hers up onto his plate.

"I left France a long time ago," he told Mark, "but France never left me." He took a sip of the Bordeaux. "Excellent," he commented. "Nineteen eighty-nine, it was a good vintage."

Mark wanted to remain sober but the wine was beguiling, as was Semra. He took another generous sip and stared at her.

Semra returned his gaze. She picked her tooth with a long fingernail and said to Mark, "I hear you are a secret agent." She regarded him expectantly, her ornately shaded eyes searing Mark's cheeks into a blush.

Embarrassed, Mark hoped that maybe his red cheeks would be blamed on the wine. "No, I'm not. I'm just a doctor, like Mahmut."

Semra turned to her lover, puzzled. "Didn't you tell me"— pointing her fork at Mark—"that he was sort of like…a James Bond?" She turned back to Mark. "They said that you took care of some pretty atrocious gangsters in Hungary."

Mark was taken aback. Gazioğlu seemed to know more about Budapest than Mark had expected.

Gazioğlu glanced nervously at Mark. "Okay, baby, that's enough." He gently placed his hand on Semra's. "He said he was just a doctor. He is just a doctor. Now, finish your meat." He sounded like an impatient father quieting a wayward child.

Semra did as she was told, but not before giving Mark another quizzical glance. Her face lit up with a smile, this time lips closed. It captivated Mark.

Mark kept throwing furtive glances at Semra for the rest of the meal. Her elongated figure appeared to him like a creature from a Manneristic post-Renaissance painting. He had never quite encountered such a woman, so coarse and yet elegant, so childish and yet mature, so awkward and yet sexy.

They journeyed back to Turkey with dessert, *künefe*, shredded phyllo with melted cheese within, served with a healthy wallop of sugary syrup. This one came with a generous helping of *kaymak*, giving Mark his second delightful encounter with the clotted cream.

Afterwards Gazioğlu invited Mark to retire to a spacious study off the living room. It too had picture windows that opened to the Sea of Marmara. Semra brought them Turkish coffee, proudly announcing that she had made it herself. She leaned over and kissed Gazioğlu, who had settled into a deep couch facing the windows. It was a long, sultry kiss. She then gave Mark a playful wave as she exited the study to retire to her bedroom.

Mark sat on another couch and turned around, craning his neck after her fading figure, his gaze fixated on her bare back.

"Exquisite, isn't she?" said Gazioğlu.

Mark barely heard him. He was hypnotized by Semra. He gawked after her until she completely disappeared. When he finally turned around, Gazioğlu had extended a box at him. "Cigar?"

Mark politely refused.

"Do you mind if I smoke?" Gazioğlu asked.

Then, without waiting for an answer, he lit one up and took a couple of puffs, staring ahead at the dark horizon. Afterwards he took the cigar between two fingers, smelled it, and inspected it.

"She is a diamond in the rough," he continued about Semra. "I am still polishing her, as I'm sure you noticed."

Mark nodded and didn't know how to answer. He was much taken by Semra, aroused in a way that for some reason made him uncomfortable.

Gazioğlu rested back into his couch and murmured audibly. "There is one thing in which she needs no refinement," he began. He leaned forward and locked eyes with Mark.

"She gives an amazing blow job."

His dark eyes twinkled behind his wire-rimmed glasses.

CHAPTER 12

TUZLA, MARCH 29

The room filled with the earthy, floral aroma of cigar smoke. Out in the distance, a ferry was making its way from Büyükada back to the mainland. Gazioğlu's study was dimly lit. They both sat silently, their sights on the sea, the only sound in the room that of an occasional puff Gazioğlu took from his cigar.

"Smells nice." Mark eventually broke the silence.

"Cuban," said Gazioğlu. "Cohiba."

Mark was not impressed. He knew nothing about cigars. Tipsy from the Bordeaux, full from the heavy meal, and with Semra's exotic figure dancing in his mind, Mark momentarily forgot what he was here for. He closed his eyes.

"So," Gazioğlu said loudly, startling Mark. He opened his eyes to find the surgeon standing in front of his chair, towering over him. "It's time to fill me in on what happened in Budapest."

Abruptly awakened, Mark was annoyed. "You tell me. You obviously know most of it already."

This provoked a quizzical look from the surgeon.

"Semra," Mark explained, referring to the comment she had made about Mark being a secret agent. "How did she know?"

Gazioğlu withdrew toward the windowsill and sat on the edge, blocking the view. "I have my own spies," he said arrogantly, and took another puff of his cigar.

"I figured," Mark responded, himself quite firm. "You must be well connected with local police. How else could you circulate in the city with an Interpol Red Alert in your name?"

Gazioğlu stiffened but did not respond.

"I bet they provide you with intelligence, too."

"It costs me dearly," Gazioğlu acknowledged.

"No doubt."

Gazioğlu leaned back and crossed his legs. "You know, I am beginning to think that what they say about you is correct. You're not just a radiologist, are you?"

Mark smiled. "Can't you tell, after all your research about me?"

The earlier collegial tone of the evening, two doctors socializing, had evaporated. Gazioğlu seemed eager to spar with Mark. "What I don't understand," he said, "is where exactly you deviated from being a regular doctor."

"My sentiments exactly!" Mark was fervent. "I've been wondering the same thing about you ever since I heard your name. Where did *you* deviate?"

"Hey!" Gazioğlu nearly shouted. "I never deviated. I am still a doctor, a surgeon, and a damn good one at that!"

"Really?" Mark said sarcastically. He knew he was provoking the man but didn't care.

"I am doing great service to humanity!" Gazioğlu was now genuinely shouting. "Do you know that?"

Mark fixed him with a cynical smile.

"I am the best damn transplant surgeon in the world!" He continued shouting. "Do you know that my five-year kidney survival rate is 84.7 percent? Now, you take that against any other major transplant center anywhere."

The number was meaningless to Mark. He had no idea what the benchmark was and he did not care.

"I have performed hundreds of transplants. If you count the surgeons I trained, I am responsible for thousands of successful kidney recipients. Up until now, I haven't killed or harmed anybody."

"Yeah?" Mark said in a mocking tone. "What about that young man in the airport in Kosovo?"

Mark was reminding Gazioğlu of the episode that had gotten him in trouble with international law enforcement. A Turkish man had fainted in Pristina Airport, in shock from blood loss, provoking an investigation that led to the discovery that he had been a paid donor. An illicit transplant ring was eventually uncovered, with Gazioğlu as its chief surgeon.

"That man was not harmed." Gazioğlu was defensive. "He is alive and well, to this day." The surgeon paused to contain his emotions. "*Eşek oğlu*," he said through his teeth, *son of a donkey*. It was a mild Turkish swear phrase.

Mark wasn't sure whether the cuss was meant for the Kosovo victim or him.

"It's surgery," Gazioğlu continued more calmly, finally getting a hold of himself. "Complications happen. You should know that."

Yes, of course, Mark thought, *there is no such thing as complication-free surgery*. Nonetheless, he answered with, "Speaking of complications. Let me tell you about one."

The surgeon leaned forward curiously.

"Have you heard of a man named Dima Rusu?"

Gazioğlu thought for a moment.

"A Moldovan in his twenties, a donor. His kidney was harvested in Braşov, Romania."

Gazioğlu's eyebrows furrowed. He obviously did not know the name. "When?" he asked. "I haven't been to Braşov," he thought for a moment, "in quite a long time."

"I am not sure." Mark remained composed. He had the upper hand. "Earlier this year, not too long ago."

"Go on." Gazioğlu puffed on his cigar.

Mark stood up and approached the window that Gazioğlu sat by. He looked out into the dark night beyond Büyükada. "As I understand it," he said, not looking at Gazioğlu, "this Dima Rusu was not a willing donor. His kidney was stolen."

"I never ever did that!" Gazioğlu protested.

"You may not have, but those you trained might. You trained some surgeons in Braşov, didn't you?"

Gazioğlu did not answer. He seemed to be contemplating whether to admit to that.

"Come on," Mark urged him. "I am not Interpol. I am not here to apprehend you."

No answer.

"You trained surgeons who worked for Nicolae Radu and Iancu Negrescu, right?"

Gazioğlu kept silent.

"Surgeons who worked for Cezar Kaminesky, maybe?"

That last name seemed to startle him. "How do you know all this?" Gazioğlu asked in a near whisper.

"Radu and Negrescu were both murdered in Budapest, assassinated on two different occasions. I was the one who discovered both bodies. Believe me, I did *not* want to know all this."

Now it was Mark who towered over the surgeon, whose crouched figure seemed to have collapsed into itself.

"Kaminesky," Mark continued, "I never met. But I met his wife, Olga." A very sexy woman, Mark fleetingly recalled. "He had a thing going with Ahmet." He paused and clarified Ahmet. "I mean Nicolae Radu."

"Yes, I know," Gazioğlu finally admitted. "I met Olga way back when. But I thought she and Cezar were separated."

"Olga was living in Budapest. Whether she went there on her own or was sent on a mission, I don't know." Mark was realizing that information was power, and he was enjoying the moment. "But I do know this: Olga aided Radu's assassins. My take on it is that she did it inadvertently. The police, though, are not so sure."

"Do you know who they are, the assassins?" Gazioğlu finally came to the main reason he had invited Mark.

"Their leader is one Vadim Rusu. Do you know the name?"

"No." Then a light bulb appeared to go off inside the surgeon's head. "Wait a minute!"

"Yes," said Mark. "He is Dima Rusu's father. From what I

understand, he is a former Russian operative who heads a paramilitary organization loyal to him. He lives in Moldova nowadays, in Chişinău."

Mark paused to observe his host. Gazioğlu had deposited his cigar on a nearby ashtray and sat at the window ledge looking up at Mark in amazement. This was obviously all news to him.

Mark continued. "He is the one behind the assassinations. He has somehow figured out the transplant ring in Braşov, and he seems to be systematically eliminating its members, whether they were directly involved with his son or not."

"But why?" asked Gazioğlu. "What happened to his son?"

"Dima Rusu was found dead in some shithole hotel in Braşov, presumably from complications of his nephrectomy."

Gazioğlu nervously ran his hand over his bald head. "Oh, my God!"

"So, *Doktor*," Mark used the Turkish pronunciation mockingly, "it is not all complication-free, is it? Even when it's not your own personal complication, it is still tied to you."

Gazioğlu stood up and paced back and forth between the window and his desk, his head bent down, digesting the news.

"Do you think they have a reach into Turkey?"

"I don't know," Mark said. "But let me tell you what I do know: They came after *me*."

The statement stopped the surgeon dead in his tracks.

"You? But why?"

"Well, obviously I'm not involved in all this transplant business. But I landed smack in the middle of their plans and foiled some of them. I am a fly in their ointment. They don't know who I am and why I am meddling. They tried to kidnap and fly me to Moldova. I escaped, and during my rescue, their two operatives, who happened to be the same ones that assassinated Radu, were killed by Hungarian police."

Gazioğlu listened to all this with a slack jaw.

Mark continued. "Now they really want me." He smiled sardonically. "You see, Mahmut"—the first time Mark had addressed Gazioğlu by his first name—"I am also a wanted man. Just like you."

Mark sat at the window ledge, where Gazioğlu had been. He crossed his legs, acting blasé about his predicament. "And I don't have any police protection."

A new silence descended upon them as Gazioğlu absorbed the news. "So, what are you going to do about it?" he asked Mark.

"I have no idea. I am taking it day by day, hoping that Rusu's organization is not tracking me in Turkey."

"Why are you here?"

"To see old friends, one in particular, an old high school classmate."

"You mean you don't have any Interpol-related plans here in Istanbul?"

"No." The question surprised Mark. "Why? Did you hear that I was connected to Interpol?"

"Yes, I did." Gazioğlu was more forthcoming. "I heard you were pretty tight with them. A certain French agent in Hungary."

"Gérard," Mark said with a slight smile, fondly recalling the avuncular Frenchman. "Yes, I suppose I am. But I am not here on any official mission for them."

Gazioğlu repeated his earlier question. "Are you sure you are not a secret agent yourself?"

Mark laughed. This annoying impression bordered on the ridiculous. "Yes, I am sure. I am *not* a secret agent."

Mark looked at his watch. It was getting late and he had a long drive back to his hotel. He asked Gazioğlu if it was possible to summon the chauffeur. The surgeon fired off a text message and beckoned Mark to the front entrance of the villa.

They waited in the spacious foyer, Gazioğlu deep in thought. Mark saw the headlights of an approaching vehicle through the stained glass windows of the magnificent door. Gazioğlu put his arm in Mark's once again and led him toward the door. The tension between them had evaporated as soon as they left Gazioğlu's study.

"Thank you," he said to Mark, "for your candor."

"No problem," Mark responded, eyeing the doctor's hand resting on his forearm. "You needed to know all this."

"I'm sorry you're leaving so soon," said Gazioğlu, as he opened the ornate door. The BMW was already parked in front.

"Me too." Mark shook hands with him. He had meant it. "By the way, you never told me when you went astray."

Gazioğlu let out a hearty laugh. "*You* never told me when *you* went astray."

Mark unclasped his hand and became serious. "In Budapest," he said. "When I discovered the dead body of my best friend from high school." He turned and walked toward the waiting car. "Maybe another time, we can discuss all this and more."

"Yes, most certainly."

Gazioğlu nodded to the driver. As Mark fastened his seat belt, Gazioğlu leaned in for one more word. "This Rusu," he said anxiously, "do you think he is after me too?"

"I don't know. But I doubt it," Mark answered.

This seemed to calm Gazioğlu. Mark swept his arm around. "Besides," he added, "you have nothing to worry about, with all this personal protection and connections to the local police."

"Yes, I suppose," said Gazioğlu. He began closing the door.

Mark got the parting shot. "You're good as gold."

CHAPTER 13

ISTANBUL, MARCH 30 ... EARLY MORNING

Mark arrived back in Istanbul around midnight. The trek back was easier, with light traffic on the Bosporus Bridge. His driver was as taciturn as before, leaving Mark to his thoughts. By now fully sober, Mark relived the evening in his mind. Gazioğlu had been gracious and charming as a host, not the heartless, arrogant monster that he had imagined, although he did have his moments.

The man obviously thought that he was on a mission, same as all good doctors. Never mind that it was a warped mission. True, he did serve those who desperately sought a new life, those who yearned to break the debilitating chains of dialysis. They paid dearly and received a cure. On the other hand, Mark thought, Gazioğlu's mission exploited and abused donors, mostly poor, ignorant men from lower echelons of society.

Furthermore, Mark did not agree with the mechanics of it all, running illicit, unlicensed operating rooms. It created a Wild West free-for-all with virtually no quality control, putting both donors and recipients at risk. Gazioğlu was proud of the high-quality care he provided. He said so repeatedly, both in the *New York Times* article and to Mark's face. In this regard he was probably a rarity.

So if he did good by his patients—clients was a better word—
did Gazioğlu deserve to be punished for it, to be ostracized as he
was, to live a fugitive life? Before meeting the man, Mark was
certain that doctors like him should go to jail. Now, he was not so
sure.

As the BMW climbed the steep hill from Beşiktaş towards
Taksim, his hotel five minutes away, Mark's thoughts turned to
Semra. What a strange, beguiling woman!

Mark wondered why he found her so attractive. She was
awkward in her impossibly tall, flat figure—well, except for her
obviously artificial boobs. Yet she was so feminine in her allure. She
clearly was an Anatolian peasant, one of millions who had migrated
to Istanbul in past decades. Most did not shed their rough-hewn,
rustic stock. Semra was obviously trying to do so, with the aid of her
rich lover. But she was, as her lover pointed out, a work in progress.

The BMW pulled up to the driveway of the hotel, where a
private security guard scanned the car for explosives before letting it
in. Afterwards, as they drove up to the entrance, Gazioğlu's words
about Semra reverberated in Mark's ears. She was skillful with oral
sex. Gazioğlu had described it in vulgar terms, one teenage boy to
another, as Ahmet would have done—as Ahmet had indeed done
years ago, with that prostitute, Yıldız. Ahmet's had been more
shocking, describing anal sex.

In a peculiar way, Gazioğlu's "blow job" comment had further
endeared him to Mark. They were roughly the same age, and under
different circumstances could have been high school mates, as Mark
and Ahmet had been. Mark bet he would have liked the guy back
then.

* * *

He awoke from a deep sleep. His mobile phone was ringing.

"Metin Bey." Mark heard a female voice hurriedly whispering
into the phone.

He did not recognize her. He hesitated, trying to wake up.

86

"Doctor Mark, please don't hang up!" The voice was louder now and equally as rushed. Mark detected a note of fear.

"Who is this?"

"Semra," said the voice. "Remember me from tonight's dinner with Mahmut?"

Suddenly Mark was wide awake. He glanced at the bedside clock. Three-thirty a.m. How had she gotten his number?

Semra continued. "You need to come here and save me. They have invaded the house. They're fighting with Mahmut."

"Who?" said Mark, stunned.

"I don't know. I did not see them. I just heard them." She continued whispering loudly.

"What about your security?"

"I don't know."

"Where are you now?"

"I escaped through my window. I am in the tool shed by the side of the house."

Mark remembered the tool shed.

"Please," Semra pleaded. "Please, I am afraid. I have no one else to turn to."

Mark wondered what to do. He couldn't very well ignore the woman's plea, hang up and go back to sleep. But go back to Tuzla? He had no idea what he would find there or how he would deal with it.

"Okay," he said, as he hurriedly got out of bed. "Stay put. I'll be there as soon as I can."

He did not hear Semra's praise to God and profuse thanks before he hung up. All he could think of was, *Here we go again.*

CHAPTER 14

BRAŞOV, MARCH 31

Andrei Costiniu stared at his blank computer screen. He was to prepare a report on a string of nighttime assaults that he and Boboc were investigating, but his mind kept drifting to the supposed suicide scene he had come upon two days earlier.

He could not let go of the notion that the victim was unlikely to have hung himself. There was something peculiar about the apartment, with Enver's sweater, coat, and keys piled on the dining table, thrown there as if he had just arrived. The refrigerator and pantry were nearly empty. The cat was unfed. It was as if the man was in a hurry to kill himself as soon as he returned home. It didn't make sense to Andrei.

Boboc had convinced him that this was a non-case. How could one guess what people did when the impulse to commit suicide came along? Who knows what they would do?

"Let it go," Boboc had said. "We have more important stuff to work on."

Andrei began typing up what he knew so far about the assault cases when the desk officer downstairs called him.

"There is a woman here, a foreigner. I think I need to send her to you."

"What for?"

"Well," the officer had an apologetic tone, "I have a hard time understanding her, but I gather she has something to do with that suicide you and Boboc looked at the other day."

"Who is she?"

"Some relative of the victim. I can't tell. She insists on speaking with a detective."

Andrei was intrigued. "Send her up."

* * *

The young woman sat across from Andrei, head bent low, eyes on the ankle-length skirt that covered her legs. She wore a dark scarf decorated with floral patterns, knotted under the chin.

"This is Emina Bekic," announced the desk officer, an older man, bald and stocky. He stood directly behind her seat.

The woman stared at Andrei. She looked to be in her late twenties. Her face, devoid of makeup, was bony and gaunt, with sharp angular features. Her dark eyes stood out prominently in her colorless face. They were red and swollen.

"*Zdravo*," she said.

Andrei locked eyes with the desk officer, puzzled. The officer handed him a passport. "Bosnian," he said.

Andrei leafed through the passport, uncertain how to proceed. "*Stii sa vorbesti romaneste?*" *Do you speak Romanian?*

The woman answered with another question in another language. "Do you speak English?"

"Yes."

The young woman's thin lips curved to a slight smile.

"What can I do for you?" Andrei continued, in English.

"I am told that you saw my brother."

"Your brother?"

"His name is Enver Muratovich."

"Oh!" Andrei suddenly put two and two together. This was the woman Ana had treated in the hospital, the one that had led Ana to meet Enver. "I am so sorry," he added respectfully. He asked her how she knew that he and Boboc had been to his brother's apartment.

"The landlady," said Emina. "She told me that the police had been there."

The officer, satisfied that the two of them had established communication, withdrew and disappeared.

"My brother did not kill himself," Emina blurted emphatically, in a near shout. "Suicide is against our religion."

Andrei momentarily ignored this. He needed some clarification. "Where exactly did you come from?"

"Mostar. That's where I live, with my mother and husband." She paused to make sure Andrei understood. "I came to bring my brother home."

"My condolences," said Andrei kindly. "I am sorry for your loss."

"Did you find out who killed him?"

Andrei was taken aback by the young woman's bluntness. He did not answer. She continued without interruption.

"Enver supported us. Sent us money. He visited us every year." Tears welled up in her eyes. "He was coming to visit us next month."

"You know," Andrei said, breaking from his professional demeanor, "we knew him. Me and my wife…"

She looked at him, surprised. She wiped her eyes with a tissue.

"My wife, her name is Ana. She is a nurse. She took care of you the year before last, at the County Hospital. Ana met your brother, when he came to pick you up."

A smile appeared on her face. "Yes, I remember," she said. "She was a very kind lady. I was so scared then. She put me at ease."

"Your brother lives in the same neighborhood as us." Andrei cleared his throat and corrected himself. "Well…lived."

Emina's smile disappeared. She bowed her head and stared at her skirt.

"We ran into him from time to time." Andrei waited for her to look at him again. "We weren't friends or anything. But we did know him."

Her eyes locked on to his. "Well then," she said, firm and serious. "You should know that Enver did not kill himself."

Andrei agreed, but he could not say so. He changed the subject. "When are you going back to Mostar?"

"This afternoon. I have made the funeral arrangements. He will be buried at home, near us."

"Can I have your address and phone number?" He handed her a pen and pad of paper.

Emina scribbled hastily and slid the pad to Andrei.

Andrei handed her a business card. "Here. This is how you can contact me." He stood up and extended his hand. "Thank you for coming here and letting us know."

"Do you know who did this to Enver?" She was emphatic again. She did not rise from her chair.

"No," said Andrei, pulling his hand back. He returned to his chair. "But we will investigate." He felt a pang of guilt. He was making a promise he could not keep.

"Please do, and let me know."

"Can you tell me a bit about Enver?" asked Andrei. He felt a need now to extend the conversation, investigating, he supposed, as he had just promised.

"He was a good man, my brother." She wiped some more tears. "He was the only man left in my family."

"How is that?"

"My father," she said, her voice quavering, "and my two brothers, Enver's older brothers…" She stopped to compose herself. "They were killed during the war. In Srebrenica."

"The massacre?"

She burst into sobs. Andrei was sorry about his blunt choice of words. He knew about the atrocity in 1995, during the Yugoslavian civil war, when eight thousand Muslim men were killed by Bosnian Serbs in Srebrenica.

"I was a little girl then." She continued through her sobs. "Enver was my older brother but he was still a boy. My other brothers were much older."

"How did he come to Romania?"

"My mother," she said, more calmly. "She had a second cousin in Bucharest, Iancu Negrescu. She sent Enver away from the war, to Iancu."

Andrei jotted down the name. "So he has been in Romania for a long time."

Emina nodded. "Yes. Iancu was good to Enver. Like a father. He regularly wrote to my mother and assured us that all was well with him. When he grew up, after the war was over, Iancu sent him back home to visit us. We used to live in Sarajevo but we moved to Mostar after the war, closer to my grandparents."

"What did Enver do here in Romania?"

"You mean work?"

Andrei nodded, pen in hand.

"He worked for Iancu."

Andrei did not jot anything down. He looked at her expectantly.

Emina understood his expression. "Business," she said. "Iancu was in business."

Sensing Andrei's dissatisfaction, she added, "I don't know what business. But Iancu was rich and he paid Enver well. Enver supported us. He regularly sent us money."

"Does your brother have any family here in Romania?"

"Aside from Iancu, no."

"How about friends? A girlfriend?"

"I don't know about that," she said. "But my mother has been searching for a suitable wife for him for years. A good Muslim girl from Bosnia."

"Did Enver have any enemies? Anyone who might want to do him harm?"

"Not that I know of."

"What about this Iancu Negrescu? How can I get in touch with him?"

Emina reached for Andrei's notepad and scribbled a phone number and address under hers.

"We've been trying to call him," she said, as she slid the notepad back to Andrei. "To let him know about Enver. But so far he hasn't answered."

Andrei read what she had written. "Bucharest," he mumbled.

"Yes, Iancu lives in Bucharest."

"Any family? Next of kin?"

"He has a son and daughter there, grown up. My mother may have some contact information for them. I don't."

"All right. Thank you." Andrei got up again, and this time, to his relief, so did she. She quickly searched a pocket in her dress and removed a mobile phone. She handed it to Andrei.

"Here, you might want to take this."

Andrei turned the phone over in his hands. A Samsung Galaxy. He tapped the screen but it did not turn on. He looked at Emina quizzically.

"It is Enver's," she said. "I turned it off."

Andrei thought for a moment. He did not recall seeing a phone in Enver's apartment. "Where did you find this?"

"It was in his coat pocket."

Andrei felt stupid for not searching the coat on the table. But then, Boboc had hurried him, and besides, they did not treat the apartment as a crime scene. "Did you find anything in it? Any note or message to you?"

"I don't know the passcode. So I couldn't get into it."

"Thank you," he said. "We'll look into it." He placed the phone on his desk. "Would you like it back when we're done? It looks like an expensive device."

"No," she answered, her eyes tearing again. "It will be nothing but a reminder…" She trailed off.

"Okay. I'll let you know as soon as I have some information." Andrei once again extended his hand to her. This time she shook it, firmly.

"Please send my regards to your wife. I have never forgotten her kindness."

* * *

Forensics kept a small office in the Sector 1 police station, their main labs being off-site at the coroner's. Andrei Costiniu found a single technician busy at her computer.

"*Salut*," said Andrei.

Katrina Popescu did not look up from her screen. "*Salut*," she answered in a murmur.

She was a waif-like figure, small, thin, and flat. Despite being in her forties, she looked like a teenager. Her sinewy red hair was always in disarray, her green eyes, haunting. She wore no makeup except for some awkwardly applied red lipstick that never quite looked right.

At first Andrei waited patiently for Katrina to finish whatever she was doing. Sensing that this would not happen, he finally said, "Do you have a minute to spare?"

Katrina looked at Andrei, surprised, as though he had just popped in. "Costiniu! What's up?"

"That suicide case in Schei, the other day…"

"Oh, yes. I heard about it."

"Was there any forensics investigation of the scene?"

Katrina raised her eyebrows, surprised at the stupidity of the question. "No," she said disdainfully. "You should know that."

Andrei responded with a downcast look.

"Wasn't it you and Boboc who ruled it a suicide? No foul play?"

"Yes, but I think I am changing my mind."

Katrina's eyes widened. "Does the boss know that?" A shift of this sort required the approval of Traian Dalca, chief of Sector 1.

"No," said Andrei sheepishly.

"Boboc?"

Andrei gave Katrina a helpless look. Boboc, as expected, had been adamant about the issue. Emina Bekic was a distraught family member, he had said, obviously in denial. Didn't all family members go through denial at the initial news of a death? What was the matter with Andrei? Why could he not let this thing go?

Katrina stood up from her desk and approached Andrei.

"Are you doing this in secret?" she whispered, amused. She had to reach up on her tiptoes, her head held high, to get to Andrei's ear.

Andrei smiled and nodded.

Katrina clapped her hands, ran to the door of her office and closed it. She then ran back to her desk and sat down expectantly.

"Okay. Tell me all about it." Her lips were parted into a wide red smile, revealing tobacco-stained teeth.

Andrei did not know Katrina well. She had a reputation around the station as an eccentric genius, aloof but useful. He had not had any close professional dealings with her.

"Why are you so interested all of a sudden?" asked Andrei suspiciously.

"I love a naughty bit of investigation. Come. Tell me." She motioned him to a chair.

"Well," said Andrei, sitting down. "See if you can crack this. It's the guy's phone." He pulled it out of his pocket and handed it to her.

Katrina recoiled in refusal. "How come it's not in an evidence bag?"

Andrei shook his head. "I just got it from a family member, his sister. It's been through who knows what hands. Dusting it for prints will be useless." He rolled the phone in his hand. "Besides, it's not a crime scene. Remember?"

Katrina told him to place the phone on her desk. After giving it a doubtful look, she said again, "Tell me about this case."

"It's mostly a hunch, but I think this guy—his name is Enver Muratovich—may not have committed suicide. He may have been murdered."

"What makes you think that?"

"For beginners, my wife Ana and I kind of knew him. He lives in our neighborhood and we used to run into him. He didn't seem like the type to kill himself."

Katrina shook her head. "Not good enough."

Andrei continued. "Then there was the scene at his apartment. It looked as though he came in from a trip away from home and as soon as he arrived, he killed himself."

Katrina looked at him skeptically. "This is the guy who hung himself, right?"

"Right." Andrei was getting concerned that he wouldn't be able to sell this to Katrina. "Then, today, this guy's sister showed up. From Bosnia. And she tells me the same thing. That he was not the type to even contemplate suicide, let alone do it."

"So how can I help?"

"I don't know," said Andrei, feeling stupid. "How can you?"

Katrina thought for a moment. "This was not treated as a crime scene. No evidence was collected; no photos, no prints, no DNA."

"Correct."

"Well," she said hopefully, "we can see what we can find on our own. Did he own his place?"

"No. He rented."

"In that case we'd better hurry up and check the place out before they clean it and rent it to someone else."

Andrei nodded.

"What about his possessions?" Katrina asked.

"I don't know."

"You're not much of a detective," she said, half-mockingly.

Andrei hung his head and nodded in agreement. "I know, I know."

"Come on, then," she said, standing up. "Let's go. Where did you say this was? Schei?"

She hefted a heavy evidence bag onto her shoulder and was at the door before Andrei was out of his chair. How, he wondered, could this tiny woman haul such a huge bag? Katrina ignored Andrei's stare and gestured for him to exit first. As he passed through the door, she gave him a slap on the bottom. "Happy to help a handsome detective like you."

Startled, Andrei hurried down the stairs and ran to fetch his car. She was right behind him, and as she slid into the passenger seat, she said, "Don't get your hopes up too high."

CHAPTER 15

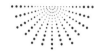

BRAȘOV, MARCH 31

The two-story white clapboard house blended indistinctly with other old ones in Strada Sforii. The street was narrow and curvy. Andrei Costiniu parked his unmarked Škoda a few houses behind. He and Katrina stayed in their seats and stared ahead at the house. It had a pair of windows on each floor.

"First floor is the landlady," said Andrei. "Muratovich lived on the second floor."

"Tell me about the scene again." Katrina craned her neck behind the windshield, intently observing the house. The street was quiet, the house showing no signs of activity.

"No forced entry," Andrei began. "No signs of struggle. He hung himself at the kitchen door. Rope tied to the doorknob on the other side."

"Who found him?"

"The landlady. Apparently she is in and out of the apartment regularly to feed his cat. He goes away on business a lot." Andrei opened the door. "Come on, let's go."

"Any suicide note?" Katrina asked as she exited the car.

"No, none." Andrei glanced at Katrina shouldering her heavy

evidence bag. "You'd better leave that in the car for now. I don't want to spook the landlady. Let's talk to her first."

They had to ring the bell three times before an old woman peeked behind a partially open door. She was short and slightly hunchbacked, her white hair running below her shoulders in an unruly, knotted mess. She had a crooked aquiline nose. She looked at Andrei with baleful blue eyes that stood out on her pale, wrinkly face.

"*Salut,*" said Andrei, giving the woman a military salute.

"*Cine ești tu?*" she responded in a raspy, hoarse voice. *Who are you?*

"*Politie.*" Andrei took out his identification. The woman threw a cursory glance at it. She then fixed her eyes on Katrina, who stood smiling beside Andrei. She looked at Andrei, then Katrina, then Andrei again, obviously in disbelief that Katrina was a police officer.

Andrei pushed on. "Elena Rădulescu?"

The woman was startled to hear her name.

"You own this building, correct?"

She pondered the question a while. "I thought you were all done with your investigation."

She made a gesture to close the door. Andrei pushed back with his hand. Rădulescu glared at Andrei, affronted.

"We need to take another look at the apartment upstairs," Andrei said assertively. Then he added, in a more pleasant voice, "If you don't mind."

The old woman obviously did mind. She glowered.

"Do you have a new renter in there?" Katrina's gentle voice broke the impasse.

The landlady turned her attention to her. There was something childish and non-threatening about Katrina. "No," she said.

"All we want to do is take a brief look around," Katrina said reassuringly. "We won't disturb anything, I promise."

The door slowly opened. Elena Rădulescu wore a white nightgown with Mickey Mouse prints all over. It draped her slender body and wiped the floor. She turned around and shuffled in, not looking back, and began laboriously climbing up a dim staircase. A collection of heavy keys clanged in her right hand.

Andrei and Katrina exchanged glances, Katrina giving him a proud nod.

"Wipe your feet before you enter," the landlady ordered them.

The act seemed futile, considering that Andrei, Boboc, the coroner's people, and who knows who else had trampled through the area two days earlier. Nevertheless, they humored the landlady and did as she asked.

Inside, as Andrei and Katrina took in the apartment, she stood by the door and keenly observed them, her head bent up on her hunched body.

The apartment looked pretty much the way Andrei remembered it. Enver's parka and sweater were still on the dining table but in different spots. The kitchen door where Enver's body hung was open, almost in the same position as when Andrei had inspected it. Enver's sister had obviously not straightened up much.

"He was away for some time before he died, wasn't he?" Andrei asked the landlady.

"Yes," she answered hoarsely. "He frequently went on business trips. He was gone for three days." She stayed put, as if guarding the door. "I fed his cat."

"Did anyone try to break into the place?"

"No." Her blue eyes seared into Andrei as if he were crazy to ask a question like that.

"Did anyone ask you to let them in while he was gone?"

The woman looked down at the floor and did not answer.

"Like, say, a family member?"

"No," she said quietly, still avoiding Andrei's eyes.

When she looked up again, she waved her keys at Andrei. "Come on," she ordered him coarsely. "Do whatever you need to do and get out of here."

"What happened to the cat?" Katrina had quickly encircled the apartment, and sensing the rising tension, she interjected.

Elena Rădulescu's expression softened. "I gave it away," she said. "To a neighbor two doors down. I can't take care of it all the time."

Katrina approached the woman and put an arm around her shoulders. She was about the same height as the stooped, craggy woman. "But you like cats, don't you?"

The woman nodded silently. "She was a nice cat," she said. "I could have kept her if I was not so..." She seemed on the verge of tears.

Andrei found her grief over the cat rather peculiar considering what had happened to the cat's owner. He said nothing. Katrina obviously had a way with her. He tried not to spoil her magic.

"Now," said Katrina, her arm still around the woman. "We are going to look at a few things here." Her voice was gentle. "We won't take long."

The landlady nodded.

"Would you mind leaving us alone and let us do it privately?"

The woman hesitated.

"I promise we won't disturb anything."

* * *

"The bitch is lying," Andrei said testily.

"You guys," said Katrina, inspecting Enver's coat and sweater. "You policemen are brutes. You don't know how to talk to people. All you do is scare them."

"Not if they don't have anything to be scared about," Andrei protested. "I am telling you. That old woman is lying."

Andrei inspected the tabletop. Enver's keys were no longer there. He pushed on with Katrina. "There was no forced entry. How did the killer gain access to the apartment?"

Katrina looked at him skeptically. "Killer?" she asked. "We haven't yet established that there was a murder. Aren't you jumping to conclusions, Mr. Detective?"

"I think she let someone in and she's hiding it."

"Good luck getting that out of her," said Katrina. "What'll you do, torture the old woman into a confession?"

Andrei realized the futility of arguing with her and quieted down.

"Now," she said, "this Enver, he came here from a trip away from home and proceeded to hang himself, right?"

"That's the story."

She approached the kitchen door.

"That's the door," Andrei confirmed.

"And he did it with what?"

"A rope," said Andrei.

"I wonder if it is still here." She looked around. "Let's look for it."

It wasn't hard to find. They spotted the rope in the kitchen, on a counter.

"I guess the coroner's people who picked up the body had no use for it," Andrei commented.

"Yeah," Katrina was excited. "Why would they? No investigation, right?"

"Let someone else dispose of it."

"That old woman you so dislike is proving to be useful," Katrina admonished Andrei. "Didn't clean up the place right away."

Andrei didn't take her bait for another argument. "So what do you think of the rope?"

The rope was at least a centimeter and a half thick. It snaked around the counter; its free end, the one that had been attached to the doorknob, was hanging down with an untied knot. At the other end, the loop that killed Enver was turned around as if the snake's head was lying on its body. Its noose was thick and long, with at least eight coils.

"Wow," Katrina exclaimed, examining the noose. "This looks pretty professional."

"So, what do you think?" Andrei asked her again.

Katrina ignored him and inspected the loop and noose closely, running the rope on her open palm once this way, then another. Here and there she stopped and inspected sections of the rope more carefully.

Andrei stood a few steps back, puzzled by Katrina's interest in the rope itself rather than the noose and loop.

She finally looked up at Andrei. "What exactly was this guy's profession?"

"We don't know yet. Why?"

"Well, this is a pretty professional job," she said, holding the noose in her hand. "Of the kind that boaters, sailors, and such might practice."

Andrei chuckled. "Boaters in Braşov?"

The city was landlocked in the heart of Transylvania.

"Who knows," said Katrina. "You and the old lady said that he went away for work. Maybe…"

Andrei got the point.

"You'd better go to the car and grab my evidence bag," she told Andrei. "I'll look around some more."

As Andrei turned around obediently, she shouted after him. "Make sure you leave the front door ajar. The old lady might not let you in a second time."

* * *

When Andrei returned with the heavy bag, he found Katrina standing atop a chair she had pulled by the kitchen door, leaning on her tiptoes, her head straining to look at the top of the door. She appeared precariously close to falling down.

"Hey, what are you doing?" Andrei dropped the bag and grabbed her by the waist.

"Oh good, you're back."

She jumped off the chair and pushed it out of the way with her foot. Andrei observed her diminutive figure with amusement. Katrina looked like a playful child.

"Put me up on your shoulders."

Andrei looked at her blankly.

"Come on!" She was impatient. "Stop looking like a dummy and pick me up."

"What for?"

"Will you just do as I say?"

Andrei let out a big sigh and squatted down, turning his back to her. Katrina leaped up on his shoulders and locked her feet around his chest.

"Okay," she said, and clapped her hands with delight. "You can get up now."

She giggled as Andrei rose up, and commented about how big his manly shoulders were. She weighed nothing.

"Okay, this way." Katrina directed him to the door. She stretched her body up, trying to inspect the top of the door.

Curious, Andrei too looked up, his gesture destabilizing Katrina. She held on to the door to avoid falling.

"Stop it, will you?"

"What are you doing?" asked Andrei.

"Be patient, I'll tell you when I am ready."

Soon she asked to be let down, went to her bag, and pulled out a giant magnifying glass. She then jumped back on Andrei's shoulders, this time inspecting the door longer.

When she came down a second time, she placed the magnifying glass back in her bag. She fell into deep thought.

Andrei waited expectantly.

She finally turned around to him, her expression no longer that of a bouncy child. "You'd better seal this place and get a forensics team in," she said. "It may be too late, but who knows? They may find more."

"More what?"

She slapped Andrei's butt for the second time that afternoon. "Congratulations, Detective," she said. "You were right. This guy did not commit suicide. He was murdered."

CHAPTER 16

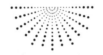

BRAŞOV, MARCH 31

Andrei sat by the living room table, mobile phone in hand, hesitating.

"What are you waiting for?" Katrina was impatient. "Make your calls."

"Look," Andrei said. "It was Boboc and I that ruled this case a suicide. Now you're asking me to abruptly reverse that?"

"That's right."

"I am doing no such thing until you explain why." Andrei beckoned Katrina, who was practically bouncing off the floor with excitement, to sit by him. "Here, calm down and sit."

She reluctantly complied, but her legs and feet kept fidgeting. Andrei wondered whether the woman needed medicine for attention deficit disorder.

"Okay," she began. "This guy comes in from a long trip and the first thing he does, before he even feeds his cat, is to commit suicide by hanging himself."

"Right." Andrei waited expectantly.

"Now, that's what I would call an impulsive suicide. Would you agree?"

"Yes," said Andrei. "Tell me something I don't know."

"Will you cut it out and listen?" Katrina playfully slapped Andrei's thigh. "You're a brute," she said, "but so handsome."

Andrei squirmed in disapproval.

"All right." Katrina settled back into her chair, her legs calm. "People who kill themselves on an impulse—if they are going to do it by hanging—they hang themselves with whatever they can find around the house, a phone cord, electrical cord, that sort of thing. Agree?"

Andrei raised his eyebrows, recognizing where she was going. "The rope," he said.

"Riiiight!" Katrina's voice was that of an approving teacher. "That rope, so thick and with such a professional looking noose. Let's say the guy is a sailor and knows how to make that sort of noose. Unlikely, but let's say it."

"I doubt he is a sailor."

"Whatever. Even if he was," Katrina's voice rose, "he still had to buy and prepare that rope. He had to have planned to commit this suicide. Do you get it? He couldn't have done this on an impulse, produced a rope and noose such as that." She pointed to the kitchen where the rope still sat on the counter.

Andrei let that point sink in. "I follow you," he said. "Nice conclusion."

Katrina sat up erect, with a satisfied smile. Now she was a proud student accepting a compliment from her teacher.

"But," Andrei continued, "I can't call the chief and reverse our earlier finding on this sort of hunch. I need solid evidence."

Katrina exhaled. "I know."

For a moment, as Katrina sat silent, Andrei felt rising disappointment.

She waited until his dismay was clearly obvious before slapping him on the thigh again. "Don't be silly. Of course I have more."

"Katrina, you're impossible. I am going to slap you myself," said Andrei.

"The rope," she said, ignoring the threat. "I will have to examine it more closely in the lab." She turned back toward the kitchen. "By the way, we'd better get it into an evidence bag soon, before that old lady returns and throws it in the trash."

"What about the rope?"

"There is a small segment of the main rope that was stretched over the top of the door."

Andrei remembered Katrina running the rope carefully on her palm. "Yes?"

"It has a wear pattern that points toward the dead body, away from the door knob."

"So?"

"And at the top of the door, where the rope was stretched, there are splinters, the door's own wear pattern. They point toward the door knob. Do you get it?"

"No."

Katrina shook her head, frustrated with how dense Andrei was. "Look," she said, going over to the door. She stood by the doorknob on the side opposite to where Enver was found. "If he was murdered, his killer would have pulled the rope toward this knob, right?"

Andrei too got up and came by the door. He stared at the doorknob without saying anything.

"So the rope would have pulled this way." Katrina mimed a killer pulling Enver's rope toward the doorknob on the other side of the door. "And it would have created the wear patterns on both the door and the rope that I just found."

Andrei moved toward the other side of the door where Enver had been hanging. Katrina joined him.

"If he committed suicide," she continued, "the dead guy would have been pulling the rope himself, in this direction." She pointed to where Enver had been found. "So the wear patterns would have been the exact opposite."

Katrina's point finally dawned on Andrei.

"So, you see," she concluded, "the wear patterns on the rope and door prove that he did not hang himself. Someone hung him by pulling on the other side of the door."

"There is one thing I still don't understand." Andrei was not ready to congratulate Katrina quite yet. "How did Enver, a healthy young guy, allow this to happen without putting up a fight?"

"Like a lamb being slaughtered," Katrina agreed. "I don't know. That's up to you to find out."

She examined the doorknobs on each side of the door. They were intact. "One more thing that makes your point even more mysterious." She looked at Andrei. "All this wear stuff could only happen if one person was pulling from the other side. If the killer had an assistant who hoisted Enver up while the killer pulled on the rope, there would be no wear stress on the rope or door."

"Yes, I get it." Andrei thought for a moment. "Enver had to have been incapacitated somehow."

"Yes, but there is no evidence of that in this apartment."

"I still can't believe that one person alone could have neutralized and incapacitated the man and then hung him. This had to be some sort of team effort."

"Agreed." Katrina thought for a moment. "Maybe the teammate let his partner do the hanging while he tended to something else."

"Right." Andrei looked around the room as if he would discover something new. "And that would only have happened if Enver was effectively neutralized while he was being hung."

"Maybe they drugged him," said Katrina. "We'd better get the body for an autopsy."

"Good luck," Andrei answered. "He is already gone. To Bosnia. His sister took him back home for burial."

"Can't you bring him back? Exhume the body?"

Andrei considered Katrina's proposal for a moment. "It would be difficult. Paperwork across international frontiers...there would be a lot of red tape."

"So where do we go from here?" asked Katrina.

"I think I'll have a hard enough time convincing Boboc, let alone the chief to initiate an investigation." Andrei took out his mobile and got ready to call. "I won't even think about an autopsy until I get across that hurdle."

Katrina stopped Andrei from dialing. "One more thing," she

said, getting to a point Andrei had made earlier. "If there was a team of killers, how did they gain access to the apartment?"

Andrei smiled at her. "You tell me."

"That old bitch let them in?"

Andrei turned around and playfully slapped her bottom.

"Ouch," she cried in delight. "Go ahead and make your phone calls," she ordered him. "I'll bag the rope as evidence."

CHAPTER 17

TUZLA, MARCH 30

Mark crossed the Bosporus Bridge again, this time in a taxi. At four a.m., bridge traffic was light. The suspension cables of the bridge were colorfully lit, the glare obscuring the view of the Old City in the dark distance. On this occasion Mark did not reminisce about the past. He was too apprehensive for that. He kept asking himself the same question over and over. What the hell was he doing? And why?

He was on his way to the luxurious villa at Tuzla where he had spent an interesting evening with the transplant surgeon Mahmut Gazioğlu and his exotic girlfriend. He had been much taken by both, but for different reasons. Gazioğlu was a fellow doctor, of the same age and background. His professional morals notwithstanding, Mark had found him appealing.

Semra, his girlfriend, was something else. Mark couldn't quite figure what about this peculiarly attractive woman so fascinated him. Or was it Mark's own vulnerability?

Mark's second marriage was in the midst of dissolution in San Francisco. He had not been with any woman in a while. Well, that wasn't entirely true. There had been Jasmin just last week, a young policewoman in Budapest who had practically thrown herself at him in her apartment, attempting to have sex with Mark. To his own amazement, Mark had refused. His friend, the late Ahmet, would have been appalled with what Mark had done, letting a gift like that go.

Mark now wondered whether Semra's appeal was simply a result of his own drought.

He was on his way to Semra's aid in a chivalrous gesture of infinite stupidity. He had no idea what he would find in Gazioğlu's house. If the attackers, whoever they were, were still there, how would he deal with them? In Budapest, when he had gotten himself in trouble, he had had two guardians who came to his rescue. One was Mustafa, a retired Turkish policeman, now private eye. Mustafa had proved himself crafty and cunning, and a loyal friend. The other was Jasmin, who mobilized the Budapest police force against a whole host of bad guys. That may well have saved Mark's life.

As the taxi left the bridge and plunged into the Asian side of the city, Mark reminded himself that he was all alone. Mustafa was somewhere in Istanbul, but Mark had not established contact with him. There was another person Mark could have used for help. Leon Adler was an Israeli Interpol liaison stationed in Istanbul. In a peculiar coincidence, he was another high school mate. Commissaire Gérard had mentioned Leon back in Budapest and asked Mark to pass on information to Leon if he uncovered any. Mark now regretted not calling Leon as soon as he arrived in Istanbul.

Staring at passing headlights on the freeway, Mark thought about his old life, the one he'd left behind in the US a scant seven days ago. It had been cautious and safe. He could not imagine being so foolhardy back then. Yet, scared as he was, Mark felt battle-hardened. He told himself that he had survived Budapest. He would somehow survive this, too. Wouldn't he?

* * *

The taxi driver was spooked by the dark, deserted road that led to Gazioğlu's villa. Mark figured his first hurdle would be to get through the main gate. He recalled that it required an electronic opener. To his surprise, the gate was wide open. A large chain hung from one end, the gate askew on its hinges.

Mark felt a sinking feeling as he observed the scene. It had obviously been forced open, most likely by some vehicle pulling on the chain. It would have made quite a ruckus. But in this isolated corner of Tuzla, the noise would have gone unnoticed. Mark doubted that even the inhabitants of the villa would have heard it. The house was set back far from the road, separated by an orchard that was part of the property.

The taxi driver too noticed the door. He stared at it sternly. Mark pulled his window down and listened. He ignored the driver, who asked him, in Turkish, what business he had out here.

All was quiet. Nothing stirred. Mark asked the driver to wait for him; he'd be returning to the Hyatt soon. The man refused and asked Mark to get out.

As the taxi sped away, Mark slid by the gate, eyeing the closed-circuit cameras mounted on each side. When he first arrived here, he figured it was natural for such a place to be equipped with surveillance. Now, the same cameras seemed menacing. He wondered if anyone inside was watching him. He cautiously walked onto the packed dirt driveway that cut through the orchard. Thankfully, it was still lit by the lanterns.

Before stepping on the paved driveway in front of the villa, Mark hid behind some bushes and observed the scene. He looked for a large pickup or SUV that might have forced the gate open with a chain. Nothing. The driveway was free of vehicles.

The house was lit as though a major party was going on, yet it was eerily quiet. The front door was wide open, with no one visible. Mark eased up. He was safe so far. He stepped out and cautiously inched along the driveway toward the house.

He did not notice the dark figure lying on the driveway until he almost tripped on it. Startled, he came to a sudden stop. A motionless body lay sprawled out by his feet. Mark bent down for a closer look. It was the guard he had seen earlier, the one who chatted with his BMW driver.

The man was dead, shot in the face near his left eye. The eye was a mangled mess. Next to him lay his rifle.

Mark's dread rose again, but he did not panic. He wondered if he should grab the weapon, just in case. He took another look around and listened. There was no sound aside from sea breeze susurrating through the trees.

He decided not to take the gun. He didn't know how to use it, and putting his fingerprints on it could potentially get him in trouble when law enforcement eventually arrived.

Mark moved around the house toward the tool shed. As expected, the gate that allowed access to the side yard was closed and locked. He recalled Gazioğlu doing that during their stroll back from the seaside. Mark would have to reach Semra, whom he presumed was still in the tool shed, by going through the inside of the house and the seaside garden.

As he entered the house, Mark wondered where the Turkish surgeon was. He decided to find Semra first. The vast open living room was brightly lit, making his task easier. There was no one there, all still and quiet. He quickly made his way to the porch doors, slid one open and made a beeline to the side yard. By now, Mark was confident that he was alone.

The tool shed was closed. He knocked softly on the door. "Semra," he whispered. "It's me, Mark." He then realized how stupid this was, and he nearly shouted, *"Aç kapıyı!" Open the door*!

Semra was crouched inside, shivering. She remained stationary and did not acknowledge Mark. He had to get her out forcefully, pulling her by the arms. She had been in there a while and it took her time to loosen her joints. She appeared in shock and did not utter a word.

Mark looked Semra up and down. She wore a flimsy nightgown that came down to her knees and exposed her shoulders. No wonder she was shivering, thought Mark. He put his arms around her and Semra readily accepted his hug, her head resting on his chest. They stood like this for a minute or two as Mark surveyed his surroundings, dimly aware of how intimately he was holding on to her.

Semra began sobbing. Her head shook against Mark's chest.

"We need to get you inside," he said to her quietly. "You need more clothes."

They silently limped into the house, where Mark discovered that Semra had her own bedroom on the first floor, a small room with two windows facing the side yard, by the tool shed. The room was cool with night air, the window through which she escaped still open. Mark closed it.

Semra first went into a nearby bathroom. When she returned, Mark told her, "You stay here and get dressed. And put together a small bag, clothes, toiletries, whatever."

She nodded amid new sobs.

"And do it fast."

Mark looked around Semra's room. A queen-size bed, side tables, closet door closed, everything was in order here. "I'll take a look around the house."

She looked at him pathetically. "Don't leave me," she pleaded.

"I'll be back soon," he said, and gave her a quick hug.

* * *

Mark made his way back to the main living room via a small hallway, and for the first time examined the place more carefully. The bar, living room, and kitchen area, all one big room, were totally undisturbed. He moved on to the foyer. Here, under the harsh light of the interior lamps, he noticed dirty footprints. In his earlier haste he had not seen them when he entered the house. They seemed to be leading out of the main door.

Mark had no idea how to read footprints. He kneeled down and took a closer look. They were shoe prints, not bare feet. There were multiple prints, definitely more than one person, but Mark could not tell how many. He was certain, however, that they all led out, none in. They had a reddish, brownish hue.

Blood.

He looked around and noticed the same prints on the majestic staircase that led to the second floor. There, amid the lushly carpeted steps, the dirty footprints stood out even more, maroon blotches on beige. Once again they were all one-way, toward the foyer. Mark carefully ascended the stairs, taking care not to step on the prints.

The staircase led to an interior balcony that encircled the open floor plan downstairs, affording an impressive view below. There were several doors off this area that Mark presumed were bedrooms. He found it odd that Semra was sleeping downstairs instead of up here, but he had no time to contemplate this.

The dirty footsteps were coming from the only double door in the area. Mark gathered it must be the master bedroom. The door was open. Mark entered the room and found a mess.

As he had expected, it was a spacious room with a huge, round bed, its covers partially off and strewn about. Two small armchairs were askew, and a foot table was turned over. Clothing items discarded from the foot table were scattered here and there. There had obviously been a struggle here. The attackers most likely came upon Gazioğlu while he was sleeping.

The floor was covered with the same lush carpet as the stairs. Mark noted that there were no foot stains here. Instead, the footsteps seemed to be emerging from another big room toward the double doors of the bedroom. A master bath?

Mark had a premonition of doom. He had a flashback to an evening a week ago when he had explored a similarly quiet, luxurious suite at the Gresham Palace hotel. There he had found Ahmet's strangely peaceful dead body in the master bathtub.

He cautiously followed the footsteps to the bathroom door. It was open, beckoning him in. He hesitated a moment, trying to contain his apprehension. The carpet here had a large mess of footsteps, all jumbled into each other.

Mark got a bad feeling that what he would find inside wouldn't be as peaceful as what he discovered in Budapest.

CHAPTER 18

TUZLA, MARCH 30

The first thing that Mark noticed was the smell, that metallic, sickeningly sweet scent of blood. It took him back to his medical school days where he had experienced cases of copious hemorrhage in the emergency room and operating theater. It was a unique smell that one never forgot. Mark knew that it took a great deal of spilled blood to create such an odor.

The bathroom was expansive, with a large tub on one side and a modern, spacious walk-in shower on another. The walls were lavishly finished with white marble, the ground tiled in beige. Yet the predominant color in the room was red.

Two walls that formed a corner of the bathtub were full of large, irregular splats of blood, with small rows of droplets in between, sprayed more neatly. Mark recognized the latter as high-speed squirts from arteries. The floor tiles near the bathtub were almost completely covered in blood, all except for a peculiarly prominent, rectangular spot that was totally clean, pure beige amid all the red.

The bathtub itself was filled with blood, most of it still liquid. Mark figured it was at least an inch thick, with small areas of clot floating on the surface. Amid this crimson pool lay a body wearing only a pair of briefs that were once white. Now they, too, were soaked, cherry red. The body lay supine within the tub, splatters of blood all over it, especially on the torso.

Mark stood in shock as he surveyed the ghastly scene. At first he did not notice that there was something odd about the body. Mark's eyes fixated on a prominent towel rack next to the bathtub, near the top of the body. It held two large bath towels somewhat askew. They, too, had prominent blotches of red, but these were not random splatters. It appeared to Mark that the assailants had used the towels to wipe their weapons clean. These towels, more than anything else in the room, caused Mark's hairs to stand on end.

A week ago, when Mark had come upon Ahmet's dead body, he had run out of the bathroom and immediatcly called for police. That's what any sane person would do.

That bathroom in Budapest had been equally luxurious, the scene clean and intact, peculiarly placid. Now Mark stood amid a true bloodbath. Horrific as it was, Mark did not feel the urge to run out.

Was he going insane? Who would he call, anyhow? He knew no one in this forsaken corner of Istanbul. He was not even sure what the Turkish equivalent of 911 was.

Mark moved toward the bathtub for a closer look at the body. His shoes slipped on the bloody tiles and he almost fell. As he regained his balance, Mark was dismayed to realize that he too would be carrying bloody footsteps out of the bathroom and down the stairs. He had no choice.

The top of the body, near the towel rack, had the most blood splatter, both on the body and on the wall behind. Mark felt a need to confirm that this was indeed Gazioğlu. It couldn't be anyone else. But still, he leaned in to see the man's face. This was to be his only opportunity to identify him. Once Mark left this bathroom, he would not return for a second look.

That's when Mark noticed that there was no face. He stood there, momentarily puzzled, trying to clarify what he was seeing amid the bloody mess. Mark realized that he was actually staring at a bloody stump of a neck. A vertebral body stood out prominently on its cut surface, its unstained grayish color the only blood-free area. The body was headless.

Mark quickly surveyed the bathroom again, looking for the head. He couldn't find it. He moved toward the walk-in shower situated some distance from the bathtub. It had been spared from the splatter, its glass door still transparent. Mark looked in. No head.

Puzzled, Mark did a 360 survey of the room. His eyes again landed on the strangely clean, rectangular spot on the otherwise totally blood-stained floor tiles. He stared at it, wondering what it was. It then dawned on him that something had stood there while Gazioğlu was being butchered.

The clean spot was a narrow, elongated rectangle, about the same size as a tote bag, the kind one might take to a gym. They had come here, Mark recognized, with a bag. They had intended to decapitate the man and take the head away with them.

CHAPTER 19

TUZLA, MARCH 30

Mark found Semra in the foyer, small suitcase in hand, staring at the bloody footsteps. As he descended the stairs, Semra's eyes caught the stains that Mark's own shoes were creating on the carpet. She looked up at him in despair.

Mark quickly came down and, grabbing her arm, took her away to the clean living room. They sat down on a couch close to each other.

Semra was no longer the elegant lady that had captivated Mark the night before. In cut-off jeans and a bulky T-shirt with red and yellow stripes—the colors of Galatasaray, the soccer team—she looked younger, boyish. Her dark hair was down to her shoulders, poorly combed. She wore no makeup. In the absence of eyeliner and lashes, her dark eyes took on a new allure as she stared at Mark with apprehension.

Mark reached out and held her hand tightly between his two hands. He waited for questions. None came.

"Is there a car we can use to get out of here?" he asked, grateful that Semra did not ask about Mahmut or the footsteps.

"No," she said. "But we can call the chauffeur." At that moment, all things considered, she was surprisingly composed.

The chauffeur was out of the question. So was another taxi. No need to invite fresh witnesses. Mark looked at his watch. It was past five a.m.

Mark took out his wallet and removed a card from it. He then walked toward the bar, mobile phone in hand, out of Semra's earshot.

* * *

"They killed him, didn't they?" Semra uttered in a monotone. It was a statement rather than a question.

"I called for a ride," said Mark, ignoring her comment. "It'll be here in half an hour."

She did not acknowledge him. She sat on the couch and stared at the dark windows facing the Marmara.

"Semra." Mark tried to break her spell. "Do you have anyone that I can take you to? Any family, friends?"

Semra silently shook her head no, her gaze fixed on the dark beyond.

Mark contemplated Semra's predicament and realized that hers was now his. "Okay, then. You're coming with me to my hotel."

She turned and gave him an expressionless stare.

Mark clasped both of her arms. "The cameras," he said. He tilted his head in the direction of the front door. "The video cameras." He gently shook her. "Do you know where they feed?"

"Where is Halil?" she muttered.

"Who?"

"Halil, our guard."

Mark shook his head. Halil, he realized, was the corpse at the front driveway, the one with the rifle. "Shit!" he exclaimed under his breath.

"Him too?"

Mark nodded yes.

Semra's head sank. She stared at her own lap, hands tucked between her legs. "Laptop. In his office."

"What?"

She looked back at Mark. Some expression had returned to her face. "The video feed," she said slowly. "It goes into a laptop in his office."

"Is there some security company that manages it?"

"No," she said. "He didn't trust them. He didn't trust the cloud either, or any other external storage. It went into his personal computer. He reviewed it from time to time."

"You didn't see the attackers, did you?"

"No," she said. "They came after the chef left and we went to bed. I woke up to a lot of noise. I think I heard popping, like a firecracker. Then there were loud footsteps, some banging and loud talk."

"What language?"

"I don't know, but it was not Turkish." Semra gave Mark a puzzled look. "How did you know they weren't Turks?"

Mark could not explain what he'd already been through with Hungarians, Slovaks, and Moldovans. "Never mind," he said. "What did it sound like?"

"Orders," she answered. "Sounded like someone was shouting orders and others obeying."

"Others? Were there more than two?"

"I think so. I'm not sure." She thought for a second. "I was sleepy and the front door is distant from my bedroom." She paused.

"You know," she said finally, "Mahmut told me many times that this might happen. That he might be attacked."

Gazioğlu's premonition surprised Mark. At the beginning of their evening together, he had sounded cocky and secure, as if he had always been that way. Mark's account of Vadim Rusu had punched a hole in this perception. But even then, when they parted, he seemed reassured by Mark's final words.

"That's why he wanted me to sleep in a separate quarter of the house," she continued. "He always told me that if anyone broke into the house, I should run away. I should not mind him. He would take care of himself." Her eyes teared. "So I ran."

"Tonight," asked Mark, "why did you choose to call *me*?" This had intrigued him ever since he had received her phone call.

"I told you already," she said sternly. "I have no one here in Istanbul. Neither does he."

She noticed Mark's surprise. "You see all this luxury here. But Mahmut has been living like a hermit, away from family and friends. He was always watching his back. He didn't even totally trust his own security guards."

"What about the police? He told me he had contacts with Istanbul police."

Semra gave a sarcastic chuckle. "Not them, either. He told me the police were completely unreliable. They would hang him in a second if it wasn't for all that he paid them. I was never to call the police. Besides," she said, her voice softening, "I had asked him for your phone number after you left last night. I thought you looked honest, and brave." A slight smile broke on her lips. "I thought you were more trustworthy than anyone else."

So that's how she knew my number, Mark answered himself. He stared at her.

"A handsome foreign agent," she was saying, "just like in the movies." She placed one hand over his. "Courageous." She leaned in toward him.

Mark drew back.

"I was correct, wasn't I?" she said.

Mark abruptly stood up. "The laptop," he said. "Show me."

* * *

Mark got a more detailed look at Gazioğlu's office than earlier. Fully lit, the office was quite large and had a spacious desk facing the picture windows. The couches he and Gazioğlu had sat in were between the desk and windows. They revolved so that those who sat in them could face either way.

"Which one?" asked Mark. There were three laptops on the desk, each hooked up to various wires.

Semra pointed to the smallest one with the Apple insignia.

Mark quickly disconnected it. Semra opened a drawer in a

credenza behind the desk and produced a bag that the laptop fit into.

"Did he keep any external hard drives as backup?"

There were two in the middle drawer of the desk. Mark tucked those into the bag.

A text message chime from his mobile startled them both.

"Our ride is here," he told Semra. "Let's go."

CHAPTER 20

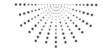

TUZLA, MARCH 30

Tarık stared at the dead body illuminated by his headlights as Mark and Semra rushed into his compact Toyota Verso SUV. Mark tucked Semra into the back seat, then entered the front.

"Thanks a lot," he said to Tarık, breathlessly. "I owe you a big one."

Tarık nodded. He pushed up his glasses, which had slipped down his nose, and threw the vehicle into gear. As Tarık curved around the driveway, careful to avoid Halil's body, Mark eased the computer bag off his shoulder.

They remained silent until they reached the D100 freeway, Tarık shooting frequent curious glances at the back seat, where Semra sat in a sideways fetal position, her seat belt unfastened. Her muffled sobs were occasionally audible above the din of traffic, already heavy with morning commuters.

"Do you mind telling me what's going on?" Tarık finally broke the silence.

"Gazioğlu, the doctor that invited me to dinner last night," Mark answered. "They broke into his house and killed him."

"Was that him on the driveway?"

"No. He was inside, in his bedroom."

Traffic came to a halt before the Bosporus Bridge. Tarık threw the gear into Park and shut off the engine. "At this time of day, crossing the Bosporus is hell." It was now past six a.m. "May as well save gas."

He turned around and took a closer look at Semra. She had fallen asleep, still in a fetal position.

"Who is that?" Tarık nodded his head toward the back seat.

"His girlfriend. Her name is Semra."

Tarık slid another glance at her, this time turning his whole body around. Traffic began moving again and Mark reminded him to start his engine.

They crawled along toward the bridge. "Did you call the police?"

"No."

Mark could tell that his reply startled Tarık, but he did not comment.

"What's in that?" He pointed to the computer bag.

"His laptop," Mark said. "And a couple of external hard drives."

Tarık shook his head in disbelief.

"Look, Tarık," Mark said firmly. "I don't want to get you in any trouble. As far as I'm concerned this drive never happened. Okay?"

Tarık gave Mark a stern look. "What about her?"

"She won't say anything."

They were finally on the bridge. Mark spotted the high-rises of the modern city lined up behind the hills, on the horizon.

"I don't get it," said Tarık. "If they stormed the house, how come you and she are unharmed?"

Mark briefly explained what had happened—his dinner with Gazioğlu, and being awakened in the middle of the night by Semra's pleading call. He did not go into the details of Gazioğlu's condition when Mark found him.

"Let me get this." Tarık shut off the engine again in the middle of the bridge. He looked at Mark, incredulous. "You re-entered the compound, saw two dead men there, probably left fingerprints all over the house, and stole the man's computer. Correct?"

"Yes."

"And you did not call the police."

"That's correct."

Tarık raised his voice. "Are you out of your mind?!"

He re-started the car.

"I have a plan." Mark stared straight ahead, his voice full of conviction.

"Oh, please, let's hear it," Tarık said sarcastically.

"I was given the name of a local Interpol contact here in Istanbul. Someone I know I can trust."

"Interpol," murmured Tarık, shaking his head dubiously.

"I plan to contact him today. Tell him what happened and deliver this computer to him."

"What's in it, anyhow?" Tarık exited the bridge. "On second thought, no. Don't tell me. I don't want to know."

They took a steep downhill boulevard toward the seaside quarter of Beşiktaş. Semra remained asleep, snoring lightly. Mark accepted Tarık's admonition and did not discuss the computer. For a while they remained silent.

Tarık turned onto the coastal road by the grave of Barbaros Hayrettin, the great Ottoman admiral. "Tell me something," he said. "How does a radiologist in San Francisco get himself involved in all this cloak-and-dagger stuff? Dead bodies. Swiping evidence. Interpol."

Mark had no answer. He himself did not understand it.

"I am beginning to think that you are as much trouble as your good buddy Ahmet."

Mark gave the young man an alarmed look. "No," he said. "Please. I am not."

"Okay, so you are not out to exploit my mother, like he did. Still, you arrived in Istanbul just yesterday, and pronto, you're in one hell of a mess."

They passed the soccer stadium at Dolmabahçe. Tarık turned right, uphill toward Mark's hotel near Taksim.

"Look," said Mark. "I am very grateful for what you're doing. Honestly, I could not think of anyone else to call."

He was about to continue when Tarık interrupted him. "You could have called your precious Interpol contact."

"No," said Mark. "Not before situating her." He nodded toward the back seat. "I want to keep her out of all this."

Tarık looked at Semra through the rearview mirror. She did not stir.

They arrived at the Hyatt and after the security sweep, Tarık dropped them off at the entrance.

"I am sorry if I caused any trouble," said Mark, as he exited the front seat of the Verso with the computer bag and opened the back door. "Don't tell your mother. She'll be upset." He woke up Semra and coaxed her out of the car.

Tarık stared at her tall, awkward figure as she stumbled out of the car, needing a step or two before she gained her balance. She turned and looked at Tarık curiously. For a moment, the two locked eyes.

Tarık surveyed her from head to toe. Then he nodded to her and threw the SUV into drive.

"I don't believe it," he muttered to himself, shaking his head, as he sped away from the hotel.

CHAPTER 21

BRAŞOV, MARCH 31

Andrei Costiniu stared at his desk. It was messy as usual, with piles of paperwork strewn all over. He booted up his desktop computer and began shuffling through a small stack of messages that had been left for him.

"You had to make a mess of it, didn't you?"

Boboc's husky voice caught him off guard. Andrei dropped the messages and looked up at his partner. Boboc hulked behind the computer screen, his gut digging into the edge of Andrei's desk. He leaned forward and rested his hands on the desk, his eyes in line with Andrei's.

"Why? Tell me, why could you not leave it alone?"

Andrei's phone call to Traian Dalca, the Sector 1 station chief, had obviously reverberated through the station. He momentarily ignored Boboc as he entered a password into his computer. He stared intently at the screen, waiting for the slow operating system to upload the correct program.

"Look, if you don't want to deal with this, suit yourself." Andrei finally locked eyes with Boboc. "I'll follow it through."

Boboc straightened up and adjusted his pants, which were

sliding low beneath his gut. "I just might do that," he said tersely, "if Dalca will let me."

"Anyhow, there is nothing for us to do for now, until the forensics team goes through the apartment." Andrei's voice was resigned.

Boboc pulled up a chair and sat down. "So what did you find?"

Andrei disengaged from the computer and sat back in his chair. Boboc's bluster had dissipated. Andrei calmly described his encounter with Enver's sister and Katrina's findings in the apartment. When he was finished, Boboc stared at him silently, a smile gradually erupting on his face.

"Good job, Mr. Detective," he said, echoing the same moniker that Katrina had used. Boboc lumbered out of the chair and adjusted his pants again. "Yes," he said emphatically, "I think I'll let you alone on this one."

As Boboc departed, Andrei looked back at his desk. His computer was ready to go, but he was no longer interested in writing a report. He shuffled his messages and spread them on his desk like a deck of cards. One caught his eye. Its heading, where the source was inscribed, was a single word: *Anonymous*.

Andrei picked up the message. It was a phone call that had come into the station an hour earlier while Andrei was with Katrina in Enver's house.

"*I have reason to believe that Enver Muratovich did not commit suicide,*" it began. "*He was murdered. There are others who were also murdered.*"

Andrei stopped and looked around the station office. There were six desks in the room, all occupied, everyone busy on their computers or on the phone. Life was going on as usual. He looked back at the message and realized that his own life had just taken a new turn.

"*If you want to know more, please call this number.*"

Andrei stared at the number. It had a 0267 area code, a landline. It was not in Brașov; that code would have been 0268.

Andrei set the message down and considered what to do. Traian Dalca's office was two doors down the hall. Should he report this to his chief immediately? He wished Ana were here. His wife's advice was always sound and sober. But he couldn't very well call her right now, within earshot of everyone.

Andrei tucked the message into his shirt pocket and got up from his desk. Boboc was right, he thought. For now, he needed to go at it alone.

CHAPTER 22

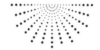

CHIȘINĂU, MARCH 31

Vadim Rusu stared out of his tenth-floor window. It was a foggy, drizzly day in Chișinău. He could not make out the details of the Nativity Cathedral below; it was just a blurry outline. The humid cold was oozing through the window into his centrally heated office. He adjusted his white turtleneck sweater higher up on his chin and buttoned his herringbone sports coat. A knock on the door took his attention away from the gloomy exterior.

Without waiting for a "come in," the door opened and Boris Petrov, his trusted second-hand man, entered. "Good afternoon, Boss."

Boris was wheeling a cafeteria cart loaded with a red and white plastic ice chest. Rusu gazed at the peculiar item, eyes squinting with curiosity. The opening of the chest was secured with a combination lock. As Boris advanced farther with the cart, the room filled with a pungent fishy smell.

"This was delivered today," Boris announced. "To be opened only in your presence."

"I don't recall ordering any fish." Rusu approached the cart with curiosity.

Boris produced an envelope that he tore open. "The

combination key." He proceeded to methodically unlock, then open the lid of the chest. Packed amid freezer bags was a brown plastic bag tied atop with a wire tie.

"I don't think this is fish, Boss." Boris removed the bag from the ice chest and gently shook it before setting it down on an empty spot in the cart. He untied the top and opened the bag, then stood back and waited for Rusu's inspection.

"What the hell?!" Rusu was staring at the bald top of a human head. "Take it out," he ordered Boris.

Firmly grabbing the content of the bag with both hands, Boris obediently removed the head, its face facing his own. He then tilted it to inspect the neck, where it had been severed. A few drops of reddish, yellowish fluid oozed out of it, causing Boris to reflexively stretch it away, onto the top of the open ice chest. He then turned the face toward his boss, tilting it so that the neck was visible.

Rusu regarded the dusky, bald figure with saggy skin and closed eyes. A goatee, wispy and white, was stained with speckles of maroon and red. "What is this?"

Boris turned the head back around to take a second look. He then set it atop the cafeteria cart. "I think, Boss, it is the Turkish doctor."

Vadim Rusu's face turned red. "The transplant doctor in Istanbul?" he asked, his voice rising.

"Yes, I think so."

"What do you mean you think so?" Rusu shouted. "It is, or it isn't! Find out right away."

Boris pulled out his mobile phone. Rusu interrupted him before he had a chance to dial.

"Get this thing out of my office!" he yelled. "Now!"

"Yes, sir."

"And don't come back," Rusu howled, "before you find out what the hell is going on."

* * *

131

When Boris returned, he knocked and waited to be allowed in. He walked with trepidation toward his usual spot on the chair facing Rusu's desk. His boss looked up distractedly from his computer screen.

"Well?"

Boris sat stiffly, his hands on his kneecaps. "That was indeed Gazioğlu," he said quietly, his voice quavering, "the Turkish doctor we were pursuing."

"So what happened?"

"He was killed in his house and his...." Boris' voice trailed off. He cleared his throat and made another try. "His head...." He cleared his throat again. "It was sent to us as confirmation that the job was completed."

Vadim Rusu punched his desk with both fists. "Goddamn it!" He erupted from his chair, sending the contents of his desk scattering. Leaning both fists on the desk, he screamed, "What the fuck do you think this is? Are we in the times of Ivan the Terrible?!"

Boris did not answer. He cast his eyes down on his kneecaps, currently covered with his white knuckles.

"Didn't I give specific instructions that this was to be a clean job?" Rusu came around his desk and pointed to the empty spot where Gazioğlu's severed head had stood. "Is this what you call a clean job?"

"No, sir," Boris answered in a near whisper.

"A simple I.D....a...a...photo would not do?" Rusu tried unsuccessfully to get a hold of himself. "Nooo!" he lifted his arms up in the air. "No," he yelled, "they had to cut his fucking head off and send it to me!" He sank into his chair, panting with fury, his face red as a beet. "I don't fucking believe this," he muttered to himself, repeating it several times.

Boris remained stone silent, frozen in position throughout his chief's outburst. He had been through many; this was as bad as any. His head remained downcast, as if he were a schoolchild getting dressed down by the principal. He waited for the storm to pass.

After a brief silence, Rusu collected himself. He asked in a calmer voice, "What happened?"

"My apologies for this fiasco," began Boris. "Apparently the Turks we contracted for the job felt that they couldn't do it. The doctor was too well connected with Turkish police."

Boris paused and eyed his boss, bracing for another outburst. But Rusu was spent. He sat in his chair and glared at his assistant, waiting for more.

"Anyhow," Boris continued, "they subcontracted the job to the Banda e Lushnjës gang."

They were both familiar with the fierce Mafia ring based in the Albanian town of Lushnjës, with a particular reputation for brutality. They were active in Italy and various Balkan countries. Rusu was not aware of their presence in Turkey.

"That figures," Rusu murmured. "Fucking Albanians. Savages."

"Yes, Boss." Boris relaxed and sat back, crossing his legs. "Savages," he confirmed.

"Our Turkish contacts were as surprised as you and I when they received the guy's head. They wanted to get rid of it ASAP. So they unloaded it right away." Boris uncrossed his legs. "To us."

"What's with that fish smell?" asked Rusu.

"They smuggled it out of Istanbul in a fishing boat through the Bosporus and Black Sea. The boat delivered it to Midia. The fishermen hid the ice chest in their cargo hold with their fish, as a precaution, you know, in case they were inspected by Turkish or Romanian Coast Guards."

"Wonderful!" said Rusu, his voice dripping with sarcasm. He was more collected now, his face returning to its usual pallor. "I can just imagine the bloody mess they left behind," he said, his voice still carrying an edge of anger.

"Not to mention the rest of the guy's body," Boris added.

"Goddamn, fucking incompetents!" Rusu shook his head. "We need to clean this up with the Istanbul police. I don't want it spilling into the news and creating some sort of international incident. You understand?"

"Yes, sir." Boris proceeded with caution. "But we are hours behind the incident. I don't know what has transpired in Istanbul by now."

"Don't you think I realize that?" Rusu was shouting again. "Do whatever you can!"

Boris stood up. "Oh, one more thing," he said.

"What now?"

Boris braced himself as he continued. "The American from Budapest."

"Don't tell me they cut off his head too," said Rusu.

"Oh, no! No," Boris said hastily. By comparison, the news was not that bad. "Our Turkish informants have reason to believe that the American established some sort of contact with this doctor." He stared at the blank spot where Gazioğlu's head had been. "Before he was killed."

"What sort of contact?"

"We don't quite know yet."

"Well, make sure they don't out that guy. Understand?"

"Yes, sir."

"I want that motherfucker alive, and here. As soon as possible."

"Yes, sir."

"And no more Albanians."

Boris turned to leave. As he opened the door, he turned around. "No more Albanians."

CHAPTER 23

ISTANBUL, MARCH 30

Mark helped Semra stumble into his hotel room. She looked out of the window at the Bosporus and behind it, at the antennas perched on Çamlıca Hill on the Asian side of the city from whence they had come. She turned back toward Mark and gave him a doleful look.

"Let's get some rest," Mark told her. "Then we'll figure out what to do next."

Semra edged past him into the bathroom while Mark took his clothes off and changed into a large T-shirt. He heard water running as he opened the sheets and collapsed onto the bed. He was exhausted from the overnight ordeal and ready for some sleep. But instead, he stared at the ceiling, Tarık's words ringing in his head. *"Are you out of your mind?"*

The police would be notified soon, most likely by a member of Gazioğlu's staff starting his workday at the Tuzla compound. Should Mark have notified the police himself? Granted, he didn't know how to contact them, but Semra or Tarık could have instructed him. How would it look when his presence in the house was discovered and he had not come forth to the police? Suspicious as hell, he thought. That's how it would look.

They might think he did it. After all, he was a wily foreign agent, wasn't he? He probably was capable of singlehandedly incapacitating the surgeon's guard and then killing him in a gruesome way. He was capable of anything. Like James Bond.

Mark cursed the entire James Bond fantasy he had harbored. After coming to America he had changed his name from Metin Özgür, the Turkish name his parents had given him, to the more American Mark Kent, a name easier to pronounce, a sexier name that had the same clipped tone as James Bond.

Then came Budapest, where a series of coincidences gave everyone the impression that he was a daring foreign agent. No one knew that the credit went to Mustafa, the Turkish private eye who had befriended Mark and secretly rescued him from various deadly binds. Then there was the episode when Mark lied to an employee of the Rudas bathhouse, telling the gullible young man that he was FBI. He did it to extract information from the youth, and got what he wanted. Hours later, after the bloodbath, with three people dead and a gang of Slovak criminals under arrest, the young man had gone on TV and declared that an FBI agent had been there, that this agent had rescued everyone.

At first the whole thing was amusing, Mark's James Bond fantasy coming to life. Then it became tiresome. Now, it was downright perilous.

Finally Mark closed his eyes. He could no longer think. He hoped that Leon, his Interpol contact, would somehow get him out of his bind. He heard light footsteps approaching the window. Eyes half mast, he saw Semra's silhouette as she pulled the nightshades, throwing the room into pitch darkness. As the sheets parted and Semra slid in bed next to him, Mark drifted off.

* * *

Mark felt a gentle electrical sensation spreading to his body from somewhere down below. It felt soothing, heavenly. The feeling grew, ballooning into an intensity Mark had not felt in a long time. *What a wonderful dream*, Mark thought, still asleep. He felt himself hardening, the sensation now more focused.

Was this going to be a wet dream, of the sort he used to have when he was young? An image appeared in his mind, that of a young woman, nubile, straddling him naked, about to take Mark inside her. He felt himself get harder. Jasmin!

Mark regretted rejecting Jasmin, when she had been about to give him long-awaited bliss. *Oh, Jasmin*, he thought, *go ahead, finish what you started*. It had not happened in real life; it may as well happen in a dream.

Mark was worried that he would soil the bedsheets, but he didn't care. The sensation, the desire was too strong. He had to go through with it. To hell with the hotel staff and whatever they found in the bed.

Mark felt a coolness as the sheets parted and his briefs began sliding off. His erection, hot and sweaty under the covers, took on a new life in the fresh air. He felt Jasmin's hand grasping him firmly, sending shock waves of pleasure through him.

What a wonderful dream. After all he'd been through, he deserved this.

Then he was engulfed in something warm and moist, firm in its grip. *Oh, Jasmin, please, go ahead. Please!*

Mark was on the verge of a climax but he had to hold on, didn't he? He had to please her too, and not be like a clumsy teenager finishing too soon. He shifted in the bed, trying to hold on, as Jasmin slowly pulled out, letting another whiff of cool air invigorate him.

Mark did not want this dream to end. The ecstasy of what was happening, the anticipation, was surely better than the ending. Jasmin slid back in, firm and determined, more moist than before. Mark relaxed and surrendered himself to her.

For someone so young, Jasmin surely knew what she was doing, exciting Mark in a manner he had never felt before. But then this was a dream, wasn't it? It was not real.

Mark didn't care. Dream or not, he needed it. He had not

experienced any such pleasure in a long while. Jasmin settled into a smooth rhythm, maintaining a firm grip on Mark.

For a moment Mark felt a strange pain down there, as if he were being scratched with fingernails up and down. It caused a new concern. Would this become one of those frustration dreams where it all derailed?

As the pain disappeared and Jasmin returned to her routine, Mark decided he could no longer wait. He had to end this now, before the dream turned into a nightmare. He willed himself, still asleep, into a release.

It came in cascades, like multiple waterfalls, forceful and determined, frenzied and ecstatic. Finally! Mark's whole body shook and shivered, while Jasmin, thrown off rhythm by the abrupt eruption, tried to hold on.

Suddenly a loud sound woke Mark into consciousness. It was the harsh sound of someone hacking, clearing their throat as though choking. The bed shook to a new rhythm, that of coughing. Mark sat up, terrified, his bliss snapped off. He stared at darkness as the coughing subsided into hoarse breaths and the bed settled down.

He saw a silhouette rise next to him and scatter to the bathroom. Light creeping from the edge of the closed bathroom door brought Mark to his senses. He realized that he himself was out of breath. What had just happened? Was it real? It couldn't be.

What a strange dream!

Mark realized that he was still hard under the covers. He slid a hand down below and felt himself. He brought his hand back up and rubbed his thumb and forefinger against each other. They were slippery and moist. *Oh my God.*

The bathroom door opened, casting a bright glare into the room. Mark had to momentarily close his eyes. When he opened them again, still trying to process what had just happened, the lights were off, the room once again pitch dark. He felt Semra rustle back to bed and pull the covers over her.

"Sorry," she said, voice still hoarse. "You surprised me."

Mark sank back on his pillow. Semra threw an arm around his

chest as she quickly fell asleep, commencing a new rhythm of delicate snores. Mark closed his eyes, deflated. The aftershocks of what had just happened held him back from sleep. It was a good dream after all.

CHAPTER 24

BRAŞOV, MARCH 31

"Hotel Sugás."

Surprised, Andrei hesitated.

"Hello, Hotel Sugás. This is *Subinspector* Andrei Costiniu, of Sector 1, Braşov Police."

"We've been expecting you." The voice was calm and polite, a well-trained receptionist. She sounded young. "Would you please stay on the line?"

Andrei quickly interjected before he lost her. "Where exactly am I calling?"

"This is Hotel Sugás, in Sfântu Gheorghe. Wait a moment please."

Sfântu Gheorghe was a nearby town northwest of Braşov in Covasna County. That explained the 0267 area code. Andrei had never been to Sfântu Gheorghe, never had any reason to go there. He waited expectantly.

A hoarse male voice came on the line. "Pista Szabó here."

Andrei repeated his introduction and added, "I am answering the message you left me."

"Yes, yes," the man said hesitantly. He seemed unsure about how to proceed.

"It was you who left me the anonymous message to call this number, correct?"

"Actually…no."

Andrei wondered whether he should just hang up. The station regularly received prank messages. This might be another one.

"Okay. Well then, thank you." Andrei's voice clearly indicated that he was terminating the call.

"Wait, wait!"

Andrei did not answer.

"I am just an intermediary," said the hoarse voice. "The person who sent you that message…she does not want to reveal herself."

Andrei hastily jotted down a word on a nearby piece of paper. "Woman."

"Well, whoever it was," said Andrei, "they had some information for me."

"Yes, that's right."

"So, how do I get in contact with her?"

"Come here," said the man.

"To Sfântu?"

"Yes, to our hotel. We're in the center of town, not far from the train station."

Andrei didn't need directions. He was quite sure he could find his way there. "When?"

"How about tomorrow?" said the man. "Any time. Pick your time."

"Okay, ten a.m." Andrei randomly picked a time.

"See you then," said the man. "Come to reception and ask for Pista Szabó. I am the manager."

* * *

Ana watched her husband with curiosity as he dried his sweat with the towel by the door.

"Are you all right?"

Andrei was returning from his regular early evening run. He had been gone longer than usual. "I needed time to think," he mumbled.

He placed the towel around his neck and bent down to remove his shoes.

"Think about what?"

He didn't answer. Ana waited for him to remove his shoes and followed her husband to the kitchen. After downing a big gulp of fruit juice, Andrei sat at the kitchen table where Ana had been patiently waiting.

"The baby. Asleep?"

Ana nodded yes.

He took a deep breath and began. "Remember the Muratovich suicide?"

Ana observed him expectantly and did not respond.

"I met his sister, Emina."

Ana smiled with surprise. "How is she?"

"Pretty distraught, as you might guess." Andrei took another sip of juice, emptying his glass. "She demanded that I investigate his case."

"What is there to investigate?"

"Well," Andrei said, letting out a big sigh, "that's what I had to think about." He hesitated.

Like all police officers, he refrained from discussing his cases with family members. But this one, the supposed suicide of Enver Muratovich, somehow felt different. It was more personal to both him and Ana, not only because Ana knew Enver and his sister, but also because of the threat the case posed to their lives.

Andrei then opened up about his conversation with Emina, about Katrina from forensics and her revelations in Enver's apartment, and the anonymous informant who had contacted him.

"What does Dalca think of all this?" Ana asked.

"He will be reopening the case, pending a formal forensics report. He hasn't assigned anyone to it yet. "

Dalca was a newcomer, a relatively young guy that Andrei did not know well. "Dalca does not know about the informant. I haven't approached him yet."

"And Boboc?"

"He is still irate that I persisted with this case. He told me to go at it alone."

"So no one knows about this informant?"

"Correct." Andrei continued with his former thought. "And you know Boboc. He is all bluster. If push comes to shove, he will help out."

"So, what are you going to do?"

Andrei took the towel off his neck and wiped his forehead. "I ran long and hard, thinking about it and weighing my options." He covered his face with the towel for a second. When he lifted it off, he had a somber expression. "For now I'll go at it alone. I'll go to Sfântu Gheorghe tomorrow and meet this informant. See what she has to say."

Now it was Ana's turn to sigh. "Andrei, this is the SRI all over again."

"I know," said Andrei, in a gloomy voice. "I know."

The episode that had ended his career in the secret service had also started with an informant who gave Andrei a tip that he could not let go. It led to a prominent politician whose corruption Andrei exposed. The politician made sure that Andrei was taken care of. It was an ugly affair.

"What if this one also ends up costing you your job?" Ana asked anxiously.

"I'll sell groceries at the Sanpetru Market?" Andrei sported a forced smile.

"This is no joke." Ana was stern.

Andrei played with his empty juice glass and did not answer.

"You still think you're a hot-shot soldier."

Andrei gave his wife a resigned nod. He had served with the elite *Vulturil*, special forces battalion of the 6th Special Operations Brigade, headquartered in Târgu Mureş. It was a sleepy Transylvanian town two-and-a-half hours northwest of Braşov. His service record was a matter of special pride. His father, who had been an army officer, was particularly delighted that his son had made it into the elite unit. Andrei had served well and been recruited to the SRI directly from the *Vulturil*.

"You cannot keep being a hero anymore," Ana continued. "You were young then, and single. You almost died—how many times?"

"Twice." Andrei recalled his harrowing experiences with a malfunctioning parachute and with friendly fire in a live ammo exercise. "Looking back," he said, "it was a lot of fun."

"You actually mean that, don't you?" Ana raised her voice. She waited for her admonition to sink in. "Then you go to the SRI and try to be a hero there."

Andrei extended his hand to Ana across the table. "Baby, I know what you're saying."

His gentle squeeze defused Ana. "You are a family man now," she said softly. "You have her to think about." She nodded her head toward the bedroom where the baby slept. "And the other one we are going to make."

Andrei stood up and came across the table, offering a hug. They stood silently, their heads wrapped around each other.

"I promise I won't let it get out of hand," he whispered into her ear.

They separated. "I'll just check this lead and report the whole thing to Dalca, hand it over to him."

CHAPTER 25

ISTANBUL, MARCH 30

The tiny yellow taxi stopped in front of a twelve-story apartment building with a small pharmacy, coffee shop, and barber at its ground level. Mark looked up, out of the open window, with surprise. The building seemed residential above those businesses, a common arrangement in Istanbul. He turned to the driver, eyed the meter, and prepared to pay.

"Are you sure this is the right place?" he asked in Turkish.

The young driver peered at his mobile perched on a dashboard stand. "12 Selçuklar Sokak," he mumbled in a thick Anatolian accent. "Yes, this is it." He turned back and put his hand out for Mark's cash.

Mark shouldered Gazioğlu's computer bag and entered the building. The four-and-a-half-mile drive from Taksim, supposedly thirteen minutes according to his phone map, had taken nearly an hour. He cursed Istanbul traffic. He worried about leaving Semra alone at the hotel. He hoped she would not bolt and disappear.

Mark pulled out the business card he had received from Commissaire Gérard, back in Budapest. "Third floor," he mumbled to himself as he pressed to summon the elevator.

"Hello." Leon Adler offered a firm handshake at the door. He was tall and lean, his long, curly blond hair an unruly mess, the way it had been back in high school. He wore a rumpled white shirt, collar open, sleeves pulled up. His slacks seemed oversized on his slim waist. He had somehow preserved a youthful, boyish appearance.

Mark took a step in and looked around. He was at the foyer of a small apartment. "Is this your office?"

Leon opened a closet and pulled out a sports coat. He put his index finger on his lip in a "shhh" sign. He blocked Mark's advance into the apartment and placed his palm on his back, gently pushing him out. "Let's go," he mouthed to Mark.

"What's going on?" Mark eyed Leon curiously as they descended in the elevator. Leon shot a quick glimpse at Mark's computer bag, then buttoned the front of his coat and watched the numbers on the elevator monitor with keen interest.

They exited to the curb where Mark had been minutes before. "Let's go get some coffee," said Leon. He pointed to the right and began walking. Mark hurried to catch up. "Have you been to Akmerkez?" he heard Leon ask.

They walked hurriedly through the residential street, Leon taking huge strides with his stork-like legs. Mark struggled to stay abreast, repeatedly readjusting the strap of the computer bag that kept falling off his shoulder. It was a sunny afternoon. He felt sweat breaking out on his face and underarms.

"Sorry," Leon said loudly, looking ahead. "My place is not the best for these kinds of meetings."

"Why?"

Leon turned and looked at Mark, surprised at his naïveté. "We worry about bugs. You know: listening devices."

Mark felt stupid for not guessing. "Is that actually your office back there?" Mark managed to keep pace with Leon, at least for now.

"Yes," he answered, still looking ahead. "It's a nice, low-profile spot. I share it with Europol."

They came upon a huge boulevard and across it, a giant shopping mall with three cylindrical, blue glass towers jutting out of it. It was as if the high-rises were nails that planted the mall firmly onto the ground.

"Akmerkez," Leon announced. "Come on." He began jaywalking across busy traffic. Mark hesitated. "Come on!"

The mall was in the shape of a giant triangle, those blue towers one at each corner. They passed through a grand entrance with multiple automatic doors into a slick, modern four-story atrium. "This way," Leon directed.

They mounted sleek escalators that afforded an open view of a wide array of luxury stores and a vast food court. At the top floor Mark followed Leon into an opulent coffee shop. It was dark, elegant, and cavernous, nothing like Mark had ever seen before. They passed through displays of deluxe confections, spacious stands that offered fancy coffee-making gear, and gift boxes that presented different flavored coffee cans and stylish cups.

Finally Leon stopped at a small set of tables in a quiet corner, plopped himself down at an empty bistro table, and offered Mark a seat. Mark hesitantly placed the computer bag upright on the floor, leaning on the leg of the table. He sat down.

"*Selamlique*," said Mark with a chuckle. It was the name of the coffee shop, a Europeanized version of the Turkish word, *selamlık*. It meant the male part of the traditional, segregated Ottoman house, the female part being the harem. That's where coffee was consumed in centuries past.

"Metin Özgür!" exclaimed Leon, as he picked up one of two vertical cardboard menus tastefully arranged on the table. He seemed more relaxed. "I remember you."

Mark picked up the other menu and did not answer.

"You were a lousy football player." Leon's eyes gleamed as they peeked at Mark above the menu. "Or as you Americans call it, soccer."

"Don't remind me," answered Mark, forcing a smile.

"I was your captain in Dean House. Remember?"

Dean was one of four sports teams that all the kids in the English High School were assigned to. They were named after British forests, and each had its own iconic color.

"Yellow," said Mark. That's all he remembered. He had suppressed most of his sports memories a long time ago.

A young waiter appeared, politely asking for their choices. Mark was surprised to see that the place offered Turkish coffee in five different flavors. He knew of only one, just coffee.

Sensing Mark's quandary, Leon pitched in. "May I suggest the cinnamon-flavored. It is excellent."

Mark agreed.

"And let's have a plate of your assorted delicacies."

The waiter nodded and disappeared.

"So," said Leon, leaning back on his chair. "When your name came up, I must say I was rather surprised."

"Me too," said Mark. He sat stiff and upright. "I mean, when I heard *your* name," he clarified.

"Gérard?" said Leon.

"Gérard," confirmed Mark, recalling the avuncular Frenchman. "A very nice man. We became good friends."

"I can't believe that a fellow EHS alum got himself mixed up with someone like Gérard." Leon clasped his hands behind his head and leaned back in his chair.

"I can't believe that a fellow EHS alum became a policeman," countered Mark.

Leon chuckled. "Yes," he said, "that school did not strive to produce cops."

"So what's your story?"

Leon straightened up. "After I graduated," he said, "we—my family—we all emigrated to Israel. I didn't want to go to university. I ended up serving a long stint in the army and after that, jumped into the police force in Tel Aviv as a detective. Over there you don't have to be a patrolman first, as in the US."

"And Interpol?"

"I got tired of the streets. The filth. The scum." Leon paused for a moment, his face serious. "Interpol was a nice office job and it allowed a good deal of travel. I was stationed all over Europe and in Central America. And now here I am, back in my birthplace, in Istanbul."

148

The waiter arrived with their orders: two ornate oversized cups of Turkish coffee, each presented on its own rectangular silver tray, with a glass of water and a Turkish delight. Mark stared at his tray and leaned in for a smell. It was a uniquely strong scent with ample hints of cinnamon.

As the waiter departed, Leon said, "What about you? What's your story?"

Mark briefly summarized how he, like Leon, had emigrated after high school, going to the US; how he lived first in Chicago, then in San Francisco; his education as a doctor; his work as a radiologist; his first wife, whom he lost in a diving accident; and his second wife, whom he was currently divorcing.

"Then," he continued, "I ended up coming to Europe to meet another old EHS classmate, my best friend in those days, and found him dead in Budapest."

"Ahmet Gürsen." Leon leaned in and examined his tray. "I remember him. Sherwood House. Center fielder. *He* was a good football player." He took a sip of coffee. "How did you get embroiled in all this?"

Mark looked at his watch anxiously. All this socializing was a waste of time. "It's a long story," he said with an abrupt edge to his voice. "I'd rather tell you some other time. That's not why I came to see you."

Leon did not push Mark. "Drink your coffee," he said. "It's getting cold."

Mark did. It was thick and strong, the cinnamon flavor lasting long after it had gone down. He took another sip. For the moment, he thought, this was the right Turkish remedy for the sleepless adventure he had just been through.

"So," Leon brushed his hair with his fingers, leaving his curls yet wilder. "What do you have for me?" He leaned sideways and gazed at Mark's bag curiously.

Mark looked at the bag and then at Leon. He was unsure about revealing its contents right away. "Do you know a doctor named Mahmut Erkan Gazioğlu?"

"Yes." Leon shook his head with some disdain. "Only recently, though, because of you."

Mark looked at him quizzically.

"We don't deal with the sort of stuff he is involved in," Leon explained. "We have our hands full with drug runners, terrorists, and Syrians."

"But you do know something."

Leon nodded. "Illegal transplant surgeon, wanted by the French and Kosovar." He straightened himself. "We have a Red Alert on him. But unable to apprehend."

"Police protection, here in Istanbul," Mark added.

"Right." Leon threw the Turkish delight into his mouth. "So," he said as he chewed. "What about this guy?"

"He's dead."

Leon choked on his confection. His coughing alarmed the waiter, who rushed over, leaving the plate of delicacies he was bringing at a nearby table. "Are you all right, *beyefendi?*"

As Leon took a sip of water and tried to regain his composure, Mark continued.

"I found his body," he said. "Early this morning, in his Tuzla compound."

He hoped that Leon would not choke on his water too.

CHAPTER 26

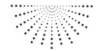

ISTANBUL, MARCH 30

Mark took a bite of pistachio delicacy from the assorted plate, which the waiter had retrieved. It was a croquante, a French-style cookie covered with avocado-colored pistachio paste. Rich, tangy, and sweet, the confection had nothing to do with traditional Turkish cuisine. Neither did this rather pretentious, faux-Ottoman coffee shop. He wondered how much all this would cost. Expensive, he bet.

Leon was recovering from his coughing spell, the solicitous waiter still hovering, no doubt concerned about the ruckus Leon was causing in the otherwise august ambiance.

"What exactly were you doing in Tuzla?" asked Leon in a hoarse voice.

"The surgeon invited me to his house," said Mark. "For dinner."

"And you found him dead?"

"Well, not exactly." Mark explained how Gazioğlu had sought him out at his hotel, and the subsequent dinner at the Tuzla compound.

"How did he know that you were at the Hyatt in Harbiye?" Leon asked, more to himself than Mark.

The question gave Mark an occasion for thought. "I don't know.

I never asked him the specifics. He seemed to know a lot about my activities."

"Through his local police contacts, I presume." Leon had recovered his composure. He threw a croquante in his mouth.

Mark relayed how Gazioğlu's girlfriend summoned him back to Tuzla in the middle of the night and his discoveries of the two dead bodies. He did not give any details of how they had died.

"So, did you notify the police?"

"No," said Mark.

Leon was taken aback by this answer. "Why not?"

"I was kind of..." Mark began answering sheepishly, "waiting for your help with that?"

Leon looked at his watch. "About what time did you discover him dead?"

"Four-thirty a.m. or so."

"So," said Leon. "It's been near twelve hours and the police have not been notified."

"Gazioğlu has a staff of servants and security people," Mark explained matter-of-factly. "I presume they have already found him and activated the police." He took a sip of coffee. "You know, when they came to work this morning."

"Oh, wonderful!" Leon said sarcastically. He eyed the computer bag again. "So what's that?" he asked, nodding toward it.

"One of Gazioğlu's laptop computers." Mark lifted the bag to his lap. "It was in his study at the Tuzla house. He had three computers there. This one contains surveillance videos from his CCTVs. I also have a couple of back-up drives."

He placed the bag atop the bistro table. "I figured if you guys reviewed it, you might identify the killers."

Leon sat back in his chair. "Let me get this straight," he said. "You made contact with an international fugitive and visited his house without ever notifying us or the Turks."

Mark nodded.

"Then you returned there to find him and his bodyguard dead. Murdered."

"Assassinated, probably," Mark corrected Leon.

Leon ignored the comment. "You failed to notify the police—or any other law enforcement." Leon's voice was rising.

Mark did not answer.

"And you removed crucial evidence from the crime scene."

"That just about summarizes it," Mark said with a slight grin.

"Are you out of your fucking mind?!" Leon shot out from his chair, his voice a near scream.

"Calm down, will you?" Mark said, startled.

"Are you okay, *efendi*?" The waiter reappeared, also alarmed.

Mark instinctively pulled back the computer bag onto his lap, covering it with his arms as if revealing it to the waiter would cause some harm. He felt stupid for doing so.

Still reeling from Leon's outburst, a phrase he heard the second time this morning, he pulled himself together. "We're quite fine, thank you," Mark lied, his voice trembling. Then, with more assurance, "Can you bring us another round of coffee? The same."

"Good move." Leon was simmering down.

"Gérard was easier to deal with." Mark muttered under his breath, as the waiter departed. It was audible enough. He stared at Leon with a stern expression. "He didn't have a temper."

Mark didn't wait for Leon to respond. He leaned across the table. "Look, I cannot involve myself with Turkish police."

"Why not?" Leon was calmer.

"My passport."

"What about it?"

"It's not kosher."

Leon raised his eyebrows quizzically.

"I don't have an entry stamp into Turkey."

"Why not?"

"I was smuggled into the country." Mark hesitated. He knew how this would sound. Weary of another outburst, he proceeded cautiously. "I crossed the border at Edirne hidden in a truck."

Leon waited for more.

"It was with a group of Turkish car thieves in Budapest. They run a chop shop there. I sought refuge with them." Mark was encouraged by Leon's expressionless face. "They smuggled me in along with their car parts."

Leon wiped his face with his palm and looked around the coffee shop, visibly trying to contain another eruption. He leaned across the table. "You are a real piece of work, you know that?" He said this gritting his teeth.

* * *

"So what do you want me to do?"

They sat amid a row of empty tables at the McDonald's in the food court one floor below. They had hastily finished their second cup of coffee at Selamlique in silence, the waiter fluttering around them with much curiosity. Leon had paid the bill—it was pretty stiff, as Mark had expected—and suggested they go somewhere else.

"I need you to be a bridge to Turkish police. Can you do that?"

They spoke in hushed tones.

"Look," said Leon sternly. "My job here depends on my good relations with the police. The reason I am effective is because I speak their language, know their values, and stroke their backs. You probably don't understand how Interpol liaisons function."

Mark had a decent understanding of it, having seen firsthand the relationship between Gérard and Kárpaty, the corrupt Budapest detective. Nevertheless, he stayed quiet.

"I do well with them," Leon concluded.

"All the better," said Mark. "You will know how to keep them at bay."

Mark handed Leon the computer bag he had been carefully protecting until now. "Here," he said. "I am sure this will help with the police."

"I presume you have some idea who the killers are." Leon unzipped the bag, looked inside, and zipped it back up.

"Not really, but I do know that this guy Vadim Rusu is behind all this."

"The Moldovan?" Leon was more engaging. "Gérard's memo did mention him. Tell me, what do you know about him?"

"As far as I understand, he is some sort of Russian operative, or maybe he trained in Russia. He runs a security company out of Chișinău. Ahmet's transplant organization." Mark stopped to correct himself. "You know he called himself Nicolae Radu in Romania."

Leon nodded.

"Anyhow, Ahmet's team somehow killed Rusu's son. They stole his kidney. So Rusu is out for revenge. He is eliminating everyone involved with this operation. In Budapest he used both his own operatives—they killed Ahmet—and local gangsters, who killed Ahmet's partner, a guy named Iancu Negrescu."

Mark waited for all this to sink in. Leon listened attentively.

"So, to answer your question, I am not sure who assassinated Gazioğlu. It could have been either."

"You mean Rusu's own agents or locals they contracted with."

"Right."

"If it is locals," Leon mused, "Turkish police would definitely be interested. It might help."

"Well, let's hope so."

But then Mark had another thought. "Let me tell you something," he proceeded with assurance. "As far as I can see—and I do have firsthand experience with this—Rusu's men are professionals. They're sharp and clean. Surgical."

"So?"

"Gazioğlu," Mark continued. "The way he was killed was real messy." Mark cringed as he recalled the horrific scene in Tuzla. "They cut his head off. Blood all over the place."

Leon made a face. After letting that sink in, he commented. "You mean it couldn't have been Rusu's men?"

"Correct." Mark was relieved that they were finally conversing without tension. "Want to know something weird?"

"You mean there's more?" Leon asked dryly.

Mark ignored that. "I looked for his head, but I couldn't find it."

"What do you mean?"

"I mean, Gazioğlu's body was there, in a bathtub full of blood, the floor full of blood. But no head."

Leon made another face.

"I think whoever did this, they took the head with them."

Leon pondered for a moment. "We need to convey all this to the police as soon as possible."

He took the computer bag and got up. "Let's go." He grinned sardonically at Mark. "Who knew that a lousy football player like you would one day turn out playing our game." He shook his head in disgust. "And equally lousy."

* * *

They exited onto the same busy boulevard. This time, much to Mark's relief, Leon chose to cross at a crosswalk by a traffic light. "How long do you plan on being here in Istanbul?" Leon asked him, amid the racket of passing cars.

They got a green light and hastily crossed the wide intersection into a quieter residential street. "I have a few loose ends to tie up," Mark said, trying to keep up with Leon's brisk pace. "Slow down, will you?"

Leon stopped and turned back. "What loose ends?" He sounded apprehensive, as if expecting another provocation from Mark.

"I am here to visit an old friend, a classmate. Her name is Günsu." Mark hesitated, realizing that he had never confirmed Günsu's surname, whether she had kept hers or adopted her late husband's. "In the old high school, she used to go by Günsu Aksoy."

The name clearly did not ring a bell with Leon. He turned forward and began walking at a distinctly slower pace. Since Leon was uninterested, Mark decided not to elaborate on Günsu and Ahmet. Instead, he said, "I also want to visit Latif Gürsen, Ahmet's father."

This drew a curious look from Leon. "He too was involved with that transplant business, wasn't he?"

Gérard appeared to have filled in Leon with plenty of detail.

"Yes," Mark answered. "He helped bankroll it, at least initially, and he was the one who introduced Gazioğlu to his son."

They turned a corner amid low-rise apartment buildings to a

street Mark recognized. Leon's office was a few buildings down the block.

"I knew Latif Bey well, back in high school," Mark continued. "I feel I owe him a visit to pay my respects." He paused. "And my condolences."

"He lives in Bodrum, right?" asked Leon.

Mark was impressed that Leon knew the details. "Yes."

"We'd be interested in any intelligence you can give us about him."

This surprised Mark. "Oh, now you're interested in this kidney transplant business." It was Mark's turn to be sarcastic.

"No," Leon answered. "We've had our eyes on Latif Gürsen for years. So has MIT." MIT was the Turkish internal intelligence service, the equivalent of the FBI.

"Why?" asked Mark.

"His activity along the southeastern border is something we do care about."

Mark recalled that Latif Bey was involved in numerous smuggling operations along the Syrian border. In fact, before sending Ahmet to Romania, he had first groomed his son in this specific business. Mark did not know that the old man was still involved in it.

"I can fill you in on whatever I find," Mark said, "if you can help me with one little detail."

Leon gave Mark a sly glance, as if saying *in your dreams, buddy*.

Mark ignored him. "I need his address. Now, that wouldn't be a big bother, would it?"

Leon relaxed. "Sure," he said. He looked relieved. "I'll text it to you later this afternoon. How are you going to get to Bodrum?"

Located in the southwestern corner of Anatolia, Bodrum, a popular Aegean seaside resort, was a long drive from Istanbul. Most traveled there by air. With his passport problem, Mark felt that air travel was out of the question. While there were no passport checks on domestic flights, this was his only valid identification, and Mark could not risk having it scrutinized by anyone, including airline staff.

"I don't know yet," said Mark. "I'll have to figure that out."

They had come to the door of Leon's office building. Leon stopped in front of the pharmacy and adjusted the strap of the computer bag he had shouldered since Akmerkez. He was about to say goodbye when Mark interrupted him.

"I have one more loose end."

"What's that?" Leon asked in an exasperated tone.

"Gazioğlu's girlfriend."

"What about her?" Leon looked like he was expecting the other shoe to drop.

"I am stuck with her," Mark said. "She is in my hotel room and I don't know what to do with her."

Leon smiled. "That, my friend, is something I can't help you with." He stuck the tip of his index finger onto Mark's chest. "Why don't you go for it? Give her a good fuck. You look like you could use it." He laughed.

Mark didn't find this funny. He hadn't expected Leon to be helpful, but it didn't hurt to try.

Leon slapped the computer bag by his side. "In the meanwhile, I'll see what we can do with this." He extended his hand to Mark. "You know, Metin Bey," he said mockingly, "I never liked you back in the English High School. You were of no use to me in Dean House."

Mark gave him a firm handshake.

"Now that we have reconnected, I like you even less." Leon took his hand back, turned around, and disappeared into the apartment building.

CHAPTER 27

ISTANBUL, MARCH 30

Semra rushed to him in relief, throwing her arms around Mark's neck. "My hero is back!"

She gave him multiple kisses on both cheeks, smearing lipstick all over. Then she stopped, her lips facing his, and leaned in. Mark withdrew his head. "Please." He tried to break free from Semra's grip.

Semra stepped back, sporting an exaggerated pout. Mark eyed her up and down. She had carefully put herself back on. Gone was the distressed, disheveled urchin he had pulled out of a freezing tool shed. The oddly eccentric, elegant model he had first encountered in Tuzla was back.

"I spent all day making myself up." She looked down at herself, running her hands along the outline of her body. "For you!"

She did indeed look ravishing in her simple get-up. A white sleeveless shirt was open a few buttons too far, generously displaying her cleavage. She wore tight cut-off jeans that gave enticing glimpses of her smooth, pale skin. She was barefoot, her long toes cleaned up and repainted. Mark marveled that in her agitated state when they left Tuzla, she had remembered to pack nail polish.

She slithered slowly toward Mark and placed an open palm on

his thigh, gradually running it toward his groin. Mark smelled the same floral perfume on her that he recalled from their encounter in the seaside garden the night before. He felt her hand on his arousal. She gently squeezed.

"How did you like your treat this morning?" she whispered seductively. Her lips were again close to Mark's.

This time Mark did not resist. As she gently pressed her lips onto his, her mouth slightly open, she squeezed with her hand, hard. Mark shuddered.

"It was good," he mumbled when he pulled back. "Very good."

She deftly unbuckled his belt and unzipped his pants. She kissed him again, her tongue exploring his, while her hand glided through his briefs. The touch of her bare fingers gave Mark new shivers. She moved her mouth across his cheek, chin, and neck, and nibbled on his ear. "Would you like another?"

Mark let himself go.

* * *

They lay on the bed, partially clothed, Mark with his shirt on and nothing below but socks. Semra lay sideways, her shirt off but her bra and jeans still on. She caressed Mark's chest under his shirt.

"That was awesome," Mark murmured, staring at the ceiling, still in the afterglow of his release.

He had tried to undress and penetrate her, but she had stopped him short, allowing only her shirt to come off, and had firmly stuck to her own agenda.

"Mahmut told me that you were an expert at this."

Semra chuckled and pinched one of his nipples. "He should know," she said. "He certainly asked for it all the time."

Mark looked at her. "I don't get it," he said. "He's been gone for, what? Less than a day. Aren't you upset?"

Semra took her hand out from under Mark's shirt. "To be honest, I was getting really tired of him."

She sat up and crossed her legs. "He wasn't very nice to me.

Treated me like a whore. Demeaning all the time, except when he wanted sex. Then he was demanding all the time."

"You two looked like a pretty good couple," Mark said, surprised by her declaration.

"Yeah, well…we weren't." She reached for her shirt lying nearby and put it on. "Besides." Her expression was dead serious. "I was sick and tired of Tuzla. I felt like a prisoner there."

She quickly buttoned up, this time fully covering her cleavage. "I longed for Istanbul. The people, the restaurants, the night life. I begged him to bring me here. And he wouldn't."

Mark could understand why Gazioğlu would be hesitant about being seen in public with her. He listened as she continued.

"Then you came." Her face brightened. "The moment I saw you, I knew that you were my salvation. My ticket out of Tuzla."

"Is that why you called me?"

She again became a playful girl and jumped on him with a vivacious hug. She pressed her lips hard against his. "Why, of course, my gallant knight!"

She pulled back, gave him an admiring look, and kissed him again. "And I was right. You did come to my rescue. You got me out of Tuzla."

Mark sat up and looked for his briefs. Semra quickly produced them from a fold in the sheets.

"Look, Semra," he said after he put them on. "I am in deep trouble."

She looked at him, bewildered.

"Those people who killed Mahmut and Halil," he continued. "They are also looking for me. They are after me, do you understand?"

A pout returned to her face, this one genuine.

"I cannot drag you into all this."

"But I want to be with you." She rested her face on his chest. "I want you to take me with you. To America."

Mark ran his fingers through her hair, baffled by how she could be a seductive vamp one minute and an innocent little girl another. He patted her back. "I still have some business to take care of here in Turkey, and all the while I have to be a step ahead of my pursuers."

Semra lifted her head and looked at him with fear in her eyes. He reached over and gently kissed her on the lips. It was the first kiss he had initiated.

"I have grown fond of you in this short time," he said seriously. "And that's why I have to find you some safe refuge."

They were interrupted by his phone ringing. It was Günsu. Mark abruptly got up and took the call in the bathroom, out of Semra's earshot.

"Tarık told me what happened last night." Günsu sounded anxious.

"He shouldn't have. I told him not to. I did not want you to worry." Mark spoke in a hushed voice.

"Are you okay? Tarık told me you were going to seek help from a friend in the police."

"I did," Mark told her calmly, hoping that she, too, would calm down. "I'm fine."

"Let's have dinner tonight. What do you say? You, me, and Tarık."

Mark looked at his watch. It was close to dinnertime. "Yes, but I don't want to stray too far from my hotel."

"How about Borsa? It's a short walking distance from you."

Mark remembered Borsa as an upscale restaurant in the Old City, serving financial bigwigs. The title meant stock market in Turkish. "In Eminönü?"

"It's no longer there. It's at the old *Spor ve Sergi Sarayı.*"

"Oh, okay." It was the old indoor sports arena that also doubled as a convention center. The place was indeed a short walk from his hotel.

"Good. See you in an hour."

They were about to hang up when Mark interjected. "Oh, there is one more, small matter."

When he returned, Mark found Semra watching music videos on TV, her head bobbing in synch to the rhythm. She looked up at him with curiosity.

"Good news," he said. "We're going out to dinner. At a fancy restaurant. Isn't that what you wanted?"

She threw the TV remote onto the bed and jumped up on Mark, arms around his neck. "I love you!" She gave him numerous giddy kisses.

Mark fervently hoped that she didn't mean it.

CHAPTER 28

SFÂNTU GHEORGHE, APRIL 1

The sky was clouding up as Andrei set out for Sfântu Gheorghe. A rainstorm was coming. Traffic in Braşov was slow. He figured it would take longer than half an hour, the usual drive time. Andrei had chosen to go there as a civilian, out of uniform. He drove his own Dacia Logan instead of the unmarked Škoda assigned to him and Boboc. He was playing hooky from work, at least for the morning. The only professional icon he took with him was his badge. He left his service revolver at home.

The Dacia cleared Braşov traffic and headed out into a wide valley on Highway 11. The Carpathian Mountains on the distant horizon blended with the dark clouds. It was a two-lane road, and soon he was stuck behind a slow-moving truck. He thought about passing it but decided not to. He had plenty of time. Besides, he needed to think.

Here I go again, he said to himself. The last time he had followed a hunch that took him on a personal mission was also via an informant. It had ended in the public disgrace and downfall of a colorful government minister and, soon thereafter, his own downfall from a promising career in the SRI.

Rain began pelting the windshield. Andrei turned on the

wipers. Ana was right. It would be in the best interest of his budding family for him to stick to the script and perform routine police work. He veered across the dividing line in an attempt to pass the truck, and felt a rush of adrenaline as a huge, oncoming truck came at him at high speed. Andrei swiftly returned to his lane, his pulse beating fast. The Dacia hydroplaned and skidded. Andrei compensated, slowed down, and put some distance between himself and the truck ahead. He waited for his pulse to calm.

He was not deviating from anything, he thought. Well, at least, not yet. He was simply checking out a lead. He had no idea what this informant would reveal. For all he knew, the woman might be a nutcase and the whole morning would be a waste. In that case, there'd be no harm done.

But what if she did deliver solid goods? What then? Would he take them and run, as he had while investigating a software licensing scandal at SRI? It had sidetracked him toward the politician whom, prior to that, he had known only as a tabloid figure in gossip columns. Once targeted, the politician had eventually targeted him back.

He followed the truck through the villages of Prejmer and Chichiş and finally got rid of it when he made a left turn onto Highway 12, while the truck continued on. Andrei now picked up speed. The hearty squall beating up his Dacia didn't matter. The road was flat and lightly traveled.

A ring on his mobile interrupted Andrei's thoughts.

"Hey man, where are you?" It was Boboc.

"What's up?"

"We need your report on those assault cases. Is it ready?"

"Shit!"

"Where are you?" Boboc repeated.

"I'm out to interview a witness," said Andrei. "On my way to Sfântu Gheorghe. Why do you need that report?"

"I don't know." Boboc was irritated. "Dalca has got something up his ass. Who knows what? He just asked for it."

"Damn."

"You did finish it, right?" Boboc knew that it was unusual for Andrei to delay reports.

"Sorry, no."

Boboc groaned.

"Hey, if I tell you where it is, you know...in the computer files, can you complete it? You know the case as well as I do."

There was a pause on the line. Then Boboc quietly said, "You're investigating that suicide at Schei, aren't you?"

"I thought you didn't want to be a part of it," said Andrei.

"Do I have a goddamn choice?" Boboc sighed loudly. "All right, tell me where the file is."

"Hey, thanks for covering me. I owe you one."

"I am not covering you," Boboc retorted. "I'm covering myself. I'll hand the damn report to the chief, but rest assured: I will also tell him that you've gone AWOL, running your own investigation."

He paused for a response. Andrei said nothing.

"Okay then," Boboc said. "You can deal with Dalca yourself." He hung up abruptly.

* * *

Hotel Sugás was busy with what seemed like a convention of Hungarian arts and crafts. Displays of embroidery, ceramics, and watercolors overflowed a nearby meeting room and into the lobby. Numerous women, many in traditional folk costumes, milled about. It took Andrei some time to reach the receptionist and ask for the manager.

He was directed to a garden restaurant in the back of the hotel. It was an oversized gazebo with wooden tables and stylish umbrellas that in good weather would have been quite pleasant. Now in the pouring rain, it was deserted. The furniture was soaking wet, the umbrellas weighted down by rainwater. Andrei sidled to the hotel building and stood under an awning. He patiently waited.

Soon a stocky man emerged and proceeded to the middle of the garden. He didn't seem to mind the rain. He wore a folk dancer costume, white shirt with bell sleeves, embroidered with flowery figures, and a buttonless vest. His head was covered with a plumed fedora. The Hungarian get-up was ridiculously small on the man's oversized frame, his belly protruding well beyond the vest, hanging over close-fitting black slacks.

The man circled around in place and eventually spotted Andrei in his hiding spot. "Braşov police?"

Andrei nodded yes.

"Pista Szabó," he said, tipping his hat. He had a leathery complexion and a rough stubble. "I'm sorry to send you out here in this weather. Come on in. Come with me." He spoke with a thick Hungarian accent.

Andrei followed Szabó through a side door and into a hallway that they traversed for a considerable distance. Szabó stopped at the farthest door and began searching his pockets for a master key card.

"Sorry for my appearance," he said, looking himself up and down. "Annual Hungarian Arts Fair. Have to look the part." He chuckled awkwardly. "You know," he added, "the population of Sfântu Gheorghe is almost entirely Hungarian." He kept patting his pockets.

Andrei knew, but he didn't care. He was getting impatient. "Where is the lady who wants to talk to me?"

Szabó finally pulled out the key card from a well-hidden pocket in his ill-fitting slacks. "Ah!" He gave Andrei a triumphant smile. "She's here." The door lock made a swishing sound and Szabó opened it. "Please," he said. "After you."

Andrei entered the room and found himself in a scene that best belonged in a comic opera.

CHAPTER 29

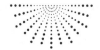

SFÂNTU GHEORGHE, APRIL 1

I t was, Andrei presumed, a deluxe hotel room, spacious, with a king-size bed, prominent TV console, and table with two armchairs. The décor, however, took him aback. Everything was yellow—walls, bedcovers, even the carpet. Andrei felt like he had entered a cave inside a giant lemon.

There was no one in the room.

The closet and bathroom doors were closed. Szabó knocked on what Andrei presumed was a bathroom door and said something out loud in Hungarian. The door slowly opened and a tall female figure appeared, walking awkwardly, as if she were on stilts.

She wore an elaborate Hungarian costume that would have stood out among those Andrei saw earlier in the lobby. It consisted of a baggy, embroidered shirt and a wide, multicolored pleated skirt with countless petticoats. It swept the floor as she waddled away from Andrei toward one of the armchairs. Strange as this was, it was her elaborate headdress that put the woman over the top. A huge tiara, at least a meter long, it swept out like the spread feathers of a peacock.

As the woman waddled toward the armchair, her skirt rustling, Andrei realized that he had not caught her face. He stood in stunned silence observing this ludicrous apparition and wondering whether his trip to Sfântu was indeed a waste of time.

Two steps short of her destination, the woman stumbled and uttered a soft cry, causing Szabó to rush to her side for assistance. She gracelessly plopped down into the armchair, her skirt spreading over the armrests. Her legs momentarily flew up, revealing a pair of bright red platform shoes that belonged in the 1970s. She hastily put her feet down and covered the shoes with the hem of her dress.

When she finally looked up at Andrei, he realized that she wore an ornate Venetian Day of the Dead mask that covered her entire face. The discordance of it all was too much. Andrei broke out into a laugh as Szabó and the woman stared at him silently.

Recomposing himself, Andrei approached the other armchair and cautiously drew it away from the woman. He introduced himself as he sat down. "I am Subinspector Andrei Costiniu, Braşov Police, Sector 1."

"I know," said the woman calmly.

"And who are you?"

"Magdalena."

"Magdalena what?"

"Just call me Magdalena."

The woman did not have a Hungarian accent. She spoke like a Bucharesti. Szabó remained standing next to her like a guard dog.

"How do you know me?" asked Andrei.

"I saw you," she answered, "coming out of Enver's apartment on Saturday. You and another plainclothes officer were leaving the building. The other one was older. A big guy."

She reached into the folds of her skirt and produced a business card, extending it to Andrei.

Andrei recognized his own card. Despite her strange get-up, the woman was legitimate. "How did you get a hold of that?"

"A neighbor," she said. "You handed it to her before you left."

Andrei vaguely remembered an old inquisitive woman he had given his card to. He took out his notebook and began writing.

"Why didn't you approach us then?"

"At the time, I wasn't quite sure what was going on. The whole thing, Enver's death along with the others, it was so shocking. I had to process it all."

Others? Andrei jotted that down with a question mark.

"Why this costume and the alias?" asked Andrei.

"That's my work," Szabó proudly interjected. "Traditional Transdanubian wedding dress."

Andrei seriously doubted that Hungarian folklore included platform shoes or Venetian masks. But he had to hand it to the two. Outlandish as it was, they had put together a costume that successfully thwarted any description of the woman. Andrei could not tell if she was tall or short, thin or fat.

"What's your relationship?" he asked.

"Family," said Magdalena, looking up at Szabó, still standing guard. She squeezed his forearm.

"What sort of family?"

"I am her sister's ex," Szabó explained. "I no longer stay in touch with my wife, but…" he almost uttered her real name, stopping at the last minute as the woman squeezed his forearm, "*Magdalena* and I are still friends. "

Andrei turned to the witness. "Why do you need to hide your identity?"

"Several reasons." She adjusted her mask, which was obviously uncomfortable. "For now, let's say that I am afraid for my life."

"Explain that, please."

"Whoever killed Enver and the others might also be after me."

Andrei was very interested in *the others*, but first he had to resolve a more important question.

"What's your relationship to Enver Muratovich?"

"We were co-workers," she answered readily. "Friends, too."

"What sort of work?"

"Medical," she said.

This puzzled Andrei. He stopped and stared at his notebook.

Noticing his perplexity, the woman added, "It is not a legitimate medical enterprise."

"You mean it's illegal?"

"Yes."

Andrei understood that this was why she was concealing herself. "So what is it?"

"Kidney transplant."

The answer caught him by surprise. He knew that an illegal organ trade existed, but he knew nothing about it. He certainly had no idea something like that might be operating in Braşov, in his jurisdiction.

"It's a pretty elaborate network," she said. "They run several branches here in Romania and others in nearby countries."

"So what exactly did Muratovich do for them?"

"He recruited donors."

"You mean he procured organs from brain-dead people in hospitals?"

"No, no. He recruited people who were paid to donate their kidneys. Poor people, peasants mostly."

Andrei hastily wrote this down. "Where are these donors?"

"Some in Romania. But most are from other places. Moldova, Bulgaria, Kosovo, Macedonia."

This, Andrei realized, was consistent with what he knew of Enver's movements, his frequent absences from home.

"Can you name any specific donors?"

"No," she said. "I don't have access to such records."

"So they kept records?"

"Naturally," she said, and added, without a hint of irony, "You can't engage in a medical enterprise without them."

"Who has access to the records?"

"Again, that's up to you to find out."

Andrei realized that his persistence in investigating the Muratovich suicide was leading him into a complex maze. It was reminiscent of his days at the SRI.

"So why do you think that Muratovich did not commit suicide?"

"I know him well," she answered with conviction. "He was not the type to take his own life."

Andrei instinctively nodded. This was a point that everyone seemed to agree on—he, Ana, and Enver's sister Emina.

"Do you know who might have wanted to kill him?"

The woman hesitated and proceeded in a more cautious tone of voice. "No," she said. "This is mainly why I contacted you. I was with him the morning of the day he died. Enver told me that two high-echelon people in his organization had died in Budapest. He seemed to think these were assassinations."

"Who?"

"Nicolae Radu and Iancu Negrescu."

Andrei jotted down the names. "Are they the ones you were referring to when you earlier said 'others'?"

"Yes."

"Just those two? There are no others who have been murdered?"

"Correct. I don't know of any others besides Radu and Negrescu."

One of those names sounded familiar but Andrei could not place it. "Do you know these people?"

"Peripherally," she said. "Not well. But I do know that they were executives in this international organ enterprise."

Andrei stopped to collect his thoughts. The woman continued. "Enver told me there had been rumors in Moldova that there was a plot against one of them."

"Who?"

"Nicolae Radu."

Andrei jotted this down. "Where in Moldova? And who from?"

"I don't know." There was fear in her voice now. "That's another reason I am contacting you."

"What's your role in this organization?" Andrei asked.

"For now, I'd like to keep this to myself."

"Are you a medic or a secretarial worker, an administrator?" Andrei persisted in the same line of questioning.

"As I said," she persisted right back, "I don't want to discuss this now."

"Look," Andrei said firmly. "I don't know if you can count on Braşov police to assist you if you're not forthright."

"But I am," she protested. "You can confirm everything I've told you so far. You'll see."

Andrei stared at her and did not answer.

"I'll tell you more in due course, I promise."

Andrei tried another approach. "Why do you think you are a target?"

"Because," said the woman, "unlike Radu and Negrescu, Enver was a peon. If they killed him, they might be after me, too."

Andrei wondered why anyone would wipe out the entire organization. "Are you aware of any rivals that might have done this?"

"Not as far as I know," she said with conviction. "We were the only ones."

"How can you be so sure?"

"You may not know this, but transplant surgery does not exist in Brașov. I mean," she corrected herself, "a legitimate program."

Andrei did not know.

"Patients who need transplants go elsewhere. Setting up such an enterprise in that city is not easy. If there were others, I would have known."

Andrei did not have the first clue as to what was required to set up a transplant program. He would have to interview legitimate hospitals about this. He moved on to another issue that bothered him.

"How do you know that Enver Muratovich's death is connected with those of Radu and Negrescu?"

"I don't for sure. Someone needs to investigate this." There was an unmistakable note of urgency in her voice. "All I know," she continued, "is that it is disturbingly coincidental for Enver to mysteriously die within days after the assassination of his bosses. It is not right for Enver's death to be ruled a suicide and swept under the rug."

"Okay, thanks." Andrei had heard enough for now. As he processed the information, he was sure to have countless follow-up questions. For now, his first order of business would be to confirm what Magdalena had told him. She had not made a favorable first impression with her ridiculous outfit, but her statements were certainly worth following up on.

"How can I contact you in the future?"

"Call Pista," she said, looking up at Szabó. "He'll know where to find me."

"Do you live here in Sfântu Gheorghe?"

"No, I live in Bucharest."

Andrei stood up. "I'll be in touch."

"Oh, one more thing." She too stood up, this time more steadily. Andrei cocked his notebook in anticipation.

"Bekim Zhulati," she said. "Write that name down. He is a surgeon who performs these transplants. He should be easy to find."

* * *

It was early afternoon when Andrei got back on the road. Szabó had shown him out, warmly shaking his hand and thanking him for coming. The rain had subsided but the road was slick. He drove slowly, deep in thought, ignoring the fact that he was hungry.

A doubt had crept into his mind about the woman. She had sounded forthright, and some of her information was indeed consistent with what Andrei knew. But then, by her own admission, she was part of a criminal enterprise and she had something to hide. Who knew what her angle really was?

Andrei pulled into a roadside stop, a gas station and small grocery that also had a food counter. Inside he ordered a double espresso and a *plăcintă*, fried pastry flat bread filled with *brânză* cheese. It was best to start with the names the woman had given him. One of them had sounded familiar. The coffee arrived first and he took a sip.

He opened his notebook and reviewed the names. Iancu Negrescu. He remembered now. Emina Bekic, Enver's sister, had mentioned that name as Enver's boss. This was consistent with Magdalena's account.

The plate of *plăcintă* arrived piping hot. He recalled Emina mentioning that she had trouble getting in touch with Negrescu. If Magdalena was correct, that would be because Negrescu was dead. He jotted down a reminder, in capital letters, to confirm that Radu and Negrescu had died in Budapest.

Andrei ate the *plăcintă* with his hands. The strong smell of the *brânză*, a creamy white sheep's milk cheese, permeated the area. He liked the tangy taste of the cheese with the fatty dough. He motioned the server at the bar for a bottle of Coca-Cola.

As Andrei downed his lunch, he contemplated the international criminal ring implicated by the informant. They were engaged in a crime he was not familiar with. Furthermore, if the two Budapest assassinations were indeed tied to Enver's death, this took the investigation well beyond his own jurisdiction in Braşov. He took a large sip of Coke and shook his head in bewilderment. What was he to do with this information?

Andrei looked around at his fellow diners at the food counter, staring at their mobile phones as they ate, blissfully ignorant of the sinister world he had uncovered. He envied them, ordinary people leading ordinary lives.

Outside, the clouds were beginning to clear, the pavement drying. There was another sip left in his coffee. He looked at it as he pulled out his mobile phone. He took his last sip, and tapped the final name he had received from Magdalena into the search engine of his mobile. Bekim Zhulati.

CHAPTER 30

ISTANBUL, MARCH 30

"Oh, my! This is so sophisticated," Semra exclaimed, staring at the nighttime scene of the Bosporus in the distance. The Ortaköy suspension bridge lit the horizon in various changing colors. "I wish I had brought that dress with me." She squeezed Mark's arm. "You know, the one I wore to dinner with you."

Günsu briefly glanced at her and took a dainty sip from her water glass.

They sat at an elegant, mahogany-lined booth along the back wall of the cavernous restaurant, facing picture windows beyond several rows of tables. The view included the lights of the hilltop Maçka district on one side and the Bosporus on the other. Mark and Semra sat along the wall facing the scenery, while Günsu and Tarık sat across from each other at the sides.

"This was a good suggestion," said Mark, addressing Günsu. She didn't answer, her eyes now resting on Tarık, who kept gleefully gazing to and fro between a bubbly Semra and his somber mom.

The restaurant was quiet, with a scant smattering of customers spread across a few tables.

"My apologies, Günsu Hanım." Semra squeezed Günsu's arm. "If I knew, I would have been better dressed." She put on a downcast face. "Unfortunately, they are all in Tuzla." Semra wore the same white shirt and cut-off jeans as in the hotel room, the shirt now wrinkled. She did put her hair into an elegant bun and applied ample makeup to conceal her tired eyes.

Günsu cringed and gave Semra a passing nod. *"Estağfurullah,"* she said. It was a multipurpose word with various different meanings. In this case, she meant *no offense*. She eyed a basket of assorted rolls from which she removed one covered with sesame seeds. She carefully examined the roll and then threw Mark a stern look.

"Oh, thank you," Tarık interrupted loudly, breaking up the tension as he accepted menus from a tuxedoed waiter.

They all sought refuge in the menus.

"May I offer you something to drink, cocktails, beer, *rakı?*" The waiter, tall and stocky, bore an air of self-importance.

"Certainly," answered Tarık. Then without waiting for anyone, "Bring us a bottle of *Yeni Rakı.*"

"Thirty-five?" asked the waiter, referring to a small, half bottle.

"No, no! The full one. The seventy." Tarık was resolute. "We could all use some."

* * *

Semra helped herself to a generous serving of leeks in olive oil. They joined cigarette *böreks*, fried eggplants with yogurt, and *plaki*, a bean salad, on her overflowing plate. "I am famished."

Mark sampled the leeks, a traditional Turkish dish he had not had in America. This restaurant's version was savory and delicate. The leeks, ordinarily stringy and chewy, melted in his mouth along with perfectly cooked slices of carrots that accompanied them, with a small smattering of rice and ample olive oil.

He took a sip of milky white *rakı* and observed the changing colors of the Ortaköy Bridge. Was it just the night before that he had crossed that bridge in a BMW? It seemed ages ago.

He was jolted by an elbow from Semra. "This is really good," she said, her mouth full of leeks.

Mark threw an anxious glance at Günsu, who was preoccupied with a small bit she had picked off her sesame roll. She then turned her attention to a splash of olive oil on her plate.

The table was full of appetizer plates. Only Tarık and Semra seemed to be partaking in them.

"Save room for the kebab you ordered," Mark admonished Semra, who was rapidly shoveling in her food.

Semra pointed her fork at Tarık. "I seem to remember you from somewhere," she said with a full mouth.

Tarık adjusted his glasses and took a cigarette *börek* with his bare hands. He threw the whole thing in his mouth, his cheeks and thick moustache bulging with the oversized load inside. He smiled at Semra, opening his lips to reveal partially chewed food.

"He is the one who drove us back from Tuzla!" Semra addressed Mark, proud of her realization.

"Tarık dear, mind your manners." Günsu frowned at her son.

Just then the waiter arrived with a busboy pushing a wheeled cart full of piping hot kebab plates. Semra clapped with joy at the tastefully arranged pieces of grilled meats, with hemispheres of rice on the side and elongated green peppers, grilled Turkish style, placed just so to complete the presentations.

Günsu ignored the kebabs and dipped another tiny piece of bread in olive oil.

* * *

"I thought that you did not cavort with prostitutes." Günsu quietly reproached Mark.

"I don't." Mark looked ahead, in the direction of the picture windows where, beyond the main dining room, he could see Tarık and Semra as shadows on the balcony. Günsu had sent them there after the kebabs. "Tarık, honey. Why don't you take the young lady and show her the view?"

"She is not a prostitute," Mark protested, pushing his half-eaten *döner* kebab plate away. He stretched back in his seat. Tipsy with *rakı*, he was irritated by the guilt trip Günsu was laying on him. "She is

Gazioğlu's girlfriend. I took her from the Tuzla compound. It was a horrible mess there."

Günsu took a sip of *rakı*. "Never mind."

She looked weary, older than her age. The lights that illuminated the booth highlighted her wrinkles and a few strands of white hair here and there. She gazed at Mark with those dark eyes that had mesmerized him back in their teenage years. "Metin," she said softly, "I always thought of you as a well-behaved, polite boy."

Her tone of voice had softened, disarming Mark. "I was," he affirmed. "I am!"

"Really?" She looked out toward her son and Semra. The two of them seemed to be having a pleasant tête-à-tête.

"We were all so proud of you," she continued. "All your old classmates."

She picked up a half-eaten *pirzola*, holding the lamb chop by the tip of the bone, and examined it. Her order had been four *pirzola*, of which she fully ate only one. Semra had picked up and devoured two others. Günsu contemplated a bite from the one that remained.

"Gone to America, became a big-shot doctor." She dropped the lamb chop back on the plate. "Look at the mess you've become."

Mark didn't know how to answer. He stared at his own half-consumed *döner*.

"This is the sort of mischief I would have expected from Ahmet." Günsu was not letting up. "Hell, even he would not have gotten into such trouble."

"He would." Mark corrected her. "He did. He got himself killed. Remember?"

Günsu's eyes teared.

Mark reached for her hand atop the table. "Look, I'm sorry," he said softly. Her hand was greasy, the lamb probably, or the olive oil. Mark didn't mind. "I didn't mean to hurt you."

She squeezed back.

"I came all the way here just to see you, to soothe you."

Günsu's expression softened.

Mark continued. "I met with Leon Adler. You probably don't remember him. He was a couple of years ahead of us. A jock."

Günsu thought for a moment and shook her head.

"He is a police officer now. Interpol. I am hoping he will help me out of this mess." Mark took his hand away. "In the meantime, I really need to do one more thing while here in Turkey."

"What?"

"I need to visit Latif Bey."

"In Bodrum?" Günsu was startled.

"I feel I owe that to him."

"Do you know where he lives?" asked Günsu.

"Yes. A place called Yalıkavak." Leon had kept his promise and texted Latif's address.

"That's a nice location," said Günsu. "It has become very chic lately." She thought for a moment. "I visited Latif once or twice in Bodrum, years ago. Tarık was still a child. He didn't live in Yalıkavak then. He must have upgraded."

Mark wiped grease off his hand with a napkin. "I am not sure how I'll get there," he continued. "Not to mention what to do with her." He nodded toward the balcony.

Günsu changed the subject. "This Leon. Do you really think he'll help?"

Mark sighed. "I'm not sure," he said. "I don't think we are off to a good start, Leon and I."

He ran his fingers through his hair. "I am not sure about anything anymore," he added, exasperated.

* * *

Tarık and Semra returned, Semra staggering a bit. "Look what Tarık got me." She raised a martini glass filled with a pink cocktail, spilling some on the tablecloth.

"You better go easy on that," said Mark.

"It got chilly out there." Tarık prepared to sit down.

"Sweetheart," Günsu interjected. "Can you take Semra Hanım to the bar? Metin and I need to discuss something privately."

The bar was outside the main dining room. Mark and Günsu

watched the pair depart, Semra leaning on Tarık while he held her drink along with his.

Silence followed as the plates were cleared. Günsu shooed the waiter away, telling him they needed more time to decide on desserts.

Mark poured himself more *rakı*, filling his tall cylindrical glass with ice cubes first. He watched the clear liquid percolate through the cubes and turn white.

"I have a place in Bodrum, not far from Yalıkavak," Günsu said abruptly. "You can stay there."

Surprised, Mark at first didn't answer. "Are you sure?"

"It's not much. A modest villa. But it has a wonderful view. You'll like it. It will do you good to get away to Bodrum."

"Well, thanks a lot. I really appreciate that."

"You want to go as soon as possible, right?"

"Right. The sooner the better." Mark took a sip of *rakı*. "I can reserve a bus ticket tonight."

"Don't." Günsu was firm. "Tarık can take you."

"No, I can't do that to him. It's too much bother. And I'm sure he has to be at work…?"

Günsu squeezed Mark's forearm. "It's not a bother. And he works for himself."

Mark stared at her with alarm as a realization dawned on him.

"He needs to see his grandfather." Günsu was dead serious. "Who knows, this might be the last opportunity."

Mark contemplated the proposition. Istanbul to Bodrum, round trip. He would be spending quite a lot of time with the young man.

"You want me to tell him," Mark said somberly.

Günsu's squeeze became tighter. "I want you to tell him."

"Are you sure?"

A tear ran down one cheek as Günsu removed her hand. She looked away, trying to conceal her face. "I know I am being a coward," she said. She turned back to Mark, tears now streaming freely. "I can't," she sobbed.

Mark slid over and hugged her. As she buried her face on his shoulder, he furtively scanned the dining room to make sure that Tarık and Semra were not within eyesight.

* * *

Mark reached for his wallet. Günsu firmly stopped him. "No," she said. "My treat."

Mark ignored her and pulled it out. He reached in. "Okay, you can pay. But I have something I want to give you."

Günsu took the black-and-white photo and examined it with curiosity. It was of a young Günsu, a head shot, with her lying prone on a beach blanket. She looked at the camera, her eyes squinting in the sun, her jet black hair in partial disarray. The camera had caught her by surprise. She smiled at it with thin long lips, slightly curled.

"What is this?" She looked at Mark, eyes wide.

"I took it. In one of our outings to Büyükada. Remember those days?"

Günsu nodded as she examined the picture again. "I remember you used to have that fancy camera," she mumbled.

The photo was an intimate portrait of a beautiful girl poised to become a young woman.

"I've kept this photo all those years," Mark said quietly. "Now, it is yours."

Günsu looked at the picture, then Mark, then back at the picture. "I did not realize that you loved me that much."

Mark did not answer. Evicting this long-cherished photo felt like a load off his back. Over the years the photo had morphed from that of a pretty girl to one that betrayed the feelings of its photographer. He watched Günsu contemplate the photo with a mixture of bemusement and woe.

She looked up at Mark with glassy eyes. "I fell in love with the wrong one, didn't I?"

Mark wondered how their lives might have been, had she come to this realization back in their high school days. "It's all in the past," he said. "We can't take any of it back."

* * *

Semra and Tarık returned with empty glasses. Semra was delighted to see several dessert plates laid out at the table. "Oooh," she squealed, "I want the *künefe* and the *aşure*." She looked around the table. "Does anyone mind?"

"Be our guest," Mark said, sweeping his hand over the plates.

They all sat and watched Semra gobble up the sweets. No one else had room for more food.

At some point Semra stopped and let out a loud burp. "Oh, dear!" she said, covering her mouth with her hand. She threw quick glances at Tarık and Günsu. "I'm so sorry."

"Semra dear," said Günsu. She reached for Semra's half-eaten plate of *aşure* with a fresh spoon and scooped some up. "How would you like to come and live with me for a while?"

Günsu's lips slowly swept the *aşure* while everyone stared at her, speechless. She chewed and swallowed. "Metin Bey here and Tarık have to take an important road trip."

This was news to Tarık, Mark noted. Tarık took his glasses off and stared at his mom with wide eyes.

Günsu ignored him and continued. "You might enjoy my place in Nişantaşı better than Tuzla," she said. "At least until they come back."

PART TWO

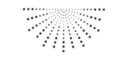

CHAPTERS 31–58

CHAPTER 31

ISTANBUL TO BODRUM, MARCH 31

"I don't know how to thank you for this."

Mark stared at the skyline of the Old City as the Toyota Verso crossed the Golden Horn toward Eminönü. The city had not changed much—the same old Istanbul of his childhood, the same domes and soaring minarets, the same men who lined the railings of the Galata Bridge with their fishing lines, the same fast-food boats bobbing up and down on the murky shores of Eminönü, selling fried fish sandwiches. Sure, there were signs of modernity, like the sleek streetcars that traversed the center of the bridge. But the Old City was still that, Mark thought. The new, expanded Istanbul had sprouted all along its periphery, for miles and miles.

Tarık turned left after the bridge. "Don't thank me," he said. "Thank my mother." His thick black moustache concealed his upper lip. His profile, with the exception of the moustache, so reminiscent of Ahmet, caused Mark to flash back to the old days in Ahmet's Murat, a Turkish Fiat, an amazing luxury for a high school boy in those days. Mark then remembered the mission entrusted to him by Günsu. He had no idea how he would break the news to the young man.

"I wouldn't want you to take on such a big chore grudgingly,"

187

Mark said, grasping at the only straw he could think of. "If you really don't want to do it, let's stop now. Your mom will understand. I'll persuade her."

Tarık waved his right hand up and down in a *calm down* gesture without taking his eyes off the road. He was navigating the small SUV through an impossible knot in traffic, weaving in and out as if in bumper cars, deftly avoiding collisions.

Soon they were on a highway along the Sarayburnu coast, at the foot of the great Ottoman Topkapı Palace, speeding under a series of white arches beyond a sign that announced Avrasya Tunnel. Traffic here was light.

Tarık took his eyes off the road and smiled at Mark. "Relax," he said. "I do want to do this."

Mark sighed inwardly, knowing he was now committed.

"What is this?" he asked, as the SUV entered the tunnel.

"The new underground tunnel across the Bosporus," said Tarık. "It takes four minutes to get across. Traffic is better here than at the bridges. Higher toll, less cars."

"Amazing," mused Mark. "In my day we had to wait in line, sometimes for hours, for ferries to shuttle us across."

Tarık chuckled. "Yeah, well. You're from the Stone Age."

The tunnel was a one-way, two-lane road. Mark did not see any oncoming vehicles. They were probably in another tunnel parallel to this one. "Allow me to pay the toll."

Tarık shook his head in disapproval. "You're our guest. No way we'll let you pay for anything."

The tunnel was initially downhill. "How deep is this?"

"One hundred six meters under the sea bed," Tarık answered proudly. "It's the deepest undersea road tunnel in the world."

Amazing, thought Mark, *such a modern convenience so close to the Old City*. Istanbul had changed after all, even at its core.

Soon they started climbing up in the direction of the Asian side. As a bright light emerged at the end of the tunnel, Tarık said, "When Mom suggested that I take you to Bodrum, I was surprised. But then I thought that a road trip with you might be interesting."

Mark looked at the young man quizzically. "How so?"

"I've never met anyone quite like you," said Tarık, steering the SUV onto the D100 freeway. "I want to get to know you."

Mark settled back in his seat and said no more.

* * *

They had set out on the road later than Tarık would have liked. Semra slept in late, lingered through a room-service breakfast, and then insisted on getting herself all primped up for that *hanımefendi*, Günsu. There was no way she would present herself disheveled, the way she had the night before.

Tarık looked impatient when they finally arrived. It was an eight-hour drive, he remarked pointedly, and it was already noon. Mark felt bad for the nuisance he was putting him through, but said nothing. Semra was too busy with bubbly excitement about her upcoming time with Günsu Hanım. She gave Mark a long goodbye hug, but to Mark's relief, refrained from kissing him in front of their hosts.

Now as they passed through the dense urban jungle of Anatolian Istanbul, Mark and Tarık remained silent. Finally, at Gebze, a small town on the outskirts, Mark said, "Your mom told me that you work for yourself. What kind of work do you do?"

"I'm a computer engineer. I do freelance work."

"So, you can work anywhere?

"Yeah, I don't need to be stuck in a fixed office." Tarık looked at Mark. "That's why I can do this trip on short notice without a problem."

"I figured you were a resourceful guy when I heard the story of how you found me in Budapest."

Tarık seemed pleased with the compliment. "Yeah, well. That was nothing, really." He then turned the question back on to Mark. "So what do you do as a doctor?"

"I read X-rays," he said, his eyes on the traffic. He paused and turned to Tarık. "Unlike you, I *am* stuck at an office all day. In a dark room, looking at computer screens."

"H'mmm," Tarık mused. "That's not how I imagine a doctor. Doesn't sound very glamorous."

Mark looked beyond the windshield and didn't answer. The young man was right.

Sensing his faux pas, Tarık quickly interjected. "Sorry, I didn't mean that as an insult."

"No offense," said Mark. "You're right. It's ho-hum. Boring." He smiled sardonically. "But you know what?" Tarık turned to him and they locked eyes. "Right now, I really miss that radiology room."

They both laughed.

"Don't you have some family in America? Anyone who misses you?"

Mark mentally scanned his friends and acquaintances back home. "No, I don't."

"Wow," murmured Tarık. "Sad." He quickly caught himself again. "I mean...I didn't mean..."

Mark cut him off. "You're right. Very sad."

"What happened?" asked Tarık. "I mean, how does a successful guy like you find yourself...." He was again lost for words.

"So lonely?"

Tarık did not want to affirm. He kept his eyes on the road.

"I had a wife whom I loved very much," Mark began his story. "College sweethearts."

Tarık looked at him as if he did not want to hear what was to follow.

"I lost her," Mark continued, "in a scuba diving accident, in the Caribbean."

"I'm sorry."

"Then I turned around and married the first cute girl that came along, an X-ray tech. Half my age."

"Sounds pretty good." He gave Mark an approving glance. "So where is she now?"

"She's pregnant," said Mark brusquely. He paused and waited for a puzzled face. Tarık gave him one. "With another guy's baby."

"Wooo!"

"Yeah, wooo. We're divorcing."

Tarık kept his eyes straight ahead.

After passing Gebze, they came upon a suspension bridge more magnificent than those that crossed the Bosporus.

"Wow!" Mark exclaimed. "What's that?"

"*Osmangazi Köprüsü*," said Tarık.

"Ha!" remarked Mark. "Named after another Ottoman Sultan."

Two of the three Bosporus bridges were named after victorious sultans from the Middle Ages—Fatih Mehmet, who conquered Istanbul, and Yavuz Selim, who conquered the holy lands of Mecca and Medina. Osman was the founder of the Ottoman Empire, which in those days was centered around the nearby city of Bursa.

"Yeah," said Tarık. "We're near Bursa. Osmangazi land. The freeway beyond the bridge is also named after him."

The bridge spanned the Gulf of Izmit, which protruded deep into Asia Minor off the Sea of Marmara, the town of Izmit at its easternmost end.

"I can't believe how modern Turkey has become," Mark marveled.

"Yeah," Tarık affirmed. "They built this to shorten the drive from Istanbul to Izmir." Izmir was the third largest city in Turkey, on the Aegean coast. They would pass by it on their way to Bodrum. "It saves two hours. It's a great shortcut."

Once beyond the bridge and through the toll gates, Tarık sped along a new tollway with scant traffic. As freshly painted lane lines whizzed by, Mark dozed off.

* * *

He awoke with a jolt as the SUV came to a stop. Tarık was sidling to a gas pump at an elaborate road stop.

"We're running low," he said as he got out.

He stuck his head into the vehicle after engaging the pump. "How about something to eat?" He looked at his watch. "It's almost four."

"Where are we?" asked Mark.

"In Susurluk, near Balıkesir." Mark realized with some dismay that they still had a long way to go.

The roadside stop, called *Karagül*, was massive. To serve the countless inter-city buses parked nearby, a large grocery store and a vast cafeteria sold a variety of foods, from snacks and sandwiches to kebabs and hot cooked Turkish home recipes.

They ate without talking. Tarık rapidly downed a hamburger with fries while Mark enjoyed a *sucuklu tost*, hot panini with Turkish sausage and melted *kaşar* cheese. He took sips of *ayran* in between, a yogurt drink.

Tarık emptied his bottle of Coca-Cola and wiped his moustache with a napkin. He regarded Mark with amusement. "You look like you're enjoying a gourmet meal," he said.

"You don't know what a treat this is." Mark pointed his half-eaten panini toward Tarık. "We don't get this in America."

"Still homesick after how many years?"

"Four decades," said Mark with a chuckle. He took another bite. "Yeah, still homesick."

"Maybe you should take a Turkish bride with you to America," Tarık said teasingly. "Might cure your sickness."

"Nooo," objected Mark with mock vehemence. "I need to lay off of marriage for a while."

Tarık opened his mouth to say something but then stopped himself.

"What? Go ahead and tell me."

"No, never mind."

"Okay," said Mark, turning the tables on the young man. "How about you? You're more eligible for marriage than I."

Tarık stuck a toothpick between his teeth and carefully examined the piece of meat he removed at the tip of the pick. "I just broke up with a long-time girlfriend," he said dolefully, his eyes on the toothpick.

"How about Semra?" Mark didn't miss a beat with a response. "You two looked like you were having a pretty good time last night."

Tarık slowly laid down his toothpick and gave Mark a strange look, with a grin that Mark could not interpret. "I don't swing that way," he said.

"What's that supposed to mean?"

Tarık looked at his empty plate, contemplating whether to answer.

"Come on, come out with it." Mark was insistent. "Is this what you didn't want to tell me a minute ago?"

"I don't care for *travesti*," said Tarık, slowly and seriously. It was a Turkish word that meant transvestite or transsexual.

Mark looked at Tarık with disbelief, mouth half open. "Nooo," he objected adamantly. "No way!"

Tarık shook his head with a sad smile. "I figured you didn't know," he said.

"Semra?"

Tarık nodded in affirmation.

"I don't believe it!"

"Last night," said Tarık, "while we were getting on so well with each other, I asked her."

Mark pushed his plate away. Suddenly he had lost his appetite.

Tarık finished. "And she confirmed."

CHAPTER 32

ON THE ROAD TO BODRUM, MARCH 31

The road was just another highway, no different than those inter-city stretches of I-5 in California, endless asphalt, not much to see. Not that Mark would have noticed anything. He stretched back, with the recliner down, and stared at the top of the windshield, sulking. His half-eaten *sucuklu tost* was giving him heartburn.

How stupid could he be? Clueless!

He raised his head up and stared at Tarık, who was concentrating on the road. Mark could swear he wore a perpetual grin on his face ever since they left *Karagül*. Tarık threw a glance at him, still grinning.

Little prick, Mark thought.

"Are you going to mope the rest of the way?" Tarık admonished him. "Because if you do, you'll take all the fun out of this road trip."

Mark didn't answer. He sank his head back in his seat, wishing he could disappear.

"It's okay," Tarık pressed him. "It's not the end of the world."

Mark groaned.

"Hey, look." Tarık took his eyes off the road for a perilously long moment. "We no longer live in the world of your generation. There is nothing wrong with liking a *travesti*."

"I feel like such a dope," Mark finally said.

"Remember Zeki Müren?" asked Tarık.

Müren was a flamboyantly gay Turkish vocalist from the 1960s and '70s who had an affinity for makeup and women's clothes on stage. These antics, along with a powerful, expressive voice, made him a superstar.

"We all loved him, didn't we?"

Tarık was correct. Despite intense homophobia and deeply conservative Islamic values, Turkish society loved and admired Müren, to this day, decades after his death.

"That's not the point," answered Mark.

Ever since leaving the bus stop, Mark had re-run Semra in his mind, like a film reel. He had realized the clues that were there all along, her strangely tall, awkward appearance, her long arms, her husky voice. He now realized why Semra had refused to go all the way when Mark had wanted to. Why had she not revealed herself?

Mark was startled out of his thoughts by a loud ring that reverberated in the SUV. Tarık tapped his mobile, mounted nearby on the dashboard, receiving the call via Bluetooth.

"*Nasıl gidiyor?*" It was Günsu. *How's everything going*, she asked.

Mark groaned again and hid his face, as if Günsu could see him.

"Fine," answered Tarık. "We're past Balıkesir, approaching Izmir." He assured her that the drive was comfortable, and that they would reach their destination sometime after eight p.m.

"You know where the key is hidden, don't you?" she asked.

"Yes, Mom." Tarık sounded annoyed by her overprotective tone. "I know what I'm doing."

"And how's Metin Bey?" She obviously was unaware that she was on a speaker phone. Mark stayed mum.

"He is a bit under the weather," said Tarık. He glanced at Mark, who was giving him a stern stare, and winked. He then continued glibly, "Either carsick, or the *sucuklu tost* he had in Susurluk is not agreeing with him."

"Oh, my goodness," Günsu remarked. "You shouldn't let your

guest eat junk like that. Promise me you'll take him to a decent restaurant when you arrive in Bodrum."

"Will do, Mom." His perpetual grin had widened. "But I don't know how long his stomach will be unwell."

"All right," said Günsu. "Let's hope not too long. Give him my best, tell him *geçmiş olsun*." It was a common Turkish well-wish to sick people, *may it come to pass.*

At that moment Mark felt like it would never come to pass.

"I'll do that, Mom. Love you."

By the time Tarık hung up, Mark had straightened up his seat. "Does she know?" he asked anxiously.

"Yes."

"What do you mean yes? How could she know?"

"I don't know," Tarık shrugged. "Women have an instinct about that. She told me, after our dinner last night, that the moment she saw Semra at Borsa she knew immediately."

"Oh my God," grumbled Mark. "I am going to kill myself. I can never face your mother again."

It's a good thing Ahmet wasn't alive, he thought to himself. Mark would never have heard the end of it; Ahmet's jokes at his expense would have lasted a lifetime.

"Easy, easy," said Tarık.

"You know that your mom already admonished me for cavorting with a prostitute at the restaurant." Mark shook his head. "And now this!"

"In a strange way, *this*," Tarık emphasized the word, "was good."

"How?"

"Mom told me that you could not possibly have knowingly done this. She figures you are just naïve. You know…gullible."

"A dupe!" exclaimed Mark. "I'm a dope *and* a dupe."

"Go easy on yourself," Tarık laughed. "At least she still believes you're virtuous."

"Well, thank God for that," said Mark, sardonically.

They fell silent for a while, both watching the road.

"You know," said Mark, "I was really beginning to fall for her."

"So, fall for her!" Tarık sounded like an older parent. "What's wrong with that? That corrupt surgeon fell for her…what was his name?"

"Gazioğlu."

"Gazioğlu," repeated Tarık. "You know, Semra told me that she expects you to take her to America." He paused and waited for a reaction. None was forthcoming. He plowed ahead. "Take her! Make an honest woman out of her. An elegant woman." He grinned broadly at Mark.

Mark looked at Tarık in disbelief.

"You just told me how lonely you are." Tarık paused as if debating whether to say what was next on his mind. "And she herself told me how much you enjoyed her *company*."

He said *company* with a special emphasis, raising and lowering his eyebrows several times. With his thick black moustache and glasses, he looked like Groucho Marx.

Mark ignored him. "From the first time I met her," he said, "I knew there was something about her. Something strange." He paused. "But I couldn't put my finger on it."

Tarık laughed uncontrollably.

"What? What?" Mark was annoyed.

"Excuse me for saying this," said Tarık, still laughing, "but you didn't put your finger on the right spot!"

Son of a bitch, thought Mark. *He is his father's son.* At that moment he could have punched Tarık, in the shoulder maybe, but they were going too fast on the freeway.

Tarık pressed his point. "I don't get it," he said. "Semra told me that you and her, you know…" he made an obscene gesture with his hand. "How did you not notice?"

"Okay, enough," answered Mark. "I don't want to talk about it anymore."

But Tarık wasn't done. "So, maybe you missed the anatomical clues. After all, you are not a real doctor. You read X-rays, right?" He continued in a mocking tone, "And now you're James Bond."

Mark gritted his teeth.

"All that aside, aren't you from San Francisco, the gay capital of the United States?"

Mark nodded. "So?"

"So, haven't you seen any like Semra in San Francisco? Surely there must have been some."

CHAPTER 33

ON THE ROAD TO BODRUM, MARCH 31

"Izmir," Tarık announced, pointing to a spot on the distant horizon. They were looking at the Aegean coast from atop a hill. The city was a speck on the hazy horizon.

"Are we going through it?" asked Mark.

"No, we'll bypass and turn south."

"How much longer?"

"Oh, about three hours or so."

Tarık had thankfully dropped the subject of Semra and turned on some Turkish pop music on his mobile. For a while he drove moving in synch to the strong techno beat of the music. Mark found it quite annoying but stayed quiet. It was better than the ribbing he had received from the young man over Semra.

"Tell me about this place you guys have in Bodrum," said Mark.

"It was my late father's. It is not in Bodrum city." Tarık pointed to his mobile. "If you look up a map of Bodrum there, you can get an idea."

Mark made the necessary entry and stared at a map of Bodrum on the screen.

"You see how Bodrum is a peninsula," Tarık explained. "The city of Bodrum is in the south side of the peninsula. Our place is north. It is in a small town called Göltürkbükü." Tarık momentarily took his eyes off the road and pointed in the general direction of their destination.

"Göltürkbükü," murmured Mark. "Strange name."

"Yeah." Tarık went on to explain. "My grandparents' place was originally in Gölköy, a small seaside village in the 1960s. In those days, the Bodrum peninsula was not very popular. Roads were bad; there was no regular air service from Istanbul. They discovered it because they got into the sponge trade."

"Sponge?"

"Bodrum used to be a big sponge-diving center. Anyhow, they fell in love with the area and bought some land with a modest farmhouse on it. Dad renovated the house into the villa you'll see. In the meanwhile the area grew, and Gölköy merged with nearby Türkbükü, and they combined the names into that weird-sounding one."

Mark reexamined the map. "I seem to remember something about you sailing there."

"My dad," said Tarık. "He was the sailing enthusiast. He belonged to the Moda Yacht Club. Mom was never into it. When we took sailing vacations from Istanbul, Dad would hire a crew to help with the boat." Tarık smiled as he thought about old memories. "Those were good times."

"So how come you didn't take it up?"

"Don't know," Tarık shrugged. "It was not in my blood, as it was in my dad's." Tarık looked at Mark and chuckled. "I guess I was not Ilhan Bey's son."

Mark was struck by the comment. He wondered if he should use the opportunity to broach the subject. He couldn't muster the courage.

His eyes on the road, Tarık did not notice Mark's quandary. "Tell me about this guy you want to visit. What was his name?"

"Latif Gürsen. Ahmet's father."

"So, what's the deal with this Latif Bey? Why do you need to see him?"

"You never knew him?" Mark asked.

"No." Tarık gave him a quizzical look. "Why would I know him?"

"I don't know," said Mark, a beat too hastily. "Your mom and Latif both had places in Bodrum. Your mom had…" he paused to find a non-provocative word, "a relationship with his son." He checked to see how this went over. Tarık seemed unfazed. Mark continued. "She told me she met Latif there on several occasions, years ago. I thought that, maybe, you met him too."

"No," said Tarık curtly. "I didn't."

"Well, I knew him," Mark began. "Since I was in high school. I admired him. He was what kids nowadays would call a cool father."

"How so?"

"He was rich and glamorous. He led a devil-may-care lifestyle. He took Ahmet and me to places other parents would not allow."

"Like where?"

"Well," said Mark, thinking of an example, "I should say he did more of this with his son, took him to bars, nightclubs, and later on, whorehouses."

Tarık looked at Mark, eyebrows raised. He then shook his head. "I would not consider that a cool father."

"*Aferin*," answered Mark. *Bravo*. He continued, "I remember one night when we went to Maksim."

"The *gazino*?" The *gazinos*, or cabarets, of Istanbul headlined the most glamorous vocalists of their day.

"You heard of it," said Mark in a congratulatory tone. "In those days, Latif Bey was carrying on an affair with Güneş Yumlu."

"The movie star?" The name surprised Tarık. He knew that in her heyday, Yumlu had been a major superstar.

"Yeah. She was a *chanteuse*, too." Mark paused. "She was so beautiful," he murmured, recalling the actress. "So enchanting."

Tarık broke into the same grin he had sported about Semra. "You are infatuated with the most unlikely…" He didn't finish his sentence.

Mark gave him a friendly punch on the shoulder. "*Kerata*," he said. *Rascal*. "You didn't know whether to say men or women, did you?"

Tarık nodded, laughing.

"Anyway," Mark continued, "one night Latif took us, me and Ahmet, for a lavish affair at Maksim. *Fasıl* group, belly dancer, then Güneş Yumlu."

Tarık seemed unimpressed.

"Turns out, for Latif this was a business outing. He was hosting this Kurdish guy from Urfa, Kara Ibrahim. The man was an infamous gangster, a smuggler along the Syrian border who had no compunction about assassinating his rivals. His name was well known. He had become a celebrity in tabloid papers."

"You were there with the gangster?" Tarık was intrigued.

"I sure was. With Kara Ibrahim and his entourage, bodyguards and all. A menacing man, but very polite. He shook my hand afterwards and told me what a good boy I was."

"Wow!" Tarık was speechless.

"Yeah, and do you know what else?"

"What?"

"On the one hand, Latif did business with dangerous characters like Ibrahim; on the other, he had the police chief of Istanbul on his payroll."

Tarık's eyes widened.

"One time Ahmet and I went to an international soccer match at Mithatpaşa." Realizing that the name of the stadium had changed, Mark corrected himself. "You know, the football stadium in Dolmabahçe."

"I know which one. Go on."

"We were guests of the police chief. Best seats."

"So what kind of work did this Latif do?"

"You won't believe it," said Mark. "He owned a factory that made women's lingerie."

"No way!" said Tarık.

"Sexy, frilly stuff. He sold to Paris. You should have seen the publicity calendars his company produced. Those models. Very sexy."

"Amazing." Tarık shook his head in disbelief. "I take it he sampled some of those models."

"Don't know for sure, but I'd say highly likely," Mark answered. "The man was an amazing womanizer. Very charming."

"Now I see where Ahmet got it," Tarık said.

"As they say," Mark nodded, "the apple doesn't fall far from the tree."

It was nearing sunset, and the Verso's headlights came on. Mark took a deep breath. "Ahmet was very charming too, just like his father."

"Yes, I noticed. He totally bewitched my mom." Tarık sounded irritated.

"That," said Mark, "goes back a long way, to our high school days."

Tarık looked at Mark in disbelief.

Mark continued. "But then, it was not just your mom. He had a strange appeal with women, a natural thing. I never quite understood it." Mark paused to think. "I mean, he was indeed handsome and carefree and funny. And he was rich. But it was beyond all that. It was as if he emitted some chemical from his body that women could not resist."

"Like pheromones?"

"Yeah, something like that." Mark turned to Tarık and spoke emphatically. "I realized when I came to Budapest that his appeal with women had not faded away. Here we were in our middle age and it was still as strong as ever."

"How so?"

"Well, there's your mom. Then there was his new wife, whom I met. But the one that really convinced me was this masseuse named Olga. I met her in Budapest."

"Did she give you a massage?"

"No, but she gave one to Ahmet, minutes before he died."

"Yoo!"

"Do you know how I became involved in this, what you call, James Bond stuff?"

"Please tell me," said Tarık.

"I went to Budapest to meet Ahmet, whom I had not seen since high school. He had summoned me there asking for my help. When

I arrived…" He paused to properly frame his story. "To make a long story short, I found him dead in his hotel room. Freshly dead. No rigor mortis. Do you know what that is?"

"Yes, go on."

"As you might imagine, I was totally shocked. As I sat in his hotel room—it was a fancy suite—I found this masseuse's business card there and realized that he must have visited her. She had given him her private phone number scribbled on the back of the card."

"So he had bewitched her, too?"

"You're getting ahead of the story," Mark reproached Tarık. "So I looked her up and she told me that they had had a long-term relationship for years."

"Amazing," said Tarık, "but I do believe it." He thought for a moment. "Wait a minute. So, Ahmet was juggling a wife in Romania, my mom in Istanbul, and this woman?"

"And," said Mark, "he was still married to Meltem, his first wife in Istanbul. They had never divorced."

Tarık swore under his breath.

"This Olga was married, too. To a dangerous character named Cezar. Their last name is the same, Cezar and Olga Kaminesky. This Cezar was somehow involved in the illicit kidney trade, but I have not quite figured out how. He is elusive."

Tarık shook his head. "What a mess."

"Here's something else that's strange: Ahmet's summons, his letter calling for my help."

"What about it?"

"It came to me as a Romanian radiology report. Ahmet had jotted his message behind it in Turkish."

"So, what's the big deal?"

"I could easily decipher the radiology report. It was of an abdominal CT scan. The medical words were similar to English. But that doesn't matter. What caught my eye was the name of the patient."

"Who?"

"It was this Cezar, Olga's husband." Mark paused to think. "I still haven't quite figured out the connection between Ahmet and some CT exam of Cezar's body."

"Strange," said Tarık. "But I bet you will."

Mark chuckled. "You have too much trust in my abilities as a detective."

"I mean it." Tarık was emphatic. "You seem to have a knack for it."

"Well, I'd like to be done with all this and return to my X-ray reading room."

The road was now following the seashore. A waning moon reflected on countless waves. A few small vessels bobbed about, their lights glittering.

"We are entering the Bodrum peninsula," said Tarık. "We'll be there soon."

Mark let out a sigh of relief. "Finally," he said. "I've had it with this drive." He was already dreading the trip back.

"You can rest and relax in our villa before we visit Latif Bey. I'll take you around tomorrow and show you our little town."

"It's a deal." Mark was thankful to this young man who had taken on the chore of becoming his chauffeur. He felt that he had established a bond with him as if he were Tarık's uncle. He hoped that Tarık felt the same. But how would he feel if Mark worked up the nerve to fulfill the errand Günsu had given him?

"Can I ask you something?" Tarık asked guardedly.

"Sure, go ahead."

"Were you in love with my mom, too?"

"How did you figure that?"

"Mom showed me that photo you took of her. The black-and-white, from way back."

Mark chuckled woefully. "That photo is like an unspoken confession."

"It is," Tarık confirmed.

They paused, letting the comment sink in.

Mark spoke. "I was indeed. At one time, I was madly in love with her. A teenage sort of thing, you know."

Tarık didn't respond.

"Then I left and she became a memory, a fixed ideal. An *idée fixe*, as Hector Berlioz, the composer, would call it."

"*Symphony Fantastique*," said Tarık, drawing a second *aferin* from Mark.

Mark elaborated. "As I said, I seem to have been attracted to most women who were drawn to Ahmet."

"Yeah, I found that a bit weird," said Tarık.

"Maybe," Mark conceded. "That masseuse Olga, in particular," Mark confessed. "She was really gorgeous. I am still a bit fixated on her."

Tarık found this amusing. "Not in a teenage sort of way, I hope."

"No." Mark became serious. "Definitely not in a teenage sort of way. Not like your mom, who I carried a torch for like the sort you'd find in nineteenth-century novels."

"So what kind of a crush is it?"

"Olga?" Mark decided to let go. "I would love to fuck her brains out."

Tarık let out a hearty laugh. It was infectious. Mark began laughing too.

They exited the highway onto progressively smaller country roads. It was dark now, and Mark could not make out anything beyond what the headlights illuminated. Tarık turned onto a poorly paved road and started uphill.

"This is the drive to our villa," Tarık announced.

The SUV bounced up and down as if on springs as they traversed ridges and potholes. Mark was jolted out of his seat as the Verso fell into a particularly deep hole, making a crashing sound.

"Sorry," said Tarık. "It's gotten worse since I last came here. I'll slow down."

Mark forgot about the rough undulations as they gained more elevation; he was captivated by the lights of the seaside village down below, twinkling on the Aegean Sea.

Tarık eventually came to a dusty stop. He turned off the engine and engaged the emergency brake.

"Finally," said Mark with relief. He reached for the door handle. "Thanks for getting us here safe and sound."

Tarık sat still in his seat, his arm bracing the steering wheel. He looked at Mark. "I have to tell you something."

Mark let go of the handle.

"I think it would have been better if you had been Mom's lover rather than Ahmet."

CHAPTER 34

BRAȘOV, APRIL 1

"Hey, you need to come and remove the guy in sixteen." The voice was angry and adamant. Zhulati looked at the screen on his mobile. The incoming number was not familiar.

"Wrong number," he murmured, wiping sweat off his forehead. He looked for his bottle of vodka. It was lying on its side on a table next to his recliner. There was a strong smell of alcohol from where it had spilled. He took the bottle and righted it. To his delight, there were about two fingerbreadths that remained inside.

"Hey, don't hang up."

Zhulati took a chug.

"It's not a wrong number. You are Zhulati, aren't you?"

Zhulati let out a loud burp. "And who are you?"

"Hotel Afroditei."

The name rang a bell. "What the fuck?"

"You guys dropped off one of your people here…" The man paused to think. "Four days ago. He was supposed to be here two days. Well, he is still here. You need to pick him up and pay me for the extra days."

"Where's Enver?" asked Zhulati. He recognized Afroditei as one of the hotels they used for the recovering donors. The guy was right. Two days was their usual routine.

"I don't know," said the man. "I've called him several times. He won't answer. I found your number from an old message Enver had left with me."

Zhulati rubbed his face and tried to clear his thoughts. It was ten p.m. He'd been drinking for…he didn't know how long. "So who is it in there, this guy in room…?"

"Sixteen. I don't know," said the hotel man, irritated. "You guys never leave me names."

That was also right. They had made anonymity arrangements with the hotels. Zhulati had never stepped foot in Afroditei. He knew about it from Enver and others who handled the donors. The place was supposed to be a shithole frequented by prostitutes and low lives.

"Look," said Zhulati. "I am a doctor. I have nothing to do with transporting these people."

"Now you do!"

"Hey, go fuck yourself!"

"No," said the guy firmly. "It's you who's fucked. If you don't come and get this guy out of sixteen, I am calling the police. And it is your name they will get."

"Okay, okay. Don't do that." Zhulati shook his head. "What's your address?"

After hanging up he took a final swig, emptying the bottle. He waited for the drink to go down and dialed Enver. It went to voicemail. "Hey man, where the fuck are you? You forgot a donor at that shitty hotel."

He then texted Enver a somewhat more polite message, urging him to call as soon as possible.

He got up to get dressed, hoping that Enver would answer. Enver didn't. Cursing him in Albanian, Romanian, and English for good measure, he left his apartment and stumbled down the stairs.

* * *

Afroditei was in a back alley not far from the Black Church square in the center of the city. Zhulati viewed the colossal silhouette of the *Biserica Neagră* from the window of his taxi. The old Gothic edifice had acquired its peculiar name centuries ago, after a fire that almost destroyed it amid a war with the Turks.

As the taxi turned into a small street leaving the Black Church behind, Zhulati slumped in his seat, well aware that his own life had just lit up into a conflagration. He did not want to burn up like the church, like Iancu Negrescu and Nicolae Radu. He wished he was more sober for what lay ahead.

The hotel was an old dilapidated wooden structure, three stories high, in a small cobblestoned street amid residential houses. A rickety neon light bearing its name flickered above the door. Zhulati met the caller, the receptionist, at the lobby. The man was surprisingly young and skinny. He brusquely introduced himself as Tomas. He wore a dirty, partially torn Rolling Stones T-shirt and oversized pajama bottoms. He threw a spent cigarette on the floor and crushed it with his slide sandal. His bare bony toes were black with dirt.

He quietly led Zhulati up a flight of stairs to room sixteen, which he opened with a key and without knocking. He turned on the light switch and returned downstairs, leaving Zhulati alone.

It took Zhulati a few seconds to adjust to the harsh light cast by a single lightbulb that hung bare from the ceiling. The room was stuffy and had a sharp, disgusting odor of feces and dried urine. It was small and sparsely furnished, a bed in one corner, a chair that also served as a bedside stand, a tiny table in another corner. There was no bathroom or wash basin. Zhulati figured the guests must use a communal bathroom.

He felt something stir in the bed. He uncovered the sheets to find an emaciated figure lying in a fetal position, his back turned to Zhulati. He wore only a pair of boxer shorts, stained with feces. They had run down to the bedsheets as well.

Zhulati gagged and headed toward the only window in the room. He opened it, stuck his head out, and took a deep breath of cool night air. He then returned to the bed and turned the figure onto his back.

"Yoet," he shook the man. "Wake up."

Yoet moaned but did not answer. Zhulati placed a palm on his back, then on his forehead. "Damn it!" Yoet was burning up with fever.

He inspected the dressing on Yoet's left flank. It was the same one he had placed on the incision four days earlier. It was heavily stained with pinkish drainage from the wound. He tore off the dressing, provoking a louder moan from Yoet. He inspected the wound with additional light from his mobile phone.

"Fuck, fuck, fuck!" Zhulati withdrew to the shelter of the open window and took several more deep breaths before searching his contacts and punching a number.

"Kyril here." Kyril Kozak, Enver's Ukrainian driver, answered.

"Kyril, thank God you answered."

"What's the matter? What time is it?" Kyril sounded like he was awakened from sleep.

"Never mind that. Do you know where Enver is?"

"No. Is that why you're calling me in the dead of the night?"

"That donor you and Enver brought in from Moldova, the last one. Enver did not take him back."

"I'm aware of that." Kyril was sharper now. "I've been waiting for a call from him. I figured there was a complication of some sort."

"There *was* a complication all right." Zhulati said angrily.

"What?"

"No one has looked after him. Not even changed his dressing. He is sick in this hellhole of a hotel. He looks septic. I think his wound is infected."

"Shit!" Kyril paused a moment. "Enver didn't check on him?"

They both knew this was unlikely. Enver took diligent care of his donors. It was the foundation of his good reputation among the villages he frequented for fresh hires.

"Something must have happened to him," said Kyril.

The thought had not occurred to Zhulati. He'd been too busy

being angry to think of alternatives. Kyril was probably right. A sudden fear grabbed him in the guts. He didn't respond to Kyril.

"Are you there? Zhulati!"

"Yes, yes." Zhulati stuck his head out of the window again. "We'll have to figure out what happened to Enver later. In the meantime, we need to get this guy out of the hotel and take him to a hospital. Are you in Braşov?"

Kyril confirmed that he was. He'd been holed up in a hotel himself, waiting for a signal from Enver. "What hospital do you want me to take him to?"

"Somewhere away from here," said Zhulati. "Can you drop him off in an ER in Moldova?"

"Yeah," said Kyril. "There is one at Ungheni, right beyond the border. Spitatul Raional."

"Sounds good. Do that."

"It's a long drive from Braşov," Kyril added. "Five and a half, maybe six hours. Do you think the guy will make it?"

"I don't know." Zhulati's fear was audible. "Let's hope so."

CHAPTER 35

BRAȘOV, APRIL 2

Andrei arrived at his desk at the police station near noon. After returning from Sfântu Gheorghe the day before, he had been preoccupied with a backlog of case reports that his partner had dumped on him as payback for the one he had missed. In the morning he decided to take advantage of the sunny early spring weather and go for a brisk run before coming to work. It gave him time to think about the Muratovich suicide that wasn't. At some point—soon, probably—he would have to present his case to Dalca, his station chief, and he needed to be ready.

As usual, his desk was full of new paperwork and messages. Amid the mess, Andrei's eye caught a transparent evidence bag with a mobile phone inside along with some paperwork. As he was about to reach up and grab it, Boboc approached with a huge sausage sandwich, half eaten, and a mustard stain by the side of his lip.

"I want you to know that your report went over well with the chief." He sat down in front of the desk. A sharp smell of mustard and onions permeated Andrei's desk. "You are permitted to thank me." Boboc took a large bite of sausage. "Did you finish the ones I left for you?" he asked with a full mouth.

"Yes," said Andrei. "And thank you very much for yesterday."

"Where have you been all morning?"

"I decided to take some time off and go for a run."

Boboc stared at his sandwich and then at his young partner, observing him with bewilderment. "Run," he said, contemplating the concept. He took a bite. "When I get the urge to exercise," he said, "I lie down a while. And it goes away." He smiled, revealing a piece of sausage stuck between his teeth.

"No doubt," said Andrei distractedly, his eyes on the evidence bag.

"So how did it go yesterday, in Sfântu?"

"I met an informant," Andrei replied, looking back at Boboc.

"What's a witness doing there?" Boboc was skeptical.

"Long story," said Andrei. "I'll tell you some other time."

"So did you get anything?"

"I am not sure." Andrei refrained from describing the strange scene at the hotel. "I need to verify the informant's claims."

"Dalca wants to talk to you." Boboc wiped his mouth with a paper napkin. "He has reviewed the preliminary forensics on that suicide in Schei."

Andrei eyed the evidence bag again. It had to be the Muratovich phone that his sister had given him. The accompanying paperwork was probably a copy of the same forensics report. "And, what did Dalca conclude?"

"I don't know. He didn't say." Boboc threw the last piece of sausage in his mouth. "He just wants to talk to you."

Andrei could not tell whether this was good or bad news.

"Was Dalca perturbed about the multiple assault cases?" asked Andrei. The investigation was stalled. There were few witnesses and no credible suspects.

"No, not really." Boboc smiled at this stroke of good luck. "It turns out he just needed an update. The news media is hounding him."

Andrei wondered what would happen if the media got wind of the explosive material Magdalena, his Sfântu informant, had handed him.

"Thanks for covering for me yesterday," said Andrei. "I'll let you know about my informant once I find out more."

"Don't bother," said Boboc as he stood up. "I am not sure I want to know."

Andrei watched his partner lumber away, then finally picked up the evidence bag. He removed the phone inside and recognized the Samsung Galaxy. There was a sticky note attached to its screen. "I rushed this through," it said, signed by Katrina.

Andrei first scanned the accompanying paperwork. There were two reports. The first was a preliminary forensics summary of Enver Muratovich's apartment. As expected, there were no signs of forced entry, no signs of any struggle, and no unexpected fingerprints. Looking through the catalogued items found in the house, one caught his eye. A nearly spent industrial tape applier was found on the floor of the kitchen close to a small pantry cabinet where Enver kept nonperishable food items, mostly cat food. Andrei wondered what that was doing there.

He moved on to the second report. This one listed the technical specs of the phone, including Enver's passcode, its registration with the phone company, and its list of contents. Andrei leafed through, briefly stopping at the contacts list. Sure enough, Iancu Negrescu and Nicolae Radu, the two names his informant had given him, were there.

He picked up the phone, removed Katrina's tag, and examined it. The phone was off. Andrei turned it on and entered the passcode. As the screen came to life he heard several different chimes. New material had come in since Enver had died. The screen lit up with two texts and a reminder to check voicemail.

The texts had come from the same source the evening before, listed in capital letters: ZHULATI. Andrei read them.

He then went to the voicemail. It was not passcoded, so he could listen. He heard an angry voice, hoarse as if it had awakened from sleep, or maybe drunk. "Hey man, where the fuck are you? You forgot a donor at that shitty hotel."

The man's number was right there, above the voicemail

message. Andrei tapped the number and the phone initiated a call. It was answered on the first ring.

"Enver!" The man did not bother to say hello. "It's about time you called." He sounded genuinely irate. "Goddamn it, man! Where have you been? We're in a shitload of trouble here."

CHAPTER 36

BODRUM, GÖLTÜRKBÜKÜ, APRIL 1

Mark awoke to a bright ray of sunshine peeking in through a crack in the curtains. He had slept soundly and felt restored. He opened the bedroom window that faced a bushy hillside. He lay down again, covers off, and enjoyed the fresh breeze that blew in. He smiled as Tarık's last words at the end of their drive reverberated in his memory.

He was a good kid, that Tarık. Straight arrow. Not like his biological father. He had to have acquired his ways from Ilhan Bey, the father who had raised him, and of course, from Günsu. She seemed to dote on him as if Tarık were still her little boy.

Mark contemplated the mission Günsu had assigned to him. He had intended to tell Tarık about his real father during their drive to Bodrum, but he had been unable to muster the courage. Instead, it was Tarık who shocked Mark with his revelation about Semra.

He momentarily relived the bliss of the sex Semra had given him with her mouth. *His* mouth, Mark corrected himself. Did this mean that Mark was gay? Semra was more feminine than many women Mark had known. He was attracted to women. He couldn't be gay. But then, what difference did it make, anyway? Tarık was correct when he told Mark that we no longer live with the morals of the 1950s and '60s. Traditional Muslim Turks would differ with Tarık, a well-educated, liberal Istanbullu. Mark himself was no longer Turkish. He was a San Franciscan, and it surely was acceptable in his own world.

He wondered about taking Semra to the United States as she desired. Aside from the obvious technical difficulties—passports, visas, immigration issues—there was a more pressing personal problem with such a plan. Mark was currently divorcing a woman he had married on the rebound, after his first wife died. Was it wise to enter a relationship on another rebound? This one with a flighty, impulsive, unpredictable character?

And then there was the issue of...Mark didn't want to face it, but he had to admit it to himself. There was the issue of her penis. How was he supposed to handle *that*?

His thoughts were interrupted by a loud creak of the main house door. It soon slammed shut. He heard Tarık yell, "Are you awake yet?"

Mark left his room and found Tarık sweaty from a morning jog. He wore contact lenses instead of eyeglasses and his eyes glistened. There were droplets of sweat at the tip of his moustache.

"I'll take a quick shower and freshen up. Then let's go into town for breakfast," Tarık said.

As Tarık disappeared, Mark walked around the villa. It was a sprawling affair, with a spacious foyer that opened onto a living room on one side and a dining room on the other. Farther back were several bedrooms and a large kitchen adjacent to the dining room. A short set of stairs off the kitchen descended to what looked like a basement. Mark did not go down.

Instead, he went into the living room and looked out at the stunning view of a hillside sprinkled with whitewashed, flat-roofed houses that sloped downhill toward a sweeping bay of azure water. The small seaside town center was flanked by barren hills that jutted out to sea and encircled the bay. It was a peaceful, idyllic scene that contrasted with Mark's image of Bodrum, overcrowded and crass, filled with super-yachts, cruise ships, loud discotheques and tacky souvenir shops.

Mark imagined Tarık's ancestors on Ilhan Bey's side coming here decades ago, how rural and raw it must have been, so different from the hustle-bustle of Istanbul. Even now, this spot was still a peaceful getaway from the urban jungle of Istanbul.

"Nice, isn't it?"

Mark turned around to see Tarık drying himself with a towel. He wore a fresh pair of gym shorts and flip flops. His young body was lean but not overly muscular. There was something strikingly different about him.

"You shaved your moustache," said Mark, surprised.

Tarık ran a finger over his smooth upper lip. "Yeah," he said with a smile.

"Why?"

"Mom texted me this morning and told me to do it."

"It's that simple?" Mark was astonished. "Mom orders, and you follow?"

"Well," said Tarık sheepishly, "it wasn't that big a deal. I had only grown it recently, after I broke up with Hülya."

"Hülya?"

"The girlfriend I told you about. We broke up recently."

Mark eyed Tarık keenly. With the moustache gone, his resemblance to Ahmet was uncanny. He turned around and stared at the Aegean Sea spreading into the horizon. He realized why Günsu had done that.

* * *

"What's down there?" Mark asked, pointing to the stairs off the kitchen.

"Come and take a look."

Five steps led down to a shallow alcove with what looked like a messy storage room littered with tools, small construction equipment, and used peasant clothes.

"My dad had a good deal of renovation work done to the house," Tarık explained. "That's what's left behind."

"Okay," said Mark, and turned back to the staircase.

219

"Hold on."

Tarık put his fingertips onto a nearly imperceptible depression in one of the wooden panels that lined the walls of the alcove. The panel slid to reveal a metal door with a key code lock. Tarık pressed several numbered buttons on the lock, entering the combination. "My birth date," he said.

He opened the door and invited Mark into a small, dark space that was cool and dry. Tarık turned on a light, and Mark was surprised to find himself in a compact, walk-in wine cellar. Old moldy bottle tops stuck out of racks that lined its walls.

"My father was a wine connoisseur," said Tarık.

Mark pulled out a random bottle and brushed the dust off its label. "1982 Chateau Latour," he said. He looked at Tarık, quite impressed.

"Unfortunately," said Tarık, "just like with sailing, I never got into wine."

Mark explored a few more bottles. There was a variety of French, Italian, and Lebanese labels, all quite impressive.

"My mom sometimes serves them to our guests."

Mark walked to the door of the cellar and looked at the mini-basement alcove. He slid the wooden panel that had covered the door, and it totally concealed the entrance. "Why the secrecy?"

"Dad didn't want others to get in here and pilfer," Tarık explained. "The house sat empty most of the year and there were various locals traipsing through, you know, workers and cleaners and such. So he had his builder install these panels to hide it."

"Very nice," Mark said. He was impressed.

"Come on," said Tarık, sliding the wood panel back open. "Let's go to the village and have breakfast."

* * *

Tarık proposed that instead of driving, they walk. After being cooped up in the SUV the day before, Mark readily agreed. It was a gentle downhill to the waterside, first on an uneven dirt path, then on poorly paved, narrow streets. They passed by the whitewashed houses that Mark had seen from the villa. Most were uninhabited.

"Vacation homes," said Tarık. "It's not the season yet. Come July and August, they will be full."

The village of Göltürkbükü extended only a few streets from the beach. "Come," said Tarık, pointing in the direction of the water.

They walked by a beach that was subdivided into different parcels, with changing rooms on the sand and raised platforms on the water furnished with lounge chairs and tables. Tent-like covers offered protection from the sun. Steps were built all around, allowing access to the water. There were no beachgoers at this hour.

"People pay for these?" Mark asked. He had never seen such raised beach amenities on stilts.

"Yes. Bodrum is full of them." Tarık walked on. "Tourists rent them by the week or month."

Beyond the beaches was a modest marina filled with fishing boats. Souvenir stands nearby sold beach clothing and gear. Tarık stopped by a man sitting on the edge of the dock surrounded by a mess of fishing nets.

"*Merhaba*, Hüseyin," he said.

The man looked up, his eyes squinting in the sun. He recognized Tarık and sprang to his feet. "Oooh, Tarık efendi." They shook hands warmly. "What are you doing here?" asked Hüseyin, obviously surprised. "It's not the season yet." He had a thick Anatolian accent.

"I have a guest," said Tarık, pointing to Mark, who was standing a few paces behind. "From America."

Hüseyin stood to attention, facing Mark. He was middle-aged, with a sun-crusted leathery complexion and days-old stubble. He wore a sideways slanted cap, an old white shirt, and a partially torn vest. He shook Mark's hand with both hands. "Hello," he said in heavily accented English, respectfully. "Welcome."

"*Hoşbulduk*," responded Mark, standard Turkish response to a welcome.

Bewildered by Mark's perfect Turkish, Hüseyin turned back to Tarık, mouth agape, hands still gripping Mark's. Tarık introduced

Mark as Metin Bey, and explained that Mark was born and raised in Istanbul. This made the fisherman gush with delight.

"Oh, in that case, please," he said in Turkish. "Come. I'll buy you tea."

They followed Hüseyin inland to a *kıraathane*, a small tea and coffee shop that was the exclusive domain of men. It was full of fishermen drinking coffee or tea, smoking *nargile* (hookas), and playing cards or *tavla* (backgammon).

Hüseyin introduced Mark to the scruffy crowd, drawing hushed greetings. They then settled at a table in a corner, where an attendant brought them tea without being asked.

"I am so glad to see you, Tarık Bey. What a pleasant surprise. And how is the *hanımefendi*, your mother?"

After the pleasantries, Tarık explained to Mark in Turkish, "Hüseyin's father, Sait Usta, was a master builder, a jack of all trades."

"Fisherman too," added Hüseyin.

Tarık took a sip of tea. "It took many years to get that villa remodeled—teardowns, additions, a lot of inside work. Sait did all of it."

"Me too," said Hüseyin. "Helped my father. I've known Tarık here since he was a little boy."

"How is the Usta?" Tarık asked.

"Retired." Hüseyin chuckled. "Still strong as an ox. He is in his eighties now. Tends to his goats."

"We used to play football together," said Tarık, laughing as he put an arm around the fisherman. "He would intentionally act like an incompetent goalkeeper. Let me score."

Hüseyin put a cigarette on his lips. "How about those times we took you fishing?"

"I was older then," said Tarık. "Grade school and high school. I had to wake up real early, in the dead of the night, and join them. It was hard work, but very exciting."

"Ilhan Bey," said Hüseyin, "*Allah rahmet eylesin*, may God bless his soul, was a true *beyefendi*, a gentleman." He stopped and lit his cigarette, taking a deep puff. "He was a wonderful father to you."

He turned to Mark. "Every year, I could not wait for the arrival of their sailboat. We always knew they were coming because Ilhan Bey sent advance notice to my dad to prepare the house."

"We stayed here a minimum of a month, sometimes up to two months," said Tarık.

Mark tried to imagine idyllic summers by a sleepy seaside resort. *Sublime*, he thought. He had to admit he was jealous. His own adult life in America had been nothing but a rat race, pursuing an education and career. He admonished himself internally for thinking that Günsu's life had derailed. Despite her folly with Ahmet, she had otherwise led a pleasant life with a good husband, a precious son, and the trappings of a wealthy Istanbul lifestyle.

As Hüseyin ordered another round of tea, Tarık commented that they needed breakfast. Soon they had fresh baked bread and plates of cheese, black olives, and sliced tomatoes. It was a classic, simple Turkish breakfast—a modest *sofra*, a spread.

Mark and Tarık quickly got to work on the offerings while Hüseyin quietly finished his smoke. Afterwards, as Tarık took his last sip of tea, Hüseyin asked, "So are you here to show Metin Bey the sights?"

"Actually, no," Tarık answered. "He came here to visit an old acquaintance of his. In Yalıkavak."

Hüseyin turned to Mark quizzically. "Who might that be?"

"Oh, you wouldn't know him," Mark said dismissively. "An old Istanbul gentleman. His name is Latif Gürsen."

This drew a laugh from the fisherman. "Don't know him?" He shook his head in disbelief. "Of course I know him. Everyone knows him!"

"How so?" asked Tarık.

"He has been a fixture here for years. Big spender. A playboy."

Mark and Tarık looked at each other. "Sounds like him," said Mark.

"He used to have this big yacht, sixty meters long," said Hüseyin. "We all competed to work on it as crew. It was seasonal work, and every year his captain would put out a notice for fresh crew."

"Isn't your job good enough income?" Tarık asked.

"My job was fine," Hüseyin said. "Fish are plenty in these seas." He chuckled. "We just wanted to be around the women Latif Bey had on that yacht." He put his fingertips on his lips and made a loud smooching sound.

"That's definitely him," said Mark, also laughing.

"He is no longer into all that," continued Hüseyin. "The yacht is gone and we never see him out and about."

"What happened?" asked Mark.

"I don't know. He got too old, I suppose." Hüseyin drew up another cigarette but didn't light it. "He is holed up in that massive new villa he bought, the old Koç property."

"Koç?" Mark turned to Tarık.

"It's a wealthy family. The late Vehbi Koç used to be the richest man in Turkey."

Mark nodded. Now he remembered the name.

"He is entrenched in there," Hüseyin continued. "Big property. Eight bedrooms, I think. Indoor, outdoor swimming pools." He lit his cigarette. "He lives there with this foreign woman. Good-looking from what I've heard. She takes care of him."

"Any idea how we can get a rendezvous with Latif?" asked Tarık.

"You haven't arranged it yet?" Hüseyin was surprised.

"I figured we'd just go over and ring the bell," said Mark. That's what he had done as a teenager whenever he went over to Latif's Istanbul apartment in Şişli to meet Ahmet.

Hüseyin gave Mark an incredulous look. He turned to Tarık. "These Americans," he said. "I don't understand how it became such a great country."

Tarık laughed. "Don't mind him. Can you help us?"

Hüseyin pulled out a mobile phone and took a couple of puffs from his cigarette while dialing. He then spoke with the cigarette dangling on his lips.

"When do you want to visit?" he asked Mark amid a haze of smoke.

"This afternoon would be nice."

A few minutes later, it was all arranged.

"That was Serdar," Hüseyin explained, referring to the person he had called. "He moonlights as an *uşak* for the lady who runs the house." *Uşak* meant servant or lackey.

"He calls himself some fancy title these days." Hüseyin hesitated. "What was it?"

"Valet," offered Mark.

"That's it! *Vale.*" He took another puff and shook his head skeptically. "The *Vale*," he said, emphasizing the title with mock importance, "will take you there. Meet him in Palmarina at three o'clock sharp."

CHAPTER 37

BODRUM, YALIKAVAK, APRIL 1

"Palmarina," said Tarık as he pulled his SUV into a parking spot. For a moment Mark was disoriented. Was he in Turkey? They were in front of a massive marina-resort complex, the boats moored here very different from those in the sleepy marina of Göltürkbükü. Fancy sailboats, yachts and superyachts. The resort featured restaurants, swimming pools, elaborate water slides, and numerous upscale shops, all encircled by spacious pedestrian walkways.

They got out of the SUV and Tarık fiddled with his mobile, mumbling something about texting Serdar, while Mark took in the scenery. Yalıkavak was another valley spreading to a breathtaking bay amid low-lying hills. Compared with Göltürkbükü, just ten minutes away, it was a different world. The whitewashed, flat-roofed houses that populated the landscape were more dense, extending well into the hills. The craggy peninsulas bordering the bay were not barren. They were full of the same houses, as well as beaches and resorts rimming the shorelines.

"Come," said Tarık, motioning Mark in the direction of a nearby promenade. He noticed Mark taking in the sight. "It used to be just like Göltürkbükü," he said. "Then they built this damn marina, and it attracted big money. It spoiled the whole place."

They met Serdar in front of Mudo, an upscale clothing store near the entrance of the marina. *"Merhaba,"* he said, *hello,* shaking hands with Mark and Tarık in a businesslike fashion.

Serdar was in his early thirties, of medium height, and very slim. He wore a tight-fitting silk shirt and jeans, shirt buttons open almost halfway, revealing several gold necklaces. His hair was trendily cut, nearly bald along the sides, and a thick dark patch atop. He sported a suitably stylish stubble.

Serdar led them to a large Land Rover SUV and opened the back doors for his guests. Mark and Tarık settled into spacious captain's chairs as Serdar slid into the driver's seat, turned on the ignition, and adjusted the volume of the techno beat that suddenly blasted the vehicle.

Gliding through afternoon traffic effortlessly at high speed, Serdar addressed them over the bass beat of the music. "So, how is my cousin Hüseyin?" he asked, looking at Tarık in the rearview mirror.

"You two are related?" Tarık was dumbfounded.

Serdar laughed. "Yes," he said. "Although I try not to think about that too much."

"Why?" said Tarık.

Serdar turned the volume up as a new song began and hummed along with the first few lines. He turned the Rover uphill onto a narrow curving road. "I decided not to become a working stiff like the rest of my clan," he said, shouting over the music.

The comment struck Mark as odd. After all, he was Latif's *uşak,* wasn't he?

"So what do you do?" asked Tarık. "Besides working for Latif."

"I don't work for Latif," Serdar corrected him. He turned the music down. "I am, shall we say, an independent contractor. I provide valet services for the rich. I do whatever, for whomever, as long as they pay me well."

The road rapidly gained elevation, affording striking views of the town and bay on every switchback.

Serdar continued. "It bought me this." He slapped the dashboard of the Land Rover. "And a small restaurant in town that doubles as a disco at night."

"So, you don't know Latif Gürsen that well then?" Mark interjected.

"Oh yes, I do." Serdar corrected again. "I've been helping out Ileana for years."

"Who is Ileana?"

"The Romanian who takes care of him."

They were now high on the hill, past the whitewashed houses, on mostly empty, bushy land with an occasional villa here and there.

"She is older now," he explained. "But still a nice piece of ass." Mark and Tarık looked at each other.

The Land Rover stopped in front of a gate mounted onto a concrete wall. Serdar searched his glove compartment for the remote opener and pressed it. As the gate slowly opened with a loud squeak, he turned back to face his passengers.

"Ileana takes care of him," he said with a grin on his face. "And I take care of her from time to time."

A short uphill drive took the Land Rover to a circular driveway with an ornate fountain in the middle. There, at the foot of a set of stairs, a woman was waiting for them. She looked to be in her forties, a full-figured woman whose loose-fitting dress nonetheless revealed prominent curves in her hips and breasts. Her dirty blonde hair was shortly cropped.

Serdar swiftly exited the SUV and let his passengers out. He embraced the woman and gave her a peck on each cheek, a Turkish-style greeting. He then formally introduced Ileana to Mark and Tarık. Ileana led them onto the stairs.

Climbing the steep stairway left Mark short of breath, but when they reached the top, he saw that the effort was worth it. They were at the entrance of a vast property, high upon a hill, and the first thing that struck the eye was a large infinity pool fronting the property, overlooking Yalıkavak and its spectacular bay. Behind the pool was a single-story, red-tiled building that curved around in a semicircle. It was attached to the main house through a covered corridor. The main house was a two-story, flat-roofed villa, built as an array of irregularly shaped rectangles in a modern architectural design. Unlike the rest of Bodrum, it was gray stucco, not whitewashed.

They stopped as Mark and Tarık took in the view. Ileana smiled and waited patiently. She was accustomed to this reaction from guests.

"Wow," said Mark. "Very nice."

"Yes," she agreed. "Beats Bucharest." She beckoned them inside. "Latif is waiting for you," she said to Mark, who was momentarily taken in by her brilliant blue eyes. "The news of your visit was a pleasant surprise. He remembers you well."

They entered the semicircular building adjacent to the outdoor pool. Mark was surprised to find himself in a vast indoor gym with a long lap pool. On one side were slick exercise machines, on the other, luxurious lounge chairs. Everything was neatly arranged and looked unused.

"How is Latif Bey?" asked Mark, his words echoing in the vast space.

"Not so good," said Ileana. She wore light makeup that allowed her natural beauty to stand out on its own. "He doesn't take care of himself. Very stubborn."

They traversed the gym into the corridor that connected to the main house.

"How long have you been with Latif?" asked Mark.

"This summer it'll be twelve years," she said.

Mark imagined her a decade younger and a bit less heavy. She would indeed have been a perfect fit for Latif. "Iancu sent me here," she added.

They entered an imposing, high-ceilinged living room with two-story picture windows that looked out at the bay and the hills behind. It was luxuriously furnished as if in a page from *Architectural*

Digest. Like the indoor pool and gym, it also looked unused. They stopped again to take in the view.

"Iancu Negrescu?" asked Mark.

"Yes," said Ileana, also looking out the window. "Did you know him?"

"I met him in Budapest," said Mark. "Nice man." He shuddered as the image of Iancu's severed hand flashed back, on the steps of a giant rooftop Jacuzzi, his dead body floating inside.

Ileana did not notice Mark's distress. "It's a shame," she said, still staring out, "what happened to him."

"How did Latif take the news?"

Ileana turned to Mark and Tarık and gave them a stern look. "He doesn't know."

Mark was surprised. "And Ahmet, his son?"

Ileana shook her head no. "Do not tell him!"

They moved on to a large open space behind the living room, where an open floor plan revealed a vast kitchen and adjacent dining area. Ileana pointed to a set of imposing marble stairs nearby.

"He will greet you in his bedroom," she said, inviting them up the steps.

"So, how did you happen to come to Turkey?" asked Mark.

"Latif's wife had divorced him," she answered as she led them up without looking back. "He was lonely." She paused and then continued. "He went through his usual series of girlfriends—you know." She turned back to Mark, who was immediately behind. Mark nodded with a knowing smile. "Then he got his heart attack."

Mark remembered this from Iancu's account back in Budapest. That's when Gazioğlu had come into the picture as the doctor who mediated Latif's care, subsequently becoming the principal consultant to their kidney transplant enterprise.

They were at the top of the stairs. "He needed someone," said Ileana. "And in those days I was drifting, aimlessly." She sounded like she was describing centuries ago. "So, Iancu came to rescue us both."

"Come," she added, motioning them to the left. "He's here."

Just before opening the door to the bedroom, she turned to Mark. "He was a good man, Iancu. I am very sorry about what happened to him."

She did not seem to know that Mark had witnessed it all, and Mark was reluctant to tell her. "How did you hear?" he asked.

"I got a message from Vasile," she said, "his son."

The bedroom was cavernous but simply decorated in neutral beige. Decorative mahogany beams highlighted a low ceiling. A king-size bed on the far side had mahogany posts that matched the ceiling beams. An open door on the wall behind the bed revealed a master bathroom. Mark noticed some scaffolding and construction equipment inside.

Along the far wall, under a large mirror were a couple of armchairs. On the other side was yet another picture window, its view of Yalıkavak reflecting off the mirror.

Latif sat in front of the picture window, on a well-padded lounge chair with wheels, facing away from them. The back of his head was hazy amid a cloud of smoke. Sitting next to him was a stocky, bald male attendant.

"You have guests, dear," said Ileana.

The attendant stood up. He was very tall. He turned the chair around, toward the guests. Mark was struck by the shriveled up, dusky old man that was dwarfed by the fancy wheelchair he sat in, his legs covered by a blanket. He had gone completely bald aside from a few wisps of white hair here and there. His eyes were dull and squinty, lost within a maze of wrinkles that crisscrossed his face. He handed his lit cigarette, mounted on an onyx holder, to his attendant and waved away the smoke that still hovered around his face.

Ileana beckoned Mark to approach closer. Tarık stood in the background.

"It's Metin," she announced.

The creases in the old man's face parted to reveal a faint smile. He extended both hands toward Mark. "Oh, my boy!" he said in a croaky voice. "What a great pleasure. Welcome."

Mark approached Latif, bowed down respectfully, and took

Latif's right hand onto his. He kissed the back of Latif's hand and placed it on his forehead in a traditional Turkish expression of respect.

Latif responded by petting Mark's head in a reciprocal gesture. "Come now," he said. "No need for that."

He tried to reach up to Mark with his arms extended, drawing alarm from his giant attendant. Mark understood and came closer, leaning down to receive a hug from Latif.

As he released Mark, Latif searched and found Ileana, who had stepped close to him. "He is a good boy," he said to her, pointing at Mark, his eyes moist with tears. Mark felt himself tearing up.

"Tell me," said Latif. "What have you been doing with your life?"

"I live in America," Mark answered. "I am a doctor."

Latif patted Mark's back. He addressed Ileana. "He was a bright boy. We knew he was destined for great things."

Tarık remained in the background and observed the scene with interest.

"I knew your father," said Latif. "I met him when you and my son were graduating from high school."

Mark knew. His father, a very different man from Latif, had surprised Mark many years later with an account of this meeting, in which Latif expressed gratitude for what a good influence Metin had been to his wayward son Ahmet.

"He was a great man, your father. A scholar and a gentleman. How is he?"

"He passed away several years ago."

Latif contemplated the news. "I am sorry to hear that," he said. "We're all dropping like autumn leaves." He looked up at Ileana standing by him and put his arm around her waist. "I too should have been dead years ago. But this woman refuses to let me go."

Ileana smiled at Latif affectionately.

"She is a good woman," said Latif. He then slapped Ileana's bottom. "And a nice piece of ass, don't you think?"

Ileana did not seem to mind. She and Mark exchanged glances. He figured she was accustomed to this sort of treatment. Mark wondered whether Serdar's boast about himself and Ileana was true. If so, Mark could understand why. Ileana's position here wasn't all that different from Semra's in Tuzla, a gilded cage from which she needed occasional escape.

At that moment Latif's attention fell to a point behind Mark. Mark turned to notice that Tarık had approached closer.

"Oh, my God!" exclaimed Latif, thunderstruck, his voice nearly a scream. "Come here, my son!" He extended his arms out enthusiastically.

Realizing that the old man was addressing him, Tarık froze with surprise.

"Come and give your old man a hug!" Latif shouted with delight.

Tarık looked at Mark quizzically.

Mark made a concealed waving motion with a hand by his side. "Just go with it," he whispered to Tarık.

Tarık cautiously approached Latif and attempted to kiss the back of his hand, as Mark had done. The gesture was cut off with an abrupt slap on his face.

"Oh, don't be silly," said Latif. He drew Tarık into his arms with surprising force and gave him a tight hug, kissing Tarık's cheeks more times than the usual Turkish courtesy.

CHAPTER 38

BODRUM, YALIKAVAK, APRIL 1

"**M**y God!" exclaimed the old man, holding Tarık's cheeks between his hands. "You have not aged one bit." He peeked at Mark standing behind. "Look how old your friend Metin looks." Then he released his hold on Tarık, who sprang back with relief and turned to Mark and Ileana for guidance. None was forthcoming.

"Tell me, my son: how are your children, and that wife of yours, Meltem? Why don't you ever bring them around?"

"They're good, sir," Tarık mumbled uneasily. "They are in Istanbul. Busy."

Latif turned to his attendant. "Hüsnü, fetch me another cigarette," he ordered.

Hüsnü looked at Ileana, who nodded yes. As Hüsnü drew up a cigarette from a silver box on a small side table, she said, "Now dear, you should not be smoking so much."

"So what?" objected Latif. "Is it going to kill me?" He turned to Mark and Tarık. "Look what an old heap I have become. I can't get around without the help of that *deve*"—calling Hüsnü a camel— "and I can no longer enjoy this beautiful woman." He pointed toward Ileana.

He took the unlit cigarette at the tip of the deluxe holder and waited for Hüsnü to light it. "Do yourselves a favor," he said to Mark and Tarık, "and don't get old."

"You have a gorgeous view here," said Mark, trying to change the subject. He moved toward the picture window and nodded to Tarık to join him.

"What's going on?" Tarık whispered.

"He thinks you're Ahmet. Just play along with it," Mark murmured, being careful not to look at Tarık.

"Why would he think that?"

"It's a nice view when you first see it," exclaimed Latif behind them. "But when you're here in this room, on this damn chair every single day, you get sick and tired of it."

Mark returned to Latif's side. "Don't you take him out?" he asked Ileana.

"We used to," she said. "But not in the last few months, after he became unable to walk."

"My back," Latif explained. "I have terrible arthritis."

"They advised surgery when he became too weak. But he refuses," Ileana explained.

"You think I am going to let those hacks cut on me?" Latif raised his voice in anger.

"I told you," said Ileana, addressing Mark, "he is stubborn. The older he gets, the more pigheaded he is."

Latif turned his attention to Tarık, who was pretending to examine the view. "Come here, my son," he pleaded. "We haven't seen each other in years. Don't stay distant." He ordered Hüsnü to bring a chair near him.

"Why didn't you tell me you were coming to Bodrum?" he said to Tarık, his bony hand tightly grabbing the young man's forearm. Latif's skin was like thin parchment, blue veins bulging beneath. "Where are you staying?"

"In Göltürkbükü," Tarık answered honestly.

The old man spat into a cup on his armrest. "Shithole!" he exclaimed. He looked up at Ileana. "Can you believe this?"

Ileana regarded him without a response.

"We have this magnificent mansion here and he goes out to…" He stopped as he realized something.

"When did you become friendly with peasants?" he asked Tarık suspiciously. "Was it that hoodlum Ibrahim who taught you to love peasants? Ha? In Urfa?"

Mark finally came to Tarık's rescue. "It's my property," he lied. "I invited him there. My family has a fancy villa on the hills overlooking the bay. It is not a peasant place."

"Well, this is unacceptable," said Latif. "If you're here, you're my guests." The croak in his voice momentarily cleared as he expressed an executive decision. "Mine. Is that clear?"

"Yes, sir." Mark figured arguing with him was futile.

"Ileana dear."

"Yes, my love."

"Prepare two guest rooms for the young men and have that *pezevenk*, what's his name?"

"Serdar?"

"Yes, him." Latif had called him a pimp. "Have him help my son and his classmate move over to our house."

Ileana pulled out her phone and proceeded out of the bedroom to call Serdar.

Latif pulled Mark's arm and beckoned his ear to his lips. "She is fucking that *pezevenk*," he whispered. "But what can I do in my helpless state?"

Mark did not know how to answer.

"I need you to take me away from here," he said more loudly. "You and my son. Take me back to Istanbul."

Tarık looked at the old man, startled by the suggestion.

"I want to see my birthplace one last time before I die," he said pathetically, as he sank his head into the plush pillow of his wheelchair.

* * *

"I am so sorry. I hope he didn't offend you." Ileana walked behind Mark and Tarık as they descended the outside steps to the driveway with the fountain. "Serdar should be here soon."

"No offense taken." Mark was gracious. "We will humor him and come back tomorrow to stay overnight."

Tarık shot an alarmed look at Mark.

"But I am afraid we cannot stay more than one night," he said, as he glanced back at Tarık with a *calm down* expression.

"It used to be better when he could get around," Ileana said. "We would take him down to the town, sometimes to Bodrum City. But his back condition——."

The sound of tires screeching interrupted her. Serdar, Mark figured, was approaching fast around the curves.

"His legs gradually got weaker," Ileana continued, "until he couldn't walk anymore. That's when I hired Hüsnü. I couldn't lift him and take him around myself."

The Land Rover shot into the driveway and came to a dusty stop.

"And that construction right by his bedroom has aggravated him further."

Mark recalled the scaffolding and construction equipment in the master bathroom. "I noticed," he said. "What is that all about?"

"Faulty plumbing," Ileana answered. "We had a broken water line within the walls that flooded part of the house. Now they are tearing up walls and replacing the bad pipes. It is dirty and noisy. And Latif hates having strangers around."

Serdar had opened the back doors. Tarık entered quickly. Serdar beckoned impatiently to Mark. He was wearing a different outfit, a formal one with white shirt and black bow tie, but no jacket.

"Anyhow, thank you," said Mark to Ileana. He extended his hand to her.

Ileana surprised him with a sudden hug. She held on to him a bit too long and gave him a single kiss on his cheek. "No," she said, her lips close to his ear. "I thank you." She separated from him. "Thanks for visiting and agreeing to come back. You can't imagine how lonely and bitter it's been here, at this mountaintop."

Serdar tore off in the Land Rover with his charges, saying how he had expected Mark and Tarık to stay for dinner with Latif. He complained about being called back too soon, taking him away from his restaurant.

They didn't speak much. Mark and Tarık held on to their armrests, Mark hoping that Serdar would not throw them off a cliff along with his precious Land Rover.

* * *

"What the hell was that about?" shouted Tarık as he himself tore out of the parking lot in Yalıkavak in his Verso.

"Slow down, will you?" Mark held on to the dashboard. He hadn't quite recovered from the roller-coaster ride Serdar had just put them through.

Mark waited until Tarık obeyed him. "Apparently Latif thinks you are his son, Ahmet."

They were on a two-lane road toward Göltürkbükü. To their left the sun was moving down toward the Aegean horizon, promising a scenic setting.

"Why would he think that?"

"He is old and senile," said Mark.

Traffic was light and Tarık picked up speed. "And now we have to stay there," he protested. "That place gave me the creeps. With that woman and the giant attendant."

"Humor him," said Mark.

Tarık shot him a skeptical glance.

"He was wrong about you, but not by too much."

"What's that supposed to mean?"

"He thought you were his son." Mark stared straight out of the windshield and maintained a monotonous tone. "You aren't." He turned toward Tarık. "You're his grandson."

"What?!" Tarık abruptly turned to Mark, momentarily losing control of his vehicle. The SUV swerved into the dirt by the side of the road.

"Careful!"

Tarık overcorrected and the Verso shot out into the oncoming lane, barely missing a pickup truck. He corrected again and brought the SUV to a screeching stop on the side of the road.

"Say that again!" he shouted at Mark.

"You heard me," Mark answered calmly. "You are Ahmet's son. Latif is your grandfather."

"No way!" He was still shouting. "How would you know that?"

"Check with your mom," said Mark.

"My mom? What about my mom?"

Mark ignored the question. "You are the spitting image of Ahmet, when Ahmet was your age," Mark explained calmly. "Especially with that moustache gone."

Tarık instinctively ran his fingers over his upper lip.

"Heck, I noticed it immediately when we first met, in Nişantaşı, even with your thick moustache. I am not surprised that the old man did not miss it."

Tarık's fingers tightly gripped his steering wheel and his head collapsed into it.

"You'd better get going," Mark said. "It'll get dark soon."

Tarık set out on the road, this time cautiously. Mark stole a look at him. Tarık appeared stunned, driving his SUV like a robot. Mark admonished himself for having been so abrupt with the revelation, but Latif had created the perfect opportunity, and Mark felt he had to take it before it passed.

Mark waited and made sure that the young man had it together. "So," he continued. "On that day, in your mom's place in Nişantaşı, after you left, I asked her."

"And?"

"And your mom confirmed."

"Why would she keep something like that from me?" Tarık objected.

"That, you need to take up with her." Mark turned his face toward the window. As he did, he noticed a movement on his outside mirror. It distracted him for a second. He couldn't quite make it out. He continued. "She did it for your own good, I think.

Ahmet would have been a terrible father to you. Look what a good man you've become under the tutelage of Ilhan."

Tarık did not answer. He was keenly observing his rearview mirror.

"What is it?"

"Police," said Tarık.

Mark turned around to see a patrol car rapidly approaching them with its lights flashing but no sirens.

"Better pull aside." Tarık brought the Verso to a gentle stop by the side of the road, to allow the police to pass. Much to his consternation, the police car also came to a stop, behind them. "Shit," he said. "Must be that move back there, when I lost control of the car."

The policeman was young and polite. He asked for identification.

"I am sorry about that skid earlier," said Tarık, as the policeman examined his driver's license.

He turned toward his patrol car and nodded to his partner. Soon a uniformed woman appeared, also young, resting her right hand on her sidearm.

"We need you to come to the station with us." The policeman was polite but firm. "Please exit your driver's seat," he ordered Tarık.

"Is that really necessary? Why don't you just give me a ticket?" Tarık argued.

"Exit now, please," the man insisted. "My partner here will drive your vehicle to the station."

The policewoman settled into the driver's seat, adjusted the mirrors, and asked Mark and Tarık to put on their seat belts. She then made a U-turn back in the direction they had come from. The patrol car followed closely, lights and sirens off.

"Where are we going?" asked Tarık, sitting behind the woman in the back.

"Bodrum City," she answered. "Central police station."

CHAPTER 39

BRAŞOV, APRIL 2

Traian Dalca entered his office in full dress uniform, the epaulettes on his crisp blue jacket bearing three small stars, the golden strands of his aiguillette forming an ornate arc on his right chest. Dalca was in his early forties but looked younger. He was tall and slim. He took off his peaked blue cap and hung it on a hook on the wall, revealing a prematurely balding scalp.

Andrei Costiniu sat uneasily on a chair in front of Dalca's desk and watched as his station chief struggled with a jacket button caught in his aiguillette. Andrei had never seen the Sector 1 chief in formal uniform. Dalca swore under his breath, managed to free the button and took off his uniform coat. He then loosened his thick blue tie, opened the collar button of his shirt, and sat down with a loud sigh.

Inspector principal de poliţie Traian Dalca's office was small and smelled dank. He nonetheless kept it clean and well-ordered. His desk was tidy, a computer screen to the right, a few papers neatly arranged in the middle, a framed photo to the left of Dalca and his wife, when he was younger and had a full head of hair.

Dalca regarded Andrei sternly with his small, dark eyes and noticed Andrei curiously observing his uniform jacket, now hanging on a hook. "Police Academy," he said. "I was giving a lecture there." He turned on his computer. "Pain in the ass," he muttered.

Andrei wasn't sure whether his chief was referring to what he had just done in the academy or the business for which he had summoned Andrei to his office. This was his first one-on-one with Dalca.

There was an awkward silence as Dalca stared at a blank computer screen, waiting for it to boot up. Once it did, he made a few clicks with his mouse, then opened a desk drawer and pulled out a file. He put on eyeglasses that made his eyes look even smaller and shuffled through the papers in the file.

"Costiniu," he said finally, regarding his subordinate through bare eyes above the glasses, "how long have you been with us?"

"About a year and a half, sir."

"Not much longer than me," said Dalca. He studied the computer screen, his index finger rolling the mouse. "SRI," he murmured. He took off his glasses and leaned forward on his desk. "You're no ordinary rookie cop," he said.

"If you say so, sir."

"It's not often that we get detectives joining us from the SRI."

Andrei knew this, but did not answer.

"So, what happened? Coming into the Braşov police force is not exactly an up career move," said Dalca mockingly.

Andrei was sure that his chief had some inkling of the answer. He tried to gather his thoughts for a suitable reply. Finally he said, "Politics."

Dalca leaned back on his chair. "Politics," he repeated knowingly. "Yes. It's all about politics, isn't it?"

Andrei nodded.

"Same with me," he proclaimed. "That's why I am here. Politics."

"What do you mean?" Andrei was genuinely curious. Talk around the station was that Dalca was too young for his post and had acquired it through connections.

"I too was on a different career path, in the General Directorate for Organized Crime." It was a fast track toward high rank in the national police.

Andrei wondered why Dalca was talking about himself. He had been summoned here, as Boboc had told him, to report his findings on the Muratovich suicide case.

"Instead," the chief continued, "I was sent here, from Bucharest, on a mission to clean up this department."

Andrei had heard about rampant corruption under Dalca's predecessor, a seasoned cop who had held the job for many years. He had allowed his men to run amok with bribes and shakedowns, creating unrest among disgruntled citizens in Braşov.

"I thought it was a worthwhile effort." Dalca stopped and contemplated his statement. "Well," he said, dismissively, "we also wished to be closer to my elderly parents. They live here in Braşov."

Andrei nodded.

"Is this why you switched from SRI? A worthwhile effort? Family in Braşov?"

"No, sir." Andrei was firm. "I was fired."

Dalca turned back to his computer and scrolled his mouse again. "Ah," he said knowingly, "the Emilia Sala affair." He took off his glasses and turned to Andrei. "Tell me, were you the one who brought her down?"

Emilia Sala was the country's former tourism minister, currently serving a six-year sentence in jail. Previously she had been a fixture in newspapers and magazines, a sexy young blonde with movie-star good looks, spouting fiery rhetoric. She had rapidly risen through the ranks of PMP, the People's Movement Party, and served in the Chamber of Deputies. She dominated headlines not only with controversial proclamations but also with her tight black leather dominatrix outfits and the occasional bikini-clad shot. Before her downfall, she had been considered a future contender for prime minister.

"In a manner of speaking," said Andrei.

"How so?" Traian Dalca clasped his hands and rested them on his desk, expectantly awaiting Andrei's answer. "Your file is rather scant on details."

Andrei was momentarily silent, contemplating how much he should reveal. "We were not after her," he said. "It was an investigation of the Microsoft corruption scandal. There were a lot of us in SRI who worked on that."

"Really?" Dalca seemed pleased with Andrei's disclosure.

"You know the Microsoft business, right?"

"Of course. Who doesn't?"

It was one of the largest corruption cases that rocked Romania, involving Windows licenses destined for use in schools being sold at inflated prices, the proceeds going to various intermediary politicians.

"She popped up in the middle of that investigation," said Andrei. "I was the one who discovered it."

"How so?"

"We were helping the National Anti-Corruption Directorate with the case. They were the principal investigators. Initially, her name was not on the list of targets." Despite himself, Andrei was warming to his story. "She was too clever to place herself directly on the take."

"Yes," said Dalca. "I've followed her career closely. Clever woman, but greedy, correct?"

"She lived a lavish lifestyle. Dorin, her second husband, was portrayed as a successful businessman, but he wasn't. When we looked into it, we discovered that he was perpetually on the verge of bankruptcy. She was forced to subsidize his failures."

"Interesting," commented the chief. "I did not know that. So how did you come to look into her?"

"An informant," said Andrei. "A secret informant that actually appeared from Dorin's direction."

"And he found you?"

"She," Andrei corrected the chief. "A woman who was having an affair with Dorin. Turns out, he was a prolific womanizer."

"Funny. I would have thought it was Emilia who had the proclivity for that."

Andrei nodded. "That was the image she projected. But actually, she was not promiscuous at all. Her quest, in my opinion, was mainly for power."

"So what about this woman? Dorin's lover."

"She was jilted and pissed off. Classic story." Andrei chuckled. "Anyhow, I had been assigned to investigate the Microsoft matter in Sala's district. So this woman contacted me. She provided intelligence connecting Emilia and Dorin to the Microsoft affair, with evidence to back it up."

"Did anyone else know about this?"

"Not at first. Just me."

"So what did you do with it?"

"It put me in a bind," Andrei admitted. "This material was not in our principal line of investigation. We already had our hands full with plenty of easy targets whose capture would have satisfied our superiors. We really did not need to go after a figure like Emilia Sala. I knew from the start that she would create trouble."

"But you did go after her, didn't you?"

"Believe me," said Andrei, "it was not an easy decision. I spent sleepless nights over it. I knew that Sala would not take it lying down. She'd retaliate."

"Were you single at the time?"

"Newly married. My wife is a nurse. She was all against it."

"But you didn't let go."

"I couldn't," said Andrei. "And when Sala found herself in a shit storm, I'm quite certain that she had her people dig down and look for who had started it."

"I can just imagine what they did to you," said Traian Dalca. "Speaking of political, SRI is the worst."

"It was a fucking cesspool," Andrei answered bitterly.

"Everything is a fucking cesspool," Dalca said blandly. "We're waist-deep in shit right now, as we speak." He closed Andrei's file and turned off the computer.

"Look, Costiniu," he said seriously. "I knew most of this. I just wanted to hear your version of it. "

Andrei smiled. He had not expected such a frank admission from the chief.

"You're no bullshitter," said Dalca.

"No sir! I'm not."

"Good. Neither am I." Dalca stood up, took off his tie and threw it on the hook above his uniform coat. It landed accurately but then slid off and fell on the floor. Dalca ignored the fallen tie and rolled up his sleeves.

"Now, why don't you tell me about this Muratovich affair?" He sat back down and regarded Andrei with a serious expression. "And no bullshit."

CHAPTER 40

BRAŞOV, APRIL 2

"It was not a suicide," said Andrei. "It was set up to look like it."

The chief pulled out another file from his drawer. "I read the preliminary forensics," he said. He shuffled through the papers. "Not much there." Dalca looked up firmly at Andrei, holding up a paper from the forensics report. "Why do you think that it's not a suicide? Please tell me that you have more than some strands askew on a rope."

Andrei figured the paper was part of Katrina's report on the rope and door impressions at the Muratovich apartment. "That's pretty compelling evidence," he argued.

"Be that as it may," contended Dalca. "Do you have anything else?"

"I have a witness."

"Who?"

"An informant," said Andrei. "She is keeping herself anonymous for now."

This made Dalca laugh. "Back to your SRI days!"

Andrei smiled and nodded. "If this informant is right, not only is the suicide an actual murder—an assassination, to be more precise—but it is part of a larger conspiracy. An international one."

This made the chief sit up straight in his chair.

"According to her, Muratovich was part of an international organ transplant team, an illicit one. She claims that two of its leaders were recently assassinated in Budapest."

"What does that have to do with us in Braşov?" asked Dalca. "I mean, aside from them leaving us a dead body here."

"If this informant is correct, the transplant enterprise is operating here in Braşov. I mean, literally, *operating*. Harvesting and transplanting kidneys here."

Dalca took a deep breath and leaned back in his chair, absorbing the news. For a moment they were both silent. "Do you think she is credible?"

Andrei answered cautiously. "I don't know yet. There is a lot to check out."

"Have you done any preliminary work on it?"

"A little," said Andrei. "She gave me a name to pursue, Bekim Zhulati. He is a surgeon, a Kosovar. So far as I can tell, he is an itinerant surgeon, a bottom feeder."

"Do you think he is doing the transplants?"

"Possible."

"Who are these two executives killed in Hungary?"

Andrei pulled out a notepad from his pocket. "Two Romanians. Nicolae Radu and Iancu Negrescu."

"Did you check their criminal records?"

"Not yet," said Andrei. "I was waiting for some direction from you before I did more."

Dalca seemed pleased.

"But I did verify from news reports on the internet," Andrei continued, "that these two did indeed die in Budapest last week. Neither are Braşov residents. They are from Bucharest."

Dalca ran his hand over his forehead, contemplating a plan. "So how do you think we should proceed?"

This was not a question ordinarily posed by a chief to a rookie subordinate. It made Andrei uneasy. He did not answer right away.

"Well," he finally said, "if the information I have checks out, we're looking at an elaborate conspiracy, both here in Braşov and outside, in and out of the country."

"If it is mostly outside our jurisdiction," added Dalca, "normally we would pass it on."

"To SRI?"

"To SRI." Dalca made a disgruntled face.

"If this outfit is as sophisticated as the informant implies, they are likely to have connections within SRI," said Andrei. His implication was clear. Forwarding the case to SRI might risk having it quashed.

"True." Dalca understood. "But then, we don't have much to go on yet, do we? I have to present a credible case to our prosecutor."

Andrei concurred. Every police sector in the city had its own prosecutor who oversaw the criminal investigations, issued search and arrest warrants, and mediated their handling in criminal courts. While the prosecutor was not Dalca's direct superior, all police actions had to be handled in a manner that satisfied him.

"For all we know, these may be wild allegations by a crazy person," Dalca continued.

"Right."

"So," said Dalca, "it would be premature to pass it on."

"Definitely," Andrei agreed. "We need to dig deeper and build a credible case."

Dalca silently sifted through the file. Finally he said, "Costiniu, I will go out on a limb."

"How so?"

Dalca stood up and went over to where his tie had fallen down. He picked it up and set it neatly atop his uniform jacket. "I will open an investigation," he said, still facing the hooks on the wall. He then turned and walked back to his desk. "But it will be in the form of a special task force. We'll keep it quiet until it bears fruit, that is, if it bears fruit at all. And that's a big if."

He sat down and leaned back in his chair. "I'll put you in charge of it."

"Thank you, sir. But won't that rub some others in this station the wrong way?"

"As I said, Costiniu, it'll be discreet. I don't want people running around spouting crazy ideas about deranged organ thieves in Brașov. If it is true, we'll announce it with proper evidence after it has been handed over to the prosecutor and meets his approval."

"Understood."

"But make no mistake about it," Dalca continued. "You're on a leash. Is that clear?"

"How tight a leash?"

"We'll see," said Dalca. "Depends on what you find."

"Who will you assign to this team?"

"You and Boboc. I can't spare others full time. You know we're short-handed."

Andrei did. Dalca's corruption cleanup of Sector 1 had depleted its manpower. That's why he and Boboc happened to be sent to Enver's suicide scene in the first place, a task well below their pay grade.

"I'll assign others on a rotating basis if you need help," Dalca added.

"Boboc is pretty skeptical. He hasn't been terribly helpful so far."

"Boboc is an ass," said Dalca. "But he is a loyal officer. He'll do as he is told. He is also comparatively clean." He paused. "As clean as anyone gets around here," he concluded facetiously.

Andrei was impressed with Dalca's insight.

"Where do you plan to start?" asked Dalca. "Maybe you should bring in this surgeon Zhulati for questioning."

"If I may," Andrei interrupted, "before we do that, it might be better to place him under surveillance and see if it yields new leads."

Dalca shook his index finger at him. "I can see the SRI in you," he said with a sly smile.

Andrei was pleased with the chief's confidence. "We'll see what he is up to, whom he contacts, where he works."

"Boboc would be ideal to run that operation," said Dalca.

Andrei cautiously advanced his next proposal. "I have an inside connection at SRI. An old friend."

Dalca didn't seem surprised.

"He is in signals intelligence, but has connections within the organization. He is reliable. I'd like to contact him and see if he can help."

"Careful with that," said Dalca. "It needs to be done discreetly. If it reaches the wrong ears, you might have another Emilia Sala affair to deal with, except that this time it would bring you and me, all of us, down."

"Understood."

"All right, then. Go with it."

Andrei stood up to leave.

"One more thing, Costiniu."

"Yes." Andrei turned back.

"Remember that you're working for the Braşov police force. Work on digging up the Braşov angle first and foremost. See if there really is an illegal transplant operation going on here. If so, our first priority is to terminate that. The rest, this supposed international conspiracy, is ultimately none of our business."

"Yes, sir. I thank you for your confidence in me."

"As I said." Dalca was firm. "I am taking a risk with you. Don't disappoint."

"I'll do my best, sir."

CHAPTER 41

BODRUM, APRIL 1

The Bodrum police station was an old, two-story Art Deco structure enclosed within a brick fence and rimmed by trees. It looked like a miniature fortress. The young female officer driving Tarık's car exchanged a few words with a colleague who emerged from a guard hut. A wooden gate lifted, and they drove by a tall communications antenna to enter what probably used to be a courtyard, and was now a cramped parking lot.

Tarık looked up out of the window and for the fourth time asked what this was all about. Mark quietly stared ahead, resigned to whatever awaited them inside. The polite but taciturn officer opened the door for Tarık while her partner, following closely behind, did the same for Mark. They were hastily led to a room in the basement.

The room was sparse, a table and some chairs, no windows. An outdated wall telephone next to a large mirror clashed with modern video equipment near the table and CCTV cameras at each corner of the ceiling.

"What is this?" asked Tarık, quite irate.

"An interrogation room," said Mark. He'd been in a simpler one the week before, in Budapest, and handled his questioner deftly. He no longer found the surroundings intimidating. "I doubt that this is about your little mishap on the road," he added.

Tarık looked at his watch. "Damn," he said. He was still reeling from the shock that Mark had delivered before being detained by the police. "I was hoping to talk to you some more."

"Not now, and not here," said Mark.

"And I'm hungry too. I was craving pizza."

Mark gave Tarık a stern look. *He is behaving like a little kid,* he thought. A Turkish police station was not exactly an appetite stimulant. "Take it easy," he said calmly. "Let's see what this is all about. We'll get you some pizza later."

They waited another fifteen minutes, Tarık pacing the room, until the door opened and a tall civilian entered in haste. The man had an imposing build, a square jaw, and an old-fashioned American crew cut. He was dressed in shorts, an untucked sleeveless shirt, and running shoes. He looked like he had been plucked from a beach bar. He stopped and briefly stared at Mark.

"Dr. Mark Kent." He addressed Mark. His deep, loud voice was as commanding as his physique.

Mark did not stand or answer.

"My name is Yusuf Bozkurt." He dug into his shorts pocket, pulled out a business card and extended it to Mark.

Mark calmly examined the elaborate emblem that dominated the card, a gray wreath that encircled a color photo of Atatürk against a red backdrop of a stylized Turkish flag. Surrounding the photo were the words, *Milli İstihbarat Teşkilatı,* National Organization of Investigation.

"MIT," murmured Mark. The phrase caught Tarık's attention. He stopped pacing and observed the curiously dressed man with some alarm.

Like the FBI, MIT dealt with high crime and national security. Unlike the FBI, it was also a tool of government suppression. It was therefore considered intimidating by many law-abiding Turks. Mark knew this but wasn't bothered much. He was no longer a Turkish citizen and besides, he had no history of political activity that might attract Turkish attention.

"My apologies for the way you were brought here." Bozkurt sat down and crossed his legs. "And for my appearance. I too was brought here unexpectedly."

Mark noted the man's lean, muscular legs. He looked to be in his fifties, yet physically very fit, certainly more so than Mark.

"We brought you here because we have a few questions about Latif Gürsen."

"Aha," said Mark, quietly nodding his head several times. They must have had Latif under surveillance, he figured. "What would you like to know?"

"What was the purpose of your visit with him?"

"He is an old acquaintance from Istanbul," Mark answered truthfully. "Father of a classmate of mine. I was visiting Turkey and thought I'd drop by and pay my respects." He then smiled. "It was also an excuse to visit Bodrum," he lied.

Bozkurt turned his attention to Tarık. "And who are you?"

Tarık froze like the proverbial deer in the headlights.

Mark quickly interjected. "His name is Tarık Polat, and he has nothing to do with what you're looking for." Mark was more assertive now. "He drove me here from Istanbul."

The MIT agent briefly considered Mark's statement, still staring at Tarık.

Mark continued. "Your business is with me," he said firmly. "Not him. Let him go."

Tarık gazed at Mark wide-eyed, surprised by his audacity.

"All right," said Bozkurt. He stood up, went to the wall phone, and barked some orders.

* * *

Tarık was released from the interrogation room after giving the MIT agent his name, place of residence in Istanbul, and his address in the Bodrum Peninsula. Bozkurt ordered the local officers to take a more detailed statement from him.

Mark and Bozkurt were alone now, facing each other.

"Let's cut to the chase," said Mark. "What do you really want to know?"

The sophisticated recording equipment had not been turned on. Bozkurt took notes in a small pocket notebook. "We are investigating Latif Gürsen."

"For what?"

"We are interested in his ties to the Kurdish community in southeastern Turkey, and some of his activities with them, weapons smuggling and people trafficking in particular."

"I figured you have him under surveillance if you came after us so soon after we visited." Mark sounded self-assured.

Bozkurt didn't respond.

"I have nothing to do with Gürsen's business, or businesses," Mark continued. "As I said, I was just visiting as a friend." He hoped he came across forthright. "But I have to tell you an interesting anecdote about his Kurdish connections."

Bozkurt leaned forward, all ears.

"I once met one of Latif's business associates, many years ago. A Kurd, a gangster from Urfa named Kara Ibrahim. Do you know him?"

Bozkurt tried to maintain an unemotional demeanor but his surprise was unmistakable. "He was before my time. But yes, I've heard of him. Nasty guy. Fortunately he was knocked off by one of his rivals. Saved us a lot of grief."

"I found that out many years later," Mark confirmed.

"So, how did you meet him?"

"Oh, it was in a *gazino* in Istanbul, Maksim. I am sure you've heard of it."

"Of course."

"Back when I was in high school I attended a soirée at Maksim as Latif's guest, along with his son Ahmet. Ahmet was my best friend. Kara Ibrahim was there, at our table, with his entourage. He was a scary looking guy but well mannered. He patted my back afterwards and told me what a good boy I was."

Bozkurt could no longer help himself. He let out a laugh. "That Latif Gürsen is a real piece of work," he said. "You mean to tell me that he was conducting business out in the open, and with two underage kids at his side?"

"Yes," Mark chuckled. "Now that you put it that way."

The exchange defused the tension between the two.

"So you were good friends with his son, Ahmet Gürsen."

Mark nodded.

"And you found him dead in Hungary last week."

Leon Adler had obviously briefed his Turkish counterparts. Mark realized that MIT must have been anticipating his presence in Bodrum. "If you're interested in the transplant network that Ahmet Gürsen ran in Eastern Europe, I'll be happy to tell you what I know."

"Go ahead."

Mark summarized his impressions of Ahmet and Iancu, and how their network was being systematically decimated by a Russian/Moldovan character named Vadim Rusu, who was avenging their inadvertent killing of his son. Bozkurt listened but did not take any notes. He seemed more interested when Mark described his encounter with Gazioğlu and the surgeon's subsequent death.

"Do you think that his girlfriend was involved in his assassination?"

"No way," said Mark. "A total innocent bystander."

"Do you have any idea who might have committed the Gazioğlu hit?"

Mark was surprised that the lofty MIT needed his help with this question. "My guess is that it was done by locals hired by Rusu's organization."

"What makes you think that?"

"I've seen Rusu's own people and their handiwork firsthand, the way they killed Ahmet Gürsen. Later, when his killers apprehended me, I saw them in action."

Bozkurt did not react. Mark figured he already knew this.

"They are paramilitary, clean and sharp. Surgical." Mark paused to gauge the impact of his opinion.

Bozkurt took notes and did not make eye contact.

"I also saw the locals they contracted in Budapest," continued Mark. "Sloppy and messy."

Bozkurt looked up at him. His lips parted in a subtle hint of an amused smile.

"The way Gazioğlu was killed," Mark said. "Super messy!"

Bozkurt nodded.

"So, a local job, I would say. But I have no idea who they might be."

"Dr. Kent." Bozkurt leaned back in his chair, his legs spread apart. "You are a doctor, am I correct?"

"Yes, a radiologist."

"There seems to be some ambiguity about whether you are a member of intelligence or law enforcement in the US."

"I am well aware of that," said Mark.

"I don't care if you are FBI, or CIA, or neither."

This, Mark thought, must be the agent's personal opinion, not an institutional one. Nevertheless, he was relieved to hear it.

"You're well informed," continued the MIT agent. "And that's all I care about." He paused to gauge the impact of his statement. Mark remained silent. Bozkurt continued. "You seem to have a knack for putting yourself at the right place, at the right time, if you catch my drift."

Mark nodded in agreement. He wasn't sure how he'd acquired this knack, but he was quite certain that he didn't want to keep it.

"Do you intend to visit Latif Gürsen again?"

"Yes," said Mark. "He invited us to stay with him. We'll be going there tomorrow morning."

"Good," said Bozkurt. "We will debrief you afterwards."

He wasn't asking for a favor, Mark realized. This was an order and Mark knew he had to obey.

"I want you to take note of everything inside his residence, in as much detail as possible. The interior of the house, those who are working for him, any contacts he has with others. I want you to tell me whatever you hear from Gürsen and his crew."

"But, as I said before," Mark objected, "I don't know anything about his businesses."

"That's beside the point," said the agent. "You don't need to pry or make him suspicious. Just tell us what you see and hear."

"Fair enough," said Mark. "How do I contact you?"

"You don't need to." Bozkurt stood up. "I'll find you."

Like you just did, thought Mark. He was uneasy about informing on Latif, but he had no choice. He had made a decision to come down to Bodrum and visit him, and it had inadvertently led him into this MIT trap. He regretted dragging Tarık into it. At this point, his foremost concern was getting out of the trap safely, and with Tarık unharmed.

Mark stood up and shook hands with Bozkurt, who towered over him. "See you soon," he said, as the female officer who had driven them opened the door to let him out.

CHAPTER 42

BODRUM, GÖLTÜRKBÜKÜ ... APRIL 1, NIGHT, APRIL 2, EARLY MORNING

"What did MIT want from you?" Tarık's words were nearly imperceptible with a mouth full of pizza.

Mark examined the *meze* plates crowding their small table. He picked a *sigara börek* and ate it in two quick bites. It was fried just right, a small cigar-like cylindrical phyllo roll stuffed with melted cheese and dill. He washed it down with a sip of beer.

"Information about Latif," he answered. "They most likely had local police keeping Latif under surveillance. When we showed up, they notified Bozkurt."

Tarık took a long chug of beer. He had been rapidly devouring a pizza for two, on his own. This was his second bottle of *Efes* beer. He let out a loud belch. "Sorry."

Mark stared at the calm sea. The small restaurant near the marina was nearly empty this late at night in the off-season. A half-moon reflected on glassy waters, its glitter interrupted by a single fishing vessel that glided nearby. He took a bite of grilled calamari and observed Tarık carefully. The day's events had clearly spiked Tarık's appetite, which surprised Mark.

They had driven back to Göltürkbükü, proceeding directly to the seaside restaurant. Tarık told Mark that the local police had not given him a hard time. They just took down basic information about his identity, background, residence, and contact number.

"Easy on the beer," Mark advised. The young man was already glassy-eyed and spoke with a hint of a slur. Mark figured his alcohol tolerance was low.

Tarık ignored him and took another chug, emptying the bottle. He waved the waiter for another.

"I was really impressed by how you handled that MIT guy," he said with exaggerated awe, his words garbled. "Like...as though... you two were equals."

There was one wedge of pizza left on the tray. Mark slid it onto his plate. He poured some of Tarık's third bottle of beer into his own glass. "I have no reason to be intimidated by them," he said quietly.

"You are so brave." Tarık fixed his shiny eyes on Mark with admiration. "Are you going to help them?"

"Do I have a choice?"

Tarık served himself the last pieces of feta cheese and melon from the *meze* plates. "I don't know how they expect us to help them," he said. "We don't know anything about Latif's activities."

"That's right," Mark agreed. "We'll act friendly and cooperative and shake them off as soon as possible."

Tarık pointed an empty fork at Mark's face. "You are a sly fox, you!" The fork wavered in the air.

Mark gently lowered Tarık's forearm and took a small sip of beer. He had been pacing himself. This was not an appropriate time to lose control with alcohol.

"I still can't believe that Latif is my grandfather," said Tarık, leaning back in his chair. He looked out at the dark horizon. "I mean, really!" He shook his head in disbelief. "A guy like that, playboy, gangster..."

He took a last sip of beer. "I have his genes!" He cried out loud.

"And those of Ahmet," Mark gently reminded him. *For you, Günsu,* he thought, suddenly weary.

"Ahmet, who I've hated for so long." Tarık slumped his head on the table and beat it with his fist, causing the empty plates of *meze* to skitter. "Why me?" he howled.

Mark stood up and came around the table. "Come on, time to go home."

He lifted the young man by his armpits. Tarık came to an unsteady stand, wavering as he took a first step.

"Shit," said Mark. "You're in no shape to drive."

"No," agreed Tarık.

"We'll walk up to the villa. Maybe it'll sober you up."

"We'll walk," repeated Tarık, surrendering himself to Mark's clumsy embrace as they stumbled out of the restaurant.

* * *

Mark was awakened from an uneasy sleep by the distant sound of a loud crash. He checked his mobile phone at the bedside. It was around 4 a.m. He sat up and listened. At first he heard nothing. Then there were hurried footsteps as Tarık burst into his room in the dark.

"We have visitors," he whispered excitedly.

Tarık was wearing a large T-shirt and boxer underwear. He was barefoot. "Did you hear that crash?"

"What was that?" Mark got out of bed and donned a T-shirt himself.

"The big pothole in the road up here," said Tarık. "Somebody hit it."

They now clearly heard the loud engine of a vehicle approaching the front of the house.

"Let's check it out," said Tarık.

"Don't turn on any lights," Mark warned him. "And don't make noise."

They tiptoed to a living room window with a view of the landing. Through a slightly parted curtain they observed the bright headlights of a minivan in front of the villa. There were no outside lights on. In the partial moonlight, Mark noted that the van was a commercial vehicle with no windows except for those in the front. There was no insignia on its dark, monochromatic paint.

Two figures emerged, one from each side. At first it was impossible to make them out except that they were tall silhouettes. The driver came around to the front and squatted down, leaning under the bumper. As he did so, Mark could clearly make him out in the brilliance of the driver's side headlight.

"Oh, fuck!" Mark exclaimed.

"What is it?" asked Tarık, alarmed by Mark's expletive.

The man outside stood up, and himself shouted what sounded like a curse in a foreign language.

"The pothole got his van," said Tarık, amused.

The timed headlights of the vehicle suddenly turned off. They saw the figures, once again dark silhouettes, stand by and examine the house.

"Is there any way out of here other than the front door?" asked Mark in a whisper.

"No."

"How about a place to hide?"

"This way," said Tarık, leading him toward the kitchen.

They scampered gingerly on bare feet, trying to make minimal sound. As Tarik led him to the shallow basement alcove, they were startled by the doorbell.

"Who are they?" asked Tarık.

"Never mind. Just go."

Tarık quickly slid the wood panel that hid the entrance to Ilhan Bey's wine cellar and punched in the code. As the bell rang again, they were in the cellar, wood panel slid back, door closed. Tarık turned on the light.

The cellar was dry and fifty-five degrees Fahrenheit, suitable for long-term wine storage. Barely dressed and in bare feet, they both felt the chill of the place, Mark getting goosebumps all over.

"Vadim Rusu's men," said Mark. "They've come for me."

"How do you know?"

The dark paramilitary uniform that Mark saw in the headlight, with dark combat boots and a sidearm holster, were unmistakable.

The man was not one of the pair that had kidnapped him in Budapest. Those two were dead. But he certainly resembled them.

"I know them," said Mark. "I've seen them before. They are capable and efficient."

"How did they know to come here?" asked Tarık.

"Who knows." Mark could not analyze the situation. He had to figure a way out. He knew that they wanted him alive and they wouldn't harm him. But he had no idea what they would do to Tarık.

"Can they see this light from outside?" Mark asked, referring to the light within the cellar.

"No, it is well sealed."

They were both startled by several loud knocks on the door.

"Did you leave any open windows anywhere?"

Tarık assured him that all windows were closed. "Do you think they'll break in?"

"I don't know," said Mark. "We'll have to stay here, and wait and see what happens."

They heard loud footsteps of the men's boots outside as they walked around the house, one set of footsteps in one direction, the other in another. Mark instinctively reached for the light switch and turned it off. There was no sense in taking any chances.

They stood inside the cold cellar for what seemed like a fortnight while the footsteps circled back to the front. Then they heard the engine of a vehicle come to life, and the van departed.

They cautiously inched out of the cellar, making sure to remain quiet. There was another loud crash of the van as it hit the same pothole on the way down the hill. They opened the living room curtain and surveyed the front landing. All was clear.

"They'll be back," said Mark, out loud.

"So, what do we do?" asked Tarık, nervously.

"We wait until they leave the village," said Mark calmly. "I doubt that they are staying here."

He turned around and began walking toward his bedroom. "We then sneak out and fetch your SUV from the marina before daybreak."

Tarık followed like a loyal dog.

"After that, we gather our stuff and move over to Latif's. It's a good thing that he invited us over. His place is much more secure."

Tarık nodded.

"Now go pack your luggage. Let's get it all ready. When we return with the car, we don't want to spend more time here, just in case they come back sooner."

CHAPTER 43

BODRUM, YALIKAVAK, APRIL 2

"These clothes stink," complained Tarık, as he took a back way to Latif's Yalıkavak villa, a little-traveled road along the foothills, bypassing the town.

"Awful," agreed Mark. "But do we have a choice?"

They were both wearing peasant clothes discarded by past workers in the basement alcove of Tarık's house. Mark had found a baggy pair of pants, torn and patched here and there, that he tied to his waist with a crude rope belt. His traditional Turkish shirt was collarless and featured flowery patterns on a red background. He wore a vest several sizes too small. The outfit was complete with a cap worn low on the forehead to conceal his face. It all reeked of stale sweat. Tarık's was similar.

"Do you think Ileana will take us in at this hour?" asked Tarık. He turned the Verso left and began climbing the mountain road with switchbacks.

"We'll have to try," said Mark.

They had packed their bags, donned the worker clothes, and slipped into town at dawn, incognito. For all anyone knew, they were two locals going to work. They had walked fast, surreptitiously checking their surroundings for any hint of Rusu's men or the menacing van. Then they picked up Tarık's SUV from the marina and returned to Günsu's villa to fetch their luggage. They were now heading for the safety of Latif's compound, away from the exposed and vulnerable villa at Göltürkbükü.

"It's better that we wait outside Latif's than at your place. The police surveillance provides an extra layer of safety. If we need to, we can call the MIT agent." Mark reached into his pocket. "I still have his card."

Tarık nodded in agreement.

As they took the third switchback, the SUV still low on the hill, Mark caught a glimpse of the summit. "Smoke," he said.

Tarık could not look up. He was too busy negotiating the curvy road. "Where?"

"High up." Mark pointed with his finger. They had already turned in a different direction and he could no longer see it. "At the top of the hill."

"Brush fire probably," said Tarık, trying in vain to spot the smoke. He sounded anxious.

"It was white smoke, and not much of it."

"Good." Tarık was relieved. "They probably put it out. Let's hope we don't have another wildfire disaster around here." Forest fires, widespread along the Mediterranean coast, had wreaked much havoc in recent years.

Mark kept looking up to see if he could spot the smoke again. Nothing.

Tarık's next words startled him.

"I'm looking forward to some one-on-one time with Latif," said Tarık. "Check out and see what, if anything, I have acquired from him."

"I bet he'll appreciate that," said Mark, as nonchalantly as he could. "But make sure you don't blow your cover."

"What cover?"

"You're his son, Ahmet. Remember?"

"Son of a bitch." Tarık all but spat out the words. "I've despised him for so long. It'll take time to get used to the idea that he is my father."

"Why do you dislike him so much?" Mark asked. The question had been bothering him since they first met. He figured he could dare ask now, after their newfound intimacy.

"I didn't care about my mom's affair with him. It's her life after all." He stole a glance at Mark. "But I hated the misery and unhappiness he brought to her life." Mark looked ahead and did not respond. Ahmet had indeed been guilty of that. Tarık continued. "I especially saw it after my dad died. You know…" He hesitated. "My real dad, Ilhan." He did not realize the irony in his comment. "That's when Mom's relationship with Ahmet came out into the open for me."

"It's a shame," Mark said, "that Ahmet died without ever being a father to you."

"Do you think he knew?"

"I don't know. Your mom didn't tell me. But it was you who didn't, and now that he is gone, it's a moot point."

"Yeah," Tarık agreed. "I suppose Latif is my only conduit to him now."

"Yes, and unfortunately, with his dementia, you can get only so much from him."

They cleared the whitewashed houses and passed by a few more exclusive villas. Closer to their destination, the road came to a straight uphill stretch where, high atop, they could see a vehicle with two figures standing on each side. Farther up, behind the vehicle, more wispy columns of white smoke came into view at the hilltop.

"What's *that* smoke?" asked Mark, pointing to the vehicle.

"No idea."

As they approached closer, they made out the distinct figures of two uniformed gendarmes in light gray shirts and characteristic green berets, their automatic rifles slung on their chests, muzzles pointing down. They stood erect, one on each side of a military Jeep that was parked sideways, fully blocking the road. One of them extended his right hand to Tarık in a universal gesture to halt. Tarık obeyed, stopping the SUV at a safe distance.

"Shit," said Mark. "You stay here. Let me check this out."

He ambled up the hill and spoke with the gendarme who had raised his hand. Tarık watched Mark gesticulate, no doubt arguing with the gendarme. He returned to the SUV in a huff.

"No use arguing with them," Mark said, annoyed. "Local kids, these gendarmes. They obey orders, like dogs."

"What is it?"

"Roadblock," said Mark, searching his pockets. "They're not letting any vehicles up beyond this point."

"Because of the brush fire?"

"Who the hell knows! They won't tell me anything." Mark pulled out what he was looking for. He examined the phone number on the business card. "Let's see if we can recruit some help."

* * *

They waited in the Verso, the SUV also blocking the road, tensely eyeing the gendarmes who remained at attention by their Jeep. They worried about other vehicles coming uphill behind them, but none did.

Presently a small police car descended at high speed, carrying a cloud of dust with it. The car came to a screeching halt behind the Jeep and a tall civilian figure hurriedly emerged. He exchanged a few words with the lead gendarme and looked in the direction of Tarık's Verso. He then waved his arm, beckoning them over.

"I'll handle this," said Mark.

Yusuf Bozkurt no longer looked like he had been plucked from a beach. His tired face was creased with furrows, his sleepless eyes sporting dark bags beneath. He wore dark slacks and a wrinkled, dirty white shirt, sleeves rolled up. He stood in front of the Jeep and watched the peasant walking uphill toward him with curiosity.

Mark took off his cap and waved at him. Bozkurt smiled. He walked over to Mark, grabbed him firmly by the arm and led him to the side of the road, behind a tree.

"Why are you wearing those?" he asked Mark.

"Never mind that. Long story." Mark shook himself loose from Bozkurt's grip. "What's going on? Why the roadblock?"

Before the MIT agent had a chance to answer, Mark threw out another question. "And why are you here?"

When Mark had called Bozkurt, he'd been pleasantly surprised to hear that he would meet them right away at the roadblock. But he had expected the agent to come up from behind them, not downhill.

"Big problem at Gürsen's compound," said Bozkurt in a near whisper.

"What?"

"Bombing."

Mark was stunned. He realized that the smoke they saw was not a brush fire. "Is Latif all right?"

"No," said Bozkurt. "He is dead."

"Oh, my God!" Mark covered his face with his hands.

One of the gendarmes approached them and asked Bozkurt if everything was okay. The agent answered in the affirmative and shooed him off. He then pulled Mark farther away from the road, deeper into a thicket of trees.

"How about the others?" Mark asked. "Ileana, his caretaker, and the male attendant, Hüsnü."

"The woman will be fine. A fractured arm, some bruises and scratches. She was not near where the bomb went off. She is in a local ER. But the male attendant was more seriously injured. They've airlifted him to a medical center in Muğla."

"When did it happen?" asked Mark.

"Sometime between midnight and one a.m."

Mark realized that's why the man looked so harried and tired. He probably had been up all night at Latif's compound.

"Look," said Bozkurt. "Normally we do not divulge details of such an incident to the public."

Mark understood and nodded. He hadn't expected much.

"But I do not consider you an ordinary member of the public," Bozkurt continued. "I would like your opinion on this."

"Okay," said Mark. Back in Budapest he would have burst with pride to have law enforcement ask for his help. Now he was just weary.

"The bomb was planted in Latif Gürsen's bedroom," said the agent. "Strategically placed beneath his bed. It was not a powerful device. Didn't do much damage to the house. Just enough to destroy the room and kill Gürsen."

"Wow." Mark had not expected this. He thought it would have been a Middle Eastern-style, diffusely destructive affair.

Bozkurt continued. "That's why the female attendant was not badly harmed. She sleeps in a distant room. The male attendant, however, was nearby."

"Do you have any idea who might have done this?" asked Mark.

"That's why I'm talking to you. I want to hear your ideas."

"Vadim Rusu's men," said Mark firmly. "They also visited us last night."

Bozkurt raised his eyes. Mark summarized what had happened at Tarık's villa and how they had escaped. "They came for us around four a.m., obviously after they finished up here."

"They would not have needed much time here," said Bozkurt. "We have a bomb squad in there, investigating, but I bet this will turn out to be a time-release device or a remote control explosive activated from outside."

"What makes you think that?"

"I reviewed the CCTV footage at the compound from the evening and night," said Bozkurt. "There was no suspicious activity in the place."

"So, it was planted earlier?" Mark fell into deep thought.

"Seems that way."

"An inside job," commented Mark.

"An inside job," Bozkurt affirmed.

"The workers," said Mark, in an excited voice.

"What workers?"

"Did you see the repair work going on in Latif's master bathroom? It's right behind the wall where his bed is."

"No," said Bozkurt. "That area is a big mess right now. We have to sort it out methodically. It'll take time."

"Ileana told me that there had been some old water pipes that burst and flooded parts of the house. They were tearing down walls and replacing the pipes. Currently they were working in the master bathroom."

Mark paused and considered his next thought. "But how would Rusu's men have known that?"

"What makes you so certain it was them?" asked Bozkurt.

"Remember what I told you about clean versus messy jobs?"

Bozkurt nodded.

"When they contract it out it's invariably messy. When they send their own men it's clean and surgical. What you're telling me, a strategically planted, remote-controlled device of limited power—it doesn't get any more surgical than that."

"And then they showed up at your place," added Bozkurt.

"Yes."

"How did you know it was Rusu's men?"

"Oh, believe me, I know!" said Mark. "I've seen them before. They're like clones, operating in pairs, wearing the same paramilitary uniforms."

They fell silent for a minute as they each digested the other's information.

Bozkurt broke the silence. "Seems to me that you are in some jeopardy," he said. "If they came looking for you and were unsuccessful, they will come again."

"Agreed," said Mark. "We had come here, to Latif's, hoping for some refuge from them." Mark cast his eyes down.

"No refuge here," said Bozkurt quietly.

"I am not worried about myself," Mark continued. "They want me alive, although I have no idea what they will do to me once they get what they want. I am worried about Tarık Polat, my companion. They have no use for him. He is a witness. They might harm him."

"If you want my advice," said Bozkurt, "you should leave the Bodrum Peninsula as soon as possible. Istanbul would be safer, at least for now."

Mark again agreed with the MIT agent. "Yes, but how?" he

said. "We drove here. We'd have to drive back. Much of the road is desolate. We're vulnerable if they come after us."

"You're even more vulnerable if you fly," added Bozkurt.

Mark didn't tell him that flying was out of the question because of his passport problem. In their first encounter, Bozkurt had never asked for any identity, perhaps because he had been well briefed by Leon Adler.

"Can you provide some support for us if we drive?" asked Mark. "Some security to accompany us?"

"No," said Bozkurt. "We don't have the resources here." Seeing the look on Mark's face, he added, "It would take several days for me to gather a team together. We were just running a small, long-term surveillance operation here that had not yielded much. Recently it shrank to a bare minimum. Gürsen had gotten too old and infirm to do anything incriminating for us to catch. We were about to close the operation down when you showed up. We simply don't have the manpower."

"So, I'm on my own. Is that right?"

"I am afraid so."

"All right." Mark turned back and took a step toward the road. Just then, a thought flashed through his mind. "By the way," he said, turning back to the agent, "there is someone that might be of interest to you, someone that might have helped with the inside job."

Bozkurt looked at him expectantly.

"His name is Serdar," said Mark. He was recalling Serdar's words as he drove them up to Latif's compound: *I do whatever, for whomever, as long as they pay me well.* Serdar would surely be the best candidate to mediate an inside job.

"He is a highly paid gofer for Latif," Mark continued. "He does errands and odd jobs. I don't know his last name but I am sure Ileana can provide you with it."

Bozkurt took a small notepad from his shirt pocket and jotted the name down.

"Rumor has it that Ileana is having an affair with him."

"So do you think that she's involved, too?"

"I doubt it," said Mark. "But that's for you to find out."

Bozkurt shook Mark's hand firmly. "Thank you," he said. "You've been very helpful."

Mark accepted the gesture with some bitterness. He had been helpful, but there was no reciprocation from MIT.

"May God be with you," added the agent.

"Yes," Mark muttered. "We'll need all the help we can get."

CHAPTER 44

BRAŞOV, APRIL 4

Andrei entered the colossal Spitatul Martinu via a modern, glass-enclosed entrance reminiscent of the Louvre Triangle. As with the Parisian museum, the slick, newly built entrance clashed with the hospital's original six-story red brick structure. The older building, which occupied several city blocks, was bland in architecture.

Once inside, Andrei navigated past an information desk and through several corridors, getting lost once or twice until he found the administration offices. He identified himself at a bank of secretaries and sat down, waiting while various medical personnel came and went. They were all clad in plain white shirts lined with red stripes, chatting business-like with the secretaries. Some—doctors, Andrei presumed—were motioned inside the offices.

Finally a tall, stocky man with a graying goatee approached Andrei and offered a formal handshake. Dr. Alexandru Coman, Chief Medical Officer of the hospital, was not dressed in medical uniform. He wore an expensive-looking blue suit, jacket buttoned, and a crisp tie. He beckoned Andrei into a spacious, well-accoutered office.

Coman sat down at his desk, put on half spectacles, and studied

Andrei's business card. "*Subinspector* Costiniu," he said. "What can I do for you?"

Andrei sat on a plush armchair, one of two in front of the doctor's desk, and examined the library of ornate books on an elaborate bookshelf lining the wall. A bank of framed diplomas formed a backdrop to the handsome, middle-aged administrator.

"Alexandru Coman," he said. "Any relation to the footballer?" The man bore the same name as a famous soccer player who played in Bucharest.

Coman smiled wearily, the question obviously one he had fielded before. "I am afraid not," he said. "I was never able to kick a ball or dribble very effectively." Andrei could tell he was trying to be self-effacing, albeit unsuccessfully.

Andrei plunged in. "I am investigating a murder committed here in Braşov," he said.

"Who?"

"A man named Enver Muratovich."

"I don't recall this," said Coman. "And I follow the news regularly. Was it something recent?"

"It's not in the news."

"So what does this have to do with us?"

"There is a person of interest in connection with this murder, a doctor, who I believe works in this hospital."

Coman was taken aback. "One of our doctors committed a murder?" he said incredulously.

"No, sir. I did not say that this doctor is a murderer. He is merely a person of interest in connection with our investigation."

"Oh, all right." Coman sat back in his tall chair and unbuttoned his jacket. "So who is it?"

"A Bekim Zhulati. He is a surgeon."

"H'mmm." Coman was thoughtful. "That name does not ring a bell. I believe I know most of our regular surgeons here."

"Exactly what is your role in this hospital?" Andrei asked.

"I am the Chief Medical Officer. I provide liaison between Administration and the medical staff. I help oversee the credentialing of doctors, their proper functioning—disciplining if necessary. I oversee quality assurance in delivery of care."

"Sounds like you have a lot on your plate."

"I do," said Coman proudly.

"How many doctors do you have on your staff here?"

"Over four hundred."

Andrei was impressed. "Big hospital," he mumbled.

"Big hospital," Coman affirmed firmly, with pride.

"So isn't it possible that you may not know every name on your medical staff?"

"Certainly," said Coman. "Exactly why are you interested in this Doctor...what was his name again?

"Zhulati. Bekim Zhulati."

"Yes, Dr. Zhulati." Coman turned to his desktop computer. "Let me look him up."

Andrei waited a minute and decided to change tack. "Mr. Coman," he said.

Coman interrupted him tersely before he had a chance to finish. "*Doctor* Coman!" He emphasized *doctor*. "I am a pulmonologist, and believe it or not, I do still practice." He pushed back from the computer screen. "When I have time from my administrative responsibilities."

This guy is a pompous ass, thought Andrei. Coman's annoyance was rubbing on him. Andrei restrained himself and continued.

"Dr. Coman," he said, placing a respectful emphasis on *doctor*. "Do you perform kidney transplant procedures in your hospital?"

Coman chuckled. "Well, I certainly don't."

Andrei did not find this funny. He waited for a proper answer.

Coman leaned back. "To be exact," he said, "no, we don't. No one does in Braşov. Patients who need transplants go to Bucharest, Fundeni Hospital."

Andrei jotted down the information into his notebook. It was consistent with his informant's statement.

The question had aroused Coman's curiosity. "Why do you ask?"

"We have reason to believe that transplants are occurring here, in Martinu, your hospital."

The answer left the doctor speechless. Coman seemed genuinely stunned. "No," he said, quietly at first. Then, with more assurance, "You are seriously mistaken, *Subinspector*. We do not have the capability to support such an endeavor in our facility."

Coman returned to his computer while Andrei, jotting down the answer, decided not to push the issue.

"Ah, there!" said Coman, looking at his screen. "Bekim Zhulati." His goatee parted into a smile. "He is indeed listed on our staff." He leaned over and looked at Andrei triumphantly. "No wonder his name wasn't familiar."

"Why?"

"He is a locum tenens."

"Explain that, please."

"He is not a regular member of our staff. He is what you might call a temp. You know, like any other temp, hired from an agency to fill in for temporarily vacant positions."

"There is something like that for doctors?" Andrei was not familiar with medical staffing. He had heard of temp agencies providing secretaries, but not doctors.

"Yes, sir! We do have a need for locum tenens physicians from time to time—say, if someone goes on a long vacation and his or her colleagues are unable to cover call."

"Okay," said Andrei. "So when was the last time he worked for you?"

"I'm afraid I do not have that information quickly at hand. I would have to consult our human resources department."

"What is it that you are looking at?" Andrei pointed to the computer.

"Oh, this?" Coman also pointed to the computer. "It's just a list of physicians on our staff."

"How many are locum tenens?"

"None in surgery, aside from Zhulati," said Coman, scrolling through the file. "We need them more in the Emergency Room and in Ob-Gyne."

"To your knowledge, does Dr. Zhulati perform kidney transplants?"

Coman shook his head in disapproval, but he leaned into his screen. After a few clicks of his mouse, he said, "No. That procedure is not listed under Zhulati's list of his privileges." He sat back, sporting a smug expression. "And it should not be, because we do *not* perform transplants here."

Andrei closed his notebook and placed it in his pocket. "Thank you, doctor, for your time."

"Who exactly was this murder victim? Enver…what?"

"Enver Muratovich."

Coman wrote the name down.

"He is not a medical person," Andrei explained. "Not associated with your hospital." He stood up.

"Good," Coman answered.

They did not shake hands. Andrei left the administrator's office with no more useful information than when he had entered. *You win some, you lose some,* he thought, as he navigated back to the main entrance with better success. He would have to find a different way to access Zhulati's activity in this hospital.

* * *

"How is it going out there?" Andrei asked Boboc on his mobile as he drove back to the station.

"Not a whole lot of activity," said Boboc. His words were garbled; he was obviously eating something. There was a pause as Boboc swallowed and took a gulp of drink. "At least there is a good café, a French bakery nearby with a clear sightline of the guy's apartment building. Cuts down on the boredom."

To Andrei's surprise, Boboc had taken their role reversal in stride. Andrei was suddenly the coordinator of the investigation and Boboc a gofer. Traian Dalca had been correct with his assessment of Boboc. The man obeyed commands, did his job, and didn't seem to mind the new pecking order of this mission.

"Have you set eyes on the man?" asked Andrei.

He waited until Boboc swallowed his next bite. "Croque-monsieur," said Boboc. "Delicious! You really should come by and try this café."

"I'm on my way back from the hospital." Andrei drove on.

"Any news there?"

"No, unfortunately. I met with a high-level administrator, a guy who oversees the doctors. He confirmed that Zhulati is on their staff but could not tell me anything else. He categorically denied that transplants were taking place there."

"Do you think he is on the up-and-up?" Boboc came in clearly. *He must have finished his sandwich*, thought Andrei.

"He seemed so. He was genuinely shocked when I threw the transplant issue at him."

"Maybe he is not in on it."

"Maybe," said Andrei. "It is a massive hospital with a lot of activity. They seem to have a whole bevy of administrators."

"One of them has to be in on it."

"Yes. Who knows who. I doubt, though, that the guy I interviewed is involved."

"Well," said Boboc. "From the way it looks here, I seriously doubt that this Zhulati is doing any useful work for them."

Boboc had been staking out the doctor round the clock for nearly two days, along with others assigned on a rotating basis. "We saw him only once," Boboc said. "Yesterday." He chuckled. "He went shopping nearby and returned to his apartment with four bottles of vodka and some snacks. He has not been out since."

"Alcoholic," Andrei mused.

"I should say so. I wouldn't want this guy cutting on me." Boboc laughed. "How are you doing with that warrant?"

Andrei had tried to get the Sector 1 prosecutor to issue an electronic surveillance warrant for Zhulati's residence.

"No luck," said Andrei. "Not enough evidence to justify it."

"Shit," said Boboc. "We're sitting here wasting time."

"Do we have any other choice?"

"Yes, we do."

Andrei listened to his partner's proposal, which employed a

routine method used before the Revolution, in the old Communist era.

"Do whatever you need to," Andrei finally said. "But I know nothing about it."

"Don't worry," Boboc assured him. "You don't."

CHAPTER 45

BRAŞOV, APRIL 5

Bekim Zhulati awoke to the sound of his ringing mobile. He rubbed his sweaty forehead with the back of his hand and searched blindly in the direction of the shrill sound. It was on a stand next to the recliner where had had been sleeping—passed out, to be more exact. He leaned forward in an attempt to rise and promptly slumped back, woozy and with a headache.

"Goddamn it," he murmured, as the phone stopped ringing.

Zhulati rubbed his eyes, then his face, his thick stubble nearly abrading the skin of his palms. He tried to make sense of the time but he wasn't sure. The room was dark. He mustered all his remaining energy to push himself off the recliner. Successful, he stumbled toward the window and pulled the curtains open. Bright daylight flooded the room.

Turning his irritated eyes away, he looked inside. The room was a mess. A pizza box with its contents half eaten by the recliner, the stand covered with two vodka bottles, one empty, another half full, his vodka glass nearby, shattered. Clothes were strewn about, along with an empty box of peanuts, candy bar wrappers, and a half-eaten stalk of romaine lettuce. He must have had the munchies.

Zhulati waddled to the bathroom for a much-needed piss,

missing the bowl with half of it. When he returned, he searched the area near his recliner for his phone. Finally, there it was, under the empty bottle. A sharp sting on his big toe stopped him dead in his tracks.

"Fuck!" He looked down to see the blood pooling by his foot, on the carpet. He limped on his heel toward the window, and under the sunlight pulled out a shard of glass from the meaty part of his toe. He licked the blood off his fingers and turned his attention to the phone, ignoring his bleeding foot.

The number that rang was that of Spitatul Martinu, the main operator. The call could have come from a thousand places. Anyone who dialed out of any hospital phone registered on the receiving end with this number.

"What the fuck?" He had no idea who had called. He had not been to the hospital since the last transplant with Yoet and, much to his dismay, had no further business there.

He checked the current time on the phone. Three p.m. He had slept most of the day. He was hungry. He decided to raid the pantry and fridge for whatever he could scrounge.

* * *

Zhulati bit into a fried chicken leg generously dipped into ketchup to conceal its disagreeable flavor. It had been in the fridge for over a week, its batter no longer recognizable. He was nonetheless grateful to have found it. With a nasty hangover, he was in no shape to go out in search of food. The phone rang again.

It was Kyril. "Hey, Bekim, how are you?"

"Not so good." Zhulati did not recognize his own voice, too throaty. He coughed several times in hopes of clearing his sound. Zhulati had a bad omen about Kyril but in his mental haze, he could not recall their last interaction. "Where are you?" he asked.

"Back home, in Odessa." Kyril sounded chirpy, well rested. "Have you heard from Enver?"

"Son of a bitch has disappeared. I thought maybe something had happened to him but you won't believe this."

"What?"

"He gave me a prank phone call a couple of days ago. It was his phone, I know. He didn't say anything. Just called and hung up."

"That's really strange," said Kyril. "That's not like him."

"Who knows," said Zhulati. "He seemed under a lot of stress on that last job, after his bosses were whacked in Budapest. Maybe he went off the deep end."

"So who contacts us for the next job?"

"There is no next job." Zhulati was irate at how clueless Kyril was. He felt a sudden need for vodka. "Hold on a second," he said. He walked over to his recliner, carefully watching for more shards of glass. He grabbed the half-consumed bottle and took a swig, thankful that this time his feet remained free of broken glass.

The drink partially cleared his cobwebs, and it came back to him. "Did you dispose of that guy as I asked you?"

"Well," Kyril was hesitant. "Yes and no."

"What's that supposed to mean?"

"I mean I did dispose of him...to a hospital. But not in Moldova."

"Where then?"

"Iaşi."

"Iaşi?!" Zhulati screamed. It threw him into a coughing fit.

Iaşi was the second largest city in Romania, located northeast, near the Moldovan border.

"Goddamn it!" Zhulati resumed screaming. "Couldn't you drive a bit more and get across the fucking border?"

"I couldn't," said Kyril. "The guy got too sick. I thought he was going to die."

"So where did you leave him?"

"Saint Spiridon. I dropped him in the ER."

Zhulati tried to contain his temper. He was familiar with the hospital. He had done some locum work in Iaşi, although not in that hospital. "What did you tell them?"

"Nothing," said Kyril. "I just put him in a wheelchair and dropped him off by the triage desk. Then I left."

"Well, thank Jesus for that!" Zhulati said sarcastically. "Listen," he said firmly. "Don't call me anymore. Do you understand? Find another job for yourself. We're done."

* * *

Zhulati lay flat on his bed, vodka bottle and phone by his side. He felt the burning pain of acid reflux deep in his chest as he stared at the ceiling. It seemed to be swaying this way and that. He tried to think a way out of his predicament. He had only a week left in this apartment, paid by those who had hired him to do several transplants in Braşov, none of which would materialize. He had no other job prospects, was running low on cash, and now he had to deal with the likelihood of trouble with Kyril's clumsy handling of the donor.

If Yoet died in Iaşi, things would not be too bad. But if they managed to save him and he talked, there was certain to be trouble. Zhulati took a final swig from the bottle and ignored the pain in his esophagus as it went down. He had to get out of Romania, soon.

The phone rang again. Zhulati checked the screen: Martinu Hospital. He hastily answered.

"Listen," said the voice on the other line. "Braşov Police is nosing around in our offices asking about you and kidney transplants."

Zhulati's pulse went up. He recognized the voice.

"You'd better hightail it out of here. Soon."

The voice hung up.

Zhulati sat up in a panic. He hurried to the living room and paced back and forth, his thoughts jumbled. On several occasions he stopped and stared out of the window. Were the police following him?

Outside, life seemed to go on as normal, the usual cars passing by, people going in and out of the small mom-and-pop grocery across the street, people sipping coffee on the sidewalk tables of the French café across the street.

"That does it," he said to himself. He grabbed his phone and dialed.

It was picked up after several rings, but there was no *hello*. "Cezar," Zhulati shouted into the phone, "is that you?"

"I told you not to call me directly," said Cezar Kaminesky, calm but firm.

"I know, I know! But I am in trouble here and I need help."

"What is it?"

"I assume you know that Nicolae Radu and Iancu Negrescu are dead."

"Yes."

"Well, since then, things have gone to hell here. Enver Muratovich has been behaving irresponsibly. He has disappeared and left our latest donor, a Moldovan kid...he has left him to rot. The kid is now sick, septic with a wound infection. He is in a hospital in Iaşi."

Cezar cut him off. "Iaşi? How the hell did he get there?"

"Never mind the details. Kyril Kozak, the driver, screwed up."

"I'll have to take care of him," said Cezar, his tone ominous.

"Never mind Kyril. We have a bigger problem." Zhulati explained that he had gotten word of police investigating Spitatul Martinu.

"How did the police find out?" Cezar paused to think. "They had to have been tipped off. Did you say anything to the police?"

"No, of course not."

"How much have you been drinking?" asked Cezar suspiciously.

"I swear, Cezar, I did not have any contact with the police. I've been holed up in my apartment the entire time."

"Kyril then?"

"He tells me he talked to no one. Just dropped off the kid and crossed the border, back home."

"What about the others? The nurse Irina or that young nurse anesthetist we hired."

"I don't know. I haven't spoken with them since the surgery."

Zhulati again felt the panic rising within. "Look," he said. "You've got to get me out of here. Back into Albania maybe. I need a safe place to lay low for a while. I have no money, no transportation. I need your help."

"All right, okay. Calm down." Cezar sounded reassuring. "You know we take care of our own. It'll take me some time to assemble a rescue mission," he said. "A day or two. Meanwhile, I want you to stay in your apartment and keep your eyes and ears open."

"Yes, Cezar, I'll do that."

"And lay off the alcohol. Stay sane."

"Whatever you say."

"Don't call me again," Cezar said. "Just be patient. I'll send some men and money right away."

"Oh, Cezar, I can't thank you enough," gushed Zhulati. "I'll make it up to you."

Cezar had already hung up.

CHAPTER 46

BRAȘOV, APRIL 7

Andrei was back in the main lobby of Spitatul Martinu, this time trailing behind Ana. His wife had no trouble navigating the intricate hallways of the huge hospital, which hadn't changed since she had worked there early in her nursing career. She headed for the elevators and pressed the button for the basement. There Ana led Andrei through dim, dank hallways, past central supply, the laundry, and the morgue, through a series of more brightly lit doors where Human Resources resided. They were swiftly ushered into the office of the head of Human Resources.

Dorina Fieraru stood up from her desk and greeted Ana with a hug and kisses on each cheek. A smart-looking woman in her early fifties with wavy red hair and ample makeup, she was dressed in a well-fitting suit that emphasized her slim figure. In her very high heels, she stood with the self-assurance of a professional model.

Smiling, Dorina looked Ana up and down. "Look how you've grown up and filled in! You used to be such a scrawny teenager."

Ana smiled graciously. "Thank you, Auntie Dorina. You look good too. It's been a while since we've seen each other."

Dorina was not Ana's real aunt, but rather, a close friend of her mother's. When Ana was a young girl, Dorina was so close to her mother that Ana and the other children took to calling her auntie.

Dorina looked behind Ana, spotting Andrei for the first time. "Oh, my! And who is this handsome hunk of a man? Your husband?"

Ana turned to the blushing Andrei and proudly introduced him.

Dorina extended a hand. "You have done well for yourself, my dear," she exclaimed to Ana, smiling flirtatiously at Andrei. "I can only dream of such a specimen of masculinity."

"And how is Uncle Iosif?" Ana asked.

Dorina huffed back to her desk. "He is no more," she said sternly. "I kicked that son of a bitch out." She sat down and motioned her guests to the chairs in front of her desk. "I found him with a twenty-two-year-old. Can you believe that? Younger than his daughter. The lech!"

"I am sorry, I did not know." Ana was shocked. She would have to tell her mother the startling news.

"Never mind," said Dorina, adjusting the hem of her skirt. She looked at Andrei. "So what can I do for you?"

Ana cut in. "You know that Andrei is a policeman now, a *Subinspector* in Sector 1. He needs information about an employee here at the hospital, a doctor."

"What sort of information?" Dorina asked Andrei guardedly, all flirtation gone.

"I am interested in a surgeon who works as a locum here," said Andrei.

"We don't have many locums in surgery."

"That's what everyone seems to think. In actual fact, you do have one. I simply need to know when he has worked here and in what capacity."

"What's the name?"

"Bekim Zhulati."

"Oh, him!" Dorina began tapping on the keyboard of her desktop.

"You know him?"

She stopped and looked at Andrei. "Look," she said. "What I'll tell you stays with us, okay? I am doing this as a favor to Ana and her dear mother."

Ana interjected. "Thank you, Auntie. We will keep this confidential."

"I remember the name because this guy is bad news," said Dorina. "His personnel file has numerous red flags."

"What does that mean?" asked Andrei.

"Hints that maybe he should not be working for this hospital, records of discipline in other hospitals, two separate medical board actions against him, and more. There is also plenty to raise concern about a substance abuse problem."

"Where did these complaints originate?" Andrei was jotting down Dorina's information.

Dorina studied her computer screen. "Other cities in Romania, Bucharest, Iaşi. Some from Pristina, in Kosovo." She looked up at Andrei and Ana. "We have reciprocity arrangements for this sort of information within the country and with many of our Balkan neighbors. Precisely to avoid troublesome doctors like Zhulati."

"Is it possible to get a copy of these?" Andrei knew he was pushing the woman, but it didn't hurt to ask.

"Not right this minute," said Dorina. "These files are all confidential. Leaking them could get me in trouble. I'll do it for the public good. This Zhulati should not be working here. But I'll have to be discreet about it."

"Thank you."

"And so will you," she admonished Andrei. "You cannot reveal the source of the information."

Andrei nodded. "So, how come you hired him?"

"It is not I who makes hiring and firing decisions of doctors," said Dorina. "We have a credentials committee that reviews new doctor applications, scrutinizes them and advises the hospital's medical executive committee on whether they should be allowed to work here."

"Sounds pretty rigorous," said Andrei.

"It is." Dorina was clearly proud of the way Martinu sorted its doctors.

"How come Zhulati slipped through?"

"I don't know for sure," said Dorina. "Rumor has it that there was some pressure from Administration to get him in. Assurances were given that he would not be a regular part of the surgery department's clinical activities."

"And is that true?"

"Yes," said Dorina. "To my knowledge, Zhulati has laid low here."

"What exactly is his activity?"

"Let's see." She scrolled through. "He was admitted to the staff as a locum nearly four years ago. He has done some emergency room coverage and he filled in for a surgeon or two when they were on vacation. I don't know how many cases he has done here, but it couldn't be very many."

"Maybe that's why there hasn't been any trouble with him," commented Andrei. "Not much activity."

"Maybe," agreed Dorina. "But with folks like him, it is a matter of time before he causes horrendous complications. It'll eventually happen."

Andrei recalled Zhulati's phone message to Enver. It was already happening. But this woman didn't need to know that. "When was the last time he worked here?"

"Nine months ago." Dorina read from the computer file. "He filled in for Dr. Inveanu."

"Nine months?!" Andrei was surprised. "We have reason to believe that he worked here last week."

"Not according to our records."

"What is the likelihood that Zhulati is performing procedures here without anyone's knowledge?"

"Undercover, as you might say in your world?"

"Call it undercover."

Dorina gave the question some thought. "It's pretty far-fetched. What sort of procedure did you have in mind? Maybe if he was removing skin moles; it would be different than, say, gallbladder surgery."

"Kidney transplants."

Dorina let out a loud laugh. She looked at Ana with an *is this guy for real* expression. "My dear," she said to Andrei, "that is major-major surgery. Do you understand that? There is no way it can happen without anyone's knowledge. Besides, there are no kidney transplants performed here in Braşov."

"So I understand," said Andrei. "They go to Fundeni in Bucharest."

"Correct."

"But humor me for a second, if you will." Andrei persisted. "Let's say, hypothetically, that some well-organized group assembles a team to perform such procedures. Where and how in Spitalul Martinu could these possibly occur?"

"Not in our main OR, for sure," answered Dorina. "That place is busy day and night. It would not go unnoticed."

"Are there any other operating facilities on the premises?"

"Well, there are two rooms in Labor and Delivery used for C-sections, and there is the Outpatient Surgery Annex."

"Labor and Delivery would be impossible," Ana exclaimed.

"Okay," said Andrei. "What about Outpatient Surgery?"

"That facility is open from six a.m. to six p.m., on weekdays only. I suppose after-hours cases are possible."

"But such surgery takes a long time, doesn't it?" Andrei asked, not waiting for an answer. "Also suppose that they bring a donor along, to harvest a kidney from. So they have two procedures to perform."

Dorina shook her head. "You're really going into fantasy-land."

"Indulge me."

"Well, yes. I suppose it would be difficult to accomplish all that after hours without it spilling over to the routine workday, and leave no traces behind." She brushed her hair back. "Wait a minute," she said suddenly. "There is a section of Outpatient Surgery that was decommissioned several years ago when they renovated the area and added on new operating rooms. There are some old, obsolete rooms there, unused."

"So, if a sophisticated team brings in their own personnel and equipment, could they possibly perform surgery there out of sight?"

"That area is really out of the way now. Yes, that's possible, but there is another impediment."

"What's that?"

"No one is allowed in and out of those premises unless they are employed or in some way associated with the hospital. We are all given badges." She pointed to hers hanging down from her smart lapel. "The operating suites cannot be accessed without them."

"But Zhulati *is* associated with the hospital, correct? He would have such a badge."

"Yes, but what about the others needed, anesthesia, circulators, scrubs?"

"Is it possible to hire them from existing OR staff?"

"Anesthesia, yes. There's a lot of them and it's a revolving door. They come and go all the time, especially the nurse anesthetists. But the nurses and scrubs, I doubt it. I know them because I have two good friends among that group. They are a small, tightly knit group. They would know if something like that was going on."

"Wouldn't Administration be aware of it too?" asked Ana.

"That's right," said Dorina, gazing at Ana approvingly.

"Okay, let's talk about Administration." Andrei turned a page in his notebook. "How is it organized?"

"Well, there is the CEO, Mr. Lazarescu—he is the big boss—and then there is the COO. Then there are several deputy administrators who oversee different service lines, like ER or Ob-Gyne."

"I met an Alexandru Coman."

"Oh, him. The CMO." She shook her head right and left. "That guy is a pompous ass, but he is the best CMO we've had. There is no way he is involved. Besides, he has no purview over any specific facilities."

"Can you give me the names of those that do have such purview?"

"Sure, there aren't that many. There is Mr. Lazarescu, of course, but you can cross him out. The man has been here for a quarter century and done a great deal to turn this hospital into what it is today. This hospital is his baby. He would not jeopardize it with such a harebrained scheme."

"Who else?"

"The COO and the deputy administrator in charge of surgical services. I'll provide you with names and access information."

"Let's get back to the surgical team," said Andrei. "Is it possible that they are employing locum tenens staff, such as nurses, as they might with Zhulati?"

"For nursing, the hospital refrains from locums, so-called *travelers*. They are too expensive."

"Can you look anyway, and see if you have any on staff?"

Dorina scrolled through several screens. "Well, what do you know! We do have one in surgery. Only one."

"Who?"

"Her name is Irina Cernea," said Dorina, reading off the screen. "She comes from Bucharest."

Andrei stood up and walked over to Dorina, leaning down to read her screen. He jotted down the name and address. The profile also included a photo, an attractive middle-aged woman.

"Can you print this out for me now?" said Andrei, this time ordering rather than requesting.

* * *

When Andrei and Ana returned to their Dacia Logan in the Martinu parking lot, Ana in the driver's seat, Andrei reached over and gave her a long kiss.

"You are a godsend," he said to a radiant Ana. "You pulled that Human Resources lady out of a hat like a magician."

"I owe her one," said Ana as she started the car.

"Give her whatever she desires," said Andrei gleefully.

Ana smiled as she drove off the lot. "Be careful with that," she responded teasingly.

Andrei looked at her quizzically.

"The only way I can truly repay her is by loaning you out for a few nights. How would you like that?"

"Dorina would chew me alive and spit me out with a wilted dick," said Andrei. "She looks horny."

Ana laughed loudly. "She complains about her husband, but she has had some flings of her own. I think she's angry at him because he did better with his lovers than she did with hers." She turned onto the main road. "So what now?"

"This opens up a lot of work." Andrei leafed through his notes. "Interview the administrators and OR staff, get a warrant to inspect the Outpatient Surgery suite." He shut the notebook. "And most important." He beamed at his wife. "Find this Irina Cernea. There is a good chance she is my informant in Sfântu Gheorghe."

* * *

Ana was navigating the narrow streets of Schei when Andrei's phone rang.

"Boboc," he said to his wife.

"Hello, boss," said Boboc, putting a mocking emphasis on *boss*.

"What's up, partner?"

"Those listening devices we planted at the boozer's apartment."

Andrei cut him off. "I know nothing about that, remember?"

"Yeah, yeah…"

Andrei could envision Boboc shaking his head in amused disapproval.

"So do you have anything for me?"

Boboc started again, in a mocking tone at first. "Yes, sir! On Saturday we, *by accident*, intercepted several phone calls that our subject engaged in. They are one-sided, mind you. The transcripts are only of his side of the conversations. I just reviewed them."

"And?"

Boboc continued speaking as though he were an actor in a comic opera. "And…they might be of interest to the investigation of our special secret task force."

"Is that so?"

"Okay," said Boboc, now stern and serious. "Cut the bullshit and get your butt to the station. You really need to hear this stuff."

CHAPTER 47

BODRUM, APRIL 2

Hüseyin broke into a loud laugh at the sight of Mark and Tarık sitting in the SUV in their ill-fitting peasant clothes.

"Tarık Bey," he said, still laughing. "If your mother saw you like this, she would have a stroke."

Tarık looked down and examined himself. He was not in a humorous mood after the news that Mark had broken about his newly found grandfather. Still, he couldn't help joining Hüseyin in his infectious laughter.

"Come on," said Hüseyin. "Hurry. Let's hustle you out of here before anyone notices those ridiculous clothes."

Tarık followed behind Hüseyin's pickup truck to a poorer part of Göltürkbükü, by the foothills near the Milas-Bodrum Yolu, the main northbound road out of the peninsula. Hüseyin led them to a carport, where he covered the Verso with an old, tattered tarp. The three then packed into the pickup for a long and bumpy ride into the countryside.

"Tarık tells me that you're in a bind." Hüseyin addressed Mark, yelling loudly over the sound of the engine.

Mark sat by the passenger window while Tarık was in the cramped middle seat, next to a floor-based gear shift. The pickup bounced them up and down at regular intervals. Mark periodically turned back to inspect their belongings in the bed of the truck through a narrow back window. Already unrecognizable with dust, they too bounced vigorously.

"Did you tell him what happened?" Mark asked Tarık discreetly.

"No," he whispered back. "Just that we're in trouble and we need refuge."

"Is where we are going safe?" Mark asked Tarık quietly.

"Absolutely," said Tarık. "Trust me."

Hüseyin didn't seem to mind not being answered. He drove on silently.

The man is going out of his way to help us, thought Mark. *We've placed him in jeopardy, too.* He needed to know the nature of their trouble.

"Latif Gürsen is dead," Mark shouted back at Hüseyin. "They bombed his house."

"I know," said Hüseyin, unfazed, concentrating on the road.

Mark and Tarık both turned to him, mystified. Hüseyin glanced at them and smiled, revealing his tobacco-stained teeth. "News travels quickly here," he said. "Everyone in Yalıkavak heard the explosion. The fishermen out at the bay saw the fire atop the hill. The firefighters, some of them are sons of our fellow fishermen." He changed gears. "So," he glanced at them, "no secrets around here."

They all fell silent as Hüseyin came to a busy roundabout and took an exit onto what soon became a poorly paved uphill rural road with hardly any traffic.

More relaxed now, Hüseyin asked, "I don't understand how Latif Gürsen's demise got you in trouble,"

Tarık turned to Mark for an answer.

"The people who killed Gürsen are professional assassins," Mark explained. "And they are also after me."

Hüseyin almost lost control of his pickup as he stared incredulously at Mark.

"They actually came to my house last night," Tarık added.

"Did they do any harm?" asked Hüseyin.

"No, we hid from them," Tarık answered. "In the basement cellar."

Hüseyin nodded.

Mark realized that the wine cellar was not a secret for him. "They left this time, but we're worried they'll come back."

Hüseyin threw Mark a stern gaze. Mark took it as a rebuke for the trouble he had attracted.

Hüseyin then cheered up and slapped Tarık's thigh. "Well," he said reassuringly, "you'll be safe with my father. No one will come up there looking for you."

* * *

They went up the narrow, rough road, passing some ancient Greek ruins scattered on the fallow, rocky landscape with only a few olive trees here and there. At times they caught glimpses of the Aegean Sea far below. They finally arrived at a hilltop compound drastically different from Latif's.

Greeting them in front of several makeshift structures was a saddled-up donkey, grazing lazily on nearby bushes. Mark was glad to exit Hüseyin's pickup and stretch his aching back. The air was cool and fresh here.

He surveyed the rocky scene speckled with scrubs and scrawny trees. The main house was crudely built, constructed on one side with whitewashed cinder blocks and on the other, with lumber. It had a corrugated metal roof with a large brick chimney protruding from it, this being the only robust structure of the house. To the left of the house, an open-air animal shed was made of slender tree trunks joined together by wooden planks. It was topped by a green canvas fluttering in the wind. Inside were several goats, lazily lounging on the dirt. Two cats were curled asleep near them.

To the right was another open-air structure, an outdoor seating area similarly constructed from sinuous vertical tree trunks and horizontal wooden planks. Its timber roof appeared sturdier than that of the house. Furnished with a divan, a long wooden table and some chairs, it looked like an open-air living room.

A corral for animals on one side, thought Mark, *and humans on the other side.*

A young woman emerged from the house and ran toward them. She was slim, early twenties, wearing no makeup, her short hair concealed under a cap-like scarf. Her tight-fitting T-shirt revealed a flat-chested body like a teenage boy's. She gave Hüseyin a hug and welcomed Tarık warmly.

"Hayriye," said Tarık to Mark, as she took their dusty luggage from Hüseyin. "Mutlu's wife."

"Who is Mutlu?"

The woman marched back into the house carrying an impossible load of luggage all at once.

"This way." Hüseyin jumped off the truck and directed them to the human corral. Mark was surprised to see a diminutive figure sitting there, on the divan. He had been concealed by the planks that lined the place. He sat cross-legged, peacefully rolling his worry beads, and did not notice his guests until they approached closer.

Hüseyin bent down and took the man's hand, kissing it and placing it on his forehead. Tarık, not far behind, shook hands with him.

Sait Bey was a balding man with a thick white moustache and ruddy complexion. A prominent Buddha belly protruded from his otherwise lean frame. He wore simple clothes, a white shirt and a pair of dark, well-worn trousers. He did not seem bothered by the scant protection they afforded from the cool weather. He lumbered up onto his bare feet and greeted Mark.

"Welcome to our humble abode." He spoke with a throaty voice.

"Thank you for having us," said Mark in Turkish.

They heard footsteps and turned to see a slim man approaching from the house with Hayriye in tow, carrying a tray of tea glasses with his left hand. He walked with a limp and moved stiffly, his right arm motionless, hanging down.

The traditional Turkish tray was held by three curving bars that rose up, converging onto a holding ring. It swayed to the awkward rhythm of the man's gait and yet, to Mark's astonishment, the tea did not spill.

The man entered the enclosed area and gave everyone an asymmetric smile. "*Hoşgeldiniz*," he said in a slurred voice. *Welcome.* He held the tray aloft as Hayriye served the tea.

"This is Mutlu, my grandson," said Sait Bey. "And his wife, Hayriye."

Mark recognized Mutlu's disability as cerebral palsy, probably a birth injury. "Your son?" he asked Hüseyin.

"No, my nephew," he answered.

The tea was yellowish, with thin, dark stems floating within. Sait and Hüseyin sat next to each other on the divan, both cross-legged. They each threw two cubes of sugar into their glasses and stirred, clinking loudly. Mark, sitting at the table, placed the sugar aside and took a cautious sip. It had a mild, herbal flavor. He examined his glass curiously.

"*Adaçayı*," Hüseyin explained.

Mutlu and Hayriye stood behind, observing everyone with keen interest.

Still puzzled, Mark turned to Tarık for clarification. Tarık stood near Sait Bey, holding his saucer and glass with one hand. "Sage tea," he said. "It's a tradition around here."

Hüseyin quietly recounted the goings-on in Yalıkavak to his father. Mark heard a gasp from Hayriye when the news of Latif Gürsen's death was announced. Sait listened calmly and did not react to any of it.

"We had to escape," Tarık interjected.

"That's perfectly fine," said the old man graciously. "You can be my guest here for as long as you need."

He looked up at Mark. "I am afraid our accommodations are not what you may be accustomed to in America."

"That's all right," Mark answered. "I'm sure we'll be fine. Many thanks for your hospitality."

Hüseyin rose. "I have to return," he said, stretching. He kissed his father's hand again, and told Tarık he'd be back later that night to check up on them.

As the noisy engine of his pickup receded, Sait Bey rose up. "Let's go for a walk, shall we? Stretch our legs a bit."

* * *

It was near dusk when Hüseyin returned. By then Mark and Tarık had taken what Mark estimated to be a two-mile hike around the rocky hilltop where, from time to time, they encountered spectacular views of hills descending onto the sea. Sait Bey hiked with surprising vigor, obviously well-conditioned. He was quiet most of the time, every so often pointing out a landmark as if he were a tour guide.

When they returned to the house, Mark and Tarık each took outdoor sponge baths and changed out of their smelly peasant clothes into their own before going inside. The interior of the house was strikingly sparse, a single room with scant furniture. Various kilims were laid on the floor with folded bedding. A large stove by one wall, on the cinder block side of the house, connected to the elaborate chimney. A corner of the house served as a kitchen, with a small wood-burning oven and a couple of wash basins atop a wooden table.

To Mark's amazement, on another corner was a sizeable plasma screen TV with some folded chairs resting on the nearby wall. It was the only sign of modernity in this otherwise rustic Anatolian décor.

Mark eyed the kilims with apprehension. He did not look forward to sleeping on one of them atop the hard floor. He realized that the outdoor living area was where Sait spent most of his life during daytime. He wondered what he did in inclement weather.

Hüseyin handed Mutlu a bunch of whole fish in a paper wrapper. "*Çupra*," he said. Sea bream. "Freshly caught."

As Mutlu hobbled toward an outdoor barbecue at the back of the house, Hüseyin beckoned Mark and Tarık. They walked a few paces away from the house, out of earshot.

"Serdar," he said, his face twisted with concern. "They found him dead."

CHAPTER 48

BODRUM, APRIL 2

"What happened?" asked Mark.

"Apparently he disappeared last night. Never closed his restaurant," Hüseyin recounted. "According to his bartender, he always does it himself. They went searching and couldn't find him."

Hüseyin paused to light a cigarette.

"So, what then?" asked Tarık, impatiently.

"Earlier today, while we were driving up here, his body washed up on a beach not far from his restaurant."

"He drowned?" asked Mark.

"Serdar, drowned? No way," Hüseyin said emphatically.

Mark and Tarık waited for an explanation.

"Look," said Hüseyin. "The man put on airs as if he was a Bodrumlu from the big city. But he was one of us, a boy of the sea. He grew up in the boats, fishing. He could out-swim anyone."

"What happened then?"

"The police have him now," Hüseyin continued. "But from what I've heard, those who found him said that there were no cuts or bruises or bullet holes on his body."

"It's too much of a coincidence that Serdar met his fate within hours of Latif's death," said Mark.

The man might have been a great swimmer, but he did not stand a chance against Rusu's operatives if they were behind this, thought Mark. He had seen their handiwork with Ahmet, whose body had also not borne any signs of trauma. They had wrapped him up in industrial tape, like a mummy, and asphyxiated him with argon gas pumped into a bag over his head. If Rusu's men needed a clean job, they knew how to do it.

Hüseyin raised his eyebrows in resignation. "It's a shame," he said, "that our cousin lost his way. He got involved with the wrong people."

The smell of grilling fish wafted in the air. Mutlu was barbecuing their supper.

"Will you tell your father?" asked Tarık.

"Eventually," said Hüseyin. "Let's first have you two squared away."

"Are you going back to town tonight?" asked Mark.

"No," answered Hüseyin. He walked to the cab of his pickup and removed a hunting rifle. Raising it up in the air, he said, "I'll stay here and keep watch."

* * *

Mark sat in the outdoor seating area and watched Sait and Hüseyin perform their fourth *namaz* of the day. The sun had just set. Father and son, sharing the same prayer carpet, were silhouettes facing southeast, toward Mecca. They had recently finished a delicious supper of grilled sea bream with rice and *piyaz*, a simple bean salad. For dessert, Hayriye had served fresh fruit, slices of apples and pears. No alcohol was consumed. Sait Bey, a devout Muslim, ran his household according to the strict tenets of his faith.

Mark watched the two men bow up and down, praying silently. Occasionally they sat up on their bent knees and rubbed their faces with their palms, their heads turned up to the heavens.

It was a clear night, a half moon rising in the horizon amid distant dark clouds. As a sea breeze took hold, it brought a delicious, salty scent and along with it, a slight shiver. Mark zipped up his jacket and contemplated his predicament.

Latif's death was a tough pill to swallow. The man had grown old and decrepit. He clearly didn't have much time left in this world. Still, he did not deserve to die the way he did, blown to pieces in his own bed. Mark recalled how much he had venerated this man once, wishing that Latif had been his own father. Tarık had not considered Latif's antics admirable. He belonged to a new generation, a more sober one.

Mark wondered whether his visit to Bodrum was what led to Latif's death. First Gazioğlu, now Latif. They had both been murdered after Mark visited them. Were Rusu's people cleaning up after him? He couldn't be certain.

One thing was for sure. Rusu's people were, at the very least, following him. Their unexpected visit at Tarık's place was a clear warning sign.

Sait and Hüseyin bowed up and down, in synch with each other. They then placed their foreheads on the carpet, praying. The *namaz* was almost over.

The news of Serdar's demise was ominous. Mark had no doubt that it was connected to Latif. If, as he theorized to the MIT agent, Serdar was the insider who gave Latif's assassins intelligence and access, he was a witness and they may have wanted him silenced. But what did Rusu's men, in and out of Turkey in a flash, care about leaving a witness behind?

Maybe Serdar had blackmailed them for money. He was certainly the type capable of doing that, foolhardy as this was against someone like Rusu. The Moldovans may have realized that Serdar would be a thorn in their side. This was certainly a good enough reason to eliminate him. Serdar had been his own worst enemy.

With Latif and Serdar out of the way, Mark realized that the only loose end for Rusu in Bodrum was Mark himself. As Bozkurt, the MIT agent, had recommended, it was best to leave the Bodrum Peninsula as soon as possible. But how? The road trip they took to come here loomed ominous in reverse. They would be sitting ducks on the highway if Rusu's operatives came after them.

Mark was once again more concerned for Tarık than for himself. He felt a certain paternal responsibility for the welfare of the young man. Mark had no children of his own and this was a source of regret for him. If he did have one, he would have liked a son like Tarık. He also felt remorse for thinking that Günsu had withered away a promising life. She had produced a fine son, a son she could be rightfully proud of.

Mark had to find a way to get himself and Tarık back to Istanbul and throw Rusu's men off the chase, at least temporarily.

Hüseyin and Sait stood up, Sait rolling up his prayer blanket. He would need it again near midnight for the final *namaz* of the day. Hüseyin left his father and approached Mark at the corral. "Where is everyone else?"

"Inside," said Mark. "Watching TV."

Earlier in the day, after noticing Mark's astonishment at the presence of a TV in the house, Mutlu had shown him cables that snaked up the hill, allowing it to run.

Hüseyin sat next to Mark. "You don't like TV?"

"I'd rather enjoy the fresh air out here," Mark said. "It's not often that I visit a place like this."

Hüseyin stood up. "Well, I do like TV. I think I'll join them inside."

Mark pulled him back down by the arm.

"Wait a minute," he said. "I have a plan I want to run by you."

CHAPTER 49

BODRUM, APRIL 2

"He was an immoral man," said Sait in his raspy voice. He took a drag from his cigarette, the bright red fire at its tip briefly lighting up the otherwise darkened corral.

Mark sat across from him at the table and looked up at the half moon high up in the sky. He listened as Sait continued talking about Latif Gürsen.

"He was like the rest of them, all those who have flocked into this land." He extended his hand outward toward the imaginary sea below. "Greedy, gluttonous, lecherous." He spat on the ground.

"I know them well," he continued. "I built many a luxurious house for them. Years ago I was a contractor for that palace Latif bought in Yalıkavak. Helped build the addition that houses his gym and indoor pool. I told him then that the piping in that house was defective, that it needed to be totally overhauled. But he didn't listen. He didn't have the money, he said. He was spending it all on that garish yacht of his and the slutty women he filled it with."

He took a final drag from his cigarette and threw it on the ground, extinguishing it with his shoe.

"I could have built myself the same sort of luxury temple, like all the others. It wouldn't have cost me as much, because I—my family—we would have done the work. Put our own sweat into it."

The man may be old, thought Mark, as old as Latif, but he still had a fiery spirit. He let Sait talk without interrupting him.

Sait swept his arm in the direction of his property. "No," he said emphatically. "I chose to retire to this house where my own father lived, the house where I was born." He stopped a second. "Well," he corrected himself, "I did build that cinder block addition with the chimney, and I did bring electricity to the property." He sounded apologetic about the modifications he had enacted.

"I am sick about what's going on downhill," he continued, referring to the Bodrum Peninsula. "In the little time I have left, I'd rather withdraw from it all and enjoy some peace with my grandson."

"Mutlu seems happy here," said Mark, recognizing the pun. The word *mutlu* meant happy in Turkish.

"Mutlu is my best grandson," said Sait. "Do you know how many grandchildren I have?"

Mark figured the man had a whole bunch.

Sait did not disclose. He continued. "That disability that *Allah* gave him, the brain injury, everyone thinks it is a curse."

Mark nodded in agreement.

"It isn't," said Sait. "It's a blessing. It has allowed him to eschew the temptations of the coast and enjoy a simple life, with a good wife. Unlike my other offspring, who are all after the money and materialism of the tourists."

"Hüseyin doesn't seem that way," objected Mark.

"Yes, you're right, mostly." Sait chuckled. "But he has had his moments. Did he tell you how he used to scramble for a job in that asshole Latif's yacht, wagging his tongue like a dog for his nude women?"

Mark laughed and agreed.

"He had the bug too," said Sait. "Except that he didn't catch the disease as badly as others."

"Like Serdar?"

Sait had a coughing spell. As it subsided he shook his hand in protest. "Don't mention that *köpek* to me," he said sternly. Calling someone a *köpek*, or dog, was a profanity. "He is not part of our family any more. We have excommunicated him."

Mark paused and wondered whether he should tell the old man. He decided to go ahead. "Serdar died last night."

Sait Bey stopped and contemplated the news. "What happened?"

"No one knows for sure, but he was most likely murdered."

"*Yazık*," said Sait, *a shame*. "He got what was coming to him." He murmured a prayer in Arabic and rubbed his face with his palms. "May *Allah* forgive his sins."

Mark heard the distant sound of a truck engine. He checked his watch. "We'll be departing soon," he said. Hüseyin was returning from a mission Mark had sent him on.

"It was good to have you here," said Sait Bey. "You take care of that boy Tarık," he ordered Mark. "You know that we love him as if he were our own."

"I see that," Mark acknowledged. "He is the son of a dear friend of mine. I too have grown fond of him."

Sait nodded in approval.

They heard the squealing brakes of Hüseyin's truck as he came to a stop by the compound.

"God be with you," said Sait.

Mark stood up and greeted Hüseyin. They briefly conversed in hushed tones. He then entered the house in search of Tarık. The house was dark and had a musty smell. He heard snoring and made out the figures of Mutlu and Hayriye in one corner, sharing a blanket over a large kilim. Tarık was on another, near the TV set.

Mark shook Tarık. "Wake up," he said in a hushed tone.

Tarık instinctively shooed Mark's arm away and groaned. "Whaat!"

"We're leaving," Mark said. "I have a plan."

Tarık sat up and rubbed his eyes.

"You're not going to like it much," Mark warned Tarık. "But it's all I could come up with."

CHAPTER 50

BRAŞOV, APRIL 7

Traian Dalca stood up to greet Andrei at his office. This time, instead of a formal uniform, Dalca wore an Adidas track suit. It made him look even younger.

"Just back from a short run," he said, smoothing whatever hair remained on his head with his fingers. "I hear you are a runner, too."

"I run longer distances," responded Andrei.

"I got into the habit while in the military," said Dalca. "Never quit since."

"Where did you serve?"

"Army. Tank unit. I was in the Moldovan War in 1992."

Andrei countered. "I was Army, too. *Vulture*. We were briefly deployed to Afghanistan."

Dalca made a face demonstrating that he was impressed. He sat down and shuffled through some uncharacteristically disordered papers at his desk. He picked one up and as he examined it, his congenial mood faded.

"Costiniu," he said, sternly staring at the paper. "I don't know what you've been up to, but you're already causing me grief."

"How so?" Andrei remained standing. He craned his neck in a futile effort to glimpse the contents of the document.

"This is a memo from the Governor." He waved the paper in the air. "It formally states what he said when he called me this morning and personally chewed me out."

The Governor of Braşov County, as the overseer of police forces within its jurisdiction, was Dalca's ultimate boss.

Dalca stared hard at Andrei, clearly expecting some response. Not knowing what this was about, Andrei remained silent.

Dalca continued. "Somebody named Lazarescu called him complaining that an officer from our Sector has been nosing around his hospital, making wild allegations about illicit transplant operations."

"The CEO of Spitatul Martinu," said Andrei.

"Was that you? Did you harass this guy?"

"That was me," said Andrei. He sat down. "But I did not talk to Lazarescu. And no, I did not harass anyone."

"Would you mind explaining this to me?"

"I interviewed the hospital's chief medical officer, a guy named Alexandru Coman. He must have told Lazarescu about it."

"What for?"

"I was working the Zhulati lead," said Andrei. "That's the only hospital in Braşov where he has privileges."

"So did you get anything?"

"Not from Coman."

Dalca rubbed his forehead in frustration. "You mean to tell me you stirred up some shit for nothing?"

"Not necessarily," said Andrei. "I now have a general idea how this transplant network might be operating."

"I'm all ears."

Andrei went on to explain that it probably was occurring at a decommissioned, abandoned corner of the Outpatient Annex, and they were most likely using employees marginally associated with the hospital. Somebody in Administration had to be facilitating, but Coman was not the one.

"I thought you said you didn't get anything from him."

"I didn't. This came from another source, a more productive one."

"Who?"

"Chief, you don't want to know that."

"Goddamn it!" Dalca threw the document onto his desk. "Tell me you didn't coerce or torture someone for the information."

Andrei laughed. "Torture? No, sir! It was a source who wants to remain secret."

"Oh, no! Not another informant! A woman, I presume?"

"How did you guess?"

"Costiniu, I hope you are aware that any evidence brought forth by illegitimate means will not pass muster with the prosecutor."

"I am well aware of that, sir. The material I have gathered so far is preliminary. Nothing solid yet, but I have some promising leads. By the conclusion of this investigation, I'll provide you with better evidence."

"All right, but be careful with Martinu Hospital," said Dalca. "You've stirred up a hornet's nest there."

"I will eventually need to inspect certain areas of that hospital with a CSI team."

"Not until you have enough to justify a warrant," Dalca warned him. "In the meanwhile steer clear of there. When you're ready to request a warrant, let me know. I'll have to pacify higher powers first."

"Yes, sir."

Dalca stood up. "I'm thirsty. Want a Coke?"

"Sure."

Andrei breathed a sigh of relief as his station chief left for the vending machine. He had not expected Coman to cause such trouble. Interviewing him was a misstep. He should have conducted a preliminary survey of the hospital's administration and focused on the right target to interrogate. Instead he had willy-nilly hit the first door that opened and botched it.

Andrei wondered whether he had lost his old SRI touch.

* * *

They quietly took sips of Coke, the atmosphere once again congenial.

"So, tell me about those two dead executives," said Dalca, referring to Nicolae Radu and Iancu Negrescu. "Any criminal records?"

"No, they are both clean."

Dalca thought for a moment. "Strange," he said.

Andrei nodded in agreement. "If they were running an outfit like this, you'd think they'd have some priors."

"Unless they were well-connected and avoided prosecution."

"Possibly."

Dalca change the subject. "Did you get anything from Budapest?"

"I did and it was strange."

"How so?"

"I spoke with an international liaison officer at their National Bureau of Investigation. He confirmed that Nicolae Radu and Iancu Negrescu were murdered in Budapest. He gave me the name of a Slovak gangster whom they arrested for Negrescu, a Tibor Bognár." Andrei studied his notes. "This guy and his gang are also accused of killing Negrescu's bodyguard."

Andrei flipped a page and looked at his chief. "With Radu, on the other hand, it was rather hush-hush. Bognár is not a suspect in that killing. I had the impression that they have a credible suspect, but they are reluctant to release that information."

"Maybe he is not apprehended and they are still on the case. That might make them cautious."

"Maybe," Andrei agreed. "But there still something fishy about the Budapest angle. I may be reading too much into it, but I have a sneaking suspicion that there may be some high-level police corruption with the Radu investigation."

"Let's hope you're correct," said Dalca facetiously. "It would be nice if it wasn't just us Romanians."

"There is something else funny about Budapest," Andrei continued. "The news accounts I initially read mentioned American law enforcement, possibly FBI, also involved with Radu and

Negrescu. Some eyewitnesses reported that an FBI agent foiled Tibor Bognár's scheme and helped with his apprehension."

"H'mmm." Dalca thought for a moment. "This conspiracy is getting really wide." He shook his head. "Across the Atlantic? Seems improbable."

"I don't get it, either. I can't imagine that this organ procurement gang would operate in that wide an area."

"Do you have a name for this American?"

"That's it," said Andrei. "All I have is a firm denial from Budapest Police."

"Well, let's hope that they are right and you are wrong," said Dalca. "I sure don't want any Americans involved in this." He took a sip of Coke. "Self-righteous pricks," he added amid a burp.

Andrei shuffled through his notes.

"What about Interpol?" Dalca asked. "Maybe they can clarify some of this."

"I thought so, too, but they are a tough nut to crack." A bit weary, Andrei rubbed his eyes. "Here's another weird thing: Budapest Police recommended that I contact French Interpol."

"The French?" Dalca was also surprised. "Why?"

"They wouldn't say. They just told me that I would know when I made contact."

"Shit," said Dalca. "Worse than the Americans."

"I contacted the French Interpol liaison at their embassy in Bucharest. So far, no response. It's a slow bureaucratic process."

"We are small fry for them here in the boonies," said Dalca. "Be persistent. Don't let them go."

"I'll keep at it."

"What about your inside connection at SRI?" asked Dalca. "They might have better luck than you with Interpol."

"Haven't had a chance to work that one yet."

"So let's see." Dalca looked at the ceiling as he tallied Andrei's accomplishments so far. "Aside from an irate hospital administrator, you have zilch." His expression once again turned stern. "What have you been doing, Costiniu?" he asked sarcastically. "Besides pissing off VIPs."

Andrei ignored the dig.

"I have picked up several decent leads, here, in town."

"Let's hear them."

"Well, for starters, there is our tail on Zhulati, the surgeon. Boboc is running it."

"Any evidence that he is doing transplants?"

"Yes and no. Currently this guy is doing nothing. He is a serious alcoholic. He is holed up in his apartment, drinking day and night."

"A drunk surgeon," said Dalca. "Wonderful!"

"He doesn't seem to have any prospects for a surgical job—at least in the near future. That may be part of the reason why he has hit the bottle so hard."

"How do you know that?"

"Boboc is listening in on him."

"Did you finally get that electronic surveillance warrant from the prosecutor?"

Andrei cleared his throat and paused a moment, trying to formulate an answer.

"Forget it," said Dalca, realizing what was going on. "Just tell me what you have."

"Okay. Zhulati is distraught. He feels trapped in Braşov. He came here to do some work and now there is none."

"Why?"

"It appears that the death of Radu and Negrescu halted the business."

"Interesting."

"He called a man named Cezar. We don't have a last name. But this Cezar seems to be the one who hired Zhulati. I'll be working on a more definite identity."

"So what's the *yes* part?" asked Dalca. "You said *yes and no* about evidence of transplant surgery."

"Well, first of all, there is no legitimate transplant program here in Braşov."

"I know," said Dalca. "They go to Fundeni in Bucharest."

Andrei was surprised by his chief's knowledge of that fact.

Sensing this, Dalca explained. "My wife has a cousin who had to go to Fundeni. Something called nephrotic syndrome destroyed her kidneys."

"Oh, okay." Andrei continued. "Our audio surveillance on Zhulati suggests that there may have been a recent transplant here in Braşov, a live donor transplant. Do you know what that is?"

"Tell me."

"They bring the donor and recipient together the same day and they remove the donor's kidney, which they then transplant immediately."

"All right."

"Well, our man Zhulati seems quite upset about a neglected donor who is sick. Once again, like Cezar, we have a first name for this donor, but not a last name. This, to me, is the most promising angle on Zhulati. If we can find this donor, it is likely to yield the best evidence that a transplant did take place."

"Why was the donor neglected?"

"As far as I can tell, Enver Muratovich, our dead guy in Schei, takes care of the donors. Enver's death left the donor in the lurch. Zhulati seems unaware that Muratovich is dead."

"What are you doing about this donor?"

"I've issued a bulletin to all police districts in the country to be on the lookout for a male, dead or seriously ill, who may have had recent abdominal surgery."

"Any takers?"

"Not so far. I am also having our team check local hospitals and clinics for such a case. In the meanwhile, Iaşi came up as a possible place where this donor might be."

"Iaşi? How does a sick guy get three hundred kilometers from here?"

"Don't know. We're listening in through bugs in Zhulati's apartment. So we only catch his side of the phone conversations. It's like a jigsaw puzzle with missing pieces. It's possible that they have a driver who took the donor away from Braşov."

"I told you I did not want to know what Boboc is up to!"

"Sorry," said Andrei. He decided to get off the subject. "Here's another good lead."

314

"Pray tell."

"I have a pretty good idea of who my Sfântu informant is."

"Who?"

"An Irina Cernea. She is a nurse, Bucharest based. I have a photo and address."

"Do I dare ask how you got that information?"

"My secret informant at Martinu. This Cernea is the only nurse there, working surgery as a locum or what they call a *traveler*. She is an outsider to their OR, a most likely suspect to assist in transplant cases."

"You'd better bring her in."

"If Irina is indeed the same person I met in Sfântu, she is very jumpy," said Andrei. "A scared animal, if you know what I mean. It would be better to leave her where she is and for me to approach her gently. If we abruptly pull her into the police station, she may clam up."

"What did you have in mind?"

"A trip to Bucharest," said Andrei. "I might convince her to talk. I think she wants to tell more. She just needs reassurance and some sense of security. A face-to-face in a non-threatening environment might do it."

"Okay, go for it," said Dalca. "But this Zhulati, he seems to be going off the deep end. Do you think it's wise to still keep him out there?"

"You're right, Boss," said Andrei. "The guy is self-destructing, drinking himself to death. Further surveillance is of no use. It's time to bring him in."

"Bring him in and don't be gentle. Lean on him. He'll crack easily."

"Consider it done," said Andrei.

CHAPTER 51

BODRUM: APRIL 3 ... EARLY MORNING

"**M**eet Cengiz," said Hüseyin. "He will be driving your car."
A short, lean teenager, looking to be not much older than fifteen, Cengiz waved hello to Mark and Tarık.

"This better work," said Tarık anxiously. "I have a bad feeling about it."

"But he is a child," objected Mark. "Does he even know how to drive?"

"Yes, sir," Cengiz responded with conviction.

They were assembled at the Akyarlar minibus stop, a clearing on the side of the Bodrum-Muğla road with a series of thatched bus stops, all empty at nearly two a.m. Tarık's Toyota Verso and Hüseyin's truck were well concealed in the dark and desolate stop. The road itself was empty, except for an occasional car that sped past.

"Cengiz is a monkey," said Hüseyin. "Show them."

Cengiz rapidly engaged in a series of somersaults that would be the envy of an Olympic gymnast.

"Believe me," said Hüseyin. "He'll do a good job."

They had left Sait Bey's hilltop compound and driven back to Göltürkbükü to pick up Tarık's SUV while it was dark. Then they rendezvoused at the minibus stop with a cousin of Hüseyin's, who dropped off Cengiz and left with no compunction about the mission assigned to his son.

Cengiz took Tarık's keys and started the Verso. Mark and Tarık piled into Hüseyin's pickup and the two vehicles began their brief northbound journey.

"I picked a spot just south of the Swissôtel resort," said Hüseyin. "Nice, sharp curve. The side rail is missing there. It was damaged last month."

Cengiz drove slowly and maintained mobile phone contact with Hüseyin. "Looks clear," he said confidently.

"Why was the side rail damaged?" asked Mark.

"Nasty accident. They are frequent around here." Hüseyin grimaced. "Made national headlines. Fifty-meter drop. One dead, one seriously injured. Lots of posturing among local politicians about making the road safer. Nothing happens, of course."

"We're almost there," they heard Cengiz say on the phone. Hüseyin instructed him to pull over to the side.

They both did. Hüseyin had one final conversation with the youngster. Cengiz gave him his mobile and got back into the Verso.

They watched from inside the pickup as the Verso took off at high speed. It quickly disappeared, swallowed by the darkness. For a brief moment there was dead silence as they anxiously watched the road for any passing vehicles. None. Then, a series of loud crashes and a splash.

"Okay," said Hüseyin. He started the engine and began slowly driving to the spot, climbing toward a sharp curve along the coastal road. The headlights soon illuminated Cengiz, who waved at them.

"Are you okay?" asked Hüseyin.

Cengiz nodded and deftly climbed into the back of the pickup in a single jump, holding on to the side of the cab and rolling his legs over.

Hüseyin pulled a powerful flashlight out of the glove compartment and crossed the road to inspect the boy's work. His light beam skittered over the sea surface and soon came to rest on the Toyota Verso, sinking rapidly, driver's side up. Mark and Tarık watched the SUV tumble one last time before it disappeared into the water.

"I told you he'd do a good job," said Hüseyin, in a self-congratulatory tone.

He started the pickup and made a U-turn. "And now for the finale."

* * *

Around three-thirty a.m., they arrived at a deserted marina at Göltürkbükü. They bade farewell to Cengiz, who seemed downcast that no one had witnessed his thrilling stunt, tumbling out of a fast-moving vehicle as it hurled off the cliff and into the sea.

"Thanks for your help," said Mark, shaking the teenager's hand.

"Yeah, thanks for destroying my car so skillfully," said Tarık sarcastically. He had been taken aback by Mark's suggestion that they stage their own demise with the stunt, but Mark had convinced him that the loss of his SUV was better than that of his life at the hands of Rusu's men.

As Cengiz walked away to meet his father, who was to pick him up in the parking lot, Mark and Tarık hurried into Hüseyin's fishing boat. Its engines were already chugging. They soon pulled off their mooring and floated out to sea.

"Where are we headed?" asked Mark, standing by the transom at the back of the boat.

"Didim," said Hüseyin. "About two hours with this *külüstür*." He fondly slapped the wooden deck rail of his boat, which he had called a jalopy. "It would be half the time with a modern speedboat."

Tarık looked weary. Lack of sleep, Mark figured, and distress over his lost SUV. He soon went below deck to find a bench to sleep on.

Mark stood beside Hüseyin on the port side gunwale, enjoying the fresh cool breeze while the boat slowly chugged on. The half-moon was a giant bright plate, low in the western horizon, getting ready to set.

"What a beautiful sight," said Mark.

Hüseyin took a deep breath, savoring the scent of the sea. "Yes," he said. "I see it all the time."

"Lucky you." Mark pointed to the setting moon. "I've never seen anything like this." He chuckled. "It has taken a catastrophe and fear for my life to experience it."

Hüseyin didn't laugh. "If I may say so," he said, nodding to where Tarık had been standing a moment ago, "you put that young man in considerable danger. I don't know these people who killed Latif Gürsen and Serdar, but I have seen enough of the kind who frequented Latif's yacht. Some were real nasty."

"You're correct," said Mark soberly. "These people are foul and dangerous. I have had firsthand experience with them."

"All that I've done to help you," said Hüseyin sternly, "I did out of respect for Ilhan Bey and Günsu Hanım. They are good people. Kind and civilized. They were good to us, my family."

"I understand and I thank you," said Mark. He had a feeling that Hüseyin didn't like him much. *That makes two*, he thought, *first Leon Adler, now Hüseyin*. "When we set out here from Istanbul, I had no idea that all this would happen." Mark was reluctant to divulge the revelation that Latif was Tarık's biological grandfather. He figured the news would jeopardize the fisherman's respect toward Günsu's family.

He also refrained from mentioning that sending Tarık to Bodrum was Günsu's idea. In Hüseyin's eyes, Mark was the bad guy, and it was best that this be so. On the other hand, he was thankful for Günsu's suggestion, as Tarık had managed to recruit Hüseyin's aid. Mark shuddered to think how he would have coped with Rusu's men had he come to Bodrum by himself.

The moon became pinkish as it approached the horizon, its outlines distorted by the atmosphere, its brightness fading. It would soon disappear.

"Once I realized the trouble we're in, Tarık's safety did become my main concern," Mark said emphatically. "Believe me, I want to get him back to Istanbul and to his mother safely and as soon as possible."

Hüseyin nodded. "They tell me that you're an American secret agent," he said. "I heard you met your counterpart from MIT in the Bodrum *Karakol* and later at Latif's, after the bombing."

"How did you hear that?"

"The gendarmes guarding the road," said Hüseyin. "They are local boys. They saw you giving advice to that MIT man."

"There are no secrets around here!"

"I don't understand how a guy born in Turkey becomes an American secret agent. It wouldn't happen the other way around."

Mark held himself back from denying that he was FBI or CIA. It was futile.

"We don't like the MIT," Hüseyin continued. "I hope that with Latif's death, they will leave us alone. And with you gone, that too will help."

"What happens when we get to Didim?" Mark asked, ignoring Hüseyin's dig.

Earlier at Sait Bey's compound, when Mark had suggested a plan to stage the auto accident, Hüseyin had assured him that this was doable. He had indeed managed to pull it off with surprising efficiency. Hüseyin had also promised to arrange their getaway, but there had been no time to discuss its details. Mark had had to simply trust him.

"We'll dress you up in peasant clothes," Hüseyin said. "I brought along better ones than those ridiculous things you wore before."

"And then?"

"Then we'll put you on the bus to Istanbul." Hüseyin looked at his watch. "There is one that comes by a little after six a.m. You should be able to catch that. I have a friend waiting for us at the port in Didim. He'll drive you to the bus station."

"Sounds good."

"I suggest that you keep a low profile. Don't talk to anyone. Your Istanbul accent does not go with the clothes you'll be wearing."

Mark smiled. This unassuming fisherman was not as simple as Mark had initially thought. Hüseyin was cunning and clever.

"In the meanwhile," added Hüseyin, "my cousin, Cengiz's

father, is announcing the tragic accident by the Swissôtel to the newspapers and TV channels, as we speak."

Mark raised his eyebrows in surprise.

"Yet another heartbreaking crash on that curve," said Hüseyin, imitating a TV announcer with mock importance. "And this time no one survived. Tarık Polat, a promising young man from Istanbul, and his American guest swallowed by the sea."

"Do you think they'll buy it?" asked Mark.

Hüseyin laughed. "You don't know the Turkish press. They'll have a field day with it. Mark my words, by sunrise you two will be famous."

This gave Mark cause for concern. What if Günsu saw this news before they arrived?

"In Istanbul too?" Mark asked.

"Possibly," said Hüseyin. "Depends on what else is on the news."

With the moon gone, the vast sea blended with the sky in pitch darkness. It was quiet except for the pat-pat-pat of the boat's engine and the rhythmic swoosh of the wake it created. Hüseyin pulled out a pack of cigarettes and drew one out. He tapped the tip of the cigarette on the deck rail before placing it on his lips.

As he searched for his lighter, he had one last piece of advice for Mark. "Your photos may be all over TV news. Leave your caps on at all times and your visors low. Keep your heads down and don't look people straight in the eye. Don't let anyone recognize you."

CHAPTER 52

ARCADIA, ODESSA, APRIL 4

The spacious penthouse was brightly lit by the morning sun. Vadim Rusu donned his sunglasses and stepped out to his airy balcony facing the beach, a coffee mug in one hand, unlit cigar on the other. The Black Sea by the shores of Arcadia spread wide and vast from this high perch, already exhibiting whitecaps in a stiff breeze. Down below, there was little activity along the beachside promenade. Vadim expected a big throng of sun-seekers later on.

He took a seat on a high chair and surveyed the stunning seascape. The breeze, a virtual storm this high up, was no problem. The ledges of the balcony were lined with Plexiglas just for this purpose. Vadim lit his cigar and regarded the three piers below, spreading out into the sea by a nearby luxury resort. It used to be a sanitarium back in communist times. Most of Arcadia, Odessa's own little Riviera, had been lined with sanitariums serving the sick. *Look at it now*, he thought, *another Miami Beach.*

The grating sound of the patio door brought him out of his reverie. Standing before him was a marvelous apparition regarding him with piercing blue eyes. She was slim and tall, her blonde hair catching the breeze blowing over the balcony barrier. A nearly transparent gown was loosely tied at her waist, revealing long, shapely legs and small, firm breasts.

"It's chilly here," she said, her Russian heavily tinged with a Scandinavian accent.

Vadim took off his sunglasses and stared at her admiringly. "That's because you're not wearing anything."

Ingrid approached him lithely, a barefoot feline, and wrapped an arm around his neck. "Come back to bed," she purred into his ear.

Vadim moved his cigar away, knowing how disagreeable it was for her, and kissed her on the cheek. He lifted the lapel of her gown and looked down at her petite breast, nipple stiff and erect. "M'mm," he said in a husky voice, "the chill agrees with you." He loved flat-chested women, the Siberian women of his childhood having all been buxom babushkas.

Ingrid pulled on his arm. "Come on, come back."

"In a minute," he said. "I have to check my phone."

"That," Ingrid waved a long, well polished fingernail at the phone, "won't fuck you like I will."

Vadim chuckled. "That's for sure." She had won. The enticement was irresistible.

But as he rose from his chair, his phone chimed, the tone of the doorman downstairs. "We have a guest," he announced.

Ingrid was in full pout. "Who?"

"Oh, nobody. Just Boris."

* * *

Boris Petrov burst onto the balcony, barely registering the nearly nude nymph next to his boss. He'd seen many come and go. As usual, he had let himself in—Vadim had provided him with a key to his Ukrainian getaway.

Ingrid shot a knowing smile at Boris as she brushed by, readjusting her gown, opening and closing and tightening the strap. Split second as it was, she managed to give Boris a generous glimpse inside.

Boris grinned at Rusu. "Very nice."

"What do you have for me?" Vadim relit his cigar.

"Good news and bad news."

"Give me the good one first."

Boris settled into a second high chair that he rearranged toward the seascape. "The old man in Turkey, Radu's father." He readjusted his chair just so. "It's done."

"Did you send out our own crew this time?"

"Yes, sir. Clean job, Turkish police will never figure it out. So the guy gets whacked. Who knows? He had plenty of enemies."

"And the snitch?"

"We took care of him too."

"Good," said Vadim. "That guy was bad news."

"Stupid son of a bitch. Greedy."

"So what's the bad news?"

"The American agent. As you know, we had located him in Istanbul, but then he disappeared. Our team discovered him in Bodrum by chance, while working on the old man. Later, they attempted to capture him but it didn't work out."

"They didn't create an incident, I hope."

"No, no," Boris said hastily. "Very quiet. Stealthy."

"This American is real slippery." Rusu puffed thoughtfully on his cigar. "We've lost him—what, three times now?"

"Something like that."

"So we'll catch him next time. That's not bad news."

"There's more, Boss."

Rusu regarded his deputy silently, his expression neutral. Bad news was not uncommon in his line of business.

"The guy is dead."

"The American?" This was a surprise.

"There are reports in the Turkish media about him."

"What happened?"

"Car accident. Went off a cliff."

Vadim took a sip of coffee and spat it out. It had gotten cold. "That's too much of a coincidence," he said. "There must be others who are after this guy. Maybe it was a hit."

"Maybe," Boris responded. "But it's quite possible that it was a real accident. Apparently the spot where he went off has been the site of several such accidents."

"Yeah, well," said Vadim, still skeptical. "If he's dead, he is dead." He pointed a finger at Boris. "But don't take it for granted. I'm telling you, this guy is crafty. He may still be alive. If so, he'll surface somewhere. Keep an eye out for him."

"Consider it done." Boris stood up. "Don't want to take up too much of your time," he said, looking inside the apartment. "Looks like you have a busy morning."

Vadim shook his head. "She's a beast," he said. "A lovely beast, but she'll kill me one of these days."

Boris laughed. "I'm sure you'll be fine," he said. "But if the missus finds out," he paused for dramatic effect, "she'll be the one who'll kill you."

Vadim chortled in agreement and promptly launched into a coughing spell.

"One more thing." Boris buttoned the front of his suit jacket. "There are a few leftovers. Small fish. A nurse, a surgeon. Regulars on the team."

Vadim understood the question. "Did any of them work on my son?"

"I don't believe so," said Boris. "The doctor is a Kosovar named Zhulati. We're quite certain he was practicing in Pristina at the time of Dima's," he paused again, this time looking for a suitable word, "incident. The nurse, I don't know. She may have assisted."

"Leave them alone," Vadim ordered. "We're done."

"If you say so, Boss." Boris tried not to look surprised.

"This thing has taken a lot out of us. Those two hits in Budapest got us in trouble with Hungarian police and Interpol. I am still smoothing things politically on that."

"We lost two of our best in Budapest," added Boris.

"Yes. Thanks to that American bastard." Vadim spat into his coffee cup again. "Then there is the gaffe in Istanbul." He shook his head, still in disbelief. "Decapitating that doctor." He pointed his finger at Boris. "I hold you personally responsible for that fiasco."

"Sorry, Boss." Boris hung his head slightly.

Much to their surprise, there had been no repercussions from Istanbul police about the incident. They did not know why, but for Boris it had been a bonus. Nevertheless, he remained contrite about the gaffe.

"I wanted the old man," said Vadim emphatically. "He's the one that started it all. But now I'm done. Finished."

He put out his cigar in the cold coffee. "So much for revenge," he mumbled to himself. He looked up at Boris and raised his voice. "We wasted all this time and money, we put our business at risk, and for what?"

Boris didn't answer.

"It won't bring my son back," said Vadim. His eyes were red; he held back tears. "Revenge," he said. "It does not feel good this time."

"There's no closure?" asked Boris.

"No closure." Vadim turned away from Boris, facing the Plexiglas barrier, and wiped away tears. As he waited for Boris to leave, he stared at the choppy waves of the Black Sea. Then he opened the patio door, reached into his pocket for an aerosol can of breath freshener, and gave himself three generous puffs. He swallowed the minty, refreshing air and headed toward the bedroom.

CHAPTER 53

ON THE ROAD TO ISTANBUL, APRIL 3

The half-empty bus disgorged its passengers at a road stop near Kemalpaşa, three hours north of Bodrum. It was past eight in the morning and everyone headed toward the cafeteria, seeking breakfast. Two peasants hung back, loitering near the bus until their fellow passengers disappeared. They were dressed in well-worn, bulky clothes, their heads covered with caps pulled down to the eyebrows. They appeared to be father and son.

The bus driver, who stood by the front passenger door enjoying a long overdue smoke, observed them curiously, for the pair, who had boarded two hours ago in Didim, had not pulled out their own cigarettes. It was unusual for peasants in his bus to remain smoke-free during such breaks.

The older man nodded to the driver and, noticing the suspicious glance he was receiving, pulled the younger one by the arm toward the cafeteria. They sat in a lonely corner, heads hung low, and silently ate cheese *poğaça* with tea. Far to the side, behind a bar filled with coffee drinkers sitting on stools, two TVs blared, one showing a soccer game in rerun, the other TRT news.

"This is really good," said the old one to the younger. He had not eaten a *poğaça* in many decades. It was a Turkish breakfast pastry somewhat akin to American biscuits, often filled with cheese or meat.

The younger one suddenly tapped his arm. "Look!" He pointed to the TV monitors.

The news had cut away from the stylish anchorwoman and to an image of a cliff that was familiar to the pair. Beneath the short video was a chyron that announced a deadly accident in the Bodrum peninsula. Another car had plunged into the sea near Akyarlar. The image shifted to a still photo of a young man from Istanbul, a voiceover declaring him to be one of two victims, the second being an American guest.

"Shit," said Tarık. "That's me." The voiceover announced the names of the pair who had perished.

"Look away," said Mark.

Tarık turned away from the TV toward the wall and pulled his cap down further. "I'd better call my mom," he said, hastily searching his pockets for his mobile. "If she sees this she'll freak out." TRT news went out nationwide.

"Don't," said Mark. "Wait until we're done here. You can text her in the bus."

They wolfed down their pastries and hastily returned to the bus, nodding once again at the puzzled driver, who rarely saw his passengers come back this soon.

* * *

The steady sway at the back of the bus was like a rolling crib, lulling a weary Mark into an uncomfortable sleep. He and Tarık tucked behind the last row of double seats on the driver's side, slumped forward so that they were hidden from sight.

Tarık, who sat by the window, had hastily texted his mother that they were all right and would be back in Istanbul later in the day. He too dozed off, his breath leaving a mist on the window.

Mark was startled awake by the vibrations of his mobile phone. He took it out and looked at the screen: Ben Allen.

"Oh, shit," he exclaimed, louder than he would have liked. He then peered around the seat in front, to see if any passenger had noticed his gaffe. No one turned back to look.

"What is it?" Tarık spoke, whispering in Turkish, tinged with a fake Anatolian accent.

"My boss," said Mark, also responding in Turkish. "Chief of Radiology at my hospital." He checked his watch. "Strange," he added. "It's past seven p.m. in San Francisco."

"So what?"

"He is calling me after regular work hours. This can't be good."

"Well, why didn't you answer?"

"Are you kidding?" Mark was incredulous. "And have everyone in the bus listen to me, a hick from Didim, converse in perfect English?" He put his phone away. "I'll call him back at our next stop."

It was a brief bathroom break in a large service station, about an hour later. Mark hid behind a different bus and rang Ben Allen. He had not heard from his boss since Budapest. Allen had not been pleased about Mark's request for what was then a brief trip to Hungary. They were short on staff and Allen had only reluctantly given Mark time off. After discovering Ahmet dead and the problems afterwards, Mark had asked for an extension, causing further displeasure.

Then there was the unfortunate episode of an FBI visit to his radiology department seeking documents requested by Interpol. An unnerved Ben Allen had clearly been irate, asking Mark what the hell he was up to. That was their last contact. Mark had not checked in with his boss since. He should have.

"Ben," said Mark, trying to keep his voice calm. "How are you?"

"Where are you?" Allen was curt.

"In Turkey. What's up?"

Ben was clearly annoyed with Mark's cavalier attitude. "Listen, Mark, we have a big problem."

Mark's stomach sank.

Allen continued. "As of earlier today, you are suspended."

Mark paused to consider the news. "Are you firing me?"

"First of all, it's not me. The medical staff took this action."

Right, thought Mark angrily. *Upon your instigation, I'm sure.* Aloud, he said nothing.

After an awkward pause, Allen continued. "You are not fired... yet." The *yet* came stiffly. "Your extended absence is being seen as a dereliction of duty. Do you catch my drift?"

"I do."

"So, if you return soon." Another pause. "Say, within three days, I'll see what I can do to reinstate you."

Mark thought about the proposal. It was a reasonable time interval to finish up in Istanbul and fly back. Turkish Airlines had direct flights to San Francisco. "What is the likelihood of my being reinstated?"

"I can't make promises. You've skirted the rules, and you've pissed off some higher-ups."

Mark could not imagine who these higher-ups would be. He'd had a congenial relationship with most. It had to be Ben behind all this.

"I'll see what I can do, Ben," said Mark, unconvincingly.

"Good." Ben was terse. "There are plenty of others vying for your job. You wouldn't be a big loss."

Mark hung up and quietly said, "Fuck you!"

This was the gratitude for the years he had put in for them. He angrily strode back to the bus and, adjusting his cap up on his forehead, nodded a salute to the driver enjoying his smoke. Mark no longer cared about being recognized. To his surprise, the driver no longer eyed him with suspicion. He saluted back with an index finger on his forehead.

* * *

As the bus approached closer to Istanbul, Mark and Tarık became more relaxed.

"How did it go with your boss?" asked Tarık.

"Not good," Mark replied. He and Tarık continued to talk in

Turkish. "I am about to be fired if I don't get back to San Francisco soon."

"So why don't you?"

Mark looked at Tarık. It was a reasonable question. He struggled for an answer.

"To tell you the truth, I'm not sure I want to return."

"Why? Weren't you the one who told me you missed your radiology reading room?" Tarık recalled their conversation on the way to Bodrum.

"Actually, I said that in jest," said Mark. He sighed. "My old life in the States is over," he said. "My marriage is gone, I lost my house, and now my job...." He trailed off and looked out the window. They were on that magnificent bridge over the Gulf of Izmit. "To tell you the truth, I have become addicted to this new way of life."

"What new way?" Tarık asked, incredulous. "You're running around Europe afraid for your life. Is that what you're addicted to?"

Mark swallowed hard. "One night, in Budapest, soon after I found your father dead, I was chased by two thugs who were intent on killing me. They were shooting at me. It was the scariest experience I've ever had. But then, when I escaped and arrived at safety, there was this exhilaration. I can't describe it, a sort of post-adrenaline rush."

Tarık shook his head in disbelief.

"I have now experienced that rush several more times since, and I'll tell you, it's addictive."

"What you're telling me is that instead of going back to your safe and calm life, you seek more danger."

Mark realized how senseless it all sounded. "I don't know, I suppose." He hesitated. "Besides, this guy Rusu will never stop searching for me. I am not sure that he'll buy this stunt we pulled in Bodrum, faking our deaths."

"Why did we do it, then?"

"Well, we bought time to leave Bodrum safely. Here we are, almost in Istanbul, and no one is accosting us."

Mark knew that Tarık was upset about losing his SUV. "Look,

I'll make it up to you with your car," he said. "It was my fault that you lost it. I'll reimburse you."

As he said that, Mark had no idea how he would keep that promise. With no job and with the divorce draining his reserves, he wasn't sure he had enough to dish out for a new car.

"Don't worry about that," said Tarık. "The money is no problem. We'll take care of it." Mark knew he was referring to his mother.

Mark stared at the front of the bus, embarrassed by his predicament.

"Do you know what I really think?" Tarık started up again.

"About what?"

"About your thirst for danger and adventure."

Mark looked down at the floor. All of a sudden Tarık was being the adult and he, in his fifties, the adolescent.

"I think that you're going through some sort of midlife crisis."

Mark chuckled. The kid was probably right. "Most men my age act out their midlife crisis with sexy twenty-somethings and leave their wives."

"Maybe that's what you should have done," said Tarık. "Let's see," he pondered with a teasing voice. "Who would qualify for such a role? The right woman to fix your predicament."

"Not Semra," said Mark.

Tarık laughed. "Semra would be perfect. Young, sexy, and how shall I say it?"

"Don't!"

"A bit offbeat?" He had that same mischievous smile Mark had seen on their drive to Bodrum. "A perfect balm for a midlife crisis."

"Uh, I don't know about that."

"Yeah, well. We're almost back in Istanbul and you'll have to face her. I think she admires you more than you can imagine. You'll have a hard time shaking her loose."

Mark looked out the window. Traffic was getting heavier as the bus passed by high-rise housing developments at the outskirts of the metropolis. The young man was right. This could all be just a midlife crisis. Mark wondered if he would be behaving like this if he were still with Megan, his first wife. He felt a pang of pain as he recalled the accident that took her. He missed Megan so much.

The bus passed by a road sign announcing the turn-off to Sabiha Gökçen Airport, Istanbul's second airport near Pendik. They would soon arrive at the heart of the city.

"You know," said Mark thoughtfully, turning to Tarık, "all of a sudden, I'm not sure I want to arrive in Istanbul."

CHAPTER 54

ISTANBUL, APRIL 4

"Glad to know you, sir," said the middle-aged Turkish man with graying hair and moustache as he effusively shook Mark's hand. His English was heavily accented.

Leon Adler, decked out in a fancy suit and tie, stood by Mark and observed the greeting with a smile. He had spiffed up his appearance, all except his mop of blond hair, which remained unruly as ever.

"Please, have a seat."

Mark and Leon sat next to each other on comfortable armchairs surrounding a coffee table laid out with tea and pastries. Their host sat across from them and crossed his legs. Behind him loomed a massive desk and a giant emblem on the wall. It featured a police star with the Turkish flag at its center, decorated by wreaths, and a round blue band that announced *Istanbul Emniyet Müdürlüğü*.

"It is not always that we encounter such a capable agent from the United States," said Ayhan Aydın, the police chief of the city. He leaned over and took a sip of tea.

Dressed in an ill-fitting suit and with a loose tie around an unbuttoned collar, Aydın looked more like an overworked school principal than a powerful law enforcer of a grand metropolis. His soft-spoken manner that betrayed a lifetime of bureaucratic ascendance left one with an erroneous impression that he was harmless.

At a loss for an answer, Mark turned to Leon, who sat erect, his hands clasped by his waist, staring proudly at the Turkish policeman. Mark had contacted Leon the day after he and Tarık arrived in Istanbul, and quickly discovered that Leon knew the highlights of what happened in Bodrum. He had obviously been briefed by Bozkurt, the MIT agent. Leon had hastily cut off Mark's own breathless account and told him that they had to meet someone. Without any explanation, Leon had picked him up and taken him to the colossal seven-story headquarters building of Istanbul Police in the Old City's Fatih district. Now, here they were, at a spacious top-story office, in a private meeting with the chief.

"I am told that you are Turkish," said the police chief.

Mark replied in Turkish that yes, he had been born and raised here but now he lived in California.

"Oh, he speaks Turkish so well." Aydın addressed Leon with delight.

Leon nodded in agreement.

The police chief continued in Turkish. "We should not let you out of our country."

The statement alarmed Mark despite the friendly tone in which it was uttered. The chief probably meant that as a compliment, but Mark wasn't sure.

"You would be such a wonderful asset for us," added Aydın.

"And he is a doctor, too," said Leon, piling on.

"Our loss, America's gain," said Aydın.

"So, what is this all about?" Mark asked Leon in English.

"It's about the great favor you have done for us," interjected the police chief, in his Turkish-accented English.

Leon nodded in the chief's direction, urging Mark to listen.

"The evidence you handed us via our valuable Interpol liaison here," Aydın pointed to Leon.

"What evidence?"

"Gazioğlu's laptop," said Leon.

It had been only six days since Mark's fateful foray into the surgeon's Tuzla compound, but the ensuing events had made it seem like months ago. He had forgotten about that computer.

"It allowed us to round up a dangerous gang of Albanian criminals who have been operating in our midst," said the chief. "We were on their trail but did not have enough to make arrests. Then came your data. It was like a Christmas gift—as they would say in your adopted country." The chief laughed at his own jest.

"Albanians?" Mark was puzzled.

"You know," said Leon, as if trying to jar Mark's memory. He made a face at Mark, eyebrows lifted, head nodding in the direction of the chief. *Come on, get with it,* he seemed to be saying.

"Oh! Them." Mark pretended he knew. "Those bastards!"

"An offshoot of the *Banda e Lushnjës* gang, operating here in Istanbul," explained Aydın. "They've been a thorn by our side for several years now."

Mark turned to Leon for an explanation. "A prominent Mafia group that operates out of the town of Lushnjës in Albania," explained Leon. "Our own Israeli law enforcement has also been interested in them."

The coin finally dropped. "So, they're the ones who killed Mahmut Gazioğlu," said Mark.

"That's right," said the police chief. "The CCTV footage you provided allowed clear identification. There were four of them. Once identified, we quickly traced them to the remainder of the group. And now they are all cleared up, those cockroaches."

He picked up the plate of Turkish pastries and offered one to Mark. Mark took a *halka*, a bracelet-like baked dough pastry covered with black sesame seeds. "Did you find the head?" he asked.

"The head of the *Lushnjës* organization resides part-time in Albania and part-time in Bari, Italy. It is up to our European colleagues to apprehend him."

"No, that's not what I meant," said Mark. "The head," he repeated. "The dead doctor's head. It was missing."

"Oooh!" The police chief laughed at the confusion. "No sir. We didn't. One of the apprehended prisoners declared that the head was sent out of the country, possibly to Romania."

"Moldova," Mark corrected the chief. The thought of the surgeon's decapitated head being sent to Vadim Rusu made his hairs rise on end.

"That's right. My apologies for the mistake." The chief turned to Leon, acknowledging Mark's astuteness with approval.

"There's more," said Leon to Mark, prompting Aydın.

"Yes, indeed," said the police chief. He waited for Mark to finish his pastry and take a sip of tea.

"We were also able to shut down a corrupt cell within our organization that operated out of Tuzla."

"You mean within the police?"

"Mr. Kent," said the police chief. "As you know, Istanbul is a very large and diverse city. If you take all the towns around your San Francisco Bay and their environs and turn them into one giant city—that's what we are."

Mark nodded. He was aware of the geographic similarity between the San Francisco Bay Area and Istanbul, and that while one operated as a single city, the American counterpart was chopped up into numerous different municipalities.

The chief continued. "We therefore have different police chiefs that operate in our different districts. It is a very complex organization."

"And you administer all that."

"Yes, sir, I do," Aydın said proudly. "But by the same token, you can see how rogue elements can easily take up shop here and there, like cancers growing on our body."

Mark nodded.

"Well, as it turns out, we had a small tumor growing in Tuzla that we were not aware of. Thanks to you, we have removed it, surgically."

Leon explained it more succinctly. "Gazioğlu was receiving protection from certain elements of the Tuzla police," he said. "The reason the Albanians were so brazen in their attack was because they expected their police connection to arrive soon afterwards and mop up after them."

"And you foiled that plan," added Aydın.

"So that's why Gazioğlu stuck to his compound in Tuzla so obstinately," Mark realized out loud. If only Semra, who had complained about her gilded Tuzla prison, knew.

"So you see, Mr. Mark Kent," said the Istanbul police chief, "you have done us a double favor. We do not tolerate such corruption in our midst." He turned to Leon. "We also express our gratitude to our fine Israeli colleagues."

Leon beamed.

"We would like to give you a token of our appreciation," said Ayhan Aydın to Mark. "You name your desire and we'll see to it."

Stunned by the gesture, Mark first looked at Leon, then at Aydın as if the police chief were a genie out of a bottle.

"Well," he said hesitantly. "There is this one thing you can help me with…"

* * *

"Nice guy," said Mark after they left the Fatih headquarters, their taxi passing by the grand Hagia Sophia mosque.

"Son of a bitch was probably displeased because he was not getting a cut of the proceeds from Tuzla," said Leon quietly, out of the driver's earshot.

"That guy Aydın is corrupt?" asked Mark loudly, in disbelief.

Mindful of the driver, Leon put his index finger on his mouth, shushing him. "Quiet."

"He seemed on the up-and-up," Mark whispered.

"None of them are." Leon looked out of the window as the taxi traversed the old Byzantine Hippodrome, nowadays a plaza dotted with a series of ancient Egyptian obelisks.

"And they are not friendly to us Israelis any longer. Not since the current Turkish government took over in 2003."

"He seemed friendly enough," said Mark naïvely. "You looked like you liked him."

Leon turned to Mark. "I have to act that way," he said quietly. "I need to keep in their good graces to do my job."

The taxi turned downhill toward the Marmara coast.

"You know, I owe you an apology," said Leon, now out loud.

"How so?"

"You ended up doing me a big favor with that crazy stunt you pulled in Tuzla. It produced a good deal of goodwill with the Istanbul police. Last time we met, I was rude to you. I am sorry about that."

"Oh, it's no big deal," Mark said dismissively. "I wasn't offended."

"No, really!" insisted Leon. "I still think that you suck as a soccer player," he said, grinning. "But you are a pretty good intelligence operative."

The taxi picked up speed on the coastal road beneath the Topkapı Palace. Mark admired the deep blue waters at the mouth of the Bosporus, passenger ferries crisscrossing around giant merchant ships back and forth from the Asian side at Üsküdar and Kadıköy.

"Did I do all right with your friend Bozkurt?" Mark asked in a provocative tone.

Leon gave him a side glance and hesitated to answer.

"You know," Mark egged him on. "The MIT guy."

Leon looked out the window. They were in the bustling business district of Eminönü by the mouth of the Golden Horn. He examined the large mosque that dominated Eminönü square as if he were seeing it for the first time. "That matter is closed," he said quietly. "End of story."

"You mean they are not investigating the bombing in Bodrum? The assassination of Latif Gürsen?"

Leon turned back and faced Mark eye-to-eye. "What is there to investigate? Latif was a major nuisance for them, and a slippery one at that. Whoever did it, they did the Turks a favor."

"It was Vadim Rusu!" Mark nearly shouted in frustration.

Leon gave him an evil eye, nodding in the direction of the driver.

"Isn't anyone going to do anything about Rusu?" Mark whispered this time, his voice still dripping with ire.

"Not the Turks." Leon was firmly convinced. "You heard Aydın. They captured suitable perps for the Gazioğlu hit and they are happy. Case closed. With MIT, it is also case closed."

"What about Interpol?" Mark asked. "Are they doing anything to apprehend Vadim Rusu?"

"To my knowledge, not much."

The answer shocked Mark. "I don't get it. Isn't there enough evidence to put him away?"

"It's not up to us to put people away. It's up to local law enforcement."

"That would be the Moldovans, right?"

"I suppose."

"So why aren't they doing anything?"

After a long wait at a traffic light, the taxi finally turned onto the Galata Bridge to cross the Golden Horn.

"Look," said Leon. "This guy Rusu is pretty powerful. He runs a security company that provides mercenary soldiers for the Russians. He is well connected and well protected, especially by Moscow. He is not easy to get."

Mark stared out the window at the line of people fishing off the bridge. The news was disturbing.

Leon continued. "Besides, I am not sure the Moldovans have been adequately informed. From what I understand, Interpol has put the Rusu file on the back burner."

"Why? Don't they think this is important?"

"No," said Leon. "I think that Rusu's influence goes deep, even within our organization."

"Wonderful," said Mark sardonically.

"Why do you care?"

"I have the feeling that Rusu is following me," Mark said. "And don't tell me I'm paranoid. Wherever I've gone, assassinations have followed. Did Bozkurt tell you that Rusu's men came after us at Tarık Polat's house?"

"No," answered Leon. "I didn't hear about that."

"A small detail compared to the bombing of Latif Gürsen." Mark shook his head reproachfully. "They tried to kidnap me and take me to Chișinău once, back in Budapest. They are still trying. I don't think they'll ever quit."

"I think it's best for you to return home to America as soon as possible."

The taxi left the Karaköy quarter on the other side of the Golden Horn and approached the pier in Kabataş, where old car ferries connected the two continents before the advent of the Bosporus bridges.

"Who's to say that he won't reach out across the ocean to nab me?" asked Mark.

Leon had no answer to that.

"Sometimes I think it might be best for me to head on to Moldova and confront Rusu myself. Get it over with."

"Don't you dare!" Leon was alarmed. "That would be the craziest thing you've done so far."

"I don't want to go back to the States until there is some conclusion to all this."

"What will you do?" asked Leon. "Stay here in Istanbul?"

"I don't know," murmured Mark. He looked out the taxi window toward the iconic Hilton Hotel perched on the Harbiye hillside, not far from where he had stayed at the Hyatt. The old *Spor ve Sergi Sarayı* where he had had a memorable meal at Borsa was nearby.

Günsu had repeated her invitation, and this time Mark had accepted. As the taxi crested the hill and turned into the Nişantaşı quarter, Mark knew that he could stay at Günsu's for a while. But this, too, made him uneasy.

When the taxi stopped and Mark got out, Leon stayed inside for the rest of the ride to his office. He rolled the window down as Mark headed toward Günsu's apartment and called after him. "Hey, I forgot to ask you something. Gazioğlu's girlfriend."

Mark stiffened.

"Remember you asked me about her before leaving for Bodrum?"

Mark shook his head, pretending not to recall. In fact, he remembered the conversation well. Leon had blown him off and told him to give Semra a good fuck; Mark, he had said, looked like he could use one.

Leon beckoned Mark closer to the taxi window. "Did you fuck her?" he asked quietly, again mindful of the driver.

Mark stared at him, annoyed. "Why do you want to know?"

"Oh, nothing," said Leon in a peculiar tone. "It's just that, from what I've heard, the Gazioğlu murder investigation revealed some interesting facts about *her*." He put a special mocking emphasis on *her*.

Mark waved his arm in a *go on, get out of here* gesture and hurried toward the apartment door.

CHAPTER 55

ISTANBUL, APRIL 4

The queen-size bed in Günsu's apartment was comfortable. Still exhausted from his Bodrum escape, Mark pulled up the heavy covers and hoped for a rejuvenating night of sleep. Günsu had offered him her own bed, with the two of them together. Mark had declined. The offer had come several decades too late. Besides, even if he wanted to, Mark was too weary for what Günsu had in mind.

Semra was still staying at Günsu's apartment, but Mark had not run into her yet. According to Günsu she had gone to stay with some friends in Beyoğlu, news that caused Mark to be concerned. Beyoğlu, along with its environs, was a traditional hub for the oldest profession, the one with which Semra had begun her days in Istanbul. Günsu had reassured him that it was a brief absence and that Semra had been a polite, well-behaved guest. Mark was thankful for that.

As Mark dug under the covers, he contemplated his next move. Should he stay in Turkey longer? Enjoy a real vacation maybe? He also contemplated a return to Budapest. Visit Jasmin, the young police officer who had befriended him and with whom he had had an unfulfilled night of love.

He was frustrated by his tenaciously arid love life. His failed marriage had sapped everything. He had then squandered his subsequent opportunities, Jasmin being the biggest. Was he ever to find a suitable lover?

Günsu wasn't it. Semra? Alluring as she was, Mark was uncertain about stepping over that line.

He thought of Olga, the masseuse in Budapest whose business card in Ahmet's hotel room had initiated his misadventure. Olga, wife of the notorious and elusive Cezar Kaminesky, had had a longstanding affair with Ahmet. On the two occasions Mark had met her, he had found Olga irresistibly attractive. As he drifted into sleep, the image of Olga in her tight, revealing masseuse uniform remained fixed in his imagination. Now *that* was a woman he could dig into, even if it entailed more perils.

But it was just a fantasy. Who knew where Olga was now? She had left Budapest shortly after their second meeting. It didn't matter, the fantasy was a good enough accompaniment into slumber.

* * *

Mark didn't hear his bedroom door open and the subsequent light footsteps. The covers parted and a cool body lay down by him. He thought he was dreaming as he felt being hugged from behind. It was the scent that woke him up, that unmistakable floral perfume that took him to the Marmara shore in Tuzla.

"Semra?"

She nuzzled her head by his neck. "I just heard that you're back. I missed you," she murmured.

Her arms firmly encircled his chest. He tried to free himself and rise but he couldn't. He was being held captive.

"I'm so glad." She kissed him lightly at the nape of his neck.

"Semra, you can't do this! Not with Günsu Hanım across the hall."

"Shh," she ordered him. "You'll wake her up." She kissed him several times on the cheek and giggled.

Mark tried to turn around and face her. She loosened her grip and let him, only to smother him with a full-on kiss on the lips. Mark smelled alcohol on her breath.

"What have you been drinking?"

"Oh, nothing," she said. "Just a couple of cocktails in Beyoğlu. Went out with old friends."

"Why are you back in Beyoğlu?" Mark raised his voice.

"Quiet, will you?" Semra playfully slapped Mark's cheek. "Just having a good time with some old friends. That's all."

Mark finally freed himself, got up, and turned the room light on. She instinctively pulled the covers above her chest. Her long black hair was loose, all over her face. She shook it off with a turn of the head and refrained from looking at him, her eyes downcast.

"Why didn't you tell me?" asked Mark sharply.

She gradually lifted her eyes back up. "I didn't think you could handle it," she said in a grave tone. Her voice was huskier, betraying her former self.

"What!" said Mark. "Were you scared that I'd harm you?" He was hurt by her insinuation.

"It's been known to happen." She sat up, body wrapped in the covers, and wiped her hair back in a nervous gesture. "To me, too."

Mark could just imagine her ordeal in the rough streets of Beyoğlu. He felt a pang of sympathy, but his sense of affront was stronger. "I'm the one who saved your life, remember?!" He had raised his voice again, this time too loudly. It caused them to both stop and listen for any sign of Günsu.

"Look," said Semra, in a resigned voice. "I am an acquired taste. Remember those insects you and Mahmut were eating? Disgusting things."

"Escargot," Mark corrected her. "They were snails, not insects."

"Whatever." She let go of the covers, revealing her ample breasts beneath a nearly transparent silk gown. "A Mardin boy like me..." She looked for the right words. "Didn't have a taste for escargot. Do you understand?"

Mark didn't answer. He was struck by Semra referring to herself by her former gender.

"Where did you learn such fancy phrases?" he asked dubiously. "'Acquired taste'!"

"Mahmut told me. He told me that all the time, that I was an acquired taste and oh, how delicious he thought I was." Her eyes got glassy and a lone tear flowed down her cheek.

His outrage deflated, Mark came back to the bed and hugged her, letting her head rest on his shoulder as she quietly sobbed. They were the tears of an angst-ridden childhood, of the fearful streets of Istanbul, of her imprisonment in Tuzla, and ironically, of the loss she had suffered there. Mark clung to her tightly and patted her head.

When she finally calmed down, she pleaded with him. "Take me with you, please."

"I don't know where I am going," he whispered.

She separated and faced him eye-to-eye. Her face was a mess, mascara flowing down both cheeks, her lipstick in pink blotches here and there. "I don't care," she said in a nasal voice. "I'll go anywhere with you."

She quickly stood up and went for a tissue dispenser atop a drawer. She blew her nose, facing away from Mark, while he regarded her tall, slim figure. Her buttocks, visible beneath her sheer gown, were alluringly outlined with dark thong underwear that disappeared between her cheeks.

Could he acquire this taste? At that moment Mark thought it might be worth a try.

CHAPTER 56

BRAȘOV, APRIL 7

The Sector 1 police station was a beehive around five p.m. Andrei ignored the steady din of the room and leaned his elbows on his desk, rubbing his eyes. It had been a long day, first with Dorina at Martinu Hospital, then with Boboc listening to the Zhulati recordings, and finally his meeting with his station chief in the afternoon. That last one had him mentally exhausted, and his day was not over yet. The constant background noise was getting on his nerves. He needed a quieter place for his upcoming phone call. He decided to try the parking lot.

He walked downstairs and gave a quick salute to the officer at the reception desk who was taking down a report from an elderly woman going on about a dog incident. Once in the parking lot, Andrei randomly picked a patrol car, entering the driver's side. He leaned back in the seat and closed his eyes for a brief rest.

Andrei considered his current predicament. His meeting with Dalca had not gone well. Spitatul Martinu, as a line of investigation, was temporarily shut off. Until he developed his other leads—Yoet, the donor, and Cernea, the nurse—he had just a single avenue toward some solid evidence: Dr. Zhulati. The doctor needed to be brought in and interrogated. Andrei checked his watch. It was getting late to do that today. Anyway, the man did nothing besides stay in his apartment. He could be there one more night. Andrei would have Boboc apprehend him in the morning. Let Zhulati enjoy one last night of inebriated bliss.

Andrei wasn't so sure that Zhulati would break down as easily as Dalca seemed to think, certainly not about his illegal surgeries. Yoet, the sick donor, was a more promising lead. Zhulati had sounded very concerned about him, both on Andrei's trick call with Enver's mobile and subsequently on the listening devices Boboc had planted in his apartment.

Andrei considered his efforts to identify the donor, so far fruitless. Local emergency rooms Andrei had contacted didn't yield much. He had run down a list he had compiled of several patients who recently turned up with complications of abdominal surgery. None fit. Some were women, many were elderly. Andrei doubted that Braşov would yield more clues. He hoped that his nationwide bulletin to police districts might do the trick. There was nothing to do but wait.

Andrei rubbed his eyelids. He was a long way from delivering on what he had promised Dalca. His current prospects looked bleak, and he did not have high hopes for his next move, a phone call to Corneliu, an old friend.

Corneliu Balaş was a Hungarian from western Transylvania near the Hungarian border. Andrei had met Corneliu in his early army days, and they had become tight buddies. They then parted ways, Corneliu having no interest in the elite force that Andrei transferred into. Years later they ran into each other while both were serving in the SRI and rekindled their friendship. Andrei used his friend's expertise in signals intelligence in several of his cases, including the fateful Emilia Sala affair. But after Andrei's departure from SRI, they had not been in contact. He hoped that the phone number he had for Corneliu was still active.

"Andrei Costiniu!" exclaimed Balaş when Andrei identified himself. Corneliu had a characteristic high-pitched voice that Andrei recognized immediately. "Hello, stranger. You're still alive!"

"Alive and well."

"And how is that sexy girl of yours? Are you still with Ana?"

"We have a baby girl now, ten months old. How about you?"

"Not so lucky. Still on the prowl." Balaş had been persistently unsuccessful in maintaining long-term relationships. "So what's up?"

"I am with Braşov Police nowadays, Sector 1."

"Yes, so I've heard. Braşov must be the safest place in Romania." Balaş laughed at his own joke.

Andrei wasn't surprised that his friend knew. Rumors and gossip traveled fast within SRI. "I need help with a murder investigation."

"Wow, they have you doing that already? You're rising fast in the world, my friend."

"Just like I did at SRI," said Andrei sardonically.

"Yeah. I hope you have a better grip on yourself nowadays."

Andrei ignored the comment. "This murder here in Braşov seems to be tied to a couple of back-to-back assassinations in Budapest two weeks ago. I am having trouble getting adequate info from the Hungarians. Interpol is also involved, but so far they are a dead end."

"Hungarians," said Corneliu, "my specialty."

"I know. That's partly why I called you."

"So what do I get for my efforts?" asked Corneliu teasingly.

In their army days, they had rewarded each other by paying for prostitutes, usually Roma Gypsies.

"No more Roma," said Andrei. "I am out of that business."

"Aww, damn!"

"Whiskey," Andrei offered, knowing it would entice his old friend. "Single malt Scotch. You name the brand."

"That'll do. Give me the names."

＊ ＊ ＊

Andrei walked back to the station with confident steps. He had been worried that Corneliu Balaş might turn him down. Much to his relief, he was still the same old army buddy, as if all those years had never passed.

"Hey, Costiniu." The watch officer at the front desk yelled after him.

Andrei waded through a gaggle of people gathered in front of the officer's desk.

"This just in for you."

He handed Andrei an email printout. It was from the Iaşi police. Andrei folded the paper and flew up the stairs two steps at a time. Once at his desk, he quickly read the message and reached for his phone.

"Hello, Funar here." Chief Inspector Geofri Funar of Iaşi Police, Sector 3, had a deep baritone voice.

"This is *Subinspector* Andrei Costiniu, Braşov, Sector 1. I am calling you about your email."

There was a pause. "So you're the officer who sent that bulletin about a sick young man with abdominal surgery?" Funar sounded puzzled.

"That's right. That was me."

"And this person is of interest in a murder investigation?"

"Yes."

"Are you the one in charge?"

Andrei smiled as his colleague's quandary dawned on him. "Yes."

Another pause. Andrei could envision the man on the other side wondering how Braşov Police was being run, placing such a low-ranking detective in charge of a high-level investigation.

"Well, all right then." Funar seemed to get himself together. "We have an individual here who fits the profile you sent."

"Where exactly?"

"Saint Spiridon County Hospital, here downtown. Young man in his twenties, presented to the Emergency Room very sick. Sepsis, the doctors said, complication of a recent operation."

"What sort of operation?"

"It appears that he had a kidney removed."

Andrei pumped a fist in the air. This had to be the man. He had a million questions. He contained his excitement and put on a calm, professional voice. "That might be him. What is the man's condition?"

"Very sick. On a ventilator."

"How were you notified?" Andrei wondered what had led the hospital to contact the police.

"Apparently he was dropped off in the Emergency Room under suspicious circumstances. The head doctor treating him notified us when they realized he was missing a kidney. She suspected foul play."

"Do you have an ID on the man?"

"Yoet Tcaci," said Funar. "He is from Moldova."

Andrei tried not to sound elated. "What have you found in your investigation so far?"

"We haven't initiated an investigation yet," said Funar. "The tip from the hospital coincidentally came in at about the same time as your bulletin. If this is your case, we'll be happy to let you lead."

Andrei figured that his counterpart in Iaşi did not want any extra work if he could help it. He couldn't blame him for that.

"It sure sounds like the guy I am looking for," said Andrei.

"So who did he murder?"

"No one," said Andrei. "He is not a suspect. He might be a crucial witness."

"Okay. I get it."

"Listen, I'll be over to Iaşi as soon as I can. In the meanwhile can you put a guard on the guy?"

"Will do," said Funar.

"Thank you so much." Andrei was truly grateful.

"One more thing," said the officer.

"Yes."

"Did I hear correctly? Are you a *Subinspector*?"

"Yes."

"And you're in charge of the investigation?"

Andrei chuckled. "I'll explain that when we meet."

CHAPTER 57

ISTANBUL, APRIL 5

The call came in as Mark was on his way back from his second visit to police headquarters. This time he was alone, his appointment inside the colossal building having been brief.

"Dr. Mark Kent?" said a quiet, hesitant voice on the line. He was hard to hear in the back seat of a taxi, amid the din of the Old City.

"Yes, that's me. Can you speak up, please?"

"My name is Vasile Negrescu. I am Iancu's son." His English was thick with an Eastern European accent. He then added, "*Merhaba*," *hello*, in Turkish.

Mark removed his mobile from his ear and stared at its screen in stunned silence, as if the screen held an explanation for this unexpected call.

"Are you there?" Vasile sounded anxious.

"Yes, yes." Mark held the phone back to his ear. "Sorry, I am in busy traffic."

"I believe you met my father recently."

"Yes, I did. In Budapest. Very nice man." Mark recalled the tall, bulky, imposing figure of Ahmet's Romanian partner. "My condolences on your loss," he added.

"That's why I am calling," said the younger Negrescu. "I wanted to invite you to my father's funeral. It will be held two days from now, here in Bucharest."

"Well, thank you, but…"

Vasile cut him off. "I know that this is a last-minute request and I believe you're currently in Turkey. We can make all the arrangements for you. We will cover your expenses, organize your flight, and a luxury hotel here."

Mark hesitated. "Why?" he said. "Why do you want me to attend?"

"From what I was led to believe, you were one of the last people who saw my father. Dumitru, his chauffeur, told me."

Mark recalled the young bodyguard with a military countenance who had driven him to a rendezvous with Iancu at a large indoor market in Budapest. He later learned that Dumitru had escaped the attack that killed his boss and a fellow bodyguard.

Vasile continued. "I am trying to piece the facts together. Budapest Police has not been helpful. I hoped that maybe you could shed some light into my father's death."

"All right," said Mark. "Thank you for the invitation. I'll be happy to come and meet you and your family."

They spent a few more minutes on the phone with details of the travel arrangements.

The taxi crawled across the Golden Horn through the Galata Bridge. Mark stared beyond the wall of people fishing off the railings toward the Bosporus, busy with innumerable vessels. The suspension bridge in Ortaköy loomed in the backdrop. A sleek modern streetcar at the center of the bridge passed them, impervious to the congestion.

Mark patted the inner pocket of his jacket. Reaching in, he removed a small blue book with the seal of America on its cover. He flipped through the pages and found what he was looking for: the missing entry stamp into Turkey. He regarded it with a smug smile.

He then looked out toward the iconic Genovese tower of Galata as the taxi exited the bridge, plunging into the Karaköy quarter. The sturdy tower had stood guard over the city for nearly seven hundred years, its conical roof soaring into the sky. He thought about his perilous trip to Mahmut Gazioğlu's compound in Tuzla to rescue Semra. Foolhardy as it was, the effort had yielded fruits beyond his imagination.

He closed the passport and slapped the cover, silently thanking Ayhan Aydın, the police chief, for the favor he had bestowed. He could leave Turkey now, with no impediments. And he no longer was at a loss for what to do next.

CHAPTER 58

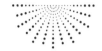

BRAȘOV, APRIL 8 ... EARLY MORNING

It was a warm night and the inside of the van was dank, the odor of stale sweat sticking to everything. Mihai Vasilescu jolted out of a snooze with a sharp pain in his neck. He removed his bulky earphones and rubbed the perimeter of his ears, trying to clear the moisture they left behind. He then massaged his neck.

The laptop screen connected to the audio equipment displayed the same sound traces it had recorded for the last two hours. There were three simultaneous waveform lines, each corresponding to a listening device Boboc had planted in the apartment. The waves came in with heartbeat-like regularity. Vasilescu opened the back doors of the van and stepped out onto the street. It was dark and deserted. He took several deep breaths of fresh air and stretched his limbs. He turned toward the French café he was parked in front of. It was closed at this hour. He could have used a big cup of coffee and a couple of croissants just about now.

He looked up at the apartment complex across the other street, at the sixth-floor windows that were the target. They were dark, as were all the other windows of the building. He checked his watch. Two-fifteen.

"Shit," he murmured. He had another four hours and forty-five minutes to spend in this prison of a van, listening to the loud, throaty snores of the surveillance subject. What had he done to deserve this? Their station chief had announced that Boboc and that young upstart Costiniu would need periodic help in an investigation none of them cared about. No one volunteered to take the twenty-four-hour stakeout that was soon announced. So Boboc, in his infinite wisdom, devised a lottery. Vasilescu drew one of the unlucky picks.

That fucking rookie Andrei Costiniu should be the one here, thought Vasilescu. He couldn't believe that Dalca had made him lead investigator on whatever this case was. Vasilescu imagined the young, handsome officer tucked in his comfortable bed, having probably fucked his cute wife real good, sleeping soundly. Middle-aged, stocky, and married to a woman he no longer cared for, Vasilescu returned to the van with a sharp pang of jealousy. He closed the back doors and sat at the console.

The computer screen continued its endless display of snores in waveform. The main line with the largest amplitude came from a listening device planted near a recliner in the living room. The other two—Vasilescu did not know their exact location—echoed the same snore forms in synch, but in lower amplitude.

Vasilescu drew a deep sigh and put on the earphones. The clock-like regularity of the snorts and wheezes were perfect for inducing sleep. He soon slumped over, eyes closed, his neck in an impossibly contorted posture beyond the edge of his seat. This time he would not wake up until the day crew arrived. Now Vasilescu's own snores matched those of the subject under surveillance.

Had the unfortunate officer remained awake, he would have soon noticed a disturbance in one of the accessory waveforms on the screen. Recording from a bug near the door of the apartment, it would have displayed waves that represented irregular mechanical sounds as the lock was picked. Then would come low-amplitude waves on all three recording lines, interspersed with the snore waves, corresponding to soft footsteps. These may not have been enough to arouse his suspicion, for soon thereafter it was back to the unaccompanied snores.

However, had Vasilescu not been dulled into deep sleep, he would have definitely been aroused by the next set of sounds that caused greater disturbance in the waveforms. The snores interrupted by gags and gurgles, two sharp, piercing, high-pitched cries, and then some banging around, a train of discordant sounds that interrupted the calm rhythm of the night. They ended with soft footsteps and the door of the apartment creaking as it closed.

Then there was nothing, the computer displaying flat lines for the remainder of the night.

Vasilescu awoke to the earsplitting sound of a siren that passed by the van. His neck pain was intense, radiating toward the back of his head and into his shoulder blades. The interior of the van was dark; he could not tell if it was morning yet. He looked at the computer screen. No more snore waves. He did not recognize the irregular patterns displayed by the listening devices. He put on the earphones. He heard cars and trucks, horns blaring, and a distant siren. The apartment was emitting the street sounds of a city starting a workday.

For a moment he wondered about the lack of sound in the apartment. The guy was obviously no longer sleeping. There was no other noise, of the toilet being flushed, kitchen activity, or any other of a hundred things people did in the morning after waking up. *Who cares*, he thought. Maybe the guy silently meditated at this hour, or maybe he was messing with his mobile phone, quietly checking out news and social media. There was only one thing Vasilescu cared about, that this cursed shift was over and relief would soon arrive.

He took his earphones off and patiently waited until sunlight flooded the interior of the van as the doors opened. Vasilescu stared, squinting as the bulky figure of Maries Boboc entered the van, his hulking footsteps shaking it like a boat in choppy waters. Boboc glanced at the computer console.

"Anything happen last night?" asked Boboc.

"No," said Vasilescu, rubbing the back of his neck. "So peaceful, you'd think he was dead."

PART THREE

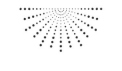

CHAPTERS 59–91

CHAPTER 59

ISTANBUL, APRIL 6

The articulated airside transfer bus was half full. Mark was surprised that the modern airport in Istanbul did not provide a jetway to the plane. As the bus took a sharp turn away from the terminal building and onto the vast tarmac, Semra lost her balance and fell onto Mark.

"You need to hold on to the handrail." Mark grabbed her firmly by the waist.

Semra smiled, her face inches from Mark's. She wore a tight-fitting jumpsuit that amply exposed her bosom, her hair neatly up in a chignon, her thin lips striking in thick red lipstick. "Why, when I have you to support me?" She leaned into him for a kiss. The two defects in her dentition were as alluring as when Mark had first spotted them in Tuzla.

"No, please. Not here." Mark drew his head back and eyed the other passengers with concern. They were mostly middle-aged businessmen with blank faces and austere dispositions. They did not seem to take notice of the tall, exotic woman in their midst.

"I am so excited," said Semra. She clapped her hands and bent down, looking out at the underbellies of massive jets that they passed by. "My first time in an airplane."

Mark was surprised. He didn't know anyone who had never flown. "How did you come to Istanbul from Mardin?" he asked her.

"From Mardin? Are you kidding?" She threw him a side glance as if he were an adorable fool. "I hardly had any bus money, let alone airplane. It took me more than a week, hustling in bus stops for each leg of the trip."

"Were you...?" Mark wasn't sure how to ask the question.

"No," she said firmly. "I was a boy then. I couldn't afford doctors either."

Earlier, in the terminal, they had said goodbye to Tarık, who had insisted on accompanying them. He remarked dryly that he would have liked to drive them himself, but he no longer had a vehicle. There were hugs and Turkish-style kisses all around, and a few tears, mostly by Tarık. He admonished Mark to come back and visit him as soon as possible, and told Semra to take good care of him, the comment causing all three of them to laugh.

In the check-in line at the Tarom airlines counter, Mark had examined Semra's passport. He had been surprised that she had one. Semra explained that Mahmut helped procure a passport for her with promises of London, Paris, and Rome. She pouted when recounting that none of it came true.

The passport had a surprisingly decent photo of her in full makeup, hair down to her shoulders. She explained that she had insisted on nearly a dozen different takes before selecting just the right one. The document listed her gender as male and her name as Selim Karacan.

"Selim," Mark said out loud. He glanced back and forth from the photo to Semra.

"Don't call me that," she said tersely.

Later, at passport control, they had a tense moment as a young officer with a steely face caught the discrepancy. He repeatedly stared back and forth between the passport and Semra, seemingly uncertain how to proceed. Semra gave him a seductive smile, her head tilted just so. The officer shook his head in disbelief, broke eye contact with her and loudly stamped a page. He then fixed his eyes on Mark with a discomforting glare.

Afterwards, as they headed to the gate on a people mover, Semra put her arm around Mark's and chuckled. She was used to it. Mark, however, still felt a fast heartbeat, the nasty stare of the officer lingering.

The airside transfer bus came to a halt aside a small plane with the Tarom insignia, the national airline of Romania. Mark and Semra exited into a brisk breeze and squinted as they looked up, taking in the airplane with unease. It was a twin turboprop with wings atop the fuselage and a single propeller on each wing. The blades of the propellers were curved, giving them a menacing look.

"Is this our plane?" Semra was shocked.

"Apparently." Mark nudged her on. They were holding up the line of passengers still exiting the bus.

They settled into cramped seats, Semra at the window, looking out with curiosity. Mark sat on the aisle and examined the interior with apprehension. A young flight attendant walked by confidently and gave him a pleasant smile, setting him somewhat at ease.

They put on their seat belts and listened to announcements in Romanian, English, and Turkish about their one-hour flight time to *Bucureşti*.

Semra gave Mark a slightly disappointed smile. "Bucharest is not Paris," she said, "or London."

Mark squeezed her arm in encouragement and did not respond.
She then added, "But it'll do."

CHAPTER 60

BRAŞOV, APRIL 8 ... MORNING

Andrei donned a white Tyvek bunny suit, blue bouffant head cover, and shoe covers. He nodded to the uniformed patrolman keeping guard outside the apartment while slipping on a pair of rubber gloves. He momentarily hesitated by the open door, reining in his dismay before entering.

Inside, the small apartment was a hub of activity. A forensic technician was lifting fingerprints while another was taking photos, the recurrent strobe-like flashes of the camera adding to the surreal scene. Several figures huddled around a recliner in the living room. Andrei spotted the rotund outline of Boboc among them and headed in that direction.

The figures parted to allow Andrei a view. There, slumped in the recliner, was the motionless figure of Bekim Zhulati. He wore a white T-shirt speckled with food stains and a pair of soiled boxer underwear. His disheveled hair partially covered his eyes. His arms were by his side, his hands covered with transparent evidence bags. The leg of the recliner was up and his outstretched legs were contorted into each other. A pungent odor emanated from the dead man: dried urine. Andrei restrained a wave of nausea.

"Well, if it isn't our handsome detective," said a short figure in a shrill voice.

Andrei nodded to Katrina as she sidled next to him. They hadn't seen each other since their fateful visit to Enver's apartment that kicked off the investigation.

"So, what do we have here?" asked Andrei, standing by the foot of the recliner.

"It appears that he was strangled by garroting," replied Katrina. "Here, let me give you a tour."

Andrei locked eyes with Boboc who stood at the other end of the recliner with a sheepish look. Boboc quickly broke his gaze and yelled at the technician with the camera. "Can you stop that for a second?" Andrei could tell that he was annoyed, but probably not at the flashing camera.

Katrina moved over to the dead man's head. She strained to lift his chin. "Rigor mortis is setting in," she murmured to herself.

She then shone a slender medical flashlight on the neck, illuminating thin circumferential lines of abrasion. Andrei came over and leaned in for a closer look.

"Notice," she said, "that there are several abrasion lines in the vicinity of the strangulation."

"He struggled," Andrei stated.

"Very good, *Doctor*." Katrina put a mocking emphasis on *Doctor*.

Andrei looked up from the neck to Zhulati's bloated face. Above the abrasion lines, it was bluish and duskier than the rest of his body. Despite a thick stubble, Andrei could spot numerous purplish spots speckling the face.

"What are these?" he asked.

Katrina's light scanned the dead man's face. "Cyanosis and fine petechiae above the strangulation line."

Andrei looked up at her quizzically.

"The oxygen deficiency before he died causes more bluish discoloration above the strangulation line. That's what cyanosis means."

Andrei nodded.

"Those spots are little blotches of bleeding—petechiae." She brushed the hair away and shone her light at the closed eyelids. The petechiae on the eyelids were coarser, more prominent. She parted a lid to reveal the same blood spots on the white of the eye. "These are all common findings in this sort of strangulation," she said.

"But look at this." She shone the light back on the abrasion lines on the neck. "Come closer." She pointed to crescent-shaped abrasion marks concentrated at a certain area of the garroting line.

"What's that?"

"Fingernail marks," said Katrina. "He struggled to free himself from whatever was squeezing his neck."

"H'mmm, that's a bit surprising," Andrei said. "The guy should have been in a drunken stupor."

"A thin object like a rope crushing your neck is pretty stimulating," said Katrina. "A perfect cure for drunken stupor."

Andrei turned his attention to Zhulati's bagged hands. Before he could ask a question, Katrina jumped in. "With any luck we can extract DNA from the nailbeds," she said, lifting the right hand up and shining the light on his fingernails. They were overgrown and dirty.

"Won't that be his own DNA?" asked Andrei. "The nail marks on the neck are his. So what use will that be?"

"You never know," she answered. "If he struggled, he may have scratched his assailant. We might get lucky and also find the killer's DNA."

Andrei stood up. "What do you estimate the time of death to be?"

"Three-sixteen a.m.," said Katrina crisply.

Andrei's eyes widened. "How can you be so precise?"

She nodded her head toward Boboc, who had been silently observing their exchange.

"The audio recordings," said Boboc.

"Did you listen to them?"

"Yes," said Boboc. "The bugs recorded a brief struggle. Then at three-sixteen, it all went silent."

"Why weren't we notified at the time?" Andrei demanded. He still did not yet know the details of what had transpired. He had been summarily summoned out of his bed by Boboc, who told him to come to Zhulati's apartment right away, that there was a big problem. Boboc did not fill him in on any details except that their surveillance target was dead, most likely murdered.

"Where was the guy in the van? Who was it?"

"Vasilescu," said Boboc. "He fell asleep."

"Asleep!" shouted Andrei. Katrina flinched and drew away from him. "Goddamn it!" He continued shouting, causing the bunny-suited technicians to stop and stare. "How do you suggest I explain this to Dalca?"

"Let's discuss that later," said Boboc in a calm voice.

Andrei rubbed his forehead and took a short time-out to calm his temper.

"Are there any other signs of struggle?" he asked in a more even voice.

"Not as far as we can tell." Boboc beckoned him toward the door. "The lock was picked," he said. "That's how the assailant entered the apartment. We found the door ajar when we busted in here."

"How many assailants, do you think?"

"I'd say it was a solo job," said Boboc. He directed Andrei's attention to the carpet, where a narrow passage from the door to the recliner had been roped off with yellow evidence tape. "Dirty footprints," he said, "more prominent incoming than outgoing."

Andrei walked alongside the prints and observed them closely. It did indeed look like a single individual. He knew that these prints would be analyzed and matched to known shoe brands. But their likelihood of yielding the identity of the killer was low.

Boboc continued his account. "The bugs recorded the lock being picked. Then there's a brief silence before the struggle. As you can see," he pointed to the footprints, "the assailant came right in front of him, perhaps face-to-face. Zhulati was probably passed out but as Katrina said, he woke up and struggled. But not for too long."

"How did you discover that there was a problem?" Andrei asked.

"I came in at seven a.m. Vasilescu looked like he had just woken up. The bugs were recording nothing but street sounds. So I quickly ran the soundwave traces and discovered…" He stopped to find the right words. "Well, I heard the guy getting killed."

Andrei's ire rose again. This time he held himself. "First Enver Muratovich, now Zhulati." His female informant in Sfântu Gheorghe was justified in being fearful for her life. Andrei now knew of a total of four murders.

"It doesn't look like the same modus operandi as the Muratovich killing," Boboc commented. "Forced entry, single assailant, no attempt at cover-up."

The two stepped outside the apartment. Andrei removed his Tyvek suit and shoe covers. "My informant," he said, "stated that someone is systematically eliminating those involved in the transplant ring. We have to assume that this is somehow tied to Muratovich, regardless of how it might look."

Andrei took his gloves off. "Shit," he said. "This creates yet more work. I was planning to head off to Iaşi today, to check out the donor."

"Go," said Boboc, his body covers still on. "I'll handle this here. I'll keep you posted if anything important comes up."

"I have to clear that with Dalca first," said Andrei.

"For once," said Boboc, "I am really glad that you're the one in charge instead of me."

Andrei shot him a piercing glance. He then turned to the elevator. "Has this been dusted for prints?"

"Yes," said Boboc. "The guys did the outside first, before working the apartment."

Andrei stepped into the elevator and impatiently pushed the button. Now that they had lost Zhulati, it was all the more important that he go to Iaşi.

* * *

Outside, a crowd had gathered around the police cordon at the sidewalk by the apartment. A pair of uniformed officers stood guard, letting in only the residents of the apartment. Andrei nodded to them as he left the sealed-off area. He spotted two TV news trucks parked across the street near where their surveillance van had been. A female reporter stood behind one of them, holding a microphone and speaking to a camera. Andrei lowered his head and tried to blend in with the crowd.

He then saw several police vehicles farther down the street, parked surprisingly far from the crime scene. He took a few steps in their direction and soon made out the tall figure of Traian Dalca, dressed civilian, speaking with an equally tall stocky figure in full rank uniform. Andrei's heart sank as he recognized the man as the city's police chief.

Before Andrei could make a move, Dalca spotted him and walked briskly toward him. He grabbed Andrei by the arm and led him to the corner of an alleyway near the French café. They stood face-to-face amid overflowing garbage cans, away from the eyes of TV news.

"Didn't we agree to bring him in?" asked Dalca sharply.

"I was going to do that this morning." Andrei met the angry gaze of his boss courageously.

"Well, he is coming in all right. In a fucking body bag!" Dalca took a step back and looked at a garbage can nearby. It was topped with towering bags, one of them busted, emitting a revolting odor.

"I screwed up," Andrei confessed. "I have no good excuse. I should have had him in as soon as we agreed."

"Costiniu," Dalca's voice was somber, "I have a good mind to take you off this case right now. Give me a reason not to do that."

Andrei could not stand the stink of the refuse. He moved deeper into the alley. Dalca stood his ground.

"I have two more leads to work on," he said, speaking louder. Dalca relented and came closer. "And one of them will only speak to me."

Andrei reminded his boss of Irina Cernea, the previously mysterious Sfântu informant. He then recounted the news from Iași about the donor Yoet Tcaci. He told Dalca that he needed to leave town and work Bucharest and Iași. He would, in a manner of speaking, be off the Brașov investigation for a while.

Dalca glared at Andrei in silence for what seemed like an eternity. "All right," he finally said.

Andrei quietly let out a sigh of relief.

"What did you find in there?" Dalca asked.

"He was strangled early this morning by a single assailant while he was passed out."

"Does it look like it's tied to the Muratovich hanging in Schei?"

"The MO is not the same," Andrei answered, "but it has to be, somehow."

"I will look into the details later," said Dalca. "I am going to be more involved with this investigation from now on."

"Was that the chief you were talking to out there?" Andrei asked.

"Yes," said Dalca. "*My* boss." He shook his head with frustration. "First the complaint from Spitatul Martinu, now one of its doctors is murdered."

"Does he know about Muratovich?"

"No," said Dalca. "And don't go around blabbing it to others in the force. I don't want him to know yet. Not until we have some solid evidence to back up this crazy notion of local transplant criminals and an international conspiracy."

"Understood." Andrei started to walk away.

"Costiniu," Dalca called after him. "Remember, shit rolls downhill!"

Andrei stopped, turned back, and stood at attention.

"I catch grief from him." Dalca nodded in the general direction of where he had been standing with his chief. "And I dish it out to you."

"Yes, sir."

Andrei emerged from the alley to find Boboc waiting for him at the corner. He smiled at Andrei sympathetically; he had heard the exchange. He grabbed his partner's arm firmly and led Andrei toward the French café. "You look like you need a stiff cup of coffee and a croque monsieur," he said. "My treat."

CHAPTER 61

BUCHAREST, APRIL 6

"Oh, wow!" exclaimed Semra as she surveyed the presidential suite of the Athénée Palace Hotel. It was essentially a small apartment, with a smartly furnished living room, a bedroom, and two bathrooms. She fiddled with some buttons on the wall that turned out to control the curtains electronically. As they whirled open, a view of neoclassical buildings in nearby Revolution Square caught her attention.

"Look!" She ran over to the window and pointed to the view. "I don't have to be in Paris."

Mark joined her, casually draping his arm around her shoulder. Paris it was not. The small square was a curious assortment of faux classical buildings, monotonous Communist apartment blocks, and a prominent, peculiar statue, meant to be heroic, of a tall white obelisk spearing what appeared to be a giant truffle atop.

Semra gave him a tight hug. "Oh, this is so romantic. Everything I ever dreamed of."

It was early evening and Mark was tired. They had been picked up at the airport by Vasile's driver in a late-model Mercedes and delivered downtown to the hotel. While Semra buzzed with excited energy, Mark yearned for a quick dinner and a good night's sleep.

Semra turned and ran into the bedroom, flinging her shoes off and throwing herself on the king-size bed. She kicked her legs up and down childishly. "Wow, this bed is so comfortable."

Mark followed, observing her with an amused smile.

She raised her arms. "Come," she said, "lie down with me."

Mark turned away. "We'd better unpack."

While he bent over his suitcase she snuck from behind, her lips close to his ear. She whispered, "I always dreamed of an American boyfriend."

Mark stopped and straightened up. He turned and gave her a peck on the lips. "Now, remember what I am here for," he said. "A funeral."

Semra listened wide-eyed, like an obedient dog.

"I expect you to behave yourself when we're in public." Mark spoke as if he were a teacher addressing a wayward student. "None of this hugging and kissing. And wear something conservative."

Semra pulled her shirt together, covering her cleavage. She pouted. She then tore her shirt open and jumped on him, pulling Mark onto the bed. As they tumbled together, she said, "Anything you say, my master."

* * *

Mark stood up eagerly to answer the knock on the door, expecting room service. Instead there were two men facing him with staid expressions. One was middle-aged, tall and burly, with a rich head of salt-and-pepper hair and a prominent gut protruding through a crisp business suit. He wore dark sunglasses. The other man was young, wide, and brawny. He had a bushy beard and wore a dark windbreaker with an insignia that Mark could not decipher.

The older man spoke. "Dr. Mark Kent?"

"Yes, that's me."

The man produced a badge from an inner pocket. "Marco Radovich, SRI," he said.

Mark examined the badge. It looked official, like that of a policeman. "What's SRI?"

"Internal Security Service of Romania." Radovich was polite and businesslike. "May we come in?"

Mark stood aside and let them in.

Radovich pointed to the younger man with the thick beard. "This is Milan, my assistant."

Milan bore a steely expression. He looked more like a bodyguard. He did not make eye contact with Mark but rather stared beyond him into the room.

Semra was standing there, gazing at the visitors. She wore a partially buttoned shirt and nothing else, her long legs and feet bare. Radovich saw her, too. He seemed surprised.

Mark ordered Semra in Turkish to retreat to the bedroom and put more clothes on.

"We're sorry to barge in on you," said Radovich. He stood in the middle of the living room and made no attempt to sit. "We won't be long."

Milan stared in the direction of the bedroom.

"We were made aware of your arrival in Romania." Radovich was formal.

Mark wondered about that name. It did not sound Romanian, but rather, Serbian. He remained silent, wondering—with some dread—why the Romanian secret service was interested in him.

"We are here to ensure your security," continued Radovich. "We know that there were attempts at your life in Hungary about two weeks ago. We do not wish anything to happen to you while you are a guest in our country."

"Well, thank you," said Mark. "But I wasn't expecting any problems. I am here to attend a funeral."

"Regardless, we would like you to keep us informed of your whereabouts and activities." Radovich presented Mark with a business card. "If necessary we will accompany you to ensure your security."

As Mark examined the card, Semra returned in a pair of jeans, her shirt buttoned. Radovich threw her a passing side glance, while Milan openly stared.

Mark rolled the card in his hand, pretending to examine it while he collected his thoughts. "Thank you for your concern. I'll do that. But right now I don't exactly know where and when this funeral will be held."

Radovich was not fazed. "That's all right. We will wait for word from you."

He turned to Milan, who was still fixated on Semra. Radovich acknowledged her for the first time. "And who is the lovely lady?"

Semra responded with a toothy smile while Mark wished that she had not reemerged. He went to her side and put his arm around her shoulder. "A friend," he said curtly. He whispered into her ear, again in Turkish, ordering her to disappear.

As she turned around, he extended a hand to Radovich. "Now, may I see you out?"

*   *   *

Soon there was another knock on the door. This time it was room service. Mark stared at the ornate china and cutlery, the warm dishes covered by silver domes. He had lost his appetite.

The visit by Radovich had shaken him up. Mark did not want any more involvement with spies or law enforcement. He had an uneasy feeling about these two visitors. They made a strange pair. He wondered if they really were who they said they were. He had no way to confirm. Mark reexamined Radovich's card. Should he do as he promised, he wondered, and inform Radovich of his activities? Did he have a choice? He needed guidance.

Mark sat down at an armchair and texted Leon Adler. *Just arrived in Bucharest. At Athénée Palace Hotel. Received two visitors as soon as I arrived. SRI. What do you think of that?*

Leon's response came promptly: *Do not contact me from within Romania.*

Mark was annoyed. *Why not?*

Not secure.

Shall I email or call directly?

No. Not secure.

Mark looked at his mobile screen, frustrated. *So what do you suggest I do?*

French embassy. Contact Interpol liaison.

Mark rubbed his forehead with his fingertips, staring at the message. He didn't know if he could do this. For now he would have to wing it.

"Are they gone? I am famished!" Semra peeked out of the bedroom door.

"Sorry," said Mark, rising to his feet. "Come. Let's eat."

* * *

"We have an absolute policy of guest confidentiality."

The hotel manager, a youthful, bespectacled man, looked at Mark coolly. He was smartly dressed in a dark suit adorned with the hotel's insignia.

"Then how could two men come to my door as soon as I arrived here?" Mark demanded, just as coolly. It was late at night and he should have been in bed. He crossed his legs as he sat opposite the manager at his desk and tried to look nonchalant, even though he was fuming.

"Let me make a call," said the manager. He picked up the phone and had several heated conversations in Romanian with his employees. He then hung up with a satisfied smile. "I checked with our reception desk, our telephone operator, and security. No one inquired about you and no employee of this hotel gave out any information about you."

"In that case, how did these people find me?"

The manager leaned forward on his desk. "Who exactly were they?"

"They claimed to be from SRI."

The manager stiffened. "Oh!" he said. "That explains it."

"Explains what?"

"Sir," said the manager, in a condescending tone, "this is not the United States of America." He paused to let that statement sink in.

"In our country, when it comes to state security, privacy is not valued as sanctimoniously as in yours. It is trespassed all the time."

Mark felt foolish as he listened. The man was pointing out what should have been obvious.

The manager continued. "Let me remind you that the SRI emerged not that long ago from the *Securitate*, Ceausescu's much-feared secret service." He sat back and now crossed his legs. "Look at Russia. It is being run by former KGB. We are not so far off from them."

Mark stood up. "I understand," he said. "Thank you for the explanation."

Mark had wasted his time with this man. As he walked to the elevators, he felt exposed, defenseless. In Budapest he had had Mustafa, the Turkish private eye, and Jasmin, the police officer, who had looked after him. In Turkey he could count on Leon, and eventually the police chief of Istanbul. Here he had no one.

As Mark had told Radovich, he had come to Romania merely for a funeral. He had not come here seeking trouble. But trouble, Mark feared, seemed to have a way of finding him. The uninvited visit by these SRI operatives was a bad omen.

CHAPTER 62

BUCHAREST, APRIL 7

The Mercedes wound through a wide avenue lined by stately nineteenth-century buildings, and entered a giant roundabout into which massive boulevards converged like rays from a star. It had a colossal triumphal arch at its center.

"Look!" said Semra. "Paris."

Gazing at the ornate arch, Mark began to doubt his earlier skepticism about Semra's impression. This was indeed very much like Place de l'Étoile in Paris, with its Arc de Triomphe.

Their driver gingerly negotiated the gaggle of vehicles that merged into the giant circle and moved on to Aviatorilor Boulevard, into an exclusive leafy neighborhood of splendid villas. Iancu's family obviously lived in a well-off area.

It was late morning and they were headed to a meeting with Iancu's children before the funeral service. Semra was, for once, dressed appropriately, in a conservative black outfit that covered her knees and cleavage. She wore minimal makeup and jewelry, her hair in a simple ponytail. By contrast, Mark, who could not have imagined any need for formal clothes when he set out from San Francisco to Budapest and had not brought any, wore a simple shirt, dark slacks, and a brown windbreaker. As the Mercedes pulled into a spacious, well-kept garden and passed by numerous luxury cars parked near a majestic home, he realized that he might be too casual.

A young maid dressed entirely in black, who spoke only Romanian but managed well with body language, greeted them. She guided Mark and Semra through several rooms populated by gloomy mourners and into a capacious, dimly lit room. It was a study, with a voluminous array of books shelved floor to ceiling and a prominent desk, where a tall funerary candle provided the main source of light. The walls were adorned with large oil paintings, two among them covered with black cloth.

Off to one side, in a dark corner by a curtained window, were an assemblage of armchairs and a couch. A young man and woman rose up from there to greet them. "Dr. Kent, we are so glad you joined us." The young man enthusiastically shook Mark's hand.

"Vasile?"

He nodded, his hand still firmly gripping Mark's. He was tall and stout, like his father, and had Iancu's bushy eyebrows. He looked ghostly in the flickering shadows of the candlelight, reminiscent of his father as he floated lifeless in the crimson waters of the rooftop Jacuzzi. The flashback momentarily overwhelmed Mark.

Everyone in the eerily darkened room froze as if Mark's emotions were contagious. Semra slid closer to Mark, putting her arm firmly around his. The maid remained in the shadows, near one of the covered paintings.

"Hello, I am Sorana." Vasile's older sister stepped out of the shadows and broke the impasse.

Mark shook himself out of his reverie. "I am glad to meet you, Sorana. Your father spoke very highly of you when he told me about his family." He turned to Vasile. "You, too." The two siblings looked pleased.

The tension having eased, Semra took a step toward the covered painting and lifted the edge of the cloth, peering into what was behind. It wasn't a painting after all. Semra turned toward Mark, lifting the cloth higher to reveal a mirror, its ornate frame similar to those of the paintings.

Suddenly the maid sprang into action and batted Semra's hand off, uttering several agitated words in Romanian. Sorana intervened with a few stern words, and the maid exited the room with her head down.

"I'm sorry," said Sorana, addressing Mark and Semra. "During the funeral mirrors have to be covered, as do all open water containers. It prevents the deceased from returning to haunt those left behind."

Mark gave Semra an icy stare, admonishing her for her gaffe.

Sorana chuckled awkwardly. "Superstition!" she said. "We have a lot of them here in Romania, especially around funeral rituals. After all, we are the home of Dracula, aren't we?"

Semra's eyes widened with fear as she stepped away from the mirror and once again clung to Mark.

"This is Semra Karacan, my Turkish companion." Mark tried to dissipate the discomfiture.

After a second round of handshakes, Sorana asked if they were hungry. There would be plenty of food at the reception after the funeral service, but for now, if they could not wait, there were some snacks, here in the house. Mark took advantage of the opportunity to dismiss Semra from what he hoped would be a private conversation with the siblings. The maid was recalled. Sporting a friendlier demeanor, she guided Semra out of the study.

Sorana beckoned Mark toward the sofa and armchairs. As they sat down she opened the curtains, allowing bright sunlight to flood in. Apparently windows were not part of the macabre ritual that applied to mirrors.

Mark now got a better look at Iancu's daughter. Sorana was an exotic beauty, dark-skinned and dark-haired. She was dressed in a baggy black outfit and, like her brother, looked older than the thirty-two years Mark knew her to be. She wore no makeup, and in the harsh sunlight Mark noticed how weary she looked, with bags under her eyes as if she had not slept.

"Excuse my appearance," said Sorana, aware of Mark's gaze.

"After the Trisagion service last night, it was my turn for the night watch."

Mark looked at her quizzically.

"The Trisagion is an Orthodox Christian prayer service," Vasile explained. "It is performed the night before a funeral. Tradition calls for three days of night watch."

"Allow me to express my sincerest condolences." Mark was embarrassed for not having said this earlier. He mentally cursed Semra for the distraction she had caused. "Is your father...here?" he asked gingerly.

"Not any longer," said Vasile. "He is on his way to the church. The casket has to be there before anyone enters." He clasped his fingers together. "Another tradition."

"Your father told me that you are the accountant for the business." Mark addressed Sorana. He then turned to Vasile. "And that you were being groomed to take over."

"Not quite." Sorana crossed her legs and assumed an authoritative posture. "I am the chief financial officer and Vasile is the chief executive officer."

Vasile observed his older sister deferentially.

"We are restructuring the company," Sorana continued. "And our first order of business is to cleanse it."

"How do you mean?" asked Mark.

"Our father left us a well-diversified business. Retail chains, import-export, construction."

"Yes," said Mark. "He told me that."

"Well," said Sorana, "we will focus on those and jettison the other elements."

She might be the CFO but she is clearly in charge, thought Mark. "You mean the kidney transplants?"

"Yes, that and others," said Sorana.

Mark knew that Iancu and Nicolae had been into various illicit lines of business, but Iancu had not elaborated on the details, and Mark had been reluctant to pry.

Vasile interjected. "This organ business was lucrative," he said, "but look what it did to our father and his partner."

"It has shaken our family to the core," said Sorana.

"I understand," said Mark. "Your father, when I last spoke with him, seemed to be leaning in the same direction."

"Tell us about that," said Sorana. "How did you happen to meet him? What happened in Budapest?"

"I met your father through Miruna, Nicolae's wife. He was there to help her collect Nicolae's body from the morgue. I don't know how much you know, but I was the one who found Nicolae dead in his hotel room."

"Our father told us," said Vasile.

"Your father wanted to know more about what happened. So he and I had a conversation in his car after he dropped Miruna off at the airport. We then had a second meeting at the central market in Budapest."

"The pickle shop in the basement?" asked Sorana.

"Yes." Mark chuckled. "An unusual place, if I may say so."

"He frequently used that pickle business for discreet meetings."

"It was discreet all right. Anyhow, that's when he told me about the transplant business and how Nicolae had received a credible threat. Nicolae was reaching out to me to help him escape to the United States."

Mark paused to search their faces for a reaction. The siblings were eagerly waiting for more. "All this was a complete surprise to me. Shock is a better word."

"We heard about this threat," said Vasile, "but we don't know where it came from."

"It was from a man named Vadim Rusu," said Mark. "He is a former Russian intelligence officer who currently resides in Moldova."

"I've heard the name," said Sorana. Her declaration surprised both Mark and Vasile. "He runs a highly regarded security business—Hercules Group, I believe it's called. They have a branch here in Bucharest. They provide security for the rich and famous. High-priced, as you might imagine. There are rumors that he also runs a side business of mercenary soldiers, mainly for Russia."

"Interesting," said Mark. All this was news to him. "But how do you know him?"

"I don't," said Sorana. "It's just that we're well connected with our local business community and we hear things." She flicked a glance at her brother. "At least, I do."

Vasile turned to Mark. "How did *you* learn about Rusu?"

"An agent of the French Interpol told me," Mark answered, "after they rescued me from Rusu's men—the same ones, it turned out, who had assassinated Nicolae."

"We heard that you are an American agent, FBI," said Vasile.

Mark did not answer. He was tired of both pretending to be an agent and denying it. He continued with his story. "Rusu is also responsible for your father's death."

This seemed to surprise the pair. "But we heard that it was a local Slovak gangster who killed him."

"Tibor Bognár," Mark affirmed. "I met him, too." Mark recalled the respect with which the fierce gangster treated him, considering Mark a suitably adroit adversary. "Bognár was merely a contractor. Rusu had hired him to track me in Budapest. Rusu had no idea who I was and why I was interjecting myself into his plans. When Bognár's people spotted me with your father, who happened to be on Rusu's hit list, Rusu engaged them on the fly to assassinate your father."

"That's what we really don't understand," said Sorana. "Why? Why all these murders?"

"It is a vendetta," said Mark. "Your father and Nicolae's kidney operation inadvertently killed Rusu's only son."

"How so?' asked Vasile.

"Apparently they used him as a donor. Stole his kidney. Afterwards the young man died of complications."

"Oh, my God!" Sorana covered her mouth with her hand, in shock. "I can easily see that man launching a vendetta," she murmured. "Rumor has it that Rusu used to be a high-level OMON operative in Communist times."

"What's OMON?" asked Mark.

"The Soviet internal intelligence agency. They went after rebels, dissidents, and other troublemakers. They were ruthless."

"But that can't be," Vasile interrupted. "My father and Nicolae ran a clean operation. They would never have taken a kidney from a donor without their consent."

"That's exactly what your father told me," Mark agreed. "But that's apparently what happened. I don't know how, but it did."

The siblings fell silent. Mark paused, allowing the gravity of the news to sink in.

"So." Mark broke the silence. "Now, Rusu's organization is systematically eliminating yours."

Vasile and Sorana looked at him with wide-eyed horror.

"You may have heard of a Turkish surgeon named Gazioğlu," Mark continued.

Sorana nodded. "Of course," she said. "We all met him."

"He is dead, too. Assassinated in Istanbul."

"Rusu?" asked Sorana.

"Most likely," said Mark. "And do you know Latif Gürsen, Nicolae's father?"

"Yes," said Vasile. "We heard that he recently passed away. His girlfriend Ileana is back here in Bucharest. I believe she will be at the funeral."

"A charming man," Sorana added. "I believe he had become infirm."

"Have you spoken with Ileana?" asked Mark.

"No, why?"

"Latif's death was another assassination," said Mark. "A bomb. Unfortunately, I was there to witness the deaths of both Gazioğlu and Latif."

"That makes four," said Sorana.

"Enver!" Vasile suddenly exclaimed.

"Oh, my God!" Sorana covered her cheeks with her hands as tears began flowing down.

"Who is that?" Mark asked.

"Enver Muratovich. He was like an older brother to us," said Vasile. "We grew up together. He too is dead."

Sorana was now sobbing uncontrollably.

"Is he somehow connected to the transplant business?" Mark was still puzzled.

"He was our main recruiter," said Vasile.

"Recruiter?"

"Of live donors."

"What happened to him?"

"We heard that he committed suicide. They found him in his Braşov apartment. He hung himself."

"When?" asked Mark.

"Just last week."

"Are you sure it was a suicide?"

"I don't know," answered Vasile, his voice tremulous. "That's what we were told."

"Enver would never have committed suicide," said Sorana firmly.

"In that case, it was probably Rusu," Mark said. "They may have made it look like suicide."

"Who else is left?" asked Vasile, addressing his sister. "Do you think they'll come after us, too?"

"The main person that's left is me," said Mark. He was trying, in an odd way, to allay Vasile's fear.

"How so? You weren't involved in the transplant business."

"True, but as I said, I am in the thick of it. I've witnessed four assassinations in Hungary and Turkey, and foiled some of Rusu's Hungarian efforts. To add to that, I've caused the death of two of his men. He is pursuing me. His men came after me in Budapest and then in Turkey."

"So he wants you dead, too?" asked Sorana.

"Not really." Mark could not believe he was so matter-of-fact about his status as a hunted man. "He just wants to know who I am and what I am up to. Bognár told me that Rusu wants me alive."

"Maybe you should return to the United States," Vasile suggested, echoing Leon Adler's recommendation. "You might be safer there."

"I doubt it," said Mark with certainty. "The world is much smaller nowadays. If he is determined to find me, he'll do so no matter where I am."

"Maybe you should just meet this Vadim Rusu and give him what he wants," Sorana said thoughtfully.

Vasile's eyes widened with alarm. "Are you crazy?"

"Actually, that thought did cross my mind," Mark said to Sorana. "It would be the surest way to shake him off my back. But I don't know what he would do after he gets what he wants. If he is as ruthless as he is reputed to be, it would be a risky move."

"I would say so," Vasile affirmed.

"Well," said Sorana, "if you need to reach out to Rusu, I am quite certain I can arrange an introduction through our business contacts here in Bucharest."

"Thanks, I'll keep that in mind." Mark looked back toward the door of the library. It was closed. "I have another problem," he said. "My companion."

"You mean the young Turkish lady, your girlfriend?" Vasile asked.

"She is not my girlfriend," Mark answered. "Actually, she was Gazioğlu's partner. I rescued her from his home. If I approach Rusu, I don't know what I would do with her. She has become my responsibility."

* * *

Mark found Semra in a spacious solarium in the back of the house. It looked out onto a well-kept garden with a central fountain that spouted water from a Cupid's mouth. Inside was a generous spread of sandwiches and an assortment of pickled vegetables. Semra approached him with a full plate and a big smile, pieces of food showing between her teeth. "Delicious stuff," she said.

There were others in the solarium congregated in small groups. Semra pointed in the direction of a group with their backs turned. "Friendly people," she said.

Mark ignored the group and examined the offerings on the table.

"And guess what?" Semra prodded him.

"What?" Mark eyed her with an amused smile.

"They speak Turkish," she said. "Her husband was your friend."

CHAPTER 63

BUCHAREST, APRIL 7

A s Mark stared at Semra, he heard a familiar voice in heavily accented Turkish. *"Merhaba." Hello.*

He turned around to face a diminutive buxom figure looking up at him with hazel eyes. "Miruna!" Mark gave her a hug. He saw tears streaming down her face.

"We have to stop meeting like this, on tragic occasions," he said awkwardly. Mark then noticed two children that flanked her skirt. "Are they…?"

"Yes," she said, wiping her tears with a napkin. "Our children."

Nazlı, the four-year-old, tugged on her mother's pleats, pleading with her in Romanian. Latif, the ten-year-old, peered at Mark stoically through thick eyeglasses. Mark extended a hand to him as if he were an adult. "Hello, young man," he said in Turkish. "I am an old friend of your father's."

The boy instantly shook Mark's hand. "My father is gone," he said. "To Heaven."

Put a moustache on him and a receding hairline, and the boy would be a spitting image of Tarık, Mark thought, *the Turkish half-brother he knows nothing about.*

"Did you hold his funeral already?" Mark quietly asked Miruna.

"No," she said sadly. "He was cremated as soon as I got back from Budapest. We had a small private memorial, that's all."

This was not Turkish tradition. But then, Mark thought, his old mate Ahmet was not traditional. He wouldn't have cared what they did with him after he died.

"I'm sorry I missed it," said Mark. "I would like to have been there."

"It has all been too much of a shock, all these deaths." Miruna pulled out a pair of dark glasses from her purse and covered her eyes. She seemed to have aged since Mark had last seen her, even though it was just over a week ago.

"How are you holding up?" Mark asked.

"As well as I can." She looked down at her little ones. "I have no choice, do I?"

"Are you moving to Bucharest?"

When they met in Hungary, Miruna had told Mark that they lived in Constanta, a port town on the Black Sea. Now that she was widowed she had intended to move.

"No," she said. "We'll stay put." She turned around and searched those gathered around the food table. She beckoned a tall woman in the distance who began limping toward them.

Ileana greeted Mark with a bittersweet smile. She had abrasions on her forehead and cheeks, and her right arm was splinted. The light had gone out of her captivating blue eyes.

"Ileana!" Mark exclaimed. "They told me you were here in Bucharest. How are you?"

She shrugged and did not answer.

"Hüsnü," Mark asked about Latif's tall attendant. "Is he okay?"

"Still in the hospital," she said. "They told me he will survive."

"I am so sorry about what happened," said Mark.

"Serdar is dead, too. Did you know?" Ileana had not mentioned her affair with the young hustler. His departure obviously weighed heavily on her, as much as Latif's, perhaps.

"Yes," he said. "I did hear. They said he drowned."

Ileana shook her head in disbelief. "I don't think so."

Mark debated whether to tell her what he knew. He decided that this was not the right occasion.

Miruna interrupted. Wrapping an arm around Ileana's waist, she proclaimed, "Now that Latif is gone, Ileana will look after his grandchildren."

Mark raised his eyebrows in surprise. Ileana looked down at little Nazlı and her lips parted into a smile.

"I asked her to come live with us," Miruna continued. "She's part of our family. That's why we're not leaving Constanta. We have a large property there, away from the hustle-bustle of Bucharest. Better for the kids."

Mark was impressed that despite the tragedies that had befallen her, Miruna was in charge of her life.

Miruna looked at her watch. "We should start on our way to the funeral service," she said. "Come sit with us at the church, will you?"

* * *

Saint Spyridon the New Church backed up onto an enormous boulevard, but its front entrance was in a nearby residential street, where the funeral cortege had created a major traffic jam. Their chauffeur suggested that Mark and Semra exit the car and walk the last block to the church. He spoke a broken but understandable English. When Mark wondered why they had not entered Saint Spyridon from the grand boulevard, he explained that Orthodox tradition called for worshippers to enter a church from the west, the sinful side, and when inside, move toward the east, into the light of Truth. All churches were east-west oriented. The big boulevard happened to be east, on the wrong side.

"Come on. Let's see if your sins will be cleansed," Mark said in jest, as he offered Semra a helping hand, ushering her out of the car. They walked with other mourners on a narrow sidewalk. "I've never been in a church," Semra said, leaving Mark momentarily speechless.

The sight of this one caused them to pause and stare, mouths agape. It was a magnificent white marble structure, with two graceful towers flanking the entrance and numerous cupolas behind, all topped with oblong domes bearing Orthodox crosses. Its ornate façade was captivating, with vertical ornamental columns and tall arched windows, some faux, others real, highlighted with orange and red accents.

Inside, everything was gold. Byzantine and Renaissance paintings adorned the walls and ceilings. Ornate Corinthian columns glistened in rich light that emanated from an enormous chandelier in the middle of the church. Iancu lay beneath the chandelier in an open casket. As they slowly walked past him, Mark threw a side glance at his late friend's partner. He had been carefully embalmed, looking as if he were peacefully asleep. His arms were folded on his chest. His right hand, still bearing a prominent pinky ring, protruded from the sleeve of his suit with no indication that it had been severed.

They sat by Miruna and Ileana during the lengthy Greek Orthodox ritual, which a tall, dark, bearded priest in flowing robes and a black headdress conducted. Ushers passed down the aisles and gave male mourners ritual handkerchiefs called *homages*. At one point the priest anointed Iancu's body with oil and prayed loudly.

Semra observed the proceedings with curiosity. Mark scanned the crowd that had completely filled the church. Iancu's family sat up front. Aside from them, he did not recognize any of the attendees.

Several minutes after the start of the service, a latecomer disrupted the monotonous chant of the priest with loud footsteps. Several heads turned toward the entrance, including Mark's. He momentarily spotted a strikingly attractive woman in high heels slip into one of the last pews. She quickly disappeared from sight.

No, it could not be her! Mark craned his neck several more times in her direction, his heart beating fast, but he could not catch another glimpse of Olga Kaminesky.

* * *

Iancu was to be interred in a family crypt in nearby Bellu Cemetery, the largest and most famous in Romania. Already filled with spacious crypts and august gravestones, the cemetery was not conducive to a crowded burial ceremony. Thus, while the immediate family accompanied the casket to Bellu, the remaining mourners filed out slowly and headed back to the villa on Aviatorilor for the reception.

It took a while for Mark and Semra to make their exit. Mark squinted in the bright sunlight as he stepped out onto the church steps. He did not notice the man until he grabbed Mark's arm and pulled him aside.

"Remember me?"

"Dumitru!" Mark started to give him a hug but then realized Dumitru's left arm was in a sling that cradled a cast. Instead, he firmly squeezed Dumitru's good arm.

"Of course I remember you," he said to Iancu's bodyguard and chauffeur, a handsome young man with a military haircut and brawny physique whom he had met in Budapest.

"I heard that you were the one who found the boss…" Dumitru's voice trailed off.

"Yes, at Rudas," Mark confirmed. "He and Iosif." Iosif was Iancu's other bodyguard. "Iosif died in my arms." Mark recalled the strapping young man horrifically bludgeoned with a machete, lying at the edge of the giant outdoor Jacuzzi in which Iancu's dead body was floating. "The last word he uttered was your name."

Dumitru's eyes teared. "We were army buddies," he said, wiping his eyes with his free hand. "We went back a long way."

"I am so sorry."

"I heard that you caught the son of a bitch who did this to them."

"Well, yes and no."

Dumitru looked at him quizzically.

"I mean, Tibor Bognár and his gang have been arrested. They were the ones you fought at Rudas. But Bognár was contracted to do the job by someone else. A powerful guy in Moldova named Vadim Rusu. He is still out there."

"I should get the bastard. Kill him myself." Dumitru's face was contorted with rage.

"It's not that simple," said Mark. Sheer bravado would be futile with Rusu. Mark touched Dumitru's cast. "I suggest you concentrate on your own rehabilitation."

Dumitru nodded silently.

Mark was curious about something. "How did you escape that rooftop? I was there too, probably a few minutes after you left, and I didn't see any way out."

"I rappelled down," Dumitru replied. "I used a hose I found that they probably kept there to water down the rooftop." He looked at his casted arm. "It wasn't good enough. As you can see, I fell the last few meters."

"I am still impressed," said Mark.

"You know that I was the one who alerted the family and Brașov to the attack that killed the boss."

Mark did not know. "Brașov?" he asked.

"Yes, I called Enver and let him know."

"Enver Muratovich?" This was the second time Mark was hearing this name.

"Yes. Enver is our main contact in the Brașov branch of the business."

"I heard that he is dead, too," said Mark.

"He supposedly hung himself," Dumitru said gloomily. "I don't believe it."

"Probably Rusu," Mark affirmed.

"Promise me that you'll find this Rusu and deal with him like you did with Bognár," said Dumitru sternly.

It was a tough promise to keep. Mark shook the bodyguard's good hand firmly.

As Mark took Semra by the hand and proceeded to the narrow street, he noticed a tall, bearded figure in a dark windbreaker observing the exiting mourners. He was at some distance beyond the church. Mark briefly locked eyes with Milan from SRI, sidekick of Radovich. Milan nodded.

Mark ignored him and continued walking, telling Semra that they should hurry to their car.

* * *

Mark was quiet during the short drive back to Aviatorilor. He was nervous about Milan. Mark had agreed to notify the SRI about his whereabouts but had not done so. Milan's presence by the church suggested that their main purpose in asking Mark to check in with SRI was to follow his movements. Why, Mark did not know.

Unlike the MIT, the Turkish intelligence service with which Mark was remotely acquainted, SRI was a complete unknown. He wasn't sure what the cost of non-cooperation would be.

As the car rounded the triumphal arch for the second time that day, Mark figured that sooner or later he would find out. Radovich was certain to make contact with him again. In the meanwhile, he still needed advice on how to deal with SRI. He looked at his watch. This funeral was taking all day. There would be no time for him to contact the French Embassy as Leon had suggested.

Mark looked at Semra, who was taking in the sights of Bucharest with much glee. She had been fascinated by everything they had done that day as if she were in an amusement park. There was nothing to do now but attend the reception that Semra anticipated with much excitement.

CHAPTER 64

BUCHAREST, APRIL 7

The villa was more crowded than earlier. Various food tables were set up in different rooms, including an outdoor one in the back garden. Mark and Semra found themselves back in the solarium, which was quieter than earlier, most guests preferring spacious settings elsewhere.

Semra began eagerly exploring the offerings while Mark sipped some fruit juice and stood quietly in a corner, observing the mourners milling in the back garden. Judging from the size of the crowd in the villa, Mark gathered that Iancu was an important personage in his own world. It was a shame how he was prematurely cut down. And for what? A mistake that was not of his making.

Mark thought about those who had fallen and the carnage he had witnessed. He took a sip of his drink and shook his head in disbelief. What a waste.

He was startled out of his thoughts by a woman wearing a dark scarf tied beneath her chin. "Mr. Mark."

At first he could not make out the woman's features until she came closer and looked up at him. She was in her twenties, wore no makeup on her gaunt, bony face, and stared at him with dark, probing eyes.

Mark smiled politely. "Do I know you from somewhere?"

"No," said the woman firmly. "My name is Emina. I come from Bosnia, Mostar."

"Nice meeting you." Mark extended her his hand.

She stood firm and did not shake his hand. "I heard that you are an American agent, FBI."

Mark's face darkened. *Here we go again*, he thought, wondering what this strange woman wanted.

Emina continued. "I'd like you to look into the death of my brother, Enver."

Mark raised his eyebrows in surprise. "Enver Muratovich?"

The woman's stern face softened and Mark discerned her sadness. "Yes. I'm glad that you already know of him."

"I heard that he was found hung in Braşov."

"They say he committed suicide," said Emina. "But he didn't. He wouldn't."

That's what everyone seems to think, thought Mark. "I understand he worked for Iancu and Nicolae."

"Iancu was like his father," said Emina. "We lost our own father in the war, when we were young." She looked down at the floor.

"My condolences," said Mark. It seemed a trifle to offer for such a tragedy.

She remained silent for a minute, trying hard to maintain her composure.

Mark pushed on. "Have you contacted the police?"

"Yes," said Emina. "And they promised to investigate." She pulled a card from her pocket. "Here. This is the man in charge of the investigation. His name is Andrei Costiniu. He is a nice man, not a brute like the others."

Mark examined the Romanian words on the card and gathered that it was of a Braşov policeman—a detective, he presumed. He wondered how to tell this young woman that she was terribly misguided about him and his capabilities.

"I heard that you caught Iancu's killers and handed them to justice." Emina fixed her dark, penetrating gaze on him. "I would be very grateful if you can do the same for my brother, may God rest his soul." She turned and motioned to a short young man supporting a hefty old woman who was hunched forward, gripping a cane.

The young man was as gaunt as Emina, his face dark with an unkempt stubble. He wore an ill-fitting, oversized suit. Emina said a few words to him in an unfamiliar language—Bosnian, Mark presumed—that caused him to start bowing repeatedly as if Mark were royalty.

The old woman wore a scarf over her head like Emina's. Her outfit was that of a peasant. It was difficult for her to look up at Mark but she did. She had pudgy red cheeks and bloodshot eyes from crying. She let go of her cane and put her palms together as if praying for Mark.

"My husband and my mother," said Emina, introducing them. She continued speaking to them in Bosnian. They listened attentively and nodded their heads emphatically. The old woman began to wail and plead with Mark in Bosnian.

"I told them that you would bring our family some justice," said Emina. "We have been wronged so many times. But this one with my brother, this has been the worst. I don't know how much my poor mother can take."

The old woman nodded as if she understood English. She looked like she was about to fall and instead leaned harder on her son-in-law.

At that point Mark spotted Semra approaching with two plates of food. He could not have been happier to see her.

"I'll see what I can do," he said to Emina. "How can I contact you?"

She gave him her mobile number and then, finally, shook his hand in a signal that she was finished. "I am so grateful that you have come to our aid," she said, continuing to squeeze Mark's hand. "I am eager to hear from you."

The three slowly shuffled away.

"What was that?" asked Semra, gazing at the departing figures with disgust.

"Bosnian relatives of the deceased," said Mark.

"They remind me of my brood in Mardin." She continued to gaze at them until they exited the solarium. "*Tövbe, tövbe*," she muttered, a Turkish expression of repentance also used as a denunciation.

Mark did not wish to explain the tortured history of these Bosnians. He stared at the plates she held.

Semra's face brightened. "Here," she said, "you have to try this." She cut a piece of cake with her fork and fed it to him. "It's called koliva. It's only served at funerals."

It was a sweet cake with the consistency of wheat, filled with cinnamon, walnuts, and raisins. "M'mmm," Mark said. "Very good." He devoured the rest as he contemplated the irony of such a delicious offering at a time of such immense sorrow. It was obviously a ritual designed to counter the bitterness of the occasion.

"One of these days you'll have to tell me about Mardin and your family," he said to Semra, his mouth half full.

Semra set down her empty plate with a clatter. "It'll take many more sweets than this to make me relive those bitter days," she said. Apparently she had noticed the significance of the koliva, too.

"Who were they, anyway?" asked Semra.

"The old woman was the younger one's mother. Her son was apparently a protégé of Iancu Negrescu. He also died recently."

"Was he involved with what Mahmut was doing?"

"Yes, the transplant business."

Semra shuddered. "What exactly is a protégé anyway?"

Mark explained how Enver was under the tutelage of Iancu, brought up and groomed by him.

"Ooh," said Semra. "I too am a protégé. I used to be Mahmut's, now I am yours."

Mark laughed. In an odd way, she was correct. As he set down his empty plate, a movement outside caught his eye. He froze and gazed intently in the direction of a rosebush in the back garden, near the fountain, where the vision he had spotted at Saint Spyridon reappeared.

"You stay here and wait for me," he said to Semra, as he hastily departed the solarium.

* * *

The back garden had the smell of freshly cut grass. Mark cautiously approached the Cupid fountain among the beds of multicolored roses. He nodded to various mourners, none of whom he knew, while his eyes scanned their faces. Then he saw her. Olga's wavy mane of blond hair, sailing atop the rest of the guests, was hard to miss. So was her tall, curvaceous figure clad in a dark jumpsuit with a stylish jacket atop. She was quietly chatting with a couple at a food table that had been set up outside.

Mark stood and watched as Olga left the couple and looked around, as if she were searching for someone. Then she slowly headed toward the house, gracefully balancing on overly high heels. Mark stealthily moved in the same direction.

They almost collided, as if by chance. She apologized in a language he did not understand. Then she looked up, saw him, and froze. Mark did not say anything. He opened the door for her and gestured her in. They walked together through a large, noisy kitchen where various workers were preparing food trays, and then into the main living room. As they passed the entrance to the solarium, Mark spotted Semra watching them intently. He motioned to her with a raised hand to stay away.

They passed by numerous mourners, accidentally bumping into one or two. Neither said a word. To any stranger, they looked like a couple exiting the reception. Mark felt as if he were in some strange dream, walking in synch with this woman he had been obsessed with, and whom he had never expected to see again.

They exited the villa just as Iancu's immediate family pulled up from the cemetery in a large SUV. Hoping to avoid them, Mark hastily grabbed Olga's arm and tugged her to a dirt path that led into some bushes.

Alone at last, they stood in a cramped space amid tall bushes, their faces nearly touching each other.

"Hello," said Mark, looking intently into her hazel eyes. "I did not expect to see you here."

She blinked and puckered her sultry red lips the way he had first seen her do at the spa of the Gresham Palace Hotel in Budapest. She looked down at her jacket and straightened its hems, then looked back up at him. "I did."

Mark raised his eyebrows in surprise. Olga leaned in and planted her soft lips on his, an enchanting kiss that slowed time to a halt. Stunned and delighted, Mark relished the kiss, hoping that she would never stop.

She did.

Mark remained stone still, eyes closed, enjoying the aftershocks of the surprise. When he opened his eyes again, Olga had withdrawn a safe distance and was watching him with amusement.

"Come on," she said. "Let's get out of here. We have to talk."

CHAPTER 65

IAŞI, APRIL 8

I t was late afternoon when Andrei arrived in Iaşi. His drive from Braşov had taken longer than usual because he had stopped at Putna-Vrancea Natural Park in the Eastern Carpathians. It had been a good time for a break after a lengthy stretch of mountainous road. He had sat at a streamside clearing and enjoyed the crisp fresh air while he listened to chirping birds and ate the lunch Ana had prepared for him.

He was excited by the prospect of investigating the witness in Iaşi, yet concerned about how productive it would be. He hoped that Yoet Tcaci's condition had improved and that the young man would provide useful testimony. This would be a wonderful break. But then, it was equally possible that the witness might not be alive by the time Andrei arrived. For the remainder of the drive, Andrei listened to music and tried not to think about his mission. He would have to deal with whatever he encountered.

Iaşi was a charming historic town, with Gothic and neoclassical buildings and the lively street life of a university town with numerous cafés and restaurants. Funar had suggested they meet at the Emergency entrance to Saint Spiridon County Hospital, so he headed straight in that direction.

The hospital turned out to be an old, dilapidated, three-story building with the exterior paint peeling in various places. Spitatul Martinu it was not. Andrei flashed his badge at a security guard who opened the gate leading to the Emergency Room.

Funar was upon him surprisingly fast, almost as soon as Andrei exited his car. He was late-middle-aged, tall and broad-shouldered, with thinning white hair and a squinty gaze. He reminded Andrei of an old general he had encountered during his time in the army.

"Welcome to Iaşi," said Funar in a deep baritone voice, firmly shaking Andrei's hand. "I hope you had an easy drive."

Andrei completed the exchange of pleasantries and asked about Yoet Tcaci.

"Still very sick," said Funar. "Come, I'll take you to him."

The ICU of the hospital was on the second floor, directly above the ER. It was like no ICU that Andrei had ever seen—an old inpatient ward converted into an ICU, with a distant nursing station and patients housed in individual rooms, mostly out of sight of the nurses. Andrei wondered how well the witness was being cared for.

Funar seemed quite familiar with the place and quickly found the correct nurse to lead them to a double room where both patients were on ventilators, with a forest of medical tubes all around. Funar motioned Andrei toward the patient by the window and departed to look for a doctor.

Andrei gazed at his witness. The young man lay motionless, eyes closed, complexion dusky, chest rising and falling to the bellowing sounds of a ventilator. He was skin and bones, reminding Andrei of World War II concentration camp photos. His wrists were secured to the bedrails with soft restraints.

"Why is he being restrained?" asked Andrei, hoping that the need for control indicated some sign of life.

"To prevent him from extubating himself," he heard a female voice behind him. "He sometimes exhibits purposeful movements and has pulled out IVs."

Andrei turned to face a young, bespectacled woman who bore a businesslike countenance. The insignia on her white coat declared her to be Dr. Violeta Hofer. She took a step forward and shook his hand.

"You're the policeman from Braşov?" she asked.

Funar introduced them to each other.

"So, what the hell is going on over there?" she asked abruptly.

Andrei was taken aback. "What do you mean?"

"I mean, sir," she pointed toward her patient, "that young, healthy people are having their kidneys stolen and being discarded like used toilet paper."

"That's what I am here to investigate," Andrei answered hesitantly.

Funar interjected. "Let's get out of this room. As you can see, there isn't much to discern from the witness." He turned to Dr. Hofer. "Is there a place where we can talk confidentially?"

"Yes, the conference room. Follow me," she ordered.

They sat in what was probably an old patient room converted awkwardly into a doctor's conference room. It was cramped with chairs and a small table. An old fashioned X-ray board hung on the wall.

"What's his condition?" Andrei asked Dr. Hofer.

"Critical," she said. "Very ill. He has been septic and has had renal failure to the point that he might need dialysis. Now he is showing signs of DIC." Seeing Andrei's quizzical look, she added, "Disseminated intravascular coagulation."

Andrei partially understood. "What do you think caused all this?"

"He had an abdominal operation, a nephrectomy, and developed a wound infection that went untreated."

"Why untreated?"

"Who knows! That's for you to find out, isn't it?" Dr. Hofer glared at Andrei behind her glasses.

"Would he have been so sick if it had been properly treated?"

"Certainly not. Surgical wound infections are rare but happen. A young man like this, if promptly treated, it would not have come to this."

Andrei took some notes. "What's the prognosis?"

"There is a high likelihood that he will die within the next few days," she said bluntly.

Andrei's heart sank. He tried not to show it. "In the event he survives, when do you think he could talk to us, give an account of what happened?"

Dr. Hofer emitted a sarcastic laugh. "I doubt, sir, that that will ever happen."

"We would like to requisition his medical records. This is part of a serious crime investigation."

"You can take that up with Administration."

The two policemen left the doctor and walked back to the Emergency Room courtyard. Funar lit a cigarette. "We'll get you the records," he said to Andrei.

"How did this man get here?" asked Andrei.

"It appears that he was dropped off at the ER triage desk by a male individual."

"Did this person tell anyone what happened?"

"No, that's it. The guy put Tcaci, who was passed out, in a wheelchair and dropped him off at Triage. Then he disappeared without talking to anyone. It spooked the hospital staff. After examining him, they promptly called us."

Andrei looked around the ancient cloister, now a parking lot for ambulances and police cars, and took in the walls of the old hospital. *What a crappy place,* he thought. He cursed his bad luck.

"Any idea who this person might be? Are there any CCTV cameras around here that recorded him?"

"Yes, they do have cameras at the Emergency entrance." Funar pointed to one in the distance. Then he took a deep drag from his cigarette and, keeping it on his lips, pulled out a notepad from his inner pocket. "His name is Kyril Kozak, a citizen of Ukraine. Residence, Odessa."

Andrei's face brightened.

"We traced him with the aid of Ukrainian police. He holds a professional driver's license. We also have a photo of him, both from his driving records and the CCTV here at Saint Spiridon. This

Kozak did not make any effort to conceal his identity from the cameras."

"Can I see the footage?"

"Certainly," said Funar. He threw his spent cigarette on the ground, extinguishing it with his foot, and continued his recounting. "Soon after dropping off Yoet Tcaci, Kozak crossed the border to Moldova and then Ukraine. We've received license plate ID's from border guards. Their timing confirms the timeline."

Andrei was impressed. Funar had told him that the Iaşi police were not going to investigate the case, hoping that Andrei would do all the work. He was grateful that some preliminaries had been done.

"Any chance this Kozak might be extradited to Romania?" Andrei hoped that the driver might provide some useful information. Yoet Tcaci's condition left him with little to go on.

"We've already initiated proceedings with Odessa," Funar replied. He pointed to an unmarked car parked behind a couple of ambulances. "That's mine," he said. "Follow me to the Sector 3 station."

"It's all very disappointing," sighed Andrei, dejectedly.

Funar gave him a slap on the back. "Cheer up, friend," he said. "I have a surprise at the station that I think you'll like."

CHAPTER 66

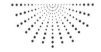

IAŞI, APRIL 8

"It was all my fault. I made him do it!" The woman bellowed, her eyes on the ceiling as if seeking redemption from a higher power. When she looked back at Andrei and Funar, tears flowed down her chubby, cherry cheeks, dripping down to an ample bosom partially covered by a paisley dress.

The two detectives remained silent, letting her purge her grief.

"What am I going to do now?" she cried. "There are no men left in his family!"

They were in a drab interrogation room, seated across an empty table from the lone woman, a young female uniformed officer observing them in a corner.

The woman pulled out a dirty, wrinkled handkerchief stashed in the armpit of her short-sleeved dress and loudly blew her nose. The interruption in her wailing gave Andrei an opportunity to pose his first question.

"What did you mean when you said it was your fault?"

She fixed her gaze on Andrei, her blue eyes misty, her mouth half open, on the verge of another sobbing jag. She looked middle-aged, in her late forties, her overweight body bursting at the seams of her well-worn dress. Her face was ruddy, her long stringy hair tightly pulled back into a ponytail.

Andrei was surprised. He had expected someone younger.

On the way to the police station, Funar had told him that the hospital had located Yoet Tcaci's wife and summoned her to Iași. She had arrived at his bedside that same morning, a few hours before Andrei. Evelina Tcaci now sat in front of the two detectives, bewildered and dejected.

"There were three others in the village that did it and were well paid." She rearranged her wrinkled handkerchief, readying it for the next round of tears. "We needed the money."

"Had done what?"

"Given their kidneys."

Andrei felt a pang of triumph. *Finally*, he thought. He looked up at the uniformed officer in the corner and directed his eyes onto a video monitor above her. She nodded in affirmation. The interview was being recorded.

"How much did they offer?" Andrei asked.

"One thousand dollars," she said. She blew her nose again. "That's a fortune." She continued gazing at her handkerchief. "My neighbor Svetlana put a down payment on a new pickup truck with that money. I wanted one too." She began sobbing again. "I was tired of hauling our family in that old Dacia that kept breaking down. Tired of pulling the car to the mechanic with a mule."

"Svetlana donated her kidney?" Andrei asked as he took notes.

"No, Ilia did. Her husband. They don't ask for kidneys from women. Men only."

Andrei looked at Funar, puzzled.

"I've heard that, too," Funar said. Earlier he had told Andrei that being close to the Moldovan border, he had heard plenty of anecdotes about the thriving organ trade in that country. "The recipients pay a lot for those kidneys," he continued. "And they prefer them from men only."

Evelina nodded in affirmation, issuing several hiccups. "Yes, that's well known in our village."

"Who offered you money for your husband's kidney?" asked Andrei.

"The Bosnian," she said. "Enver."

"Enver Muratovich?"

"I don't know his last name. He is a Bosnian who comes from Braşov. Sweet-talks everyone into giving away kidneys."

"If I were to show you a photo, would you recognize him?"

"Of course," she said.

Andrei realized with some consternation that he did not have a photo of Enver. He quickly text-messaged Boboc, requesting one.

Evelina continued her story. "You know, Yoet got cold feet at the last minute. He didn't want to go. Enver and the Ukrainian came to me for help." She started wailing again. "And I foolishly led them to where he was hiding." Her sobs melded in with the hiccups.

The comment caught Funar's attention. "Ukrainian?"

"Kyril," she said amid her sobs. "The driver."

The two detectives looked at each other and Andrei realized that Kyril Kozak was Funar's catch. Andrei was happy to let Funar have him. The rest of this woman's testimony was good as gold, firmly establishing the existence of the kidney trade and tying it in with Enver Muratovich. It was just what Andrei needed to prove his case to his boss, Dalca.

Andrei's mobile pinged. He opened the photo Boboc had sent him and showed it to Evelina Tcaci. "Is this Enver?"

She paused and studied the photo quietly. She then burst out, "Yes. That's him. I hope he rots in hell!"

Andrei changed the subject. "What is the name of your village?"

Funar answered. "Răspopeni," he said. "I'll send you some info about it later."

"Why?" Evelina wailed. "Why?"

"Why what?" asked Andrei.

"They all came back healthy and happy. They all got their money. Why did my Yoet turn out like this?"

Andrei did not answer. He could not tell the woman that Enver was unable to look after her husband because he had been assassinated.

Funar answered instead. "It happens," he said. "These outfits, they are not legitimate medical establishments. Submitting oneself to underground surgery is risky business."

Evelina Tcaci paused her weeping and stared at Funar wide-eyed. She then erupted again. "Oh, may God take me, too! Look what I have done!"

The uniformed officer approached the pitiful woman and handed her a glass of water. She stroked Evelina's hair and whispered a few consoling words into her ear. She then gave Funar a dirty look.

They waited for Evelina to calm down, then Andrei resumed his questioning. "I need to understand something," he said. "You can't just come and ask for a kidney as if you're buying livestock."

Evelina nodded.

"So was there a preliminary to this? Were you approached earlier?"

"Oh, yes." Evelina looked angry. "Enver came by months ago. Svetlana introduced him. He talked to us for hours. There was no pressure, he said. Think about it, he said. He would come back later, he said. He did come back, a month later. By then I had convinced Yoet to go through with it."

"So then Enver came and took him away?"

"Oh, no!" She looked at Andrei as if he were crazy. "He arranged blood tests. A whole bunch of them. Afterwards he called us and told us he had good news. Yoet was eligible. He was now on a waiting list. We waited three more months with anticipation."

Andrei realized that he was getting a glimpse of the tip of the iceberg. The organization that Enver's bosses had set up was quite elaborate. They screened potential donors and entered them into a database to match with recipients. When the right recipient appeared, they activated a suitable donor. Uncovering the layers of such a complex organization would be a challenge.

"We will need you to sign a sworn statement to the testimony you just gave," said Andrei. "Are you willing to do that?"

Evelina considered the question with fearful eyes.

Funar came to the rescue. "The officer here will prepare the statement and help you with it."

He gestured to the female officer, who approached Evelina and put an arm around her. For the first time in the session Evelina's lips parted into a thin smile. "Oh, all right," she murmured. She rose up from her chair and buried her head in the officer's shoulder.

The two detectives also rose. As the female officer led a shuffling Evelina toward the door, Andrei called out.

"I'm sorry," he said. "I have one more question."

The two women paused and stared at Andrei, the officer's arm still firmly around Evelina.

"You said that there were no men left in the family. What did you mean by that?"

Evelina looked at the floor and paused before she answered. "My first husband," she said in a barely audible voice, "was Yoet's brother, the oldest. I had two children with him, a son and a daughter. We lost him in a road accident."

She looked at the female officer, tears flowing again. "Yoet was the youngest of five boys, the only single one. So he had to step in."

"Common tradition in rural areas," Funar whispered into Andrei's ear.

"He turned out to be a better husband than his older brother," continued Evelina. "We had a child together, my two-year-old."

Evelina was spent. She turned around, head slumped, shoulders hunched, and let the officer help her out of the interrogation room.

* * *

"There you have it," said Funar. He crossed his legs and sat back, one arm dangling from the back of his chair.

They remained in the interrogation room, just the two of them.

Andrei finished the notes he was jotting down and closed his notebook. "Tragic," he said.

"These peasants. Stupid people," said Funar with disdain. "They deserve what they get."

Andrei did not feel that way and considered arguing with his counterpart. But Funar had been helpful, and he did not want any friction between them. He would need continued cooperation from the Iaşi police.

"This is the first decent break I've had in the case," said Andrei as he put his notebook in his jacket pocket.

"Hopefully we'll give you another one with that Ukrainian son-of-a-bitch driver."

"I want to thank you," Andrei said. He extended his hand to Funar.

"Glad to oblige." Funar shook his hand firmly.

They stood up and walked out of the room.

"So," said Funar, patting Andrei's back. "How come a *Subinspector* like you is in charge of such a big investigation?"

Andrei chuckled. "I had promised to tell you, hadn't I?"

"I am dying to hear."

They strolled out to the parking lot. "This Enver Muratovich," said Andrei, "was written off as a suicide. I was the one who figured out that it was a murder. So my chief assigned the investigation to me. At the time we had no idea that we were about to uncover a conspiracy concerning illicit kidney transplants."

"So, that's it? As easy as that?" Funar was not satisfied.

"Well," said Andrei sheepishly, "that, and the fact that I have prior experience in the SRI."

Funar stiffened at the mention of SRI. He looked Andrei up and down as if he were seeing him for the first time.

"Don't ask me why I went from SRI to Braşov Police," said Andrei, anticipating Funar's next question. "It's a long story."

"I bet." Funar opened Andrei's car door. "So what's next for you?"

"I am headed to Bucharest in pursuit of another lead." Andrei settled into the driver's seat.

"Good luck," said Funar. "I'll keep you abreast of what happens here." He closed Andrei's door.

410

CHAPTER 67

IAŞI, APRIL 8

The drive from Iaşi to Bucharest would take nearly six hours, and it was already sunset. Andrei decided to go part way and stay overnight in Tecuci, a small town about two hours down the road.

He was full of excitement about his first useful witness. As tragic as her circumstances were, Yoet's wife had been clear and convincing. Evelina had unequivocally confirmed the existence of a kidney transplant ring and placed Enver Muratovich in the middle of it. This was information Andrei had hoped to obtain from Dr. Zhulati, whose murder had set back the investigation. Now he hoped that Irina Cernea, his masked informant from Sfântu Gheorghe, would help rip a wider opening in the case.

As he left metropolitan Iaşi in his rearview mirror his mobile rang. He took it on a speaker.

"Hey, Chief." It was Boboc, placing a comic emphasis on *Chief*. "Did you get that photo of Muratovich I sent you?"

"Yeah, thanks."

"Was it useful?"

"Indeed."

"Did that donor identify him?"

"The donor is very sick," said Andrei. "He will most likely die soon."

"So your trip to Iaşi was a waste then, huh?"

"No, not at all." Andrei summarized for him Evelina Tcaci's testimony. "We have her on record," he added. "Geofri Funar, my contact in Iaşi, will forward us her sworn statement."

"Good work," said Boboc.

"Thanks. Any news at your end?"

"We have a surprise," said Boboc.

Andrei braced himself for bad news.

"The forensic guys lifted a partial from Zhulati's doorknob that does not belong to our good doctor."

"Really?" Andrei had not expected Zhulati's killer to be so careless as to leave fingerprints behind.

"It matches a certain Alin Barbu, a well-known drug dealer and street thug. He has a long list of priors. The narcs know him well, and so do I. I arrested him once or twice in the past."

"The Zhulati job, a common drug crime?" Andrei was puzzled. "Do you have a toxicology report yet?"

"Preliminary results are what you'd expect. High alcohol level, 0.32. No drugs."

"Have you interviewed this Barbu?"

"No, not yet. The fingerprint news is brand new."

"Just because Barbu's fingerprint is on the door doesn't mean that he killed the doctor," Andrei said.

"Right. Here's something else. They are telling me that there was DNA recovered from Zhulati's fingernails that does not belong to him."

"Aha! Any ID on that?"

"Not yet. They submitted it to SNDGJ."

SNDGJ was a national forensics DNA database created in 2016. Romania was a latecomer to the DNA game. While it had grown rapidly, the database wasn't always useful in producing hits. Nevertheless, it was becoming more and more indispensable.

Boboc continued. "If Barbu shows up in Zhulati's nails, then we can nail him." He laughed at his own pun. "We'll know by tomorrow or the next day."

"Is Barbu in town?" asked Andrei.

"Yes, he is out and about. Business as usual. He has no idea we're on to him."

"In that case, you may as well wait until the DNA results come in."

"That's what I figure."

"Does Dalca know any of this?"

"Yes," said Boboc. "The chief has been on my ass like he's glued to me. It's a good thing you're gone."

"Tell him about the donor's wife. Maybe he'll ease up."

"I will. Thanks."

Andrei hung up, surprised that a common street criminal was turning out to be the main suspect in Zhulati's murder. Maybe the fingerprint was a false lead. He would have to wait and see how the investigation unfolded.

In the meantime, he needed a good night's rest and a clear mind to prepare a strategy on how to approach Irina Cernea. He pulled into a roadside hotel just outside Tecuci.

It was a cramped, dank room. At least the bedsheets were clean. Andrei threw his small suitcase on a torn armchair, removed his shoes, and plopped onto the bed. The springs of the mattress creaked loudly in protest. He closed his eyes and tried to wipe out the thoughts racing through his mind. For a moment all he heard was his heartbeat throbbing at his temple. A chime of his phone interrupted his reverie. It was a text message from Corneliu Balaş. "Call me when you have a chance."

So much for sleep, thought Andrei. He dialed his old army buddy with a loud sigh.

"Andrei, how are you?" Balaş sounded chipper.

"Let's see," Andrei said. "I have been driving all over Romania and now I am in some shithole motel in Tecuci. No dinner, no Ana."

Balaş chuckled. "That murder investigation weighing you down?"

"How did you guess?"

"Are you making any headway?"

"Yes," said Andrei. "I have a new corpse and another one that will die soon. Great progress."

"And no suspects?"

"Nothing definite yet."

"Woo, buddy. That sucks."

"So do you have anything for me?" Andrei braced himself for yet another dead end.

"Well, for starters," said Balaş in a promising tone, "the investigation into your two dead Bucharestis is being driven by the French Interpol."

"I already heard that," said Andrei. "Any idea why?"

"It seems that they knocked off a French citizen with a botched kidney harvesting. The guy was an arms salesman who disappeared from Tiraspol and popped up a few days later in some low-class hotel in Braşov, sick as a dog and with a surgical wound on his flank. He went on to die."

"Holy shit," Andrei murmured to himself. "Yoet Tcaci!"

"What?"

"Oh, never mind," said Andrei.

"No, no. Tell me."

"The guy I just told you about, the one who's about to die. Same story. Young guy, found sick in Braşov with a flank wound, suffering severe complications from kidney removal."

"How did you get so lucky to stumble upon these bad actors?"

Andrei ignored that. "What else do you have on the Frenchies?"

"The lead agent on the case is a certain Jean-Claude Gérard. The guy is an old fox with a storied career, decades in the Sûreté, and now with Interpol. I've heard the name before on several occasions. It seems that Gérard had some prior interest in those two dead guys, Radu and Negrescu."

"Why?" asked Andrei. "I checked their criminal records. They have none."

"Andrei, my friend, don't go naïve on me now!"

Andrei did not answer.

"These guys were too well connected to receive trouble from law enforcement."

"I figured," said Andrei. "I just wanted to hear it from you."

"Attaboy."

Andrei waited for more.

"Anyhow, your two dead clowns were into all sorts of shit besides the organ trade. That's where Gérard and French Interpol caught the scent of their trail."

"Like what?"

"Well, smuggling, for starters, mostly from Turkey and the Middle East."

"Drugs?"

"Interestingly, no drugs. Goods and women: you know, human trafficking. They had numerous legitimate businesses as fronts— retail, construction, financial services. They probably ran a pretty sophisticated money laundering operation, too."

Andrei scratched his head. This case was ballooning well beyond any scope he had imagined.

"But lately, their most lucrative venture was the transplant trade. They hit a gold mine with rich Israelis who were willing to pay a premium for kidneys. You know that they don't do transplants in Israel."

"No, I didn't. Why?"

"Harvesting organs from a dead body is against the Jewish religion."

"Oh, so they don't mind others getting killed in the process."

Balaş chuckled. "That's the way of the world, my man. As long as your compadres are kosher, who cares about the rest?"

"Okay, so who is killing them?"

"Iancu Negrescu was killed by a Slovak gang headed by a hood named Tibor Bognár. The gang operated in and around Budapest."

"I already know that," said Andrei. "Bognár and his

accomplices have all been apprehended. What about Nicolae Radu?"

"Ah! That's the million-dollar question."

"What do you mean?"

"I mean everyone is all hush-hush about that."

"That's exactly the impression I had. That's why I asked you to nose around." Andrei sounded impatient.

"Hold your horses, will you?"

"Sorry."

"I don't have a name for you, but I do have some credible information."

"Go ahead."

"It is some Russian bigwig, from what I understand, well connected with the Kremlin. There is a lot of reluctance to go after this guy."

"Why?"

"I don't know." Balaş sounded honest. "This guy is tied in with some elements of the Russian secret service."

"Which one?"

"Don't know. Listen, will you? Don't cut me off."

"Okay, all right."

"Rumor has it that he runs a security company of some sort. I don't know the name. He has men, former military, former agents, you catch my drift? Men who are pros. He sent his men to do a clean hit on Nicolae Radu. Rumor also has it that this Russian contracted Bognár to whack Negrescu and Bognár botched it. He managed the hit but got himself caught."

"Why would this Russian want to kill these guys?"

"I am not certain." Balaş paused to think. "Maybe he is into the same transplant game as they are and he is eliminating rivals. Maybe these clowns gave him the same treatment as the French arms salesman and your donor guy."

"If so, he would have been pretty sick."

"Maybe he was and he recovered. Maybe it was not him, but one of his colleagues or employees, someone he valued."

"I catch your drift."

"If I come across the name, I'll pass it on."

"Thanks," said Andrei.

"That might be worth a second bottle of Scotch." Balaş laughed.

Andrei had one last question. "I heard that the FBI was also present in Budapest. Did you come across anything relating to that?"

"Yes," said Balaş. "There is an American in the midst of all this, but no one is clear about who exactly he is. One thing is for certain. This American reported both of your dead guys to the police. In other words, he was the first one on both crime scenes—at the Gresham Hotel for Radu and at Rudas Baths for Negrescu. He was also responsible for the arrest of Bognár and his gang. He has since mysteriously disappeared."

"How can that be? The guy would be a key material witness."

"My sources are mum about that. If you ask me, he either cut some secret deal with Budapest Police, or he, too, was whacked and they haven't found the body."

"What agency does he actually belong to?" asked Andrei. "Seems a bit far-fetched for FBI to have such an operative in Hungary."

"As I said, it is unclear. He is supposed to be a doctor, but this may very well be a cover."

"Do you have a name?"

"Wait a minute." Balaş paused to look it up. "Mark Kent," he said.

Andrei wrote the name down.

"He is an immigrant to America," Balaş added. "From Turkey. His Turkish name was Metin Özgür."

"Interesting," Andrei remarked. "Nicolae Radu is also a Turkish immigrant."

"Right. These two supposedly knew each other back in Turkey, decades ago. School friends or something."

"Do you think this Mark Kent was also involved in Radu and Negrescu's criminal activities?" Andrei asked.

"If he was, he has presided over a spectacular destruction of it, hasn't he?"

"Yeah, you're right." Andrei drifted into silent thought.

"Sorry I can't be any more specific," said Balaş.

"No, no. This is very useful stuff."

"I'll pass on more if I come across anything."

Andrei thanked his friend and hung up. He took a long, hot shower and then got into the creaky bed, the mysteries of his case creaking around in his head. Who was this Russian and why was he on a killing spree? Why was the modus operandi in the Zhulati killing so different from that of Enver Muratovich? How could young, healthy people subject themselves to illicit surgery for what amounted to a pittance?

And who was this mysterious Mark Kent?! What was his role in all this?

Finally he drifted into sleep, hoping that the next day a new witness would shed more light into the mystery. Andrei intended to arrive early in Bucharest and stake out Irina Cernea's residence and workplace. Afterwards, he would decide how to intercept her.

CHAPTER 68

BUCHAREST, APRIL 7

Olga blasted out of the Negrescu compound with Mark in the passenger seat of her Audi sports car. Mark hastily fumbled for his seat belt as he prepared for a perilous ride in the fast lane. Up ahead was a single parked vehicle that conspicuously faced the wrong side of the road. Mark spotted a colossal figure cramped at its driver's seat, biting into a sandwich. Milan.

Mark glanced at Olga, who was focused on racing ahead of traffic, oblivious to Mark's rising alarm. He suddenly ducked under the dashboard and stayed there, pretending to fuss with his shoes.

"Is everything all right?" asked Olga.

Mark straightened up and looked behind him at Milan's car as it rapidly disappeared. "My shoe," he stammered. "Too tight." He adjusted himself in his seat, now more relaxed. "My feet are swollen. I think I stood on them too long."

She threw a momentary glance at the dark area under the dashboard where Mark's feet were hidden. "You need a massage," she said, her eyes back on the road.

"Is that advice or a promise?" Mark asked flirtatiously.

"Whatever you wish."

"You never gave me that massage I signed up for at Gresham Palace." Mark continued his flirtatious tone.

In Budapest, Mark had engaged Olga as an excuse to meet and question her. At the time, she was on staff at the hotel's spa. Realizing Mark's intentions, Olga evaded him. Mark persisted and tracked her down to a seedy strip club where she was hiding. There she surprised him with an admission that she and Ahmet had been long-time lovers. Their conversation was interrupted by two thugs who were intent on killing Mark. Olga helped him escape.

The thugs had pursued Mark into the street, guns blazing. It was Mark's first brush with death, and it occurred in the midst of an irresistible desire Mark felt for this sultry woman. Just before dashing away from the thugs, Mark had leaned into Olga for a kiss that never happened.

"Well, that massage is long overdue, isn't it?" Olga lowered her sunglasses and eyed him seductively. "I won't charge you."

"Not just my feet?" said Mark in jest.

"Not just your feet."

Mark grasped the dashboard with both hands as the Audi suddenly accelerated. He tried to ignore the discomfort of the rising bulge in his pants.

* * *

Olga lived in the Crângaşi district, in a spacious ninth-floor apartment that overlooked Lacul Morii, a large lake on the northwest side of the city. Mark gazed at the lake out of the living room windows while she changed. The sun was low on the opposite shore, its golden light glistening on crystal-calm waters. It was quiet and peaceful here, a refuge from the turmoil.

The sound of soft footsteps drew his attention back inside. Olga was barefoot, wearing a red silk gown loosely tied at the waist, carrying a folded table. She gave him a brief smile and put the table down.

"Nice place," said Mark.

She approached the window and looked out. "Yes, isn't it?"

"What do you do here in Bucharest?"

"I have my own massage practice." She leaned down and began unfolding the portable table. "It's going well."

A glimpse of her generous breasts amid the loose folds of her gown left Mark momentarily speechless. "Very well indeed, for you to have this apartment."

Olga straightened up and tightened her gown. "Not that well," she smiled somewhat ruefully. "All this," she swept her arm around the apartment, "that's money from my husband."

Mark wanted to ask more but her massage table was ready. "All right. Clothes off!" Olga placed her hands on her hips and eyed Mark expectantly.

Discombobulated, Mark turned back to the window as if concerned that someone might look in.

She chuckled. "Don't worry, no one will see you this high up. Come on, let's go."

Mark began peeling his clothes awkwardly. "Uh, should I shower first?"

"No," she said unwaveringly. "I'm a professional, remember? I am accustomed to body odors." She turned toward a nearby cabinet and removed a plastic spray bottle. "Besides," she added, "this will soon make you smell like a fresh flower."

"A fresh flower," Mark mumbled as he peeled off his socks. "I've never felt that way before."

She laughed and watched him fuss with his briefs. "This too?" he asked.

"Everything!" she commanded, like a drill sergeant.

Soon he was prone on the massage table, his bare buttocks covered with a towel. The oil she sprayed on him did indeed smell like fresh lilacs. Her fingers were soft but firm as they found achy knots and stiff muscles on his back and shoulders.

Mark tried to raise his head and tell her how wonderful this was. She pushed him down before he could open his mouth. "Relax," she said firmly.

He let himself fall into a state of semi-consciousness where all that mattered was the power of her palms and electrifying touch of her fingertips. She skipped his covered derriere and moved down to his thighs and calves, and eventually to his feet. "There," she said quietly as he moaned with pleasure, her fingertips steady on his toes. "The foot massage." Mark did not want it to end.

"Okay, turn over."

When Mark clumsily rolled around, somehow successfully keeping the towel at his waist, she let out a big laugh. He raised his head and looked down at the sharp peak in the center of the towel.

"Sorry," he said haplessly.

She ignored him and worked the front of his legs, then his stomach muscles and his chest. She was close to his face now, her barely covered breasts dangling over him, her loose blonde hair tickling his skin.

Mark lifted his head off the table and sought her lips. This time the gesture was not thwarted. She responded lightly at first with her moist, meaty lips, and then with more resolve. She untied the knot on her belt and let her gown slide off. Her right hand slipped below the towel in a firm grasp that sent shivers up his body. She slithered over him and pressed herself onto his chest.

"Stop," said Mark suddenly. "Not here, not on the massage table."

She stood up and extended a hand, helping him off the table. Mark followed her to the bedroom, limping. The massage had loosened him all over except for his erection, which at that moment felt like the strongest bone in his body.

It was beyond anything Mark had imagined. His awkward efforts with Jasmin in Budapest and Semra in Istanbul were only a prelude to Olga. She was resolute and methodical, unwavering despite his premature release soon after they plunged into bed. She pressed a finger on his lips as he mumbled apologies, silencing him. She then planted herself on his face, quietly demanding her turn. Mark eagerly rose to the challenge and as she shook uncontrollably, wetting his face, Mark felt a new wave of desire that he soon put to work.

Now atop her, with her legs firmly clenched around him, Mark released years of frustration with a surprising surge he never knew he possessed. He continued for a while before he concluded, provoking her into numerous aftershocks. She clenched her fingertips on his back, her sharp nails biting into his flesh in fits of pain that further stoked his fury. With his next release, loud and volcanic, he was spent.

He pulled away and lay down, sweaty and panting. She lay on her side and watched, amused. "Wow," she said, gently stroking his hair, "I never imagined…"

He looked at her with weary, grateful eyes. "Me neither."

CHAPTER 69

BUCHAREST, APRIL 8 ... EARLY MORNING

Mark awoke sweaty from the heat of Olga's body on his. He pulled his covers off and sat up. He had no idea what time it was. He wondered about Semra. Had she made it back to the hotel? She would be wondering where he was. Should he call her?

Olga turned and extended her arm to him, pulling him back in. His face between her breasts, Mark forgot everything. They started again, this time more methodical, not as passionate. She gently pushed Mark's shoulders down toward her legs. "Do it again," she murmured, as Mark buried himself between them. "M'mmm...so good."

Once she finished, he tried to enter her. "Easy," she said. "It's sore." He took heed and moved gingerly. She directed his pace with her hands on his buttocks. He did not take long.

Afterwards she slipped off to the bathroom, leaving a light on at her bedside table. Mark admired her silhouette as she disappeared. He eagerly waited for her to return, for another glimpse. She ran back into bed and pulled the covers up. "Uuh, cold!"

Mark rested on one elbow, partially sitting up, and silently eyed her. She looked back at him. "What? What are you looking at?"

"I'm wondering what a beautiful woman like you is doing with a guy like me."

She repositioned herself, her covers slipping down to reveal her shoulders. "You're not so bad-looking yourself," she said teasingly.

"No, seriously," said Mark. "What were you doing at that funeral?"

"Paying my last respects. I knew Iancu from way back."

"You weren't looking for me?"

She turned away, reaching up to turn the light off. Mark grabbed her arm and stopped her. "No, please. Answer me."

"Do we have to do this now?"

"Yes," he said. "I'll have to leave soon. I need to know."

She pulled her mobile phone from the night table and lit its screen. "Leave now? It's three in the morning."

Mark didn't answer. She was right.

"Are you eager to get back to your Turkish girl?"

The question caught him by surprise. "You saw her?"

"I watched you since you arrived at the church."

"So you *were* after me."

She nodded.

"How did you know I was in Bucharest?"

"Martina," she said.

"Who?"

"Sorana's maid. You met her, you and your girl."

Mark remembered now, the woman clad in black who had been appalled when Semra uncovered the mirror. He looked at Olga quizzically.

"We are old friends," she said. "Back in the day, we worked together."

"As maids?"

"No," she said brusquely. "A different job."

Mark knew what that was. Iancu had told him that Ahmet, who had an insatiable appetite for prostitutes, had first met Olga when she was a young one.

"Let's say I moved on and up, and helped Martina with that new job. Nicolae made it possible." Olga continued. "Martina knew that you were coming to Bucharest from the moment Sorana and Vasile invited you."

Mark wondered if that was how the SRI had also been informed about his arrival.

"So, why did you look me up?"

"We had unfinished business, remember?"

Mark pondered what she meant by that. Was she referring to their last encounter in Budapest that was interrupted by thugs?

"I thought we had finished that conversation," said Mark. He had followed up the next day with a phone call that he considered fruitless. All he had learned was that she would be leaving Hungary soon.

"You didn't get what you wanted to know, and neither did I."

"I didn't know that you wanted..." Mark trailed off.

She set her phone back on the table. "What, that I wanted you?"

"Well, yes! That's for sure, but that you wanted information."

"Men are openly attracted to me all the time. I, on the other hand, can easily conceal mine." She looked at him with her beautiful hazel eyes. "Yes, I did find you attractive, but the situation in Budapest was not ideal, to say the least. That last moment before you fled, when you tried to kiss me..."

"You noticed that?"

"How could I not? It was a shame it didn't happen."

For a moment Mark wanted to stop talking and plunge into yet another session of lovemaking. But he restrained himself. "So what was it that you wanted to know?"

"You go first. Ask what you want to ask."

"All right," said Mark. "Let's start with Nicolae...Ahmet. Did you give his killers access to the hotel?"

This was an issue that he and Budapest Police had speculated about. The hotel had strict security procedures that Ahmet's killers had deftly bypassed. The killers had to have had inside help. Olga was the obvious suspect since, soon after his death, she fled with no explanation.

Olga lowered her eyes. "Yes," she said quietly.

Mark had witnessed Olga's despair about Ahmet's death when

they spoke at the strip club. This did not jibe with her role as an assistant to the assassination.

"What happened?" asked Mark. "Were you somehow tricked into it?"

"Do you believe that I am innocent?" she asked with surprise.

"Of course I do," he answered. "I saw your grief back in Budapest. It was obvious that you could not have intentionally helped them."

She let out a sigh of relief. "Yes," she said. "That son of a bitch tricked me." She sat up and brushed her hair back. "And I fell for it."

"Cezar?"

She nodded in affirmation. "He told me that he was sending a pair of emissaries to meet with Nicolae and they needed free access to the hotel. Could I leave them a master key card? This sort of secretive stuff was common in his world. So I didn't think much of it. Besides, he and Nicolae were on good terms. I couldn't have imagined that Cezar would help get him killed."

"Those people who were sent," said Mark, "they were recorded by the lobby cameras."

"I'm not surprised. I was told to leave a master card for them at the lobby. I left it at a corner of the reception desk in an envelope. The receptionists didn't know."

"Did you mention these emissaries to Nicolae when you gave him a massage?" Ahmet had received a massage from Olga immediately before he was killed.

"No. He didn't want to talk. He wanted sex. So I gave him some. Then he wanted more. I told him, later. I gave him my phone number."

"Why did he need your number? Weren't you two still having an affair?"

"I did not see Nicolae after I moved to Budapest. He had heard that I was working at Gresham Palace and sent me a message there that he would be coming. I could not have the sort of sex he wanted in the spa, at work, as you can imagine. So I gave him my new mobile number. We planned a rendezvous later, when we were both free."

"Did you know why Nicolae came to Budapest?"

"No, not really. Nicolae and I did not discuss his business much. We just made love."

Funny, thought Mark, how this was exactly what Günsu had told him about her and Ahmet.

Mark explained. "He was there to meet me. He was looking for a way out of Romania, and wanted my help to get him to the US."

"I want you to know," Olga said in a firm voice, "that I left Cezar after Nicolae died. This time for good."

"Tell me about it." Mark touched her face lightly.

She propped her pillow on the headboard and sat up, the covers falling down to her waist, leaving her chest bare. She seemed oblivious to how distracting this was to Mark.

"I should never have fallen for him," she said. "I was young and naïve."

"Was he your…boss at one time?" Mark wanted to say *pimp*, but he held back.

"I was very young when I met him," she said. "In Gdańsk."

"Poland?" Mark was baffled.

"Yes, we're both Polish."

Mark realized that the last name, Kaminesky, now made sense. It had not sounded Romanian.

"I was fourteen," she said. "I had run away from home, in Poznań." She stopped to collect her emotions. "Abusive stepfather," she said. "Started when I was ten."

"I'm sorry," Mark said hesitantly.

"Gdańsk is a port city," she continued. "Lots of sailors."

Mark understood where the story was headed, but did not interrupt.

"He was just nineteen at the time, a small-time hustler, dealing drugs and robbing drunken sailors. He had just begun running girls. I became his best. I boosted his business."

I'll bet, Mark thought to himself. Aloud, he asked, "How did you end up in Romania?"

"I was living with him. He got busted several times and did short stints in jail. That was not a problem. He had taught me how to run his business—the girls, not the other stuff. But then he got in trouble with a local gangster, a guy well connected to the Polish Mafia."

"What happened?"

"They got into some stupid fight. I don't remember what it was about. A bar fight. Cezar stabbed him to death. He didn't mean to do it, he told me; it just happened. He knew this would bring big trouble. We left soon after that. He had friends in Bucharest and so he set up shop there."

"I heard that he is a dangerous man, into various different crimes."

"You heard right. He has a bad temper, and when he loses it he can be irrational, wild and violent. That guy he killed in Poland was the first of many to come."

"How come you married him then?"

"What did you expect me to do? I was sixteen when I ended up in Romania with him, a foreign country where I knew no one. He was my sole source of support. I worked diligently for him and helped him run his girl business. We became partners of sorts. So marriage was not too big a further step."

"Wasn't he jealous of the men you were with?"

"No, it was just business."

"What about Ahmet? He surely was not a routine customer."

"At first that's all he was," said Olga. "But I started falling for him. He had a special allure, an irresistible charm. And he was so good with sex. I usually did not get attached to my customers, but with him…it was different. I looked forward to the next time, and there was always a next time, and then another."

"Cezar must have surely known."

"He did and he didn't care. Ahmet paid well. He was a good customer. That's all that mattered to Cezar. Years later they went into business together. By then I was no longer working and I was seeing Ahmet secretly. Cezar knew but he turned a blind eye to it."

"You were no longer working?"

"I was in my late twenties and I got tired of it. We were well off and Cezar agreed that I no longer needed to do it. That's when I went to school and learned to become a masseuse."

"How did you end up in Budapest?"

"It was my initial separation from Cezar. Our relationship had deteriorated. He was abusive, he would hit me at times, and he had his own affairs that he openly flaunted."

"He let you leave, just like that?" Mark knew that men like that tended to not let go.

"He was quite controlling in years past. When I tried to leave, he threatened me. But two years ago I had this job opportunity in Budapest, at the Gresham Hotel. I told him that I wasn't really leaving him. We would still be partners. I really wanted this job."

"And he bought that?"

"He did." She laughed mirthlessly. "Because he himself had fallen for some teenager and was totally infatuated with her. A Russian girl. He wouldn't let her turn tricks. He set her up in her own apartment in Braşov, away from us in Bucharest." She shook her head. "As if I wouldn't know."

"Tell me about Cezar and Ahmet," Mark prompted.

Olga yawned and stretched. She checked the time on her mobile. "Can we sleep now? I promise I'll tell you more in the morning." She slid under the covers. "Come, cuddle me." She turned off the nightlight.

CHAPTER 70

BUCHAREST, APRIL 8 ... MORNING

Mark awoke first. He quietly slipped out of bed and went to the picture windows of the living room, watching dawn break over the peaceful lake. He contemplated his situation. The night with Olga had been beyond anything he had dreamed of. He was amazed that Olga found him attractive.

Mark had a history of being attracted to Ahmet's girls. None had returned the favor, Günsu being the prime example. She had come around now, but Mark no longer possessed the youthful crush he had harbored for her. It had deflated like a popped balloon when they reconnected in Istanbul.

With Olga, on the other hand, it was not that sort of a crush. As he had explained to Tarık during their drive to Bodrum, Mark's desire for her had been mainly lustful. Now it was fulfilled. Well, not quite. Maybe he could have a bit more this morning, before he departed.

Mark smiled. What a stroke of good luck. This past night alone made coming to Romania worth his while.

He wondered whether he would see Olga again. He was doubtful. They lived in very different worlds. Reconciling them would be an enormous effort. It was time to move on and get back to the United States, time to put his life back in order. A new job perhaps, a fresh start, and eventually a new woman.

Mark rubbed his forehead. All this was wonderful fantasy, but first he had to extricate himself from Europe, from Vadim Rusu and his long reach. He had to figure out what to do with Semra, not to mention his newest prickly problem, the Romanian secret service.

"What are you doing up so early?"

Mark turned back to see the alluring silhouette of Olga, wearing a gown and slippers.

"I couldn't sleep," he said.

She approached closer. "Considering how much you exerted yourself, I would have thought the contrary." She reached up and kissed him.

"Maybe I need another workout," he answered in jest.

She broke away and started for the kitchen. "I'll make you coffee."

They sat at her small kitchen table in tall chairs and silently sipped instant Nescafé.

"You promised to tell me about Ahmet and your husband."

"He is no longer my husband," Olga said. She shuddered and closed her gown tighter around her chest.

"So you and Cezar are divorced?"

"Not officially, but we may as well be. We haven't physically seen each other in two years, and we communicate only occasionally."

"Does he know that you're back in Romania?"

"Yes," she nodded.

"And he leaves you unmolested?" Mark was skeptical.

"He no longer has any use for me." She took a long sip of coffee. "I have grown old. I am no longer attractive to him. He is into teenagers."

"He is an idiot," said Mark. "You're gorgeous. Any man would be lucky to have you."

She gave him a doleful look. "Thanks. But I haven't found a new one that I want to be with."

Mark wondered if this was a proposition in disguise. He sidestepped the comment. "Back to Ahmet," he said. "Tell me about him and Cezar."

"Yes." She sat up more erect. "Ahmet...Nicolae. At first, as far as Cezar was concerned, he was a good customer. Then he became a distant friend. When Nicolae started his kidney business and it took off, Cezar wanted part of it. Nicolae was all too glad to have Cezar help out. You see, Nicolae was a visionary, a deal maker, but he did not have enough patience for the small details, the nitty-gritty. Cezar did. Cezar also had connections with which he could create an infrastructure—secretaries, testing labs, recordkeeping, and so on, to keep all this on the up-and-up."

"You mean, so the authorities wouldn't question it?" asked Mark.

"You don't know Romania," she said. "Nothing happens here without greasing someone's palm."

"Turkey is the same way," Mark responded, trying to sound worldly.

"That's nothing compared with what happens here. Cezar had already built all the necessary connections with the powers that be. So it wasn't that difficult for him to set up and run this kidney business."

"There is something that baffled me from the very beginning," said Mark, setting his coffee mug down. "Ahmet contacted me in America via a radiology report he used as a ruse. He scribbled a message to me in Turkish in the back of the report."

"What's puzzling about that?"

"The report was of a CT scan, of the abdomen."

Olga waited expectantly.

"The strange part is that the name of the patient, the one who had been scanned, was Cezar. Cezar Kaminesky. Now, why would Ahmet be in possession of a medical report that belongs to your husband?"

Olga smiled knowingly. "It wasn't just his name, was it? There was a number next to it."

"Yes, fifty-eight. How did you know?"

"The patient who was scanned was not Cezar. It was some live donor they screened with a CT. They could not keep legitimate medical records on these people, so they came up with a secret set of records where each donor was named after Cezar with a number after it. That number could be used to trace the donor."

"So Cezar ran the CT?"

"No, a technician did. A technician hired by his organization. It was all part of that infrastructure I told you about."

"How did Ahmet—Nicolae—come to possess that report?"

"Cezar was an independent contractor running all this for Nicolae and Iancu. So they got copies of all these records."

Mark had finished his coffee. He put the mug down and stood up. "Now I get it," he said.

"There's something you need to know," said Olga.

Mark ignored her comment and knelt down in front of her. Grabbing her right foot, he began massaging it.

"Oh, that feels good," she purred.

He kissed her big toe and continued. "I'm all ears."

She leaned forward and looked down at him. "Do the other one, too?"

He did as told. "What do you think?" he asked. "Could I join your profession?"

She opened her gown and spread her legs. "Not until you prove yourself with this." She pointed toward her stylishly cropped pubic hair.

"Whatever you say, mistress." Mark marched his hands up her legs and began working on her with his fingers, and later, once she was aroused enough, with his mouth.

They ended up on the kitchen floor, their bodies entangled in a complex knot, and Mark received what he had hoped for, one last time.

She held her back as he helped her up afterwards. "You animal," she said. "You hurt my back."

"It wasn't me. It was the way you were arching yourself."

They limped together to the bedroom, Mark supporting her.

They tumbled under the covers and relaxed in each other's embrace.

Afterwards Mark lay back and stared at the ceiling. "You were going to tell me something and I interrupted."

She slapped his chest playfully. "Bad boy."

"All right, what is it?"

"I was going to tell you that Cezar eventually started his own transplant business."

"Separate from Nicolae and Iancu?"

"Yes. It was too lucrative for him to remain an accessory. He wanted more."

"How did Nicolae and Iancu feel about it?"

"I have no idea," she said. "But on the surface there was no friction between them. It was all business as usual."

"Iancu told me that there was plenty of business to go around," Mark said. "He and Nicolae started the same way, taking business from others."

"Right, but Cezar had no scruples about the way he ran it. His was a factory. He didn't care what the results were. He charged less than others and got more customers. He figured they got what they paid for."

"H'mmm," said Mark. "That's totally different than Ahmet and Iancu. They tried to run it as safe and clean as they possibly could."

They paused momentarily and considered what they had revealed to each other.

Olga broke the silence. "Now my turn," she said.

"No, thanks, I am exhausted. I can't do more."

She laughed. "Not that, silly! I had questions too, remember?"

"Okay, go ahead."

"Do you know why Nicolae and Iancu were killed?" Olga asked, her voice catching.

"Is this why you came for me at the funeral?" Mark asked, rising up and leaning toward her.

Olga pressed her head deeper into her pillow. "Well, yeah," she said hesitantly. "And..."

"And what, sex?" Mark sounded skeptical. "Were you that eager to make love to me?"

Olga sat up and propped her pillow behind her. "All right, no. Not at first. But after that kiss in the garden…well…I changed my mind."

Mark was flattered. He pushed on. "So what did you originally have in mind?"

"I heard about what happened in Budapest after I left and I wanted to know more. I wanted to hear your version of it." She avoided eye contact with Mark, keeping her gaze downcast.

Mark stroked her hair. "Well, for what it's worth, I really don't care why you sought me out. I am glad you did." He planted a soft kiss on her lips. "What we did last night, I will cherish it for the rest of my life," he whispered.

It was Olga's turn to look skeptical.

"No, really. I mean it."

"Look," she said. "I am a whore who is mixed up with gangsters and criminals. You are a respectable doctor from America. Why would you honestly want to have anything to do with me?"

"You're not a whore. Didn't you say that yourself?" Mark caressed Olga's cheek. "You are the most beautiful woman I have ever met."

She leaned into his hand and kissed his palm.

"Honestly," Mark continued. "From the first moment I saw you at that spa, I've had an irresistible crush on you."

Olga's sultry lips parted into a slight smile. "Does this mean that we might have a future together?"

Mark lay down and gazed again at the ceiling. "I don't know," he said slowly. "My life is such a mess right now." He explained his predicament in San Francisco, losing his marriage, about to lose both his job and his house. "I don't know where I am going from here. I have no idea what tomorrow holds."

"I understand," said Olga. "Plus you already have that Turkish girl."

"Yes," he said. "We look like we are a couple but we are not. I am more like a guardian to her."

"A guardian with benefits?" Olga smiled dubiously.

Mark did not wish to explain Semra's secrets. He changed the subject. "What do you know about what happened in Budapest?"

"I heard that Nicolae and Iancu were killed by a Slovak gang and that you helped with their capture. But I don't know why they were murdered."

"It's not quite like that."

She looked at him quizzically.

"Have you heard of a Vadim Rusu?" he asked. "A former Russian intelligence operative."

"Rusu," she said, giving it some thought. "Sounds familiar but no, I don't think so."

"As it turns out," Mark explained, "Nicolae and Iancu's organization used his son as a kidney donor, and this young man ended up dying of complications. So Rusu is out for justice, in his own way."

"Dima Rusu," she suddenly uttered.

"Yes, how did you know?"

She sat bolt upright. "Oh, my God!" She put her hand on her mouth and repeated more loudly, "Oh, my God!"

"What? What is it?"

"Dima Rusu was an involuntary donor. They drugged him and stole his kidney," Olga blurted out excitedly.

"How do you know that?"

She did not answer him. She rocked back and forth, coming to grips with what she had just realized.

"Olga," he took her face in his hands and turned her toward him. "Tell me, what is it?"

"Sylvia," she said.

"Who?"

"Sylvia," she blurted out, in a shaky voice. "An old friend, a co-worker, like Martina."

"Let me guess," said Mark. "Was Sylvia the one who lured Dima into the transplant trap?"

"Yes," Olga confirmed. "She called me and told me about it. She was very upset when she found out how it turned out."

437

"I'm glad to know she had some conscience," Mark said sardonically.

"But that's not all of it," Olga pleaded.

"What else?"

"Sylvia did not work for Nicolae and Iancu," she said, now unwavering. "She worked for Cezar."

CHAPTER 71

BUCHAREST, APRIL 8 … MORNING

"Are you sure about that?" Olga's revelation struck Mark like lightning.

"Yes, of course I am. Sylvia and I go a long way back. We both worked for Cezar. There were times back then when I managed her myself."

Mark shot out of bed and began pacing back and forth in the bedroom, stark naked.

"What's the matter?"

"Don't you get it?" he said, speaking loudly enough to startle her. "If Sylvia was the woman responsible for trapping Dima Rusu, then it was Cezar and his organization that took his kidney, not Nicolae and Iancu."

"That sounds about right."

"It makes sense in another way," Mark continued.

"What way?"

"Iancu himself told me that they ran a clean operation. They did not engage in dirty tricks like involuntary kidney harvests. I believed him."

"Cezar did," Olga interrupted him.

"Cezar did," Mark confirmed. "That was part of his modus operandi."

They both fell silent, contemplating the implications.

Olga spoke first. "So then why did Dima Rusu's father seek vengeance from Nicolae and Iancu?"

"Not just them; that's not the half of it. Rusu also targeted others in their organization. Believe me, I've witnessed too many killings since I arrived in Europe." He stopped and shook his head in disbelief. "And if what you're telling me is right, it was all for naught."

"What I told you *is* right."

She put her dressing gown back on and went into the bathroom. Mark scooped his shirt and underwear from a messy pile at the foot of the bed and put them on. He waited for Olga to reappear.

"Why would Vadim Rusu believe that Nicolae and Iancu's organization killed his son?" he asked her.

"Because Cezar misled him to think that?"

"Is Cezar capable of misleading a veteran operative like Rusu?"

"Yes," said Olga. "He absolutely is."

"Maybe Cezar realized who Dima was, and by then it was too late. So he decided to deflect attention away from himself."

"That would not be the first time he has done something like this," Olga confirmed.

"I need to process this," said Mark excitedly. "I need to figure out what to do with this information."

"What can you do? All those people are dead already."

"I don't believe Rusu is done yet," Mark said. "He needs to know this. He needs to stop coming after Nicolae's organization. He needs to stop coming after *me*."

"How do you propose to convince him?" Olga asked doubtfully.

"I don't know." Mark scratched his head. "Do you have any proof that connects this Sylvia to Cezar?"

"Sure," said Olga. "I've kept all sorts of paperwork, letters, emails, photos and texts related to Cezar's business."

"You have?" Mark was stunned.

"Insurance, in case he tried to harm me." She smiled. "Why do you think he still supports me financially, lets me live like this?"

"He needs you to stay silent."

Olga nodded.

Mark gave her a tight hug. "You are a clever woman!"

She kissed him. "Come," she said. "I'll fix you some breakfast. You can figure out what to do later."

CHAPTER 72

BUCHAREST, APRIL 9

Andrei left Tecuci early. His night in the lumpy motel bed had been restless, full of thoughts about his upcoming encounter with his next witness in Bucharest. He had traced Irina Cernea through her CNP number, a personal numerical code assigned to each citizen by a national registry. He had then obtained driver's license and vehicle information via ARR, the Romanian Road Authority, and RAR, the Romanian Automobile Registry. He discovered that Irina lived in the Colentina district in northwest Bucharest and worked in nearby Fundeni Hospital.

Fundeni, Andrei realized, would be an appropriate place for the Braşov transplant ring to source nursing staff from, since it was a major referral center for legitimate transplants. Andrei had no doubt that Irina would turn out to be working either in the operating room or transplant service in that hospital.

He arrived in Bucharest mid-morning and headed straight to Irina's place of residence. Colentina was full of eight- to ten-story apartment buildings inhabited mostly by Chinese and Arab immigrants. Irina's housing block, however, stood out. It was a complex of two-story townhouses with open carports. Matching the apartment number to the parking space, Andrei found Irina's carport empty.

He returned to his car and called Fundeni Hospital, asking the operator to connect him to the OR. Soon he had a friendly female voice on the line. "Fundeni OR, Luiza speaking."

"Hello, Luiza, I am looking for Irina Cernea."

Luiza answered quickly. "Irina is in a case right now. Is it urgent? I can get her out."

Andrei quietly pumped a fist. He had guessed correctly. "No," he said calmly. "It's not urgent. I can look her up after work. When does she get off?"

"Let me check."

Andrei waited patiently.

"Her shift ends at nineteen-hundred." Seven p.m. He had some time.

Andrei stopped at a nearby café for a late breakfast before heading to Fundeni. The hospital was located on a sprawling campus across several city blocks, concrete-fenced and lined with tall trees, accessible via a single main security gate. Off to the side, another gate provided egress for parked cars. Andrei flashed his police identity and asked the gate guard for directions to the employee parking lot.

It was an open-air area, rather small considering the size of the hospital and the number of people it must employ. Andrei figured that many took public transportation to work. He parked outside the lot and walked among the parked cars looking for Irina's vehicle, a blue Renault with a license plate number he already knew. It took a while, but he found it.

Andrei made a mental note of its location and returned to his car. He would come back at the end of Irina's shift and follow her back to her house. He preferred to surprise her at her own carport, a quieter, more isolated spot than this busy hospital campus. He considered simply waiting for her at her apartment but decided against it. What if she didn't come back and went elsewhere first? It would be best to follow her out of the hospital.

There were several walking paths that led from the parking lot to the hospital building. Andrei explored these and repositioned his car at a suitable spot from which he could furtively spot Irina as she arrived. It was a good location that also allowed a decent view of the two-way vehicle access to the lot. He could not see Irina's parked car from this vantage point, but this did not matter. There was only one way out. He would wait for the Renault and follow it after it exited.

Andrei noted that the hospital had private security with cars that patrolled the premises. This might be a problem if he was spotted loitering around the parking lot entrance. He did not want a security car intercepting him just as Irina was walking to the lot. It might catch her attention and spook her. They seemed to pass by infrequently, but even so, Andrei decided to warn security that he would be on the premises.

His plan set, Andrei left Fundeni and returned to Irina's neighborhood. He drove around and got the lay of the land, spotting a rickety shopping center nearby and several restaurants. He searched for a suitable hotel on his mobile and found one about two miles away. He secured a room and took a long nap to make up for the night before. He needed to be sharp and alert for what he expected to be a busy evening.

At six-thirty p.m., Andrei returned to Fundeni. Again he flashed his badge, and then told the guard at the security gate his intention to interview a witness in the vicinity of the employee lot. The guard took down the description of Andrei's car and promised to notify the private patrol that he would be there.

Andrei pulled into his pre-determined spot as the sun was setting. He parked and waited patiently. The pathway that he expected Irina to take was poorly lit at dusk. He eventually spotted her walking briskly to the lot. As she passed by a light, Andrei made out her face, definitely the same as in the personnel photo he had secured from Ana's Aunt Dorina. As soon as she disappeared, he turned on his car engine and prepared to drive off after her.

The Renault failed to appear as expected. After a while Andrei opened his car door and vainly looked in the direction of the lot, wondering what was going on. Had Irina returned to the hospital via another path? Maybe she'd forgotten something.

While he contemplated his next move, flashing yellow lights caught Andrei's attention. A tow truck with a Motor Assistance insignia on its doors appeared and drove into the lot at high speed.

Maybe there was a mechanical problem with Irina's car. But Andrei could not be sure that the tow truck was for her. It had appeared far too soon after Irina's arrival. After a call for help, most tow trucks took at least half an hour to arrive, if not longer. The speed of the truck was suspicious; they usually lumbered at a slow pace.

Andrei turned off his car engine and with the noise gone, he carefully listened. He could hear the grumble of the tow truck for another minute or two before the sound ceased. After a brief spell of total silence, a loud scream pierced the sky. It was a woman's voice.

She was screaming, "*Ajutor, ajutor!*" *Help!* The second *ajutor* was abruptly cut off.

Andrei quickly got back in his car, turned on his engine, and roared into the parking lot.

CHAPTER 73

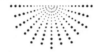

BUCHAREST, APRIL 9

The parking lot was dark. Andrei's headlights illuminated two men who were forcing a woman into the cab of the tow truck. Their faces were covered with balaclavas. One of them had his hand tightly around her mouth while the other lifted her up by the waist and danced around her kicking legs.

Momentarily blinded by Andrei's headlights, the two men froze in surprise. At that moment the woman bit the hand covering her mouth, causing one of them to scream and recoil. He forcefully slapped her in the face with his other hand.

With her face free, Andrei confirmed that the woman was Irina. He rushed out of his car, his service weapon drawn, and yelled, "Stop, police!"

The man grabbing Irina's waist let go and brandished a knife from his pocket. Andrei responded with a shot aimed at the winch of the tow truck. It made a loud metallic noise and ricocheted off the truck, smashing the back window of a nearby parked car.

The two men let go and began running, the knife falling to the ground. They wove around the parked cars and were soon swallowed by dark shrubbery along the edge of the parking lot.

Another pair of headlights appeared behind Andrei's car. Hospital security. Andrei rushed to Irina, who was lying on the ground, looking dazed. He extended her a hand. "Are you all right?"

She looked up at him, eyes wide with surprised recognition. A small stream of blood was trickling from her nostril down to her chin. She wiped it with the back of one hand while with the other she accepted Andrei's and stood up.

"What's going on here?" asked an excited security guard, an overweight young man who looked like he still belonged in high school. "Was that a shot I heard?"

Andrei flashed his badge. "Police," he said with authority. "This woman was being kidnapped. Call for help. Call 112. We need more police here."

The guard spotted the blood on Irina's face and backed away, frightened. He waddled to his car and fumbled with his two-way radio.

"What are you doing here?" asked Irina, her voice hoarse from the loud scream she had just uttered.

Andrei offered her some tissue he had fetched from his car. "Saving your life."

The lot was filled with flashing lights of the tow truck, two hospital security vehicles, and police cars from Bucharest, Sector 2. Andrei summarized the situation to a uniformed officer while another took Irina's statement in the back seat of a patrol car. Officers were sent to search the perimeter guided by additional hospital security. A forensics van arrived and Tyvek-suited technicians began examining the tow truck. The dropped knife was photographed and bagged as evidence.

Andrei gave Bucharest Police the contact for Boboc and asked them to forward their findings to Braşov, Sector 1. He then called Boboc and explained what had happened. He didn't have much time to discuss things right now, he told him. He needed to get his witness out of this scene before she totally freaked out.

The search party returned empty-handed. The two kidnappers had disappeared. Andrei gave additional statements describing the two men. There was not much to tell.

Finally, Andrei ushered Irina into the passenger seat of his car and slowly backed out of the crime scene.

"You must be hungry," said Andrei, as he drove out of the hospital campus. "Would you like something to eat?"

Irina stared at him in disbelief. "How did you find me?"

Andrei turned onto Strada Pescarilor, heading toward Irina's house. "There's a pizza joint near your place," he said, ignoring her question. "How about that?"

"You know where I live?"

Once again, Andrei did not answer. He kept driving, while Irina silently stared out the window. With each turn he took, she became increasingly agitated, realizing that he indeed did know.

"Am I under arrest?" she demanded.

"No."

"Well then, just drop me off at home." She opened her purse and searched for her house keys. "Thank you for saving me from those thugs."

Andrei gave her a side glance. "Do you live with anyone?"

"No, just myself."

"I don't think that you should stay at your home."

"Why? What do you mean?"

"What happened to your car at the parking lot?"

"It wouldn't start."

"Did you call for roadside assistance?"

"Yes."

"Did you wonder about how quickly they arrived?"

Irina paused and pondered the question. "What are you getting at?"

"I think those guys probably tampered with your car. They set you up."

"You mean this was not a random mugging?"

"Wasn't it you yourself who told me you were afraid for your life?"

They were at the small shopping center near her residence. Andrei slowed, looking for the pizza place.

"I didn't expect anything at my own workplace," said Irina.

Andrei stopped by the restaurant and turned off his engine. "Come on," he said. "Let's grab a bite and we'll talk." He exited and came around to open her door. "Then you'll gather some stuff from your place and come with me."

Irina hesitantly rose out of the car. "Is that an order?" she asked tersely. "You can't make me do it!"

"Dr. Zhulati is dead," said Andrei. "Murdered in Braşov."

"What?!" Irina stumbled and held onto the open door to avoid falling. "Oh, my God!"

"It seems to me you were next," he continued. "I got there just in time."

Andrei helped her onto the sidewalk, his hand firm around her arm. She was still off balance as they walked into the restaurant.

"You need to tell me everything you know," he said. "That's the only way I can help you."

* * *

"What happened to Zhulati?" asked Irina, toying with a slice of pizza she barely ate.

Andrei was hungry, his appetite stoked by the adrenaline surge at the parking lot. He swallowed a massive mouthful. "As I said, he is dead, murdered. I can't tell you much beyond that. It is being investigated."

"What about Enver?" she asked. "Did you look into it?"

"Yes," said Andrei. "It was not a suicide."

Irina lowered her eyes, staring blankly at a fleck of pizza crust on the table. Ordinarily it should have been Andrei asking the preliminary questions, but Andrei felt that she needed to be softened up.

"Who did it?" asked Irina, her eyes glassy.

"We don't know yet," said Andrei. "We're working on it."

Irina took a sip of beer from a can. "Such a shame," she murmured, gazing at the can.

"What?"

She picked a piece of sausage off her pizza and rolled it between her fingers. "I should have never gotten into this. Never."

Andrei did not respond. He waited for her to continue.

"The money was good. Extra cash to spend." She grimaced. "Little good it did me."

"What did you get into?" Andrei asked quietly.

"Helping them with transplants."

"How exactly?"

"I was a jack of all trades. I did the pre-op assessments, assisted in the surgeries and acted as the scrub. I then recovered the patients." Seeing Andrei's quizzical look, she explained, "Meaning that I attended to them while they were in recovery." She hesitated, then added, "It was actually the donors I recovered. Many of the recipients brought their own nurses with them for their post-op care. It was better for them, for obvious reasons."

"Who did you work for?"

"That's a complicated question."

"Why?"

"Well, it was Iancu Negrescu and Nicolae Radu who oversaw the whole business, but they used an independent contractor for a lot of the details, a third party."

"Who?"

"Someone named Cezar Kaminesky."

Andrei had begun jotting down notes as Irina spoke. When he heard that name he paused. "Did you say Cezar?"

"Yes. Do you know him?"

Andrei did not answer. He remembered one of Zhulati's recorded phone calls. It had been with a Cezar. "What exactly did Cezar do?"

"He provided personnel and infrastructure—all the bureaucratic work that was needed to keep track of tests and to match donors with recipients."

"Was Zhulati employed by Cezar?"

"The surgeons were not employees. They were independent contractors. Cezar found them and arranged their schedules. I believe they received their payments from Cezar, but the money actually came from Negrescu and Radu."

"How many doctors were there?"

"Not a lot." She thought for a moment. "Two or three maybe. Then there was the Turkish one who trained them; he was really good."

"Turkish?"

"His name is Gazioğlu. Rigorous. Cares for his patients. Excellent surgical technique."

"And the others?"

"I no longer remember their names. Recently we've been mostly working with Zhulati."

"Did all this happen at the outpatient annex at Spitatul Martinu?"

Irina looked at him with amazement. "How do you know that?"

"Why wouldn't I?"

"They did their utmost to cover their tracks."

"Who?"

"Everyone. Cezar's crew, the hospital…" She trailed off.

"You? Enver?"

She lowered her eyes again. "How did you find all this out?"

"Same way I found you," said Andrei. "Investigative police work."

She took a long gulp of beer and finished the can. "I don't know how I could imagine that we were failsafe, that we wouldn't get discovered. I was such a fool."

"Come," said Andrei as he paid the bill. "Let's go to your house."

"Then what?"

"Then you come with me, to Braşov. We'll put you under police protection and get a formal statement from you."

"What if I refuse?"

"I can have you arrested as an accessory to the crimes you just admitted. That would be the good-case scenario."

"What's the bad one?"

"I can let you go back home and leave you alone. You can wait there for the assassins to come back."

CHAPTER 74

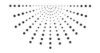

BUCHAREST TO BRAŞOV, APRIL 9

I t was nearly eleven when Andrei began driving to Braşov with Irina on board. They would arrive well past midnight. After the pizzeria, Andrei took her home to pack a suitcase. Standing guard by her carport, he kept a vigilant eye on the surroundings. All was calm.

While he waited, Andrei called the station for them to arrange a hotel in Braşov and police cover for his witness. He wasn't sure if this would happen on such short notice in the middle of the night. The alternative was to place Irina in a jail cell for her own protection, an option Andrei did not relish, given how fragile and distraught she was.

Andrei also called Ana, waking her up. She had been worried about him, having had no contact with Andrei since Iaşi. He told her about the witness he was bringing in and that it would be a long night, to not wait up for him.

Traffic on the highway was light. Irina was sulky and silent, staring out into the darkness.

"That was a crazy outfit you wore in Sfântu Gheorghe." Andrei tried to coax her into conversation with a light subject.

Irina nodded in agreement. "Our original plan was to do the interview as an internet video connection, with my face hidden."

"Yeah. That might have been less ridiculous."

"But Pista changed my mind. He said that it was not safe, that the Wi-Fi could be traced by the police."

"Pista Szabó, the hotel manager?"

"Yes."

"What is his role in the transplant business?"

"None." Irina became more animated. "He is innocent. He was just trying to help me. Leave him alone!"

Andrei did not respond. He would have to interview Szabó and decide for himself. "Are you two...?"

"Lovers?" She turned toward him. "Heavens no!"

Andrei gave her a sideways glance. "Just asking."

"I told you, didn't I? He is family." She paused. "Well...ex-family, but family nonetheless. He is a nice guy. He would be devastated if he knew that I was involved in all this."

He was also an accessory to a crime, thought Andrei. The assistance he had provided to conceal Irina, herself a criminal, exposed him to prosecution.

Andrei decided that this line of conversation was a mistake. He plunged into the heart of the matter.

"Tell me," he said. "How did one of these transplant operations happen? Describe it to me step by step."

"What do you want me to tell you? Where they cut and how they remove the kidney?"

"No, I don't need to know the technical details. Just tell me what your experience was."

"To begin with, I was notified in advance that there was a case."

"How far in advance?"

"Not far enough. Usually a week or so. I figured that's when they signed a deal with a recipient and activated an available donor. They then got a crew together in haste."

"Was there a problem with that?"

"Yes. My schedule at Fundeni was set farther in advance. So I frequently had to come up with excuses to get time off. It was a hassle."

"How often did these happen?"

"It was very random. Sometimes we'd get five or six in a row, at other times we'd go for weeks with none."

This made Andrei wonder. The bug on Dr. Zhulati seemed to indicate that he had expected several jobs. He needed to ask Irina if she knew of any upcoming jobs, but he held the thought. He was more curious about something else. "Who was the crew?"

"We did not have a normal OR crew."

Andrei had no idea what that might be. Before he had a chance to ask, she continued.

"It was just the surgeon, anesthetist, and me. That's all."

"That doesn't sound right for a complex operation like a transplant."

Irina snickered. "Well, it wasn't exactly Fundeni!"

"Okay, I get it. Who was the anesthetist?"

"A nurse anesthetist, not a doctor. They varied from case to case. They came from locum companies."

"That doesn't sound good."

"You'd be surprised," said Irina. "They were quite experienced, higher in quality than some of the surgeons."

"What was the problem with the surgeons?"

"Think about it," she said in a condescending voice. "Would any decent, successful surgeon be involved in all this?"

Andrei nodded in agreement. "But what about that Turkish guy? You said he was good."

"Gazioğlu was an exception. I think he was a founder of the enterprise. I don't know for sure, but I had an inkling that he helped set it up with Radu and Negrescu."

"All the others were no good?"

"Did you investigate Zhulati?" Irina asked dryly.

Despite his concern for discretion, Andrei could not help but chuckle. "I get your point."

She continued. "First we got the donor, early in the day. They had to get some last-minute testing before they came to me."

"Like what?"

"Some blood tests, but most important, a CT scan."

"Why a CT?"

"They had to know the renal anatomy and rule out any unexpected problems like a tumor."

"Why wasn't that done in advance?"

"These donors came from poor, rural areas—places like Moldova, Bulgaria, or Kosovo. There were no CT scans there."

Andrei thought of Yoet. He fit the bill for what she was describing.

"So I prepared the donor for kidney harvesting and then helped with the operation. As I said, I was the scrub, the circulator, and the assistant."

Andrei had some inkling of what that entailed, thanks to Ana. "How can that be?"

"You need a surgeon who is adept at working in such circumstances. For instance, if the surgeon needed some instrument that was not in the field, I'd have to break scrub, become a circulator and get it for him, then scrub back."

"Sounds cumbersome."

"It was. But what choice did we have? The more people involved in the case, the more risky it was. Right?"

Andrei nodded.

"Zhulati was a drunk and a slob. He was a pig, too. Always hitting on me. But believe it or not, he was a slick surgeon. He worked well in those circumstances."

"Then you—how did you phrase it—recovered the donor?" Andrei asked.

"Correct, I got them settled in recovery. After that, we turned our attention to the recipient. In the meantime, we stored the kidney in a special solution."

"Did you have much contact with Enver Muratovich?"

"Oh, yes, on every case."

"How so?"

"He was the one who brought in the donors, looked after them, and took them back home."

"When you say looked after them, was he a nurse? Did he know about post-op care?"

"No, of course not." She paused and stared into the darkness.

Andrei noticed that she was wiping her eyes with the back of her hand.

"He was a good man, Enver." She covered her mouth, stifling a sob. "He did his best under the circumstances. He cared about those young men. Really cared."

"You and Enver…" Andrei was hesitant. "Did you?" He was risking another rebuff as with Szabó, but he had to ask.

"A while back," she confessed. "While my life was in turmoil." She wiped her eyes again, this time with tissue she pulled out of her pocket. She collected herself and looked straight at Andrei with a serious expression. "It was all in the past."

"But you were friends?"

"We were friends, yes."

"So, once again," said Andrei, returning to his line of questioning, "how could Enver provide post-op care in some shitty hotel in a bad quarter of Braşov?"

"Oh, you know about that too?"

"Hotel Afroditei? Yes."

"How did you find *that* out?"

The name of the hotel had popped up in Boboc's audio transcript of Zhulati's phone conversations, a detail that Boboc had passed on to him. "Your last donor. He was removed from that hotel in a critical condition and taken away."

"Yoet?"

Andrei nodded.

Irina drew a loud sigh. "Oh, my God! How is he?"

"Very sick. In a hospital in Iaşi."

"Iaşi! What is he doing there?"

"Long story. Don't ask. They are not expecting him to survive."

Irina began sobbing, this time uncontrollably.

Andrei waited for her to calm down. "I gather that when Enver died, no one stepped in to care for Yoet."

"Enver saw to it that the donors were fed, their dressings were properly changed, and that they got antibiotics and pain medications." Her voice was still trembling.

"It appears that none of that was done. Yoet Tcaci became septic."

"Of course," she said. "They put too much on Enver because he was so reliable. There was no substitute for him."

"You could have done it, couldn't you? Stayed in Braşov and looked after the donor?" Andrei tried not to sound accusatory. "After all, you were the only one on the team who knew that Enver was dead."

Irina stared at him, speechless. Despite Andrei's soft tone, the accusation hit her like a slap in the face. She bent her head down and wept quietly.

"You're right," she said, avoiding his gaze. "I should have." She then looked up at Andrei, her wet eyes illuminated by the bright light of an oncoming car. "Honestly, the thought never crossed my mind. I panicked. All I thought about was my own safety. I fled Braşov as fast as I could."

Andrei had not meant to shake her up. "It's okay," he said. "Sounds like the aftercare of the donors was never your responsibility. I can understand why you did what you did."

"Now that you brought it up," replied Irina, "I can't." She covered her face with her hands.

Near midnight, Andrei stopped at a gas station where he bought espressos for the two of them. They stood alone at a dimly lit bar, the attendant busy at the cashier with another motorist.

"Do you know anyone outside the crew that you so far described who may have knowledge of this transplant operation?" Andrei asked, sipping his coffee.

Irina thought for a moment. "Well, there is Nicoleta."

"Who is that?"

"The radiology tech. She runs the CT scans."

"Nicoleta who? Do you have a last name?"

"No, I'm afraid not. I only met her occasionally. Enver knew her, though. He was always there for the CT scans. I believe she kept a special log of the donors. As you might imagine, these were not part of the hospital's regular charts."

Andrei pulled out his notebook and jotted the name down. "Is she a regular there, or is she a locum like you and Zhulati?"

"Nicoleta? Oh, she's a regular. But she does this on the side. Gets paid separately, like I do."

Andrei felt a pang of excitement. Finally, he thought, a solid link to the functional apparatus of Spitatul Martinu. "What about Administration? Someone in Administration had to know and permit access to the premises."

"I believe you're right, but I don't know who it might be. I never worked in that hospital regularly."

They finished their espressos and walked back to Andrei's car. The midnight air was cool and crisp. Irina seemed calmer, the break having helped her recover from the emotional turmoil of Andrei's questioning. As he opened the car door for her, a thought occurred to him. "This Nicoleta, the CT technician. Would she have advance knowledge of upcoming transplants?"

"She would have to," Irina answered. "Just like me, her job took her away from her regular schedule to do these."

"But she still would have to make special time for the secret pre-op scan, wouldn't she?"

"Yes. It happened at off-hours. What are you getting at?"

Andrei started the car. "Nothing. Just wanted to know."

CHAPTER 75

BUCHAREST, APRIL 8 ... MORNING

Mark took a taxi from Olga's apartment to the Athénée Palace Hotel. Traffic was light this early in the morning. Mark was still reeling from his discovery that it was Cezar Kaminesky—not Ahmet and Iancu—responsible for Dima Rusu's death. This preoccupied his thoughts, superseding the earlier pleasures of the night.

How could a supposedly wily, experienced intelligence operative like Vadim Rusu be hoodwinked by a false accusation? Mark could not fathom this, especially after having witnessed the deaths of Ahmet, Iancu, Iosif, Gazioğlu, Latif, and Serdar. What a waste of so many lives.

Mark recalled the conversation he'd had with the Commissaire of the French Interpol at an outdoor café in Budapest, where Cezar Kaminesky's name had first come up. "He is a bad character," Gérard had told him about Cezar. "A gangster."

That was for sure. But the man was also a mass murderer, whether he knew it or not. He had not only Dima Rusu's blood on his hands but those others' as well.

Mark was surprised that Cezar was letting Olga live freely in Romania. Given all that Olga knew about his activities, and certainly aware of her resentment about being made an accessory to Ahmet's murder. One would think that Cezar would be more careful with Olga. Olga's explanation that Cezar was preoccupied with a younger mistress did not convince Mark. He worried about Olga's safety. But then, she was shrewd and seasoned, experienced in her husband's crime world. Surely she could take care of herself.

They had parted with the understanding that they would keep in touch with each other. Neither, however, expected another encounter. They had received what they needed from each other, Olga's needs surprisingly similar to Mark's. Nevertheless, Mark hoped that he would somehow run into her again. After last night, Mark was no longer sure that all he harbored for Olga was pure lust.

As the peculiar obelisk at Revolution Square came into view, Mark's thoughts returned to Vadim Rusu. Someone somehow had to inform him of his deadly mistake, set him straight, and send him in pursuit of Cezar Kaminesky. Cezar, who had successfully evaded law enforcement for years, was more vulnerable when it came to Rusu and his organization.

Mark's first thought was to seek help from Interpol. Leon in Istanbul would have been helpful, but he had made it clear that he was out of reach. If Mark went to the French Embassy as Leon had suggested, he would be dealing with characters he did not know or trust. Besides, if there were elements within European law enforcement secretly allied with Rusu, who was to say that there weren't others protecting Cezar?

What about SRI? After all, he had an SRI agent readily available to discuss the matter. Mark quickly dismissed this notion, too. He found Marco Radovich and his sidekick Milan shifty and untrustworthy. Who knew what they might do with such information. Mark didn't even know why they were tailing him in the first place. No, SRI would not do.

As the taxi pulled up by the hotel's driveway, Mark decided that there was only one option. He paid the driver, exited the cab, and entered the lobby, where he settled into an armchair. He pulled out his mobile phone and dialed Sorana.

* * *

Mark found Semra sulking on a couch in the hotel suite. She was wearing her baggy red and yellow T-shirt and had her hair down. She stared stonily at a muted TV screen.

"Good morning," he said awkwardly, trying to sound chipper.

She looked up at him and did not answer. Her face was plain, with no makeup. Mark could see dark rings around her eyes. Abruptly she pointed the remote at the TV and shut it off, then swiftly got up and disappeared into the bedroom without giving Mark a second look.

Mark let out a big sigh and undressed. He headed to the shower, luxuriating under the hot stream and wondering if he had made the right decision by calling Sorana. As he dried himself off, he heard Semra moving around in the bedroom. She was obviously upset at him, and he could understand why. But he was not in the mood for an argument, although there was no way around it. He put on a hotel robe and reluctantly opened the bathroom door.

"Where have you been?" demanded Semra in an accusatory tone. She was sitting up in bed, her legs under the blanket.

Mark did not answer. Instead, he opened the unruffled covers on his side of the bed and tried to get in. Semra extended an arm and pushed him away. "Don't," she said.

Mark moved to the far edge of the bed and sat down.

"You were with that blonde, weren't you? Who is she?"

"An acquaintance from Hungary," said Mark calmly.

"Did you fuck her well?" Semra shouted. "Was she a good fuck?"

Mark looked down at his bathrobe and adjusted its edges. "I had some important business with her."

"Oh, I can just imagine!"

Semra's anger began rubbing off on Mark. "Look," he said tersely. "What I did with her is none of your business."

The comment stopped her dead in her tracks. She stared at him silently. "I knew it," she whispered.

"You knew what?"

Semra collected herself and took charge of her anger. "Remember when I told you that I am an acquired taste?"

Mark nodded. He could see where this was going.

"You obviously have no intention of acquiring it," Semra said dolefully. She scanned his face for a reaction.

Mark stayed silent, expressionless.

"You prefer *real* women, like that blonde bombshell." She put a special emphasis on *real*.

"But I *have* acquired a certain affection for you," Mark said meekly.

Semra laughed caustically. "Oh yeah?" She threw her covers off and lifted her T-shirt. "Then why don't you come and get this?" she said, spreading her legs.

She wore slim panties that left no doubt about what was within. Mark hesitated a moment, then gently pulled the covers over her. "You're right," he said, resigned, "I can't do it."

Semra looked straight ahead, avoiding Mark's gaze, and began crying quietly. "This is my lot in life," she murmured. "I'll never find the right man."

Mark edged closer to her. She did not push him away. He gently grabbed her wrist. "I don't know whether you're right about that," he said in a conciliatory tone. "All I know is that we are stuck with each other in this foreign country and we are in a perilous situation."

"How much worse can it be than Tuzla?"

"This one is more sinister," he said solemnly. "We have to leave here soon and embark on a risky journey."

"Where?"

"I don't know yet," he said. "But you have no choice. You have to come with me, unless you want to return to Istanbul by yourself."

"I can't," said Semra. "I can't go back to Beyoğlu and start all over again."

"I thought so."

They stayed silent for a while, Semra's storm fading as fast as it had erupted. Finally she broke the silence. "Are you in love with her?"

"Who, Olga?"

"Is that her name, that blonde?"

"Yes. And no, I am not," said Mark. "In fact, I don't believe I'll see her again," he added, hoping there was no telltale regret in his voice.

Semra wiped her face with the back of her hands. Her expression softened. "Good," she said.

Mark pulled back the covers again and this time slid in with no resistance. "I've had a long night," he said. "I need a nap." He yawned.

Semra too slid in. "I had a long night, too," she said, "waiting for you."

They lay under the covers side-by-side, looking at the ceiling.

"I may not be the right man for you," Mark said calmly, "but I am all you have." He turned and looked at her. "Until we find a suitable new life for you, you'll have to put up with me."

Semra giggled. "That might be for the rest of your life."

Mark turned back and stared at the ceiling again. *Let's hope not*, he thought, as he closed his eyes.

CHAPTER 76

BRAȘOV, APRIL 10

The baby's cries woke him. Wearily, Andrei eyed the bedside clock. He had slept only about two hours. Ana's side of the bed was empty. He stumbled out of bed and shuffled into the kitchen in his pajamas, eyes half-mast.

"Who was she?" asked Ana. She sat across from the baby, who was eagerly leaning into a spoonful of formula in her high chair.

Andrei yawned, kissed the baby and his wife, and headed toward the steaming coffee pot. "The traveler nurse from Bucharest," he said. "The one that your Auntie Dorina told us about. Her name is Irina Cernea."

He had deposited Irina in a hotel not far from Afroditei, in surroundings that were only slightly better. A uniformed officer assigned by the station had met them there.

"Why did you bring her to Brașov?" asked Ana, as she continued to feed the baby.

"She needs protection," said Andrei. "She was attacked yesterday by people intent on killing her. I thwarted the attack."

Ana stopped, a full spoonful in her hand, and turned to Andrei, who was leaning on the kitchen counter, sipping coffee. "Oh, my God, are you okay?"

"Yes." Andrei smiled at her. "Two guys. They weren't very good. One had a knife, I had a gun. They scrambled pretty quickly when I fired a warning shot."

The baby protested, leaning toward the food Mom held up. Ana hastily shoved the spoon into her mouth. "Is this related to the kidney business?" she asked.

"I don't know for sure," said Andrei. "I think so."

"So what now?"

"I'm going to the station," Andrei answered. "All of a sudden there is a lot going on. This case is beginning to crack open."

Ana stood up and approached him. "Be careful, will you? I don't like hearing that you fired your gun."

Andrei gave her a hug and a gentle peck on the lips. "You're a good sport for putting up with all this," he said. "And your help has been invaluable. Without your connection to Dorina, I would not have discovered this witness."

Ana returned to the baby. She lifted her up and began burping her.

"She was friends with Enver," Andrei continued. "She's pretty distraught about what happened to him."

"Poor thing." Ana softly patted the baby's back.

"She is a pretty experienced nurse," he added. "Works at Fundeni in Bucharest."

"And she moonlights here at Martinu? Why?"

"For the extra money," said Andrei. "Now she regrets it."

Ana left the kitchen to put the baby down. She returned and began washing her hands at the sink. "Are you going to get in trouble with this investigation?"

Andrei poured himself more coffee. "I don't think so." He took a sip. "So far, Dalca is backing me up. But let me tell you, it's been tough. There was pushback from the Governor's Office with my investigation of Martinu. Then, when Dr. Zhulati was murdered, that was also on me. Dalca made it clear that if there were any more screw-ups, I would be in trouble."

"You'll be selling groceries at the Sanpetru Market?" Ana said in jest, caressing Andrei's cheek.

"I have a better idea," said Andrei. "I'll stay home and take care of our babies, and you can support us."

"What babies?" Ana shook her head skeptically. "We only have one."

Andrei put his coffee down and lifted her up. She was light as a feather. He started toward the bedroom.

"What are you doing?" Ana giggled.

He didn't answer. He deposited her onto the bed. "We'd better hurry up and make another," he said, as he removed his pajamas.

* * *

Boboc was exceptionally sarcastic. "Why, if it isn't our own Sherlock Holmes and Hercule Poirot, all in one!" He gave Andrei a forceful slap on the back, jolting him forward.

"Cut it out, will you?" demanded Andrei, annoyed.

They had run into each other outside the station, in the parking lot. Boboc was gobbling a bulky breakfast sandwich in one hand, a coffee cup in the other.

"After the Zhulati fiasco and your slip-up at Spitatul Martinu, I thought you would be toast." Boboc grinned and took a sip of coffee. "But look at you now, good as gold."

Andrei raised his eyebrows, startled by the remark. "What do you know about Martinu?" The complaint that the hospital's CEO issued was supposedly confidential between Dalca and Andrei.

"I hear that they were upset about your interrogation of that bigwig in Administration."

"Who told you that?"

Boboc took a big bite of his sandwich and let Andrei remain in suspense as he chewed slowly. "Silviu Vulpe," he said finally. "He called me yesterday."

"Who the hell is he?"

"The hospital's security chief," said Boboc. "He and I go back a long way. Army buddies back in the day. He was in the police force for a short while but was injured; shot in the spine and ended up with a weak leg. He's worked private security since."

"What did he say?"

"That you accused them of conducting illicit transplants." Boboc took another sip of coffee. "He told me that we were not allowed in his hospital unless we had a warrant."

"Yes," said Andrei, eyes downcast. "That is a roadblock to the investigation."

Boboc gave Andrei a friendly slap on the back. "No worries, *boss*." He polished off the rest of his sandwich as Andrei gave him a skeptical look. "The other reason Vulpe called was to tell me that if I needed any special favors at Martinu, he would see to it."

Andrei exhaled in relief. "Good to know. But right now we have enough on our hands without needing to step into that minefield."

"So I hear," said Boboc. "What was all that in Bucharest yesterday?"

"Did they send you any information?"

"No, not yet. But I haven't checked today's incoming messages yet."

They saluted a pair of uniformed officers heading to their patrol car. Boboc waited for them to get out of earshot. "So, you have a second witness?" he asked.

"Yeah," said Andrei proudly. "And this one can link Muratovich to the illegal transplant operation."

"Does that tie in with that donor's wife in Iaşi?"

"In some ways it does. They are both credible witnesses who link Muratovich to the transplant business."

"Wonderful," said Boboc. He took his last sip of coffee. "Where are they?"

"Evelina Tcaci is in Iaşi. I left her with Geofri Funar. He will forward a formal transcript of her testimony to us."

"And the other one, the Bucharesti?"

"Here, downtown, in a hotel. She is ready to sing."

"Sing what?"

"The details of how the transplant ring operates at Spitatul Martinu."

Boboc took a step back. "Woo," he said. "You got that nailed?"

"She doesn't have all the specifics, but it is a long way toward putting the puzzle together."

"What about Muratovich? Does your witness know who whacked him?"

"No," said Andrei, as they headed toward the station entrance. "That is still a blank." He was reluctant to reveal what Corneliu Balaş had told him about the mysterious Russian connection. Andrei's contact with SRI was a secret between him and his boss. He would reveal this information solely to Dalca. "But we're coming along. What about you? Anything new on the Zhulati murder?"

"The DNA matched," Boboc said, as he climbed the stairs ahead of Andrei with surprising agility. When they arrived on the second story landing he stopped and waited for Andrei to catch up. "Alin Barbu is our man."

Now it was Andrei's turn to raise his eyebrows.

Boboc continued. "Dalca is happy as a clam," he chuckled. "We are bringing Barbu in."

"Good news," commented Andrei. "Still, quite puzzling, isn't it?"

"I know," Boboc confirmed. "Doesn't jibe with Muratovich."

"Doesn't," murmured Andrei.

Boboc pulled his pants up. "Maybe Barbu can explain it. I am hoping to interrogate him soon. Do you want to be there?"

"Certainly," said Andrei. "But I seriously doubt that he'll explain anything."

CHAPTER 77

BRAȘOV, APRIL 10

"You look like you've been working hard," said Dalca, leaning back in his chair.

It was late morning and Andrei indeed looked haggard, hair askew, face pale, and eyes lined with dark rings. He sat in front of his chief and nodded in agreement. "Yes, sir."

"I've heard bits and pieces of what you've been up to," said Dalca. "Fill me in on the details."

Dalca was civilian and casual, wearing a crisp white shirt with an open collar and slacks. His demeanor matched his appearance. Andrei gathered that his boss's opinion of the case had improved since their last meeting in the garbage-strewn alley near the Zhulati murder scene.

But before Andrei had a chance to speak, Dalca interjected. "Start with Bucharest, will you? I got a call from the police chief there about an assault and kidnapping attempt."

"Did they get the two assailants?" asked Andrei.

"He didn't say. Actually he mostly had questions about what you were doing in their turf."

"I was picking up Irina Cernea, my informant. She works at Fundeni. "

"Right. I recall giving you the green light on that."

"As it turned out, I intercepted two guys who were abducting her in the parking lot. They scrambled away fast."

"The Budapest chief said shots were fired."

"One warning shot," said Andrei. "Nothing serious."

"It damaged a car that belonged to a doctor who works there. We're on the hook for that."

"Shit." Andrei recalled that his bullet ricocheted off the tow truck, shattering the back window of a car. In the heat of the moment he had not paid much attention to it.

"Never mind," said Dalca. "So, was the witness helpful?"

"Yes," Andrei answered proudly. "She confirms that there indeed is an illicit transplant ring in Braşov. She worked their surgeries. She linked Enver Muratovich to the enterprise."

"Is she credible?"

"Absolutely," said Andrei. "She is ready to give us a statement under oath."

"What do you make of this abduction attempt?"

"I don't think it was random," said Andrei. "It appeared to have been planned. I think they intended to kill her, like Zhulati. She is part of the same enterprise that is being decimated. It was her turn."

"Is that why you're asking for protection for her?"

"Yes. We need her." Andrei was adamant. "She is a better witness than Zhulati would have been. More reliable and better yet, sober."

"I'll provide the cover," said Dalca. He folded his arms and regarded Andrei. "You realize that all this is good news but also bad news."

"What's the bad news?"

"Now that this local transplant ring is confirmed, I'll have to announce it to my chief and the Governor."

"And the news media," Andrei added glumly.

"It has the potential of igniting a firestorm," Dalca said.

Andrei did not respond. This was Dalca's problem, not his.

"In some ways I wish we had left that suicide alone," Dalca continued, referring to Enver. "I know we couldn't, but…"

"We've opened a big can of worms," Andrei conceded.

"So what else do you have in that can of worms? What happened in Iaşi?"

"I located the donor," said Andrei. "He is very sick and is expected to die. If so, this will be yet another murder in our jurisdiction related to this case."

"That will make three," said Dalca. "Muratovich, Zhulati, and this man."

"His name is Yoet Tcaci," Andrei said. "And he has a wife who appeared on the scene. Moldovan peasants. The wife is also a decent witness. She confirmed that Enver Muratovich recruited them with promise of monetary reimbursement. She shed some light onto the recruiting process and pre-surgical arrangements."

"Where is this witness now?"

"With Iaşi Police. I have a helpful counterpart there, a guy named Geofri Funar. He is handling the Tcacis. He will forward us a formal report of her interrogation."

"I know Funar," said Dalca. "A salty old dog. A bit callous, but a good investigator."

"That's him all right." Andrei smiled at Dalca's dead-on description. The chief was obviously well connected with the greater world of Romanian law enforcement.

"We also seem to be making some headway with the Zhulati fiasco," said Dalca.

"So I hear," Andrei replied. "Alin Barbu's DNA matched the blood on Zhulati's fingernails."

"What do you think—did this scumbag whack Muratovich, too?"

Andrei hesitated, searching for a suitably worded answer. "Let's see how his interrogation goes."

"You don't think so, do you?"

"I hate to pass premature judgments on the case. The guy isn't even apprehended yet."

"Come on, Costiniu. I thought you were not a bullshitter. Cut it out and tell me your hunches."

"Okay," said Andrei with a sigh. "The Muratovich job was a sophisticated hit. It is more akin to the assassination of Nicolae Radu in Budapest, a clean hit with an attempted cover-up. Zhulati, on the other hand, was sloppy. The killer left significant evidence at the scene, as one might expect from a junky street criminal. I don't think Barbu is capable of the better planned, fake hanging of Muratovich. Heck, I even doubt that the old witch, his landlady, would allow a guy like Barbu onto her property."

Dalca nodded, and signaled for Andrei to continue.

"Then we have the attempt on Irina Cernea in Bucharest," said Andrei. "Clearly also planned but once again, sloppy. Not a very professional job."

"Did you have anyone else in mind that might be behind all this?"

"My SRI contact gave me a hint." Andrei said this nonchalantly.

Dalca's eyes widened. He leaned forward on his desk and clasped his hands together.

Pleased with the chief's reaction, Andrei continued. "A Russian operative. Former secret service. He now runs a security company and has the apparatus to dispatch assassins."

"Whoa!" Dalca recoiled into his seat with a puzzled expression, trying to absorb the news. "I don't get it," he said. "What do the Russians have to do with this?"

"This guy is super-secret," said Andrei. "The info on him is still hazy. But I have the impression that this is not an official Russian government sting. It's personal."

"Why? What's his motive?"

"Don't know," said Andrei. "My SRI guy doesn't, either."

Dalca rubbed the sides of his chin with his hand. "This is too big for us in Braşov," he said.

"Chief, I am being guided by the instruction you gave me at the beginning."

"Which one? 'Don't fuck up'? 'You're on a leash'?"

Andrei chuckled. "No, sir!" He said it in jest, with military emphasis. "The one about keeping the investigation close to Braşov. So, for now I am not pursuing this Russian business."

"Good man."

"But I do have a couple of avenues to explore, if you permit me."

"Costiniu, are you fucking with me?"

"No, sir. Just saying…"

They were both smiling now, Dalca onto Andrei's ruse. "What? What avenues?" Dalca asked with mock austerity.

"I do have the names of the French Interpol and American FBI connections in Budapest."

"Who are they?"

"The French guy is an old veteran from the *Sûreté*. His name is Claude Gérard. I might be able to contact him."

"And the American?"

"His name is Mark Kent. He also is a mysterious figure. The guy vanished from the scene soon after the Negrescu hit. No one knows where he is. I might have a shot at him if I contact the FBI, through the American Embassy."

"So, one or both of these guys could put this together for us, right?"

"The outside part of it, perhaps," said Andrei. "Budapest, and this Russian that may be ordering the hits. I am not sure they would help much with the details of what's happening in Braşov."

"Except for the Muratovich hit?"

"Maybe."

"Are you going to go for it?" asked Dalca.

"Who, the Frenchman or the American?"

"Either."

"Do you want me to?"

"It is enticing," said Dalca. "But it seems to me that you should stick to my instruction to keep it close to home."

"Right. I'll have my work cut out for me, with Cernea, the Tcacis, and Alin Barbu. If some opportunity comes up to contact these others, I'll see what I can do."

Dalca stood up, came around his desk and leaned back on it. He looked down at Andrei. "You know, Costiniu, when you screwed up with Zhulati, I began doubting myself about trusting you with this assignment. But now, you have redeemed yourself. We are back on track."

"Thank you, sir." Andrei also stood up and took a couple of steps back, facing his boss directly. "Do you want to hear something funny?"

Dalca stiffened. "I don't think so. I'm not in any mood for jokes."

Andrei hesitated.

"Come on, out with it." Dalca sat on the edge of his desktop and dangled his legs. He wore fancy Italian loafers with no socks.

"This American, Mark Kent. He is originally Turkish. He immigrated to America when he was young."

"What's so funny about that?"

"Nicolae Radu, the first one to be murdered, is also originally Turkish. He immigrated to Romania."

"A coincidence." Dalca wasn't impressed.

"I don't think so." Still standing, Andrei leaned forward, resting his arms on the back of his chair. "My source at SRI says that these two, Kent and Radu, were schoolmates in Turkey. They were friends. I don't know what to make of that," he added, "but it is very intriguing."

"We'll probably never know." Dalca stood up and returned to his chair. The meeting was over.

But Andrei wasn't finished. "Chief, we need to come up with a plan to apprehend the transplant ring and charge those who allowed it to operate at Spitatul Martinu."

Dalca looked up at Andrei, who could tell his boss was annoyed. "How do you propose to do that? The gang is defunct, isn't it?"

"Not quite," said Andrei. "The gang that Radu and Negrescu ran may be out of business, but there is another element that is still in operation."

"What element?"

"A guy named Cezar Kaminesky. He's originally Polish. I looked him up. A gangster with a long rap sheet that goes back decades. Drugs, smuggling, prostitution, human trafficking. He was implicated in a couple of murders but escaped conviction."

"Is he local? I never heard of him."

Andrei saw that Dalca was intrigued. "No. Bucharest mostly, although he operates in other locales."

"So, what does he have to do with the transplant business?"

"According to my informant Cernea, he was an independent contractor for Radu and Negrescu who provided infrastructure for their transplants. Lab work, secretarial work, hiring doctors and technical staff, that sort of thing. Apparently he went into the business himself, for the whole shebang. The transplants."

"At Martinu?"

"I believe so."

"Shall we bring him in?"

"As far as I can gather, this Cezar is a slippery guy. Currently there are several warrants for his arrest out of Bucharest, but he has gone underground."

"Wonderful," said Dalca, facetiously. "So why are you bringing this up?"

"I think that there will be more illicit transplants at Martinu. If we lay low and wait for one, we might be able to catch them in the act, in flagrante delicto."

"Exactly how do you propose to do that?"

"Through Irina Cernea. She was their main nurse. She is likely to receive advance notice."

"How is she supposed to do that when she is under our protection?" objected Dalca. "Besides, she is Bucharest-based. She would have to return there if we put her up to that ruse. In that case we would have to arrange protection with Bucharest Police. I spoke with the chief there and I don't like the guy. It's too complicated."

"I agree," said Andrei. "We need to keep her here, under our eyes."

Andrei approached the desk and leaned on it. He was now facing down his chief, who looked up at him from his chair.

"I can use Irina's connections to make this happen."

"What connections?"

"Give me some leeway, Chief, and I'll produce results."

Dalca looked skeptical. "I don't like it," he said. "But what the hell. I already went out on a limb with you. I may as well go all the way."

"Thanks." Andrei took a step back from the desk.

"But if the bough breaks," said Dalca ominously, "we will both fall."

He reached for his desk phone and, before tapping a number, added, "And there is no safety net below."

CHAPTER 78

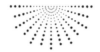

CHIŞINĂU, APRIL 8

"Good afternoon, Boss."

Boris barged into Rusu's office unannounced. Rusu sat on one of several armchairs arranged around a coffee table in a corner of his spacious office, receiving a manicure from a woman on a low stool.

"What is it?" Rusu asked abruptly, right hand extended as the woman, black hair covering her bent face, worked a cuticle pusher on his index finger. He was preoccupied with a mobile phone in his free hand.

Boris settled into an armchair facing Rusu and crossed his legs. He was dressed impeccably as always—crisp blue Italian suit, open-collared shirt with his trademark earphone-shaped cuff links. He observed the manicurist.

"New girl?" he asked.

The woman stopped and looked up at Boris. She was a slender, dark-skinned young woman, barely an adult.

"Dika's daughter," said Rusu, patting her hair with his unfinished right hand. Dika was Rusu's regular. "Who do you get yours from?" He looked up from his phone. "Do you still prefer those cute boys?" he asked mockingly.

Boris's sexual proclivities were well known, dating back many years. It was a source of gossip within the macho military culture of their social milieu. Rusu, who placed more importance on meritocracy, didn't care. Boris's competence mattered more than his personal tastes.

Boris ignored the question and plunged into why he was there. "We received a referral from Bucharest for a new client, a Turk."

Rusu did not look up from his phone. "Is that why you are disturbing me?" he murmured. "Just refer them to our client relations department."

Boris nervously played with a cuff link and watched the manicurist as she worked a cuticle nipper on Rusu's hand. Rusu turned to her and said, "There's a small hangnail here; really annoying." He pointed to his ring finger. "Can you get that?"

The young woman nodded.

"Boss, believe me, you want to know about this client. His name is Metin Özgür." He pronounced the name in proper Turkish.

"Doesn't ring a bell," said Rusu, watching the manicurist.

"I checked out the name. He lives in America. He also has an American name."

Boris looked pleased with the removed hangnail and relaxed his hand, leaving it in the care of the manicurist as he looked up at his assistant, annoyed.

Boris continued. "His name is Mark Kent."

Rusu suddenly jerked his hand and almost bolted out of his chair. The manicurist screamed as the nipper cut into his finger.

"Oww!" Rusu looked at a thin stream of blood running down his nailbed.

"Oh, I'm so sorry," cried the young woman, in a panic. "So sorry." She pulled Rusu's hand back and pressed a small cotton swab on the tip of the finger.

"Never mind," he said gently to her. "I've been through worse. It's not your fault." Rusu turned to Boris. "I knew it!" he shouted. "Didn't I tell you that the son of a bitch was not dead?"

"Yes, Boss. You're right, as usual." Boris was at his obsequious best.

"Where did you say the referral came from?"

"Bucharest Chamber of Commerce."

"How the hell did he manage that, approaching us this way?"

"Who knows?"

"What do you suppose he is after?"

Boris raised his eyebrows and lifted his hands in resignation.

"Well, you'd better find out before we let him in here," Rusu barked.

"Do you want me to engage the guy?" asked Boris. "We could just ignore the request."

"Are you kidding? Of course we will engage him!"

"All right, Boss. Just asking."

"After all the trouble we've been through to apprehend him, do you think I'll pass up this chance?" Rusu removed the cotton from his finger. It was no longer bleeding. He motioned for the manicurist to continue with the cuticle job.

"Just find out what his intentions are. If he plays this client game and pretends to engage our services, go along with it. Make sure you bring him here to Chişinău. I want him on my turf."

"Understood."

"And no fighting, no violence. He comes here alive!"

"Yes, sir." Boris stood up to leave.

As the door closed and Rusu was alone again with the manicurist, she asked, "Would you like some varnish on your nails?"

"No," he said distractedly. "No need to make them shine right now."

CHAPTER 79

BUCHAREST, APRIL 8

Mark and Semra took an outdoor table at the rooftop restaurant of the Athénée Palace Hotel. It was late for lunch and most tables were empty.

Mark looked at his watch. "I slept too long," he said. He still felt tired.

"You needed it, after your *expedition* last night." Semra placed an icy emphasis on *expedition*.

A waiter brought them menus. Mark was thankful as they both fell silent, examining the offerings.

After a few minutes, Mark pushed back his chair and stood up. "Order me a salade niçoise and a beer," he instructed Semra. "I have to go to the bathroom real quick."

It was a small, splendid men's room, extravagantly renovated with modern fixtures. There were two urinals with a marble divider in between. One was occupied by a corpulent old man who was doing his business slowly. Mark took the other and eyed the bald, bearded old man through his peripheral vision. He was thankful that he did not have prostate problems yet. He'd be done quickly. He concentrated on himself.

A sudden sigh, loud as if gulping for air, broke him out of his

481

reverie. He looked aside and was surprised that the old man was no longer there.

Mark heard shuffling steps and a cry of protest behind him. He quickly zipped his pants and turned around to find Marco Radovich facing him, well within his personal space.

"Hey, stop that," yelled the old man as Mark saw a tall figure pushing him toward the restroom door by the lapel. The man was unsuccessfully struggling to zip himself up. Milan opened the door and shoved the man out. He then turned back and stood in front of the door, keeping guard.

"What is this?" asked Mark in protest. He tried to appear aggrieved despite the butterflies in his stomach.

"Mr. Kent," said Radovich. "Doctor," he corrected himself. "I thought we had a deal."

Radovich was close enough that his protruding belly almost touched Mark. He raised his dark glasses and looked up at Mark with squinty eyes. Mark noted that one eye, the right one, had a discolored cornea. He had suffered some sort of injury to it. Mark realized that maybe this was why he wore dark glasses indoors.

"We did," said Mark, trying to appear blasé. He took a step back toward the urinal and felt it press against the back of his leg. There was no room to retreat.

"Then why did you not inform us that you were to attend a funeral yesterday?"

Mark looked beyond Radovich toward the door. Milan stood there, arms folded at his chest, and gave him a menacing smile.

"I didn't think I needed to," he answered Radovich, "since your big bear here"—he pointed to Milan—"was following me."

Mark tried to evade the violation of his personal space by stepping aside. This activated the electronic flush of the urinal, water flowing copiously and loudly. It momentarily distracted all three and caused Mark to look behind. When he turned back, Radovich had finally stepped away from him.

Mark took immediate advantage of the breathing room and sidestepped further, toward a sink. "He was quite noticeable," he added. He then turned around to wash his hands. He took his time, observing the two SRI operatives through a mirror.

Radovich waited patiently for Mark to finish and when he turned around, said, "Dr. Kent, perhaps you don't know us Romanians. We are very bureaucratic people. We like to adhere to rules."

Really? Mark wanted to say in mock disbelief, but he held his tongue.

"Regardless of whether we knew where you were, we still needed you to register your whereabouts with us."

"This is ridiculous," Mark protested. He raised his voice. "What do you really want from me? Just come out and say it!" Mark made a move toward Radovich to push him away.

"There is no need to get aggressive, sir." Radovich put an arm up to stop him, while with his other hand he opened his jacket to display a gun within a shoulder holster.

Milan had taken a step forward toward Mark. Radovich stared him down, causing him to halt.

"Let me just warn you that if you don't do as we ask, there will be consequences." Radovich closed the flap and buttoned his jacket. "And you won't like them."

"Like what?" Mark was still in protest mode.

"We can place you under arrest, you and your lady friend," he said, gritting his teeth. "You might tolerate our interrogation methods but I doubt that she will."

Milan chuckled.

The threat worked. Mark loosened his stance. "All right. I will try to be more cooperative from now on."

Someone tried to open the bathroom door, knocking loudly when Milan held his hand against it. Milan opened the door slightly and barked at the man that it was occupied.

When the door closed again, Radovich asked, "Doctor, where were you last night?"

"Here at the hotel, where else?"

"Please don't treat us like fools." Radovich was exasperated. He looked down at his feet and rubbed his forehead. "We know from the surveillance cameras that you weren't here. You returned around half past six this morning."

Mark felt his face flush. It was a clumsy, stupid answer. He should have known better.

"Once again, Doctor, where were you?"

"I was with a prostitute," he blurted out. "It's a private thing, if you catch my drift. I don't want to broadcast it to the world."

Radovich and Milan exchanged glances. "What about your lady here?" asked Radovich. "Isn't she enough for you?"

"Well…you know how it is. When you're familiar with someone…you maybe want a different taste."

Mark had never been a liar. In his youth, his inability to tell a believable lie had gotten him in trouble. Now, since arriving in Europe and experiencing a series of life-threatening events, Mark had become quite adept at lying. He was particularly proud of an episode where he had lied through his teeth to a Hungarian detective named Zoltán as he was being interrogated about a street fight. He had been quite convincing.

"My God," said Milan loudly. "That woman of yours is gorgeous. Refusing her for another woman is a crime."

Milan's outburst surprised both Radovich and Mark. They stared at him in silence. Radovich lifted his glasses and gave him a dirty look. Milan hung his head like a scolded dog. He stepped back and leaned on the door, eyes downcast.

"A prostitute all night long," said Radovich. "That is quite expensive. Can you afford that?"

"I am here as a guest of Iancu Negrescu's children," answered Mark readily. "They are paying for all this." He swept his arms around the room. "I discreetly asked Vasile to make some arrangements for me and he was glad to oblige. Their chauffeur drove my lady back to the hotel from their residence."

Mark felt on firm footing. The tale he was spinning made sense. He hated to involve the Negrescus in it, but he figured they knew how to deal with characters like Radovich.

"What was the name of this prostitute?" asked Radovich. He pulled a small notepad from his inner pocket.

"Bridgette," said Mark, a name he had picked off the top of his head. "I don't know her last name."

Radovich had begun writing but stopped and looked at Mark, dissatisfied.

"She was quite good," Mark added quickly. "Especially if you are into S&M. Are you?"

Radovich ignored the bait. "Where did you spend the night with her?"

Mark thought for a moment. "I have no idea," he said. He needed to pick a place far from Olga's neighborhood. "It was a hotel near the airport." He thought for a second. "Doxa," he said. He had seen ads for this hotel at the airport when he arrived.

Radovich jotted that down. "All right," he said calmly. He handed Mark another business card. "We expect to hear from you soon." He then nodded to Milan, who opened the door for him.

* * *

Mark slid into his chair at the restaurant and let out a loud sigh.

"Where have you been?" demanded Semra.

"Don't ask. I got hung up at the restroom." He looked at the huge salad in front of him. Semra had already finished a hamburger and was working on the last of her fries. Suddenly he no longer had an appetite. Mark waved at the waiter and asked that the salad be boxed for him.

"What's the matter with you? Are you all right?" Semra sensed a change in Mark's demeanor.

"No, I am not all right," he said. "We need to leave Romania as soon as possible."

CHAPTER 80

BUCHAREST, APRIL 9 ... EARLY MORNING

The knock on the door came past one a.m. "Laundry service."

Mark and Semra were dozing off in the living room of their suite with their street clothes on. Mark stumbled up and opened the door to two men in white coveralls, pushing two laundry carts partly filled with towels and sheets.

The men scrambled into the room and closed the door. They were young, slender, and quick. Mark noted that they wore dark outfits beneath their bunny-suit coveralls with black military-style boots protruding beneath. They each had a right-sided bulge on their waist that outlined a holstered weapon.

The two men brought their laundry carts into the middle of the room and rapidly disgorged their contents. "Hurry, get in!" one of them ordered.

Semra looked at Mark quizzically. Mark had told her that they would be picked up and transported to a different country, but he had not known how. Mark stared into one of the laundry carts. It was large enough to accommodate a single person. He nodded to Semra to get into the other. She hesitantly complied.

"Your luggage?" asked the man.

Mark pointed to their bags by the edge of a sofa. As the two men quickly gathered them up, he slipped into the laundry cart.

Soon they were covered with towels and sheets, their luggage also within, awkwardly pressing on their bodies as the carts exited the suite and rolled down the hallway. It was a claustrophobic experience, and Mark was thankful that he did not suffer from it. He knew that Semra didn't either, since she had previously endured Gazioğlu's tool shed.

As they stopped and waited by an elevator, Mark's apprehension about what they were doing was amplified. Would the SRI characters he was trying to evade somehow track him down anyway? Were his rescuers likely to be worse than Radovich and Milan?

His thoughts were interrupted by the ding of the arriving elevator. He again concentrated on the sounds and feel of where the laundry cart was going. He hoped that this would end soon.

Mark and Semra emerged from the laundry carts in the back of a large van soon after it departed the hotel premises. Mark figured that it had been parked by a loading dock in the back of the building, where it would not have been noticed at this time of the night.

The van momentarily stopped to allow them easy footing out of their hiding spots. It was spacious, filled with several empty laundry carts in its cargo area. Up front was a row of seats behind the driver. One of the men, still in white coveralls, guided them onto the seats. The other one drove.

The van slowly made its way through deserted streets, obeying traffic lights and speed limits. It then stopped on a dark roadside beyond the outskirts of Bucharest.

"All right," said the driver. "Time to get out."

Mark and Semra emerged into the chilly night guided by their rescuers. Mark got a first look at the van that had hustled them out of the Athénée Palace. It was a large Mercedes-Benz Sprinter bearing the insignia of what he gathered was a commercial laundering company.

They walked a short distance down a dirt road, guided by the two men, to where they could see red taillights. It was another van, its engine alive and humming, white smoke emanating from its exhaust.

There were two men waiting for them there, both also in white coveralls. This pair looked different from the ones accompanying Mark and Semra. One was older and corpulent, the other merely a teenager. Their coveralls were authentic and featured the same insignia as the ones on the Mercedes Sprinter.

The two pairs of men exchanged words in Romanian. The real launderers then headed for their van while Mark's rescuers removed their bunny suits at the roadside. One of them invited Mark and Semra into the new, smaller van. It looked familiar, similar to the one that had come searching for him in Tarık's Bodrum villa.

The men themselves, stripped of their bunny suits, now looked fearfully familiar. Nimble in their dark paramilitary uniforms and bearing the same side arms Mark had seen in his Budapest abductors, they were undoubtedly Vadim Rusu's men.

* * *

The new van took off at high speed and was soon on a highway.

"Where are we going?" asked Mark.

"We will change vehicles at the Moldovan border," answered the man on the passenger seat. He turned around and examined Mark and Semra's silhouettes. "We have almost five hours until then," he said. "You may as well get some sleep."

Semra dozed off right away, quietly snoring with her head sharply tilted. Mark was tired, but in his apprehension sleep did not come easily. He slept in brief spells full of vivid, frightening dreams. Otherwise his thoughts were occupied with what he was doing. He was surprised by how swiftly Vadim Rusu's organization had sprung into action after he called Sorana. There had been a few back-and-forth text messages between Mark and Sorana's contact at the Bucharest Chamber of Commerce. By that evening he had received notice to pack up and be ready for a transport that would arrive after midnight.

The road was dark and nearly deserted. The men up front remained quiet. Mark was impressed with their efficiency. Their ruse had been perfect. The laundry company was most likely one that regularly served the Athénée Palace. They had not aroused any suspicion.

And so here he was, thought Mark, on his way to Chișinău, a fate he had heretofore fearfully dodged.

He had no idea what kind of a man Rusu would turn out to be, how he would receive the news that Mark was bringing, or what he would do with Mark afterwards. Still, throwing himself into the arms of Rusu seemed like a better option than remaining exposed in Romania to the likes of Radovich. In Hungary and Turkey, he had had protectors he could count on. In Romania, he had none.

A sudden jolt of the van startled him. Mark opened his eyes and realized that he had indeed drifted into a brief spell of deep sleep amid his thoughts. A bright ray of sunshine at his window forced his eyes shut. He heard one of his rescuers, the man on the passenger side, exit the van. Soon the side door of the van slid open.

Semra stretched and yawned. She looked outside with curiosity. "Where are we?"

They were on an isolated roadside again, this time well lit by the morning sun. Traffic was scant, mostly commercial trucks.

The man gave Semra a helping hand out of the van. "We're at the border," he said. "A few kilometers from the Albita checkpoint."

Mark exited next and stretched his stiff legs. He breathed in the crisp country air and examined the surroundings. Not much here. Flat, arid landscape as far as the eye could see. He wondered what they were doing here. The driver was also out of the van now, quietly conversing on his mobile. Mark remembered being told that they would exchange vehicles at the border.

Sure enough, a car appeared on the horizon and rapidly approached them, coming to a halt behind the van. It was a dark, late-model S-Class Mercedes. A man emerged from the passenger side and stood smiling, his eyes glued on Mark. He did not have the cloned look of Rusu's paramilitaries. He was older, forties perhaps, with a hint of white at the temples. His rich, well-coiffed hair was slicked back with oil. He was tall and slim, handsome, with deep-set eyes and a square jaw. He wore an obviously expensive suit, with a crisp, open-collar shirt.

He approached Mark and courteously extended his right hand. "Dr. Mark Kent," he said in a thick Slavic accent. "Such a pleasure to finally meet you."

Mark noticed a peculiar cuff link on the man's wrist, shaped like an earphone. He hesitantly shook hands.

"My name is Boris Petrov," he said, shaking Mark's hand firmly. "I'll be your host in Moldova."

Semra came beside Mark and gazed at the man, catching his attention. Boris froze and gazed back at her, forgetting to pull his hand back from Mark's. They momentarily stood there, an awkward threesome, the men arrested in a handshake.

Boris finally took his hand back and said, "And who might this young lady be?"

"Semra Karacan," said Mark. "From Istanbul."

Boris gave her a keen look over, prompting Semra to bashfully check herself. He took a step toward her and gently grabbed her hand. "*Memnun oldum,*" he said, in near-perfect Turkish, *so happy*. He bowed and lifted the back of her hand to his lips.

"Oh," said Semra, surprised. She nervously combed her hair with her free hand while observing Boris's lips on her hand. "*Merhaba.*" *Hello*, she managed, in a lame response.

Boris straightened and placed his palm on Semra's back. "Please," he said politely in English. He pointed to the Mercedes. "Be my guest."

His driver had opened the back door and stood at attention. Semra turned to Boris, their faces close to each other. "Thank you," she said, and let him lead her into the car.

Mark stood on the side of the road, amused at having been momentarily forgotten. He watched Boris fuss over Semra. After she entered the car, Boris leaned in and said a few words to her that Mark could not discern. Boris then stood by the open back door and stared inside, totally entranced.

The scene reminded Mark of his own initial reaction upon

encountering her in Tuzla, except that then Semra had looked glamorous in a sexy cocktail dress and full makeup. Mark was impressed that she could elicit a similar reaction after a half-sleepless night, with rumpled clothes and an unmade face.

Boris finally turned back to Mark. "Oh, so sorry," he said. "Your companion here is quite captivating."

"I know," said Mark.

Boris invited Mark into the car.

"Where are we going?" Mark asked.

"To Chişinău," said Boris. "But first we will pass the border checkpoint. Then we will have a nice breakfast in Moldova."

"Do you need our passports?" Mark asked as he stepped in.

"No need," said Boris. "The border guards are taken care of." As he closed the door, he added, "On both the Romanian and Moldovan sides."

CHAPTER 81

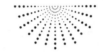

BRAȘOV, APRIL 10

The young prisoner limped into the interrogation room with his hands cuffed in front, a jail guard holding him by the arm. He stumbled twice and almost fell forward before he was plopped down on a chair. He looked up at the guard with disgust. "Thanks for nothing," he hissed.

"Well, well...Alin Barbu!" Boboc stood up from behind a desk facing the prisoner. "Good to see you again, Alin." He examined the prisoner's face. "Looks like they roughed you up a bit."

Alin was tall and scrawny. His gaunt face revealed bruises and abrasions, partially concealed by a scraggly stubble. His red hair was cropped short. He fixed his dark eyes on Boboc in a fury. "Your guys did this to me," he screamed. "Is this the way you treat people?"

Boboc chuckled. He grabbed Alin's chin and turned it right and left. "Doesn't look too bad." He stepped back and sat on the edge of the desk. "Nothing to worry about. You're still as ugly as ever."

"What is the meaning of this?" Alin cried. "Why did you pull me in?"

The door of the room opened and Andrei stepped in. He was stiff and formal in his shirt and tie under a partially zipped police windbreaker. Alin and Boboc stopped and observed him. Andrei came around the desk and unzipped his jacket, revealing a large shoulder holster with a prominent gun within. He took his jacket off, wrapped it around the back of the chair that Boboc had occupied, and sat down. He opened a dossier he had brought with him and shuffled through some papers.

Alin's watchful eyes went back and forth between Boboc and Andrei. "Who is this?" he asked Boboc.

"My new boss." Boboc smiled and crossed his arms, still perched at the edge of the table.

"Mr. Barbu," Andrei spoke calmly, "my name is Andrei Costiniu. I am the chief investigator in the matter concerning the death of one Bekim Zhulati, a doctor."

Barbu's eyes widened. "Never heard the name," he said nervously.

"We have convincing evidence that you murdered this doctor." Andrei's dry monotone was intimidating.

"Alin," Boboc cut in. "You seem to be moving up in the world." His tone was mockingly friendly. "How many times have you been busted for possession and theft?"

Alin gave Boboc a nasty look. He did not answer.

Boboc continued. "But murder! Congratulations. You are in the premier league now."

"I didn't kill anyone," Alin protested, looking first at Boboc, then at Andrei.

"Oh, come on, Alin," Boboc objected. "We know that you broke into the guy's apartment in the dead of night and strangled him."

Alin started to rise from his chair. "I did no such thing!" The jail guard, still close by, pushed him back down by the shoulder.

Boboc continued. "You picked the guy's lock. It was not a slick job. You left footprints all over the apartment. Just come out and say it. You killed the guy."

Alin eyed his jail guard and decided to stay in his chair. He turned to Andrei in a pleading tone.

"Look," he said. "I am innocent. I don't know what you're talking about. You got the wrong guy. Let me go."

"Mr. Barbu," Andrei maintained his official voice, "can you tell

493

us where you were on the night of April seven and early morning of April eight?"

Barbu hesitated, giving the question some thought. "I was with my old lady, at her place."

"Can you give us her name and address?"

"I don't recall much of that night. We were pretty plastered."

"You mean to tell us," Boboc interjected, "that you don't remember the name of your girlfriend?" He let out a loud laugh.

Barbu glared at Boboc, trying to contain his annoyance. He then turned to Andrei. "Do I need a lawyer? I think I need a lawyer," he shouted, leaning forward.

Andrei looked at the papers scattered on his desk and pondered the question. "That is your prerogative if you so wish, Mr. Barbu." He gradually lifted his eyes toward the prisoner.

Barbu recoiled and checked Boboc for guidance. He was clearly more intimidated by this young cop, a new face, than Boboc. Boboc smiled and did not respond. He leaned in toward Alin's neck and gently touched some scratch marks below his chin. "What are these, Alin?"

Barbu withdrew his neck and made a futile attempt to push Boboc away, forgetting that he was handcuffed.

"They don't look fresh," Boboc continued in mock curiosity. "Surely, the police didn't give you these." He placed his hand on Barbu's chin and assumed a theatrical pose, as if in deep thought. "Could it be that Dr. Zhulati did that?" His voice rose as he posed the question.

He then shot out of his seat, bringing his face close to Alin's. "While you were strangling him!" he screamed. Some of Boboc's spittle inadvertently splattered Alin's face.

"I told you, I did not kill him!"

Andrei interjected in a calm voice. "Then perhaps you have a plausible explanation for how your DNA came to be found under the doctor's fingernails?"

"And your fingerprints on the lock you picked!" Boboc added loudly.

Barbu was deflated. He stared down at his shoes.

Andrei changed the line of questioning. "Mr. Barbu, do you know a man by the name of Enver Muratovich?"

"No," said Alin quietly. He paused for a moment. He seemed to be scanning his mind for the name. "Who is that?"

Andrei and Boboc exchanged split-second glances. Barbu's demeanor seemed authentic. Boboc gave Andrei a subtle nod.

"A man who was found hung in his apartment in the Schei district, about a week ago," Andrei said. "A Bosnian."

Barbu was calm. "No," he said. "Haven't heard that name." His prior bluster was gone. "What?" he continued. "Did he kill himself?"

"We just wanted to know if you knew this man, that's all." Andrei shuffled the papers on his desk, taking time to clear his thoughts. "Mr. Barbu," he added in a friendly tone, "if you cooperate with us, there might be room for leniency."

"What is it that you want?" asked Barbu.

"Let me put it to you simply," said Andrei, in a more stern tone. "We have unassailable evidence that you committed the murder of Dr. Bekim Zhulati. Whether you confess or not doesn't matter. Either way, you are going to prison for a long time."

Barbu's eyes widened. He leaned forward in his chair.

"Yeah," added Boboc. "A long, long time. And you know how hard it is to get a fix in there." He let out a laugh. "Hey, maybe this will do you good. You'll be clean and sober for the first time in your life."

Barbu shot him an anxious side glance and tried to keep his eyes on Andrei.

"Did you know this Dr. Zhulati?" Andrei asked.

Barbu shook his head no.

"Could you have come in contact with him in any drug deal?" Andrei was quite certain that Zhulati was solely an alcoholic and not into street drugs, but he posed the question nonetheless.

"I told you, didn't I?" Barbu was once again agitated. "I don't know the man."

"So," said Andrei. "If you had nothing to do with Dr. Zhulati, why would you kill him?" Andrei seemed to ponder the question. "There clearly was no drug deal. Nothing was stolen from him..."

A wave of fear passed though Alin Barbu's face as he now realized the intent of the interrogation.

Boboc interjected. "Who put you up to it, Alin? How much did they pay you to do the hit?"

Alin's eyes darted between Boboc and Andrei. He looked like a ferret.

Boboc did not let up. "I hope they didn't pay you much, because you did a real lousy job!" He let out another laugh. "Heck, if it was me I would ask for my money back."

"Fuck you, Boboc." Alin seethed.

"Mr. Barbu." Andrei regained Alin's attention. "Were you approached by any foreigners to do this job?"

Barbu was confused by the question. "Foreigners? What foreigners?"

"Russians, Moldovans, Turks?"

"No, no! No foreigners." He shook his head violently. "I don't know any foreigners."

"Then who was it?" Boboc screamed, his face again closer to Barbu's.

"I think I want a lawyer," Barbu said again, his voice shaking. "Get me a lawyer."

"Mr. Barbu, we know that you did not do it for your own sake. Someone must have hired you to kill Dr. Zhulati. We are more interested in prosecuting this person, not you. If you reveal who it is, we'll see to it that the prosecutor goes easy on you."

Barbu sat back and looked away. He did not answer.

"Come on, Barbu," Boboc chimed in. "Tell us who it is and this won't be a nightmare for you."

"I want a lawyer," Barbu hissed at Boboc.

They tried a few more times in different ways, to no avail.

After the jail guard took Barbu away, Andrei collected his papers and rose up. "Well," he said, "at least we know that he didn't do Muratovich."

"Agreed," said Boboc. "Did you see how calm he was with

Muratovich as opposed to Zhulati? He definitely did not do Muratovich."

"I also believe the part about no foreigners," Andrei added.

"Yeah, what was that all about?" Boboc asked.

Now that he had briefed Dalca, Andrei felt it was time to let Boboc in on it. "I uncovered some intelligence that a Russian bigwig might be behind these murders."

"Where the hell did you get that?" Boboc was taken aback.

"SRI," said Andrei. "A contact I have there."

Boboc lowered his eyes and contemplated the news. "Interesting," he said quietly. "I suppose that's why the boss put you in the lead, didn't he?"

Andrei did not answer. He let his partner's realization hang in the air.

After a while, Boboc spoke. "So who is this Russian?"

"I don't have a name yet; nor do I have a motive." Andrei explained what he knew, that the Russian had the apparatus to dispatch assassins and that he had contracted kills outside of Romania related to the Braşov transplant ring.

"Woo!" Boboc raised his eyebrows. "This thing is ballooning into something very big."

Andrei agreed. "But we still have a lot to uncover," he added.

"Yeah," said Boboc. "Like who did Muratovich versus Zhulati."

"I am quite certain that Muratovich will be traced to the Russian." Andrei rubbed his forehead. "But I really don't get Zhulati. The Russian, whoever he is," he said, "he doesn't strike me as the type who would hire someone like Alin Barbu for a kill."

"Russian Mafia?" Boboc suggested. "They would do it themselves."

"I don't think it was a Mafia hit," said Andrei. "I think it is something different."

"What?"

"I don't know." Andrei pursed his lips in resignation. "I don't know if we'll ever know."

"The issue of motive is even more complicated," said Boboc. "If

Muratovich and Zhulati have different killers, there might be different motives."

"Correct," said Andrei. "I doubt that Alin Barbu would know, or care."

"What a fucking mess," said Boboc. "How are we going to untangle all this?"

Andrei chuckled. "Maybe a genie will magically appear and show us the way."

Boboc slapped Andrei's back, laughing. "Keep hoping for that, partner."

CHAPTER 82

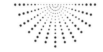

BRAȘOV, APRIL 10

I t was late afternoon when the station's duty officer brought the young woman to Andrei's desk. She wore tight blue scrubs that revealed the folds of her plump figure. Her curly red hair, long and disheveled, partially covered one eye. She looked bewildered as she took in the disorderly array of desks and busy plainclothes officers.

Andrei rose up. "Nicoleta Ciobanu?" He extended her a hand.

She cleared the hair from her eye and examined Andrei up and down. Impressed by his good looks, a bashful smile appeared on her lips. She shook his hand hesitantly.

"Thank you for your cooperation," said Andrei. "I am *Subinspector* Andrei Costiniu." He pointed toward the door. "Please, this way."

He led her downstairs to the ground floor and into a starkly lit corridor. She followed a few paces behind, silent, eyes on the ground. Andrei stopped at a closed door and waited for her to catch up.

"What is this all about?" she asked, her voice cracking.

"You'll see in a minute." He opened the door. "There is someone here whom I believe you know."

It was a cramped conference room that the cops used for

meetings with each other or with lawyers. Andrei had intentionally avoided the nasty interrogation room where they routinely grilled the likes of Alin Barbu. He needed Nicoleta to cooperate, but not with blunt coercion. He had chosen this room for this reason.

An oversized table left little wiggle room between its chairs and the walls. At the far end, a dirty window let in some partial sunlight.

"Hello, Nicoleta." Irina sat by the window and smiled. She looked weary.

Nicoleta froze like a deer in the headlights. Andrei pulled back a chair. "Please, sit down." She awkwardly squeezed herself into the tight space and sat down.

Andrei came around and sat opposite to her. "I believe you know Irina Cernea."

Despite Andrei and Irina's friendly demeanor, Nicoleta was rattled. "Am I in trouble?" She looked straight at Andrei, acting as though Irina was not in the room.

"Why do you think you may be in trouble?" asked Andrei coyly.

Nicoleta's eyes darted to Irina for a split second, then back to Andrei. "Why is she here?"

"You are a radiology technician at Spitatul Martinu, am I right?" Andrei leaned forward and clasped his hands, placing them atop the desk.

Nicoleta nodded.

"You work there full time?"

"Yes."

"And what is it that you do as a radiology tech?"

"Mostly run the CT scanner. Sometimes I pitch in with regular X-rays if they are short on staff."

"And Irina works with you at Martinu?"

Nicoleta brushed her unruly hair off her forehead. She looked at Irina again, this time longer, trying to gauge her. Irina smiled back.

"No," she said hesitantly. "Not quite."

"You know her from your side job, don't you?" Andrei asked abruptly.

Nicoleta stiffened. "Look," she said, with a slight surge of courage. "I came here because I was asked to answer some questions about my job at Martinu. I was not expecting this!" She pointed at Irina.

She then addressed Irina. "Do you mind telling me what's going on?"

Irina looked at Andrei, who nodded his approval. "They know about it, Nicoleta," she answered simply. "All of it."

Nicoleta raised and lowered her eyebrows, trying to fathom this.

Irina continued. "They need to shut it down and catch the leaders."

"Ms. Ciobanu," Andrei took over, "you might not know this, but the side business you engaged in has resulted in a number of deaths. Murders, to be more specific."

"I didn't kill anyone!" Nicoleta nearly shouted.

"I know you didn't," said Andrei. "But in the eyes of the law, you are an accessory."

"How do you know that? You can't prove that!"

"I have a willing and credible witness here." Andrei pointed to Irina. "She has already testified to that under oath."

Nicoleta looked at Irina in disbelief.

"The extra money wasn't worth it, Nicoleta." Irina sounded surprisingly calm. "We're both in trouble."

Andrei stood up and gestured toward Irina, who took his cue and began negotiating around the chairs toward the door. As she passed Andrei, she nodded to him.

"Thank you Ms. Cernea," he said loudly, and waited for her to leave the room.

Nicoleta's face was beet red. She quit fighting with her hair and faced Andrei, eyes wide with fear. "What do you want from me?"

"We need you to tell us the details of what you did for the transplant outfit."

Nicoleta's eyes watered. She lowered her head.

"And we need the secret log book you kept. I believe it is somewhere in the radiology department."

Nicoleta looked up again, surprised that Andrei knew this. Tears began flowing down her cheeks.

"There is one more thing," Andrei continued. "If you cooperate with us, I promise I will seek lenience for you with the prosecutor. And we will not place you under arrest."

Nicoleta wiped her tears with the back of her hand. "Help?" she asked. "How?"

"You will continue on with your job as though this meeting never happened." Andrei added, "And do not tell anyone about it."

Nicoleta nodded.

"At some point I will approach you for that log book. You'll cooperate." Andrei was treading sensitive territory, since he could not step foot into Martinu without higher authority. But he needed to make sure that the log book did not disappear. "I want you to keep your eyes and ears open. If you catch any hint that a new transplant is scheduled, I want you to report it. I will use Irina as an intermediary. She knows the hospital and the routines of the enterprise. She'll help us with it."

"What if nothing happens?" asked Nicoleta. "I hear rumors that the leaders of the operation are dead."

"So is Enver Muratovich," said Andrei. "Did you know that?"

Nicoleta let out a surprised cry. "No! That can't be true."

"The death of Enver Muratovich is one of the murders that I just mentioned, associated with the transplant enterprise."

"Oh my God." Nicoleta was still in disbelief. "He was such a nice man."

"Did you two know each other well?"

"Not really," she said. "It's just that he visited my CT scanner regularly. He was always polite and personable."

Andrei was pleased with Nicoleta's candor. She was already cooperating. "Why did he visit your scanner so often?" he asked.

"For the pre-op scans of the donors." Nicoleta suddenly froze and placed her hand on her mouth.

"That's the sort of cooperation that will reduce your trouble," said Andrei, encouragingly.

Nicoleta slackened in resignation. "All right," she said. "I'll do as you say."

CHAPTER 83

LEUŞENI, APRIL 9 ... MORNING

"If you'll excuse me, I will freshen up a bit," Semra said, standing by her luggage at the edge of the room. She then departed with some clothes and toiletries.

Mark and Boris watched her disappear from their perch at the breakfast table. They were in a small inn in the village of Leuşeni, on the Moldovan side of the border. As promised, the border crossing had been a breeze. The subsequent breakfast, hearty country fair, was devoured by all.

"Lovely creature," commented Boris, placing a toothpick between his front teeth. Mark was struck by his glistening teeth. Artificially whitened, he figured.

"I bet she is amazing in bed, ha?" Boris gave Mark a friendly punch in the shoulder.

Mark ignored the gesture and picked at a piece of sausage on his plate. "Oh, she is full of surprises."

"You're a lucky guy," said Boris, looking expectantly at the door where Semra had disappeared. "I can just imagine."

Mark lifted his head and smiled. He felt a strong need to change the subject. "How come you speak Turkish so well?"

"My mother, bless her soul, was Azeri," said Boris. "She spoke good Turkish as did her parents, my grandparents."

Mark gave him a quizzical look; most Azeris lived in Azerbaijan.

Boris explained. "My father was a Soviet soldier, in the army, stationed in Azerbaijan's capital, Baku. That's where my parents met."

"Did you follow in your father's footsteps?"

"Yes," said Boris. "But I did not stay in the army long. I joined special forces and then…" He stopped, reluctant to give his full curriculum vitae. "Well," he said, "and then, Rusu."

The owner of the inn, a tall, corpulent man with a giant black moustache, collected plates and poured them fresh coffee.

"So," asked Boris, as he blew on the hot coffee and took a sip, "what news are you bringing us?"

After Mark's initial message, amid the various back-and-forths mediated by the Chamber of Commerce, Boris had identified himself as the main intermediary for Vadim Rusu and indicated that they knew who Mark was. What were Mark's intentions in contacting them? Mark had messaged the truth, that he would be bringing important information concerning the death of Rusu's son. This had the desired effect; Mark's offer was accepted. When Mark requested assurance for safety, Boris had readily acceded to it.

"If you don't mind," said Mark, "I'd rather wait to discuss this with Mr. Rusu."

Boris smiled. "Very prudent of you," he said. He took another sip. "I have to tell you, Dr. Kent—you are a doctor, aren't you?"

"Yes, a radiologist."

"Well, I have to tell you that Mr. Rusu and I have acquired much respect for your capabilities. You are a wily and resourceful operative."

"Thank you," said Mark. He wasn't sure what to make of this compliment, considering that he was responsible for the death of two paramilitaries in Rusu's stable.

Mark decided to respond in kind. "I should tell you that I am very impressed with your organization. The way you have conducted your hits and the way you extricated me out of Bucharest were clean and efficient."

Boris put his coffee down and played with one of his cuff links. "Our hits?" he murmured, as if he did not know what Mark was talking about.

Mark ignored him. "But the hits you contracted out to locals were a mess."

The comment momentarily startled Boris.

"That Turkish doctor," Mark continued. "He lost his head. Literally."

Boris returned to fiddling with his cuff link.

Mark decided to keep baiting him. "I came upon the scene, you know. A bloody mess. I looked all over for his head and could not find it."

Boris finally looked up at Mark with a sly smile. "My boss Mr. Rusu also lost his head," he said. "Over this affair."

Mark chuckled. "I hope he's okay." He was pleased to extricate the admission.

Boris shuddered as if trying to eject the episode from his memory. "He is," he said. "But it took a while."

Semra reappeared at the door. She had transformed herself. Her hair was up in a sophisticated chignon held by a Japanese stick. Her makeup, expertly applied, gave her a regal bearing. She wore a revealing low-cut dress and high heels that accentuated the lovely curves of her calves.

Boris stood up in amazement, his chair falling behind him in a loud thump. "Oh my God!"

He took her hand again, this time holding it in both of his, and surveyed her up and down, his eyes notably delayed at her cleavage. He then kissed Semra's hand several times. "You look ravishing, my dear," he said elegantly.

"Oh, Mr. Petrov, you're so kind." Semra, clearly delighted, gently adjusted the back of her hair with her free hand.

"Come," said Boris, still holding her hand. He led Semra to the table. "Would you like anything else?"

"Oh, no thank you." Semra was at her flirtatious best. "You

have been so gracious so far, so *misafirperver*." The last word, uttered seductively, meant *hospitable*.

"This is just the beginning, my dear," said Boris. "Your stay in Moldova will be unforgettable, I promise you."

* * *

They started off on the ride to Chișinău, Mark and Semra in the back of the Mercedes, Boris up front, head craned back, trying to maintain idle chat with Semra. It wasn't a long drive, Boris had told them, an hour or so.

Ignoring Boris and Semra, Mark dozed in the soft comfort of his leather seat. It had been a long night and the heavy breakfast added to his lethargy. The idle banter nearby did not faze him as he drifted off.

Mark wasn't sure how long he was out when he was jolted out of his sleep by a text message chime. Another soon followed. Mark quickly muted his phone and looked around, dazed. Boris and the driver were looking ahead, both silent. Semra stared at him quizzically. "What was that?"

Mark turned on his screen. "Olga," he murmured quietly.

"Oh, her!" Semra's voice was icy.

Mark ignored her and scrolled through the incoming material. It was what Olga had promised. He looked up at Semra.

"Another rendezvous? In Moldova?" she asked sarcastically.

"No, no," Mark said hastily. He put his index finger on his mouth. "Shhh," he admonished her, nodding his head toward the front of the car. She turned away from Mark in a huff and observed the scenery out of her window.

Mark returned to his mobile and scrolled through the material again, this time more slowly. As he was doing so, another text arrived from Olga.

"Be careful," she wrote. "I think Cezar is on to you."

CHAPTER 84

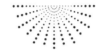

CHIŞINĂU, APRIL 9

Boris came for Mark early in the afternoon for the short walk to Skytower. Earlier he had deposited Mark and Semra at the Royal Boutique, a luxury hotel close to the modern glass tower. Mark had a chance to clean up and, despite his rising unease, catch up on sleep. Boris remained overly solicitous toward Semra. He promised to send his chauffeur to take her shopping at Malldova, an upscale shopping mall. It would all be on his account.

Semra gave Mark an apprehensive hug. "Be careful," she said, unknowingly echoing Olga, as she planted a kiss on his cheek. Mark had not let her in on the nature of his mission, but she could sense that it was risky.

The afternoon sky was overcast and Mark felt a slight chill as he and Boris entered Skytower, passing through an airport-style metal detector. Some change in Mark's pocket set off the detector, unnerving him further. Upstairs, outside the penthouse office, he was frisked by two dark uniformed, side-armed paramilitaries, what Mark now came to call *Rusu clones*. He no longer found them fearsome.

Inside, Vadim Rusu rose from behind a gargantuan desk. "At last," he said, extending a hand to Mark. "I was tired of the cat-

and-mouse game." His voice was a deep baritone, his English heavily tinged with a Slavic accent.

Mark shook the hand of this man he had fearfully evaded for so long. Rusu looked older than he expected. Nearly bald and with a whiting goatee, his face was lined with numerous creases. His dark eyes, small and deep-set, like those of a bear, were squinty and weary. He was nonetheless tall, erect, and imposing.

"When I left San Francisco for Budapest, I never expected to become a mouse," Mark retorted.

The remark drew a laugh from Boris, who stood back and observed the pair. Rusu did not react. He showed Mark to a chair and asked him if he wanted coffee, tea, or Scotch. Mark sat down and momentarily surveyed the surreal scene of the ruthless pair, Rusu and Boris, responsible for so many killings, as solicitous hosts. He asked for tea and reminded himself not get too at ease.

Boris served Mark from a nearby samovar while he and Rusu took Scotch on the rocks. The formalities complete, the three men sat in chairs facing each other, Boris and Rusu with legs crossed, Mark grabbing his armrests. They silently took their first sips.

Mark broke the silence. "May I extend my sincere condolences on the passing of Dima."

The gesture seemed to startle Rusu, whose eyes widened for a split second. He awkwardly re-crossed his legs. "Thank you," he said. He took another sip of Scotch. "How did you come to know about him?"

"Credible rumors," said Mark. "I did not know Dima personally." He wasn't about to mention Claude Gérard of the French Interpol, who had given him the intelligence soon after a Hungarian SWAT team killed two of Vadim Rusu's men while rescuing Mark.

"A real shame," Mark added. "It should never have happened."

"A real shame indeed," echoed Boris.

Rusu gave Boris a sharp look. "Mr. Kent," he said to Mark quietly, "you have interjected yourself into our business quite unexpectedly. Would you care to explain who sent you here and what your mission is?"

"I came to Budapest to meet Ahmet Gürsen, whom you know as Nicolae Radu. He happens to be a childhood friend from Istanbul."

Rusu cast his eyes on his glass of Scotch. He stirred it, the ice inside making loud clinking sounds. He lifted the glass to his lips but then changed his mind and set it down. He turned slightly to Boris.

"Come now, Doctor," said Boris, taking the cue from his boss. "You don't expect us to believe that, do you?"

"You can believe what you want," said Mark firmly. "That's the truth."

"We don't care which American intelligence agency you belong to," Boris continued. "What we would like to know is why they are interested in this."

Mark was quite sure that if he denied being a secret agent, these two would never believe that either. "What do you mean by *this?*" he asked.

Boris and Rusu exchanged glances. A brief silence followed; they each seemed to be searching for an answer.

Mark decided to take the initiative and boldly declared, "We have no interest whatsoever in the activities of the Hercules Security Group."

Mark was on thin ice. He had woven tall tales before and gotten away with them. This would be the tallest of them all. "On that, I can give you the personal assurance of the Deputy Attorney General of the US Department of Justice."

Rusu and Boris absorbed the comment. It implied that Mark was FBI, most likely a high-ranking officer.

"So what is it, then?" asked Boris.

"Actually," Mark said, crossing his legs and leaning back in his chair, "you probably won't find it terribly interesting." He tried to act calm even though his pulse raced and the butterflies in his stomach nearly heaved him out of his chair.

Boris examined a cuff link. Rusu stared at Mark, expressionless.

Encouraged by the lack of objection, Mark continued. "I am a member of a secret task force, organized by the DOJ—Department of Justice—that is investigating the illegal organ trade worldwide. Our aim is to bring the more egregious leaders to prosecution."

"That's quite ambitious," said Boris. It looked like he believed it. "It is happening in numerous corners of the world, many of which are out of your jurisdiction."

"True," said Mark. He then chuckled nervously. "But you know us Americans. We sometimes go on quixotic crusades and celebrate whatever little success we attain as big triumphs."

Rusu's lips parted into the slightest hint of a smile. "I am glad," he said, "that you can admit to that."

Mark nodded in acknowledgment and took a sip of tea. His mouth was dry from anxiety. He mentally forced himself to push on.

"Nicolae Radu and Iancu Negrescu came to our attention as ringleaders of an elaborate Eastern European transplant scheme. When my connection to Radu was discovered..."

Mark paused to check for reaction. Boris nodded knowingly.

"Well then. You can imagine." Mark uncrossed his legs and leaned in for a few more sips of tea.

"You were assigned to the investigation because you and Radu were childhood friends?" Boris filled in.

Mark gestured to Boris as a teacher might acknowledge a perceptive student. "Imagine my surprise when I arrived in Budapest and found Radu dead."

Rusu nodded. *He's buying it,* Mark thought.

"At the time I had no idea what was going on and why he had died," Mark said. This was indeed the truth, and he felt more comfortable stating it. "And so, I investigated it. And I stumbled into your organization inadvertently." Mark placed special emphasis on *inadvertently*.

"Where does this investigation stand at present?" asked Rusu.

"I am glad you asked." Mark extended his empty glass of tea toward Boris. He obligingly stood up and refilled it from the samovar. Mark continued. "With Radu and Negrescu gone, we are now focusing our interest on a certain Cezar Kaminesky," he said. "Do you know him?"

Boris abruptly turned back from the samovar upon mention of the name. Rusu remained expressionless. Neither spoke.

Mark paused, letting the name sink in.

"Go on," Rusu said finally.

"Well," said Mark, "he is also running a transplant operation, and a dirty one at that."

Boris returned with Mark's tea and interrupted him. "What about the killers of Radu and Negrescu? Aren't you interested in them?"

Mark exchanged a knowing glance with Boris. Mark and Boris had touched upon the subject of Rusu's assassinations earlier, at breakfast, but this question had not come up. Boris had saved it for his boss.

"That's none of our business," Mark readily answered. "Nor are some killings that have occurred in Turkey recently, in Istanbul and Bodrum." He blew on the hot tea and took a sip.

"Aren't you sharing your intelligence with European law enforcement?" asked Boris.

Mark smiled. "I was in contact with them while in Hungary," he said. "They shared more with me than I did with them." He set his tea down and looked directly at Rusu. "Since then I haven't had any communication with them. Frankly, at this point it is no longer up to me. When my mission is complete and I issue a report, my superiors can decide what to do with the intelligence."

Mark figured that a belated bureaucratic action from the FBI would be less threatening to Rusu than those of a rogue agent loose in Europe.

He continued in a different vein. "May I express my regrets for the losses your organization suffered in Budapest."

Once again, Rusu remained stone silent.

"They were, shall we say, collateral damage in the hands of Hungarian law enforcement," Mark explained. "I did not have anything to do with it directly."

"In battle," Rusu said, his words deliberate and emphatic, "you take your wounds and you lick them."

Mark nodded in understanding.

"And," continued Rusu, in the same measured delivery, "you try to inflict worse wounds on your enemy in return."

The remark startled Mark. The teacup he was holding began to shake, some tea spilling on the side. He nervously set it down and examined the faces of his adversaries. Rusu was expressionless, his bear eyes holding Mark's gaze. Boris gave him a meaningless smile while he played with a cuff link.

"I am not your enemy," Mark said quietly.

"That," said Rusu, "is up to us to determine." He stood up and walked toward a nearby cabinet by the wall. His gait was plodding, his demeanor stern.

As Rusu opened a drawer, Mark sank into his seat, foolishly hoping that he could disappear. He feared the worst. Rusu pulled out an ornate wooden box and lumbered back. He sat down and opened the box, examining its contents.

Mark exchanged a nervous glance with Boris, who observed his boss with amusement.

Rusu turned the box around and tilted it so Mark could see its contents. "Cigar?" he asked.

Mark was not a smoker, but at that point, in his infinite relief, he acceded. Mark shuddered as he watched Rusu decapitate the tapered end of a plump stogie with a double guillotine-style cutter.

"Cohiba?" Mark asked nervously.

Rusu turned to Boris, two fingers still in the cutter, and nodded knowingly. Boris then expressed his boss's feelings. "Our compliments. You know your cigars."

Mark took a cautious puff from the cigar, which Rusu himself lit. He hoped it would not launch him into a coughing fit. As his vision became murky with the smoke he exhaled, Mark had a flashback to Tuzla, where Mahmut Gazioğlu had enjoyed an identical Cohiba hours before he was decapitated. Mark shivered within, as if the act of smoking this cigar were the equivalent of drinking the unfortunate surgeon's blood.

The room was filled with a sickly sweet, cherry-apple scent of two Cohibas alight. "What do you think?" asked Rusu, as he filled the room with more smoke.

Mark held the stogie between his index and middle fingers and examined it as if he were a long-time aficionado. He leaned his nose into the smoke. "Outstanding," he said, holding back a cough.

As Rusu gave Boris an approving nod, Mark suddenly stood up and asked if he could use a restroom. With Rusu's approval, Boris called one of the Rusu clones to accompany Mark to the men's room down the hall. As the paramilitary sentry stood guard outside the bathroom, Mark relieved his lungs with a muffled coughing fit that caused him to vomit. He waited a few minutes to regain his composure and for his reddened face to return to pale.

He then opened the door and nodded to the guard for a walk back into the cauldron.

CHAPTER 85

CHIŞINĂU, APRIL 9

When Mark returned to Rusu's office, he asked for a shot of Scotch.

"Is everything okay?" asked Boris.

"The breakfast," said Mark. "It didn't agree with me."

Boris handed him a Scotch on the rocks. Mark handed it back. "Add some water, please."

"Those country sausages," said Boris, as he sprayed a splash of water into the glass. "They can be hard on uninitiated stomachs."

Mark let out another cough as he eyed his unfinished cigar on a nearby ashtray, its smell still pungent. Currently there was a lot that was hard on the uninitiated. He pushed the ashtray away.

They settled back into their chairs. Rusu, who had been quietly observing Mark, spoke. "I understand," he said, "that you bear some news for us, news of importance."

Mark took a sip of the Scotch and let the burn in his gullet replace that of the vomit. "Yes," he said. He took out his phone and hastily scrolled through his messages, checking to make sure that Olga's texts were still there. It didn't hurt to double-check the back-up before launching his bombshell.

Mark then looked up at Boris and Rusu. "It concerns this Cezar Kaminesky," he said. "I have reliable intelligence that it was he who entrapped your son Dima and stole Dima's kidney."

Vadim Rusu's eyebrows went up. He looked at Boris, who had frozen in the act of playing with a cuff link. Neither responded. They waited for more.

"I thought that this might be of some importance to you." Mark took another sip of Scotch. He needed the chemical boost of the harsh drink.

"Where did you get that information?" Boris finally responded.

"Cezar's wife," said Mark. "Her name is Olga." He paused for a reaction. Rusu was impossible to interpret. Boris's face betrayed disbelief. "I believe you know her," Mark added.

"What makes you think so?" asked Boris.

"Well," said Mark, a bit more relaxed as the alcohol surged through his system. "She was the one who helped your men with the Radu hit. Gave them access to the hotel in Budapest. Afterwards, Tibor Bognár's men interrupted a meeting I had with Olga and chased me. You surely know that, since you hired Bognár."

"How did Olga Kaminesky give you this information?" Rusu interjected.

"I met her again," said Mark. "Two days ago, in Bucharest. At Iancu Negrescu's funeral."

"Do you have any proof to support this claim?" asked Boris.

"Yes, I do," Mark answered. "But before I present it, I would like some assurance from you that there will be no reprisals."

"Against whom?" asked Boris. "Why would we retaliate against Olga Kaminesky?"

"It is not her that I am worried about," answered Mark. "You see, the evidence comes from the woman Cezar used to entrap Dima. I would like you to leave her alone."

The exchange of glances between Rusu and Boris was different this time. They were both clearly intrigued.

"No reprisals." Rusu was firm. "You have my word."

"All right, then," said Mark. He was uncertain about Rusu's

reliability, but he couldn't ask for more. "I have some data in my mobile phone that Olga forwarded to me. This material is communication from Sylvia—that's the name of the woman—that Olga kept. The two of them were friends, and Sylvia confided in her."

Mark raised up his cell phone. Boris took the phone and connected it to a laptop on Rusu's desk. Within a few minutes the material in the phone was downloaded. Boris invited his boss to his seat and pulled up a chair next to him so that they could scroll through it together. Mark stood behind them.

This was the first time Mark himself was reading the communication in detail. Previously he had skimmed over it. They were mostly text messages and a few emails. Sylvia's tone was fearful and contrite. She clearly had not understood what the consequences of her actions would be when she was sent out to flirt with Dima in an upscale bar in Bucharest.

"That's the name of the bar," Boris murmured as he studied the screen. "The details look correct."

Sylvia's act had been brief. It was clear from her texts that she was routinely assigned the task of hunting for healthy young men in specific bars, where she first lured them by flirting. Once she determined that they were the right fit, she slipped a sedative into their drink. The rest was apparently taken care of by Cezar and his men.

Sylvia was not bothered by any of her other conquests because there had been no adverse outcomes. But when Dima Rusu turned up dead, everything changed. It was clear from her texts that she was not only remorseful but also fearful of law enforcement, and of Cezar. She intended to stop working for Cezar and disappear, possibly to another country.

Toward the end, an image appeared that Mark had not noticed before. Olga must have included this by mistake. It was a faded photo of a young man standing in front of a ship. He was smiling at the camera. The image was murky and had nothing to do with Sylvia or Dima Rusu. Boris ignored it. He quickly scrolled past and closed the laptop.

Rusu moved away from the desk and headed to the window, leaving Mark and Boris by his desk. He seemed deep in thought. Boris stood and moved toward the other end of the room, gesturing to Mark that he should follow. He then gave Mark a hand gesture to remain quiet, bracing himself for the explosion.

It came within seconds. Vadim Rusu erupted in Russian with a torrent that came in waves of screams. Boris stood at attention, his head downturned, and repeatedly nodded at his boss. Mark was taken aback. He had never seen an outburst so severe. Rusu waved his arms this way and that, at one point accidentally hitting the window. Somehow it withstood the blow and did not shatter.

Finally spent, Rusu spoke in English. "How the hell did this happen?" His voice was hoarse.

"I am not sure, Boss," said Boris quietly, cautiously raising his eyes.

"That son of a bitch fooled us and we bought it like amateurs?" Rusu managed to raise his voice again.

"The information he gave us seemed quite credible at the time," Boris said meekly.

"Goddamn it, Boris!" Rusu reached another climax. "I hold you responsible for this."

At that moment, Mark almost pitied Boris. He looked at him sympathetically.

"I will look into it, Boss," Boris said, with a composure that surprised Mark.

"It's too late, isn't it?" screamed Rusu. He was breathing rapidly, exhaling with a wheeze. He made an effort to control his anger. As his breathing returned, he said bitterly, "All that effort. It was all a waste."

He seemed more concerned about the needless energy his organization had spent rather than the lives lost for naught. He turned back and walked to his desk, his face beet red, his cheeks swollen with anger. "Out!" He pointed to the door. "Both of you. "

Boris grabbed Mark's arm and pulled him to the door. As the two hastily departed, Rusu sank into his chair, spent.

* * *

"So, what happened?" ask Mark.

They had retreated to a nearby cavernous conference room that dwarfed the two of them.

"You saw it, didn't you?" said Boris. His voice echoed from the far walls of the room. "The boss lost his head, just like when he discovered the decapitation of that Turkish doctor."

"No," said Mark. "That's not what I'm asking. What happened with Cezar?"

"Oh. Well, soon after Dima's death, he contacted us," Boris answered. "We didn't know who he was. We had had no prior interest in this organ business." Boris pulled out a chair and sat down.

"Did he contact you in person? Did you actually meet him?" Mark stood on the opposite side of a large conference table.

"No," said Boris. "It was by phone. He later sent a courier with paperwork from Radu and Negrescu that pertained to Dima's operation."

"What sort of paperwork?"

"Medical records, lab reports, X-ray reports." He paused to think. "An operative report. They all had Radu's signature beneath, as if he had read and approved the reports."

This puzzled Mark. "I am not fully certain, but I don't believe that Radu and Negrescu placed signatures on their medical records," he said. There had been no such signature on the radiology report that Ahmet had summoned him with.

Boris looked at Mark. He raised and lowered his eyebrows in a resigned gesture. "Well, he managed to fool the boss." He shook his head in disapproval. "The boss was not in a discerning mood at the time. He was grieving Dima's death and was very angry." Boris pointed towards Rusu's office. "You see how he gets. You can't reason with him."

Mark, too, shook his head. "I don't know how you put up with it."

"I'm used to it," said Boris, with a sigh. "I've been with him for many years." He paused and inspected his cuff links. "Anyhow, when he got this intelligence from Cezar, he had a knee-jerk reaction. He issued orders to find and kill Radu, Negrescu, and whoever else was involved in his son's death. We never checked to confirm the veracity of the information."

"Do you realize how many lives you've wasted with this mistake?" Mark demanded bitterly.

"We don't think that way." Boris was cold and detached. "The assassinations we engineered in Budapest and Turkey are nothing compared with what we did in Russia and Moldova in years past."

Mark was shocked by the admission. He had come to like Boris as a charming rascal. This was a ruthless side he had not seen before.

"You should know," Boris continued, "that recently the boss ordered a stop to the assassinations, after the Bodrum hit, the one on Radu's father."

"Was there anyone left?" Mark asked sarcastically.

"Yes," said Boris, ignoring Mark's tone. "Small fry: surgeons, nurses, anesthetists. They all worked at Spitatul Martinu."

"What's that?"

"A hospital in Braşov." Boris turned over a cuff link. "That's where they took Dima's kidney."

"Why did Rusu stop?"

"He got tired of it. We spent a lot of time and money and energy on the project. He realized after a while that it wasn't helping with his grief. It would not bring his son back."

Mark contemplated this for a moment. "It's all very sad, isn't it?" he said. "All around, for everyone concerned."

"I suppose." Boris's tone was again cold.

"Does this mean that you were no longer after me?" asked Mark.

"You were supposed to be dead, remember?" Boris smiled and shook his index finger at Mark.

"Did you buy that?" Mark asked.

"No, not really."

They both laughed.

"Come on," said Boris. "Let's get out of here." They exited the conference room to the hallway, where Boris summoned two guards.

"So what happens now?" asked Mark.

"I don't know for sure," said Boris. He nodded to the guards to move a few steps away. "But if the boss behaves as he usually does, he will soon issue an assassination order for Cezar Kaminesky."

"From what I've come to know of Cezar," said Mark, "he is quite slippery, not that easy to get."

"Look," said Boris. "This is the boss's only son we're talking about. He will make us pursue the bastard to the ends of the earth." He motioned to the guards. "These guys will accompany you to your hotel."

He shook Mark's hand. "Thank you for approaching us," he said. "Enjoy the hotel and Chişinău. You can stay as long as you like."

Mark smiled. "Thank you, but I'd like to leave as soon as possible."

"For where?"

"I don't quite know yet."

Boris handed Mark a business card. "Let me know," he said. "I can facilitate travel arrangements for you."

Mark examined the card. It displayed only Boris's name and a phone number.

"That's my personal mobile," said Boris.

Mark guessed that he did not hand out the card frequently. "Thanks," he said. "I will definitely do that."

"Take care of that delightful girl of yours," said Boris. "I am so jealous."

"You know," Mark said hesitantly, "she is not really a girl."

"Of course I do, my friend." Boris placed a hand over Mark's shoulder and squeezed it. "How could you not notice?"

Mark stared at Boris, his cheeks reddening in embarrassment. For a moment he was back in Tarık's car on the way to Bodrum.

"As I said," Boris continued, his hand still squeezing Mark, "I envy you."

Mark departed Skytower flanked by a pair of black uniformed paramilitaries, their side arms prominent on their belts. He marveled at the change of circumstances, these deadly killers that he feared so, now his protectors.

CHAPTER 86

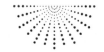

CHIŞINĂU, APRIL 9

Mark returned to his hotel suite in late afternoon, tired but pleased. His uncertain mission to confront Vadim Rusu had succeeded beyond his expectations. The man was a tempestuous brute prone to rash decisions. *Not surprising*, Mark thought, *given his background.* He had expected a more rational, calculating mind based on Rusu's extensive intelligence experience. Instead, it turned out that Boris was the more rational, moderating influence, keeping his boss's excesses in check.

At this point, Mark didn't mind if Rusu went ballistic in finding and eliminating Cezar Kaminesky. This shadowy figure had managed to turn people's lives upside down unbeknownst to them. He deserved whatever Rusu had in store for him.

Mark saw that Semra had not yet come back—probably still shopping, he decided. She would be spending as much as she could on the blank check that Boris had offered. Mark chuckled as he thought about Boris's crush on Semra. The man was more complex than he initially appeared. He certainly had diverse penchants. Mark himself could not acquire the taste, as Semra had put it, but others did: first Gazioğlu, now Boris. *Well, let them be,* thought Mark.

He went into the bedroom and undressed, letting out a huge

yawn as he got into bed. The collective fatigue of everything he had done since arriving in Romania bore down on him. He closed his eyes with a huge sense of relief. Vadim Rusu was off his back. When he awoke, he would figure out his exit strategy.

* * *

It was pitch dark when Mark woke up. His mind was cloudy as he reached for his phone to check the time. It was close to ten p.m. Semra was not in the bed. He turned on the light and called out for her. No answer. He got up and searched the large hotel suite. Not only was she not there, but there were no packages or bags that he expected to see after her shopping spree. It looked as though she had never come back.

Puzzled, he sat down and thought the situation out. He decided to call Boris. When he turned on his mobile to dial him, the phone's screen opened to Olga's text messages. There, facing him again, was the curious photo that she had included. The poor resolution had made the picture appear blurry when magnified on Boris's laptop screen. It was not as blurry on the smaller screen of his phone. Something struck him about the smiling young man. He isolated the photo and examined it more carefully.

Intrigued, he sent a text message to Olga asking what the picture was. There was no immediate answer. Mark then messaged Boris. Had his chauffeur returned yet?

Boris's prompt response caused Mark to forget about the photo. Yes, he said, the chauffeur had indeed come back several hours ago. He had dropped Semra off at the hotel.

Mark scratched his head. Where was she? He decided to go downstairs and check with the reception desk.

The lobby was quiet at this hour, the reception desk staffed by a single, smartly dressed young woman. Mark explained the situation to her. She tapped a few keys on her computer and said, "Aha."

She looked up at Mark. "Wait a second," she said. "Roman will explain." She summoned Roman with a walkie-talkie.

Roman turned out to be the bellman. He was middle-aged, tall, and stocky. After a brief conversation with the receptionist in Romanian, he motioned Mark to come with him. Mark looked at the receptionist quizzically. She instructed him to follow Roman.

Roman mumbled in Romanian as he unlocked a small back room where they kept luggage and other guest possessions. He pointed to a pile of bags and boxes and said something that Mark did not understand. The pile looked like what Mark would have expected from Semra's shopping spree.

As Mark examined the bags, Roman produced an envelope from his pocket and held it out to Mark. Just then Mark's text message chimed and he saw that it was Olga. He disregarded Roman and read Olga's brief message. It was her answer to his query, and it caused Mark to freeze and stare at his phone screen, stunned.

Roman gently tapped Mark's shoulder and broke his trance. He spoke to Mark in Romanian and forced the letter into Mark's hand. As the bellman stepped back, Mark tore open the envelope. He could feel the blood drain from his head as he read the message. He looked at Roman, who was tapping a number into his phone.

"Wait a minute," Mark yelled at him, but it was in vain. Roman didn't speak English.

Mark rushed out of the baggage room and back to the reception desk. The young woman's eyes widened as she sensed Mark's panic.

"Quick," said Mark. "I need to use your phone."

The woman froze.

"Come on, come on! It's urgent."

She hesitantly handed him a desk telephone while Mark searched his pockets for Boris's business card. He quickly called him again. Much to his frustration, it went to voicemail.

"Boris, this is Mark Kent," he said hastily. "Semra has been kidnapped from the Royal Boutique. They now want me, too. They are monitoring my mobile phone. So I can't use it. I will leave it at reception for you. Please, help…" His voice faded as the dial tone of the voice message cut him off.

The receptionist, having overheard Mark's message, handed him an empty manila envelope. Mark quickly dropped his phone into it, sealed the envelope, and instructed her to give it to Boris

Petrov. He then rushed to the front door of the hotel, past a bewildered Roman, and descended the outside stairs to the driveway.

The message Roman had handed him said that the bellman would alert Semra's kidnappers when Mark received the note. Within five minutes a car would arrive for him. Mark needed to be there promptly. It also advised Mark not to notify anyone, that they were monitoring his mobile phone.

Mark felt the chill of the night air. He had come to the lobby in jeans and a long-sleeved T-shirt. He had no time to return upstairs and fetch a coat. He surveyed the dark driveway, panting.

A pair of headlights appeared, turning into the driveway from the street. It had to be them. Mark cursed himself for not taking precautions with his mobile, especially since he had gotten in trouble with kidnappers who tracked him the same way in Budapest.

The headlights approached closer and a small, nondescript sedan pulled over. The front passenger window opened and the driver, a face Mark didn't recognize, ordered him to get in.

Mark tried to enter through the back passenger door. It was locked from within. "Get in the front," the driver ordered in a rush. Mark did.

As soon as he closed the door, the car took off. Mark turned to the driver to say something but was instantly cut off by a strong arm that grabbed his collar bones from behind and pinned him to his seat rest.

"What's going on?" he began to shout, but he could not get it all out. He was cut short with a sharp jab into his neck. It was a needle. The injection burned as it went into the side of his neck in the vicinity of his external jugular vein.

When the needle came out, the arm that pinned him down relaxed. The man in the back seat said, "Give me your phone."

Mark recognized the voice. He turned around to see the bulky figure of Milan in the back seat.

"It's not with me," Mark said. His voice sounded funny, as if it were someone else talking. Suddenly Mark was no longer fearful. He made a move toward Milan with his right arm, but the arm did not appear to be his.

"Search him," Milan ordered the driver.

The car pulled to a sudden stop by a curb. As the driver began frisking him, Mark started feeling woozy. "What's going on?" he tried to ask again, but his voice trailed and his head slumped.

He barely heard the driver reply. "Nothing."

As the car started off again, Mark lost consciousness.

CHAPTER 87

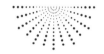

BRAȘOV, APRIL 11

"Here," said Traian Dalca, as he handed Boboc the fax he had just received. Andrei and Boboc put their heads together and examined it. It was early in the morning, before their shifts began. Dalca, who had called this special meeting, rubbed his chin and watched his two officers in front of his desk.

"Interesting," said Andrei.

The fax was from the Bucharest police chief regarding the attack on Irina Cernea. One of the assailants, the one bearing the knife, had been arrested after a brief investigation. It was a slam-dunk case because his fingerprints on the knife he dropped matched a known database of local criminals. Aurel Pichler was well known to Bucharest police, a common drug addict and thief. He had failed to take the simplest of precautions: wear a glove.

"Another Alin Barbu," said Boboc, looking at Dalca. "The Bucharest version."

"Did they get the second guy?" asked Andrei.

Boboc flipped to the second page. "Still at large." He read on. "It appears that the other guy is a tow truck driver. His company confirmed his employment. He apparently fled."

"Aha," said Andrei. "That explains how they got hold of the truck."

"This Pichler is a canary," Dalca interjected. "He came right out and told them everything. The police chief called and told me so before he sent the fax." He turned to Andrei. "You were right. It was not a mere kidnapping. They intended to kill the nurse."

Andrei grimaced, imagining Irina in the hands of those two thugs. It had been a close call.

Dalca continued. "This Pichler apparently named a certain Cezar Kaminesky as the one who hired him."

"Really?" Andrei suddenly sat up straight.

"Where did I hear that name?" asked Boboc.

"It's the other transplant organizer," said Andrei. "The shadowy one." He refreshed Boboc and Dalca on Cezar's role in Radu and Negrescu's transplant business, information that Irina Cernea had provided.

"Does this mean that this Cezar is behind Zhulati's murder?" Boboc wondered aloud.

"It could very well be," said Andrei.

"You'd better have another go at Alin Barbu," Dalca ordered his officers. "See what he does when you throw Cezar Kaminesky at him."

"There is something I don't understand," said Andrei. "These people, Zhulati, Irina Cernea, even Enver Muratovich in a roundabout way—they all worked for Cezar. Why would he want to kill his own people?"

"Doesn't make any business sense," Boboc agreed.

"Yeah, well," said Dalca, "we're progressing in fits and spurts. Let's hope that we eventually get to the bottom of all this."

"I don't believe that will happen until we have a better grasp of the overall context," said Andrei.

"You mean the international angle?" asked Dalca.

"Correct."

"We may never get there," said Dalca. "As I've said all along, let's clear the Braşov side of this case and I'll be happy with that."

"What we need is a witness who can put the whole picture together," Andrei mused.

"Dream on," said Boboc, chuckling.

Dalca, too, laughed. "Wait for Christmas," he said mockingly. "Maybe Santa Claus will deliver you the witness."

"That's seven months from now," said Andrei soberly. "How many more will die by then?"

Dalca and Boboc stared at Andrei.

Andrei ignored them and stood up. "This is too much to fathom before breakfast." He left without asking the others to join him.

"That hotel is disgusting," said Irina. She took a sip of cappuccino. "Do you know how many cockroaches I am sharing my room with?"

Andrei was about to bite into a croissant but changed his mind. "I am sorry that we couldn't get you a better place," he said.

They were in the French café across from Zhulati's apartment building.

"I have a friend here, a male nurse, I can stay with."

"I don't know if that's safe." Andrei took a bite.

"No worries. He is gay."

Andrei laughed. "That's not the point." He sipped his latte. "I meant security. It would jeopardize you *and* him."

"Well, if I stay in that hotel much longer, my health will be jeopardized." She was firm.

"I understand." Andrei used a soothing voice. "I promise I'll figure out a different place for you. Just hang in there a while longer."

"Hurry up, will you?" Irina said crossly, as she cut into her croque monsieur.

Andrei needed to change the subject. He looked out the window and pointed to an apartment building across the street. "Did you know that Dr. Zhulati lived there?"

Irina shuddered. "No, thank God." She glanced at the building.

"He sure tried hard to get me there," she said, shaking her head. "Is that where he died?"

"Yes."

"I can't believe that all this is happening." She stared at her coffee cup.

They both fell silent as they worked on their food. Andrei furtively eyed Irina. Despite her complaints about the hotel, she looked more rested. He wasn't surprised to hear that Zhulati had tried to get her into bed. She was strikingly attractive. Her blonde hair was down now, and framed vivid blue eyes with just the right amount of makeup.

Now those eyes were looking at Andrei expectantly. "So, why did you bring me here?"

Andrei surveyed the café to confirm that they wouldn't be overheard. He spoke quietly. "Bucharest Police caught one of your assailants."

Irina lifted a single eyebrow.

"He is a local street criminal by the name of Aurel Pichler. Do you know him?"

"No," said Irina without hesitation. "What did he want, did he say?"

"Yes." Andrei paused and thought about how to break the news. "To kill you."

"Oh." Irina's reaction was muted. She was already familiar with the notion since Andrei had repeatedly mentioned it. "Why?"

"Pichler testified that he was hired by Cezar Kaminesky."

Irina covered her mouth and turned her eyes toward the street. When she looked back at him they were full of tears.

Andrei continued. "We are currently theorizing that it was Cezar who contracted out the Zhulati murder."

"How so?"

"There are similarities between the two cases, yours and Zhulati's."

Irina wiped her tears before they flowed down her cheeks.

"Any idea why Cezar might want to do this?" asked Andrei.

"No," she said. "None." She pushed her unfinished plate away from her. "As far as Cezar was concerned, Zhulati and I were good employees." Her eyes squinted as she gave the issue some thought. "Do you think he was behind Enver, too?"

"I don't know," Andrei admitted. "I wonder if the complication with Yoet Tcaci spooked Cezar. You, Zhulati, and Enver were all involved in that operation. You are witnesses. If that's the case, there might be others he plans to eliminate."

"There aren't many more," said Irina. "Just the nurse anesthetist." She had given the police his name and they were tracking him down.

"There was also a driver, by the name of Kyril Kozak, a Ukrainian. Did you know him?"

"Not personally," she said. "Enver mentioned him once or twice. He used to say Kyril was reliable." She took a sip of coffee. "Have you located him?"

"Yes," said Andrei. "Iaşi Police is having him extradited from Odessa."

"So Kyril is safe," said Irina. She smiled ruefully at the irony of what she had just said. "What about Nicoleta?" she asked.

"We're keeping an eye on her, as we are with you," said Andrei. "But she doesn't know any of this. I do not want to spook her."

"She is spooked alright," said Irina. "But not by Cezar."

"Have you spoken with her?"

"Yes," said Irina. "That's what you asked me to do, isn't it?"

"I figured she'd be more comfortable with you than with us."

"You figured right," said Irina. "But she is very worried. You see, she is not unattached like me. She is a single mom raising two children. This affair threatens to upend her entire life."

Andrei already knew Nicoleta's personal circumstances. "I realize that," he said. "That's why I need you to keep her calm until we can enact my plan."

"I'll do my best, but I don't know how long she can stand the tension," said Irina. "We certainly should not tell her this news about Cezar. It would totally break her down."

"I agree," said Andrei. "Do your best to keep her calm. I appreciate what you're doing," he added.

Andrei looked up at Zhulati's apartment building and pondered the situation. The alcoholic surgeon had been a fragile link in the case. Now he was replaced by Nicoleta, on whom Andrei had placed all his hopes for a breakthrough. She, too, could easily crumble.

"Come on, let's go," he said to Irina. "I'll take you back to your luxury suite."

CHAPTER 88

UNKNOWN LOCATION, APRIL 10

Mark awoke woozy and nauseated. He felt a discomfort in his pelvis; his bladder was full. His nose itched. He tried to scratch it and discovered that he couldn't. His right arm would not move. He opened his eyes and surveyed his surroundings, his blurred vision slowly clearing.

He was lying on a hospital bed spread-eagled, his arms and legs in leather restraints. He checked his right arm. The sleeve of his T-shirt had been cut open from wrist to shoulder and an IV was running into a vein near his elbow. He tried to bend the arm and free himself. He couldn't. The restraint was well secured.

The room was dimly lit and he could not see much beyond his immediate bed. Mark spotted a silhouette at the edge of the darkness who murmured something in Romanian.

"Let me out!" Mark yelled.

The figure came closer and he realized it was a young, austere-looking woman dressed in blue scrubs, her black hair tightly bound. She looked down at him, placed her index finger over her lips and said, "Shhh." She then inspected the IV line and fiddled with the flow regulator.

"Who are you?" Mark shouted at the woman. "What are you doing to me?"

"Calm down, Dr. Kent." Mark heard a male voice in the darkness.

The woman turned back in the direction of the voice, nodded, and walked away. Soon the tall figure of Marco Radovich emerged from the shadows. He wore his characteristic dark glasses. "I don't want to sedate you again so soon."

"What did your goon inject me with?"

"Ketamine," said Radovich. "Effective, wouldn't you say?"

Mark's neck throbbed at the site of the injection. Radovich approached closer. "Don't worry; we know the right dose and how to titrate it."

Mark's head sank back on his pillow. "Yeah," he said, in a resigned tone. "After all, you run an elaborate medical organization, don't you?"

Radovich smiled and did not answer.

"Agent Radovich of the SRI," Mark said sarcastically. "Or should I call you Cezar?"

CHAPTER 89

UNKNOWN LOCATION, APRIL 10

"How do you know that?" Cezar hissed, his face contorted. He was clearly taken aback. He slid off his glasses and fixed his gaze on Mark. His damaged right cornea glistened in shades of beige and gray.

"Your eye," said Mark, pleased with the discomfort he had caused his captor. "How did that happen? Street fight in Gdańsk?"

Cezar momentarily inspected his glasses, trying to regain his composure. His smile returned. "Kent," he said, "I underestimated you." He wiped his glasses with a small cloth and put them back on. "Until I met you," he continued, "I didn't think much of American operatives. An impotent lot."

"And you," said Mark, "you're a phony. It must have been easy to bribe your way into a false identity with the SRI."

"In Romania, anything is possible." Cezar was calm now. "For the right price."

"When I first heard the name Cezar Kaminesky, I never thought that I would actually meet him."

"Or my wife," Cezar added.

Mark wasn't quite sure what Cezar intended by that remark. Had he discovered their tryst in Bucharest?

"I need to pee," said Mark. "And I need some water."

Cezar called back the young nurse, whispered a few words to her, and walked away. In the next few minutes Mark endured the indignation of having his pants pulled down and a Foley catheter inserted into his penis. It was uncomfortable and burned as it went. Mark was nonetheless relieved to empty his bladder. She then held a plastic cup of water near his lips and let him drink through a straw.

When the nurse departed, Mark sank back and considered his predicament. The young man in the mysterious photo that Olga had sent had an injured right eye. When Mark discovered this in his hotel room and questioned Olga, the reply she sent shocked him. The photo was of a young Cezar. That's when Mark put two-and-two together. Despite the hazy photo, the bad eye of the young man was obvious, and uncannily similar to that of the SRI agent who had foisted himself and Milan on Mark. Radovich was Cezar.

So Cezar had been following Mark all along. If so, he had to know that Mark visited Vadim Rusu. Mark hoped that Cezar only monitored his mobile's GPS signal and not the contents of Mark's messages. He was glad to have left his phone at the hotel. That way it couldn't fall into Cezar's hands.

Mark wondered what Cezar's intentions were. Did he seek information? Mark felt the same dread that he had experienced when Vadim Rusu was chasing him. He closed his eyes and tried to relax. He would need his full wits for whatever was to come.

* * *

Mark was alone for what felt like days. He had lost track of time. He wondered how long it had been since he was kidnapped. His surroundings held no clue as to the time of day, although his body, clearly in need of sleep, told him that it wasn't yet morning. Ketamine, he knew, was a relatively short-acting drug. They had probably given him more through the IV in his arm to keep him further sedated. That's why Cezar had mentioned that they had titrated the dose, knowing just how much of it to pump into him.

The sedation was not a substitute for proper sleep. Mark figured it had to be the middle of the night.

Cezar eventually reappeared, dressed in jeans and a leather motorcycle jacket, zipped up. He sat down and crossed his legs, revealing black leather boots.

"Why are you doing this to me?" asked Mark.

"Kent," said Cezar, "you have been a major nuisance, a thorn in our side."

Cezar pulled out a pack of cigarettes from his jacket and lit an unfiltered one. He took a long drag and blew the smoke out toward the ceiling. Mark was repelled by the smoke but tried to hide it. Cezar seemed like he wanted to talk. It wouldn't hurt to engage him. "There is something I don't understand," Mark said.

Cezar picked a piece of tobacco from his lips and flicked it off, cocking his head.

Mark continued. "If you were already following me and tracking my moves, why did you go through all the trouble with that SRI ruse?"

Cezar watched the thin wisp of smoke emanating from his cigarette. "I wanted to meet you," he said, his eyes on the cloud. He then turned his gaze back to Mark. "Size you up."

"I thought you held us Americans in low regard," Mark retorted sarcastically.

"I do, indeed. But after all the trouble you caused in Hungary, I needed to see what I was up against." He took another drag from his cigarette. "You know," he said, "Tibor Bognár is an old friend."

"What a surprise," Mark said dryly.

Cezar ignored the jab. "Tibor sent me a message from jail that I should be careful with you. I must say, when I first met you at the Athénée, I didn't quite get it. You looked hapless." He flicked ashes from his cigarette onto the floor. "Now I know better."

"How did you find out that I was coming to Romania?" asked Mark. "Through the staff of Negrescu's children?"

"Good guess." Cezar nodded approvingly. "That SRI identity was not custom-made for you. I've used it in the past. It comes in handy in a pinch."

The ruse had succeeded because Mark knew nothing about the Romanian internal security service. He couldn't even confirm the authenticity of Radovich's badge. Mark regretted not contacting Interpol at the French Embassy as Leon had recommended. They might have set him straight.

"You know," said Mark, "I really did come here for Iancu Negrescu's funeral. Nothing else."

"Yeah, well, you still stuck your nose in where it didn't belong." Cezar uncrossed his legs, one boot stomping the ground. "What is it with you, Kent? How come you can't keep yourself out of trouble?"

Mark wondered the same thing. He changed the subject. "Tell me, Cezar, why did you blame Radu and Negrescu for the fiasco with Vadim Rusu's son?"

Cezar's eyes narrowed as he realized the depth of Mark's knowledge. Mark braced himself for questions about how he had discovered this. To his surprise, Cezar remained quiet, momentarily contemplative. Then he took a last puff from his cigarette. "Very good, Kent," he said, with a forced smile. "Yes, I definitely did underestimate you."

Relieved that Cezar had not pressed him, Mark stayed quiet and tried not to make eye contact with him.

"It was a good move," Cezar finally said, in answer to Mark's question. "You see, I kept myself clean and I had someone else eliminate my competition." He threw the spent cigarette on the floor and extinguished it with his boot. "Kill two birds with one stone."

"You've killed more than two birds," said Mark angrily. "You have the blood of many more on your hands."

Cezar laughed out loud, showing gnarly, tobacco-stained teeth. "Now that you reminded me, I'd better go to confession and get my sins absolved."

Mark felt stupid about trying to elicit remorse from a guy like Cezar. He changed the subject. "Where is my girlfriend? What did you do with her?"

"The Turk?" Cezar shook his head in disapproval. "A girl?!" He chortled. "Interesting taste you have, Doctor. Not my thing, but I must admit she is a pretty creature."

"She has no involvement in any of this," said Mark. "You should let her go."

"She is safe," Cezar said. "For now," he added with a grin. "I do have a few men who'd like to give her a test run." Cezar waited for a reaction. Mark remained expressionless. "You tried her, I presume," Cezar said sardonically. "How is she?"

Mark turned his head away.

Cezar pressed on. "Which do you prefer, Doctor, her or my wife?"

There it was, Olga again. Cezar had obviously discovered where Mark had been on the night he had questioned him about.

"You think I wouldn't find out?" Cezar's tone took a decidedly foul turn.

The damn mobile, thought Mark. That's how Cezar probably knew. "I gather you two are no longer husband and wife," he said.

"So she says, the bitch!" Cezar spat on the floor. "Did you enjoy her?"

"I don't understand," said Mark. "You put up with her customers, not to mention her affair with Nicolae Radu. So what if I have a one-night stand with her?"

"What did she tell you?" Cezar demanded, raising his voice.

"She told me that Nicolae was a great lover," Mark answered. "That you and I don't even come close."

"She told you about Dima Rusu, didn't she?" His voice grew louder.

Mark was relieved to hear the question. It indicated that Cezar had no knowledge of the texts Olga had sent him. "No, I got all that from Interpol," he lied. "They know a lot about you. You know they're after you, don't you?"

Cezar laughed at the comment. "Everyone's after me," he said. "But no one can catch me." The braggadocio in his voice was unmistakable.

You don't know the half of it, Mark wanted to tell him. *Wait until Vadim Rusu comes after you.* But he held his tongue. He wanted to get off the subject of Olga. "So," he said, "you now have the Braşov transplant business all to yourself. You should be happy."

"It's a tough business," Cezar responded. "I don't know how long I'll hang on to it."

"What is it?" Mark asked. "Is taking over for Radu and Negrescu turning out to be a challenge?"

"You're quite perceptive, Kent."

"Thank you." This time Mark accepted the compliment. He chuckled. "Be careful what you wish for, ha?"

"That son of a bitch Rusu did not stop with Radu and Negrescu."

"Tell me about it," said Mark. "I witnessed them in Turkey."

"I don't give a damn about the ones in Turkey. But there is one in Braşov that really hurts."

Mark pondered the comment. "Muratovich?" he asked.

"Very good," said Cezar. "You seem to know everything, don't you?"

"What was so special about Muratovich?"

"He was the best recruiter, a real gold mine. I had hoped to get him on my team. Do you know how hard it is to convince these dumb peasants? Muratovich was like a magician." For a moment Cezar pondered his business. "Besides, doctors and nurses are getting hard to come by."

"Yes, I can see that," Mark said. "The assassination of the most prominent surgeon can't be good for business."

"Who, Gazioğlu?" asked Cezar.

"Yes. I was there," said Mark. "Do you know how they killed him?"

Cezar waited expectantly. He obviously had not heard.

"They decapitated him. A fucking bloodbath! I saw the scene with my own eyes."

Cezar's eyebrows went up.

"And they took his head away. Sent it to Rusu."

It took a few seconds for Cezar to absorb the news. Mark continued, "Vadim Rusu is an unforgiving man."

Cezar let out a throaty cough. "Who sent you to Rusu?" he asked.

"What makes you think I met Rusu?" Mark answered.

"Oh, come on, Kent!" Cezar said indignantly. "Why else would you come to this godforsaken corner of Europe and visit Skytower?"

Mark decided it was futile to deny he knew him. "All right, okay. No one sent me. I made my own arrangements." Now that he was certain Cezar had not seen Olga's texts, he could make headway with this lie.

"You have guts, Kent." Cezar nodded approvingly. "When I first met you, I couldn't imagine that you were tough enough to face Rusu."

"I had no choice," Mark answered, pleased with the compliment in spite of himself. "I had to do it."

"Why?" asked Cezar.

"Same as you," said Mark. "I was a thorn in his side because of what I had done in Hungary. He kept sending his men after me, trying to bring me to Chişinău. I got tired of the chase and decided to give him what he wanted."

"And what was that?" Cezar asked.

"I let him know who I was and that I had no interest in this transplant business, that I just stumbled into it through bad luck." Mark raised his head and looked at Cezar for a reaction.

He seemed to be buying it. "And what was his response?"

"Rusu might be a brutal guy," Mark said, "but he is reasonable. He had already conducted a fairly detailed investigation on me. Nothing I said was in conflict with it."

"What else did you discuss?"

"Small talk," said Mark. "How to improve relations between America and Russia."

"Come now, Kent!"

Mark laughed. "You have no sense of humor," he said. "Nothing else. We parted amicably and I am quite certain I now have him off my back."

Cezar looked at him skeptically.

"And then, just when I thought I was free, I am caught in your clutches." Mark was now being truthful. "So, now you know. Why don't you let me and my girlfriend free and we'll get out of your life. I promise you'll never hear from me again."

Cezar did not respond. He stood up and called out for the nurse in Romanian. She emerged from the shadows holding a large syringe.

"You take me for a sucker," said Cezar, his tone icy. "You feed me stupid shit lies."

Mark's heart sank. He had really thought that he had convinced Cezar as he had done with others.

"If you want to play it that way, no problem." Cezar had a muted conversation with the nurse. She nodded.

While the nurse connected the syringe to Mark's IV line, Cezar faced Mark with a sinister grin. "Goodbye, Kent. Before you leave for good, you might as well make yourself useful."

The nurse depressed the plunger and opened the flow regulator on the IV. She attached a pulse oximeter on Mark's fingertip. Cezar briefly observed her, then began walking away.

As the medicine ran in, Mark wondered what Cezar's last comment meant. "No, please don't," Mark wanted to scream at Cezar before he disappeared. But the medicine was already taking its hold. Mark drifted off, hoping that it was a sedative dose of Ketamine and not a fatal one.

CHAPTER 90

BRAȘOV, APRIL 12

Andrei was awakened by the shrill sound of his mobile phone. He had taken to sleeping with it at his bedside. Ana stirred. "What is it?"

Andrei turned on a lamp and picked up the phone. "Irina," he whispered. It was shortly past five a.m. After a brief conversation, Andrei hung up and slid his covers off.

"What's going on?" asked Ana.

"She just got word," Andrei answered. "A transplant, scheduled for later today. Nicoleta was put on standby for a screening CT."

* * *

"Are you absolutely certain about this?" Dalca asked Andrei.

It was another pre-breakfast meeting, Andrei seated in front of the chief's desk. The second floor of the station was partially dark, with only a skeleton crew at work. Dalca looked disheveled in rumpled jeans and T-shirt, sporting a thick stubble. He had obviously come in straight out of bed.

"Yes, sir," said Andrei. "It's coming down sooner than I expected."

"We don't have much time," said Dalca. "I have to alert the Chief and the Governor." Dalca rubbed his eyes with the palms of his hands. "I am not looking forward to this."

The Governor and police chief were Dalca's problem; Andrei was eager to get on with it. "We also have to obtain urgent warrants from the prosecutor."

They were interrupted by Boboc, who lumbered in noisily.

"You're late," said Dalca.

Boboc held up a paper tray of three coffee cups and a white paper bag. He laid out the piping hot coffee and fresh croissants on Dalca's desk. "From the French café by Zhulati's," he said.

They quietly sipped the freshly brewed coffee. "Excellent," said Dalca, Boboc's tardiness forgiven.

Boboc took two croissants onto his lap and sat down. He spoke with a full mouth. "What's the layout of the place?"

They pored over floor plans of the hospital that Andrei had previously procured, concentrating on the outpatient annex. Boboc examined the document intently, dropping crumbs of flaky dough onto it. "This will take more than the two of us," he said. He looked up at Dalca. "Will this be a stealthy operation or do we go in with guns blazing?"

Dalca sipped more coffee and pondered the question. "If we go in there with visible force and this turns out to be nothing," he said, "it will be a huge fiasco, a major PR disaster."

"I don't believe we need a lot of muscle for this operation," commented Andrei. "After all, we're going after medical personnel. It is highly unlikely that we will encounter armed resistance."

"I agree," said Boboc. "Still, we should be cautious and have some uniforms for support."

"You two will do it." Dalca made a command decision. "You enter plainclothes. Once you secure cooperation within, you can bring in the uniforms before raiding the target. But the uniforms remain out of sight until then. Is that clear?"

"Yes, sir," Andrei said. "How do we get cooperation within?"

"We will have to give someone in that hospital advance notice," said Dalca. "Someone who won't raise a stink."

Boboc wiped his mouth with the back of his hand and smiled. "Yeah," he said in a mocking tone. "We're in trouble with that hospital, aren't we?" He playfully slapped Andrei's shoulder. "Thanks to someone in Sector 1."

Andrei ignored the dig. "How about your old friend, the security chief? What was his name?"

"Vulpe," said Boboc. "Silviu Vulpe."

"What's this about?" Dalca had not heard about Boboc's connection.

Boboc explained that he had received an assurance of assistance from his old colleague, now the security chief at Spitatul Martinu, if they needed it.

"Very well," said Dalca. "Is he reliable?"

"Yes, sir, he is." Boboc stood up and shook croissant crumbs off his leg. "Once he knows what this is about, I am sure he'll cooperate."

"I'll give you six uniforms," said Dalca. "I want everyone to wear body cameras. We have to keep a record of everything for evidence and to protect ourselves against any backlash from the hospital."

Boboc sat down again and reached for his coffee. "So, let me get this straight. Andrei and I go in first. We rendezvous with security, and then let the uniforms in through some back door."

"That's right," said Dalca. "Boboc, I want you to arrange the raid plan and brief the uniform team. And let me know as soon as possible about your inside contact."

Dalca turned to Andrei. "You, Costiniu, will prepare the search and arrest warrants for the prosecutor. Pay careful attention to detail."

"Yes, sir." Andrei sensed the electricity in the air. This was to be either the biggest triumph of Dalca's career or his worst failure.

"Anything else?" asked Boboc.

Dalca reached for a croissant. "How about a doctor?" he said.

"Doctor, what doctor?" Boboc raised his eyebrows as he gulped his coffee.

"You will be raiding a surgical procedure and interrupting it.

How will you deal with the patient?" Dalca chided Boboc. "All you think about is muscle and insiders," he complained. "How will you insure that the donor is not harmed?"

"You're right, Chief," said Andrei. "We'll see what we can do about that."

Boboc gave Andrei an *are you crazy* look. Where would they find a doctor at the last minute? Andrei gave him their secret *calm down* gesture, moving his downturned palm up and down.

"And I," said Dalca, oblivious to the exchange between the partners, "will make some phone calls."

* * *

"It's happening," said Irina. "The donor is in."

It was slightly past noon when Andrei took her call. He had just forwarded his warrants to Dalca and the prosecutor's office.

Irina added, "This whole thing is unusual."

"How so?"

"Well, for beginners, it's a late start. We usually start operating in early morning. And then, Nicoleta tells me that the donor is atypical."

"What does she mean?"

"Older. And he doesn't look like the usual peasants."

Andrei did not know what to make of all that. He hung up and notified Dalca and Boboc, activating the plan. As he rose out of his desk, Irina called again.

"Nicoleta just sent me an urgent text," she said. "You need to hear this."

"What?"

"The surgeon came to the CT console to examine the scan. He commented that he was told to remove both kidneys."

"I don't get it," said Andrei. "Isn't it a live donor?"

"Yes," said Irina.

"Can he live without kidneys?" Andrei asked, incredulous.

"You can survive without one kidney, but not without both."

Irina's voice took an ominous tone. "The donor will be committed to dialysis or, if he is discarded like Yoet, he will die."

Andrei went quiet, absorbing this. Finally he asked, "Are there two recipients?"

"That's the other thing," Irina answered. "Apparently there are no recipients." She paused and then added, "That explains the late start. If they are just harvesting and nothing else, they have plenty of time to finish up. Nicoleta says that the surgeon was instructed to place the kidneys in the preservative solution and send them on."

"What do you make of that?" asked Andrei.

Irina paused. "As I said, it's unusual. I've never seen any kidneys removed and saved for later. They have all been live donor transplants at Martinu."

"Will it be the same sort of crew?" asked Andrei. "Are there any others, bodyguards and such?"

"As far as I gather, it's only a small medical team. That part is the same. But one thing is for sure," she added. "This donor is in serious trouble."

CHAPTER 91

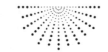

BRAŞOV, APRIL 12

The outpatient annex at Spitatul Martinu was dark and deserted.

Andrei and Boboc had been dismayed to discover that the hospital had some thirty-five different entrances. Most were locked and alarmed, including two entrances to the annex. They entered the hospital through the main building, at the Emergency Room ambulance bay.

The uniformed team waited in a van outside the annex while Andrei and Boboc met up with Boboc's old friend by the triage desk. Silviu Vulpe turned out to be a tall, slim man who looked considerably younger than Boboc, even though they were roughly the same age.

"Fancy meeting you like this," Vulpe addressed Boboc dryly. He bore a military countenance in his well-starched uniform. There were no handshakes, and he did not acknowledge Andrei.

"Nasty business," Vulpe murmured, as he led them into a small doctor's room. He motioned to a young, somewhat bewildered physician who was dictating into a medical record to leave his computer and follow the three of them.

The young doctor hastily threw a wrinkled, stained white coat over his green scrubs and obediently followed the imperious Vulpe, nodding hello to the two policemen whom he did not know. "What is this all about?" he asked Boboc, as the group departed the ER on the heels of the taciturn Vulpe. The hospital's security chief walked surprisingly fast despite a limp that caused him to drag his right leg.

The doctor had apparently been warned by Vulpe that his assistance would be needed in a police matter, but with no specifics.

"We may need your help with a victim of a criminal act," said Boboc.

"Inside the hospital?!" The doctor was incredulous.

Vulpe turned and gave him a stern look.

As they approached the annex, they passed by Radiology, where several technicians eyed the curious group with interest. Andrei spotted Nicoleta among them, wearing an anxious expression. He gave her a subtle nod but otherwise avoided her gaze.

They passed a set of double doors into the outpatient annex, where Vulpe deactivated the alarm to one of the entrances. The young doctor stood by, curious but afraid to ask. A look of alarm flooded his face as six uniformed policemen poured in, bearing side-arm pistols and automatic rifles held across their chests.

So much for no muscle, thought Andrei. Boboc had obviously disregarded Dalca's directive.

But Silviu Vulpe was pleased to encounter the armed men. His expression softened and his attitude became more hospitable. "This way," he said to Boboc in a solicitous manner, as if he were a hotel bellman.

"Wait a minute." Boboc stopped his host. He pulled out a diagram of the annex and began barking instructions to his team as to who should be positioned where. Vulpe joined in the conversation and threw in a couple of helpful suggestions.

They left one of the uniforms to guard the gate and moved on, the ER doctor now in near panic. Two more officers were left to guard consecutive turns of the dim hallway, while the rest of the team continued on to their target, two old operating rooms in a defunct, abandoned corner of the annex.

The hallways were lit solely by small fire regulation lights. They proceeded slowly, trying not to make much noise with their footsteps. Vulpe admonished the doctor, who had carelessly posed a brief question that echoed off the walls.

The first operating room they came to was dark and obviously out of commission. Farther down, a bright light emanated into the hallway, beckoning them to the second room.

Boboc quietly issued final instructions to his team and asked Vulpe and the doctor to stand behind. Andrei and Boboc stood by the door of the operating room, while the uniform officers lined each side, rifles ready. They then burst in.

"Police!" yelled Boboc. "Stop what you're doing."

The operating room was small and brightly lit with powerful overhead lights illuminating the operating table. Two pairs of eyes turned toward the police team. The anesthetist peeked behind his curtain and a woman looked up from the opposite side of the table, eyes wide with surprise.

Andrei and Boboc stared at the back of what they presumed to be the surgeon. He was bent over the operating table continuing to work, oblivious to the loud interruption. "Metz," he said, lifting his right hand up. The woman handed him a pair of Metzenbaum dissecting scissors. As he placed the instrument into the wound, she nudged him with her arm and nodded in the direction of the intruders. The surgeon turned around.

He was a young, tall man, with obviously long hair packed into a bouffant cap. A thick black beard protruded from the edges of his mask. He still held the Metzenbaum scissors in his right hand. It took the surgeon a few seconds to comprehend the scene. He then pointed the scissors toward the police team and screamed, "Get out of here. This is a sterile area."

Two uniformed officers aimed their rifles at him while a third yanked the scissors out of his hand and roughly jerked him away from the operating table. "What are you doing? You can't do this!" he protested, as he landed in the arms of the pair of uniforms. He had a heavy accent.

Vulpe crept into the room with the ER doctor in tow, just in time to witness the handcuffing of the surgeon now lying face down on the floor.

Boboc yelled, "Stop this operation. You are all under arrest."

Andrei nudged the ER doctor toward the operating table. As the doctor took reluctant steps, taking care not to contaminate the drapes, the surgeon, hands cuffed behind his back, yelled, "We can't stop! We are deep in the patient's retroperitoneum." Andrei and Boboc looked at each other perplexedly, having never heard the medical term for where the kidneys reside.

The ER doctor ignored the surgeon and leaned his head into the operating field, widely exposed by a metal retractor. He made eye contact with the nurse standing motionless across the table and asked, "What is this?"

"Nephrectomy," she replied.

"What for?"

There was no answer.

Silviu Vulpe observed the exchange, stunned and silent. He had obviously expected the police raid to be in vain.

The ER doctor turned to the police team and raised his hands in resignation. "Look," he said, "this is way above my pay grade." He boldly pushed Vulpe aside and marched out of the room.

The nurse assisting in the surgery addressed Andrei and Boboc. "Wait a minute, please." She turned toward a back table and moistened some lap sponges in a plastic bucket of saline. "I need to protect the wound." She wrung the sponges. "Just give me a minute, will you?"

While the nurse removed the retractor and began packing the wound with the wet sponges, the anesthetist chimed in. "Let her do what she needs to do," he said. "And don't take me away. I need to be here to support his breathing and give him anesthesia."

Andrei and Boboc exchanged glances with Vulpe. None of them knew how to proceed. Andrei asked the armed officers to stand away from the operating table.

The anesthetist continued. "I can't wake him up until the wound is closed."

At that moment a new figure entered the operating room. Alexandru Coman, dressed in casual slacks and a polo shirt, stopped and stared at the scene. The chief medical officer of the hospital was panting, having obviously run down the hall to get here. Beads of sweat appeared on his forehead. He surveyed the room with much surprise.

"Who are you?" he said to the nurse and the anesthetist. They stared back at him in silence.

Coman then took note of Vulpe and the police team, his gaze stopping at Andrei. As they locked eyes, blood drained from Coman's face, causing his white goatee to nearly disappear. He staggered and looked as if he were about to faint.

PART FOUR

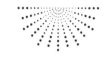

CHAPTERS 92–114

CHAPTER 92

BRAŞOV, SPITATUL MARTINU, APRIL 12

Mark awoke in a haze. He opened his eyes and raised his head to look around. His world was spinning. He gave up and waited for his vertigo to calm down. A searing pain emerged in his right side. He moaned loudly. He noticed a blurry female figure approaching him with a syringe. Oh, no! It was that nightmare. He was still in Cezar's captivity.

The nurse said something in Romanian and injected the contents of the syringe into an IV line. Mark noticed that the line was on his left arm now, not his right, as before. He tested his restraints and moved his left arm, only to have the nurse gently hold it down. He tried his right arm and his legs. They moved. No restraints!

His vision began to clear. He noticed that the nurse was not the one in the nightmare. She was blonde and middle-aged. She wore a peculiar uniform, plain white shirt lined with red stripes, white pants also striped down the side. She smiled at Mark as she fiddled with the flow regulator. "This should make you feel better," she said, in heavily accented English.

Mark tried raising his head again. The world was more stable now. He was in a well-lit room, a hospital room with a single bed, his. The nurse turned and began walking away. Mark followed her wide buttocks swinging up and down. Before leaving the room, she stopped and spoke to someone in Romanian.

Mark forced himself up further, resting on his right elbow, curious about who else was in the room. The move provoked another sharp pain in his right flank. He groaned, prompting the nurse to turn and look back. A male figure appeared beside her, intently gazing at Mark.

"It's okay," Mark mumbled as he lay back down.

The nurse left. The man approached Mark. "Easy. Don't strain yourself," he said, in remarkably good English. He was handsome, lean, and athletic. He wore a white shirt, collar open, covered by a windbreaker with an official insignia on the left chest.

The medicine was taking hold and Mark's pain was easing. He felt a peculiar, uneasy calm as he touched his painful flank. It was covered with a bulky dressing. "Where am I?" Mark asked, slurring his words. "Who are you?"

"You are in Braşov," said the man. "I am Andrei Costiniu, *Subinspector*, Braşov Police, Sector 1."

"Braşov?" Mark mumbled, confused. "How did I get here?"

"Never mind that." The policeman leaned toward Mark. He had striking, deep blue eyes. "And you are Mark Kent, is that correct? US citizen?"

"Yes," Mark confirmed. "How do you know me?"

"I've heard your name," said the policeman. "You had no ID on you. We identified you through the CT scan records."

"CT! What CT?"

"You had a CT scan of your abdomen before your surgery."

Mark was feeling woozy as the medicine reached its full effect. No ID? That was correct. He had left his wallet and passport at the hotel room. It took a few more seconds for Mark to fully register everything he heard. Surgery! He ran his hand over the dressing that covered his flank. "Is that what this is?"

"Yes," said the policeman. "They tried to remove your kidney."

"Kidney," Mark whispered. "Why?" He closed his eyes.

Suddenly he realized he knew the answer. Cezar's last words came back to him: *Before you leave for good, you might as well make yourself useful.*

*Useful, useful…*It reverberated in his mind, echoing eerily. Mark now understood. Amid his chemical haze, none of it seemed to matter. "Where is Semra?" he whimpered.

"Who?"

Mark opened his eyes. He saw two policemen overlapping each other. "Please, you need to find her."

"Who is she?"

"Boris will know." Mark's head sank into the pillow. "Call Boris."

"Boris who?"

The policeman's question faded as Mark drifted into unconsciousness.

CHAPTER 93

BRAŞOV, SPITATUL MARTINU, APRIL 12

A ndrei sat across from the patient and tried to tune out the steady drone of the monitors. It was late evening and Andrei had been up since before dawn. Despite his fatigue, he was excited to be here, staring at the elusive American agent who had become something of a legend. What a shock it had been when the donor they rescued turned out to be Mark Kent. Andrei wondered how this guileful operative had gotten himself into this predicament. Who was responsible for the operation they had raided? And more important, what did the American know? How much would he share?

The nurse had told Andrei that she had given the patient a hefty dose of morphine. He would be drowsy for a while. Andrei did not care. He would stay at the American's bedside all night if necessary, until he woke up and was able to talk.

Outside the room they had placed a uniformed guard, allowing no one in except medical personnel. The door creaked open and the guard nodded to Andrei, letting in Alexandru Coman.

The chief medical officer had regained his composure. Dressed impeccably in a suit and tie, with his fleshy complexion back to normal, he stared at the drowsy patient. "I hear he will be fine."

"Good to know," Andrei replied. "Did you know that they intended to remove both his kidneys?"

Coman's eyes widened. "No! Do you have any idea who is behind this?"

"Not with certainty," said Andrei. "We have some suspicions." He pointed to the patient. "He needs to confirm them. I am quite sure he knows who did it."

"Have you spoken with him?"

"Briefly. Just enough to confirm his identity."

"Who is he?"

"A foreigner." Andrei was reluctant to disclose details. "Like most of the other donors."

Coman did not push the point. "I owe you a big apology, both for myself and on behalf of Spitatul Martinu." He was no longer the distant, arrogant administrator Andrei had first encountered.

"Yeah, well…" Andrei was magnanimous. "What I came to you with did violate the bounds of credulity."

They both fell silent and stared at the patient.

Coman pulled out an envelope from the inner pocket of his jacket. "Mr. Lazarescu, the CEO of the hospital, and I had a meeting, just the two of us. We discussed what happened and how this was possible."

"There had to be someone within your ranks in Administration," Andrei said. "Someone reasonably high up who could facilitate it."

"Yes," Coman agreed. "And without our knowledge." He handed Andrei the envelope. "We think that this is your man."

Andrei tore the envelope open and took out a one-page Human Resources summary, complete with name, contacts, and a photo.

"Our vice president in charge of surgical services," said Coman. "Mr. Lazarescu and I have been trying to contact him since your raid, but he is not answering."

The information was a peace offering. Andrei had no time to thank Coman. This vice president was either on the lam, or worse, another victim of whoever was murdering those involved with the transplant enterprise. Andrei rushed out to raise an alert with Dalca to find the man.

* * *

"Water," the patient moaned. "I need water."

Andrei called for the nurse. "Can he have a drink?"

"Yes," she said. "He is on a clear liquid diet."

Soon the American was sitting up in his hospital bed, looking better after two glasses of water. He now sipped ginger ale from a can through a straw.

Andrei pulled a chair close to the bed. He unzipped his windbreaker and removed it. "How are you?" he asked as he sat down and crossed his legs.

The American ran his hand by his surgical dressing. "Better. Doesn't hurt as much."

"Good."

"I seem to remember something about my kidney," said Kent. "I am not certain. I was drugged."

"You had an operation to remove your kidney."

"Yes, right…" The patient put the ginger ale aside. "Did they take it?"

"No," said Andrei. "We intervened and stopped it as they got to…" Andrei pulled his notebook and shuffled through some pages. "Your adrenal gland."

"They came close," said the American, a faint smile appearing on his lips.

"They intended to take *both* your kidneys."

The patient's eyes turned down and the color drained from his face. For a while he did not respond. He then pulled himself together and looked at Andrei. "Thank you," he said, "for saving my life."

"Do you know who did this?"

"Yes. A man by the name of Cezar Kaminesky."

Andrei nodded. "That's what I thought."

"Do you know him?"

"Yes. He has been one of the suspects in our investigation."

"So you know that he runs a transplant enterprise here in Braşov?"

"So we've heard." Andrei got his notebook ready. "How did you get involved with him?"

"I didn't," said Kent. "He tailed me and kidnapped me, in Chişinău."

Andrei looked up from his notebook in surprise. "Moldova?"

"Yes."

"What were you doing there?"

"It's a long and complicated story," said the American. He reached for the ginger ale can but as he twisted, got stuck with a painful spasm. "Ow!"

Andrei handed him the can. The American waited for the spasm to calm, took a sip, and said, "I promise I'll tell you the details, but first I need your help in contacting someone. It's urgent."

"Semra?" asked Andrei.

Mark looked surprised. "How do you know that name?"

"You mentioned some names before you passed out." Andrei shuffled some pages and read out loud, "Semra, Boris."

"Boris," said Mark, with urgency in his voice. "I need to contact Boris."

Andrei pulled out his mobile phone. "What's the number?"

"I don't know," said Kent.

Andrei eyed the patient quizzically.

Kent explained, "The number is in my cell phone and I left it in my hotel at Chişinău."

"So how do you propose to contact him?"

"I need to access the Cloud," said Mark. "I can get my contacts from there. Can you do it on your mobile, or bring a computer here?"

"Sure." Andrei stood up. "Who is this Boris, anyway? What's his last name?"

"Boris Petrov," said Mark. "He is Vadim Rusu's assistant. They run a Chişinău-based security company called Hercules."

"Russians?" asked Andrei.

"Yes, Russians. But they reside in Moldova."

This had to be the mysterious Russian that Corneliu Balaş, Andrei's SRI contact, had mentioned. Andrei felt a surge of excitement. He wanted to pump his fist in the air but of course, he didn't. He first needed to assist the American.

CHAPTER 94

BRAȘOV, SPITATUL MARTINU, APRIL 12

"Dr. Kent, good to hear from you. Are you all right?"

The sound of Boris's voice was strangely comforting. Mark sat at the edge of his bed, phone to his ear, while the Brașov police officer stood nearby, listening curiously. There was no way to have this conversation in private. The phone belonged to the policeman who had helped Mark navigate through a series of passwords and security codes to gain access to the Cloud.

"No, I am not all right." Mark continued without giving Boris a chance to interject. "Did you get my message and my phone?"

"Yes."

"Semra," said Mark. "They kidnapped her. You need to find her."

The policeman leaned in, notepad in hand.

"We have," said Boris.

Mark pulled the phone off his ear. He stared at its screen in disbelief. "Is she okay?"

"Shaken a bit, but otherwise fine."

"Oh, thank God!" Mark let out a sigh of relief.

"But I have bad news for you."

"What?" asked Mark anxiously.

Boris was hesitant with his answer. "Well, you see…"

"Come on! Say it."

The Braşov policeman cocked his head like a dog, listening eagerly.

"All right," said Boris, summoning courage. "She does not want to go back to you."

"Is that so? What does she intend to do with herself?"

"She wants to stay here, with me."

Mark pulled the phone off his ear again, this time beginning to laugh. He caught himself, muted the phone, and let it out. The policeman stared at him curiously. "What's so funny?" he asked.

Mark gained his composure and unmuted the phone. "I am sorry to hear that," he said solemnly.

"I figured so," said Boris. "But I think it is for the best."

"So what happened to her?"

"We found her in an apartment not far from the hotel. The kidnapper, I am afraid, did not do well."

Mark could just imagine.

Boris continued. "A guy named Milan. Big guy."

"He works for Cezar," said Mark. "The two of them were using an SRI ruse."

"Yes, so we understand."

"How did you find her so quickly?"

"The hotel that you stayed at, the Royal—we are part owners. The bellman is our employee. He gave us a description of the man who abducted Semra from the lobby. We got a plate number of his car from our CCTV cameras outside the building."

"A small sedan," said Mark. "He came back for me later."

"Yes, we caught that on film too. Same car. We hoped that we would find you with Semra."

"He took me elsewhere," said Mark. "To Cezar. I don't know where it was."

"We didn't either. We lost track of the car after it picked you up and left the hotel premises."

"So how did you find Milan?"

"We tracked down the license plate," said Boris. "The rest was easy. This Milan, he lives here in Chișinău. We raided his apartment and found Semra there."

"What happened to him?"

"Milan is no longer with us," said Boris crisply.

"Who is Milan?" asked the policeman, who could hear only Mark's side of the conversation.

Mark pulled the phone away from his ear. "I'll explain later," he whispered.

"Did Cezar harm you?" Boris asked.

"I'm not sure yet," said Mark.

"What does that mean?"

"I am in Brașov, in that Martinu hospital that you had mentioned," Mark answered. "Cezar tried to take my kidneys, make a donor out of me."

"Oh, my! Are you okay?"

"Yes," said Mark. "Brașov Police rescued me before they removed the first kidney. But I have a surgical scar on my flank. I have to recuperate from the operation."

"*Geçmiş olsun*," said Boris in perfect Turkish, the customary response to news of illness. *May it come to pass.*

Mark thanked him in Turkish. "*Teşekkürler.*"

"So did they catch Cezar?" asked Boris.

Mark realized that he had not asked the policeman this question. "Wait a minute," he said. He muted the phone again and asked Andrei Costiniu if they had caught Cezar Kaminesky. Andrei shook his head.

"No, they didn't," Mark told Boris.

"All right," said Boris. "We're looking for him, too."

"He is elusive," Mark commented.

"Never mind that," Boris answered with confidence. "We have our own ways of finding people."

Mark had no doubt. "Can you keep me updated?" he asked.

"Sure thing," said Boris. "Oh, by the way. We took possession of your belongings in the hotel. They include your wallet and passport."

"Great," said Mark. "I thought they would get lost."

"I'll forward them to you along with your phone."

Mark hung up with a sense of serenity. How ironic, he thought, that his much-feared pursuer had turned into a protector.

"Tell me what's going on." The policeman interrupted Mark's thoughts.

Mark gave the mobile back to the officer and checked the wall clock. "Can we do this tomorrow? It's really late and I don't feel that well."

CHAPTER 95

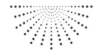

BRAȘOV, SPITATUL MARTINU, APRIL 13

Andrei arrived at the hospital room as the surgical team came by on morning rounds. Their leader, Dr. Dragavei, saluted Andrei and pushed the door open. "How is our patient doing?" she said.

Andrei had briefly met the surgeon the day before, after they rolled Mark Kent from the outpatient annex to a pre-op holding area in the main hospital. Since the ER physician turned out to be useless, the on-call general surgeon who happened to be Dr. Dragavei was summoned to deal with the extraordinary problem of cleaning up and closing another surgeon's interrupted operation.

A tall, slim young woman, seemingly fresh out of residency, Dr. Dragavei had lifted the towels covering the open wound and examined it. She had then calmly ordered an OR to be set up immediately. Her subsequent procedure did not take long.

Now Andrei watched a resident remove Kent's dressing while the surgeon conversed with the patient.

"The pain is not too bad," said Mark Kent. "What did you find in there?"

"Whoever performed the opening did a decent job." Dragavei replied in English. "Straightforward retroperitoneal dissection. No

567

major bleeders." She paused. "I understand you are a doctor too, is that correct?"

"Yes," said the American, "but not a surgeon. I'm a radiologist."

"Doesn't matter," she said. "You understand."

"I do."

"Fortunately for you, the police arrived on time," she continued. "They had not devascularized the kidney or manipulated the ureter yet. Your kidney is intact."

She inspected Kent's wound. "Looks good," she said. As a member of her entourage applied a fresh dressing, she continued. "I am sure you understand that there is a significant infection risk, given the circumstances of this surgery."

"Yes," said Kent.

"We are covering you with prophylactic antibiotics."

"Good."

"But most surgical infections don't appear right away. They tend to occur one to two weeks later."

The patient covered himself with bedsheets and listened.

"It would be beneficial for you to stay here in Braşov for a while so we can keep an eye on this wound. If it does get infected we would have to take care of it."

"What does that involve?" Andrei interjected from the corner of the room.

Dr. Dragavei turned to him. "Another surgery. Re-explore and clean the wound and follow up with stronger, intravenous antibiotics."

Andrei locked eyes with the American, who was obviously worried by the prospect.

"When will I be discharged?" asked the patient.

"You can leave tomorrow."

The patient looked at Andrei. "Where would I go?"

"I don't know." Andrei was flustered.

Dr. Dragavei laid a soothing hand on the patient's shoulder. "Don't worry about that," she said. "I'll have the hospital's discharge planners come up with a suitable placement."

She turned back and began walking out. "Administration should help," she murmured to Andrei out of the patient's earshot. "After all, those idiots are responsible for this debacle."

* * *

"I am really curious about something." Andrei addressed his ward.

They were alone and it was time for Andrei to seek the information he had been waiting for. "Americans do not send solo agents into the field in a foreign country. It's usually a team operation supported by their embassy and assisted by locals."

Kent looked at Andrei, and waited for a question.

"So, are you really alone in this operation or do you have a support team?"

"How does a provincial police officer know about the workings of a foreign intelligence agency?" asked Kent.

Andrei smiled. "Before Braşov Police, I too was an intelligence officer, in Romanian internal security."

"SRI?" asked the American. He made a face, looking disgusted.

"Yes," Andrei answered. "Don't you like us?"

"No, it's not that. You see, Cezar Kaminesky approached me with a ruse. He pretended to be an SRI officer."

"And you fell for that?" Andrei was surprised.

The patient straightened himself and sat up in his bed. "Look," he said. "I'll let you in on a secret."

Andrei leaned forward, notebook in hand, eager to hear what the American had to say.

"I am not FBI. I am not CIA." Kent spoke slowly, emphasizing each word. "I do not belong to any intelligence agency. I am just a civilian, a doctor who practices in California."

Andrei let out a big laugh. "You expect me to believe that?"

Kent's eyebrows furrowed; he looked annoyed. "When people first began thinking I was some kind of James Bond, I found it amusing. I was flattered. But it quickly got old. Now, I have given up. I can't seem to convince anyone that I am not who they think I am."

"How could that be?" asked Andrei.

"It's a long story," said the American with a sigh. "Do you have time?"

Andrei leaned back in his chair and crossed his legs. "Go ahead," he told the patient. "I am all ears."

The American looked amused. "It could be a novel."

Andrei chuckled.

Kent put up his arm, as if to interrupt Andrei. "No, let me correct myself," he said, smiling. "Two novels."

CHAPTER 96

BRAȘOV, SPITATUL MARTINU, APRIL 13

Mark pushed the call light to summon a nurse. He was tired and his wound ached. He had just finished recounting his story to the affable Romanian police officer. Andrei seemed genuinely interested in Mark's welfare. Finally, a Romanian Mark could trust for protection, something he had previously lacked.

The day shift nurse walked in. She was younger and more agile than his prior nurse, but her English was rudimentary. Mark communicated his need for a pain pill, speaking slowly and emphasizing each word. She brought him Tylenol with codeine.

As he waited for the medicine to kick in, Mark's thoughts wandered. He was apprehensive about the next day. He had yet to receive a discharge plan from the hospital and remained downcast about the prospect of a prolonged stay in Brașov.

He would be all by himself here, wherever they put him up. He realized that he missed Semra. Mark had grown accustomed to her, despite his relief upon hearing that she wanted to remain with Boris Petrov. Mark couldn't help but smile as he thought about it. He had seen the writing on the wall as soon as those two met. Regardless, Mark would have still preferred Semra's company here in Brașov.

He reached for his bulky surgical dressing. The wound was not as tender as the day before. He tried to reconstruct the timeline from his encounter with Cezar on Thursday night to the present. His surgery had occurred on Saturday. Mark had no recollection of Friday. He realized that Cezar must have kept him stored and sedated—who knew where—while he was transported from Chişinău to Braşov.

He could not believe that his European misadventure, what started as an intended rendezvous with an old friend, had led him here to an obscure hospital in an unknown city, recovering from an operation to steal his kidneys. It was a brush with death of the sort he never imagined.

In Budapest, when he escaped thugs shooting at him, Mark had felt a rush of adrenaline that became addictive. He sought more and stumbled into a kidnapping attempt that turned into a street fight, followed by dramatic encounters with Tibor Bognár's gangsters and Rusu's paramilitary operatives. He was rescued from the clutches of Rusu's men by Hungarian special forces in a dramatic tear gas attack.

This current situation, the closest he truly came to dying, was different. There was no adrenaline rush in being sedated and subsequently waking up with a surgical wound.

Mark was exhausted, physically and mentally spent. He needed a suitable place to recuperate, one that would reinvigorate him. Braşov would not do, nor would San Francisco. There was nothing left in his hometown. His boss had probably terminated him by now, anyway. His divorce proceedings were rendering him impoverished and homeless. His life was in shambles.

As the narcotic began inducing a dry mouth, Mark was overcome by the speed with which his life had disintegrated. He closed his eyes and recalled the radiology report that had summoned him to Europe. His old mate Ahmet had scribbled a note on it in Turkish. The scan, an abdominal CT, was that of a patient named Cezar Kaminesky-58. Mark never expected to meet this notorious criminal, let alone suffer a near-death experience in his hands. Mark wished that he had never seen that CT report.

His thoughts turned back to Andrei Costiniu, whom he had

conversed with for a long while. Andrei told him that Braşov Police began their investigation with the death of Enver Muratovich, the recruiter. It then expanded to another murder, that of a surgeon Mark did not know. Andrei mentioned other elements of the investigation, including a sick donor and an assault on a nurse with intent to kill.

The policeman was surprised to learn that Mark knew about Enver. Mark described his encounter with Enver's sister at Iancu Negrescu's funeral. He then recalled that Emina had given him a business card with Costiniu's name and asked that Mark contact him. They both laughed at the coincidence. Andrei remarked jokingly that if Mark wanted to meet him, he could have just phoned instead of turning himself into a kidney donor.

Andrei was particularly interested in Vadim Rusu. After explaining who Rusu was, Mark clarified a crucial gap in Andrei's knowledge, that of Rusu's motive in attacking the transplant enterprise. He told Andrei about the death of Rusu's son, another unfortunate donor, and Rusu's quest for revenge. He gave Andrei his eyewitness account of the assassinations that followed, in all their gory details.

The policeman was clearly pleased with the information Mark provided. He inquired whether Vadim Rusu was behind the Braşov murders he was investigating. This led Mark to discuss what he gleaned from Vadim Rusu in his face-to-face encounter with him. He explained that Rusu's assassinations ended with that of Enver Muratovich.

Mark could not shed any light into the killing of the Kosovar transplant surgeon or the attack on the team's nurse in Bucharest. Andrei explained that they had credible suspects for these crimes, street criminals who were most certainly contract hires. The one in Bucharest, already apprehended, had fingered Cezar Kaminesky. Could Rusu have put Cezar up to these? The policeman seemed keen in tying all the crimes to one perpetrator.

Mark told Andrei he believed Rusu's claim that Enver Muratovich was Rusu's last kill. If Cezar was behind the others, he was doing those on his own. Mark went on to describe the grand deception that Cezar had inflicted upon Vadim Rusu. It was Cezar who was responsible for Dima Rusu's death. He had subsequently taken advantage of Vadim's grief and convinced him that Radu and Negrescu's transplant team had done it.

Andrei was amazed at this turn of events. In that case, he remarked, all those assassinations in Hungary and Turkey, not to mention that of Muratovich, were for naught. Mark nodded in affirmation, saying what a waste it all was. A true tragedy. He then told Andrei about Cezar's dismay at the loss of Enver, the recruiter. Cezar had valued Enver's services. How ironic, he commented, that it was Cezar himself who had set events in motion that resulted in the recruiter's death.

Andrei inquired about Mark's encounter with Cezar. Mark described his surreal captivity in Chişinău, conversing with Cezar while physically restrained. The last thing he recalled was getting an injection. The policeman took detailed notes. He asked Mark how he discovered Cezar's duplicity regarding Rusu's son. This led to Olga. Mark kept their affair to himself, but told Andrei about his discussions with Olga first in Budapest and then in Bucharest. He described the estranged relations between husband and wife.

Andrei took in all this information and commented that Cezar had to be the most likely suspect for the crimes that had occurred after the death of Enver Muratovich. Mark wondered why Cezar would assassinate valuable people that he used in his own business. Andrei had given this some thought. He explained that perhaps Cezar was spooked by the recent donor that was dying of complications. Those he aimed to eliminate were witnesses to the operation that had caused the donor's demise.

Andrei then wondered why Cezar had also targeted Mark. It was Mark's turn to explain that Cezar had him in his gunsight ever since Mark had contacted Olga in Budapest. Mark needed to die because he had inadvertently interjected himself into Cezar's business. Mark did not divulge that there was also an element of jealousy in Cezar's motives.

Andrei said that they needed more evidence to connect Cezar to the murder of the Braşov surgeon and the donor. Nevertheless,

Braşov Police had plenty of reason to arrest Cezar based on both Mark's testimony and that of the Bucharest assailant. Unfortunately, he added, they had no leads on where to find him. Neither did Mark.

Finally, Andrei asked about Semra. Mark was not forthright about her. Just a girlfriend, he told Andrei, who dumped him for Boris Petrov. He did not mention Semra's association with Gazioğlu and made certain to emphasize that Semra knew nothing about the transplant ring.

Andrei gave Mark a warm handshake before departing. He was honored and delighted to have met him, he told Mark. Tired as he was, and with his surgical incision beginning to hurt again, Mark was nonetheless pleased by the policeman's compliment.

* * *

Mark was startled awake by someone entering his room. It was nighttime and the lights were dimmed. The silhouette that stood near his bed was not his nurse. It was a tall, male figure.

"Who are you?" Mark growled, as he sought the call light button. It was lost within the sheets.

The lights came on and Mark discovered a well-dressed middle-aged man with a receding hairline and white goatee.

"Sorry," said the man. "I didn't mean to scare you."

Mark raised the back of his hospital bed and looked up at the unexpected visitor who extended a hand to him.

"My name is Alexandru Coman," he said, firmly shaking Mark's hand. "I am the Chief Medical Officer of Spitatul Martinu. May I?" Coman pulled up the chair Andrei had used. "On behalf of the hospital administration, I would like to express our sincere apologies for what happened to you."

Mark looked at the clock on the wall. It was after nine p.m. He wearily accepted the apology.

"I understand that you, too, are a doctor, is that correct?" Coman seemed in a chatty mood. Mark wasn't. "Yes," he said, and did not elaborate.

575

"That makes it yet more embarrassing that this unfortunate incident happened."

"It's okay," said Mark. "Don't worry about it." It wasn't okay, but Mark did not wish to discuss this at this hour with a new round of codeine in his system.

"I am here to offer you a token of our apology," Coman said formally. "It's a mere nothing but it might help nonetheless."

"What?" Mark was blunt.

"I understand that Dr. Dragavei wishes to keep a close eye on you after your discharge."

"Yes, unfortunately."

"We would like to offer you an apartment here in Braşov, not far from the hospital. At no cost to you, of course. We will take care of all your charges and send you a visiting nurse, who will check up on you as needed."

Another offer for a free stay in Romania. The last one Mark had received, from Iancu's son Vasile, had turned into the current disaster. Mark shook his head in disbelief.

Coman took Mark's gesture as a rejection. "It is a very nice apartment," he said defensively. "We keep a small suite of residences nearby, for VIP patients or families from faraway places. You'll like it."

This was the only discharge plan Mark had received so far. He had no choice. "All right. Thank you."

Coman stood up. "Very well then," he said cheerfully. "I'll make arrangements so that it is ready by the morning."

As he turned to leave, Mark posed a question that stopped him in his tracks. "Did you know that these transplants were going on in your hospital?"

"No," said Coman quietly, still facing the door.

"How can that be?"

Coman turned around. Mark noticed a weary look on his face. "We're asking ourselves the same question," he said.

He then approached Mark and gave him his business card. "I know that you Americans are prone to suing your hospitals," he said dryly. "You can give this to your lawyer and have them contact me."

CHAPTER 97

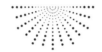

BRAŞOV, APRIL 13

"We all watched the raid at the station." Traian Dalca pulled up a chair for Andrei at the dining room table; he had summoned Andrei to his apartment for a briefing. Earlier, at the station, the unit had watched the body camera feeds of Andrei and the others on a large-screen monitor. "Congratulations. Well done."

Andrei sat down just as Dalca's wife appeared with a tray of tea and cups. "Santa Claus did come early," he said jokingly.

Mrs. Dalca gave Andrei a funny look as she set down the tray. Plump, with curly dark hair and a dour expression, she was nothing like the youthful woman in the photo on the boss's desk. Traian had clearly aged better.

"Was it really him?" Traian asked Andrei, as he gently sipped the hot liquid.

"Yes," said Andrei. "Mark Kent. And he is a wealth of information." He stirred some sugar into his tea. "According to Kent, the mysterious Russian is someone named Vadim Rusu," Andrei continued. "He runs a Chişinău-based security company called Hercules Security Group. I checked it out. It's legit."

"Never heard the name." Dalca looked expectantly at Andrei, waiting for more.

"Kent maintains that Rusu is responsible for the murder of Enver Muratovich."

"What's the motive?"

Andrei explained the debacle with Dima Rusu, Vadim's thirst for revenge, and how it resulted in a series of killings in Hungary, Turkey, and finally, Braşov.

"You got all that from this Mark Kent?" Dalca sounded impressed.

"There's more." Andrei leafed through his notebook. "Kent is quite certain that the Zhulati murder and attempt at Irina Cernea are not Rusu's jobs."

"How does he know that?"

"Rusu told him. So did his assistant, a guy by the name of Boris Petrov."

"Kent met this Rusu?" Dalca's surprise was turning into incredulity.

"Yes, in Chişinău. That's where Cezar Kaminesky abducted him and brought him here as a donor."

Dalca ran his hand over his bald head. "Unbelievable," he said.

"There are more details to the story. There is a Turkish girlfriend mixed up in all this. Then there is Cezar's wife, a woman by the name of Olga, who resides in Bucharest, also part of the story."

Dalca looked at his watch. "I think I've heard enough for now," he said. "I'll wait for your written report for the rest. We need to decide what to do next."

"How did the Chief and the Governor take the news of the transplant ring?" Andrei asked, nervously stirring his tea.

"Not bad," said Dalca, "considering that we've broken it up and apprehended some suspects." He took another sip of tea. "The news will be announced tomorrow."

"It'll be a media circus," said Andrei.

"You tell me!"

"Anything on the surgical team we arrested?" Andrei had stayed on with Mark Kent and did not know the fate of those they had apprehended.

"The nurse and anesthetist have been mum. But the surgeon is talking. He is Greek, from Corfu, a young guy. Apparently it was his first stint with an illicit job. He was underemployed in the depressed Greek economy and looking to supplement his income. So he gets himself ensnared in his first foray." Dalca shook his head. "He identified Cezar Kaminesky as the person who hired him."

"That makes three different sources implicating Cezar," Andrei commented. "The assailant in Bucharest, Mark Kent, and now this surgeon."

"We now need to focus on apprehending Cezar," said Dalca. "Once the news breaks, we'll be under intense pressure to catch him. I don't want our coup with the transplant ring spoiled by any delay in catching Cezar." Dalca seemed to stiffen as he sipped his tea.

"Did this Greek doctor or the others on the team have any idea of Cezar's whereabouts?" asked Andrei.

"No. The doctor says that his communications were conducted online. The other two are not talking."

"I have no leads, either," Andrei continued, "except for one thing: Mark Kent tells me that Cezar has a young mistress here in Braşov. But I have no name or address."

"How does he know?"

"He apparently got it from Cezar's wife, Olga."

"This Kent is a pretty resourceful agent, isn't he?"

"He claims he is not an agent, that he is just a private citizen, a doctor."

Dalca waved his hand in disbelief. "Whatever he is, can he get us more information on this mistress?"

"Possibly. He thinks he could check in with Olga Kaminesky again but this might be difficult. She might be in hiding."

Dalca said nothing, apparently pondering all that they had discussed.

"What are we going to do about Vadim Rusu?" Andrei asked. "He is, after all, the perpetrator of our original murder."

"Budapest Police and Interpol knew about Rusu. Am I correct?"

"Yes," said Andrei. "Kent confirms that."

"And they have done nothing about it?"

"We don't know what they have done."

"Doesn't matter," said Dalca dismissively. "I am sure they made some attempt to apprehend him and obviously didn't."

"Possibly."

"So, what makes you think we will have any reach? This Rusu must be very well connected."

"What's your plan?" asked Andrei.

Dalca sighed. "Well, one option is to turn the whole damn thing over to the National Directory on Organized Crime and SRI."

Andrei looked down at his notes, disappointed.

"The other, the one I much prefer," Dalca continued, "is to bury the whole Rusu angle. Lay it to rest. Catch Cezar and be done with it."

Andrei looked at his chief, eyebrows raised.

"Oh, come on, Costiniu!" Dalca raised his voice. "I told you from the very beginning that as much as possible, we needed to keep this affair within the boundaries of Braşov."

"Whatever you say," said Andrei in resignation. "You're the boss."

Dalca eyed his subordinate skeptically. "Drink your tea," he ordered.

Andrei took two large sips and contemplated his chief's demand. "There is a potential problem with that plan."

"What?" Dalca demanded, clearly exasperated.

"Vadim Rusu could get to Cezar before us."

"How so?"

"According to Kent, Rusu will place the resources of his entire organization into searching for Cezar. If he succeeds, there is a high likelihood that Cezar will be dead before we can apprehend him."

"I thought Rusu had stopped assassinating."

"Now that he knows Cezar is behind his son's death, he will make an exception."

"He did not know that?"

"It was Kent who set him straight."

"Well then," said Dalca briskly, "you have your work cut out for you." He fixed his eyes on Andrei. "Hurry up and get to Cezar first."

Andrei pushed his teacup away and stood up, preparing to leave.

"I don't want any elusive Russians complicating this case." Dalca was stern. "We'll do our best to keep the case within our jurisdiction, regardless of how it ends. Is that clear?"

"Crystal clear." Andrei turned and began walking away.

"Wait a minute!"

Andrei froze. *What now,* he thought.

"I want a detailed report of your investigation on my desk by eight o'clock tomorrow morning."

Andrei looked at his watch. "But," he said, then hesitated.

"When the news is announced tomorrow and the shit hits the fan, I need to be well informed so I can deal with the fallout."

Andrei nodded, eyes downcast. He would have to pull an all-nighter to produce that report.

"Those are the fruits of success." Dalca chortled, apparently reading his mind.

Mrs. Dalca was friendlier as she saw Andrei out. Perhaps she was grateful for the end of the evening interruption. Andrei headed to his car for his own overnight interlude.

CHAPTER 98

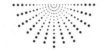

BRAŞOV, APRIL 14

Mark awoke to bright sunshine streaming through the hospital window as his nurse raised the shades.

"Good morning," she said, wheeling a portable vital-signs monitor close to his bed. "How are you feeling today?" She was the same nurse who had first cared for him.

As Mark held an electronic thermometer under his tongue, his right arm firmly in the nurse's possession, he noticed a large cardboard box near the entrance. "What's that?" he asked. It came out as an unintelligible mumble with his tongue pressing down on the thermometer.

"Stay quiet!" she admonished him, as she recorded his pulse, blood pressure, and oxygen saturation. When she finally removed the thermometer, Mark asked again. "What's that?"

She went over and opened the box. "This came early in the morning by courier." She strained as she pulled out a familiar object. "We could not give it to you until the police inspected its contents."

It was Mark's luggage that he had left behind at the Royal Boutique Hotel. Judging by the way the nurse held it, the suitcase was full. She placed it at the foot of his bed and opened it, inspecting the contents. "Good. Looks like you will have something to wear when you leave the hospital."

Mark threw his covers off and began searching the luggage himself. He didn't care much about clothes. "Yes!" he shouted triumphantly, as he pulled out his wallet, passport, and mobile phone from an inner compartment. He silently thanked Boris Petrov and inspected the contents of his wallet. Nothing was missing. He then jumped out of bed and felt an immediate pain on his side.

"Careful," said the nurse. "You're only two days post-op."

"When do I get out of here?"

"How about you take a shower and brush your teeth first? I'll help you." It was not a suggestion but an order. "Then I'll summon the discharge planner."

* * *

Mark was sitting in the guest chair previously occupied by Andrei Costiniu and Alexandru Coman, scrolling through emails on his phone, when Andrei walked in, accompanied by a woman in purple scrubs.

"Well, well," he said. "Looks like our patient is doing better."

Mark looked up at him and smiled. "You don't look all that well yourself." The policeman appeared haggard, his eyes sunken and lined with dark rings. "You look like you never went to bed."

"That's about right," said Andrei. "I had to work all night."

"So what are you doing here then? Go get some rest."

"I need to make sure that you get to your new residence safe and sound."

"I hope you're not driving in this condition," said Mark.

"No. We'll take a patrol car. The officer guarding you will drive." Andrei then noticed the luggage. "I see you got it," he said. "Is everything in order?"

"Yes, thanks."

"I had it inspected. Better be cautious. I inspected your apartment, too. Nice place." Andrei stood aside and let the woman approach Mark. She had curly red hair and her tight scrubs revealed the various lumps and folds of her body. She was holding a yellow manila envelope.

"I'd like you meet someone who was instrumental in your rescue," said Andrei, giving the woman a squeeze on the arm.

The woman smiled shyly.

"Dr. Mark Kent, meet Nicoleta Ciobanu. Nicoleta is a CT technician here in the hospital."

Mark nodded at the woman and smiled. He then turned to Andrei, puzzled.

"Nicoleta performed your pre-op CT scan," said Andrei. "She also alerted us to your arrival, thereby setting our raid in motion."

"Oh, wow!" Mark stood up and extended his right hand to the woman. "Thank you so much."

Nicoleta shyly shook his hand. "I have something for you." She gave him the envelope. "Call it a souvenir."

Mark undid the metal clasp and removed what appeared to be a medical report, written in Romanian on the hospital's letterhead. It looked familiar. As he began scrutinizing it, he sank back into his chair.

"Oh, dear God," he said quietly.

Andrei and Nicoleta observed him in silence as he perused the document. It was a radiology report of an abdominal CT. The patient's name was Cezar Kaminesky-88. From what Mark could gather, the findings were normal.

Mark looked up at Nicoleta. "That's me, isn't it?" he said in a hoarse voice.

"Yes, sir."

"We are in possession of the log book she kept," said Andrei. "It translates those numbers to the real names of those secretly scanned."

Mark's eyes teared. "This is how it started, you know."

"Yes, you told me," said Andrei gently.

Nicoleta looked at them quizzically. "The doctor was summoned from America," explained Andrei, "by a similar report onto which Nicolae Radu had placed a message."

"Never in my wildest dreams," said Mark, "would I have

imagined that I would become the subject of such an exam." He shuddered, then stood up and approached Nicoleta. "May I?" he said, as he opened his arms. She froze in his tight embrace. "That's what we do in California," he explained, laughing.

He then turned to Andrei. "Come on, Detective," he ordered with mock authority. "Let's get out of here."

CHAPTER 99

BRAȘOV, APRIL 14

Andrei sat in the front passenger seat of the patrol car with Mark in the back. It was a short drive, just two blocks from the hospital. They could have walked it, but this was more secure. Besides, Andrei wasn't sure that Mark was in any condition to walk even that far.

The apartment was in a quiet residential area set back from the main avenue on which Spitatul Martinu was located. It was an old two-story building with four units, two on each floor. This was the place Alexandru Coman had mentioned to Mark—the apartment building the hospital had bought and renovated for families of patients and guests of the hospital.

In his advance inspection, Andrei had discovered that only one unit was currently occupied, by an out-of-town family with a sick relative who were living on the first floor. Andrei persuaded Coman to give him another unit for Irina, who had happily moved in to one of the upper-floor apartments the night before. Andrei was happy, too: now he could keep both his witnesses under one protective cover.

"Welcome to your new home." Andrei opened the back door of the patrol car for Mark, who eyed the building warily. "It'll be all right," Andrei said, seeing Mark's hesitation. "It is secure." Mark was to have an upper-floor apartment, Andrei explained, a safer option than the ground floor.

They climbed a short flight of stairs, Mark lagging behind. As Andrei unlocked Mark's apartment, Irina opened her door and peeked out. "Hello."

"Oh, Irina." Andrei waited for Mark to climb the last couple of steps. "This is Mark Kent. He is from America." Mark nodded to her.

"Mark, this is Irina Cernea," Andrei continued. "She is a nurse. You two will be temporary neighbors."

It was a brief encounter with no handshakes.

"Irina," said Mark, as Andrei motioned him inside. "Is that the nurse who was assaulted in Bucharest?"

"Yes," Andrei replied curtly. He did not have the energy to discuss it further. "Let me show you around."

The apartment was surprisingly spacious. It had two bedrooms, a bathroom, and a living room, all fully furnished with modern accoutrements. It smelled of fresh paint. Mark checked the bedrooms. One was clearly the master, larger and with a side door that accessed the bathroom.

"Which bedroom shall I take?" Mark asked, as they walked to the living room.

"Whichever you want," said Andrei expansively. "The whole place is yours."

"I thought that maybe you needed one for the police guard."

Andrei stood by one of two windows that faced the street. "There won't be any guard in residence," he said. "We are short-handed in our sector. The chief cannot spare a full-time officer."

Mark looked out the window and tried to hide his disappointment. The apartment faced a small, desolate street with similar apartment buildings across.

"That's why I like this place," Andrei continued. "It is self-contained, very few windows, and there is a decent security system with an alarm at the front door downstairs. The building is hard to penetrate." He walked into the small kitchen, Mark following him.

"I expect you to stay in this apartment the whole time," Andrei said firmly. "The hospital assured me that whatever you need will be fetched for you." He opened the refrigerator. "Good," he said, as he looked inside. It was stocked with basic food items. "Besides," he added, as he checked a small pantry, also full, "you're in no shape to be out walking around."

Mark shrugged. "You're the boss." He moved toward a curious wall fixture, a red lever covered with transparent plastic. "What is this?" he asked. "I've seen it on several walls."

"A code alarm," said Andrei, "like you find in hospital hallways and rooms. They're also in the bedrooms and bathroom."

"I don't get it." Mark was puzzled. "We're no longer in the hospital."

"Dr. Coman told me that if activated, these will summon a rapid-response team from the hospital's Emergency Room. Since they have patients staying here, they thought it would be a good idea in case anything happens." Andrei looked at his watch. "Time for me to go back to the station. Is there anything else I can do for you?"

"No, thanks," said Mark. He extended his hand to Andrei. "You've been a tremendous help. Thank you very much."

"We'll be running more frequent patrols through here," Andrei said as he shook Mark's hand. "Until Dr. Dragavei clears you for discharge, we'll make sure that you're secure."

* * *

"Check this out!" Boboc pointed his mobile phone screen at Andrei. It displayed a breathless headline from one of the national news outlets. "International Organ Thieves Busted In Braşov."

Boboc scrolled to another, from a different media outlet. "We're all over the news."

Andrei nudged the phone back toward his partner. "Do they mention us?"

"No," said Boboc. "Just the Governor. But it is only a matter of time before they descend here like a flock of ravens and start pecking."

Andrei sat down at his desk and leaned back, arms folded behind his head. He closed his eyes. "I'm beat," he said. "I need to go home and get some sleep."

"How did it go with the American?"

"Fine," said Andrei. "He is jumpy, and he has every right to be, after what happened to him."

"Do you think that place is safe?"

"I hope so," said Andrei. "To tell you the truth, I would have preferred a full-time uniform in there." He opened his eyes and straightened his chair. "It's a shame Dalca did not approve that."

They were interrupted by a group of detectives and uniformed officers who came displaying their own mobile phones tuned to the news. Loud congratulations and fervent back slapping followed, intermixed with a few off-color jokes.

"We found that slimy administrator," Boboc said quietly, after they departed.

"Yeah? Where was he?"

"Apparently he has a ski chalet in Sinaia. He went into hiding there." Sinaia was a Transylvanian resort town in the southern Carpathian Mountains, not far from Braşov. "The local cops will be sending him over to us tomorrow." Boboc laughed. "We can add him to our collection in jail."

"Dalca told me that with the exception of the surgeon, no one is talking."

"That's right," said Boboc. "Give them some time. They'll eventually break."

He pulled his chair closer to Andrei and leaned in to whisper. "I saved the best for the last."

"What now?"

"Alin Barbu," Boboc pronounced softly, with a crafty smile.

"Don't tell me he overdosed...or escaped."

"No, no." Boboc leaned in closer. "He is ready to talk. He wants a deal and I've already arranged something with the prosecutor."

Andrei's face sank.

"What?" Boboc spoke more audibly now, and indignantly. "You don't like that?!"

Andrei rubbed his face with the palms of his hands. "I do, I do," he said wearily. "It's just that I am too tired to deal with it right now." He got up from his chair. "Can we do him later? After I get some sleep."

Boboc could not conceal his disappointment. "If you say so," he said. "I was looking forward to another go at that scumbag."

"Don't worry," said Andrei, as he headed toward the door. "You'll get your chance."

CHAPTER 100

BRAȘOV, APRIL 14

Mark stared at the kettle heating on the stove and tried to ignore the ache from his surgical incision. He was reluctant to take more codeine, so would have to put up with the pain. He looked around the kitchen. It had been tastefully painted in bold colors, undoubtedly with the intention of keeping spirits up for those who stayed here. It did nothing to allay Mark's dark mood. To him this apartment, nice as it was, was just a prison.

How did I get myself here? Mark wondered. He could no longer recall the details of all he had been through in Hungary, Turkey, Moldova, and Romania.

He poured boiling water over a tea bag. As he took his first sip, his eyes caught the code alarm on the wall. He wondered if it had ever been used. Highly unlikely, he thought, that such an emergency would occur.

A knock on the door interrupted his reverie. He nervously approached the peephole. It was that nurse, his new neighbor. Mark let her in.

"I was wondering if you needed company," she said. "It's lonely here."

"Certainly." Mark was pleased. "Would you like some tea?"

They sat across from each other at a small kitchen table sipping tea. "Your apartment is more spacious than mine," she said. "I only have a single bedroom and not much of a living room."

She was an attractive woman, petite and slim, with curly blonde hair flowing down to her shoulders, and an alluring smile. "I lucked out, I suppose," Mark responded.

"Oh, I don't think so. In case you don't realize, you're the VIP here."

"And you, you're not?"

"Actually," she said, eyes downcast, "I am a criminal."

"I thought you were a witness under protection."

"I am that, too. I'll be at the mercy of the justice system once this is all over."

"Why? Because you were participating in those transplants?"

Irina's eyes moistened. "I am ashamed of what I've done," she said, "and what has happened. Too many have died."

Mark reached out and gave her arm a supportive squeeze. "But they weren't your fault."

"I feel indirectly responsible," she said.

"If it's any consolation, I feel indirectly responsible for some of those deaths, too." He was referring to his inadvertent role in guiding Rusu's Slovak goons to Iancu Negrescu and Iancu's eventual murder, as well as his theory that Rusu's men followed him to Gazioğlu and Latif, both also killed.

Irina's eyes widened. "Why? You weren't part of the transplant business, were you?"

"No," said Mark. "Maybe I can explain it some other time. It's a long story."

"I understand that you're an international foreign agent." Irina looked at Mark with admiration. "That you helped crack the case."

Mark took a sip of tea. "It's not over yet."

"Not until they get Cezar," she said.

"Not until then," Mark confirmed.

Irina stood up. "Well, I don't want to take up too much of your time. Thank you for the tea."

Mark walked her to the door. "Would you like to have dinner tonight?"

Irina gave a sarcastic chuckle. "Where?"

"Right here," he said. "We can order out for something. I'm on the hospital's expense account. I think I deserve a decent meal after nothing but clear liquids."

"Are you supposed to eat solid food?" asked Irina, suddenly all nurse.

"I don't know, I didn't ask," Mark shrugged. "But what the hell."

"Actually," said Irina thoughtfully, "there is no need for you to refrain from solid food. What you had was a retroperitoneal operation, not intraperitoneal. There should be no ileus."

"You're the doctor," said Mark teasingly.

"No, but I know." Irina was serious. "I've cared for many like you."

"It's good to know that there is competent help close by."

"I know a decent sushi place nearby," Irina offered. "Within walking distance. I don't know if the police will allow delivery into the building."

"I am under orders not to leave," said Mark.

"Me too." She winked. "But I can make a tiny exception." They shook hands.

* * *

Mark heard a conversation in Romanian that echoed in the stairway outside his apartment. He recognized Irina's voice; she was speaking to a man. Soon there was the sound of footsteps climbing the stairs. Mark let Irina in before she rang his bell.

"Mission accomplished." She proudly raised a bag in one hand and, smiling broadly, raised the other to show a bottle of wine. "And a bonus." She headed for the kitchen, Mark in tow. As she pulled out plates from the cupboards, Mark asked, "The sushi place sells wine, too?"

"No." She turned back and smiled. "But there is a liquor store down the block." She started scouting drawers for a corkscrew. "Aha."

Mark removed several Styrofoam containers from the food bag, each filled with different assortments of rolls, sashimi, and one with tempura. "Looks delicious," he said. "I can't wait."

She uncorked the wine and poured some for him. "Chardonnay," she said. "From a winery near Ploieşti."

"They make wine here in Romania?" Mark was surprised.

"Sure they do." She took a taste.

Mark gave his glass a whirl and took a careful sip. "Not too different from California Chardonnay," he said. "A bit sweeter, but still as oaky."

"So you're a wine connoisseur, too."

"Living where I do, so near the Wine Country, it just happens," Mark said. He eyed the tempura. "We should work on this first before it gets cold."

They ate with their fingers. "Good, huh?" she commented. Mark nodded in agreement, mouth full.

"Who were you talking to in the hallway?" he asked her, as their plates emptied.

"A maintenance man from the hospital," she answered. "He was fixing an electrical glitch in the first floor. Apparently the family staying there complained."

"Oh, okay." Mark eyed another container. "What shall we have next?"

"The sashimi," she said firmly, and unsheathed a pair of chopsticks. Mark sipped his wine and watched Irina try a yellowtail. "It's good," she said, then sampled the salmon and tuna. Mark stood still, watching her. "Are you all right? Or don't you like this?"

"I'm okay," said Mark. He took another pair of chopsticks. "I just feel woozy already, from the wine."

Irina poured herself some more. "Good," she said playfully. "That means more for me."

Mark laughed. He noticed his incision didn't hurt as much. The Chardonnay, no doubt. "So, tell me, how did you get yourself embroiled in all this?"

Irina sighed. "I was married to a deadbeat guy who could never keep a job. I was the only steady wage earner. I worked at Fundeni Hospital in Bucharest, in a transplant service. So when Cezar recruited me, I took it. The extra money was good." She took a sip of wine. "Besides, the opportunity to get away from him—my husband—and spend time in Braşov was much welcome."

"How did the surgeries happen?" Mark asked.

Irina explained their setup at the outpatient annex in detail.

"Unbelievable," said Mark, as he chewed on a roll. Irina's account was his first look into the back end of the organization. "Did you know Nicolae Radu and Iancu Negrescu?"

"Remotely," she said. "They came by every so often."

"How about Cezar?"

"I met him once, years ago, when he first recruited me. He is a secretive guy. We mostly conducted business via text messages and an occasional email." She stared at a piece of sushi between her chopsticks. "I knew Enver Muratovich." Her face slackened and she set down the chopsticks.

"I didn't," Mark answered, oblivious to her consternation. "But I heard much about him."

"He was a decent man," said Irina. "He didn't deserve to die." She started to cry softly.

"Now, now," said Mark, flustered. He handed her a napkin. "How well did you know him?"

Irina dabbed at her eyes. "We had an affair toward the end of my marriage. I spent more time in Braşov in those days, in his apartment." She pushed her plate away and took a large sip of wine. "He helped me get through my divorce."

"So how come you two did not…"

"Get married?" She issued a doleful laugh. "No way," she said. "He was Muslim, from Bosnia. He was bound by tradition. His family would have never accepted me, a Christian."

"I met his sister and mother," said Mark.

Irina's eyes widened. "Emina? How did that happen?"

Mark told her about Iancu's funeral and his encounter with them.

"What an amazing coincidence," she said.

"You want to hear something even more amazing?"

Irina nodded.

"Emina gave me the business card of a Braşov police officer and told me to contact him in connection with Enver. I threw it in my pocket and forgot about it. Guess who that was?"

"Andrei!"

"Yes. Can you believe it?" They both laughed.

"He is so handsome," said Irina, sounding wistful, and keeping her eyes away from Mark.

"Oh, so you have the hots for him, do you?" Mark teased.

"Why not? He's a hunk. All he has to do is ask. But alas..."

"Alas what?"

"He is happily married. Besides, I am too old for him."

"No, you're not. You're a very attractive woman." Mark meant this. If circumstances were different, he might have made a move for her.

Irina smiled shyly. "Thank you," she said. "What about you? You seem to have had a James Bond life. Did you do as well with the ladies?"

"I don't kiss and tell."

"Oh, come on! Humor me. We're stuck in this prison together with nothing but memories and fantasies."

"All right, all right." Mark looked at the nearly empty bottle of wine. He poured himself a final sip. "First there was a young Hungarian policewoman who threw herself at me and I refused."

"Why?"

"Because I was stupid."

"You're not married, are you?"

"Going through a divorce back in the US." Mark was definitely tipsy now. He raised his hand in a stop gesture. "Don't interrupt me."

"Okay."

"Then there was an amazingly attractive woman in Istanbul, Gazioğlu's girlfriend." He paused, wondering how much of Semra to reveal. "I rescued her from a home invasion where he was killed. We became an item, in a manner of speaking."

"Interesting," said Irina. "How did that turn out?"

Oh, what the hell, thought Mark. "She turned out to be a man."

Irina erupted into laughter. Mark smiled and watched her. She placed her palm on her mouth and forced herself to stop. "I am so sorry," she said. "Is that really true?"

Mark told her the story of Semra and how she was now with one of Vadim Rusu's henchman. He continued. "I finally found some bliss with Olga. She was so hot and sultry." Mark hesitated. "But it was more complicated than that."

"Don't tell me she was a trans, too," said Irina, giggling.

"Olga is Cezar Kaminesky's wife."

Irina inhaled loudly. "What?! You had an affair with *his* wife?!"

Mark nodded.

"Oh, my God," she said, excitedly. "This is *better* than James Bond." Then she added, more seriously, "No wonder he came after you."

"He is an evil man," said Mark. "He spoke with me before he sent me for this operation." Mark touched the dressing on his flank. "Everything about him was sinister." Mark stopped and eyed the empty wine bottle. "You don't suppose we can get more?"

Irina stood up and scoured the cupboards. "Voilà!" She raised a bottle of clear liquid. "Vodka."

Mark knew he shouldn't but he sipped the vodka straight anyway. He continued with his saga. "I thought that Vadim Rusu was evil, too, until I met him," he said.

"What was he like?" Irina's voice was sure and steady despite the wine and vodka.

"A tough guy, for sure. But you could tell the hurt he was carrying. He had lost his only son. He was dealing with it the only way he knew how. He made it clear to me that there had been no closure with the revenge he inflicted on so many. The hurt doesn't go away."

"Do you have any children?" Irina abruptly asked Mark.

"No. You?"

"I miscarried twice and then had to have a hysterectomy." Her face slackened again. "Losing those fetuses was hard enough. I can just imagine what it must be like to lose a grown child."

"Strange," said Mark, "how, when compared to Cezar Kaminesky, Vadim Rusu's actions seem justifiable."

Irina raised her eyebrows. "If you say so." She took another sip of vodka. "What do you think will happen to them?"

"Who, Cezar or Rusu?"

"Both."

"I am quite sure nothing will happen to Rusu. He has already successfully evaded multiple European law enforcement agencies. He is well connected."

"And Cezar?"

"He should hope that Andrei catches him first," said Mark. "If not, he will fall into Rusu's hands." He looked at his partly full vodka glass. He was beginning to feel dizzy. "I think we drank too much." He stood up and stumbled back to his chair.

Irina laughed. "You certainly did." She came around the table. "Here, I'll lend you a hand." She supported Mark to his bedroom and tucked him in, clothes still on. "I'll clean up and see myself out," she told him.

"Thank you," said Mark. "I really enjoyed your company."

She leaned down and kissed Mark's forehead. "Remember," she said, pointing to the wall. "I am behind that. If you need anything, just knock on the wall."

CHAPTER 101

BRAȘOV, APRIL 14

"Congratulations." The gruff, sandy voice of Geofri Funar resonated on Andrei's phone. "You're the major news. Here at Iași that's all everyone is talking about."

The call had interrupted the afternoon nap that Andrei had been craving. He looked at his watch. He had slept only two hours, not nearly enough to make up for the prior sleepless night. "Me?" he asked, wearily. "Was I mentioned by name?"

"No," said Funar. "But you know what I mean. We all knew that it was your collar when we heard about the transplant bust."

"Good." Andrei was relieved.

"When you first described it to me, I did not appreciate how big this would turn out," Funar continued. "I am very impressed."

"Thanks," said Andrei. "But please don't mention me publicly."

"Why? Don't you want to be famous?"

"No," said Andrei firmly. "I'd rather stay in the shadows."

Funar laughed. "Once a spy, always a spy." He let out a smoker's cough. "Don't worry, my friend. Your secret is safe with me."

"Is that why you called, to congratulate me?"

"That," said Funar, "and I have other news. Yoet Tcaci died earlier today."

Andrei felt a pang of sadness upon hearing this. Even though it was expected, the news hit him surprisingly hard. He rubbed his forehead and eyes and tried to gather his emotions.

"Did you hear me?" asked Funar.

"Yes," Andrei finally answered. "Thanks for letting me know."

"We will be handling the autopsy here, if you don't mind."

"That's fine."

"Naturally, we will forward our findings as soon as they become available."

"Thanks, and thank you for the call." Andrei started to hang up.

"One more thing." Funar clearly wasn't finished.

"Yes?"

"We have Kyril Kozak, the driver who dropped off Tcaci, in custody. He was delivered to us yesterday by the Ukrainians."

"Great." Another piece of expected news. "Did he provide any new information?"

"We haven't interrogated him yet. But we'll let you know about him too."

"Good."

Funar hesitated briefly, then said, "It looks as though we'll be sharing some of the limelight of this big bust, since we have some of the players in our corner of the country."

"It certainly does."

"You can bet that we won't be as shy with the media as you are." Funar laughed.

"By all means."

"Give your boss my regards," said Funar. "Tell Dalca I said that he has a good man working for him."

This time, Andrei hung up before Funar could think of something else to say, and fell back asleep.

* * *

Alin Barbu shuffled into the interrogation room confidently, appearing to be comfortable in his handcuffs and shackles. He ignored his prison guard and did not acknowledge Andrei and

Boboc. They were waiting for him in the same spots as before, Andrei sitting behind the desk, Boboc perched at one corner of it. Barbu sat down and looked up at his attorney, a rotund young man dressed in a wrinkled suit.

"Well, if it isn't my old friend Alin Barbu," Boboc exclaimed mockingly. He examined Alin's face. "Prison suits you well," he said. "You don't look as ugly as I remember you."

"Insulting my client will not lead to a productive outcome," the attorney pronounced firmly. He dipped into his pocket for business cards and handed a couple to the policemen. "Dragos Grosu," he said. "I am Mr. Barbu's court-appointed attorney."

Boboc examined the card and began to laugh. "What an appropriate name." *Grosu* meant stout or bulky.

"It could be yours, too," the lawyer retorted, his eyes fixed on the policeman's own girth.

"Well, it isn't. My name is Maries Boboc, *Inspector de poliție*, Sector 1." He extended his hand to the lawyer. Grosu ignored the gesture.

"*Inspector*," said Barbu, spitting out the word as if it were spoiled meat. "He is nothing but a blob of shit."

"All right, that's enough." Andrei stood up and came around the desk and extended a hand to the lawyer, who knew enough to shake it. "Andrei Costiniu," he said, firmly but politely. "I am lead investigator in the matter concerning your client." He did not mention his rank. "Now please take a seat and let's discuss this in a civilized manner."

Alin Barbu and Boboc exchanged nasty glances without saying another word. Grosu, the lawyer, went straight to the heart of the matter. "I understand that you have a plea bargain offer for my client."

"We do," said Andrei. "But only if your client's statement is true so far as we can verify it." Andrei returned to his desk, removed a document from a folder, and handed it to the lawyer.

"What does this mean?" Barbu asked Grosu, shifting nervously in his seat.

"Shh, let me read it first."

"You guys promised to let me out if I gave you what you want." Barbu addressed Andrei.

The lawyer squeezed his client's arm. "Quiet for a moment, will you?"

They all fell silent. Eventually, Grosu addressed Andrei. "Is the prosecutor ready to execute this offer?"

"Execute!" Barbu shouted. "What do you mean execute? I thought you were letting me go!"

Grosu turned to his client with a sigh. "They are not going to execute you. They're using the word in a different context. This is a good offer."

Barbu stared at his lawyer blankly.

"They are offering you eighteen months, with parole for good behavior."

"What do you mean, eighteen months?!" Barbu shouted indignantly. "I thought they would let me go."

"Look," said Grosu. "You're otherwise looking at twenty-five to life, for capital murder. Believe me, this is a good offer."

Barbu remained unconvinced. The lawyer looked around the room and spotted the video cameras and audio equipment on the ceiling. "May I have a word in private with my client?" he asked.

"Certainly," said Andrei. "But the correctional officer has to be in attendance."

Boboc led them to a small side room. When he returned, Andrei admonished his partner. "Can you please not rile him up until we get through this?"

"Fucking bastard," murmured Boboc. "If I had my way he'd be singing the old-fashioned way, like we did in Ceauşescu's time."

"That's long gone," said Andrei. "Just hold yourself for a bit."

Boboc groaned and returned to his perch by the edge of the desk.

When Barbu and his attorney came back, Grosu said, "Okay, it is a deal." He addressed Andrei. "But we would like you to do the interrogating." He kept his eyes off Boboc.

"Very well." Andrei opened a dossier and shuffled some papers.

"Mr. Barbu, let me start by asking what caused you to change your mind."

"About what?"

"About testifying."

Barbu grinned. "You did."

"How so?"

"With your bust at Spitatul Martinu."

"And how did that affect your case?'

"The way I figure, he has his own hide to worry about, more so than mine."

"Who?"

"Who else? Cezar. Cezar Kaminesky."

Andrei and Boboc exchanged glances. "Why would Cezar worry about you?"

Barbu shook his head as if he were talking to a group of dummies. "Because he is the man. The one who hired me to do the hit on the doctor. Isn't that what you wanted to hear?"

"We want to hear the truth," said Andrei. "Not what you think we might want to hear."

"Well, that's the God's honest truth. That fucker Cezar put me up to it and got me into all this trouble."

"How well do you know Cezar Kaminesky?"

"He and I go way back," said Barbu, now relaxed. He leaned back and crossed his shackled legs at the ankles. "We sold pharmaceuticals together, you know what I mean?"

Andrei nodded.

"In my younger days I also provided protection to some of his whores."

Boboc looked at Barbu with surprise. "Yeah," Barbu addressed Boboc. "I don't look it now, but back in the day I was bulky. I worked out, kept myself in shape." He turned back to Andrei. "I could take on three guys and knock them down."

"Did you do any hits for him before?" Andrei asked.

"No, he usually did that himself. More recently he began using a goon named Milan."

"So, why did he ask you to do the doctor?"

"He said that he and Milan were busy with some matter in Bucharest. He could not tend to it. He told me the guy would be an easy target. A drunk. Wouldn't put up any fight."

Andrei could guess what preoccupied Cezar in Bucharest. They were closely following the American, Kent, under the ruse of being SRI agents. He recalled Kent mentioning Milan.

Barbu continued. "He offered me five hundred dollars up front and another five after the job was done. That's pretty good money for an hour's worth of work."

"Did he pay you?"

"Sure he did. I did the job, didn't I? You guys have already figured that out."

"Do you have any addresses for Cezar? Anywhere where we can locate him?"

"You mean you haven't caught him yet?" Barbu was suddenly alarmed. He turned to his lawyer. "Cezar is still out there," he said. "Fucker can get me in prison. We shouldn't have taken this deal."

"Officer Costiniu," said the lawyer, addressing Andrei in a formal tone. "How close are you to arresting Cezar Kaminesky?"

"We are very close," said Andrei, effortless in his straight-out lie, a leftover from his days in SRI. "It would help, however, if your client could give us a few tips on his whereabouts."

"Check out his girlfriend," said Barbu.

"Girlfriend?"

"Yeah, he is smitten with some pussy that he has holed up here in Braşov. He can't get enough of her."

"Have you met her?"

"Oh, yeah," said Barbu. "Nice piece of ass. Young girl. I too would be screwed if I was screwing that chick." He let out a coarse laugh, exposing a mouth ravaged by methamphetamine, his rotten, crumbling teeth teetering on discolored, receding gums.

"Name and address," said Andrei.

"Martina Erner," said Barbu. "I don't know the address exactly but I can tell you about where it is."

Andrei took down the information. "Do you know of any other

addresses that Cezar Kaminesky may be using, either here or elsewhere?"

"He has places in Bucharest and somewhere on the Black Sea shore, but I don't know those. As far as I know, Martina's apartment is where he has been hanging out lately. That's where I usually meet him."

* * *

Andrei looked at his watch. It was close to eight p.m. The interrogation had finally finished, and Grosu had hustled his client out. Andrei brushed his hair back with his fingers. "What do you think?" he asked Boboc.

"We need to run a background check on this mistress. If she is as young as Barbu claims, there is a strong likelihood that she has no priors."

"Right."

"If so…"

"Yeah, I know," Andrei cut him off. "It'll be difficult to obtain a warrant for raiding her place."

"All we can do is put up a surveillance team at the address and hope we catch Cezar going in or out."

"I agree," said Andrei wearily. "No other choice." He added dryly, "And look how well that worked out with Zhulati."

CHAPTER 102

BRAŞOV, APRIL 15 ... PRE-DAWN

Mark slept restlessly. Earlier, when he first lay down, the world was spinning from the alcohol he had consumed. He was nauseated. He recalled Irina kissing his forehead. *A nurturing woman,* he thought, even in the midst of all her troubles. He had enjoyed her company, but he really should not have drunk that much.

His sleep was marred by troubling dreams and frequent interruptions. By about two a.m. he was wide awake, his mind racing. He knew that this was an after-effect of the alcohol. He was no longer dizzy. He tried to calm himself down and doze off again, forcing pleasant thoughts into his mind. It was only partially successful. His sleep remained fragile.

Amid this turmoil a noise caught his attention and brought him back to wakefulness. It sounded like his apartment door. "Irina?" he called. There was no answer. He listened carefully. There was no other noise. He must have been dreaming.

But then he heard soft footsteps coming from the living room. Looking under the closed door of his bedroom, he spotted a light that rapidly went by, a flashlight beam.

His heart racing, Mark sat upright. Someone was in his apartment. How could anybody get in? What about that alarm system? Mark had no time to think. He quietly slipped out of bed and slid toward the wall that he shared with Irina.

The footsteps grew louder. They were clearly approaching his bedroom. Mark began loudly banging on the wall.

Suddenly the door flung open and a tall, stout figure rushed in, his flashlight scanning Mark's bed. The open door allowed some outside light from the living room windows. In the dim darkness, Mark recognized the familiar outlines of Radovich, the SRI agent— aka Cezar. He seemed frozen at the foot of the bed, his flashlight fixed on the parted covers, no doubt wondering where Mark was.

Certain that Cezar would soon find out, Mark began pounding on the wall in a panic. "Irina," he yelled. "Irina, help!"

Suddenly he was blinded by the light that shone directly on his face.

He heard an animal-like grunt as Cezar lunged for him, his strong hands wrapping around Mark's neck as he bellowed, "You son of a bitch. I should have killed you in Chişinău!"

CHAPTER 103

BRAŞOV, APRIL 15 ... PRE-DAWN

Andrei was sleeping restlessly. He was still dead tired, having been up all night the night before, preparing the report for Dalca. Even so, now he tossed and turned in bed, falling in and out of sleep, his mind working fitfully with too many thoughts.

Alin Barbu's interrogation had been a major shot in the arm. Afterwards, Andrei had hastily arranged a surveillance team for Martina Erner's residence. Boboc had taken the first overnight shift. As expected, Cezar's mistress, whom they discovered to be only eighteen, did not have any criminal history.

Her residence, in an isolated six-story apartment building, was located in a leafy area at the foot of Mount Tâmpa. It was easy to set up surveillance there since there were no other apartment buildings nearby, just greens and a children's park. So far the surveillance had yielded no sign of Cezar.

Given the urgency of the situation, Dalca himself had taken on the sensitive task of convincing the prosecutor to issue a search warrant. But with the media frenzy that had erupted when the news broke, it would have to wait until the next day.

For now, there was nothing to do but wait, and sleep. But Andrei couldn't. He worried about the American holed up in the apartment near the hospital. He had assured Mark Kent that the place was safe, but he was not entirely sure of that. He was glad that Irina Cernea was nearby, keeping an eye on their charge.

Irina had called Andrei earlier and told him about her dinner with the American. He was a pleasant guy, she said. When Andrei questioned her about the dinner, she confessed that she had disobeyed orders and ventured out to fetch sushi. Andrei was cross but had not reprimanded her. After all, he had imprisoned those two in that apartment building.

When Irina mentioned in passing that a hospital maintenance person was doing after-hours electrical work within the building, it set up warning flags for Andrei. He asked a detective on the overnight shift to check with the hospital to see if any maintenance work had been authorized. So far, there had been no answer.

Andrei somehow dozed into a deeper sleep, only to be suddenly awakened by Alexandru Coman, the chief medical officer, who had become the hospital's liaison to the police.

"I don't know why your request was so urgent," said Coman, obviously irritated. "What difference does it make if there was maintenance work or not? Could it not have waited until the morning?"

Andrei looked at the clock. It was nearly two a.m. He did not wish to offer any explanations. "Well," he demanded, "was there or not?"

"No," said Coman. "We had to track down the head of our maintenance department and have him come into the hospital to check records. There was no request for any maintenance work of any kind at that building, and no one was sent there."

Andrei sat up, now wide awake. The maintenance guy Irina had spotted was clearly a security breach. He wasn't sure what it meant and how it could be rectified at this hour. He could call the patrol car assigned to the area to see if anything was out of order. But since he couldn't sleep anyway, Andrei decided to check the apartment for himself.

As he got into his car, Andrei received another call. It was Irina, clearly panicked. "Quick, get over here. The American is in trouble. Someone tried to kill him."

* * *

Andrei arrived at the apartment building surprised to find an ambulance at the entrance, lights still flashing. There were no medics in sight. The patrol car he had alerted screeched to a stop soon afterwards, sirens and lights on. The door of the building was ajar. The family occupying the first-floor apartment was out on the sidewalk in their pajamas, looking scared and bewildered. Andrei pulled out his service weapon and rushed up the stairs, the two uniforms from the patrol car in tow.

He found Kent's apartment door wide open, all the lights on inside. The first person he sighted was a man in scrubs carrying a hand-held manual resuscitator. The man stared at the police with surprise.

"Who are you?" asked Andrei.

"Respiratory therapist with the rapid response team." The young man did not convey any sense of urgency. He fixed his eyes on Andrei's gun.

"Where is he?" asked Andrei, looking beyond the therapist.

"In there," said the respiratory therapist, pointing to the master bedroom.

Andrei and the uniforms rushed in to find Mark crumpled by a wall in a corner of the room, a doctor and two nurses surrounding him. Irina was crouched next to him. She saw Andrei and came over to him.

"Thank God you're here," she said. She was holding a dressing to the side of her neck. The left side of her face was bruised.

"Are you okay?" asked Andrei.

"I'm fine," she said. She pulled out the dressing and examined a thin streak of blood. She had a superficial cut on her neck. "This is nothing."

Andrei turned his attention to Mark, still on the floor. "How about him?"

"He was nearly strangled," said Irina. "And his surgical incision is bleeding. He says it hurts."

The doctor heard the commotion and turned around. "Someone tried to strangle him," he said to Andrei. "Fortunately it was unsuccessful. He will be hoarse for a while and he'll have bruises around his neck. Otherwise he'll be all right."

"What about his surgery?" Andrei asked.

"Oh, that." The doctor seemed unfazed. "Some of the staples got torn off during the struggle. So it bled a bit. But overall the suture line is intact. It'll be fine."

"Do you think he needs to go back to the hospital?" asked Andrei.

"No," came a raspy voice from the floor. "I don't want to." Mark raised his head and gave Andrei a determined look. His eyes were bloodshot, his hair a mess. They had placed a bandage around his neck as if he were wearing a peculiar scarf.

"Why that bandage?" Andrei asked the doctor.

"Oh, some scratch marks and abrasions, nothing major." He called out to the two nurses, one of whom was closing a crash cart, the other holding a defibrillator. "We're done here," he told them.

He then went around to the living room and inspected the premises. "Nice place," he said. "I had heard there might be emergencies here, but I have never been called to one before."

The nurses gathered their equipment and the respiratory therapist, and followed the doctor out of the apartment.

* * *

"What happened?" asked Andrei.

"Cezar," said Mark in a weak voice. "I am quite sure of that."

Irina had helped him back to bed and pulled the covers over him. She brought him a codeine pill with some water. She refused his objections and ordered him to take the pain medicine.

"I heard him bang on the wall and yell for me," said Irina to Andrei, pointing to the wall she shared with Mark. "I immediately activated the hospital code alarm and then rushed in here. The door to the apartment was open. I found a man assaulting Mr. Kent and tried to pull him off." Irina was talking faster now, as if wanting to purge every detail.

"He let go of Mark and came after me," she continued. Andrei caught the familiar reference this time of just Kent's first name. "He slapped me in the face, hard. I screamed and told him that the police and a medical team would be here soon. He came at me again and I ran out to the hallway. He followed me and hit me again. Then he took a knife from his pocket." Andrei could see that Irina was starting to tremble. He put a steadying hand on her arm.

"He told me that he wanted to kill the American with his own hands, but for me the knife would be fine," Irina said with a shudder. "I dodged but he managed to cut me in the neck. That's when the medical team arrived. When he heard them, he ran down the stairs and disappeared." Irina paused for a moment and drew a big gulp of air. "That's when I called you."

Andrei shook his head in disbelief. "What about the door alarm, the outside door. Did that go off?"

"No," said Irina, her body starting to slump as the adrenaline left it. "I heard no alarms."

"The maintenance guy," said Andrei. "That's probably what he was doing here, deactivating the alarm. Do you remember him?"

"I sure do," said Irina. "I know the man. I've seen him at the hospital before."

"Do you know his name?"

"No, but if you get me photos of those who work at Maintenance I can single him out."

Andrei turned to Mark. "Did he say anything to you?"

Mark rubbed the dressing over his throat and spoke weakly. "Just that he should have killed me in Chişinău."

Andrei scanned the apartment for any clues Cezar may have left behind. There were none, aside from multiple footprints, useless since so many had since traipsed through.

"I will have one of the officers stay here for the rest of the night," he said. He then turned to Irina. "I'd rather that you move into the spare bedroom here so that you're both together."

Irina nodded. She left to fetch what she needed from her apartment.

"I was sure I was going to die," Mark said in a thick voice, already groggy from the narcotic.

"I'm sorry about this," Andrei answered. "I'll make sure we tighten the security around here."

Mark turned on his side and curled up into a fetal position.

CHAPTER 104

BRAŞOV, APRIL 15

Mark awoke to the sound of a conversation outside his bedroom. He had a hangover from the narcotic, his mind groggy, his mouth dry. Cezar's assault had left him with a sore neck. The bandage around his neck was choking him. Pulling on its edges, he managed to loosen it, only to realize that it was of no avail. It still felt as though Cezar's powerful fingers were clamped around his throat.

Mark closed his eyes and relived the terror of the attack, how close he had come to death, his life being squeezed out as if from a wet rag by a raging Cezar. As terrifying as Mark's encounters with the deaths of Iancu and Gazioğlu had been, this was worse. This time he was the one who was Cezar's mark, and he'd been quite certain he would meet the same fate as the others.

He remembered Cezar hissing something in his ear about Olga that Mark, nearly fainting at that point, did not quite understand. But the putrid smell of Cezar's breath was vivid in his memory, as was Cezar's spit that splattered his earlobe. Somewhere in his consciousness Mark realized that this attack was not just business for Cezar; it was more primal than that. And then, as he was sure he was taking his final, choking breaths, Mark was amazed that he suddenly called up an image of Olga. She was in bed next to him, her breasts casually exposed as she leaned toward him for a kiss. Maybe, Mark had thought for the second time, what he felt for her was not mere lust after all.

The rest of the assault was a blur, Cezar's hands suddenly releasing him as Mark fell to the ground, a woman screaming—he now realized it was Irina—the medical team that had arrived tending to him. Mark let go of his neck bandage and opened his eyes wide, surveying the bedroom now flooded with sunlight, and listening to the conversation in the living room. Both affirmed, much to his disbelief, that he was still alive.

He got up and made his way to the living room, where he found Andrei, Irina, the uniformed officer, and another plainclothes officer, older and rounder. To his surprise, the hospital's chief medical officer was also there, seated across a coffee table from the group. Irina seemed to be the center of attention. She was examining some documents.

They all stopped and looked at Mark when he stumbled in. Andrei stood up. "How are you?"

Mark leaned on a nearby chair to steady himself and ran his hand through his hair. "What's going on?" he asked, his voice hoarse and barely audible.

"We're trying to identify the maintenance man from yesterday," Irina answered. She then placed a finger on a photo. "I'm quite sure that's him."

The plainclothes officer took the document with the photo and examined it. "Okay," he told the group. "I'll arrest him." He then turned to Mark and gave him a friendly squeeze on the arm. "Maries Boboc," he said. "I'm glad to finally meet you."

Mark shook his hand and collapsed into a nearby empty chair. Andrei made a more formal introduction, adding, "Boboc is my partner."

It was now Coman's turn to greet Mark. "I am glad to hear that you're okay," he said. "Our hospital's rapid response team did a good job."

"They saved his life," Irina chimed in. "Mine, too."

Coman beamed. This was the first bit of good news since the police raid in his hospital. "When we renovated these apartments, there were many who did not want a code alarm system installed. Not worth the cost, they said." He pounded his chest with his fist. "But I insisted that it be done."

After Coman and Boboc left, Andrei sank onto the couch. Mark figured Andrei looked about as bad as he himself did, except with no bandages.

Andrei rubbed his eyes and said, "I should have figured that angle ahead of time."

"What angle?" Irina asked.

"That the transplant enterprise would need some technical assistance in setting up that OR—electrical lines, gas lines for anesthesia, you name it. They had to make sure that those were in working order when their surgeries took place."

"So you think that this maintenance guy was helping them with that?" asked Irina.

"We won't know for sure until he is apprehended, but I bet that he was in cahoots with that vice president in charge of surgical services who was their link to Administration."

"So they were both associated with Cezar?"

"How else would Cezar know where to come?" answered Andrei. "And have the alarm system conveniently deactivated ahead of his arrival." Andrei shook his head in dismay. "It was a major screw-up on my part."

Mark was surprised that Andrei was openly discussing details of his investigation with a witness on the case. He was clearly exhausted and had let his guard down.

Irina approached Andrei and put her arm around his shoulders. "You're doing the best you can," she said consolingly. For a moment Mark thought she was going to kiss him.

"Thanks for the encouragement," said Andrei. "Let's hope that my chief sees it the same way." He stood up. "I'd better be going." He looked at Mark and then Irina. "Now you two are stuck with each other," he said sternly. "Until we apprehend Cezar Kaminesky, you are not to leave this apartment. Is that clear?"

Irina gave Andrei a fake military salute. "Yes, sir!"

"If you need anything, food and such, just call the hospital and have them deliver it."

He looked at Mark, who was crumpled down on his seat. "And you," he said. "You'd better get back to bed."

CHAPTER 105

BRAȘOV, APRIL 15

The setting sun was throwing an orange glow on the "BRASOV" sign high atop Mount Tâmpa as the police team assembled near a children's park. Traian Dalca was leading the charge. Dressed in a dark paramilitary uniform, complete with a sidearm, full service belt, and a dark cap low on his forehead, Dalca looked like a gung-ho rookie rather than the seasoned administrator he was.

The team huddling around him was mostly borrowed from special forces units, all wearing similar uniforms. Dalca pointed to a couple of them. "You two will take the back of the building and cover the service entrance near the garbage dump. And you," he singled out a group of four, "off to the sides." To the one carrying a sniper rifle, "You will cover the front entrance from there." He pointed toward a tree fifty meters away. As they all departed, he barked, "The rest come with me."

They had memorized their positions in a hasty drill back at the station, using a map of the premises. Dalca gave final instructions to the remaining six who would accompany him into the building. Two would cover the front entrance from the inside while the rest would take the stairs to the sixth floor.

Andrei looked at Boboc. He could tell Boboc was thankful to have received the front door assignment, spared from the climb. He looked laughably out of his element in his paramilitary uniform, his gut protruding onto his service belt, a low button on his shirt busted open.

"Let's not fuck this up," said Dalca. "I bet TV vans will soon arrive." He took a deep breath. "I can smell those wolves."

Andrei looked up at the BRASOV sign that formed a backdrop to the city amid the greenery of the scenic mountaintop. Its letters were identical to the more famous sign, also on a mountaintop, over Los Angeles. He checked his mobile phone one last time, turned it off, and tucked it into a chest pocket. He had a nagging feeling that Dalca's raid would not be as successful as in the movies produced under the HOLLYWOOD sign.

Earlier that day, the surveillance team assigned to Martina Erner's residence had called in to announce a figure they spotted entering the building that matched Cezar Kaminesky's description. But in the dim light of dawn, they had seen only the silhouette of a tall, stocky man they assumed to be their target. Despite the uncertainty, Dalca, who had managed to convince the prosecutor to hastily issue warrants, jumped at the opportunity. Now that the media were involved, he was not taking any chances. Besides, he himself wanted to collar the now famous criminal whose face was plastered all over the news.

He and Andrei would enter the apartment first, with two other officers backing them up. Unlike the raid on the hospital, they were expecting significant resistance. Thus the team was well armed, and included a sniper, just in case.

The surveillance team had summoned the manager of the building prior to Dalca's arrival. A scrawny middle-aged man with a sallow face, looking ill-tempered even from a distance, the manager opened the entrance, no doubt annoyed at being called back to work after hours.

The two accompanying officers climbed the stairs ahead of Dalca and Andrei, weapons drawn, checking for potential threats.

None. The party made it to the sixth floor uneventfully. After taking a minute to catch their breaths, Dalca nodded to one of them.

The young officer rang the bell, and banged on the door loudly. "Police, open up!"

There was no response. The officer knocked again. Once more, no response.

Dalca exchanged glances with Andrei. They both removed their weapons and Dalca approached the door. He threw it open with a single, swift, spirited kick. Andrei was impressed.

They poured into the apartment. It was a luxurious place with a wide foyer that opened into a living room affording scenic vistas of Mount Tâmpa.

There was no one there.

They swept the living room and a nearby kitchen and secured them. Then they branched out to two hallways, one on each side of the entrance that led to bedrooms and bathrooms. Dalca took one with an officer, Andrei and an officer the other.

Andrei proceeded down his hallway into the only bedroom on that side. As he opened the door, a shrill scream pierced the quiet in the apartment. It was coming from the other hallway, Dalca's side. Andrei and his companion stopped dead in their tracks. Another, shorter scream followed. It was a female.

Andrei instructed his accompanying officer to check the bedroom on their side while he took off in the direction of the scream. It came from the master bedroom at the other end of the apartment. Andrei stormed in to find a naked woman dripping wet, holding earphones in one hand. Dalca was handing her a big towel.

Mortified, the woman stared at the police officers, tears running down her moist cheeks. She was a fake blonde. Her curly hair, full of black roots, stuck to her face. She would have been quite pretty with her hair done and some makeup, but right now she looked like a soggy meerkat. Her nubile body was that of a teenager who had not yet filled out, her breasts tiny mounds on a rib-lined chest. She dropped her earphones and quickly covered herself with the towel, taking care to first conceal her dark pubis.

Dalca covered her shoulders with another towel. He then threw a sharp look at his gaping crew. "What are you looking at?" he yelled. "Go on, get out of here!"

As Andrei shuffled out with the two officers, he heard the young woman tell Dalca, amid sobs, "He is not here. I haven't seen him in two days."

They descended the stairs in slow, disheartened steps. At the second floor, an apartment door opened and a tall, stocky man emerged, surprised to see the armed officers. "What is going on up there?" he demanded.

Andrei gazed at the man. His body was similar to the description they had of Cezar's, but his face wasn't. Andrei introduced himself and asked for the man's name and whether he lived here. The man complied and confirmed that this was his apartment. Andrei realized that the man had returned to the building from work at about the time the surveillance team reported spotting Cezar.

"Is everything all right upstairs?" the man asked. "I heard a woman scream."

Andrei reassured him and told him to go back inside. There would be some additional police activity upstairs, he said, but nothing that would disturb him or his neighbors.

Andrei emerged into the cool evening air to find two TV vans near the children's park. A reporter stood by one of them, in a bright spotlight, with a camera rolling. She was interviewing the apartment manager. Dalca had predicted correctly. He would be seriously displeased.

Soon the chief emerged from the building. "Goddamn it!" he said, surveying the scene. He pulled his cap down lower on his face and stood next to Andrei. "They don't miss a beat, do they?"

"What happened in there?" asked Andrei in a near whisper.

"Can't you tell?" said Dalca crossly. "The woman was in a bath with her earphones on. She never heard us when we knocked."

A camera crew from the second van rushed toward them with a reporter close behind.

"Shit," said Dalca. "Here they come. You'd better disappear."

Andrei quickly walked away, avoiding eye contact with the TV crew. He alighted toward the tree under which he found the sniper, sitting cross-legged, hugging his rifle. Andrei took out his phone and turned it back on.

The sniper stood up and shouldered his rifle. "False alarm?"

"Something like that."

They walked together toward the transport vehicle, Andrei scrolling through his phone screen. He froze when he spotted a message, and read it twice. It had come in while they were raiding the apartment. It was from Mark Kent.

CHAPTER 106

BRAŞOV, APRIL 15

Mark was tired of lying in bed. He had slept through lunch. Later in the afternoon, Irina had awakened him, insisting that he down a watery soup she made from a can she found in the pantry. Despite his difficulty swallowing, Mark had found the soup surprisingly rejuvenating. He pushed himself up and out of bed and walked into the living room. The setting sun was sending crimson rays into the apartment.

Irina wasn't there. Probably back in her own apartment, Mark figured. He sat down and scrolled through his phone. There were no messages of interest.

Mark assessed his situation for the umpteenth time. He needed to get out of here—this apartment, this country—and soon. But how? And where would he go? A sojourn in the Bodrum Peninsula would do him good, he decided. He was certain Tarık could arrange something.

First, he had to figure a way to exit this prison in Braşov. He rubbed his face with his palms, plotting escape fantasies. Maybe Irina could help him. Or should he contact Olga? The thought of her triggered both desire to be with her and dread for what might have happened to her. Had Cezar gotten to her, too?

For also the umpteenth time, Mark recalled his night with Olga, how magnificent it had been. He then felt the bandages on his neck and right flank. Right now, even if Olga were here, he doubted he could perform as he had in Bucharest. Still, how wonderful it would be if Olga accompanied him to the Turkish coast. He envisioned himself on a yacht with her, cruising the Turquoise Coast, making love on deck under the warm Mediterranean sun.

His thoughts were interrupted by a text message. Boris. *Proceed to this address immediately*, it said. Mark didn't recognize the address, other than it was in Romania. The message continued with an instruction about an entry code, a series of numbers.

Mark stared at the curious message. *What is it?* he messaged back. There was no answer. *I have no means to get there.* Boris would not know that he was stuck in this apartment.

Mark stared at his phone screen for what seemed like an eternity. Eventually a response appeared. *Just do as I say*, it said. *Find a way.*

As Mark pondered what to do, Boris sent him another message, an emoji of a human eye, wide open, pupil dilated.

* * *

Irina stared at Mark's phone. She had been in her apartment, freshening up after a shower, when Mark fetched her. "Looks like the outskirts of Braşov," she said, as she entered the address into her own phone's GPS. "Northeast."

"Can we go there?" asked Mark.

"Did you notify Andrei?"

"I tried him both by phone and text," said Mark. "He's not answering."

Irina frowned. "Who is this Boris, anyway?"

"Vadim Rusu's assistant, the second in charge in his organization."

Irina raised her eyebrows. "Is he trustworthy? Wasn't he involved in all those assassinations?"

"At this point," said Mark with conviction, "I totally trust him."

"What do you think we will find there?" she asked.

"I have no idea," said Mark. "But I have a feeling it has to do with Cezar. Maybe a clue as to where he is."

"What if Cezar himself is there waiting for us?"

"I seriously doubt that Boris Petrov would send me into peril like that."

"All right," said Irina, putting on her coat. "I'm tired of being cooped up here, anyway." She smiled at Mark. "A little adventure will do us good."

"How will we get there?" he asked.

"Taxi," said Irina. "We'll walk over to the hospital and catch one from there. It'll attract less attention than if we call one here." She surveyed Mark up and down. "You can walk a couple of blocks, can't you?"

"Yes, I think so," said Mark.

Irina reached for the bandage on Mark's neck. "Let's remove this ridiculous thing," she said. "It will draw less attention."

CHAPTER 107

BRAȘOV, APRIL 15

Andrei surveyed the pandemonium in the children's park near Martina Erner's apartment building. The dark of the evening was pierced by bright TV lights, the camera crews augmented with two more trucks. Traian Dalca, their principal target, looked ill at ease as he issued awkward statements to each reporter one by one. He had to offer a plausible explanation for the fiasco that his raid had turned into. *No comment* would not do.

Andrei spotted a ridiculously large figure atop a child's bench, eating a sandwich. He made a straight beeline for it. Boboc looked up at him with a full mouth. "Fucked up, huh?"

"Where did you find that sandwich?" said Andrei. They had embarked upon the raid with no expectation of dinner, and there were no nearby food shops.

Boboc smiled. "I brought it with me, just in case." He looked out at the TV crews. "I was worried that this circus could go well beyond dinnertime." He took a bite. "I was right," he said with a full mouth. "But I didn't figure this." He chuckled as he pointed his sandwich in the direction of a discomfited Dalca.

Andrei gave his partner's arm a tug. "Come on, get up," he said.

Boboc reluctantly stood. "What? What is it?"

"Check this out." Andrei lit up his phone screen. "From the American, Kent."

Boboc mumbled the message as he read it, his eyes nearly popping out. *"I am proceeding to the following address with Irina. Please join us as soon as possible."*

"It came a while back," said Andrei. "While we were up there." He nodded toward the top floor of the apartment building.

"That's an industrial area, on the northeast side," said Boboc, tapping the phone screen. "What business would Kent have there?"

"I have no idea," said Andrei. "I left express instructions with both of them to stay put in the apartment."

"Looks like they have flown the coop," said Boboc, taking a big bite from his sandwich.

"Sure does." Andrei pulled Boboc by the arm. "And so should we. We need to get out of here and hit that address, pronto!"

"Wait, wait," Boboc pleaded. "Let me finish this."

"There is no time," said Andrei. "Come on, let's go."

CHAPTER 108

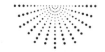

BRAȘOV, APRIL 15

As the taxi left city lights behind, forging onto a dark, desolate, country road, Mark had a strong sensation of foreboding. He flashed back to his lone taxi ride to Tuzla, in what seemed like ages ago, also during the dark and with no idea why he was doing so or what he would encounter.

The taxi driver said something in Romanian that Mark did not understand. Nonetheless the man clearly sounded uneasy. Irina answered back in a commanding voice. She then turned to Mark and grabbed his hand, giving him an encouraging squeeze.

She is one tough woman, thought Mark, squeezing back in appreciation. Her presence in this foolhardy venture was the only difference from his equally reckless journey to Gazioğlu's compound. Yet, what good would Irina do in the face of untold danger? She was not a cop, after all, and she did not carry a weapon.

"Are we going the right way?" he whispered to her.

"Yes," she said.

Mark nodded in the direction of the driver. "Why is he nervous?"

"It's an industrial area," she answered. "He doesn't take customers there at this hour of the evening."

Mark turned away. He pulled out his phone and searched its screen.

"Anything?" asked Irina.

"No." Mark put the phone away.

"It's strange," she said. "Andrei is usually prompt with responses."

The taxi driver turned into an industrial park dimly lit by scarce streetlights. After passing several large buildings, he came to a halt in front of a smaller corrugated metal structure. The area was deserted. Mark's apprehension rose as he looked out the window.

Irina had a brief exchange with the driver as she paid him. As soon as they exited, the taxi sped off.

"Isn't he waiting for us?" Mark asked nervously.

"No," said Irina. "He is spooked. He can't understand why we came here from the hospital." She looked around at the dim emptiness that surrounded them. "He told me to call for another taxi."

Mark shared the driver's sentiment but said nothing. He checked Boris's text against the prominent numbers by the door of the building. "This is it," he said. As they stepped forward, he added, "Damn, I wish Andrei was here."

Irina put her arm into his. "Come on," she said forcefully. "Wasn't it you who said that Boris would not send you into peril?"

* * *

Mark and Irina picked their way amid ventilators, operating room tables, and large gas canisters, all neatly arranged in a well-lit, well organized space. Mark examined the wares curiously. "Looks like a warehouse for medical equipment."

They had easily entered the place, unlocking the door with the code that Boris had provided, and quickly found a light switch. Irina examined a shelf full of drainage bags, bandages, and various sized syringes and needles. "It sure is."

"I wonder why Boris wanted us to come here?" Mark mumbled, his voice still hoarse. He gazed deeper inside and saw nothing but more equipment, all carefully organized, nothing out of place.

As they stepped farther in, Irina pointed to what seemed like an office at the far end of the warehouse. It was lined with large windows that allowed those inside a commanding view of the entire place. "Let's check that," she said, walking ahead of Mark.

As they came closer, they could make out a figure that seemed to be asleep by a desk. Mark's heart pounded when he realized that the figure was not moving at all. He kept a few paces behind Irina, who entered the office through an open door and searched for a light switch.

"There," she said as she flipped the switch. They froze as they examined the figure that was illuminated, sitting at an office chair pulled away from a nearby desk. It was a tall, stocky man, fully dressed, immobile, arms slumped by the side, legs spread apart. A translucent plastic bag over his head obscured his face. The bag was firmly tied around his neck. A dark, narrow hose exited from the bag on one side of his neck and led to a nearby gas canister lying atop the table.

Irina lifted the man's right wrist, his dusky hand flopping down as she did so. She felt for a pulse. "He's dead," she said. She moved the arm up and down a bit, bending it at the elbow. It moved easily. "Must be recent," she commented. "No rigor mortis." She reached toward the bag covering the man's head.

"No, don't!" Mark suddenly ordered at the top of his voice. It came out as a shrill whisper. "Don't disturb it. The police won't like that."

Mark leaned in and shone his phone light through the partially opaque bag. "It's him," he said as he straightened up. "Cezar Kaminesky."

Cezar was wearing a sleeveless T-shirt and slacks that had been stained with urine. Mark noted parallel lines on Cezar's bare forearm that appeared at regular intervals and continued onto the shirt. Similar lines were also present on his pants but less noticeable.

Mark trained his light on the gas canister. It was considerably smaller than those stored in the warehouse. He peered at the label. *Argon.* A chill ran up his spine as Mark realized what had happened.

CHAPTER 109

BRAȘOV, APRIL 15

"Where are we going?" Boboc asked.

He sat in the back seat of the patrol car Andrei had commandeered. A uniformed officer was driving at high speed, lights flashing, sirens on. Andrei sat in front. He did not answer his partner; he was busy texting Mark Kent. *We're on our way. Stay put. Do not enter the premises.*

Andrei then addressed the officer driving the car. "Do you have any idea what this place is?"

"No, sir." The officer kept his attention on the road. "But in that section of the northeast, there is nothing but scattered industrial installations."

This was not terribly helpful. Andrei had already checked his own map and concluded the same. He decided to dial the station. He gave the duty officer their target address and requested a description of where they were headed.

"Shouldn't we notify the boss?" Boboc asked.

His partner was right. But Andrei wanted more certainty before he did that. A call soon came back from the duty officer. "It is a warehouse for medical equipment," he said. "If you like, we can check who owns it and what it contains. But that'll take time."

Andrei told him not to bother. They would be there soon enough. Then he realized that a text message had come in while he was talking. It was from Mark Kent. "Goddamn it!" he shouted.

"What?" said Boboc, startled. "What is it?"

"Kent," said Andrei. He read the American's message out loud: *Too late, we're in. We found Cezar. He is dead.*

Andrei tapped the arm of the driver forcefully. "Speed up, will you?"

They were already going at high speed on a deserted country road. The driver gave Andrei a momentary glance and pressed harder on the gas pedal.

Andrei now called Traian Dalca. No answer. After three tries, he gave up. Letting out a loud sigh, he told Boboc that Dalca must still be busy with the TV crews.

"Let me try," said Boboc. He called a buddy of his on the raiding team and asked him to pull Dalca out of whatever he was doing. It's urgent, he said. He handed his phone to Andrei.

"Chief," said Andrei in an excited voice, "we found Cezar Kaminesky. We think he is dead." He gave Dalca their destination address and then handed the phone back to Boboc. "I have a feeling this will be one giant shit show."

* * *

The patrol car turned into a barren industrial complex and rapidly came upon a corrugated metal building, where its headlights briefly illuminated two figures sitting on the steps at the entrance. The driver gave a quick blast of his siren to attract attention, as if the arrival of the vehicle with lights flashing were not sufficient.

Andrei spotted Kent's head rising up. He waved at the car.

The three occupants of the patrol car rushed toward Mark and Irina. Mark greeted them. "He's inside," he said. He began tapping some numbers on a coded entry key. "We did not disturb anything in there."

The door easily gave way, leaving Andrei surprised that Mark knew the entry code. They entered a well-illuminated warehouse.

Mark and Irina seemed to know their way inside. "This way," said Irina, directing them deeper inside the building.

Andrei examined the peculiar sight of the dead man sitting on an office chair with a bag over his head. At first he didn't notice the tube sticking out of the bottom of the bag. He carefully examined the surroundings. There was no evidence of any struggle. Everything in the office seemed in order. Nor was there any evidence of violence on the body.

"What is this?" asked Andrei.

"It's an exit bag." Hoarse and weary as he was, the American seemed sure of himself.

"A what?"

Mark pointed to the tube emanating from the bag and directed the officers' attention to the gas canister. "Argon," he said. "It's an inert gas."

Andrei remained puzzled. "You mean he took his own life with one of the gas canisters here, in the warehouse?"

"I don't think so." Once again, the American spoke with conviction.

Andrei and Boboc stared at Kent.

"Those canisters in the warehouse are for medical use, oxygen and nitrogen." Mark stopped to rest his increasingly shrill voice. He let out a dry cough and continued. "There is no medical use for argon. It is usually used for industrial purposes, such as welding."

Andrei peered into the bag. "Are you sure it's him?"

"Yes, definitely," said Mark. "I've seen him many times. It's Cezar all right."

"How did you know to come here? And the entry code to this place?"

"I received a tip," said Kent.

"Who from?"

"Boris Petrov."

Andrei stiffened. He scrutinized the body as he processed Kent's response. "How did Petrov know that Cezar committed suicide here?" As soon as he said it, Andrei realized what a stupid statement this was.

"It was not a suicide," said Mark, slowly and deliberately. "They killed him and staged it to look like a suicide." Mark approached closer to Cezar's body. "This is the exact same way they killed Nicolae Radu in Budapest. Same modus operandi." He pointed to the regularly spaced lines on Cezar's arms. "See these?"

Andrei and Boboc leaned closer as the American ran his phone light across parallel horizontal lines on the forearms that continued onto the shirt and pants.

"These are industrial tape marks," Kent explained. "Nicolae Radu had them, too. His were more prominent because he was naked. They show up better on bare skin."

"You mean they tied him up?" asked Andrei.

"Like a mummy," said Kent. "That way he could not fight what followed." He focused the light on the bare skin of one forearm. "We were puzzled by these lines on Radu until Budapest Police discovered spent industrial tape appliers among the possessions of Vadim Rusu's assassins."

Andrei suddenly recalled a puzzling piece of evidence at Enver Muratovich's apartment: empty industrial tape appliers. Enver must have been neutralized the same way. That's why he had not put up any fight while being hung.

Kent pointed to the argon gas canister. "They also found similar argon canisters along with the industrial tape." He turned to Andrei. "Both Radu and Cezar were tied up and rendered helpless and then asphyxiated with the exit bag. In Radu's case, they took all the props away and left his dead body looking like he had a heart attack in the bathtub. In Cezar's case, it appears they left the bag and gas canister because they wanted it to look like suicide."

Andrei recalled the hung body of Enver. He had not noticed any lines on his body, but then he had not looked for them, either. He regretted not examining him more closely.

"Just what exactly is an exit bag?" asked Boboc.

"It's an American term for a popular, painless way to commit suicide," Mark explained. He pointed to the bag over Cezar's head. "You tie the bag over your head, airtight so no fresh air gets in. Then you run an inert gas into the bag and it asphyxiates you as the gas replaces the oxygen within the bag. It can be helium, argon, or neon. Any one of them will do."

"'Exit' because you're leaving this world," Boboc suggested. Mark nodded.

Irina had been watching and listening quietly by the office door. "It was too humane a way to dispose of Cezar," she said angrily. "They should have flayed his skin like the Turks used to do."

Andrei looked at her, startled. He turned to Kent. "How did Boris Petrov contact you?"

"Text message." Mark Kent scrolled through his phone screen, found the message, and handed his phone to Andrei.

Andrei studied the message. Dalca and his entourage would be arriving here any minute. Impulsively, he slid the message sideways and tapped the delete icon.

"I deleted it," he said, as he returned the phone to a stunned Mark Kent.

"Why?" Though hoarse, Mark still managed to sound incredulous.

"It is best that it end this way, as a suicide," said Andrei. "Without the complications of another murder by foreigners we cannot pursue." He then looked at his watch. "In a few minutes my chief will arrive here. There will be a lot of questions now and later." He tapped his finger on Kent's chest. "You will not tell them about Vadim Rusu or Boris Petrov."

"What do you want me to say?"

Andrei thought for a moment. "Tell them that you received a tip from your headquarters. Tell them the source is classified."

Kent frowned at him.

Andrei ignored the look and went on. "Tell them that after his inability to eliminate you, and with his transplant enterprise exposed, Cezar Kaminesky preferred to commit suicide rather than be caught and go to prison."

Andrei made sequential eye contacts with Kent, Irina, and Boboc. "Do we all agree that it was a suicide?"

Kent and Irina looked at each other, then nodded in affirmation.

Boboc stepped forward and gave his partner a big slap on the back. "There you go!" he shouted with delight. "I am proud of you, partner."

CHAPTER 110

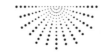

BRAȘOV, APRIL 15

Traian Dalca, still in his dark uniform, walked into the warehouse with a certain swagger, right hand resting on his holstered sidearm. His entourage, the raiding party from Martina Erner's apartment, lumbered in behind him, curiously examining the medical wares they passed by. Andrei and Boboc greeted their chief outside the door of the office. Dalca froze when he spotted Mark Kent behind Andrei. "What is he doing here?" His right hand was no longer on his gun, but rather angrily pointing at Mark.

"He is the one who discovered Cezar," Andrei answered calmly.

Dalca hastily pushed Andrei and Boboc aside and entered the office by himself. He soon emerged, still stern but puzzled. "What is this?"

"Suicide," said Andrei brusquely. "He killed himself by asphyxiation using that gas canister to replace oxygen in his bag."

The chief paused and briefly contemplated Andrei's explanation. He was then distracted by members of his team approaching the office door and peering inside. "Go away," he yelled at them. "Go! We're done. You're no longer needed."

As they departed, he ordered Andrei, "Line this all up with crime scene tape. The building perimeter, too."

"Yes, sir." Andrei knew that there was no hurry to do this since the place was totally desolate aside from the police presence.

"I called in a forensics team," said Dalca, more calmly. "They should arrive soon." He then turned to Mark and for the first time seemed to notice Mark's bruised neck and red eyes. He paused, momentarily puzzled, until he realized what these were. His eyes drifted to Irina, who stood beside Mark.

Dalca turned to Andrei with a new surge of fury. "Did they touch the body? Did they disturb anything?"

Mark took a step forward to answer but Andrei laid a hand on his chest. "No, sir," said Andrei. "I can assure you that nothing was disturbed." Dalca locked eyes with Andrei, then with Mark, his expression skeptical. He was obviously considering whether to buy this. He then changed the subject, addressing Mark directly. "How did you discover this place?"

Mark exchanged a split-second glance with Andrei, who gave him a veiled nod of approval. "A tip," he said, somewhat hesitantly, his voice a near whisper. At that moment Mark was glad that his injured throat concealed his reticence, for he was cringing inside.

"A tip?!" Dalca sounded harsh. "What sort of a tip. From whom?"

"A contact in Bucharest," said Mark, trying in vain to speak more loudly. "It was conveyed via the CIA." He waited a second to gauge Dalca's reaction and, after a dry cough, continued with more confidence. "The source is classified, sir."

"Classified, huh?" Dalca murmured to himself, staring at the American.

Boboc was standing behind his chief, grinning. The whole scene reminded Mark of episodes in his old high school in Istanbul when ill-behaved kids busted by a teacher tried to escape punishment with bullshit explanations. Irina was staring at him dubiously, but said nothing.

"Sir," Andrei interjected calmly, "there is no evidence of forced entry, no evidence of struggle, no violence or blood." His subordinate's calm seemed to finally rub off on Dalca, whose expression softened. Andrei continued. "When we check the ownership of this warehouse, I bet we'll find Cezar Kaminesky as owner or part owner."

"So what are you saying?" asked Dalca, his tone more curious than agitated.

"It's obvious," continued Andrei, with smooth conviction. "The man decided to end it rather than get caught." He swung his arm theatrically around the contents of the warehouse. "So he came here, to an out-of-the way, familiar place, and killed himself."

Dalca rubbed his forehead with his fingertips. "I seem to recall that the last time we encountered a suicide, it was you who questioned it and opened up the Pandora's Box that we are now in."

"Yes, sir."

"But you have no doubts about this one?"

"None," said Andrei firmly. "I'm sure the forensic evidence will show it was a suicide."

Andrei felt a pang of conscience about the lie he was perpetrating, but this was the clean ending that Dalca himself had demanded when they met the night before. Skeptical at first of his chief's demand, Andrei had pondered the issue and come around to agreeing with him. Pursuing a powerful and elusive, well-connected Russian that international law enforcement had failed to apprehend was a quixotic venture. It would detract from their success in Braşov. Best to end it this way, saying it was a suicide.

Andrei locked eyes with his chief. For a brief moment all was silent as Dalca's doubt turned into recognition. He gave Andrei a barely perceptible nod. "In that case," he said, his lips curling into a sly smile, "this investigation is concluded."

"Thank God!" exclaimed Boboc, his remark drawing an irate glance from Dalca.

"Stay here and guard the body until the forensics team arrives," he ordered Andrei.

Andrei gave his chief a military salute.

"Well done, Costiniu," Dalca added.

"Thank you," Andrei said quietly.

Dalca then addressed Mark Kent. "Please express our gratitude to your superiors. We cannot do so ourselves because we're small fry here in Braşov."

Mark bowed his head forward in a gesture of affirmation. He was glad his throat was too sore and that he could no longer speak.

CHAPTER 111

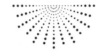

BRAŞOV, APRIL 16

Mark gave Irina a warm hug. "Thank you for everything," he said. "You've been my guardian angel."

Irina sported a bittersweet smile. She shouldered a backpack and picked up her luggage. "It's been good to know you," she said. "I will forever remember these few days we spent here in Braşov."

It was early afternoon the day after their discovery of Cezar's dead body. They stood at the landing of the staircase outside Mark's apartment door.

Mark zipped up her jacket. "Where are you headed?"

"Back to Bucharest. To my old life." Irina sighed. "But it won't be the same for a while."

"I bet."

"I need to return to work. It'll keep me sane while I deal with the fallout."

"It's good that Bucharest is not that far from Braşov."

"Far enough." She chuckled awkwardly. "Considering how often I will have to come back here to deal with my legal case."

"You've been so good to them," Mark said. "I'm sure they'll give you a break."

"Andrei thinks so." She then added sorrowfully, "But it won't bring Enver back."

Their conversation was interrupted by the sound of the main door downstairs. The alarm had not been fixed yet, the maintenance staff at the hospital still in turmoil after the arrest of one of their own.

Mark and Irina listened as footsteps climbed the stairs. Irina took a step back in surprise and stared at the statuesque blonde who appeared at the top of the staircase, her hazel eyes fixed on Mark. "Hello," she said, her sumptuous red lips parting into a broad smile.

Mark stood still, stunned and speechless. The woman opened her arms to him. "Well, aren't you glad to see me?"

"Olga!" Mark finally exclaimed, although his voice was still hoarse. He drew her arms around his waist and gave her a long kiss, generously reciprocated. Olga then stepped back a pace and ran a finger on Mark's bruised neck. "What happened to you?"

Irina interrupted. "Olga? As in Cezar's wife?"

"No longer," said Olga, arms still around Mark, smiling.

"Your husband…your ex…did that," Irina explained, pointing to Mark's neck. "Tried to strangle him."

Olga's eyes widened as she reexamined Mark. "Oh, my God. Are you all right?"

"Yes. It was nothing," he lied. He placed a hand on Olga's back and turned her toward Irina. "Olga, meet Irina Cernea. She is a nurse."

Olga raised her hand gracefully, long nails sparkling with red nail polish. "Glad to meet you."

As the two women shook hands, Olga ran her other hand into Mark's hair, raking it with her fingers. "Did you take good care of this boy?" she asked Irina, teasingly.

"She did," Mark answered.

Olga gave him another peck on the lips. "Not that good, I hope."

Irina took an awkward step toward the stairs. "I'd better be heading out."

Mark rushed to her and gave her a big hug. "Thanks for

everything," he whispered, giving her a quick kiss on the cheek. "Keep in touch."

"I will." Irina turned to Olga. "It's good to meet you. I heard so much about you."

With that, Irina descended the stairs. She did not look back.

* * *

"I see it didn't take you long to find another one," Olga teased Mark, her hand caressing his cheek. They had gone inside Mark's so-called secure apartment.

Olga sat on the sofa, shoes off, feet folded under her, Mark sitting next to her, within breathing distance. "Olga," he said tenderly, "I was worried about you."

"Never mind that. I told you I can take care of myself." She gently caressed Mark's cheek. "Now, tell me the truth. How bad was it?"

Mark sighed. "He almost killed me, twice. If it weren't for the Braşov police and that woman you just met, I wouldn't be here." He lifted his shirt and pulled back his bandage. "Look."

Olga grimaced as she examined the staples that held the surgical wound together. "You did get my warning that Cezar was on to you, didn't you?"

"Yes, I did. Thank you."

"Little good it did." She gently rubbed her hand over the scar. "Did he take your kidney?"

"Not quite." Mark told her the story of his ordeal with Cezar in Chişinău and the subsequent events in Braşov, including his rescue from the operating room and Cezar's attempt to strangle him.

Olga listened quietly, eyes wide. "My God. You *have* been through a lot."

"How did you find me?" asked Mark, suddenly curious.

"You'd have to be blind and deaf not to notice the news," she said, chuckling. "Cezar and the transplant bust are all over the papers and internet. Then last night I saw the news of his death. They mentioned an American agent who had been instrumental in helping local police. I knew that it had to be you. It wasn't hard to find out where you were from Spitatul Martinu."

"Wonderful," said Mark, facetiously. "I'm glad that they are keeping strict confidentiality."

Olga pinched his cheeks. "Sweetie," she said, "are you forgetting that you are in Romania? You are so clever and cunning and yet, sometimes so naïve." She gave him a gentle kiss. "I missed you after you left."

"Really?"

"I know that it was supposed to be a one-nighter, no strings attached. But still..." She gazed out the window.

"I would have missed you too," said Mark teasingly, "but I had no time for that."

Olga laughed. "So when I discovered where you were, I decided to come over and see if..." she trailed off again. Then she ran a hand under Mark's shirt, gently caressing his belly. "See if you needed another massage," she murmured.

"I do." Mark felt a rise within. "But I don't think I can perform in my condition."

"Perform?!" Olga objected. "Who asked you to perform?"

She lifted his shirt and leaned in to kiss his belly button. She then raised her eyes, fixing her gaze on his as she started to undo his belt. "You stay right there," she purred. "Olga will take care of you."

CHAPTER 112

BRAȘOV, APRIL 22

Andrei undid the buttons of his jacket. The aiguillette they had added to his formal uniform got caught in one of them.

"Damn it!" He struggled to free the golden rope and let out a laugh after succeeding. He recalled Traian Dalca having the same problem when he first met his boss. Andrei was as uncomfortable in the stiff uniform as Dalca had been.

They had all worn uniforms that day, Boboc too, and he looked surprisingly distinguished as he accepted a plaque of commendation from the Governor, with the city's chief of police proudly looking on. Boboc held the large frame awkwardly while photos were taken. Andrei received the same plaque and handled it more deftly.

They then looked on as Traian Dalca was given a medal of some sort and declared the hero of the entire affair. Dalca gave a stiff military salute, chest held out in pride, eyes beaming as he posed for reporters with his superiors.

"What a crock of shit," said Boboc afterwards to Andrei, when they were back at the station. "Let's go to that French café across from Zhulati's apartment and have a croque monsieur."

"You go ahead," said Andrei. "I have a few things I need to clear up."

Boboc looked at him reproachfully. "You'll have to meet me there at some point, since we're no longer going to see each other here." Boboc had announced his retirement, effective immediately. Andrei patted his partner's back and promised many meetings to come. He knew Boboc would want to keep abreast of the latest gossip.

Alone at his desk, Andrei looked around the scarcely populated station room. Most of the officers were still at the reception that followed the ceremony. He picked up an email message that had been printed and left on his desk. "Thanks for the wonderful Scotch," it read, followed by a thumbs-up emoji. "I look forward to sharing some with you."

It was from Corneliu Balaş, his old friend and SRI contact. Corneliu had called Andrei after the news about Cezar broke, telling him that he knew it was Andrei who managed to solve the case even though his name wasn't anywhere in the news. *Excellent spycraft*, Balaş had complimented him. He heard rumors, Corneliu said, that the agency wanted to rehire him.

Andrei's response was firm. What he had done was not spy work, he told his friend. It was police work. He was happy here in Braşov, away from the murky milieu of the intelligence agency. If invited back, he would not accept. Then he had sent Corneliu a bottle of twenty-five-year-old Macallan as thanks for the help he'd given Andrei with the case.

Andrei set Corneliu's message aside and took out his phone. He opened a video conferencing app and tapped a number. A gaunt young woman appeared on the screen, looking surprised by the call.

"Hello, Officer Costiniu," she said. "Do you have any news for me?"

"Hello, Emina. I do."

The young woman undid the knot on her scarf and carefully readjusted it, revealing a bit more of her forehead. "I heard about your raid on the illegal transplant outfit in Braşov. It is all over European news."

"We have terminated them," replied Andrei.

Emina silently nodded her approval. "Any progress on my brother's murder?"

"We've identified the main perpetrator, a man named Cezar Kaminesky. He is dead now." Andrei did not elaborate on the convoluted story of how Cezar had come to goad Vadim Rusu into assassinating her brother, Enver Muratovich. It was better to keep it simple.

"Good," said Emina. "Did the American agent Mark Kent assist you in your investigation?"

"He did. He was very helpful."

"I met him, you know, in Bucharest. I gave him your card and asked him to assist."

"So I discovered," said Andrei, smiling. "Thank you for doing that. In a roundabout way, you ended up helping your brother's investigation."

"This is important news for my family." Emina remained solemn. "Maybe it will bring us some closure."

"Let's hope so."

"Thank you so much for taking my plea seriously, and please convey my gratitude to the American agent."

"I will."

"And please send my regards to your lovely wife. I will never forget her kindness."

Andrei felt a sense of contentment as he hung up. Now he could go home to Ana and the baby. He had no desire to hang out with VIPs at a reception.

Once home, Ana greeted him at the door with a tantalizing up-and-down look-over. "Oh my, you look so handsome in that uniform," she said. "Just like the old days."

"They promoted me to Inspector." Andrei pushed aside his aiguillette as he attempted to unbutton his jacket.

Ana laid a hand on his arm. "No, don't," she said. "Stay like that awhile, my fine prince."

"I am no longer into uniforms," he said, his hand still on a button.

She reached up and kissed him. "Well, I am."

She took him by the hand and led him to the bedroom. "Here," she said, laying her fingers on his button. "Let *me* undo them." Andrei looked on as Ana slowly undressed him. "Just like the old days," she said, and then began slipping out of her own clothes.

Andrei pulled her to him and murmured, "Another go at a second baby?"

She playfully pushed him onto the bed and jumped over him, face atop his. "Not necessary," she said, as she readied to take him in. "He is already on his way."

CHAPTER 113

ON THE BLACK SEA, APRIL 24

A stiff breeze caught the blue and yellow flag at the aft of the boat, flapping it in a fury. She stood up and lifted her sunglasses, searching for the source of the noise. It was calm here on the aft deck, protected from the wind by a tall gunwale. She returned to her divan and reclined, eyes closed, and let the warm sun bathe her bikini-clad body.

Her reverie was interrupted by a shadow that fell over her face. "You are a sight to behold," she heard him say softly. She smiled as she accepted the mojito cocktail he handed her.

"You're up, finally," she said.

"*Semracığım*," he said to her in Turkish—*my dear Semra*—as he took a sip from his own drink. "You wore me out."

She sat up and he sat next to her. They stared beyond the Ukrainian flag flying aft, at the darkening horizon where gathering clouds cast dark shadows over Odessa. Out here, on this stretch of the Black Sea, it was sunny and calm. Earlier, they had heard an afternoon squall that passed over them, but they hadn't cared. They were busy downstairs in the main cabin, making love.

"Look," she said, pointing toward the city. "It must be raining on your boss Vadim. Do you think he is preoccupied like we were?"

"I seriously doubt it." Boris leaned in and gave her a long kiss.

"But that Swedish model he has…" She trailed off, wishing she looked as good as Vadim Rusu's girl.

"The boss likes to collect beautiful things." Boris sipped his drink. "Cars, jewelry, girls. But he does not use them much."

Semra put her arms around his neck. "But you do. Don't you?"

Boris put down his mojito and hugged her back. "You are a unique gem, my dear," he said. "But you're making me feel my age."

"Honey, you are the best lover I've ever had."

"Better than Kent?"

Semra let out a loud laugh. "Oh, so you're worried about him now, are you?" She stood up and slipped her carefully pedicured toes into sandals. She took a few steps toward the aft of the boat and looked out at the wide horizon.

"Well," she heard him say awkwardly, "he is handsome, dashing, and exotic."

Semra examined the waves on the restless sea, momentarily pensive as she recalled Mark Kent, his captivating presence in Mahmut's house when they first met, how relieved she was to receive his hug when he rescued her that horrible night, the two occasions when she made love to him. She did miss him.

"Don't you agree?" Boris pressed his point.

She turned back to Boris and sat down next to him, her expression no longer playful. "He never quite figured out how to treat me like a proper woman," she said flatly. She took a sip of her drink and stared at Boris, her expression softening. "But you do."

Boris nodded, happily accepting the compliment.

"Besides," Semra said, stretching an arm in a wide arc around the aft deck, "he never had any of this. He told me once that he was broke, nothing to return to in the US."

"Men like him tend to be that way," Boris replied dismissively. "Righteous crusaders who don't know how to monetize their successes."

"And now you're the big boss." Semra gave him another hug. "Who would ever imagine: me with the big boss!"

Soon after the hit on Cezar Kaminesky, Vadim Rusu had announced his retirement and turned over day-to-day operations to Boris. He wished to stay away from Chișinău, he told Boris, and spend more time in Odessa.

"What I wouldn't pay to have my family in Mardin see me now," Semra added.

She quietly thanked the American for making her new life possible. If it hadn't been for Mark's decision to take Semra with him to Romania, none of this would have happened. She would be stuck back where she had started, in the streets of Beyoğlu.

"Are you hungry?" asked Boris.

"Yes," she said. "What do you have?"

"How about beluga caviar?"

"How about that?"

"And champagne, Billecart-Salmon, Brut."

He supported her as they walked inside. Semra was still trying to gain her sea legs. She stared at the bubbles fulminating in the champagne flute as he poured. She took a sip of the light, smooth cuvée and again thought about her life so far. It was tranquil at last, despite all that had raged within.

"*Nostrovia*," she said, raising her glass.

CHAPTER 114

ISTANBUL, APRIL 25

"My apologies, but we are no longer serving breakfast," the young waiter, formally dressed in a black bow tie, announced in English.

Mark took a look around the vast Hyatt dining room where busboys were taking away the opulent breakfast spread. "No problem," he said in Turkish. "I had room service."

The waiter blinked as he recognized the American whose Turkish had been surprisingly good. "*Hoşgeldiniz*," he said, bowing respectfully. He repeated in English, "Welcome back, sir. I bet you wouldn't mind a bit of *kaymak*, would you?" The waiter called out to one of the busboys carrying a plate off the display.

Mark was impressed that the waiter remembered. He ordered a cup of Turkish coffee to go with it.

As the *kaymak* was laid at his table, Mark gazed through picture windows of the dining room toward the Bosporus, where a white Istanbul ferry was dwarfed by a huge Russian cargo ship sailing perilously close by. He had taken these ferries for granted all his life. Now Mark marveled at the skill and temerity it took to navigate these small vessels as they crisscrossed the narrow strait amid gargantuan Russian ships.

He closed his eyes and enjoyed a spoonful of *kaymak* as it coated his tongue with a smooth, intensely creamy flavor. He was glad to be back in Istanbul. He had high hopes that from here on his life would, as the Turkish expression went, turn out like *kaymak*.

"A penny for your thoughts."

Mark opened his eyes to see the tall, lanky figure of Leon Adler standing over him. He hastily stood up and shook hands with his old high school friend. "I am totally in awe of what you accomplished in Romania," Leon said.

"Thanks," Mark replied, as he signaled to the waiter to bring another cup of coffee and motioned to Leon to sit. "But it came at a high cost." He lifted his shirt discreetly and showed Leon his surgical scar, then tilted his head to display a fading bruise on a spot that Cezar had squeezed. "I almost got killed, twice."

"You should be awarded some sort of medal, for bravery," Leon said. "So, tell me all about it."

Mark recounted the events with Rusu and Boris in Chișinău and his subsequent run-in with Cezar. He described Cezar's two attempts to do him in. He told Leon about the grand deception Cezar had inflicted upon Vadim Rusu, who had been rendered susceptible to such a lie by his grief over his son. And finally, Mark told him how eerily similar Cezar's death was to that of their high school mate Ahmet, aka Nicolae Radu. He knew that Leon was smart enough to figure Cezar's death was not self-inflicted.

Leon took notes as he listened. "How did you find out about Cezar's lie to Rusu?" he asked.

"An informant," said Mark. He did not wish to discuss Olga with him.

"Who?" Leon pressed.

Mark took a last sip of coffee and lightly punched Leon's arm. "From one intelligence officer to another," he said, good-humoredly, "some sources need to remain secret."

Leon burst into a laugh. "Oh, so now you're one of us, are you?"

"Why not?" said Mark, smiling. "Everyone already thinks I am."

Leon put his notebook away and looked at his watch. He tapped a text message on his phone while Mark polished off his remaining *kaymak*.

"Ah!" said Leon, as he received a response to his text. He stood up. "Wait here. I'll be back in a second."

Mark looked around the vast dining room as he waited. With the conclusion of the breakfast buffet, it was nearly deserted. When Leon returned, Mark was dumbfounded to see the older man who accompanied him, taller than Leon, wearing brown-rimmed spectacles and sporting a white goatee. "*Bonjour, mon bon ami*," said Commissaire Jean Claude Gérard, shaking hands with Mark.

"Oh, my God. I don't believe this." Mark shook the Frenchman's hand with delight. He turned to Leon, smiling. "Where did you find him?"

"I wanted to come and personally thank you for the help you have rendered us." Gérard was formal but effusive. He patted Leon's back. "And thank you for taking my advice and keeping Adler in the loop."

They all sat down, Mark calling the waiter again for more coffees.

"Tell me about Cezar," said the Commissaire. "What was he like?"

"Pure evil," Mark responded. He described Cezar's ruse as an SRI agent, his menacing sidekick Milan, and his own conversation with Cezar as his captive.

"I hear you got to meet his wife again." The Frenchman uttered this with a special inflection in his voice. Leon raised his eyebrows in surprise.

"Yes," said Mark, hoping his voice betrayed nothing. "At Iancu Negrescu's funeral."

"Was she any help?"

Mark paused and squinted as he thought of a proper answer. As usual, the foxy Frenchman knew more than he let on. "Well...in a manner of speaking, yes." He quickly changed the subject. "Let me tell you about Vadim Rusu. Did you know that I met him, too?"

The Interpol men listened eagerly as Mark recounted his story.

When he finished, he addressed Gérard. "Will you be going after Rusu?"

The Commissaire clasped his hands and looked down at his lap. "*Malheureusement*, no." He removed his eyeglasses and rubbed his eyes. "It is political, coming from much higher up."

They all silently contemplated this, none of them surprised. Mark then spoke. "Well, at least he won't do any more harm."

"How so?" asked Leon.

"Boris told me that Rusu had given up on assassinations. When it came to the loss of his son, revenge did not bring closure."

Gérard raised his eyebrows. "The man has a semblance of humanity after all."

Mark continued. "Besides, from what I gather, he has retired, turned over the management of Hercules, his security company, to Boris Petrov."

"Really?" Gérard was genuinely surprised. "*Mon ami*," he added, "you never cease to amaze me with your revelations."

Mark chuckled as he recalled the first time he astounded the wily Frenchman when he pointed out that the radiology report Ahmet had summoned him to Budapest with was of a patient named Cezar Kaminesky.

"How do you know this?" asked Leon. "Or is this from another secret source?"

Mark smiled. "No, I can reveal this one. Semra Karacan told me."

"Gazioğlu's girlfriend?" Leon was startled.

Mark nodded.

"I had forgotten about her. Wasn't she your, uh…ward?" He grinned slyly at Mark.

"Yes."

"So, whatever happened to her?"

"She left me and took up with Boris Petrov." Mark shrugged his shoulders. "Love at first sight."

"There," said Leon, laughing. "Another problem solved."

Gérard looked at them quizzically. Leon explained Mark's

quandary at being stuck as the sole guardian of the murdered surgeon's girlfriend and how Mark took her to Romania.

"So," said the Frenchman. "Alone again?"

"Naturally."

Mark's answer, harkening to the refrain of Gilbert O'Sullivan's 1972 hit song, caused them all to break into laughter.

"My dear friend," the Frenchman said, "may I propose that you solve this problem soon? Perhaps a female companion could keep you out of trouble."

"You're so right," said Mark. "I'll get on it right away." He smiled in a way that puzzled his companions.

Gérard pulled out a small red velvet box. "I have a present for you," he said to Mark.

He opened the box to reveal a medal hanging from a red, white and blue silk ribbon, its suspension loop adorned with an olive branch crown. Mark and Leon leaned in for a closer look. "It's the *Médaille d'honneur de la Police Nationale*," Gérard said. *The Medal of Honor of the National Police.*

Astounded, Mark glanced back and forth between the medal and the Commissaire.

Gérard continued. "It is awarded to those who have faithfully served in long careers." He then tapped Mark's lap. "You are an extremely unusual recipient of this honor, my friend. But you deserved it."

Mark took the open box and held it delicately, as if it were a priceless jewel. He glanced at a beaming Leon, who turned his palms up and said, "Don't look at me! I wasn't the one who suggested it."

"I was," said Gérard, shaking Mark's hand. "For putting your life on the line in the service of our cause."

"Inadvertent as it was," Mark murmured. Gérard's words and deed had touched him deeply.

"What do you know?" said Leon, boisterously. "You can officially consider yourself one of us after all."

Mark looked at the shiny medal. "If you don't mind," he said to the Commissaire, "I think I will take Vadim Rusu's example and retire, before this honor does me in."

The three men bade their cordial goodbyes in the lobby of the hotel. Then Mark headed back up to his room, knowing that Olga was there taking a shower, and readying herself for a day of sightseeing in Istanbul.

EPILOGUE

OFF THE BODRUM PENINSULA, APRIL 28

A warm breeze caught the Turkish flag in the aft of the vessel, causing it to flap loudly. She sat up on her chaise longue and raised her sunglasses, searching for the source of the noise. Mark was nearby, his eyes resting on her. She wore a bikini that accentuated her sensuous curves, her bosom nearly bursting out of the top, radiant under the hot sun.

The boat gently rocked in the calm sea as it sailed farther out into the Mediterranean. Olga stood up and slipped her long, well-pedicured toes into sandals. She approached Mark, a bit unsteady on her feet, and sat next to him. "That warm wind," she said, "it feels good."

Mark moved behind her and wrapped his arms around her waist. "You," he whispered in her ear. "It's you who feels good." He gave her a gentle kiss on the back of her neck.

Olga caressed his cheek, her eyes on the coast of Bodrum, now a small fleck on the horizon. "This is such a nice treat," she said. Then she turned back as a young man wearing a captain's cap and white jacket with epaulettes approached them.

"How are you enjoying our sail so far?" he asked her.

"Wonderful, my dear. You're such a kind host."

Mark chimed in. "When did you learn to sail?"

Tarık took off the captain's cap and rubbed his retreating hairline. "I didn't," he said, smiling sheepishly. He was growing back his moustache but it was still a fleck of dirty black on his upper lip. "Let's just say I am in training. I have a real captain at the helm."

Mark and Olga had spent two days in Istanbul, keeping to themselves as they toured the Old City, the Bosporus, and some of Mark's childhood haunts. They then flew to Milas-Bodrum Airport, the flight a welcome luxury for Mark. Tarık picked them up in his new car and brought them to his family villa in Göltürkbükü, Mark relieved at not having to watch his back this time.

Then there was Olga. She drew admiring stares wherever they went, from men and women alike. Tarık himself was dumbfounded to see Mark with such an arresting woman. After a day of rest, they embarked on Tarık's yacht on a Blue Voyage, a custom private cruise of the Turkish Mediterranean Coast.

"Would you like a drink?" asked Tarık, ever the gracious host.

Mark and Olga looked at each other and nodded. Mark stood up. "Here," he said. "I'll help you." The two men went inside to a bar near the fore deck while Olga headed down below, in search of more suntan lotion.

"You never told me what happened in Romania," Tarık said as he fetched a vodka bottle from a cabinet. He looked at the scar on Mark's right flank, prominently reddish in its early healing phase. "What is that?"

"I ran into some bad guys," said Mark. "They tried to steal my kidneys."

Tarık looked away and shuddered, momentarily unable to open the vodka bottle. "Wow!"

"They didn't succeed," Mark assured him. "I was saved in the nick of time. The bad guy is dead, taken out."

"By whom?"

"Vadim Rusu."

"The Russian who was after you?" asked Tarık, startled.

"Yeah, well…" Mark didn't quite know how to explain the turn of events. "Let's just say that Rusu and I came to an understanding and became allies…sort of."

"I was worried about you," Tarık said. "I had a feeling something bad might happen in Romania." He poured vodka into glasses that Mark had prepared with ice. "And Olga," he added. "Where did you find her?"

"She is the one I told you about when we drove to Bodrum. Remember?"

"The one you wanted to…" Tarık did not finish his sentence. He broke out in a loud laugh and patted Mark's back. "Good for you."

Mark poured some club soda into the drinks. "It was quite an effort," he said. "Totally unexpected, I should add."

"But it did happen," Tarık countered. "And she is gorgeous, more so than Semra." He raised and lowered his eyebrows in the same Groucho Marx gesture he had done before.

They had already discussed Semra's happy fate. That was the first question Tarık had asked Mark when they met at the airport.

"It would have been a lot easier for your father to snag Olga." Mark stirred the drinks. "May he rest in peace."

Tarık let the remark slide, saying nothing as he and Mark walked back out onto the deck. Olga had not yet returned.

"How come your mother didn't come with us?" Mark asked.

"She is not feeling up to it," Tarık said awkwardly. He did not tell Mark that when he had informed Günsu of Mark's Romanian girlfriend, she had not taken the news well.

"I'll have to stop by and see her when I return to Istanbul," said Mark.

They set their drinks down on the aft deck and leaned on the gunwale, continuing their conversation as they stared at the sea.

"What will you do after this?" asked Tarık.

Mark stared at the foamy wake of the boat. "Go back to San Francisco and pick up the pieces of my life, see if I can patch them together."

"And her?" Tarık was referring to Olga.

"She'll go back to her own home in Bucharest. She has her own life."

"Will you see her again?"

"I don't know," said Mark. "I am taking it one day at a time. I don't want to think about that."

Olga reappeared, holding a bottle of suntan lotion she had finally found in Mark's luggage. She raised her glass in a toast.

"What are we toasting?" Mark asked, smiling.

"Cezar," she said solemnly. Seeing Mark's startled look, she quickly added, "In his evil way, he allowed us to all meet." She raised her glass. "And to Mark, for disposing of him."

Mark and Tarık looked at each other, slowly raising their glasses.

"Yes," Tarık said quietly, then grinned. "To Mark!" He took a big gulp.

Mark laughed and slid aside Olga. He gently clinked his glass on hers. "To Cezar," he said. "Glad to be his last mark."

MARK TO MURDER

A CHAPTER FROM THE FIRST MARK KENT MYSTERY

Mark's first pursuit of Olga, in Budapest, left him running for his life, as you're about to read in Chapter 19 of Mark to Murder: Death in Budapest. *Be sure to enjoy this fast-paced first book in full, and discover more about Mark Kent plus the exotic (and deadly) locales he invariably finds himself in.*

* * *

She sat behind a small desk in a moldy back office, her face illuminated by a faint table lamp. Her wavy golden hair hung loose, her face more radiant than at the spa despite meager makeup. The room was chilly and she wore a wool V-neck sweater over her dress, unbuttoned at the top, her ample bosom conspicuous. She extinguished a spent cigarette, forcefully squeezing it, and gave him a weary look.

"What do you want from me?"

Mark played with the straps atop a plastic bag containing his bottle of Lagavulin. He sat awkwardly on an uncomfortable wooden chair in front of her desk as if he were interviewing for a job.

"First," he muttered, "let me tell you that I am not a policeman, or detective, or anything like that."

She let out a hoarse chuckle. "That's obvious," she said.

Mark felt foolish. He stroked his bottle as if it were a pet. The Scotch had been effective, attracting sufficient attention from the bar. Still, he had had to wait over an hour, suffering through two more strip performances. When they presented him with the bill, Hannah long since gone, Mark realized that he would indeed pay dearly for a tête-a-tête with Olga. Eventually, after his credit card cleared, one of the bouncers that stood guard led him to the back of the bar and through a narrow, dark hallway into this office.

After a pause to collect himself, Mark began. "Why did you not tell me who you were at the hotel?"

"Is this why you took all the trouble to come here? To ask me that?" She was disdainful.

"No, no...." Mark tried a fresh start, a bit more assertive. "It's just that Ahmet was an old friend of mine, a dear friend...at one time."

"Who?"

"Nicolae," Mark corrected himself. "Nicolae Radu."

She reached over to a dark corner of the desk and slid a pack of cigarettes toward her. She shook one out and looked at him. Her hazel eyes were captivating.

"Did you know Nicolae?" Mark asked.

She nodded. "I saw him from time to time."

"You mean, he came here to Budapest and got massages from you?"

She lit the cigarette, leaning into the lighter in a seasoned move. She squinted as she let out her first drag. "No. Mostly in Romania."

Mark tried to contain his surprise.

"This was our first time in Budapest," she added.

"I wanted to know what he was like." Mark hoped he sounded nonchalant, the news of their Romanian relationship reverberating in his mind.

"He was a good lover," she said. She took another drag from her cigarette and was momentarily lost in thoughts. "He was funny. Jovial."

"Yes," said Mark.

"It's a shame," she whispered, looking down at her cigarette, avoiding Mark's eyes.

"But he was naughty too, wasn't he? Prone to trouble?"

"He didn't talk about any troubles with me. That's what I loved about him. We all have our troubles." She placed her cigarette on the ashtray and rubbed her forehead, her eyebrows raised. She looked tired in the harsh chiaroscuro of the table lamp. "He made me forget mine."

For a moment Mark thought she would tear up. Instead, she picked up her cigarette and took a longer drag.

"So how did you know him...back in Romania?" Mark felt like he had a thousand questions to ask this woman.

She suddenly sat up, alert, like a guard dog that sensed something. "You shouldn't have come here," she said.

He opened his mouth to respond and she raised her hand, shushing him. They both listened. Mark heard it too. Faint footsteps in the hallway.

"We don't have any more time," she said anxiously. "They're coming for you."

"Who?" Mark was incredulous.

Olga sprang to her feet. "Come on," she said hurriedly. "Come here, quick!"

She moved toward a dark corner behind the desk and opened a different door that Mark had not noticed. "Follow this hallway all the way. It has a few turns. It'll take you out to a back street."

Mark hesitantly got up. The footsteps outside were getting louder, sounding like more than one person. Mark came around the desk.

"Hurry! If they find you, they'll kill you."

"But I have more questions," Mark protested.

"Not now!" She was almost in a panic.

He was by the door, his face inches from hers. He could smell fresh lavender and musk in her hair. He stopped, momentarily enthralled by her. Why, he wondered, was he drawn to Ahmet's women? How could he, after all these years, feel like the awkward teen he was in Istanbul? He leaned in toward Olga.

"When you get to the street, run!" She did not notice his quandary. "And don't look back. Don't come back."

"Can I call you?"

The footsteps were almost at the door, loud, reverberating from the walls of the main hallway.

"I don't know," she said, and she shoved him out the door. "I'll be leaving soon."

The door slammed behind him.

The hallway was cold. Mark took a few nervous steps in pitch darkness. He imagined whoever they were bursting into the room, Olga holding them off for a brief while. Alone now, and free of Olga's allure, Mark came to his senses, a sudden fear swelling within. He briefly lit up the hallway with his phone screen. It was around thirty feet straight, unobstructed, then a left turn. He thought about running for it but his footsteps would be too loud. Besides, he was afraid to do that in darkness. He walked fast, trying hard to muffle his feet, his heart pounding.

After taking the left turn, he lit the corridor again and found it blocked by a door up ahead. He shoved the door open into what seemed like another building. It was warmer here, and harshly lit by one bare bulb. It smelled mustier. The door loudly clanked shut behind him. Damn!

He ran, breathless, almost slamming into a wall as the hallway took a turn. He heard the door opening. He ran faster toward another door up ahead. He could hear the same footsteps approaching behind. He slammed his body into the door and found himself in crisp, fresh air, a short set of stairs leading up to a sidewalk. He took the stairs two at a time.

He was on an empty, narrow, one-way residential street. He randomly took a right turn and ran again toward a nearby corner where he took another right turn. It was a slightly wider street, still one way, and Mark recognized it. The entrance to the strip club was only a few paces away. Traffic was scant. A man who appeared drunk stumbled on the opposite sidewalk, past a shadowy figure who stood still under a dark doorway. A couple, arm in arm, walked toward him, their eyes on the pavement.

Mark stopped for a minute and looked around the corner to where he had come from. No one in pursuit. He broke into a massive sweat. He felt a weight bearing down on his right arm. He lifted it and was amazed to see the bottle of Scotch, still in its bag, that had survived his flight. He unzipped his coat, tucked it into his chest, and zipped back up. He began walking at a brisk but steady pace, past the entrance of the club, still desolate, and toward the next corner. It was brightly lit on his side of the street. Mark recalled the *Colorado Sörbár* that he had spotted from the taxi earlier.

The building bearing the bar curved around into Almássy utca, a pedestrian mall that cut diagonally across Dohány. Mark relaxed and turned into Almássy, walking toward the sidewalk tables set up by the beer bar, well lit and occupied by a few customers. Mark intended to continue down this mall, unsure about what he would encounter farther down.

He figured heading away from the nightclub was the safest move. Then his heart skipped several beats.

Two shadowy silhouettes broke out of the dark, directly approaching him at a fast pace from the opposite end of Almássy. It had to be them. They must have taken a left turn out of where Mark had emerged and circled around the opposite direction. Mark quickly ducked onto an outdoor chair of the Colorado Bar, facing away from the pair of pursuers. He forced himself to be calm but his heart raced.

They ran right by the bar without taking a look at its patrons. Mark got a quick glimpse of the two. One was tall and heavy-set, dark and greasy, with a bushy moustache and what looked like a week-old beard. The other was short and athletic, also dark complexioned, pacing slightly ahead of his partner, his hands swinging by his side like a track athlete. Mark saw a gun in his right hand moving swiftly up and down with his arm motions. He contained his rising panic.

As the pair disappeared into Dohány, Mark felt stunned stares directed at him. Two young men and a woman sat around the table, hands on beer mugs, regarding the sweaty intruder who had suddenly occupied the only other free seat at their table. Mark smiled sheepishly and nodded hello to them. He quickly wiped his brow with a paper napkin set at his spot on the table. He stood up so abruptly that he almost knocked over his chair. After saying good night in English, he walked as nonchalantly as he could into the darkness of Almássy, away from Dohány.

The street was lined with old apartment buildings and had waist-high wooded planters down the middle, empty benches between each. Silhouettes of young trees protruded from the planters, supported by poles. Beyond the bar there was not a soul on Almássy. Mark came upon a triangular plaza where the street forked into a Y, its extensions no longer a pedestrian mall. A small park was tucked between the two diverging roads, walled and fenced, its entrance straight ahead, shuttered. There were cars parked along both streets, all facing one way, toward him. A street sign announced Almássy tér. Mark realized he was at one edge of a small, triangular square with a park in the middle. The area was dim and desolate.

Mark stood and hesitated. Should he go left or right?

He heard faint footsteps and looked behind. He recognized the shadowy figures of his two pursuers backlit by the lights of the beer bar walking quickly toward him. They must have gone back to where they started, and now backtracked.

Mark instinctively took off, running fast toward the left, tripping into the street across a step where the pedestrian mall ended. He ran along the fenced wall of the park, not looking back. Suddenly he spotted a break in the wall, an alcove, and he dove into it. He stopped, panting hard. A wooden hut was built into the alcove as a public toilet. Mark was in a narrow space between the fence and the entrance to the ladies' room, hidden from view. Trying to catch his breath, he wheezed loudly as he exhaled. The sound scared him. He held his breath and listened. No footsteps. Had they gone down the other side of the fork?

Despite his terror, Mark collected his thoughts. He could not hide here forever. Sooner or later they would discover him. He listened attentively, and hearing nothing, slid out of the alcove and onto the street.

"*Állj meg!*" The yell startled him. He stopped and looked behind. He saw the solitary figure of the tall, stocky pursuer who repeated the order in English.

"Stop!"

The man was standing at the end of Almássy út, where Mark had stood minutes ago, in front of the park entrance. He turned to his right and yelled at his partner. Mark realized that the two had split there, each searching one side of the fork.

Mark dashed forward. A shot rang out. Mark instinctively ducked and tumbled, the bottle of Scotch thumping painfully against his ribs. He almost fell down. As he recovered his balance, he realized that he was not hit. He heard loud footsteps approaching. There was an intersection fifty feet up ahead, a faint headlight of a motorcycle far beyond. A left turn there would bring him to a busier quarter, Mark hoped, back to Dohány maybe, closer to the New York Café. They could not openly shoot at him there. Could they?

Just then he was blinded by bright headlights. Mark froze and almost fell again, this time backwards. A car had come to a sudden stop at the intersection, then slowly turned into the street, facing him. The sound of footsteps behind him disappeared. They must have frozen, too. The car stood still, engine running, lights on, blocking Mark's way.

Mark panted, sweat pouring out of his forehead and neck. Was there an accomplice in this car? Is that why his pursuers had stopped? Terror, rising within, threatened to overwhelm rational thought.

Maybe it was just a random vehicle, someone lost, stopping to figure his location. Maybe that's why his followers had stopped, too. They did not want any witnesses.

The car did not budge.

Mark had two choices. He could run forward and take his chances with the car, or he could run back, into the arms of his chasers. *Goddamnit*, he thought. How would they take the news of his death back home, not far from a seedy strip club in Budapest? What would they think he had been up to? He couldn't believe he had gotten himself into this predicament.

Mark broke into a run, toward the car. He heard a commotion behind him as his pursuers also took off. Soon Mark was upon the car, a mid-sized sedan. As he tried to bypass it, the passenger door suddenly opened and he slammed into it, his arms flying through its open window.

"Get in!" A shout from within. It was too dark to make out the driver.

Breathless, with sweat-blurred eyes despite the cold, Mark turned behind and saw his followers, now within a few feet, the tall guy stationary, the short one sprinting toward him.

A loud order rang out again. "Get in! Fast."

ACKNOWLEDGMENTS

In late 2015, when I set out to write a crime story set in Turkey and Eastern Europe, I never imagined that it would balloon into a giant project comprising two novels. *Mark to Murder*, the first installment of the story, published in 2018, promised a sequel to complete the saga. This, once again, turned into a more elaborate venture than I had originally imagined.

Many thanks to Robert Lawrence, MD, an exceptional forensic pathologist, for a tip he mentioned in passing while I was writing *Mark to Murder*. It became the foundation of the initial Braşov murder that spawned Andrei's investigation in *Cezar's Last Mark*. Dr. Lawrence also provided invaluable advice on the other crime scenes of the story and their associated forensics.

A heartfelt expression of gratitude to two mates from the English High School of Istanbul. Loni Arditi of Tel Aviv, Israel, a retired police officer and Interpol agent, kept me on the realistic path regarding police matters, as he did with *Mark to Murder*. Selim Hacısalihzade, a loyal, enthusiastic reader of all that I write, continued with his candid advice without regard for my feelings: a rare gift to any writer. He also kept me apprised of details pertaining to Istanbul—most important, in placing the unfortunate transplant doctor's villa in Tuzla, a suburb I have never visited.

My longtime editor, Mim Harrison, remains a crucial element in the successful completion of my publications. Her unwavering support and encouragement are cherished and treasured.

Finally, a special note of thanks to my old high school mate Ahmet Biliktan, who assisted with some of the Romanian details, and whose mysterious disappearance in the 1990s inspired the two stories in the first place. We reconnected with each other in 2016 while I was writing *Mark to Murder*, he in Romania and I in the US, and have kept in touch ever since.

ABOUT THE AUTHOR

Just as two fictional storylines converge in *Cezar's Last Mark*, so do two real-life storylines of the author. Moris Senegor is a neurosurgeon (thus those powerful scenes in the operating room) and a native of Istanbul (hence the authentic sights, smells, tastes, and language of Turkey that Mark returns to). *Cezar's Last Mark* is Moris's fourth book, and the second in the Mark Kent series, following *Mark to Murder*. Moris is also the author of a short-story collection and a memoir of his neurosurgery residency in San Francisco.

Additionally, Moris is an accomplished photographer and a wine connoisseur, and lectures on symphonic music. He and his wife divide their time between San Francisco and Stockton, California.

More on Moris at morissenegor.com.